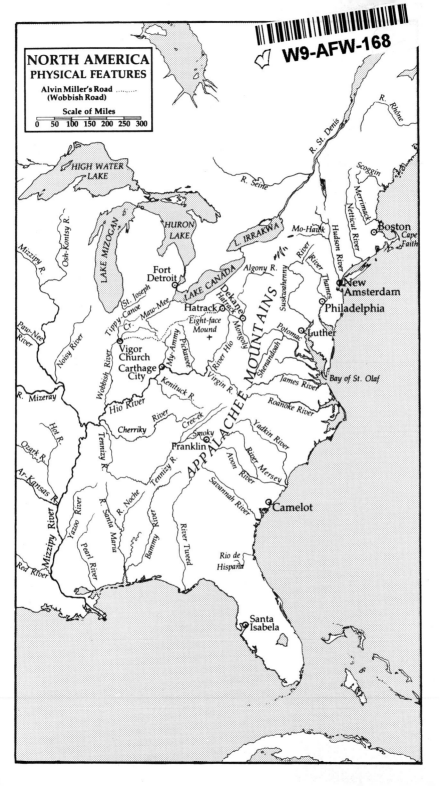

W9-AFW-168

NORTH AMERICA
PHYSICAL FEATURES

Alvin Miller's Road ....
(Wobbish Road)

Scale of Miles

0   50   100 150 200 250 300

HIGH WATER LAKE

HURON LAKE

LAKE MIZOGAN

LAKE CANADA

L. IRRAKWA

R. St. Denis

R. Rhone

R. Seine

Scoggin

Merrimack

Netticut River

Hudson River

Mo-Hauk

Boston

Cape Faith

New Amsterdam

Fort Detroit

Hatrack

Dekane

Hatrack

Algony R.

Suskwahenny

River Thames

Philadelphia

Mizzipy R.

Osh-Kontsy R.

St. Joseph

Tippy-Canoe

Maw-Mee Cr.

Eight-face Mound

My-Ammy

Pickawee

Hatrack Mongoly

River Hio

Potomac

Luther

Paw-Nee River

Noisy River

Vigor Church

Carthage City

Wobbish River

Virgin R.

Shenandoah

Bay of St. Olaf

James River

R. Mizeray

Hio River

Kenituck R.

Cherriky

River

Cree-ek

Roanoke River

Hot R.

Tennizy R.

Smoky

Franklin

Yadkin River

River Mersey

Ozark R.

R. Santa Maria

R. Noche

Tennizy River

Avon River

Ar-Kansas R.

Yazoo River

Pearl River

Bammy

River Tweed

Savannah River

Camelot

Mizzipy River

Rio de Hispana

Red River

Santa Isabela

APPALACHEE MOUNTAINS

HATRACK RIVER

HATRACK RIVER

The Tales of Alvin Maker:
Part One

Seventh Son
Red Prophet
Prentice Alvin

ORSON SCOTT CARD

SCIENCE
FICTION

Published by arrangement with
Tom Doherty Associates, Inc.
49 West 24th Street
New York, NY 10010

ISBN 1-56865-989-X

Printed in the United States of America

HATRACK RIVER
The Tales of Alvin Maker: Part One

CONTENTS

SEVENTH SON

To Emily Jan,
who knows all the magic
that she'll ever need

ACKNOWLEDGMENTS

I owe thanks to Carol Breakstone, for her help in researching folk magic of the American frontier. The material she found became a rich mine of story ideas and details of life in the frontier period of the Northwest Territories. I also made extensive use of information contained in Douglass L. Brownstone's *A Field Guide to America's History* (Facts on File, Inc.) and John Seymour's *The Forgotten Crafts* (Knopf).

Scott Russell Sanders contributed by putting in my hands a copy of his exquisite story cycle *Wilderness Plots: Tales About the Settlement of the American Land* (Quill). His work showed me what could be achieved through realistic handling of frontier life and helped keep me on the right track with my ongoing Alvin Maker project. And, though he is long dead, I owe a considerable debt to William Blake (1757–1827), for writing poems and proverbs that came so perfectly to Taleswapper's lips.

Above all, I am grateful to Kristine A. Card, for the incalculable value of her criticism, encouragement, editing, and proofreading, and for single-handedly turning our children into wise, kind, well-mannered human beings, who readily forgive their father when he is not a fit example of those virtues.

CONTENTS

1

Bloody Mary

Little Peggy was very careful with the eggs. She rooted her hand through the straw till her fingers bumped something hard and heavy. She gave no never mind to the chicken drips. After all, when folk with babies stayed at the roadhouse, Mama never even crinkled her face at their most spetackler diapers. Even when the chicken drips were wet and stringy and made her fingers stick together, little Peggy gave no never mind. She just pushed the straw apart, wrapped her hand around the egg, and lifted it out of the brood box. All this while standing tiptoe on a wobbly stool, reaching high above her head. Mama said she was too young for egging, but little Peggy showed her. Every day she felt in every brood box and brought in every egg, every single one, that's what she did.

Every one, she said in her mind, over and over. I got to reach into every one.

Then little Peggy looked back into the northeast corner, the darkest place in the whole coop, and there sat Bloody Mary in her brood box, looking like the devil's own bad dream, hatefulness shining out of her nasty eyes, saying Come here little girl and give me nips. I want nips of finger and nips of thumb and if you come real close and try to take my egg I'll get a nip of eye from you.

Most animals didn't have much heartfire, but Bloody Mary's was strong and made a poison smoke. Nobody else could see it, but little Peggy could. Bloody Mary dreamed of death for all folks, but most specially for a certain little girl five years old, and little Peggy had the marks on her fingers to prove it. At least one mark, anyway, and even if Papa said he couldn't see it, little Peggy remembered how she got it and nobody could blame her none if she sometimes forgot to reach under

Bloody Mary who sat there like a bushwhacker waiting to kill the first folks that just *tried* to come by. Nobody'd get mad if she just sometimes forgot to look there.

I forgot. I looked in every brood box, every one, and if one got missed then I forgot forgot forgot.

Everybody knew Bloody Mary was a lowdown chicken and too mean to give any eggs that wasn't rotten anyway.

I forgot.

She got the egg basket inside before Mama even had the fire het, and Mama was so pleased she let little Peggy put the eggs one by one into the cold water. Then Mama put the pot on the hook and swung it right on over the fire. Boiling eggs you didn't have to wait for the fire to slack, you could do it smoke and all.

"Peg," said Papa.

That was Mama's name, but Papa didn't say it in his Mama voice. He said it in his little-Peggy-you're-in-dutch voice, and little Peggy knew she was completely found out, and so she turned right around and yelled what she'd been planning to say all along.

"I forgot, Papa!"

Mama turned and looked at little Peggy in surprise. Papa wasn't surprised though. He just raised an eyebrow. He was holding his hand behind his back. Little Peggy knew there was an egg in that hand. Bloody Mary's nasty egg.

"What did you forget, little Peggy?" asked Papa, talking soft.

Right that minute little Peggy reckoned she was the stupidest girl ever born on the face of the earth. Here she was denying before anybody accused her of anything.

But she wasn't going to give up, not right off like that. She couldn't stand to have them mad at her and she just wanted them to let her go away and live in England. So she put on her innocent face and said, "I don't know, Papa."

She figgered England was the best place to go live, cause England had a Lord Protector. From the look in Papa's eye, a Lord Protector was pretty much what she needed just now.

"What did you forget?" Papa asked again.

"Just say it and be done, Horace," said Mama. "If she's done wrong then she's done wrong."

"I forgot one time, Papa," said little Peggy. "She's a mean old chicken and she hates me."

Papa answered soft and slow. "One time," he said.

Then he took his hand from behind him. Only it wasn't no single egg he held, it was a whole basket. And that basket was filled with a clot of straw—most likely all the straw from Bloody Mary's box—and that straw was mashed together and glued tight with dried-up raw egg and shell bits, mixed up with about three or four chewed-up baby chicken bodies.

"Did you have to bring that in the house before breakfast, Horace?" said Mama.

"I don't know what makes me madder," said Horace. "What she done wrong or her studying up to lie about it."

"I didn't study and I didn't lie!" shouted little Peggy. Or anyways she meant to shout. What came out sounded espiciously like crying even though little Peggy had decided only yesterday that she was done with crying for the rest of her life.

"See?" said Mama. "She already feels bad."

"She feels bad being caught," said Horace. "You're too slack on her, Peg. She's got a lying spirit. I don't want my daughter growing up wicked. I'd rather see her dead like her baby sisters before I see her grow up wicked."

Little Peggy saw Mama's heartfire flare up with memory, and in front of her eyes she could see a baby laid out pretty in a little box, and then another one only not so pretty cause it was the second baby Missy, the one what died of pox so nobody'd touch her but her own mama, who was still so feeble from the pox herself that she couldn't do much. Little Peggy saw that scene, and she knew Papa had made a mistake to say what he said cause Mama's face went cold even though her heartfire was hot.

"That's the wickedest thing anybody ever said in my presence," said Mama. Then she took up the basket of corruption from the table and carried it outside.

"Bloody Mary bites my hand," said little Peggy.

"We'll see what bites," said Papa. "For leaving the eggs I give you one whack, because I reckon that lunatic hen looks fearsome to a frog-size girl like you. But for telling lies I give you ten whacks."

Little Peggy cried in earnest at that news. Papa gave an honest count and full measure in everything, but most especially in whacks.

Papa took the hazel rod off the high shelf. He kept it up there ever since little Peggy put the old one in the fire and burnt it right up.

"I'd rather hear a thousand hard and bitter truths from you, Daughter, than one soft and easy lie," said he, and then he bent over and laid on with the rod across her thighs. Whick whick whick, she counted every one, they stung her to the heart, each one of them, they were so full of anger. Worst of all she knew it was all unfair because his heartfire raged for a different cause altogether, and it always did. Papa's hate for wickedness always came from his most secret memory. Little Peggy didn't understand it all, because it was twisted up and confused and Papa didn't remember it right well himself. All little Peggy ever saw plain was that it was a lady and it wasn't Mama. Papa thought of that lady whenever something went wrong. When baby Missy died of nothing at all, and then the next baby also named Missy died of pox, and then the barn burnt down once, and a cow died, everything that went wrong made him think of that lady and he began to talk about how much he hated wickedness and at those times the hazel rod flew hard and sharp.

I'd rather hear a thousand hard and bitter truths, that's what he said, but little Peggy knew that there was one truth he didn't ever want to hear, and so she kept it to herself. She'd never shout it at him, even if it made him break the hazel rod, cause whenever she thought of saying aught about that lady, she kept picturing her father dead, and that was a thing she never hoped to see for real. Besides, the lady that haunted his heartfire, she didn't have no clothes on, and little Peggy knew that she'd be whipped for sure if she talked about people being naked.

So she took the whacks and cried till she could taste that her nose was running. Papa left the room right away, and Mama came back to fix up breakfast for the blacksmith and the visitors and the hands, but neither one said boo to her, just as if they didn't even notice. She cried even harder and louder for a minute, but it didn't help. Finally she picked up her Bugy from the sewing basket and walked all stiff-legged out to Oldpappy's cabin and woke him right up.

He listened to her story like he always did.

"I know about Bloody Mary," he said, "and I told your papa fifty times if I told him once, wring that chicken's neck and be done. She's a crazy bird. Every week or so she gets crazy and breaks all her own eggs, even the ones ready to hatch. Kills her own chicks. It's a lunatic what kills its own."

"Papa like to killed *me*," said little Peggy.

"I reckon if you can walk somewhat it ain't so bad altogether."

"I can't walk *much*."

"No, I can see you're nigh crippled forever," said Oldpappy. "But I tell you what, the way I see it your mama and your papa's mostly mad at each other. So why don't you just disappear for a couple of hours?"

"I wish I could turn into a bird and fly."

"Next best thing, though," said Pappy, "is to have a secret place where nobody knows to look for you. Do you have a place like that? No, don't tell me—it wrecks it if you tell even a single other person. You just go to that place for a while. As long as it's a safe place, not out in the woods where a Red might take your pretty hair, and not a high place where you might fall off, and not a tiny place where you might get stuck.''

"It's big and it's low and it ain't in the woods," said little Peggy.

"Then you go there, Maggie."

Little Peggy made the face she always made when Oldpappy called her that. And she held up Bugy and in Bugy's squeaky high voice she said, "Her name is Peggy."

"You go there, *Piggy*, if you like that better—"

Little Peggy slapped Bugy right across Oldpappy's knee.

"Someday Bugy'll do that once too often and have a rupture and die," said Oldpappy.

But Bugy just danced right in his face and insisted, "Not piggy, *Peggy!*"

"That's right, Puggy, you go to that secret place and if anybody says, We got to go find that girl, I'll say, I know where she is and she'll come back when she's good and ready."

Little Peggy ran for the cabin door and then stopped and turned. "Oldpappy, you're the nicest grown-up in the whole world."

"Your papa has a different view of me, but that's all tied up with another hazel rod that I laid hand on much too often. Now run along."

She stopped again right before she closed the door. "You're the *only* nice grown-up!" She shouted it real loud, halfway hoping that they could hear it clear inside the house. Then she was gone, right across the garden, out past the cow pasture, up the hill into the woods, and along the path to the spring house.

2

Wagon People

They had one good wagon, these folks did, and two good horses pulling it. One might even suppose they was prosperous, considering they had six big boys, from mansize on down to twins that had wrestled each other into being a good deal stronger than their dozen years. Not to mention one big daughter and a whole passel of little girls. A big family. Right prosperous if you didn't know that not even a year ago they had owned a mill and lived in a big house on a streambank in west New Hampshire. Come down far in the world, they had, and this wagon was all they had left of everything. But they were hopeful, trekking west along the roads that crossed the Hio, heading for open land that was free for the taking. If you were a family with plenty of strong backs and clever hands, it'd be good land, too, as long as the weather was with them and the Reds didn't raid them and all the lawyers and bankers stayed in New England.

The father was a big man, a little run to fat, which was no surprise since millers mostly stood around all day. That softness in the belly wouldn't last a year on a deepwoods homestead. He didn't care much about that, anyway—he had no fear of hard work. What worried him today was his wife, Faith. It was her time for that baby, he knew it. Not that she'd ever talk about it direct. Women just don't speak about things like that with men. But he knew how big she was and how many months it had been. Besides, at the noon stop she murmured to him, "Alvin Miller, if there's a road house along this way, or even a little broken-down cabin, I reckon I could use a bit of rest." A man didn't have to be a philosopher to understand her. And after six sons and six daughters, he'd have to have the brains of a brick not to get the drift of how things stood with her.

So he sent off the oldest boy, Vigor, to run ahead on the road and see the lay of the land.

You could tell they were from New England, cause the boy didn't take no gun. If there'd been a bushwhacker the young man never would've made it back, and the fact he came back with all his hair was proof no Red had spotted him—the French up Detroit way were paying for English scalps with liquor and if a Red saw a White man alone in the woods with no musket he'd own that White man's scalp. So maybe a man could think that luck was with the family at last. But since these Yankees had no notion that the road wasn't safe, Alvin Miller didn't think for a minute of his good luck.

Vigor's word was of a road house three miles on. That was good news, except that between them and that road house was a river. Kind of a scrawny river, and the ford was shallow, but Alvin Miller had learned never to trust water. No matter how peaceful it looks, it'll reach and try to take you. He was halfway minded to tell Faith that they'd spend the night this side of the river, but she gave just the tiniest groan and at that moment he knew that there was no chance of that. Faith had borne him a dozen living children, but it was four years since the last one and a lot of women took it bad, having a baby so late. A lot of women died. A good road house meant women to help with the birthing, so they'd have to chance the river.

And Vigor did say the river wasn't much.

3

Spring House

The air in the spring house was cool and heavy, dark and wet. Some-times when little Peggy caught a nap here, she woke up gasping like as if the whole place was under water. She had dreams of water even when she wasn't here—that was one of the things that made some folks say she was a seeper instead of a torch. But when she dreamed outside, she always knew she was dreaming. Here the water was real.

Real in the drips that formed like sweat on the milkjars setting in the stream. Real in the cold damp clay of the spring house floor. Real in the swallowing sound of the stream as it hurried through the middle of the house.

Keeping it cool all summer long, cold water spilling right out of the hill and into this place, shaded all the way by trees so old the moon made a point of passing through their branches just to hear some good old tales. That was what little Peggy always came here for, even when Papa didn't hate her. Not the wetness of the air, she could do just fine without that. It was the way the fire went right out of her and she didn't have to be a torch. Didn't have to see into all the dark places where folks hid theirselfs.

From her they hid theirselfs as if it would do some good. Whatever they didn't like most about theirself they tried to tuck away in some dark corner but they didn't know how all them dark places burned in little Peggy's eyes. Even when she was so little that she spit out her corn mash cause she was still hoping for a suck, she knew all the stories that the folks around her kept all hid. She saw the bits of their past that they most wished they could bury, and she saw the bits of their future that they most feared.

And that was why she took to coming up here to the spring house.

Here she didn't have to see those things. Not even the lady in Papa's memory. There was nothing here but the heavy wet dark cool air to quench the fire and dim the light so she could be—just for a few minutes in the day—a little five-year-old girl with a straw poppet named Bugy and not even have to *think* about any of them grown-up secrets.

I'm not wicked, she told herself. Again and again, but it didn't work because she knew she was.

All right then, she said to herself, I *am* wicked. But I won't be wicked anymore. I'll tell the truth like Papa says, or I'll say nothing at all.

Even at five years old, little Peggy knew that if she kept *that* vow, she'd be better off saying nothing.

So she said nothing, not even to herself, just lay there on a mossy damp table with Bugy clenched tight enough to strangle in her fist.

Ching ching ching.

Little Peggy woke up and got mad for just a minute.

Ching ching ching.

Made her mad because nobody said to her, Little Peggy, you don't mind if we talk this young blacksmith feller into settling down here, do you?

Not at all, Papa, she would've said if they'd asked. She knew what it meant to have a smithy. It meant your village would thrive, and folks from other places would come, and when they came there'd be trade, and where there was trade then her father's big house could be a forest inn, and where there was a forest inn then all the roads would kind of bend a little just to pass the place, if it wasn't too far out of the way— little Peggy knew all that, as sure as the children of farmers knew the rhythms of the farm. A road house by a smithy was a road house that would prosper. So she would've said, Sure enough, let him stay, deed him land, brick his chimney, feed him free, let him have my bed so I have to double up with Cousin Peter who keeps trying to peek under my nightgown, I'll put up with all that—just as long as you don't put him near the spring house so that all the time, even when I want to be alone with the water, there's that whack thump hiss roar, noise all the time, and a fire burning up the sky to turn it black, and the smell of charcoal burning. It was enough to make a body wish to follow the stream right back into the mountain just to get some peace.

Of course the stream was the smart place to put the blacksmith. Except for water, he could've put his smithy anywheres at all. The iron came to him in the shipper's wagon clear from New Netherland, and the charcoal—well, there was plenty of farmers willing to trade charcoal for a good shoe. But water, that's what the smith needed that nobody'd bring him, so of course they put him right down the hill from the spring house where his ching ching ching could wake her up and put the fire back into her in the one place where she had used to be able to let it burn low and go almost to cold wet ash.

A roar of thunder.

She was at the door in a second. Had to see the lightning. Caught just the last shadow of the light but she knew that there'd be more. It wasn't much after noon, surely, or had she slept all day? What with all these blackbelly clouds she couldn't tell—it might as well be the last minutes of dusk. The air was all a-prickle with lightning just waiting to flash. She knew that feeling, knew that it meant the lightning'd hit close.

She looked down to see if the blacksmith's stable was still full of horses. It was. The shoeing wasn't done, the road would turn to muck, and so the farmer with his two sons from out West Fork way was stuck here. Not a chance they'd head home in *this*, with lightning ready to put a fire in the woods, or knock a tree down on them, or maybe just smack them a good one and lay them all out dead in a circle like them five Quakers they still was talking about and here it happened back in '90 when the first white folks came to settle here. People talked still about the Circle of Five and all that, some people wondering if God up and smashed them flat so as to shut the Quakers up, seeing how nothing else ever could, while other people was wondering if God took them up into heaven like the first Lord Protector Oliver Cromwell who was smote by lightning at the age of ninety-seven and just disappeared.

No, that farmer and his big old boys'd stay another night. Little Peggy was an innkeeper's daughter, wasn't she? Papooses learnt to hunt, pickaninnies learnt to tote, farmer children learnt the weather, and an innkeeper's daughter learnt which folks would stay the night, even before they knew it right theirselfs.

Their horses were champing in the stable, snorting and warning each other about the storm. In every group of horses, little Peggy figgered, there must be one that's remarkable dumb, so all the others have to tell him what all's going on. Bad storm, they were saying. We're going to get a soaking, if the lightning don't smack us first. And the dumb one kept nickering and saying, What's that noise, what's that noise?

Then the sky just opened right up and dumped water on the earth. Stripped leaves right off the trees, it came down so hard. Came down so thick, too, that little Peggy couldn't even see the smithy for a minute and she thought maybe it got washed right away into the stream. Oldpappy told her how that stream led right down to the Hatrack River, and the Hatrack poured right into the Hio, and the Hio shoved itself on through the woods to the Mizzipy, which went on down into the sea, and Oldpappy said how the sea drank so much water that it got indigestion and gave off the biggest old belches you ever heard, and what came up was clouds. Belches from the sea, and now the smithy would float all that way, get swallered up and belched out, and someday she'd just be minding her own business and some cloud would break up and plop that smithy down as neat as you please, old Makepeace Smith still ching ching chinging away.

Then the rain slacked off a mite and she looked down to see the smithy still there. But that wasn't what she saw at all. No, what she saw was sparks of fire way off in the forest, downstream toward the Hatrack, down where the ford was, only there wasn't a chance of taking the ford today, with this rain. Sparks, lots of sparks, and she knew every one of them was folks. She didn't hardly think of doing it anymore, she only had to see their heartfires and she was looking close. Maybe future, maybe past, all the visions lived together in the heartfire.

What she saw right now was the same in all their hearts. A wagon in the middle of the Hatrack, with the water rising and everything they owned in all the world in that wagon.

Little Peggy didn't talk much, but everybody knew she was a torch, so they listened whenever she spoke up about trouble. Specially this kind of trouble. Sure the settlements in these parts were pretty old now, a fair bit older than little Peggy herself, but they hadn't forgotten yet that anybody's wagon caught in a flood is everybody's loss.

She fair to flew down that grassy hill, jumping gopher holes and sliding the steep places, so it wasn't twenty seconds from seeing those far-off heartfires till she was speaking right up in the smithy's shop. That farmer from West Fork at first wanted to make her wait till he was done with telling stories about worse storms he'd seen. But Makepeace knew all about little Peggy. He just listened right up and then told those boys to saddle them horses, shoes or no shoes, there was folks caught in the Hatrack ford and there was no time for foolishness. Little Peggy didn't even get a chance to see them go—Makepeace already sent her off to the big house to fetch her father and all the hands and visitors there. Wasn't a one of them who hadn't once put all they owned in the world into a wagon and dragged it west across the mountain roads and down into this forest. Wasn't a one of them who hadn't felt a river sucking at that wagon, wanting to steal it away. They all got right to it. That's the way it was then, you see. Folks noticed other people's trouble every bit as quick as if it was their own.

4

Hatrack River

Vigor led the boys in trying to push the wagon, while Eleanor hawed the horses. Alvin Miller spent his time carrying the little girls one by one to safety on the far shore. The current was a devil clawing at him, whispering, I'll have your babies, I'll have them all, but Alvin said no, with every muscle in his body as he strained shoreward he said no to that whisper, till his girls stood all bedraggled on the bank with rain streaming down their faces like the tears from all the grief in the world.

He would have carried Faith, too, baby in her belly and all, but she wouldn't budge. Just sat inside that wagon, bracing herself against the trunks and furniture as the wagon tipped and rocked. Lightning crashed and branches broke; one of them tore the canvas and the water poured into the wagon but Faith held on with white knuckles and her eyes staring out. Alvin knew from her eyes there wasn't a thing he could say to make her let go. There was only one way to get Faith and her unborn baby out of that river, and that was to get the wagon out.

"Horses can't get no purchase, Papa," Vigor shouted. "They're just stumbling and bound to break a leg."

"Well we can't pull out without the horses!"

"The horses are *something*, Papa. We leave 'em in here and we'll lose wagon and horses too!"

"Your mama won't leave that wagon."

He saw understanding in Vigor's eyes. The *things* in the wagon weren't worth a risk of death to save them. But Mama was.

"Still," Vigor said. "On shore the team could pull strong. Here in the water they can't do a thing."

"Set the boys to unhitching them. But first tie a line to a tree to hold that wagon!"

It wasn't two minutes before the twins Wastenot and Wantnot were on the shore making the rope fast to a stout tree. David and Measure made another line fast to the rig that held the horses, while Calm cut the strands that held them to the wagon. Good boys, doing their work just right, Vigor shouting directions while Alvin could only watch, helpless at the back of the wagon, looking now at Faith who was trying not to have the baby, now at the Hatrack River that was trying to push them all down to hell.

Not much of a river, Vigor had said, but then the clouds came up and the rain came down and the Hatrack became something after all. Even so it looked passable when they got to it. The horses strode in strong, and Alvin was just saying to Calm, who had the reins, "Well, we made it not a minute to spare," when the river went insane. It doubled in speed and strength all in a moment, and the horses got panicky and lost direction and started pulling against each other. The boys all hopped into the river and tried to lead them to shore but by then the wagon's momentum had been lost and the wheels were mired up and stuck fast. Almost as if the river knew they were coming and saved up its worst fury till they were already in it and couldn't get away.

"Look out! Look out!" screamed Measure from the shore.

Alvin looked upstream to see what devilment the river had in mind, and there was a whole tree floating down the river, endwise like a battering ram, the root end pointed at the center of the wagon, straight at the place where Faith was sitting, her baby on the verge of birth. Alvin couldn't think of anything to do, couldn't think at all, just screamed his wife's name with all his strength. Maybe in his heart he thought that by holding her name on his lips he could keep her alive, but there was no hope of that, no hope at all.

Except that Vigor didn't know there was no hope. Vigor leapt out when the tree was no more than a rod away, his body falling against it just above the root. The momentum of his leap turned it a little, then rolled it over, rolled it and turned it away from the wagon. Of course Vigor rolled with it, pulled right under the water—but it worked, the root end of the tree missed the wagon entirely, and the shaft of the trunk struck it a sidewise blow.

The tree bounded across the stream and smashed up against a boulder on the bank. Alvin was five rods off, but in his memory from then on, he always saw it like as if he'd been right there. The tree crashing into the boulder, and Vigor between them. Just a split second that lasted a lifetime, Vigor's eyes wide with surprise, blood already leaping out of his mouth, spattering out onto the tree that killed him. Then the Hatrack River swept the tree out into the current. Vigor slipped under the water, all except his arm, all tangled in the roots, which stuck up into the air for all the world like a neighbor waving good-bye after a visit.

Alvin was so intent on watching his dying son that he didn't even notice what was happening to his own self. The blow from the tree was enough to dislodge the mired wheels, and the current picked up the wagon, carried it downstream, Alvin clinging to the tailgate, Faith weeping inside, Eleanor screaming her lungs out from the driver's seat, and the boys on the bank shouting something. Shouting, "Hold! Hold! Hold!"

The rope held, one end tied to a strong tree, the other end tied to the wagon, it held. The river couldn't tumble the wagon downstream; instead it swung the wagon in to shore the way a boy swings a rock on a string, and when it came to a shuddering stop it was right against the bank, the front end facing upstream.

"It held!" cried the boys.

"Thank God!" shouted Eleanor.

"The baby's coming," whispered Faith.

But Alvin, all he could hear was the single faint cry that had been the last sound from the throat of his firstborn son, all he could see was the way his boy clung to the tree as it rolled and rolled in the water, and all he could say was a single word, a single command. "Live," he murmured. Vigor had always obeyed him before. Hard worker, willing companion, more a friend or brother than a son. But this time he knew his son would disobey. Still he whispered it. "Live."

"Are we safe?" said Faith, her voice trembling.

Alvin turned to face her, tried to strike the grief from his face. No sense her knowing the price that Vigor paid to save her and the baby. Time enough to learn of that after the baby was born. "Can you climb out of the wagon?"

"What's wrong?" asked Faith, looking at his face.

"I took a fright. Tree could have killed us. Can you climb out, now that we're up against the bank?"

Eleanor leaned in from the front of the wagon. "David and Calm are on the bank, they can help you up. The rope's holding, Mama, but who can say how long?"

"Go on, Mother, just a step," said Alvin. "We'll do better with the wagon if we know you're safe on shore."

"The baby's coming," said Faith.

"Better on shore than here," said Alvin sharply. "Go *now*."

Faith stood up, clambered awkwardly to the front. Alvin climbed through the wagon behind her, to help her if she should stumble. Even he could see how her belly had dropped. The baby must be grabbing for air already.

On the bank it wasn't just David and Calm, now. There were strangers, big men, and several horses. Even one small wagon, and that was a welcome sight. Alvin had no notion who these men were, or how they knew to come and help, but there wasn't a moment to waste on introductions. "You men! Is there a midwife in the road house?"

"Goody Guester does with birthing," said a man. A big man, with arms like oxlegs. A blacksmith, surely.

"Can you take my wife in that wagon? There's not a moment to spare." Alvin knew it was a shameful thing, for men to speak so openly of birthing, right in front of the woman who was set to bear. But Faith was no fool—she knew what mattered most, and getting her to a bed and a competent midwife was more important than pussyfooting around about it.

David and Calm were careful as they helped their mother toward the waiting wagon. Faith was staggering with pain. Women in labor shouldn't have to step from a wagon seat up onto a riverbank, that was sure. Eleanor was right behind her, taking charge as if she wasn't younger than all the boys except the twins. "Measure! Get the girls together. They're riding in the wagon with us. You too, Wastenot and Wantnot! I know you can help the big boys but I need you to watch the girls while I'm with Mother." Eleanor was never one to be trifled with, and the gravity of the situation was such that they didn't even call her Eleanor of Aquitaine as they obeyed. Even the little girls mostly gave over their squabbling and got right on.

Eleanor paused a moment on the bank and looked back to where her father stood on the wagon seat. She glanced downstream, then looked back at him. Alvin understood the question, and he shook his head no. Faith was not to know of Vigor's sacrifice. Tears came unwelcome to Alvin's eyes, but not to Eleanor's. Eleanor was only fourteen, but when she didn't want to cry, she didn't cry.

Wastenot hawed the horse and the little wagon lurched forward, Faith wincing as the girls patted her and the rain poured. Faith's gaze was somber as a cow's, and as mindless, looking back at her husband, back at the river. At times like birthing, Alvin thought, a woman becomes a beast, slack-minded as her body takes over and does its work. How else could she bear the pain? As if the soul of the earth possessed her the way it owns the souls of animals, making her part of the life of the whole world, unhitching her from family, from husband, from all the reins of the human race, leading her into the valley of ripeness and harvest and reaping and bloody death.

"She'll be safe now," the blacksmith said. "And we have horses here to pull your wagon out."

"It's slacking off," said Measure. "The rain is less, and the current's not so strong."

"As soon as your wife stepped ashore, it eased up," said the farmer-looking feller. "The rain's dying, that's sure."

"You took the worst of it in the water," said the blacksmith. "But you're all right now. Get hold of yourself, man, there's work to do."

Only then did Alvin come to himself enough to realize that he was crying. Work to do, that's right, get hold of yourself, Alvin Miller. You're no weakling, to bawl like a baby. Other men have lost a dozen children and still live their lives. You've had twelve, and Vigor lived to be a man, though he never did get to marry and have children of his own. Maybe Alvin had to weep because Vigor died so nobly; maybe he cried because it was so sudden.

David touched the blacksmith's arm. "Leave him be for a minute," he said softly. "Our oldest brother was carried off not ten minutes back. He got tangled in a tree floating down."

"It wasn't no *tangle*," Alvin said sharply. "He jumped that tree and saved our wagon, and your mother inside it! That river paid him back, that's what it did, it punished him."

Calm spoke quietly to the local men. "It run him up against that boulder there." They all looked. There wasn't even a smear of blood on the rock, it seemed so innocent.

"The Hatrack has a mean streak in it," said the blacksmith, "but I never seen this river so riled up before. I'm sorry about your boy. There's a slow, flat place downstream where he's bound to fetch up. Everything the river catches ends up there. When the storm lets up, we can go down and bring back the—bring him back."

Alvin wiped his eyes on his sleeve, but since his sleeve was soaking wet it didn't do much good. "Give me a minute more and I can pull my weight," said Alvin.

They hitched two more horses and the four beasts had no trouble pulling the wagon out against the much weakened current. By the time the wagon was set to rights again on the road, the sun was even breaking through.

"Wouldn't you know," said the blacksmith. "If you ever don't like the weather hereabouts, you just set a spell, cause it'll change."

"Not this one," said Alvin. "This storm was laid in wait for us."

The blacksmith put his arm across Alvin's shoulder and spoke real gentle. "No offense, mister, but that's crazy talk."

Alvin shrugged him off. "That storm and that river wanted us."

"Papa," said David, "you're tired and grieving. Best be still till we get to the road house and see how Mama is."

"My baby is a boy," said Papa. "You'll see. He would have been the seventh son of a seventh son."

That got their attention, right enough, that blacksmith and the other men as well. Everybody knew a seventh son had certain gifts, but the seventh son of a seventh son was about as powerful a birth as you could have.

"That makes a difference," said the blacksmith. "He'd have been a born dowser, sure, and water hates that." The others nodded sagely.

"The water had its way," said Alvin. "Had its way, and all done. It would've killed Faith and the baby, if it could. But since it couldn't, why, it killed my boy Vigor. And now when the baby comes, he'll be the sixth son, cause I'll only have five living."

"Some says it makes no difference if the first six be alive or not," said a farmer.

Alvin said nothing, but he knew it made all the difference. He had thought this baby would be a miracle child, but the river had taken care of that. If water don't stop you one way, it stops you another. He shouldn't have hoped for a miracle child. The cost was too high. All his eyes could see, all the way home, was Vigor dangling in the grasp of the roots, tumbling through the current like a leaf caught up in a dust devil, with the blood seeping from his mouth to slake the Hatrack's murderous thirst.

5

Caul

Little Peggy stood in the window, looking out into the storm. She could see all those heartfires, especially one, one so bright it was like the sun when she looked at it. But there was a blackness all around them. No, not even black—a nothingness, like a part of the universe God hadn't finished making, and it swept around those lights as if to tear them from each other, sweep them away, swallow them up. Little Peggy knew what that nothingness was. Those times when her eyes saw the hot yellow heartfires, there were three other colors, too. The rich dark orange of the earth. The thin grey color of the air. And the deep black emptiness of water. It was the water that tore at them now. The river, only she had never seen it so black, so strong, so terrible. The heartfires were so tiny in the night.

"What do you see, child?" asked Oldpappy.

"The river's going to carry them away," said little Peggy.

"I hope not."

Little Peggy began to cry.

"There, child," said Oldpappy. "It ain't always such a grand thing to see afar off like that, is it."

She shook her head.

"But maybe it won't happen as bad as you think."

Just at that moment, she saw one of the heartfires break away and tumble off into the dark. "Oh!" she cried out, reaching as if her hand could snatch the light and put it back. But of course she couldn't. Her vision was long and clear, but her reach was short.

"Are they lost?" asked Oldpappy.

"One," whispered little Peggy.

"Haven't Makepeace and the others got there yet?"

"Just now," she said. "The rope held. They're safe now."

Oldpappy didn't ask her how she knew, or what she saw. Just patted her shoulder. "Because you told them. Remember that, Margaret. One was lost, but if you hadn't seen and sent help, they might all have died."

She shook her head. "I should've seen them sooner, Oldpappy, but I fell asleep."

"And you blame yourself?" asked Oldpappy.

"I should've let Bloody Mary nip me, and then Father wouldn't've been mad, and then I wouldn't've been in the spring house, and then I wouldn't've been asleep, and then I would've sent help in time—"

"We can all make daisy chains of blame like that, Maggie. It don't mean a thing."

But she knew it meant something. You don't blame blind people cause they don't warn you you're about to step on a snake—but you sure blame somebody with eyes who doesn't say a word about it. She knew her duty ever since she first realized that other folks couldn't see all that she could see. God gave her special eyes, so she'd better see and give warning, or the devil would take her soul. The devil or the deep black sea.

"Don't mean a thing," Oldpappy murmured. Then, like he just been poked in the behind with a ramrod, he went all straight and said, "Spring house! Spring house, of course." He pulled her close. "Listen to me, little Peggy. It wasn't none of your fault, and that's the truth. The same water that runs in the Hatrack flows in the spring house brook, it's all the same water, all through the world. The same water that wanted them dead, it knew you could give warning and send help. So it sang to you and sent you off to sleep."

It made a kind of sense to her, it sure did. "How can that be, Old-pappy?"

"Oh, that's just in the nature of it. The whole universe is made of only four kinds of stuff, little Peggy, and each one wants to have its own way." Peggy thought of the four colors that she saw when the heartfires glowed, and she knew what all four were even as Oldpappy named them. "Fire makes things hot and bright and uses them up. Air makes things cool and sneaks in everywhere. Earth makes things solid and sturdy, so they'll last. But water, it tears things down, it falls from the sky and carries off everything it can, carries it off and down to the sea. If the water had its way, the whole world would be smooth, just a big ocean with nothing out of the water's reach. All dead and smooth. That's why you slept. The water wants to tear down these strangers, whoever they are, tear them down and kill them. It's a miracle you woke up at all."

"The blacksmith's hammer woke me," said little Peggy.

"That's it, then, you see? The blacksmith was working with iron, the hardest earth, and with a fierce blast of air from the bellows, and with a fire so hot it burns the grass outside the chimney. The water couldn't touch him to keep him still."

Little Peggy could hardly believe it, but it must be so. The blacksmith had drawn her from a watery sleep. The smith had *helped* her. Why, it was enough to make you laugh, to know the blacksmith was her friend this time.

There was shouting on the porch downstairs, and doors opened and closed. "Some folks is here already," said Oldpappy.

Little Peggy saw the heartfires downstairs, and found the one with the strongest fear and pain. "It's their mama," said little Peggy. "She's got a baby coming."

"Well, if that ain't the luck of it. Lose one, and here already is a baby to replace death with life." Oldpappy shambled on out to go downstairs and help.

Little Peggy, though, she just stood there, looking at what she saw in the distance. That lost heartfire wasn't lost at all, and that was sure. She could see it burning away far off, despite how the darkness of the river tried to cover it. He wasn't dead, just carried off, and maybe somebody could help him. She ran out then, passed Oldpappy all in a rush, clattered down the stairs.

Mama caught her by the arm as she was running into the great room. "There's a birthing," Mama said, "and we need you."

"But Mama, the one that went downriver, he's still alive!"

"Peggy, we got no time for—"

Two boys with the same face pushed their way into the conversation. "The one downriver!" cried one.

"Still alive!" cried the other.

"How do you know!"

"He can't be!"

They spoke so all on top of each other that Mama had to hush them up just to hear them. "It was Vigor, our big brother, he got swept away—"

"Well he's alive," said little Peggy, "but the river's got him."

The twins looked to Mama for confirmation. "She know what she's talking about, Goody Guester?"

Mama nodded, and the boys raced for the door, shouting, "He's alive! He's still alive!"

"Are you sure?" asked Mama fiercely. "It's a cruel thing, to put hope in their hearts like that, if it ain't so."

Mama's flashing eyes made little Peggy afraid, and she couldn't think what to say.

By then, though, Oldpappy had come up from behind. "Now Peg," he said, "how would she know one was taken by the river, lessun she saw?"

"I know," said Mama. "But this woman's been holding off birth too long, and I got a care for the baby, so come on now, little Peggy, I need you to tell me what you see."

She led little Peggy into the bedroom off the kitchen, the place where Papa and Mama slept whenever there were visitors. The woman lay on the bed, holding tight to the hand of a tall girl with deep and solemn eyes. Little Peggy didn't know their faces, but she recognized their fires, especially the mother's pain and fear.

"Someone was shouting," whispered the mother.

"Hush now," said Mama.

"About him still alive."

The solemn girl raised her eyebrows, looked at Mama. "Is that so, Goody Guester?"

"My daughter is a torch. That's why I brung her here in this room. To see the baby."

"Did she see my boy? Is he alive?"

"I thought you didn't tell her, Eleanor," said Mama.

The solemn girl shook her head.

"Saw from the wagon. Is he alive?"

"Tell her, Margaret," said Mama.

Little Peggy turned and looked for his heartfire. There were no walls when it came to this kind of seeing. His flame was still there, though she knew it was afar off. This time, though, she drew near in the way she had, took a close look. "He's in the water. He's all tangled in the roots."

"Vigor!" cried the mother on the bed.

"The river wants him. The river says, Die, die."

Mama touched the woman's arm. "The twins have gone off to tell the others. There'll be a search party."

"In the dark!" whispered the woman scornfully.

Little Peggy spoke again. "He's saying a prayer, I think. He's saying—seventh son."

"Seventh son," whispered Eleanor.

"What does that mean?" asked Mama.

"If this baby's a boy," said Eleanor, "and he's born while Vigor's still alive, then he's the seventh son of a seventh son, and all of them alive."

Mama gasped. "No wonder the river—" she said. No need to finish the thought. Instead she took little Peggy's hands and led her to the woman on the bed. "Look at this baby, and see what you see."

Little Peggy had done this before, of course. It was the chief use they had for torches, to have them look at an unborn baby just at the birthing time. Partly to see how it lay in the womb, but also because sometimes a torch could see who the baby was, what it would be, could tell stories of times to come. Even before she touched the woman's belly, she could see the baby's heartfire. It was the one that she had seen before, that burned so hot and bright that it was like the sun and the moon, to compare it to the mother's fire. "It's a boy," she said.

"Then let me bear this baby," said the mother. "Let him breathe while Vigor still breathes!"

"How's the baby set?" asked Mama.

"Just right," said little Peggy.

"Head first? Face down?"

Little Peggy nodded.

"Then why won't it come?" demanded Mama.

"She's been telling him not to," said little Peggy, looking at the mother.

"In the wagon," the mother said. "He was coming, and I did a beseeching."

"Well you should have told me right off," said Mama sharply. "Speck me to help you and you don't even tell me he's got a beseeching on him. You, girl!"

Several young ones were standing near the wall, wide-eyed, and they didn't know which one she meant.

"Any of you, I need that iron key from the ring on the wall."

The biggest of them took it clumsily from the hook and brought it, ring and all.

Mama dangled the large ring and the key over the mother's belly, chanting softly:

> *"Here's the circle, open wide,*
> *Here's the key to get outside,*
> *Earth be iron, flame be fair,*
> *Fall from water into air."*

The mother cried out in sudden agony. Mama tossed away the key, cast back the sheet, lifted the woman's knees, and ordered little Peggy fiercely to *see*.

Little Peggy touched the woman's womb. The boy's mind was empty, except for a feeling of pressure and gathering cold as he emerged into the air. But the very emptiness of his mind let her see things that would never be plainly visible again. The billion billion paths of his life lay open before him, waiting for his first choices, for the first changes in the world around him to eliminate a million futures every second. The future was there in everyone, a flickering shadow that she could only sometimes see, and never clearly, looking through the thoughts of the present moment; but here, for a few precious moments, little Peggy could see them sharp.

And what she saw was death down every path. Drowning, drowning, every path of his future led this child to a watery death.

"Why do you hate him so!" cried little Peggy.

"What?" demanded Eleanor.

"Hush," said Mama. "Let her see what she sees."

Inside the unborn child, the dark blot of water that surrounded his heartfire seemed so terribly strong that little Peggy was afraid he would be swallowed up.

"Get him out to breathe!" shouted little Peggy.

Mama reached in, even though it tore the mother something dreadful, and hooked the baby by the neck with strong fingers, drawing him out.

In that moment, as the dark water retreated inside the child's mind, and just before the first breath came, little Peggy saw ten million deaths by water disappear. Now, for the first time, there were some paths open, some paths leading to a dazzling future. And all the paths that did not end in early death had one thing in common. On all those paths, little Peggy saw herself doing one simple thing.

So she did that thing. She took her hands from the slackening belly and ducked under her mother's arm. The baby's head had just emerged, and it was still covered with a bloody caul, a scrap of the sac of soft skin in which he had floated in his mother's womb. His mouth was open, sucking inward on the caul, but it didn't break, and he couldn't breathe.

Little Peggy did what she had seen herself do in the baby's future. She reached out, took the caul from under the baby's chin, and pulled it away from his face. It came whole, in one moist piece, and in the moment it came away, the baby's mouth cleared, he sucked in a great breath, and then gave that mewling cry that birthing mothers hear as the song of life.

Little Peggy folded the caul, her mind still full of the visions she had seen down the pathways of this baby's life. She did not know yet what the visions meant, but they made such clear pictures in her mind that she knew she would never forget them. They made her afraid, because

so much would depend on her, and how she used the birth caul that
was still warm in her hands.

"A boy," said Mama.

"Is he," whispered the mother. "Seventh son?"

Mama was tying the cord, so she couldn't spare a glance at little
Peggy. "Look," she whispered.

Little Peggy looked for the single heartfire on the distant river.
"Yes," she said, for the heartfire was still burning.

Even as she watched, it flickered, died.

"Now he's gone," said little Peggy.

The woman on the bed wept bitterly, her birthwracked body shuddering.

"Grieving at the baby's birth," said Mama. "It's a dreadful thing."

"Hush," whispered Eleanor to her mother. "Be joyous, or it'll darken
the baby all his life!"

"Vigor," murmured the woman.

"Better nothing at all than tears," said Mama. She held out the crying
baby, and Eleanor took it in competent arms—she had cradled many a
babe before, it was plain. Mama went to the table in the corner and took
the scarf that had been blacked in the wool, so it was night-colored clear
through. She dragged it slowly across the weeping woman's face, saying, "Sleep, Mother, sleep."

When the cloth came away, the weeping was done, and the woman
slept, her strength spent.

"Take the baby from the room," said Mama.

"Don't he need to start his sucking?" asked Eleanor.

"She'll never nurse this babe," said Mama. "Not unless you want
him to suck hate."

"She can't hate him," said Eleanor. "It ain't his fault."

"I reckon her milk don't know that," said Mama. "That right, little
Peggy? What teat does the baby suck?"

"His mama's," said little Peggy.

Mama looked sharp at her. "You sure of that?"

She nodded.

"Well, then, we'll bring the baby in when she wakes up. He doesn't
need to eat anything for the first night, anyway." So Eleanor carried
the baby out into the great room, where the fire burned to dry the men,
who stopped trading stories about rains and floods worse than this one
long enough to look at the baby and admire.

Inside the room, though, Mama took little Peggy by the chin and
stared hard into her eyes. "You tell me the truth, Margaret. It's a serious
thing, for a baby to suck on its mama and drink up hate."

"She won't hate him, Mama," said little Peggy.

"What did you see?"

Little Peggy would have answered, but she didn't know words to tell most of the things she saw. So she looked at the floor. She could tell from Mama's quick draw of breath that she was ripe for a tongue-lashing. But Mama waited, and then her hand came soft, stroking across little Peggy's cheek. "Ah, child, what a day you've had. The baby might have died, except you told me to pull it out. You even reached in and opened up its mouth—that's what you did, isn't it?"

Little Peggy nodded.

"Enough for a little girl, enough for one day." Mama turned to the other girls, the ones in wet dresses, leaning against the wall. "And you, too, you've had enough of a day. Come out of here, let your mama sleep, come out and get dry by the fire. I'll start a supper for you, I will."

But Oldpappy was already in the kitchen, fussing around, and refused to hear of Mama doing a thing. Soon enough she was out with the baby, shooing the men away so she could rock it to sleep, letting it suck her finger.

Little Peggy figured after a while that she wouldn't be missed, so she snuck up the stairs to the attic ladder and up the ladder into the lightless, musty space. The spiders didn't bother her much, and the cats mostly kept the mice away, so she wasn't afraid. She crawled right to her secret hiding place and took out the carven box that Oldpappy gave her, the one he said his own papa brought from Ulster when he came to the colonies. It was full of the precious scraps of childhood—stones, strings, buttons—but now she knew that these were nothing compared to the work before her all the rest of her life. She dumped them right out, and blew into the box to clear away the dust. Then she laid the folded caul inside and closed the lid.

She knew that in the future she would open that box a dozen dozen times. That it would call to her, wake her from her sleep, tear her from her friends, and steal from her all her dreams. All because a baby boy downstairs had no future at all but death from the dark water, excepting if she used that caul to keep him safe, the way it once protected him in the womb.

For a moment she was angry, to have her own life so changed. Worse than the blacksmith coming, it was, worse than Papa and the hazel wand he whupped her with, worse than Mama when her eyes were angry. Everything would be different forever and it wasn't fair. Just for a baby she never invited, never asked to come here, what did she care about any old baby?

She reached out and opened the box, planning to take the caul and cast it into a dark corner of the attic. But even in the darkness, she could see a place where it was darker still: near her heartfire, where the emptiness of the deep black river was all set to make a murderer out of her.

Not me, she said to the water. You ain't part of me.

Yes I am, whispered the water. I'm all through you, and you'd dry up and die without me.

You ain't the boss of me, anyway, she retorted.

She closed the lid on the box and skidded her way down the ladder. Papa always said that she'd get splinters in her butt doing that. This time he was right. It stung something fierce, so she walked kind of sideways into the kitchen where Oldpappy was. Sure enough, he stopped his cooking long enough to pry the splinters out.

"My eyes ain't sharp enough for this, Maggie," he complained.

"You got the eyes of an eagle. Papa says so."

Oldpappy chuckled. "Does he now."

"What's for dinner?"

"Oh, you'll like this dinner, Maggie."

Little Peggy wrinkled up her nose. "Smells like chicken."

"That's right."

"I don't like chicken soup."

"Not just soup, Maggie. This one's a-roasting, except the neck and wings."

"I hate *roast* chicken, too."

"Does your Oldpappy ever lie to you?"

"Nope."

"Then you best believe me when I tell you this is one chicken dinner that'll make you *glad*. Can't you think of any way that a partickler chicken dinner could make you glad?"

Little Peggy thought and thought, and then she smiled. "Bloody Mary?"

Oldpappy winked. "I always said that was a hen born to make gravy."

Little Peggy hugged him so tight that he made choking sounds, and then they laughed and laughed.

Later that night, long after little Peggy was in bed, they brought Vigor's body home, and Papa and Makepeace set to making a box for him. Alvin Miller hardly looked alive, even when Eleanor showed him the baby. Until she said, "That torch girl. She says that this baby is the seventh son of a seventh son."

Alvin looked around for someone to tell him if it was true.

"Oh, you can trust her," said Mama.

Tears came fresh to Alvin's eyes. "That boy hung on," he said. "There in the water, he hung on long enough."

"He knowed what store you set by that," said Eleanor.

Then Alvin reached for the baby, held him tight, looked down into his eyes. "Nobody named him yet, did they?" he asked.

"Course not," said Eleanor. "Mama named all the other boys, but you always said the seventh son'd have—"

"My own name. Alvin. Seventh son of a seventh son, with the same name as his father. Alvin Junior." He looked around him, then turned to face toward the river, way off in the nighttime forest. "Hear that, you Hatrack River? His name is Alvin, and you didn't kill him after all."

Soon they brought in the box and laid out Vigor's body with candles, to stand for the fire of life that had left him. Alvin held up the baby, over the coffin. "Look on your brother," he whispered to the infant.

"That baby can't see nothing yet, Papa," said David.

"That ain't so, David," said Alvin. "He don't *know* what he's seeing, but his eyes can see. And when he gets old enough to hear the story of his birth, I'm going to tell him that his own eyes saw his brother Vigor, who gave his life for this baby's sake."

It was two weeks before Faith was well enough to travel. But Alvin saw to it that he and his boys worked hard for their keep. They cleared a good spot of land, chopped the winter's firewood, set some charcoal heaps for Makepeace Smith, and widened the road. They also felled four big trees and made a strong bridge across the Hatrack River, a covered bridge so that even in a rainstorm people could cross that river without a drop of water touching them.

Vigor's grave was the third one there, beside little Peggy's two dead sisters. The family paid respects and prayed there on the morning that they left. Then they got in their wagon and rode off westward. "But we leave a part of ourselves here always," said Faith, and Alvin nodded.

Little Peggy watched them go, then ran up into the attic, opened the box, and held little Alvin's caul in her hand. No danger—for now, at least. Safe for now. She put the caul away and closed the lid. You better be something, baby Alvin, she said, or else you caused a powerful lot of trouble for nothing.

6

Ridgebeam

Axes rang, strong men sang hymns at their labor, and Reverend Philadelphia Thrower's new church building rose tall over the meadow commons of Vigor Township. It was all happening so much faster than
Reverend Thrower ever expected. The first wall of the meetinghouse
had hardly been erected a day or so ago, when that drunken one-eyed
Red wandered in and was baptized, as if the mere sight of the church-
house had been the fulcrum on which he could be levered upward to
civilization and Christianity. If a Red as benighted as Lolla-Wossiky
could come unto Jesus, what other miracles of conversion might not be
wrought in this wilderness when his meetinghouse was finished and his
ministry firmly under way?

Reverend Thrower was not altogether happy, however, for there were
enemies of civilization far stronger than the barbarity of the heathen
Reds, and the signs were not all so hopeful as when Lolla-Wossiky
donned White man's clothing for the first time. In particular what somewhat darkened this bright day was the fact that Alvin Miller was not
among the workers. And his wife's excuses for him had run out. The
trip to find a proper millstone quarry had ended, he had rested for a
day, and by rights he should be here.

"What, is he ill?" asked Thrower.

Faith tightened her lips. "When I say he *won't* come, Reverend
Thrower, it's not to say he *can't* come."

It confirmed Thrower's gathering suspicions. "Have I offended him
somewise?"

Faith sighed and looked away from him, toward the posts and beams
of the meetinghouse. "Not you yourself, sir, not the way a man treads

on another, as they say.'' Abruptly she became alert. ''Now what is that?''

Right up against the building, most of the men were tying ropes to the north half of the ridgebeam, so they could lift it into place. It was a tricky job, and all the harder because of the little boys wrestling each other in the dust and getting underfoot. It was the wrestlers that had caught her eye. ''Al!'' cried Faith. ''Alvin Junior, you let him up this minute!'' She took two strides toward the cloud of dust that marked the heroic struggles of the six-year-olds.

Reverend Thrower was not inclined to let her end the conversation so easily. ''Mistress Faith,'' said Reverend Thrower sharply. ''Alvin Miller is the first settler in these parts, and people hold him in high regard. If he's against me for some reason, it will greatly harm my ministry. At least you can tell me what I did to give offense.''

Faith looked him in the eye, as if to calculate whether he could stand to hear the truth. ''It was your foolish sermon, sir,'' she said.

''Foolish?''

''You couldn't know any better, being from England, and—''

''From Scotland, Mistress Faith.''

''And being how you're educated in schools where they don't know much about—''

''The University of Edinburgh! Don't know much indeed, I—''

''About hexes and doodles and charms and beseechings and suchlike.''

''I know that claiming to use such dark and invisible powers is a burning offense in the lands that obey the Lord Protector, Mistress Faith, though in his mercy he merely banishes those who—''

''Well looky there, that's my point,'' she said triumphantly. ''They're not likely to teach you about that in university, now, are they? But it's the way we live here, and calling it a superstition—''

''I called it hysteria—''

''That don't change the fact that it works.''

''I understand that you *believe* that it works,'' said Thrower patiently. ''But everything in the world is either science or miracles. Miracles came from God in ancient times, but those times are over. Today if we wish to change the world, it is not magic but science that will give us our tools.''

From the set of her face, Thrower could see that he wasn't making much impression on her.

''Science,'' she said. ''Like feeling head bumps?''

He doubted she had tried very hard to hide her scorn. ''Phrenology is an infant science," he said coldly, "and there are many flaws, but I am seeking to discover—"

She laughed—a girlish laugh, that made her seem much younger than a woman who had borne fourteen children. "Sorry, Reverend Thrower, but I just remembered how Measure called it 'dowsing for brains,' and he allowed as how you'd have slim luck in these parts."

True words, thought Reverend Thrower, but he was wise enough not to say so. "Mistress Faith, I spoke as I did to let people understand that there are superior ways of thought in the world today, and we need no longer be bound by the delusions of—"

It was no use. Her patience had quite run out. "My boy looks about to get himself smacked with a spare joist if he don't let up on them other boys, Reverend, so you'll just have to excuse me." And off she went, to fall on six-year-old Alvin and three-year-old Calvin like the vengeance of the Lord. She was a champion tongue-lasher. He could hear the scolding from where he stood, and that with the breeze blowing the other way, too.

Such ignorance, said Thrower to himself. I am needed here, not only as a man of God among near heathens, but also as a man of science among superstitious fools. Somebody whispers a curse and then, six months later, something bad happens to the person cursed—it always does, something bad happens to everybody at least twice a year—and it makes them quite certain that their curse had malefic effect. Post hoc ergo propter hoc.

In Britain, students learned to discard such elementary logic errors while yet studying the trivium. Here it was a way of life. The Lord Protector was quite right to punish practitioners of magic arts in Britain, though Thrower would prefer that he do it on grounds of stupidity rather than heresy. Treating it as heresy gave it too much dignity, as if it were something to be feared rather than despised.

Three years ago, right after he earned his Doctor of Divinity degree, it had dawned on Thrower what harm the Lord Protector was actually doing. He remembered it as the turning point of his life; wasn't it also the first time the Visitor had come to him? It was in his small room in the rectory of St. James Church in Belfast, where he was junior assistant pastor, his first assignment after ordination. He was looking at a map of the world when his eye strayed to America, to where Pennsylvania was clearly marked, stretching from the Dutch and Swedish colonies westward until the lines faded in the obscure country beyond the Mizzipy. It was as if the map then came alive, and he saw the flood of people arriving in the New World. Good Puritans, loyal churchmen, and sound businessmen all went to New England; Papists, Royalists, and scoundrels all went to the rebellious slave country of Virginia, Carolina, and Jacobia, the so-called Crown Colonies. The sort of people who, once they found their place, stayed in it forever.

But it was another kind of people went to Pennsylvania. Germans, Dutchmen, Swedes, and Huguenots fled their countries and turned Pennsylvania Colony into a slop pot, filled with the worst human rubbish of the continent. Worse yet, they would *not* stay put. These dimwitted country people would debark in Philadelphia, discover that the settled— Thrower did not call them ''civilized''—portions of Pennsylvania were too crowded for them, and immediately head westward into the Red country to hew out a farm among the trees. Never mind that the Lord Protector specifically forbade them to settle there. What did such pagans care for law? Land was what they wanted, as if the mere ownership of dirt could turn a peasant into a squire.

Then Thrower's vision of America turned from bleak to black indeed. He saw that war was coming to America with the new century. In his vision, he foresaw that the King of France would send that obnoxious Corsican colonel, Bonaparte, to Canada, and his people would stir up the Reds from the French fortress town in Detroit. The Reds would fall upon the settlers and destroy them; scum they might be, but they were mostly English scum, and the vision of the Reds' savagery made Thrower's skin crawl.

Yet even if the English won, the overall result would be the same. America west of the Appalachees would never be a Christian land. Either the damned Papist French and Spanish would have it, or the equally damned heathen Reds would keep it, or else the most depraved sort of Englishmen would thrive and thumb their noses at Christ and the Lord Protector alike. Another whole continent would be lost to the knowledge of the Lord Jesus. It was such a fearsome vision that Thrower cried out, thinking none would hear him in the confines of his little room.

But someone did hear him. ''There's a life's work for a man of God,'' said someone behind him. Thrower turned at once, startled; but the voice was gentle and warm, the face old and kindly, and Thrower was not afraid for more than a moment, despite the fact that the door and window were both locked tight, and no natural man could have come inside his little room.

Thinking that this man was surely a part of the manifestation he had just seen, Thrower addressed him reverently. ''Sir, whoever you are, I have seen the future of North America, and it looks like the victory of the devil to me.''

''The devil takes his victories,'' the man replied, ''wherever men of God lose heart, and leave the field to him.''

Then the man simply was not there.

Thrower had known in that moment what the work of his life would be. To come to the wilds of America, build a country church, and fight the devil in his own country. It had taken him three years to get the money and the permission of his superiors in the Scottish Church, but now he was here, the posts and beams of his church were rising, their white and naked wood a bright rebuke to the dark forest of barbarism from which they had been hewn.

Of course, with such a magnificent work under way, the devil was bound to take notice. And it was obvious that the devil's chief disciple in Vigor Township was Alvin Miller. Even though all his sons were here, helping to build the churchhouse, Thrower knew that this was Faith's doing. The woman had even allowed as how she was probably Church of Scotland in her heart, even though she was born in Massachusetts; her membership would mean that Thrower could look forward to having a congregation—provided Alvin Miller could be kept from wrecking everything.

And wreck it he would. It was one thing if Alvin had been offended by something Thrower had inadvertently said and done. But to have the quarrel be about belief in sorcery, right from the start—well, there was no hiding from this conflict. The battle lines were laid. Thrower stood on the side of science and Christianity, and on the other side stood all the powers of darkness and superstition; the bestial, carnal nature of man was on the other side, with Alvin Miller as its champion. I am only at the beginning of my tournament for the Lord, thought Thrower. If I can't vanquish this first opponent, then no victory will ever be possible for me.

"Pastor Thrower!" shouted Alvin's oldest boy, David. "We're ready to raise the ridgebeam!"

Thrower started toward them at a trot, then remembered his dignity and walked the rest of the way. There was nothing in the gospels to imply that the Lord ever ran—only walked, as befitted his high station. Of course, Paul had his comments about running a good race, but that was allegory. A minister was supposed to be a shadow of Jesus Christ, walking in His way and representing Him to the people. It was the closest these people would ever come to beholding the majesty of God. It was Reverend Thrower's duty to deny the vitality of his youth and walk at the reverent pace of an old man, though he was only twenty-four.

"You mean to bless the ridgebeam, don't you?" asked one of the farmers. It was Ole, a Swedish fellow from the banks of the Delaware, and so a Lutheran at heart; but he was willing enough to help build a

Presbyterian Church here in the Wobbish valley, seeing how the nearest church besides that was the Papist Cathedral in Detroit.

"I do indeed," said Thrower. He laid his hand on the heavy, axe-hewn beam.

"Reverend Thrower." It was a child's voice behind him, piercing and loud as only a child's voice can be. "Ain't it a kind of a charm, to give a blessing to a piece of wood?"

Thrower turned around to see Faith Miller already hushing the boy. Only six years old, but Alvin Junior was obviously going to grow up to be just as much trouble as his father. Maybe more—Alvin Senior had at least had the good grace to stay away from the church-raising.

"You go on," said Faith. "Never mind him. I haven't learned him yet when to speak and when to keep silence."

Even though his mother's hand was tight-clamped over his mouth, the boy's eyes were steady, looking right at him. And when Thrower turned back around, he found that all the grown men were looking at him expectantly. The child's question was a challenge that he had to answer, or he'd be branded a hypocrite or fool before the very men he had come to convert.

"I suppose that if you think my blessing actually does something to change the nature of the ridgebeam," he said, "that might be akin to ensorcelment. But the truth is that the ridgebeam itself is just the *occasion*. Whom I'm really blessing is the congregation of Christians who'll gather under this roof. And there's nothing magic about that. It's the power and love of God we're asking for, not a cure for warts or a charm against the evil eye."

"Too bad," murmured a man. "I could use a cure for warts."

They all laughed, but the danger was over. When the ridgebeam went up, it would be a Christian act to raise it, not a pagan one.

He blessed the ridgebeam, taking care to change the usual prayer to one that specifically did *not* confer any special properties upon the beam itself. Then the men tugged on the rope, and Thrower sang out "O Lord Who on the Mighty Sea" at the top of his magnificent baritone voice, to give them the rhythm and inspiration for their labors.

All the time, however, he was acutely aware of the boy Alvin Junior. It was not just because of the boy's embarrassing challenge a moment ago. The child was as simple-minded as most children—Thrower doubted he had any dire purpose in mind. What drew him to the child was something else entirely. Not any property in the boy himself, but rather something about the people near him. They always seemed to keep him in attention. Not that they always *looked* at him—that would be a full-time occupation, he ran about so much. It was as if they were always aware of him, the way the college cook had always been aware of the dog in the kitchen, never speaking to it, but stepping over and around it without so much as pausing in his work.

It wasn't just the boy's family, either, that was so careful of him. Everyone acted the same way—the Germans, the Scandinavians, the English, newcomers and old-times alike. As if the raising of this boy were a community project, like the raising of a church or the bridging of a river.

"Easy, easy, easy!" shouted Wastenot, who was perched near the east ridgepole to guide the heavy beam into place. It had to be just so, for the rafters to lean evenly against it and make a sturdy roof.

"Too far your way!" shouted Measure. He was standing on scaffolding above the crossbeam on which rested the short pole that would support the two ridgebeams where they butted ends in the middle. This was the most crucial point of the whole roof, and the trickiest to get right; they had to lay the ends of two heavy beams onto a pole top that was barely two palms wide. That was why Measure stood there, for he had grown into his name, keen-eyed and careful.

"Right!" shouted Measure. "More!"

"My way again!" shouted Wastenot.

"Steady!" shouted Measure.

"Set!" shouted Wastenot.

Then "Set!" from Measure, too, and the men on the ground relaxed the tension on the ropes. As the lines went slack, they let out a cheer, for the ridgebeam now went half the length of the church. It was no cathedral, but it was still a mighty thing to achieve in this benighted place, the largest structure anyone had dared to think of for a hundred miles around. The mere fact of building it was a declaration that the settlers were here to stay, and not French, not Spanish, not Cavaliers, not Yankees, not even the savage Reds with their fire arrows, no man would get these folks to leave this place.

So of course Reverend Thrower went inside, and so did all the others, to see the sky blocked for the first time by a ridgebeam no less than forty feet in length—and that only half of what it would finally be. My church, thought Thrower, and already finer than most I saw in Philadelphia itself.

Up on the flimsy scaffolding, Measure was driving a wooden pin through the notch in the end of the ridgebeam and down into the hole in the top of the ridgepole. Wastenot was doing the same at his end, of course. The pins would hold the beam in place until the rafters could be laid. When that was done, the ridgebeam would be so strong that they could almost remove the crossbeam, if it weren't needed for the chandelier that would light the church at night. At night, so that the stained glass would shine out against the darkness. That's how grandiose a place Reverend Thrower had in mind. Let their simple minds stand in awe when they see this place, and so reflect upon the majesty of God.

Those were his thoughts when, suddenly, Measure let out a shout of fear, and all saw in horror that the center ridgepole had split and shivered at the blow of Measure's mallet against the wooden pin, bouncing the great heavy ridgebeam some six feet into the air. It pulled the beam out of Wastenot's hands at the other end, and broke the scaffolding like tinderwood. The ridgebeam seemed to hover in the air a moment, level as you please, then rushed downward as if the Lord's own foot were stomping it.

And Reverend Thrower knew without looking that there would be someone directly under that beam, right under the midpoint of it when it landed. He knew because he was *aware* of the boy, of how he was running just exactly the wrong direction, of how his own shout of "Alvin!" brought the boy to a stop in just exactly the wrong place.

And when he looked, it was exactly as he knew it would be—little Al standing there, looking up at the shaven tree that would grind him into the floor of the church. Nothing else would be damaged—because the beam was level, its impact would be spread across the whole floor. The boy was too small even to slow the ridgebeam's fall. He would be broken, crushed, his blood spattering the white wood of the church floor. I'll never get that stain out, thought Thrower—insanely, but one could not control one's own thoughts in the moment of death.

Thrower saw the impact as if it were a blinding flash of light. He heard the crash of wood on wood. He heard the screams. Then his eyes cleared and he saw the ridgebeam lying there, the one end exactly where it should be, the other too, but in the middle, the beam split in two parts, and between the two parts little Alvin standing, his face white with terror.

Untouched. The boy was untouched.

Thrower didn't understand German or Swedish, but he knew what the muttering near him meant, well enough. Let them blaspheme—I must understand what has happened here, thought Thrower. He strode to the boy, placed his hands on the child's head, searching for injury. Not a hair out of place, but the boy's head felt warm, very warm, as if he had been standing near a fire. Then Thrower knelt and looked at the wood of the ridgebeam. It was cut as smooth as if the wood had grown that way, just exactly wide enough to miss the boy entirely.

Al's mother was there only a moment later, scooping up her boy, sobbing and babbling with relief. Little Alvin also cried. But Thrower had other things on his mind. He *was* a man of science, after all, and what he had seen was not possible. He made the men step off the length of the ridgebeam, measuring it again. It lay exactly its original length along the floor—the east end just as far from the west end as it should be. The boy-sized chunk in the middle had simply disappeared. Vanished in a momentary flash of fire that left Alvin's head and the butt ends of the wood as hot as coals, yet not marked or seared in any way.

Then Measure began yelling from the crossbeam, where he dangled by his arms, having caught himself after the collapse of the scaffolding. Wantnot and Calm climbed up and got him down safely. Reverend Thrower had no thought for that. All he could think about was a six-year-old boy who could stand under a falling ridgebeam, and the beam would break and make room for him. Like the Red Sea parting for Moses, on the right hand and the left.

"Seventh son," murmured Wastenot. The boy sat astride the fallen ridgebeam, just west of the break.

"What?" asked Reverend Thrower.

"Nothing," said the young man.

"You said 'Seventh son,' " said Thrower. "But it's little Calvin who's the seventh."

Wastenot shook his head. "We had another brother. He died a couple minutes after Al was born." Wastenot shook his head again. "Seventh son of a seventh son."

"But that makes him devil's spawn," said Thrower, aghast.

Wastenot looked at him with contempt. "Maybe in England you think so, but around here we look on such to be a healer, maybe, or a doodlebug, and a right good one of whatever he is." Then Wastenot thought of something and grinned. " 'Devil's spawn,' " he repeated, maliciously savoring the words. "Sounds like hysteria to me."

Furious, Thrower stalked out of the church.

He found Mistress Faith sitting on a stool, holding Alvin Junior on her lap and rocking him as he continued to whimper. She was scolding him gently. "Told you not to run without looking, always underfoot, can't never hold still, makes a body go plumb lunatic looking after you—" Then she saw Thrower standing before her, and fell silent.

"Don't worry," she said. "I'll not bring him back here."

"For his safety, I'm glad," said Thrower. "If I thought my church-house had to be built at the cost of a child's life, I'd sooner preach in the open air all the days of my life."

She looked close at him and knew that he meant it with his whole heart. "It's no fault of yourn," she said. "He's always been a clumsy boy. Seems to live through scrapes that'd kill an ordinary child."

"I'd like—I'd like to understand what happened in there."

"Ridgepole shivered, of course," she said. "It happens sometimes."

"I mean—how it happened to miss him. The beam split—before it touched his head. I want to feel his head, if I may—"

"Not a mark on him," she said.

"I know. I want to feel it to see if—"

She rolled her eyes upward and muttered, "Dowsing for brains," but she also moved her hands away so he could feel the child's head. Slowly now, and carefully, trying to understand the map of the boy's skull, to read the ridges and bumps, the troughs and depressions. He had no need to consult a book. The books were nonsense, anyway. He had found that out quite quickly—they all spouted idiotic generalities, such as, "The Red will always have a bump just over the ear, indicating savagery and cannibalism," when of course Reds had just as much variety in their heads as Whites. No, Thrower had no faith in those books— but he *had* learned a few things about people with particular skills, and head bumps they had in common. He had developed a knack of understanding, a map of the shapes of the human skull; he knew as his hands passed over Al's head what it was he found there.

Nothing remarkable, that's what he found. No one trait that stood out above all others. Average. As average as can be. So utterly average that it could be a virtual textbook example of normality, if only there were any textbook worth reading.

He lifted his fingers away, and the boy—who had stopped crying under his hands—twisted on his mother's lap to look at him. "Reverend Thrower," he said, "your hands are so cold I like to froze." Then he squirmed off his mother's lap and ran off, shouting for one of the German boys, the one he had been wrestling so savagely before.

Faith laughed ruefully. "You see how quickly they forget?"

"And you, too," he said.

She shook her head. "Not me," she said. "I don't forget a thing."

"You're already smiling."

"I *go on*, Reverend Thrower. I just go on. That's not the same as forgetting."

He nodded.

"So—tell me what you found," she said.

"Found?"

"Feeling his bumps. Brain-dowsing. Does he got any?"

"Normal. Absolutely normal. Not a single thing unusual about his head."

She grunted. "*Nothing* unusual?"

"That's right."

"Well, if you ask me, that's pretty unusual right there, if a body was smart enough to notice it." She picked up the stool and carried it off, calling to Al and Cally as she went.

After a moment, Reverend Thrower realized she was right. Nobody was so perfectly average. Everybody had *some* trait that was stronger than the others. It wasn't normal for Al to be so well balanced. To have every possible skill that could be marked by the skull, and to have it in exactly even proportions. Far from being average, the child was extraordinary, though Thrower had no notion what it would mean in the child's life. Jack of all trades and master of none? Or master of all?

Superstition or not, Thrower found himself wondering. A seventh son of a seventh son, a startling shape to the head, and the miracle—he could think of no other word—of the ridgebeam. An ordinary child would have died this day. Natural law demanded it. But someone or something was protecting this child, and natural law had been overruled.

Once the talk had subsided, the men resumed work on the roof. The original beam was useless, of course, and they carried the two sections of it outside. After what had happened, they had no intention of using the beams for anything at all. Instead they set to work and completed another beam by midafternoon, rebuilt the scaffolding, and by nightfall the whole roof ridge was set in place. No one spoke of the incident with the ridgebeam, at least not in Thrower's presence. And when he went to look for the shivered ridgepole, he couldn't find it anywhere.

7

Altar

Alvin Junior wasn't scared when he saw the beam falling, and he wasn't scared when it crashed to the floor on either side. But when all the grown-ups started carrying on like the Day of Rapture, a-hugging him and talking in whispers, *then* he got scared. Grown-ups had a way of doing things for no reason at all.

Like the way Papa was setting on the floor by the fire, just studying the split pieces of the shivered ridgepole, the piece of wood that sprung under the weight of the ridge-beam and sent it all crashing down. When Mama was being herself, not Papa or nobody could bring big old pieces of split and dirty wood into her house. But today Mama was as crazy as Papa, and when he showed up toting them big old splinters of wood, she just bent over, rolled up the rug, and got herself out of Papa's way.

Well, anybody who didn't know to get out of Papa's way when he had that look on his face was too dumb to live. David and Calm was lucky, they could go off to their own houses on their own cleared land, where their own wives had their own suppers cooking and they could decide whether to be crazy or not. The rest of them weren't so lucky. With Papa and Mama being crazy, the rest of them had to be crazy, too. Not one of the girls fought with any of the others, and they all helped fix supper and clean up after without a word of complaint. Wastenot and Wantnot went out and chopped wood and did the evening milking without so much as punching each other in the arm, let alone getting in a wrestling match, which was right disappointing to Alvin Junior, seeing as how he always got to wrestle the loser, which was the best wrestling he ever got to do, them being eighteen years old and a real challenge, not like the boys he usually hunkered down with. And Measure, he just sat there by the fire, whittling out a big old spoon for

Mama's cooking pot, never so much as looking up—but he was waiting, just like the others, for Papa to come back to his right self and yell at somebody.

The only normal person in the house was Calvin, the three-year-old. The trouble was that normal for him meant tagging along after Alvin Junior like a kitten on a mouse's trail. He never came close enough to *play* with Alvin Junior, or to touch him or talk to him or anything useful. He was just there, always there at the edge of things, so Alvin would look up just as Calvin looked away, or catch a glimpse of his shirt as he ducked behind a door, or sometimes in the dark of night just hear a faint breathing that was closer than it ought to be, which told him Calvin wasn't lying on his cot, he was standing right there by Alvin's bed, *watching*. Nobody ever seemed to notice it. It had been more than a year since Alvin gave up trying to get him to stop. If Alvin Junior ever said, "Ma, Cally's pestering me," Mama would just say, "Al Junior, he didn't say a thing, he didn't touch you, and if you don't like him just standing quiet as a body could ask, well, that's just too bad for you, because it suits me fine. I wish certain other of my children could learn to be as still." Alvin figured that it wasn't that Calvin was *normal* today, it's that the rest of the family had just come up to his regular level of craziness.

Papa just stared and stared at the split wood. Now and then he'd fit it together the way it was. Once he spoke, real quiet. "Measure, you sure you got all them pieces?"

Measure said, "Ever single bit, Pa, I couldn't've got more with a broom. I couldn't've got more if I'd bent down and lapped it up like a dog."

Ma was listening, of course. Papa once said that when Ma was paying attention, she could hear a squirrel fart in the woods a half mile away in the middle of a storm with the girls rattling dishes and the boys all chopping wood. Alvin Junior wondered sometimes if that meant Ma knew more witchery than she let on, since one time he sat in the woods not three yards away from a squirrel for more than an hour, and he never heard it so much as belch.

Anyway, she was right there in the house tonight, so of course she heard what Papa asked, and she heard what Measure answered, and her being as crazy as Papa, she lashed out like as if Measure had just taken the name of the Lord. "You mind your tongue, young man, because the Lord said unto Moses on the mount, honor your father and mother that your days may be long on the land which the Lord your God has given you, and when you speak fresh to your father then you are taking days and weeks and even *years* off your own life, and your soul is not in such a condition that you should welcome an early visit to the judgment bar to meet your Savior and hear him say your eternal fate!''

Measure wasn't half so worried about his eternal fate as he was worried about Mama being riled at him. He didn't try to argue that he wasn't talking smart or being sassy—only a fool would do that when Mama was already hot. He just started in looking humble and begging her pardon, not to mention the forgiveness of Papa and the sweet mercy of the Lord. By the time she was done with ragging him, poor Measure had already apologized a half a dozen times, so that she finally just grumped and went back to her sewing.

Then Measure looked up at Alvin Junior and winked.

"I saw that," said Mama, "and if you don't go to hell, Measure, I'll get up a petition to Saint Peter to send you there."

"I'd sign that petition myself," said Measure, looking meek as a puppy dog that just piddled on a big man's boot.

"That's right you would," said Mama, "and you'd sign it in blood, too, because by the time I'm through with you there'll be enough open wounds to keep ten clerks in bright red ink for a year."

Alvin Junior couldn't help himself. Her dire threat just struck him funny. And even though he knew he was taking his life in his hands, he opened up his mouth to laugh. He knew that if he laughed he'd have Mama's thimble hard on his head, or maybe her hand clapped hard on his ear, or even her hard little foot smashed right down on his bare foot, which she did once to David the time he told her she should have learnt the word *no* sometime before she had thirteen mouths to cook for.

This was a matter of life and death. This was more frightening than the ridgebeam, which after all never hit him, which was more than he could say for Mama. So he caught that laugh before it got loose, and he turned it into the first thing he could think of to say.

"Mama," he said, "Measure can't sign no petition in blood, cause he'd already be dead, and dead people don't bleed."

Mama looked him in the eye and spoke slow and careful. "They do when I tell them to."

Well, that did it. Alvin Junior just laughed out loud. And that set half the girls to laughing. Which made Measure laugh. And finally Mama laughed, too. They all just laughed and laughed till they were mostly crying and Mama started sending people upstairs to bed, including Alvin Junior.

All the excitement had Alvin Junior feeling pretty spunky, and he hadn't figured out yet that sometimes he ought to keep all that jumpiness locked up tight. It happened that Matilda, who was sixteen and fancied herself a lady, was walking up the stairs right in front of him. Everybody

hated walking anywhere behind Matilda, she took such delicate, ladylike
steps. Measure always said he'd rather walk in line behind the moon,
cause it moved faster. Now Matilda's backside was right in Al Junior's
face, swaying back and forth, and he thought of what Measure said
about the moon, and reckoned how Matilda's backside was just about
as round as the moon, and then he got to wondering what it would be
like to *touch* the moon, and whether it would be hard like a beetle's
back or squishy as a slug. And when a boy six years old who's already
feeling spunky gets a thought like that in his head, it's not even half a
second till his finger is two inches deep in delicate flesh.

Matilda was a real good screamer.

Al might have got slapped right then, except Wastenot and Wantnot
were right behind him, saw the whole thing, and laughed so hard at
Matilda that she started crying and fled on up the stairs two steps at a
time, not ladylike at all. Wastenot and Wantnot carried Alvin up the
stairs between them, so high up he got a little dizzy, singing that old
song about St. George killing the dragon, only they sang it about St.
Alvin, and where the song usually said something about poking the old
dragon a thousand times and his sword didn't melt in the fire, they
changed *sword* to *finger* and made even Measure laugh.

"That's a filthy filthy song!" shouted ten-year-old Mary, who stood
guard outside the big girls' door.

"Better stop singing that song," said Measure, "before Mama hears
you."

Alvin Junior could never understand why Mama didn't like that song,
but it was true that the boys never sang it where she could hear. The
twins stopped singing and clambered up the ladder to the loft. At that
moment the door to the big girls' room was flung open and Matilda,
her eyes all red from crying, stuck her head out and shouted, "You'll
be sorry!"

"Ooh, I'm sorry, I'm sorry," Wantnot said in a squeaky voice.

Only then did Alvin remember that when the girls set out to get even,
he would be the main victim. Calvin was still considered the baby, so
he was safe enough, and the twins were older and bigger and there was
always two of them. So when the girls got riled, Alvin was first in line
for their deadly wrath. Matilda was sixteen, Beatrice was fifteen, Eliz-
abeth was fourteen, Anne was twelve, Mary was ten, and they all preferred picking on Alvin to practically any other recreation that the Bible
would permit. One time when Alvin was tormented past endurance and
only Measure's strong arms held him back from hot-blooded murder
with a hayfork, Measure allowed as how the punishments of hell would
most likely consist of living in the same house with five women who

were all about twice a man's size. Ever since then, Alvin wondered
what sin he committed before he was born to make him deserve to grow
up half-damned to start with.

Alvin went into the little room he shared with Calvin and just set
there, waiting for Matilda to come and kill him. But she didn't come
and didn't come, and he realized that she was probably waiting till after
the candles were all out, so that no one would know which of his sisters
snuck in and snuffed him out. Heaven knew he'd given them all ample
reason to want him dead in the last two months alone. He was trying
to guess whether they'd stifle him with Matilda's goosedown pillow—
which would be the first time he was ever allowed to touch it—or if
he'd die with Beatrice's precious sewing scissors in his heart, when all
of a sudden he realized that if he didn't get outside to the privy in about
twenty-five seconds he'd embarrass himself right in his trousers.

Somebody was in the privy, of course, and Alvin stood outside jumping and yelling for three minutes and still they wouldn't come out. It
occurred to him that it was probably one of the girls, in which case this
was the most devilish plan they'd ever come up with, keeping him out
of the privy when they knew he was scared to go into the woods after
dark. It was a terrible vengeance. If he messed himself he'd be so
ashamed he'd probably have to change his name and run away, and that
was a whole lot worse than a poke in the behind. It made him mad as
a constipated buffalo, it was so unfair.

Finally he was mad enough to make the ultimate threat. "If you don't
come out I'll do it right in front of the door so you'll step in it when
you come out!"

He waited, but whoever was in there *didn't* say, "If you do I'll make
you lick it off my shoe," and since that was the customary response,
Al realized for the first time that the person inside the privy might not
be one of his sisters after all. It was certainly not one of the boys. Which
left only two possibilities, each one worse than the other. Al was so
mad at himself he smacked his own head with his fist, but it didn't make
him feel no better. Papa would probably give him a lick, but even worse
would be Mama. She might give him a tongue-lashing, which was bad
enough, but if she was in a real vile temper, she'd get that cold look
on her face and say real soft, "Alvin Junior, I used to hope that at least
one of my boys would be a born gentleman, but now I see my life was
wasted," which always made him feel about as low as he knew how to
feel without dying.

So he was almost relieved when the door opened and Papa stood
there, still buttoning his trousers and looking none too happy. "Is it
safe for me to step out this door?" he asked coldly.

"Yup," said Alvin Junior.

"What?"

"Yes sir."

"Are you sure? There's some wild animals around here that think it's smart to leave their do on the ground outside privy doors. I tell you that if there's any such animal I'll lay a trap and catch it by the back end one of these nights. And when I find it in the morning, I'll stitch up its bung hole and turn it loose to bloat up and die in the woods."

"Sorry, Papa."

Papa shook his head and started walking toward the house. "I don't know what's wrong with your bowel, boy. One minute you don't need to go and the next minute you're about to die."

"Well if you'd just build another outhouse I'd be fine," Al Junior muttered. Papa didn't hear him, though, because Alvin didn't actually say it till the privy door was closed and Papa'd gone back to the house, and even then he didn't say it very loud.

Alvin rinsed his hands at the pump a long time, because he feared what was waiting for him back in the house. But then, alone outside in the darkness, he began to be afraid for another reason. Everybody said that a White man never could hear when a Red man was walking through the woods, and his big brothers got some fun out of telling Alvin that whenever he was alone outside, especially at night, there was Reds in the forest, watching him, playing with their flint-bladed tommy-hawks and itching to have his scalp. In broad daylight, Al didn't believe them, but at night, his hands cold with the water, a chill ran through him, and he thought he even knew where the Red was standing. Just over his shoulder, back over near the pigsty, moving so quiet that the pigs didn't even grunt and the dogs didn't bark or nothing. And they'd find Al's body, all hairless and bloody, and *then* it'd be too late. Bad as his sisters were—and they were *bad*—Al figured they'd be better than dying from a Red man's flint in his head. He fair to flew from the pump to the house, and he *didn't* look back to see if the Red was really there.

As soon as the door was closed, he forgot his fears of silent invisible Reds. Things were right quiet in the house, which was pretty suspicious to start with. The girls were never quiet till Papa shouted at them at least three times each night. So Alvin walked up real careful, looking before every step, checking over his shoulder so often he started getting a crick in his neck. By the time he was inside his room with the door closed he was so jittery that he almost hoped they'd do whatever they were planning to do and get it over with.

But they didn't do it and they didn't do it. He looked around the room by candlelight, turned down his bed, looked into every corner, but there was nothing there. Calvin was asleep with his thumb in his mouth, which meant that if they *had* prowled around his room, it had been a while ago. He began to wonder if maybe, just this once, the girls had decided to leave him be or even do their dirty tricks to the twins. It would be a whole new life for him, if the girls started being nice. Like as if an angel came down and lifted him right out of hell.

He stripped off his clothes quick as he could, folded them, and put them on the stool by his bed so they wouldn't be full of roaches in the morning. He had kind of an agreement with the roaches. They could get into anything they wanted if it was on the floor, but they didn't climb into Calvin's bed or Alvin's neither, and they didn't climb onto his stool. In return, Alvin never stomped them. As a result Alvin's room was pretty much the roach sanctuary of the house, but since they kept the treaty, he and Calvin were the only ones who never woke up screaming about roaches in the bed.

He took his nightgown off its peg and pulled it on over his head.

Something bit him under the arm. He cried out from the sharp pain. Something else bit him on the shoulder. Whatever it was, it was all over inside his nightgown, and as he yanked it off, it kept right on nipping him everywhere. Finally it was off, and he stood there stark naked slapping and brushing with his hands to try to get the bugs or whatever they were off him.

Then he reached down and carefully picked up his nightgown. He couldn't see anything scurrying away from it, and even when he shook it and shook it, nary a bug fell off. Something else fell off. It glinted for a moment in the candlelight and made a tiny twinking sound when it hit the floor.

Only then did Alvin Junior notice the stifled giggling from the room next door. Oh, they got him, they got him sure. He sat on the edge of his bed, picking pins out of his nightgown and poking them into the bottom corner of his quilt. He never thought they'd be so mad they'd risk losing one of Mama's precious steel pins, just to get even with him. But he should have known. Girls never did have any bounds of fair play, the way boys did. When a boy knocked you down in a wrestling match, why, he'd either jump on you or wait for you to get back up, and either way you'd be even—both up or both down. But Al knew from painful experience that girls'd kick you when you were down and gang up on you whenever they had the chance. When they fought, they fought in order to end the fight as quick as they could. Took all the fun out of it.

Just like tonight. It wasn't a fair punishment, him poking her with his finger, and them getting him all jabbed up with pins. A couple of those places were bleeding, they stabbed so deep. And Alvin didn't reckon Matilda had so much as a bruise, though he wished she did.

Alvin Junior wasn't mean, no sir. But sitting there on the edge of the bed, taking pins out of his nightgown, he couldn't help but notice the roaches going about their business in the cracks of the floor, and he couldn't help imagining what it would be like if all those roaches just happened to go a-calling in a certain room full of giggles.

So he knelt down on the floor and set the candle right there, and he began whispering to the roaches, just the way he did the day he made his peace treaty with them. He started telling them all about nice smooth sheets and soft squishy skin they could scamper on, and most of all about Matilda's satin pillowcase on her goosedown pillow. But they didn't seem to care about that. Hungry, that's all they are, thought Alvin. All they care about is food, food and fear. So he started telling them about food, the most perfectly delicious food they ever ate in their life. The roaches perked right up and came close to listen, though nary one of them climbed on him, which was right in keeping with the treaty. All the food you ever wanted, all over that soft pink skin. And it's safe, too, not a speck of danger, nothing to worry about, you just go on in there and find the food on that soft pink squishy smooth skin.

Sure enough, a few of the roaches started skittering under Alvin's door, and then more and more of them, and finally the whole troop went off in a single great cavalry charge under the door, through the wall, their bodies shiny and glowing in the candlelight, guided by their eternal insatiable hunger, fearless because Al had told them there wasn't nothing to fear.

It wasn't ten seconds before he heard the first whoop from the room next door. And within a minute the whole house was in such an uproar you'd've thought it was on fire. Girls screaming, boys shouting, and big old boots stomping as Papa rushed up the stairs and squashed roaches. Al was about as happy as a pig in mud.

Finally things started calming down in the next room. In a minute they'd come in to check on him and Calvin, so he blew out the candle, ducked under the covers, and whispered for the roaches to hide. Sure enough, here came Mama's footsteps in the hall outside. Just at the last moment, Alvin Junior remembered that he wasn't wearing his nightgown. He snaked out his hand, snatched the nightgown, and pulled it under the covers just as the door opened. Then he concentrated on breathing easy and regular.

Mama and Papa came in, holding up candles. He heard them pull down Calvin's covers to check for roaches, and he feared they might pull down his as well. That would be such a shameful thing, to sleep like an animal without a stitch on. But the girls, who knew he couldn't possibly be asleep so soon after getting stuck with so many pins, they were naturally afraid of what Alvin might tell Mama and Papa, so they made sure to hustle them out of the room before they could do more than shine a candle in Alvin's face to make sure he was asleep. Alvin held his face absolutely still, not even twitching his eyelids. The candle went away, the door softly closed.

Still he waited, and sure enough, the door opened again. He could hear the padding of bare feet across the floor. Then he felt Anne's breath against his face and heard her whisper in his ear. "We don't know how you did it, Alvin Junior, but we know you set those roaches onto us."

Alvin pretended not to hear anything. He even snored a little.

"You don't fool me, Alvin Junior. You better not go to sleep tonight, because if you do, you'll never wake up, you hear me?"

Outside the room, Papa was saying, "Where's Anne got to?"

She's in here, Papa, threatening to kill me, thought Alvin. But of course he didn't say it out loud. Anyway, she was just trying to scare him.

"We'll make it look like an accident," said Anne. "You always have accidents, nobody will think it's murder."

Alvin was beginning to believe her, more and more.

"We'll carry your body out and stuff it down the privy hole, and they'll all think you went to relieve yourself and fell in."

That would work, thought Alvin. Anne was just the one to think of something so devilish clever, since she was the very best at secretly pinching people and being a good ten feet away before they screamed. That was why she always kept her fingernails so long and sharp. Even now, Alvin could feel one of those sharp nails scraping along his cheek.

The door opened wider. "Anne," whispered Mama, "you come out of there this instant."

The fingernail quit scratching. "I was just making sure little Alvin was all right." Her bare feet padded back out of the room.

Soon all the doors were closed, and he heard Papa's and Mama's shoes clattering down the stairs.

He knew that by rights he should still be scared to death by Anne's threats, but it wasn't so. He had won the battle. He pictured the roaches crawling all over the girls, and he started to laugh. Well, that wouldn't do. He had to stifle that, breathe calm as could be. His whole body shook from trying to hold in the laughter.

There was somebody in the room.

He couldn't hear anything, and when he opened his eyes he couldn't see anybody. But he knew somebody was there. Hadn't come in the door, so they must've come in the open window. That's plain silly, Alvin told himself, there isn't a soul in here. But he lay still, all laughter gone out of him, because he could *feel* it, somebody standing there. No, it's a nightmare, that's all, I'm still spooked from thinking about Reds watching me outside, or maybe from Anne's threat, something like that, if I just lie here with my eyes closed it'll go away.

The blackness inside Al's eyelids turned pink. There was a light in his room. A light as bright as daylight. There wasn't no candle in the world, no, not even a lantern that could burn so bright as that. Al opened his eyes, and all his dread turned into terror, for now he saw that what he feared was real.

There was a man standing at the foot of his bed, a man shining as if he was made of sunlight. The light in the room was coming from his skin, from his chest where his shirt was tore open, from his face, and from his hands. And in one of those hands, a knife, a sharp steel knife. I am going to die, thought Al. Just Like Anne promised me, only there wasn't no way his sisters could conjure up such an awful apparition as this one. This bright Shining Man had come on his own, that was sure, and planned to kill Alvin Junior for his own sins and not cause somebody else had set him on.

Then it was like as if the light from the man pushed right through Alvin's skin and came inside him, and the fear just went right out of him. The Shining Man might have him a knife, and he might've snuck on into the room without so much as opening a door, but he didn't mean no harm to Alvin. So Alvin relaxed a little and wriggled up in his bed till he was mostly sitting, leaning up against the wall, watching the Shining Man, waiting to see what all he'd do.

The Shining Man took his bright steel knife and brought the blade against his other palm—and cut. Alvin saw the gleaming crimson blood flow from the wound in the Shining Man's hand, stream down his forearm, and drip from his elbow onto the floor. He hadn't seen four drops, though, before he came to see a vision in his mind. He could see his sisters' room, he knew the place, but it was different. The beds were up high, and his sisters were giants, so all he could see clear was big old feet and legs. Then he realized he was seeing a little creature's view of the room. A roach's view. In his vision he was scurrying, filled with hunger, absolutely fearless, knowing that if he could get up onto those feet, those legs, there'd be food, all the food he'd ever want. So he rushed, he climbed, he scurried, searching. But there wasn't no food, not a speck of it, and now huge hands reached and swept him off, and then a great huge shadow loomed over him, and he felt the hard sharp crushing agony of death.

Not once, but many times, dozens of times, the hope of food, the confidence that no harm would come; then disappointment—nothing to eat, nothing at all—and after disappointment, terror and injury and death. Each small trusting life, betrayed, crushed, battered.

And then in his vision he was one who lived, one who got away from the looming, stomping boots, under the beds, into the cracks in the walls. He fled from the room of death, but not into the old place, not into the safe room, because now that was no longer safe. That was where the lies came from. That was the place of the betrayer, the liar, the killer who had sent them into this place to die. There were no words in this vision, of course. There could be no words, no clarity of thought in a roach's brain. But Al had words and thoughts, and he knew more than any roach what the roaches had learned. They had been promised something about the world, they had been made *sure* of it, and then it was a lie. Death was a fearful thing, yes, flee that room; but in the other room, there was worse than death—there the world had gone crazy, it was a place where anything could happen, where nothing could be trusted, where nothing was certain. A terrible place. The worst place.

Then the vision ended. Alvin sat there, his hands pressed against his eyes, sobbing desperately. They suffered, he cried out silently, they suffered, and I did it to them, I betrayed them. That's what the Shining Man came to show me. I made the roaches trust me, but then I cheated them and sent them to die. I've done murder.

No, not murder! Who ever heard of roach-killing being murder? Nobody in the whole world would call it that.

But it didn't matter what other folks thought of it, Al knew that. The Shining Man had come to show him that murder was murder.

And now the Shining Man was gone. The light was gone from the room, and when Al opened his eyes, there was no one in the room but Cally, fast asleep. Too late even to beg forgiveness. In pure misery Al Junior closed his eyes and cried some more.

How long was it? A few seconds? Or did Alvin doze off and not notice the passage of a much longer time? Never mind how long—the light came back. Once again it came into him, not just through his eyes, but piercing clear to his heart, whispering to him, calming him. Again Alvin opened his eyes and looked at the face of the Shining Man, waiting for him to speak. When he said nothing, Alvin thought it was *his* turn, and so he stammered out the words, so weak compared to the feelings in his heart. "I'm sorry, I'll never do it again, I'll—"

He was babbling, he knew it, couldn't even hear himself speak he was so upset. But the light grew brighter for a moment, and he felt a question in his mind. Not a word was spoke, mind you, but he knew that the Shining Man wanted him to say what it was he was sorry *for*.

And when he thought about it, Alvin wasn't altogether sure what all was wrong. Sure it wasn't the killing itself—you could starve to death if you didn't slaughter a pig now and then, and it wasn't hardly murder when a weasel killed himself a mouse, was it?

Then the light pushed at him again, and he saw another vision. Not roaches this time. Now he saw the image of a Red man, kneeling before a deer, calling it to come and die; the deer came, all trembling and its eyes wide, the way they are when they're scared. It knew it was coming to die. The Red loosed him an arrow, and there it stood, quivering in the doe's flank. Her legs wobbled. She fell. And Alvin knew that in this vision there wasn't no sin at all, because dying and killing, they were both just a part of life. The Red was doing right, and so was the deer, both acting according to their natural law.

So if the evil he done wasn't the death of the roaches, what was it? The power he had? His knack for making things go just where he wanted, making them break just in the right place, understanding how things ought to be and helping them get that way? He'd found that right useful, as he made and fixed the things a boy makes and fixes in a rough country household. He could fit the two pieces of a broken hoe handle, fit them so tight that they joined forever without glue or tack. Or two pieces of torn leather, he didn't even have to stitch them; and when he tied a knot in string or rope, it stayed tied. It was the same knack he used with the roaches. Making them understand how things was supposed to be, and then they did what he wanted. Was that his sin, that knack of his?

The Shining Man heard his question before he even found words for it. Here came the push of light, and another vision. This time he saw himself pressing his hands against a stone, and the stone melted like butter under his hands, came out in just the shape he wanted, smooth and whole, fell from the side of the mountain and rolled away, a perfect ball, a perfect sphere, growing and growing until it was a whole world, shaped just the way his hands had made it, with trees and grass springing up on its face, and animals running and leaping and flying and swimming and crawling and burrowing on and above and within the ball of stone that he had made. No, it wasn't a terrible power, it was a glorious one, if he only knew how to use it.

Well if it ain't the dying and it ain't the knack, what did I do wrong?

This time the Shining Man didn't show him a thing. This time Alvin didn't see no burst of light, there wasn't a vision at all. Instead the answer just came, not from the Shining Man but from inside his own self. One second he felt too stupid ever to understand his own wickedness, and then the next second he saw it all as clear as could be.

It wasn't the roaches dying, and it wasn't the fact he made them do it. It was the fact that he made them do it just to suit his own pleasure. He told them it was for their own good, but it wasn't so, it was for Alvin's benefit alone. Harming his sisters, more than harming the roaches, and all so Alvin could lie in his bed shaking with laughter because he got *even*—

The Shining Man heard the thoughts of Alvin's heart, yes sir, and Al Junior saw a fire leap from his gleaming eye and strike him in the heart. He had guessed it. He was right.

So Alvin made the most solemn promise of his whole life, right then and there. He had a knack, and he'd use it, but there was rules in things like that, rules that he would follow even if it killed him. "I'll never use it for myself again," said Alvin Junior. And when he said the words he felt like his heart was on fire, it burned so hot inside.

The Shining Man disappeared again.

Alvin lay back, slid down under the blanket, exhausted from weeping, weary with relief. He'd done a bad thing, that was so. But as long as he kept this oath he made, as long as he only used his knack to help other people and never ever used it to help himself, why then he would be a good boy and didn't need to be ashamed. He felt light-headed the way you do coming out of a fever, and that was about right, he had been healed of the wickedness that grew inside him for a spell. He thought of himself laughing when he'd just caused death for his own pleasure, and he was ashamed, but that shame was tempered, it was softened, cause he knew that it would never happen again.

As he lay there, Alvin once again felt the light grow in the room. But this time it didn't come from a single source. Not from the Shining Man at all. This time when he opened his eyes he realized the light was coming from himself. His own hands were shining, his own face must be glowing the way the Shining Man had. He threw off his covers and saw that his whole body glowed with light so dazzling he couldn't hardly bear to look at himself, except that he also couldn't bear to look anywhere else. Is this me? he thought.

No, not me. I'm shining like this because I've also got to do something. Just like the Shining Man did something for me, I've got something to do, too. But who am I supposed to do it for?

There was the Shining Man, visible again at the foot of his bed, but not shining no more. Now Al Junior realized that he knew this man. It was Lolla-Wossiky, that one-eyed whisky-Red who got himself baptized a few days ago, still wearing the White man's clothes they gave him when he turned Christian. With the light inside him now, Alvin saw clearer than he ever did before. He saw that it wasn't likker that poisoned this poor Red man, and it wasn't losing one eye that crippled him. It was something much darker, something growing like a mold inside his head.

The Red man took three steps and knelt beside the bed, his face only a little way from Alvin's eyes. What do you want from me? What am I supposed to do?

For the first time, the man opened his eyes and spoke. "Make all things whole," he said. A second later, Al Junior realized that the man had said it in his Red language—Shaw-Nee, he remembered, from what the grown-ups said when he was baptized. But Al had understood it plain as if it was the Lord Protector's own English. Make all things whole.

Well, that was Al's knack, wasn't it? Fixing things, making things go the way they were supposed to. Trouble was, he didn't even half understand how he did it, and he surely had no idea how to fix something that was alive.

Maybe, though, he didn't have to understand. Maybe he just had to *act*. So he lifted his hand, reached out as careful as he could, and touched Lolla-Wossiky's cheek, under the broken eye. No, that wasn't right. He raised his finger until it touched the slack eyelid where the Red man's other eye was supposed to be. Yes, he thought. Be whole.

The air crackled. Light sparked. Al gasped and pulled his hand away.

All the light was gone from the room. Just the moonlight now coming in the window. Not even a glimmer of the brightness was left. Like as if he just woke up from a dream, the strongest dream he ever had in his life.

It took a minute for Alvin's eyes to change so he could see. It wasn't no dream, that was sure. Cause there was the Red man, who had once been the Shining Man. You ain't dreaming when you got a Red man kneeling by your bed, tears coming out of his one good eye, and the other eye, where you just touched him—

That eyelid was still loose, hanging over nothing. The eye wasn't healed. "It didn't work," whispered Alvin. "I'm sorry."

It was a shameful thing, that the Shining Man had saved him from awful wickedness, and he hadn't done a thing for him in return. But the Red man said nary a word of reproach. Instead he reached out and took Alvin's naked shoulders in both his large strong hands and pulled him close, kissed him on the forehead, hard and strong, like a father to a son, like brothers, like true friends the day before they die. That kiss and all it held—hope, forgiveness, love—let me never forget that, Alvin said silently.

Lolla-Wossiky sprang to his feet. Lithe as a boy he was, not staggering drunk at all. Changed, he *was* changed, and it occurred to Alvin that maybe he *had* healed something, set something right, something deeper than his eyes. Cured him of the whisky-lust, maybe.

But if that was so, Al knew it wasn't himself that done it, it was the light that was in him for a time. The fire that had warmed him without burning.

The Red man rushed to the window, swung over the sill, hung for a moment by his hands, then disappeared. Alvin didn't even hear his feet touch the ground outside, he was that quiet. Like the cats in the barn.

How long had it been? Hours and hours? Would it be daylight soon? Or had it taken only a few seconds since Anne had whispered in his ear and the family had quieted down?

Didn't matter much. Alvin couldn't sleep, not now, not with all that had just happened. Why had this Red man come to him? What did it all mean, the light that filled Lolla-Wossiky and then came to fill him? He couldn't just lie here in bed, all full of wonder. So he got up, slithered into his nightgown as fast as he could, and slipped out of his door.

Now that he was in the hall, he heard talking from downstairs. Mama and Papa were still up. At first he wanted to rush down and tell them what all happened to him. But then he heard the tone of their voices. Anger, fear, all upset. Not a good time to come to them with a tale of a dream. Even if Alvin knew it wasn't a dream at all, that it was real, *they'd* treat it like a dream. And now that he was thinking straight, he couldn't tell them at all. What, that he sent the roaches into his sisters' room? The pins, the pokes, the threats? All of that would come out too, even though it felt like months, *years* ago to Alvin. None of it mattered now, compared to the vow he had taken and the future he thought might be in store for him—but it would matter to Mama and Papa.

So he tiptoed down the hall and down the stairs, just close enough to hear, just far enough to be around the corner and out of sight.

After just a few minutes, he forgot about being out of sight, too. He crept farther down, until he could see into the big room. Papa sat on the floor, surrounded with wood. It surprised Al Junior that Papa was still doing that, even after coming upstairs to kill roaches, even after so much time had passed. He was bent over now, his face buried in his hands. Mama knelt in front of him, the biggest hunks of wood between them.

"He's alive, Alvin," said Mama. "All the rest ain't worth never mind."

Papa lifted his head and looked at her. "It was water that seeped into the tree and froze and thawed, long before we even cut it down. And we happened to cut it in just such a way that the flaw never showed on the surface. But it was split three ways inside, just waiting for the weight of the ridgebeam. It was water done it."

"Water," said Mama, and there was derision in her voice.

"This is fourteen times the water's tried to kill him."

"Children always get in scrapes."

"The time you slipped on a wet floor when you were holding him. The time David knocked down the boiling cauldron. Three times when he was lost and we found him on the bank of the river. Last winter when the ice broke on the Tippy-Canoe River—"

"You think he's the first child to fall into the water?"

"The poison water that made him throw up blood. The mud-covered buffalo that charged him in that meadow—"

"Mud-covered. Everybody knows that buffaloes wallow like pigs. It had nothing to *do* with water."

Papa slapped his hand down hard on the floor. The sound rang like a gunshot through the house. It startled Mama, and of course she started to look toward the stairs to where the children would be sleeping. Alvin Junior scampered right back up the stairs and waited out of sight for her to order him back to bed. But she must not have seen him, cause she didn't shout anything and nobody came up after him.

When he tiptoed back down, they were still going at it, only a little quieter.

Papa whispered, but there was fire in his eyes. "If you think this *doesn't* have to do with water, then *you're* the one that's a lunatic."

Mama was icy now. Alvin Junior knew that look—it was the maddest Mama knew how to get. No slaps then, no tongue-lashings. Just coldness and silence, and any child who got that treatment from her began to long for death and the tortures of hell, because at least it would be warmer.

With Papa she wasn't silent, but her voice was terrible cold. "The Savior himself drank water from the Samaritan well."

"I don't recollect that Jesus fell down that well, neither," said Papa.

Alvin Junior thought of hanging onto the well bucket, falling down into the darkness, until the rope bound up on the windlass and the bucket stopped just above the water, where he would have drowned for certain. They told him he wasn't yet two years old when that happened, but he still dreamed sometimes about the stones that lined the inside of the well, getting darker and darker as he went down. In his dreams the well was ten miles deep and he fell forever before waking up.

"Then think of this, Alvin Miller, since you think you know scripture."

Papa started to protest that he didn't think nothing of the kind—

"The devil hisself said to the Lord in the desert that the angels would bear Jesus up lest he dash his foot against a stone."

"I don't know what that has to do with water—"

"It's plain that if I married you for brains I was plumb cheated."

Papa's face turned red. "Don't you call me no simpleton, Faith. I know what I know and—"

"He has a guardian angel, Alvin Miller. He has someone watching out for him."

"You and your scriptures. You and your angels."

"You tell me why else he had those fourteen accidents and not one of them so much as gave him a scrape on his arm. How many other boys get to six years old without no injury?"

Papa's face looked strange then, twisted up a little, as if it was hard for him to speak at all. "I tell you that there's something wants him dead. I *know* it."

"You don't know any such thing."

Papa spoke even slower, biting out the words as if each one caused him pain. "I *know*."

He had such a hard time talking that Mama just went on and talked right over him. "If there's some devil plot to kill him—which I ain't saying, Alvin—then there's an even stronger heavenly plan to preserve him."

Then, suddenly, Papa didn't have no trouble talking at all. Papa just gave up saying the hard thing, and Alvin Junior felt let down, like when somebody said uncle before they even got throwed. But he knew, the minute he thought about it, that his papa wouldn't give up like that lessen it was some terrible force stopping him from speaking up. Papa was a strong man, not a bit cowardly. And seeing Papa beat down like that, well, it made the boy afraid. Little Alvin knew that Mama and Papa were talking about him, and even though he didn't understand half what they said, he knew that Papa was saying somebody wanted Alvin Junior dead, and when Papa tried to tell his real proof, the thing that made him *know*, something stopped his mouth and kept him still.

Alvin Junior knew without a word being said that whatever it was stopped Papa's mouth, it was the plain opposite of the shining light that had filled Alvin and the Shining Man tonight. There was something that wanted Alvin to be strong and good. And there was something else that wanted Alvin dead. Whatever the good thing was, it could bring visions, it could show him his terrible sin and teach him how to be shut of it forever. But the bad thing, it had the power to shut Papa's mouth, to beat down the strongest, best man Al Junior ever knew or heard of. And that made Al afraid.

When Papa went on with his arguments, his seventh son knew that he wasn't using the proof that counted. "Not devils, not angels," said Papa, "it's the elements of the universe, don't you see that he's an offense against nature? There's power in him like you nor I can't even guess. So much power that one part of nature itself can't bear it— so much power that he protects hisself even when he don't know he's doing it."

"If there's so much power in being seventh son of a seventh son, then where's *your* power, Alvin Miller? You're a seventh son—that ain't nothing, supposedly, but I don't see you doodlebugging or—"

"You don't know what I do—"

"I know what you *don't* do. I know that you don't believe—"

"I believe in every true thing—"

"I know that every other man is down at the commons building that fine church, except for you—"

"That preacher is a fool—"

"Don't you ever think that maybe God is using your precious seventh son to try to wake you up and call you to repentance?"

"Oh, is that the kind of God you believe in? The kind what tries to kill little boys so their papas will go to meeting?"

"The Lord has *saved* your boy, as a sign to you of his loving and compassionate nature—"

"The love and compassion that let my Vigor die—"

"But someday his patience will run out—"

"And then he'll murder another of my sons."

She slapped his face. Alvin Junior saw it with his own eyes. And it wasn't the offhand kind of cuffing she gave her sons when they lipped or loafed around. It was a slap that like to took his face off, and he fell over to sprawl on the floor.

"I'll tell you this, Alvin Miller." Her voice was so cold it burned. "If that church is finished, and there's none of your handiwork in it, then you will cease to be my husband and I will cease to be your wife."

If there were more words, Alvin Junior didn't hear them. He was up in his bed a-trembling that such a terrible thought could be thought, not to mention being spoke out loud. He had been afraid so many times tonight, afraid of pain, afraid of dying when Anne whispered murder in his ear, and most of all afraid when the Shining Man came to him and named his sin. But this was something else. This was the end of the whole universe, the end of the one sure thing, to hear Mama talk about not being with Papa anymore. He lay there in his bed, all kinds of thoughts dancing in his head so fast he couldn't lay hold of any one of them, and finally in all that confusion there wasn't nothing for it but to sleep.

In the morning he thought maybe it was all a dream, it had to be a dream. But there were new stains on the floor at the foot of his bed, where the blood of the Shining Man had dripped, so that wasn't a dream. And his parents' quarrel, that wasn't no dream neither. Papa stopped him after breakfast and told him, "You stay up here with me today, Al."

The look on Mama's face told him plain as day that what was said last night was still meant today.

"I want to help on the church," Alvin Junior said. "I ain't afraid of no ridgebeams."

"You're going to stay here with me, today. You're going to help me build something." Papa swallowed, and stopped himself from looking at Mama. "That church is going to need an altar, and I figure we can build a right nice one that can go inside that church as soon as the roof is on and the walls are up." Papa looked at Mama and smiled a smile that sent a shiver up Alvin Junior's back. "You think that preacher'll like it?"

That took Mama back, it was plain. But she wasn't the kind to back off from a wrestling match just because the other guy got one throw, Alvin Junior knew that much. "What can the boy do?" she asked. "He ain't no carpenter."

"He's got a good eye," said Papa. "If he can patch and tool leather, he can put some crosses onto the altar. Make it look good."

"Measure's a better whittler," said Mama.

"Then I'll have the boy *burn* the crosses in." Papa put his hand on Alvin Junior's head. "Even if he sits here all day and reads in the Bible, this boy ain't going down to that church till the last pew is in."

Papa's voice sounded hard enough to carve his words in stone. Mama looked at Alvin Junior and then at Alvin Senior. Finally she turned her back and started filling the basket with dinner for them as was going to the church.

Alvin Junior went outside to where Measure was hitching the team and Wastenot and Wantnot were loading roof shakes onto the wagon for the church.

"You aim to stand inside the church again?" asked Wantnot.

"We can drop logs down on you, and you can split them into shakes with your head," said Wastenot.

"Ain't going," said Alvin Junior.

Wastenot and Wantnot exchanged identical knowing looks.

"Well, too bad," said Measure. "But when Mama and Papa get cold, the whole Wobbish Valley has a snowstorm." He winked at Alvin Junior, just the way he had last night, when it got him in so much trouble.

That wink made Alvin figure he could ask Measure a question that he wouldn't normally speak right out. He walked over closer, so his voice wouldn't carry to the others. Measure caught on to what Alvin wanted, and he squatted down right there by the wagon wheel, to hear what Alvin had to say.

"Measure, if Mama believes in God and Papa doesn't, how do I know which one is right?"

"I think Pa believes in God," said Measure.

"But if he don't. That's what I'm asking. How do I know about things like that, when Mama says one thing and Papa says another?"

Measure started to answer something easy, but he stopped himself—Alvin could see in his face how he made up his mind to say something serious. Something true, instead of something easy. "Al, I got to tell you, I wisht I knew. Sometimes I figure ain't nobody knows nothing."

"Papa says you know what you see with your eyes. Mama says you know what you feel in your heart."

"What do *you* say?"

"How do *I* know, Measure? I'm only six."

"I'm twenty-two, Alvin, I'm a growed man, and I still don't know. I reckon Ma and Pa don't know, neither."

"Well, if they don't *know*, how come they get so mad about it?"

"Oh, that's what it means to be married. You fight all the time, but you never fight about what you think you're fighting about."

"What are they really fighting about?"

Alvin could see just the opposite thing this time. Measure thought of telling the truth, but he changed his mind. Stood up tall and tousled Alvin's hair. That was a sure sign to Alvin Junior that a grown-up was going to lie to him, the way they always lied to children, as if children weren't reliable enough to be trusted with the truth. "Oh, I reckon they just quarrel to hear theirselfs talk."

Most times Alvin just listened to grown-ups lie and didn't say nothing about it, but this time it was Measure, and he especially didn't like having Measure lie to him.

"How old will I have to be before you tell me straight?" asked Alvin.

Measure's eyes flashed with anger for just a second—nobody likes being called a liar—but then he grinned, and his eyes were sharp with understanding. "Old enough that you already guess the answer for your-self," he said, "but young enough that it'll still do you some good."

"When's that?" Alvin demanded. "I want you to tell me the truth now, all the time."

Measure squatted down again. "I can't always do that, Al, cause sometimes it'd just be too hard. Sometimes I'd have to explain things that I just don't know how to explain. Sometimes there's things that you have to figure out by living long enough."

Alvin was mad and he knew his face showed it.

"Don't you be so mad at me, little brother. I can't tell you some things because I just don't know myself, and that's not lying. But you can count on this. If I *can* tell you, I will, and if I can't, I'll just say so, and won't pretend."

That was the most fair thing a grown-up ever said, and it made Alvin's eyes fill up. "You keep that promise, Measure."

"I'll keep it or die, you can count on that."

"I won't forget, you know." Alvin remembered the vow he had made to the Shining Man last night. "I know how to keep a promise, too."

Measure laughed and pulled Alvin to him, hugged him right against his shoulder. "You're as bad as Mama," he said. "You just don't let up."

"I can't help it," said Alvin. "If I start believing you, then how'll I know when to stop?"

"Never stop," said Measure.

Calm rode up on his old mare about then, and Mama came out with the dinner basket, and everybody that was going, went. Papa took Alvin Junior out to the barn and in no time at all Alvin was helping notch the boards, and his pieces fit together just as good as Papa's. Truth to tell they fit even better, cause Al could use his knack for *this*, couldn't he? This altar was for everybody, so he could make the wood fit so snug that it wouldn't ever come apart, not at the joints or nowhere. Alvin even thought of making Papa's joints fit just as tight, but when he tried, he saw that Papa had something of a knack at this himself. The wood didn't join together to make one continuous piece, like Alvin's did—but it fit good enough, yes sir, so there wasn't no need to fiddle.

Papa didn't say much. Didn't have to. They both knew Alvin Junior had a knack for making things fit right, just like his Papa did. By night-fall the whole altar was put together and stained. They left it to dry, and as they walked into the house Papa's hand was firm on Alvin's shoulder. They walked together just as smooth and easy as if they were both parts of the same body, as if Papa's hand just growed there right out of

Alvin's neck. Alvin could feel the pulse in Papa's fingers, and it was beating right in time with the blood pounding in his throat.

Mama was working by the fire when they came in. She turned and looked at them. "How is it?" she asked.

"It's the smoothest box I ever seen," said Alvin Junior.

"There wasn't a single accident at the church today," said Mama.

"Everything went real good here, too," said Papa.

For the life of him Alvin Junior couldn't figure out why Mama's words sounded like "I ain't going nowhere," and why Papa's words sounded like "Stay with me forever." But he knew he wasn't crazy to think so, cause right then Measure looked up from where he lay all sprawled out afore the fire and winked so only Alvin Junior could see.

8

Visitor

Reverend Thrower allowed himself few vices, but one was to eat Friday supper with the Weavers. Friday *dinner* was more accurate, since the Weavers were shopkeepers and manufacturers, and didn't stop work for more than a snack at noon. It wasn't the quantity so much as the quality that brought Thrower back every Friday. It was said that Eleanor Weaver could take an old tree stump and make it taste like sweet rabbit stew. And it wasn't just the food, either, because Armor-of-God Weaver was a churchgoing man who knew his Bible, and conversation was on a higher plane. Not so elevated as conversation with highly educated churchmen, of course, but the best that could be had in this benighted wilderness.

They would eat in the room back of the Weavers' store, which was part kitchen, part workshop, and part library. Eleanor stirred the pot from time to time, and the smell of boiled venison and the day's bread baking mingled with the odors from the soapmaking shed out back and the tallow they used in candlemaking right here. "Oh, we're some of everything," said Armor, the first time Reverend Thrower visited. "We do things that every farmer hereabouts can do for himself—but we do it better, and when they buy it from us it saves them hours of work, which gives them time to clear and plow and plant more land."

The store itself, out front, was shelved to the ceiling, and the shelves were filled with dry goods brought in by wagon from points east. Cotton cloth from the spinning jennies and steam looms of Irrakwa, pewter dishes and iron pots and stoves from the foundries of Pennsylvania and Suskwahenny, fine pottery and small cabinets and boxes from the carpenters of New England, and even a few precious bags of spices shipped into New Amsterdam from the Orient. Armor Weaver had confessed once that it took all his life savings to buy his stock, and it was no sure

bet that he'd prosper out here in this thinly settled land. But Reverend
Thrower had noticed the steady stream of wagons coming up from the
lower Wobbish and down the Tippy-Canoe, and even a few from out
west in the Noisy River country.

Now, as they waited for Eleanor to announce that the venison stew
was ready, Reverend Thrower asked him a question that had bothered
him for some time.

"I've seen what they haul away," said Reverend Thrower, "and I
can't begin to guess what they use to pay you. Nobody makes cash
money around here, and not much they can trade that'll sell back east."

"They pay with lard and charcoal, ash and fine lumber, and of course
food for Eleanor and me and—whoever else might come." Only a fool
wouldn't notice that Eleanor was thickening enough to be about halfway
to a baby. "But mostly," said Armor, "they pay with credit."

"Credit! To farmers whose scalps might well be traded for muskets
or liquor in Fort Detroit next winter?"

"There's a lot more talk of scalping than there is scalping going on,"
said Armor. "The Reds around here aren't stupid. They know about the
Irrakwa, and how they have seats in Congress in Philadelphia right along
with White men, and how they have muskets, horses, farms, fields, and
towns just like they do in Pennsylvania or Suskwahenny or New Orange.
They know about the Cheriky people of Appalachee, and how they're
farming and fighting right alongside Tom Jefferson's White rebels to
keep their country independent from the King and the Cavaliers."

"They might also have noticed the steady stream of flatboats coming
down the Hio and wagons coming west, and the trees falling down and
the log houses going up."

"I reckon you're half right, Reverend," said Armor. "I reckon the
Reds might go either way. Might try to kill us all, or might try to settle
down and live among us. Living with us wouldn't be exactly easy for
them—they aren't much used to town living, whereas it's the most
natural way for White folks to live. But fighting us has got to be worse,
cause if they do that they'll end up dead. They may think that killing
White folks might scare the others into staying away. They don't know
how it is in Europe, how the dream of owning land will bring people
five thousand mile to work harder than they ever did in their lives and
bury children who might have lived in the home country and risk having
a tommyhock mashed into their brains cause it's better to be your own
man than to serve any lord. Except the Lord God."

"And that's how it is with you, too?" asked Thrower. "Risk everything, for land?"

Armor looked at his wife Eleanor and smiled. She didn't smile back,

Thrower noticed, but he also noticed that her eyes were beautiful and deep, as if she knew secrets that made her solemn even though she was joyful in her heart.

"Not land the way farmers own it, I'm no farmer, I'll tell you that," said Armor. "There's other ways to own land. You see, Reverend Thrower, I give them credit now because I believe in this country. When they come to trade with me, I make them tell me the names of all their neighbors, and make rough maps of the farms and streams where they live, and the roads and rivers along their way here. I make them carry letters that other folks writ, and I write their letters for them and ship them on back east to folks they left behind. I know where everything and everybody in the whole upper Wobbish and Noisy River country is and how to get there."

Reverend Thrower squinted and smiled. "In other words, Brother Armor, you're the government."

"Let's just say that if there comes a time when a government would come in handy, I'll be ready to serve," said Armor. "And in two years, three years, when more folks come through, and some more start making things, like bricks and pots and blackware, cabinets and kegs, beer and cheese and fodder, well, where do you think they'll come to sell it or to buy? To the store that gave them credit when their wives were longing for the cloth to make a bright-colored dress, or they needed an iron pot or a stove to keep out the winter cold."

Philadelphia Thrower chose not to mention that he had somewhat less confidence in the likelihood of grateful people staying loyal to Armor-of-God Weaver. Besides, thought Thrower, I might be wrong. Didn't the Savior say that we should cast our bread upon the waters? And even if Armor doesn't achieve all he dreams of, he will have done a good work, and helped to open this land to civilization.

The food was ready. Eleanor dished out the stew. When she set a fine white bowl in front of him, Reverend Thrower had to smile. "You must be right proud of your husband, and all that's he's doing."

Instead of smiling demurely, as Thrower expected that she would, Eleanor almost laughed aloud. Armor-of-God wasn't half so delicate. He just plain guffawed. "Reverend Thrower, you're a caution," said Armor. "When I'm up to my elbows in candle tallow, Eleanor's up to hers in soap. When I'm writing up folks' letters and having them delivered, Eleanor's drawing up maps and taking down names for our little census book. There ain't a thing I do that Eleanor isn't beside me, and not a thing she does that I'm not beside her. Except maybe her herb garden, which she cares for more than me. And Bible reading, which I care for more than her."

"Well, it's good she's a righteous helpmeet for her husband," said Reverend Thrower.

"We're helpmeets for each other," said Armor-of-God, "and don't you forget it."

He said it with a smile, and Thrower smiled back, but the minister was a little disappointed that Armor was so henpecked that he had to admit right out in the open that he wasn't in charge of his own business or his own home. But what could one expect, considering that Eleanor had grown up in that strange Miller family? The oldest daughter of Alvin and Faith Miller could hardly be expected to bend to her husband as the Lord intended.

The venison, however, was the best that Thrower had ever tasted. "Not gamy a bit," he said. "I didn't think wild deer could taste like this."

"She cuts off the fat," said Armor, "and throws in some chicken."

"Now you mention it," said Thrower, "I can taste it in the broth."

"And the deer fat goes into the soap," said Armor. "We never throw anything away, if we can think of any use for it."

"Just as the Lord intended," said Thrower. Then he fell to eating. He was well into his second bowl of stew and his third slice of bread when he made a comment that he thought was a jesting compliment. "Mrs. Weaver, your cooking is so good that it almost makes me believe in sorcery."

Thrower was expecting a chuckle, at the most. Instead, Eleanor looked down at the table just as ashamed as if he had accused her of adultery. And Armor-of-God sat up stiff and straight. "I'll thank you not to mention that subject in this house," he said.

Reverend Thrower tried to apologize. "I wasn't serious about it," he said. "Among rational Christians that sort of thing is a joke, isn't it? A lot of superstition, and I—"

Eleanor got up from the table and left the room.

"What did I say?" Thrower asked.

Armor sighed. "Oh, there's no way you could know," he said. "It's a quarrel that goes back to before we were married, when I first come out to this land. I met her when she came with her brothers to help build my first cabin—the soapmaking shed, now. She started to scatter spearmint on my floor and say some kind of rhyme, and I shouted for her to stop it and get out of my house. I quoted the Bible, where it says, You shall not suffer a witch to live. It made for a right testy half hour, you may be sure."

"You called her a witch, and she married you?"

"We had a few conversations in between."

"She doesn't believe in that sort of thing anymore, does she?"

Armor knitted his brows. "It ain't a matter of believing, it's a matter of doing, Reverend. She doesn't do it anymore. Not here, not anywhere. And when you sort of halfway accused her of it, well, it made her upset. Because it's a promise to me, you see."

"But when I apologized, why did she—"

"Well, there you are. You have your way of thinking, but you can't tell her that come-hithers and herbs and incantations got no power, because she's seen some things herself that you can't just explain away."

"Surely a man like you, well read in the scripture and acquainted with the world, surely you can convince your wife to give up the superstitions of her childhood."

Armor gently laid his hand on Reverend Thrower's wrist. "Reverend, I got to tell you something that I didn't think I'd ever have to tell a grown man. A good Christian refuses to allow that stuff in his life because the only proper way to bring the hidden powers into your life is through prayer and the grace of the Lord Jesus. It ain't because it doesn't *work*."

"But it *doesn't*," said Thrower. "The powers of heaven are real, and the visions and visitations of angels, and all the miracles attested in the scripture. But the powers of heaven have nothing at all to do with young couples falling in love, or curing the croup, or getting chickens to lay, or all the other silly little things that the ignorant common people do with their so-called hidden wisdom. There's not a thing that's done by doodlebugging or hexing or whatever that can't be explained by simple scientific investigation."

Armor didn't answer for the longest while. The silence made Thrower quite uncomfortable, but he had no idea what more he could say. It hadn't occurred to him before that Armor could possibly *believe* in such things. It was a startling perspective. It was one thing to abstain from witchery because it was nonsense, and quite another to believe in it and abstain because it was unrighteous. It occurred to Thrower that this latter view was actually more ennobling: for Thrower to disdain witching was a matter of mere common sense, while for Armor and Eleanor it was quite a sacrifice.

Before he could find a way to express this thought, however, Armor leaned back on his chair and changed the subject entirely.

"Reckon your church is just about done."

With relief, Reverend Thrower followed Armor onto safer ground. "The roof was finished yesterday, and today they were able to clap all the boards on the walls. It'll be watertight tomorrow, with shutters on the windows, and when we get them glazed and the doors hung it'll be tight as a drum."

"I've got the glass coming by boat," said Armor. Then he winked. "I solved the problem of shipping on Lake Erie."

"How did you manage that? The French are sinking every third boat, even from Irrakwa."

"Simple. I ordered the glass from Montreal."

"French glass in the windows of a British church!"

"An American church," said Armor. "And Montreal's a city in America, too. Anyway, the French may be trying to get rid of us, but in the meantime we're a market for their manufactured goods, so the Governor, the Marquis de la Fayette, he doesn't mind letting his people turn a profit from our trade as long as we're here. They're going to ship it clear around and down into Lake Michigan, and then barge it up the St. Joseph and down the Tippy-Canoe."

"Will they make it before the bad weather?"

"I reckon so," said Armor, "or they won't get paid."

"You're an amazing man," said Thrower. "But I wonder that you have so little loyalty to the British Protectorate."

"Well, you see, that's how it is," said Armor. "You grew up under the Protectorate, and so you still think like an Englishman."

"I'm a Scot, sir."

"A Brit, anyway. In your country, everybody who was even rumored to be practicing the hidden arts got exiled, right away, hardly even bothered with a trial, did they?"

"We try to be just—but the ecclesiastical courts are swift, and there is no appeal."

"Well, now, think about it. If everybody who had any gift for the hidden arts got shipped off to the American colonies, how would you ever see a lick of witchery while you were growing up?"

"I didn't see it because there's no such thing."

"There's no such thing *in Britain*. But it's the curse of good Christians in America, because we're up to our armpits in torches, doodle-bugs, bog-stompers and hexifiers, and a child can't hardly grow to be four feet tall without bumping headlong into somebody's go-away or getting caught up in some prankster's speak-all spell, so he says everything that comes to mind and offends everybody for ten miles around."

"A speak-all spell! Now, Brother Armor, surely you can see that a touch of liquor does as much."

"Not to a twelve-year-old boy who never touched a drop of liquor in his life."

It was plain that Armor was talking from his own experience, but that didn't change the facts. "There is always another explanation."

"There's a powerful lot of explanations you can think up for anything that happens,'' said Armor. ''But I tell you this. You can preach against conjuring, and you'll still have a congregation. But if you keep on saying that conjuring don't *work*, well, I reckon most folks'll wonder why they should come all the way to church to hear the preaching of a plumb fool.''

''I have to tell the truth as I see it,'' said Thrower.

''You may see that a man cheats in his business, but you don't have to name his name from the pulpit, do you? No sir, you just keep giving sermons about honesty and hope it soaks in.''

''You're saying that I should use an indirect approach.''

''That's a right fine church building, Reverend Thrower, and it wouldn't be half so fine if it wasn't for your dream of how it ought to be. But the folks here figure it's *their* church. They cut the wood, they built it, it's on common land. And it'd be a crying shame if you were so stubborn that they up and gave your pulpit to another preacher.''

Reverend Thrower looked at the remnants of dinner for a long time. He thought of the church, not unpainted raw lumber the way it was right now, but finished, pews in place, the pulpit standing high, and the room bright with sunlight through clean-glazed windows. It isn't just the place, he told himself, but what I can accomplish here. I'd be failing in my Christian duty if I let this place fall under the control of superstitious fools like Alvin Miller and, apparently, his whole family. If my mission is to destroy evil and superstition, then I must dwell among the ignorant and superstitious. Gradually I will bring them to knowledge of the truth. And if I can't convince the parents, then in time I can convert the children. It is the work of a lifetime, my ministry, so why should I throw it away for the sake of speaking the truth for a few moments only?

''You're a wise man, Brother Armor.''

''So are you, Reverend Thrower. In the long run, even if we disagree here and there, I think we both want the same thing. We want this whole country to be civilized and Christian. And neither one of us would mind if Vigor Church became Vigor City, and Vigor City became the capital of the whole Wobbish territory. There's even talk back in Philadelphia about inviting Hio to become a state and join right in, and certainly they'll make such an offer to Appalachee. Why not Wobbish someday? Why not a country that stretches from sea to sea, White man and Red, every soul of us free to vote the government we want to make the laws we'll be glad to obey?''

It was a good dream. And Thrower could see himself within it. The man who had the pulpit of the greatest church in the greatest city of the territory would become the spiritual leader of a whole people. For a few minutes he believed so intensely in his dream that when he thanked Armor kindly for the meal and stepped outside, it made him gasp to see that right now Vigor Township consisted entirely of Armor's big store and its outbuildings, a fenced common with a dozen sheep grazing on it, and the raw wood shell of a big new church.

Still, the church was real enough. It was almost ready, the walls were *there*, the roof was on. He was a rational man. He had to see something solid before he could believe in a dream, but that church was solid enough now, and between him and Armor they could make the rest of the dream come true. Bring people to this place, make this the center of the territory. This church was big enough for town meetings, not just church meetings. And what about during the week? He'd be wasting his education if he didn't start a school for the children hereabouts. Teach them to read, to write, to cipher, and, above all, to *think*, to expunge all superstition from their minds, and leave behind nothing but pure knowledge and faith in the Savior.

He was so caught up in these thoughts that he didn't even realize he wasn't heading for Peter McCoy's farm downriver, where his bed would be waiting for him in the old log cabin. He was walking back up the slope to the meetinghouse. Not till he lit a couple of candles did he realize that he actually meant to spend the night here. It was his home, these bare wooden walls, as no other place in the world had ever been home to him. The sappish smell was like a madness in his nostrils, it made him want to sing hymns he'd never even heard before, and he sat there humming, thumbing through the pages of the Old Testament without so much as noticing that there were words on the paper.

He didn't hear them until they stepped onto the wooden floor. Then he looked up and saw, to his surprise, Mistress Faith carrying a lantern, followed by the eighteen-year-old twins, Wastenot and Wantnot. They were carrying a large wooden box between them. It took a moment before he realized that the box was meant to be an altar. That in fact it was a rather fine altar, the wood was tightly fitted as any master cabinetmaker could manage, beautifully stained. And burnt into the boards surrounding the top of the altar were two rows of crosses.

"Where do you want it?" asked Wastenot.

"Father said we had to bring it down tonight, now that the roof and walls were done."

"Father?" asked Thrower.

"He made it for you special," said Wastenot. "And little Al burnt in the crosses hisself, seeing how he wasn't allowed down here no more."

By now Thrower was standing with them, and he could see that the altar had been lovingly built. It was the last thing he expected from Alvin Miller. And the perfectly even crosses hardly looked like the work of a six-year-old child.

"Here," he said, leading them to the place where he had imagined his altar would stand. It was the only thing in the meetinghouse besides the walls and the floor, and being stained, it was darker than the new-wood floor and walls. It was perfect, and tears came to Thrower's eyes. "Tell them that it's beautiful."

Faith and the boys smiled as broad as could be. "You see he ain't your enemy," said Faith, and Thrower could only agree.

"I'm not his enemy, either," he said. And he didn't say: I will win him over with love and patience, but I *will* win, and this altar is a sure sign that in his heart he secretly longs for me to set him free from the darkness of ignorance.

They didn't linger, but headed home briskly through the night. Thrower set his candlestick on the floor near the altar—never *on* it, since that would smack of Papistry—and knelt in a prayer of thanksgiving. The church mostly built, and a beautiful altar already inside it, built by the man he had most feared, the crosses burnt into it by the strange child who most symbolized the compelling superstitions of these ignorant people.

"You're so full of pride," said a voice behind him.

He turned, already smiling, for he was always glad when the Visitor appeared.

But the Visitor was not smiling. "So full of pride."

"Forgive me," said Thrower. "I repent of it already. Still, can I help it if I rejoice in the great work that is begun here?"

The Visitor gently touched the altar, his fingers seeking out the crosses. "*He* made this, didn't he?"

"Alvin Miller."

"And the boy?"

"The crosses. I was so afraid they were servants of the devil—"

The Visitor looked at him sharply. "And because they built an altar, you think that proves they're not?"

A thrill of dread ran through him, and Thrower whispered, "I didn't think the devil could use the sign of the cross—"

"You're as superstitious as any of the others," said the Visitor coldly. "Papists cross themselves all the time. Do you think it's a hex against the devil?"

"How can I know anything, then?" asked Thrower. "If the devil can make an altar and draw a cross—"

"No, no. Thrower, my dear son, they aren't devils, either of them. You'll know the devil when you see him. Where other men have hair on their heads, the devil has the horns of a bull. Where other men have feet, the devil has the cloven hooves of a goat. Where other men have hands, the devil has the great paws of a bear. And be sure of this: he'll make no altars for you when he comes.'' Then the Visitor laid both his hands on the altar. ''This is *my* altar now,'' he said. ''No matter who made it, I can turn it to my purpose.''

Thrower wept in relief. ''Consecrated now, you've made it holy.'' And he reached out a hand to touch the altar.

''Stop!'' whispered the Visitor. Even voiceless, though, his word had the power to set the walls a-trembling. ''Hear me first,'' he said.

''I always listen to you,'' said Thrower. ''Though I can't guess why you should have chosen such a lowly worm as me.''

''Even a worm can be made great by a touch from the finger of God,'' said the Visitor. ''No, don't misunderstand me—I am not the Lord of Hosts. Don't worship me.''

But Thrower could not help himself, and he wept in devotion, kneeling before this wise and powerful angel. Yes, angel, Thrower had no doubt of it, though the Visitor had no wings and wore a suit of clothes one might expect to see in Parliament.

''The man who built this is confused, but there is murder in his soul, and if he is provoked enough, it will come forth. And the child who made the crosses—he is as remarkable as you suppose. But he is not yet ordained to a life of good or evil. Both paths are set before him, and he is open to influence. Do you understand me?''

''Is this my work?'' asked Thrower. ''Should I forget all else, and devote myself to turning the child to righteousness?''

''If you seem too devoted, his parents will reject you. Rather you should conduct your ministry as you have planned. But in your heart, you'll bend everything toward this remarkable child, to win him to my cause. Because if he does not serve me by the time he's fourteen years of age, then I'll destroy him.''

The mere thought of Alvin Junior being hurt or killed was unbearable to Thrower. It filled him with such a sense of loss that he could not imagine a father or even a mother feeling more. ''All that a weak man can do to save the child, I will do,'' he cried, his voice wrung almost to a scream by his anguish.

The Visitor nodded, smiled his beautiful and loving smile, and reached out his hand to Thrower. ''I trust you,'' he said softly. His voice was like healing water on a burning wound. ''I know you will do well. And as for the devil, you must feel no fear of *him*.''

Thrower reached for the proffered hand, to cover it with kisses; but when he should have touched flesh, there was nothing there, and in that moment the Visitor was gone.

9

Taleswapper

There was once a time, Taleswapper well remembered, when he could climb a tree in these parts and look out over a hundred square miles of undisturbed forest. A time when oaks lived a century or more, with ever-thickening trunks making mountains out of wood. A time when leaves were so thick overhead that there were places where the forest ground was bare from lack of light.

That world of eternal dusk was slipping away now. There still were reaches of primeval wood, where Red men wandered more quietly than deer and Taleswapper felt himself to be in the cathedral of the most well-worshipped God. But such places were so rare that in this last year of wandering, Taleswapper had not journeyed a single day in which he could climb a tree and see no interruption in the forest roof. All the country between the Hio and the Wobbish was being settled, sparsely but evenly, and even now, from his perch atop a willow at the crest of a rise, Taleswapper could see three dozen cookfires sending pillars of smoke straight up into the cold autumn air. And in every direction, great swatches of forest had been cleared, the land plowed, crops planted, tended, harvested, so that where once great trees had shielded the earth from the sky's eye, now the stubbled soil was naked, waiting for winter to cover its shame.

Taleswapper remembered his vision of drunken Noah. He had engraved it for an edition of Genesis for Scottish rite Sunday schools. Noah, nude, his mouth lolling open, a cup half-spilled still dangling from his curled fingers; Ham, not far off, laughing derisively; and Japheth and Shem, walking backward to draw a robe over their father, so they would not see what their father had exposed in his stupefaction. With an electric excitement, Taleswapper realized that this, now, is what that prophetic moment foreshadowed. That he, Taleswapper, perched atop a tree, was seeing the naked land in its stupor, awaiting the modest covering of winter. It was prophecy fulfilled, a thing which one hoped for but could not expect in one's own life.

Or, then again, the story of drunken Noah might not be a figure of this moment at all. Why not the other way around? Why not cleared land as a figure for drunken Noah?

Taleswapper was in a foul mood by the time he reached the ground. He thought and thought, trying to open his mind to see visions, to be a good prophet. Yet every time he thought he had got something firm and tight, it shifted, it changed. He thought one thought too many, and the whole fabric came undone, and he was left as uncertain as ever before.

At the base of the tree he opened his pack. From it he took the Book of Tales that he had first made for Old Ben back in '85. Carefully he unbuckled the sealed portion, then closed his eyes and riffled the pages. He opened his eyes and found his fingers resting among the Proverbs of Hell. Of course, at a time like this. His finger touched two proverbs, both written by his own hand. One meant nothing, but the other seemed appropriate. ''A fool sees not the same tree that a wise man sees.''

Yet the more he tried to study out the meaning of that proverb at this moment, the less connection he saw, except that it included mention of trees. So he tried the first proverb after all. ''If the fool would persist in his folly he would become wise.''

Ah. This was speaking to him, after all. This was the voice of prophecy, recorded when he lived in Philadelphia, before he ever began his journey, on a night when the Book of Proverbs came alive for him and he saw as if in letters of flame the words that should have been included. That night he had stayed up until dawn's light killed the fires of the page. When Old Ben came thumping down the stairs to grouch his way in for breakfast, he stopped and sniffed the air. ''Smoke,'' he said. ''You haven't been trying to burn down the house, have you, Bill?''

''No, sir,'' answered Taleswapper. ''But I saw a vision of what God meant the Book of Proverbs to say, and wrote them down.''

''You are obsessed with visions,'' said Old Ben. ''The only true vision comes not from God but from the inmost recesses of the human mind. Write that down as a proverb, if you want. It's far too agnostic for me to use it in Poor Richard's Almanac.''

''Look,'' said Taleswapper.

Old Ben looked, and saw the last flames as they died. ''Well, now, if that's not the most remarkable trick to do with letters. And you told me you weren't a wizard.''

''I'm not. God gave this to me.''

"God or the devil? When you're surrounded by light, Bill, how do you know whether it's the glory of God or the flames of hell?"

"I don't know," said Taleswapper, growing confused. Being young then, not yet thirty, he was easily confused in the presence of the great man.

"Or perhaps you, wanting truth so badly, gave it to yourself." Old Ben tilted his head to examine the pages of Proverbs through the lower lenses of his bifocals. "The letters have been burned right in. Funny, isn't it, that I'm called a wizard, who am not, and you, who are, refuse to admit it."

"I'm a prophet. Or—want to be."

"If one of your prophecies comes true, Bill Blake, then I'll believe it, but not until."

In the years since then, Taleswapper had searched for the fulfilment of even one prophecy. Yet whenever he thought he had found such a fulfilment, he could hear Old Ben's voice in the back of his mind, providing an alternate explanation, scoffing at him for thinking that any connection between prophecy and reality could be true.

"Never *true,*" Old Ben would say. "Useful—now, there's something. Your mind might make a connection that is useful. But *true* is another matter. True implies that you have found a connection that exists independent of your apprehension of it, that would exist whether you noticed it or not. And I must say that I have never seen such a connection in my life. There are times when I suspect that there are no such connections, that all links, bonds, ties, and similarities are creatures of thought and have no substance."

"Then why doesn't the ground dissolve beneath our feet?" asked Taleswapper.

"Because we have managed to persuade it not to let our bodies by. Perhaps it was Sir Issac Newton. He was such a persuasive fellow. Even if human beings doubt him, the ground does not, and so it endures." Old Ben laughed. It was all a lark to him. He never could bring himself to believe even his own skepticism.

Now, sitting at the base of the tree, his eyes closed, Taleswapper connected again: The tale of Noah with Old Ben. Old Ben was Ham, who saw the naked truth, limp and shameful, and laughed at it, while all the loyal sons of church and university walked backward to cover it up again, so the silly truth would not be seen. Thus the world continued to think of the truth as firm and proud, never having seen it in a slack moment.

That is a true connection, thought Taleswapper. That is the meaning of the story. That is the fulfillment of the prophecy. The truth when we

see it is ridiculous, and if we wish to worship it, we must never allow
ourselves to see it.

In that moment of discovery, Taleswapper sprang to his feet. He must
find someone at once, to tell of this great discovery while he still believed it. As his own proverb said, "The cistern contains: the fountain
overflows." If he did not speak his tale, it grew dank and musty, it
shrank inside him, while with the telling the tale stayed fresh and virtuous.

Which way? The forest road, not three rods off, led toward a large
white church with an oak-high steeple—he had seen it, not a mile away,
while up the tree. It was the largest building Taleswapper had seen since
he last visited in Philadelphia. Such a large building for people to gather
in implied that folks in this part of the land felt they had plenty of room
for newcomers. A good sign for an itinerant teller of tales, since he
lived by the trust of strangers, who might take him in and feed him
when he brought nothing with him to pay with, except his book, his
memory, two strong arms, and sturdy legs that had carried him ten
thousand miles and were good for at least five thousand more.

The road was rutted with wagon tracks, which meant it was often
used, and in the low places it was firmed up with rails, making a good
strong corduroy so that wagons wouldn't mire in rain-soaked soil. So
this was on its way to being a town, was it? The large church might
not mean openness at all—it might speak more of ambition. That's the
danger of judging anything, thought Taleswapper: There are a hundred
possible causes for every effect, and a hundred possible effects from
every cause. He thought of writing down that thought, but decided
against it. It had no traces on it save the prints of his own soul—neither
the marks of heaven nor of hell. By this he knew that it hadn't been
given to him. He had forced the thought himself. So it couldn't be
prophecy, and couldn't be true.

The road ended in a commons not far from a river. Taleswapper knew
that from the smell of rushing water—he had a good nose. Around the
commons were scattered several buildings, but the largest of all was a
whitewashed clapboard two-story building with a small sign that said
"Weaver's."

Now when a house has a sign on it, Taleswapper knew, that generally
means the owners want people to recognize the place though they've
never been shown the way, which is the same as to say that the house
is open to strangers. So Taleswapper went right up and knocked.

"Minute!" came a shout from inside. Taleswapper waited on the
porch. Toward one end were several hanging baskets, with the long
leaves of various herbs dangling. Taleswapper recognized many of them

as being useful in various arts, such as healing, finding, sealing, and reminding. He also recognized that the baskets were arranged so that, seen from a spot near the base of the door, they would form a perfect hex. In fact, this was so pronounced an effect that Taleswapper squatted and finally lay prone on the porch to see it properly. The colors daubed on the baskets at exactly the correct points proved that it was no accident. It was an exquisite hex of protection, oriented toward the doorway.

Taleswapper tried to think of why someone would put up such a powerful hex, and yet seek to conceal it. Why, Taleswapper was probably the only person around likely to feel the whiff of power from something as passive as a hex, and so be drawn to notice it. He was still lying there on the floor, puzzling about it, when the door opened and a man said, "Are you so tired, then, stranger?"

Taleswapper leapt to his feet. "Admiring your arrangement of herbs. Quite an aerial garden, sir."

"My wife's," said the man. "She fusses over them all the time. Has to have them just so."

Was the man a liar? No, Taleswapper decided. He wasn't trying to hide the fact that the baskets made a hex and the trailing leaves intertwined to bind them together. He simply didn't know. Someone—his wife, probably, if it was her garden—had set up a protection on his house, and the husband didn't have a clue.

"They look just right to me," said Taleswapper.

"I wondered how someone could arrive here, and me not hear the wagon nor the horse. But from the looks of you, I'd guess you came afoot."

"That I did, sir," said Taleswapper.

"And your pack doesn't look full enough to hold many articles to trade."

"I don't trade in *things*, sir," said Taleswapper.

"What, then? What but things can be traded?"

"Work, for one thing," said Taleswapper. "I work for food and shelter."

"You're an old man, to be a vagrant."

"I was born in fifty-seven, so I still have a good seventeen years until I've used up my three-score and ten. Besides, I have a few knacks."

At once the man seemed to shrink away. It wasn't in his body. It was his eyes that got more distant, as he said, "My wife and I do our own work here, seeing how our sons are right small yet. We've no need of help."

There was a woman behind him now, a girl still young enough that her face hadn't grown hard and weathered, though she was solemn. She held a baby in her arms. She spoke to her husband. "We have enough to spare another place for dinner tonight, Armor—"

At that the husband's face went firm and set. "My wife is more generous than I am, stranger. I'll tell you straight out. You spoke of having a few knacks, and in my experience that means you make some claim to hidden powers. I'll have no such workings in a Christian house."

Taleswapper looked hard at him, and then looked a bit softer at the wife. So that was the way of it here: she working such hexes and spells as she could hide from her husband, and he flat rejecting any sign of it. If her husband ever realized the truth, Taleswapper wondered what would happen to the wife. The man—Armor?—seemed not to be the murderous kind, but then, there was no telling what violence would flow in a man's veins when the flood of rage came undammed.

"I understand your caution, sir," said Taleswapper.

"I know you have protections on you," said Armor. "A lone man, afoot in the wild for all this way? The fact that your hair is still on your head says that you must have warded off the Reds."

Taleswapper grinned and swept his cap off his head, letting his bald crown show. "Is it a true warding, to blind them with the reflected glory of the sun?" he asked. "They'd get no bounty for *my* scalp."

"Truth to tell," said Armor, "the Reds in these parts are more peaceable than most. The one-eyed Prophet has built him a city on the other side of the Wobbish, where he teaches Reds not to drink likker."

"That's good advice for any man," said Taleswapper. And he thought: A Red man who calls himself a prophet. "Before I leave this place I'll have to meet that man and have words with him."

"He won't talk to *you*," said Armor. "Not unless you can change the color of your skin. He hasn't spoke to a White man since he had his first vision a few years back."

"Will he kill me if I try?"

"Not likely. He teaches his people not to kill White men."

"That's also good advice," said Taleswapper.

"Good for White men, but it may not have the best result for Reds. There's folks like so-called Governor Harrison down in Carthage City who mean naught but harm for all Reds, peaceable or not." The truculence had not left Armor's face, but he was talking anyway, and from his heart, too. Taleswapper put a great deal of trust in the sort of man who spoke his mind to all men, even strangers, even enemies. "Anyway," Armor went on, "not all Reds are believers in the Prophet's peaceable words. Them as follow Ta-Kumsaw are stirring up trouble down by the Hio, and a lot of folks are moving north to the upper

Wobbish country. So you won't lack for houses willing to take a beggar in—you can thank the Reds for that, too.''

"I'm no beggar, sir," said Taleswapper. "As I told you, I'm willing to work."

"With knacks and hidden shiftiness, no doubt."

The man's hostility was the plain opposite of his wife's gentle welcoming air. "What *is* your knack, sir?" asked the wife. "From your speech you're an educated man. You'd not be a teacher, would you?"

"My knack is spoken with my name," he said. "Taleswapper. I have a knack for stories."

"For making them up? We call that lying, hereabouts." The more the wife tried to befriend Taleswapper, the colder her husband became.

"I have a knack for remembering stories. But I tell only those that I believe are true, sir. And I'm a hard man to convince. If you tell me your stories, I'll tell you mine, and we'll both be richer for the trade, since neither one of us loses what we started with."

"I've got no stories," said Armor, even though he had already told a tale of the Prophet and another of Ta-Kumsaw.

"That's sad news, and if it's so, then I've come to the wrong house indeed." Taleswapper could see that this truly wasn't the house for him. Even if Armor relented and let him in, he would be surrounded by suspicion, and Taleswapper couldn't live where people looked sharp at him all the time. "Good day to you."

But Armor wasn't letting him go so easily. He took Taleswapper's words as a challenge. "Why should it be sad? I live a quiet, ordinary life."

"No man's life is ordinary to himself," said Taleswapper, "and if he says it is, then that's a story of the kind that I never tell."

"You calling me a liar?" demanded Armor.

"I'm asking if you know a place where my knack might be welcome."

Taleswapper saw, though Armor didn't, how the wife did a calming with the fingers of her right hand, and held her husband's wrist with her left. It was smoothly done, and her husband must have become quite attuned to it, because he visibly relaxed as she stepped a bit forward to reply. "Friend," she said, "if you take the track behind that hill yonder, and follow it to the end, over two brooks, both with bridges, you'll reach the house of Alvin Miller, and I know he'll take you in."

"Ha," said Armor.

"Thank you," said Taleswapper. "But how can you know such a thing?"

"They'll take you in for as long as you want to stay, and never turn you away, as long as you show willingness to help out."

"Willing I always am, milady," said Taleswapper.

"*Always* willing?" said Armor. "Nobody's *always* willing. I thought you always spoke true."

"I always tell what I believe. Whether it's true, I'm no more sure than any man."

"Then how do you call me 'sir,' when I'm no knight, and call her 'milady,' when she's as common as myself?"

"Why, I don't believe in the King's knightings, that's why. He calls a man a knight because he owes him a favor, whether he's a true knight or not. And all his mistresses are called 'ladies' for what they do between the royal sheets. That's how the words are used among the Cavaliers—lies half the time. But your wife, sir, acted like a true lady, gracious and hospitable. And you, sir, like a true knight, protecting your household against the dangers you most fear."

Armor laughed aloud. "You talk so sweet I bet you have to suck on salt for half an hour to get the taste of sugar out of your mouth."

"It's my knack," said Taleswapper. "But I have other ways to talk, and not sweetly, when the time is right. Good afternoon to you, and your wife, and your children, and your Christian house."

Taleswapper walked out onto the grass of the commons. The cows paid him no mind, because he *did* have a warding, though not of the sort that Armor would ever see. Taleswapper sat in the sunlight for a little while, to let his brain get warm and see if it could come up with a thought. But it didn't work. Almost never had a thought worth having, after noon. As the proverb said, "Think in the morning, Act in the noon, Eat in the evening, Sleep in the night." Too late for thinking now. Too early for eating.

He headed up the pathway to the church, which stood well back from the commons, atop a good-sized hill. If I were a true prophet, he thought, I'd know things now. I'd know whether I'd stay here for a day or a week or a month. I'd know whether Armor would be my friend, as I hope, or my enemy, as I fear. I'd know whether his wife would someday win herself free to use her powers in the open. I'd know whether I'd ever meet this Red Prophet face to face.

But that was nonsense, he knew. That was the sort of seeing that a torch would do—he'd seen them doing it before, more than a few of them, and it filled him with dread, because it wasn't good, he knew, for a man to know too much of the path of his own life ahead. No, for him the knack he wanted was prophecy, to see, not the small doings of men and women in their little corners of the world, but rather the great sweep of events as directed by God. Or by Satan—Taleswapper wasn't particular, since both of them had a good idea of what they planned to do in the world, and so either one was likely to know a few things about the future. Of course, it was likely to be more *pleasant* to hear from God. What traces of the devil he had touched so far in his life had all been painful, each in its own way.

The church door stood open, this being a warmish day for autumn, and Taleswapper buzzed right in along with the flies. It was as fine a church inside as out—obviously Scottish rite, so it was plain—but all the more cheerful for that, a bright and airy place, with whited walls and glasspaned windows. Even the pews and pulpit were of light wood. The only thing dark in the whole place was the altar. So naturally his eye was drawn to it. And, because he had a knack for this sort of thing, he saw traces of a liquid touch upon the surface of it.

He walked slowly toward the altar. Toward it, because he had to know for sure; slowly, because this sort of thing ought not to be in a Christian church. Up close, though, there was no mistaking. It was the same trace he had seen on the face of the man in DeKane who tortured his own children to death and blamed it on the Reds. The same trace he had seen lingering on the sword that beheaded George Washington. It was like a thin film of filthy water, invisible unless you looked at a certain angle, in a certain light. But to Taleswapper it was always visible now—he had an eye for it.

He reached out his hand and set his forefinger carefully on the clearest trace. It took all his strength just to hold it there for a moment, it burned so, setting his whole arm to trembling and aching, right to the shoulder.

"You're welcome in God's house," said a voice.

Taleswapper, sucking on his burnt finger, turned to face the speaker. He was robed as a Scottish Rite preacher—Presbyterian, they called them here in America.

"You didn't get a splinter, did you?" asked the preacher.

It would have been easier just to say Yes, I got a splinter. But Taleswapper only told stories he believed. "Preacher," said Taleswapper, "the devil has set his hand upon this altar."

At once the preacher's lugubrious smile disappeared. "How do you know the devil's handprint?"

"It's a gift of God," said Taleswapper. "To see."

The preacher looked at him closely, unsure whether or not to believe. "Then can you also tell where angels have touched?"

"I could see traces, I think, if goodly spirits had intervened. I've seen such marks before."

The preacher paused, as if he wanted to ask a very important question but was afraid of the answer. Then he shuddered, the desire to learn plainly fled from him, and the preacher spoke now with contempt. "Nonsense. You can fool the common people, but I was educated in England, and I am not deluded by talk of hidden powers."

"Oh," said Taleswapper. "You're an educated man."

"And so are you, by your speech," said the preacher. "The south of England, I would say."

"The Lord Protector's Academy of Art," said Taleswapper. "I was trained as an engraver. Since you're Scottish rite, I daresay you've seen my work in your Sunday school book."

"I never notice such things," said the preacher. "Engravings are a waste of paper that could be given over to words of truth. Unless they illustrate matters that the artist's eye has actually seen, like anatomies. But what the artist conceives in his imagination has no better claim on my eyes than what I imagine for myself."

Taleswapper followed that notion to its root. "What if the artist were also a prophet?"

The preacher half-closed his eyes. "The day of prophets is over. Like that apostate heathen one-eyed drunken Red man across the river, all who claim to be prophets now are charlatans. And I have no doubt that if God granted the gift of prophecy even to one artist, we would soon have a surplus of sketchers and daubers wishing to be taken for prophets, especially if it would bring them better pay."

Taleswapper answered mildly, but he did not let the preacher's implicit accusation stand. "A man who preaches the word of God for a salary ought not to criticize others who seek to earn a living by revealing the truth."

"I was ordained," said the preacher. "No one ordains artists. They ordain themselves."

Just as Taleswapper had expected. The preacher retreated to authority as soon as he feared his ideas could not stand on their own merit. Reasonable argument was impossible when authority became the arbiter; Taleswapper returned to the immediate matter. "The devil laid his fingers on this altar," said Taleswapper. "It burned my finger to touch the place."

"It never burned mine," said the preacher.

"I expect not," said Taleswapper. "*You* were ordained."

Taleswapper made no effort to hide the scorn in his voice, and it plainly irked the preacher, who lashed back. It did not bother Taleswapper when people got angry at him. It meant they were listening, and at least half believing him. "Tell me, then, if you have such keen eyes,'' said the preacher. ''Tell me if a messenger from God has ever touched the altar.''

Plainly the preacher regarded this question as a test. Taleswapper had no idea which answer the preacher thought was correct. It hardly mattered; Taleswapper would answer truthfully, no matter what. ''No,'' he said.

It was the wrong answer. The preacher smirked. ''Just like that? You can say that he has not?''

Taleswapper thought for a moment that the preacher might believe his own ordained hands had left the marks of God's will. He would lay that notion to rest at once. ''Most preachers don't leave tracks of light on things they touch. Only a few are ever holy enough.''

But it wasn't himself the preacher had in mind. ''You've said enough now,'' said the preacher. ''I know that you're a fraud. Get out of my church.''

''I'm no fraud,'' said Taleswapper. ''I may be mistaken, but I never lie.''

''And I never believe a man who says he never lies.''

''A man always assumes that others are as virtuous as himself,'' said Taleswapper.

The preacher's face flushed with anger. ''Get out of here, or I'll throw you out.''

''I'll go gladly,'' said Taleswapper. He walked briskly to the door. ''I never hope to return to a church whose preacher is not surprised to learn that Satan has touched his altar.''

''I wasn't surprised because I don't believe you.''

''You believed me,'' said Taleswapper. ''You also believe an angel has touched it. That's the story you think is true. But I tell you that no angel could touch it without leaving a trace that I could see. And I see but one trace there.''

''Liar! You yourself are sent by the devil, trying to do your necromancy here in the house of God! Begone! Out! I conjure you to leave!''

''I thought churchmen like you didn't practice conjurings.''

''Out!'' The preacher screamed the last word, the veins standing out in his neck. Taleswapper put his hat back on and strode away. He heard the door slam closed behind him. He walked across a hilly meadow of dried-out autumn grass until he struck the track that led up toward the house that the woman had spoken of. Where she was sure they'd take him in.

Taleswapper wasn't so sure. He never made more than three visits in a place—if he hadn't found a house to take him in by the third try, it was best to move on. This time, the first stop had been unusually bad, and the second had gone even worse.

Yet his uneasiness wasn't just that things were going badly. Even if at this last place they fell on their faces and kissed his feet, Taleswapper felt peculiar about staying around here. Here was a town so Christian that the leading citizen wouldn't allow hidden powers in his house—yet the altar in the church had the devil's mark on it. Even worse was the pattern of deception. The hidden powers were being used right under Armor's nose, and by the person he loved and trusted most; while in the church, the preacher was convinced that God, not the devil, had claimed his altar. What could Taleswapper expect, in this place up the hill, but more madness, more deception? Twisted people entwined each other, Taleswapper knew that much from the evidence of his own past.

The woman was right—the brooks were bridged. Even this, though, wasn't a good sign. To bridge a river was a necessity; to bridge a broad stream, a kindness to travelers. But why did they build such elaborate bridges over brooks so narrow that even a man as old as Taleswapper could leap them without wetting a foot? The bridges were sturdy, anchored into the earth far to either side of the stream, and both had roofs, well thatched. People pay money to stay in inns that aren't as tight and dry as these bridges, thought Taleswapper.

Surely this meant that the people at the end of the track were at least as strange as those he had met so far. Surely he ought to turn away. Prudence demanded that he leave.

But prudence was not strong in Taleswapper's character. It was as Old Ben told him, years before. "You'll go into the mouth of hell someday, Bill, just to find out why the devil has such bad teeth." There was a reason for the bridges, and Taleswapper sensed that it would mean a story worth remembering in his book.

It was only a mile, after all. Just when it seemed the track was about to wander into impenetrable wood, it took a sharp northward turn and opened into as pretty a holding as Taleswapper had seen, even in the placid settled lands of New Orange and Pennsylvania. The house was large and fine, with shaped logs, to show that they meant it to last, and there were barns and sheds and pens and coops that made it almost a village in itself. A wisp of smoke rising a half mile on up the track told him that his guess wasn't all wrong. There was another household nearby, sharing the road, which meant it was probably kin. Married children, no doubt, and all farming together, for the better prosperity of all. That was a good thing, Taleswapper knew, when brothers could grow up liking each other well enough to plow each other's fields.

Taleswapper always headed for the house—best to announce himself at once, rather than skulking about and being taken for a robber. Yet this time, when he meant to walk toward the house, he felt himself become stupid all at once, unable to remember what it was he was about to do. It was a warding so powerful that he did not realize he had been pushed away until he was halfway down the hill toward a stone building beside a brook. He stopped abruptly, frightened, for no one had power enough, he thought, to back him off without him realizing what was happening. This place was as strange as the other two, and he wanted no part of it.

Yet as he tried to turn back the way he had come, the same thing happened again. He found himself going down the hill toward the stone-walled building.

Again he stopped, and this time muttered, "Whoever you are, and whatever you want, I'll go of my own free will or I'll not go at all."

All at once it was like a breeze behind him, pushing him toward the building. But he knew he could go back if he wanted. Against the breeze, yes, but he could do it. That eased his mind considerably. Whatever constraints had been placed upon him, they were not meant to enslave him. And that, he knew, was one of the marks of a goodly spell—not the hidden chains of a tormentor.

The path rounded to the left a bit, along the brook, and now he could see that the building was a mill, for it had a millrace and the frame of a tall wheel standing where the water would flow. But no water flowed in the race today, and as he came close enough to see through the large barn-size door, he discovered why. It wasn't just closed up for the winter. It had never been used as a mill. The gears were in place, but the great round millstone wasn't there. Just a foundation of rammed cobbles, level and ready and waiting.

Waiting a long time. This construction was at least five years old, from the vines and the mosses on the building. It had been a lot of work to build this millhouse, and yet it was being used as a common haybarn.

Just inside the large door, a wagon was rocking back and forth as two boys grappled together atop a half-load of hay. It was a friendly bout; the boys were obviously brothers, the one about twelve years old, the other perhaps nine, and the only reason the young one wasn't thrown off the wagon and out the door was because the older boy couldn't keep himself from laughing. They didn't notice Taleswapper, of course.

They also didn't notice the man standing at the edge of the loft, pitchfork in hand, looking down at them. Taleswapper thought at first that the man was watching in pride, like a father. Then he came close enough to see how he held the fork. Like a javelin, ready to cast. For a single moment, Taleswapper saw in his mind's eye just what would happen—the fork thrown, burying itself in the flesh of one of the boys, surely killing him, if not immediately, then soon enough, with gangrene or belly bleeding. It was murder that Taleswapper saw.

"No!" he shouted. He ran through the doorway, fetching up alongside the wagon, looking up at the man in the loft.

The man plunged the pitchfork into the hay beside him and heaved the hay over the edge onto the wagon, half-burying the two boys. "I brought you here to work, you two bearcubs, not to tie each other in knots." The man was smiling, teasing. He winked at Taleswapper. Just as if there hadn't been death in his eyes a moment before.

"Howdy, young feller," said the man.

"Not so young," said Taleswapper. He doffed his hat, letting his bare pate give away his age.

The boys dug themselves out of the hay. "What were you shouting at, Mister?" asked the younger one.

"I was afraid someone might come to harm," said Taleswapper.

"Oh, we wrassle like that all the time," said the older boy. "Put her there, friend. My name's Alvin, same as my pa." The boy's grin was contagious. Scared as he'd been, with so much dark dealing going on today, Taleswapper had no choice but to smile back and take the proffered hand. Alvin Junior had a handshake like a grown man, he was that strong. Taleswapper commented on it.

"Oh, he gave you his fish hand. When he gets to wringing and wrenching on you, he like to pops your palm like a razzleberry." The younger boy shook hands, too. "I'm seven years old, and Al Junior, he's ten." Younger than they looked. They both had that nasty bitter body stench that young boys get when they've been playing hard. But Taleswapper never minded that. It was the father who puzzled him. Was it just a fancy in his own mind, that Taleswapper thought he meant to kill the boys? What man could take a murderous hand to boys as sweet and fine as these?

The man had left the pitchfork in the loft, clambered down the ladder, and now strode toward Taleswapper with his arms out as if to hug him. "Welcome here, stranger," said the man. "I'm Alvin Miller, and these are my two youngest sons, Alvin Junior and Calvin."

"Cally," corrected the younger boy.

"He doesn't like the way our names rhyme," said Alvin Junior. "Alvin and Calvin. See, they named him like me hoping he'd grow up to be as fine a specimen of manhood as I am. Too bad it ain't working."

Calvin gave him a shove of mock anger. "Near as I can tell, he was the first try, and when I came along they finally got it right!"

"Mostly we call them Al and Cally," said the father.

"Mostly you call us 'shutup' and 'get over here,' " said Cally.

Al Junior gave him a whack on the shoulder and sent him sprawling in the dirt. Whereupon his father placed a boot on his backside and sent him head over heels out the door. All in fun. Nobody was hurt. How could I have thought there was murder going on here?

"You come with a message? A letter?" asked Alvin Miller. Now that the boys were outside, yelling at each other across the meadow, the grown men could get a word in.

"Sorry," said Taleswapper. "Just a traveler. A young lady in town said I might find a place to sleep up here. In exchange for whatever good hard work you might have for my arms."

Alvin Miller grinned. "Let me see how much work those arms can do." He thrust out an arm, but it wasn't to shake hands. He gripped Taleswapper by the forearm and braced his right foot against Taleswapper's right foot. "Think you can throw me?" asked Alvin Miller.

"Just tell me before we start," said Taleswapper, "whether I'll get a better supper if I throw you, or if I don't throw you."

Alvin Miller leaned back his head and whooped like a Red. "What's your name, stranger?"

"Taleswapper."

"Well, Mr. Taleswapper, I hope you like the taste of dirt, cause that's what you'll eat before you eat anything else here!"

Taleswapper felt the grip on his forearm tighten. His own arms were strong, but not like this man's grip. Still, a game of throws wasn't all strength. It was also wit, and Taleswapper had a bit of that. He let himself slowly flinch under Alvin Miller's pressure, long before he had forced the man to use his full strength. Then, suddenly, he pulled with all his might in the direction Miller was pushing. Usually that was enough to topple the bigger man, using his own weight against him— but Alvin Miller was ready, pulled the other way, and flung Taleswapper so far that he landed right among the stones that formed the foundation for the missing millstone.

There had been no malice in it, though, just the love of the contest. No sooner was Taleswapper down than Miller was helping him up, asking him if anything was broken.

"I'm just glad your millstone wasn't in place yet," said Taleswapper, "or you'd be stuffing brains back into my head."

"What? You're in Wobbish country, man! There ain't no need for brains out *here*."

"Well, you threw me," said Taleswapper. "Does that mean you won't let me earn a bed and a meal?"

"Earn it? No sir. I won't allow such a thing." But the grin on his face denied the harshness of his words. "No, no, you can work if you like, because a man likes to feel that he pays his way in the world. But truth is I'd let you stay even if you had two legs broke and couldn't help a lick. We've got a bed all ready for you, just off the kitchen, and I'll bet a hog against a huckleberry that them boys already told Faith to set another bowl for supper."

"That's kind of you, sir."

"Not at all," said Alvin Miller. "You sure nothing got broke? You hit them stones awful hard."

"Then I imagine you ought to check to make sure none of those stones got split, sir."

Alvin laughed again, slapped him on the back, and led him up to the house.

Such a house it was. There couldn't be more screeching and shouting in hell. Miller tried to sort out all the children for him. The four older girls were his daughters, busy as could be at half a dozen jobs, each one carrying on separate arguments with each of her sisters, at the top of her voice, passing from quarrel to quarrel as her work took her from room to room. The screaming baby was a grandchild, as were the five toddlers playing Roundheads and Cavaliers on and under the dining table. The mother, Faith, seemed oblivious to it all as she labored in the kitchen. Occasionally she'd reach out to cuff a nearby child, but otherwise she didn't let them interrupt her work—or her steady stream of orders, rebukes, threats, and complaints. "How do you keep your wits together, in all this?" Taleswapper asked her.

"Wits?" she asked him sharply. "Do you think anyone with wits would put up with this?"

Miller showed him to his room. That's what he called it, "your room, as long as you care to stay." It had a large bed and a feather pillow, and blankets, too, and half of one wall was the back of the chimney, so it was warm. Taleswapper hadn't been offered a bed like this in all his wandering. "Promise me that your name isn't really Procrustes," he said.

Miller didn't understand the allusion, but it didn't matter, he knew the look on Taleswapper's face. No doubt he'd seen it before. "We don't put our guests in the worst room, Taleswapper, we put them in the best. And no more talk about *that*."

"You have to let me work for you tomorrow, then."

"Oh, there's jobs to do, if you're good with your hands. And if you ain't ashamed of women's work, my wife could use a help or two. We'll see what happens." At that, Miller left the room and closed the door behind him.

The noise of the house was only partly dampened by the closed door, but it was a music that Taleswapper didn't mind hearing. It was only afternoon, but he couldn't help himself. He swung off his pack and pried off his boots and eased himself down on the mattress. It rustled like a straw tick, but there was a feather mattress on top of that, so it was deep and soft. And the straw was fresh, and dried herbs hung by the hearthstones to give it the smell of thyme and rosemary. Did I ever lie upon so soft a bed in Philadelphia? Or before that, in England? Not since I left my mother's womb, he thought.

There was nothing shy about the use of powers in this house; the hex was right in the open, painted above the door. But he recognized the pattern. It wasn't a peacemaker, designed to quell any violence in the soul that slept here. It wasn't a warning, and it wasn't a fending. Not a bit of it was designed to protect the house from the guest, or the guest from the house. It was for comfort, pure and simple. And it was perfectly, exquisitely drawn, exactly the right proportions. An exact hex wasn't easy to draw, being made of threes. Taleswapper couldn't remember seeing a more perfect one.

So it didn't surprise him, as he lay on the bed, to feel the muscles of his body unknotting, as if this bed and this room were undoing the weariness of twenty-five years of wandering. It occurred to him that when he died, he hoped the grave was as comfortable as this bed.

When Alvin Junior rocked him awake, the whole house smelled of sage and pepper and simmered beef. "You've just got time to use the privy, wash up, and come eat," said the boy.

"I must have fallen asleep," said Taleswapper.

"That's what I made that hex to do," said the boy. "Works good, don't it?" Then he charged out of the room.

Almost immediately Taleswapper heard one of the girls yelling the most alarming series of threats at the boy. The quarrel continued at top volume as Taleswapper went out to the privy, and when he came back inside, the yelling was still going on—though Taleswapper thought perhaps now it was a different sister yelling.

"I swear tonight in your sleep Al Junior I'll sew a skunk to the soles of your feet!" Al's answer was muffled by distance, but it caused another bout of screaming. Taleswapper had heard yelling before. Sometimes it was love and sometimes it was hate. When it was hate, he got out as quickly as he could. In this house, he could stay.

Hands and face washed, he was clean enough that Goody Faith allowed him to carry the loaves of bread to the table—"as long as you don't let the bread touch that gamy shirt of yours." Then Taleswapper took his place in line, bowl in hand, as the whole family trooped into the kitchen and emerged with the majority of a hog parceled out among them.

It was Faith, not Miller himself, who called on one of the girls to pray, and Taleswapper took note that Miller didn't so much as close his eyes, though all the children had bowed heads and clasped hands. It was as if prayer was a thing he tolerated, but didn't encourage. Without having to ask, Taleswapper knew that Alvin Miller and the preacher down in that fine white church did not get along at all. Taleswapper decided Miller might even appreciate a proverb from his book: "As the caterpillar chooses the fairest leaves to lay her eggs on, so the priest lays his curse on the fairest joys."

The meal was not a time of chaos, to Taleswapper's surprise. Each child in turn reported what he did that day, and all listened, sometimes giving advice or praise. Finally, when the stew was gone and Taleswapper was dabbing at the last traces in his bowl with a sop of bread, Miller turned to him, just like he had to everyone else in the family.

"And your day, Taleswapper. Was it well spent?"

"I walked some miles before noon, and climbed a tree," said Taleswapper. "There I saw a steeple, which led me to a town. There a Christian man feared my hidden powers, though he saw none of them, and so did a preacher, though he said he didn't believe I had any. Still, I was looking for a meal and a bed, and a chance to work to earn them, and a woman said that the folks at the end of a particular wagon track would take me in."

"That would be our daughter Eleanor," said Faith.

"Yes," said Taleswapper. "I see now that she has her mother's eyes, which are always calm no matter what is happening."

"No, friend," said Faith. "It's just that these eyes have seen such times that since then it hasn't been easy to alarm me."

"I hope before I leave to hear the story of such times," Taleswapper said.

Faith looked away as she put another slab of cheese on a grandchild's bread.

Taleswapper went right on with his account of the day, however, not wishing to show that she might have embarrassed him by not answering. "That wagon track was most peculiar," he said. "There were covered bridges over brooks that a child could wade in, and a man could step over. I hope to hear the story of those bridges before I go."

Again, no one would meet his gaze.

"And when I came out of the woods, I found a mill with no millstone, and two boys wrestling on a wagon, and a miller who gave me the worst throw of my life, and a family that took me in and gave me the best room in the house even though I was a stranger, and they didn't know me to be good or evil."

"Of course you're good," said Al Junior.

"Do you mind my asking? I've met many hospitable people in my time, and stayed in many a happy home, but not one happier than this, and no one quite so glad to see me."

All were still around the table. Finally, Faith raised her head and smiled at him. "I'm glad you found us to be happy," she said. "But we all remember other times as well, and perhaps our present happiness is sweeter, from the memory of grief."

"But why do you take in a man like me?"

Miller himself answered. "Because once we were strangers, and good folk took us in."

"I lived in Philadelphia for a time, and it strikes me to ask you, are you of the Society of Friends?"

Faith shook her head. "I'm Presbyterian. So are many of the children."

Taleswapper looked at Miller.

"I'm nothing," he said.

"A Christian isn't nothing," said Taleswapper.

"I'm no Christian, either."

"Ah," said Taleswapper. "A Deist, then, like Tom Jefferson." The children murmured at his mention of the great man's name.

"Taleswapper, I'm a father who loves his children, a husband who loves his wife, a farmer who pays his debts, and a miller without a millstone." Then the man stood up from the table and walked away. They heard a door close. He was gone away outside.

Taleswapper turned to Faith. "Oh, milady, I'm afraid you must regret my coming to your house."

"You ask a powerful lot of questions," she said.

"I told you my name, and my name is what I do. Whenever I sense that there's a story, one that matters, one that's true, I hunger for it. And if I hear it, and believe it, then I remember it forever, and tell it again wherever I go."

"That's how you earn your way?" asked one of the girls.

"I earn my way by helping mend wagons and dig ditches and spin thread and anything else that needs doing. But my life work is tales, and I swap them one for one. You may think right now that you don't want to tell me any of your stories, and that's fine with me, because I never took a story that wasn't willingly told. I'm no thief. But you see, I've already got a story—the things that happened to me today. The kindest people and the softest bed between the Mizzipy and the Alph."

"Where's the Alph? Is that a river?" asked Cally.

"What, you want a story?" asked Taleswapper.

Yes, clamored the children.

"But not about the river Alph," said Al Junior. "That's not a real place."

Taleswapper looked at him in genuine surprise. "How did you know? Have you read Lord Byron's collection of Coleridge's poetry?"

Al Junior looked around in bafflement.

"We don't get much bookstuff here," said Faith. "The preacher gives them Bible lessons, so they can learn to read."

"Then how did you know the river Alph isn't real?"

Al Junior scrunched his face, as if to say, Don't ask me questions when I don't even know the answer myself. "The story I want is about Jefferson. You said his name like you met him."

"Oh, I did. And Tom Paine, and Patrick Henry before they hanged him, and I saw the sword that cut off George Washington's head. I even saw King Robert the Second, before the French sank his ship back in naught one and took him to the bottom of the sea."

"Where he belonged," murmured Faith.

"If not deeper," said one of the older girls.

"I'll say amen to that. They say in Appalachee that he had so much blood on his hands that even his bones are stained brown with it, and even the most indiscriminate fish won't gnaw at them."

The children laughed.

"Even more than Tom Jefferson," said Al Junior, "I want a tale of the greatest American wizard. I bet you knew Ben Franklin."

Again, the child had startled him. How did he guess that of all tales, those about Ben Franklin were the ones he best loved to tell? "Know him? Oh, a little," said Taleswapper, knowing that the way he said it promised them all the stories they could hope for. "I lived with him only half a dozen years, and there were eight hours every night that I wasn't with him—so I can't say I know *much*."

Al Junior leaned over the table, his eyes bright and unblinking. "Was he truly a maker?"

"All those stories, each in its own time," said Taleswapper. "As long as your father and mother are willing to have me around, and as long as I believe I'm being useful, I'll stay and tell stories night and day."

"Starting with Ben Franklin," insisted Alvin Junior. "Did he really pull lightning out of the sky?"

10

Visions

Alvin Junior woke up sweating from the nightmare. It was so real, and he was panting just as if he had been trying to run away. But there was no running away, he knew that. He lay there with his eyes closed, afraid to open them for a while, knowing that when he did, it would still be there. A long time ago, when he was still little, he used to cry out when this nightmare came. But when he tried to explain it to Pa and Mama, they always said the same thing. "Why, that's just *nothing*, son. You're telling me you're so a-scared of *nothing*?" So he learned himself to stifle and never cry when the dream came.

He opened his eyes, and it fled away to the corners of the room, where he didn't have to look right at it. That was good enough. Stay there and let me be, he said silently.

Then he realized that it was full daylight, and Mama had laid out his black broadcloth pants and jacket and a clean shirt. His Sunday go-to-meeting clothes. He'd almost rather go back to the nightmare than wake up to this.

Alvin Junior hated Sunday mornings. He hated getting all dressed up, so he couldn't set on the ground or kneel in the grass or even bend over without something getting messed up and Mama telling him to have some respect for the Lord's day. He hated having to tiptoe around the house all morning because it was the Sabbath and there wasn't to be no playing or making noise on the Sabbath. Worst of all he hated the thought of sitting on a hard bench down front, with Reverend Thrower looking him in the eye while he preached about the fires of hell that were waiting for the ungodly who despised the true religion and put their faith in the feeble understanding of man. Every Sunday, it seemed like.

And it wasn't that Alvin really despised religion. He just despised Reverend Thrower. It was all those hours in school, now that harvest was over. Alvin Junior was a good reader, and he got right answers most of the time in his ciphering. But that wasn't enough for old Thrower. He also had to teach religion right along with it. The other children—the Swedes and Knickerbockers from upriver, the Scotch and English from down—only got a licking when they sassed or got three wrong answers in a row. But Thrower took his cane to Alvin Junior every chance he got, it seemed like, and it wasn't over book-learning, it was always about religion.

Of course it didn't help much that the Bible kept striking Alvin funny at all the wrong times. That's what Measure said, the time that Alvin ran away from school and hid in David's house till Measure found him nigh onto suppertime. "If you just didn't laugh when he reads from the Bible, you wouldn't get whupped so much."

But it was *funny*. When Jonathan shot all those arrows in the sky and they missed. When Jeroboam didn't shoot enough arrows out his window. When Pharaoh kept finding tricky ways to keep the Israelites from leaving. When Samson was so dumb he told his secret to Delilah after she already betrayed him twice. "How can I keep from laughing?"

"Just think about getting blisters on your butt," said Measure. "That ought to take the smile off your face."

"But I never remember till after I already laughed."

"Then you'll probably never need a chair till you're fifteen years old," said Measure. "Cause Mama won't ever let you out of that school, and Thrower won't ever let up on you, and you can't hide in David's house forever."

"Why not?"

"Because hiding from your enemy is the same as letting him win."

So Measure wouldn't keep him safe, and he had to go back—and take a licking from Pa, too, for scaring everybody by running away and hiding so long. Still, Measure *had* helped him. It was a comfort to know that somebody else was willing to say that Thrower was his enemy. All the others were so full of how wonderful and godly and educated Thrower was, and how *kind* he was to teach the children from his fount of wisdom, that it like to made Alvin puke.

Even though Alvin mostly kept his face under control during school, and so got less lickings, Sunday was the most terrible struggle of all, because he sat there on that hard bench listening to Thrower, half the time wanting to bust out laughing till he fell on the floor, and half the time wanting to stand up and shout, "That's just about the stupidest thing I ever heard a growed man say!" He even had a feeling Pa wouldn't lick him very hard for saying that to Thrower, since Pa never had much of an opinion of the man. But Mama—she'd never forgive him for doing blasphemy in the house of the Lord.

Sunday morning, he decided, is designed to let sinners have a sample of the first day of eternity in hell.

Probably Mama wouldn't even let Taleswapper tell so much as the tiniest story today, lessen it came from the Bible. And since Taleswapper never seemed to tell stories from the Bible, Alvin Junior guessed that nothing good would come today.

Mama's voice blasted up the stairs. "Alvin Junior, I'm so sick and tired of you taking three hours to get dressed on Sunday morning that I'm about to take you to church naked!"

"I ain't naked!" Alvin shouted down. But since what he was wearing was his nightgown, it was probably *worse* than being naked. He shucked off the flannel nightgown, hung it on a peg, and started dressing as fast as he could.

It was funny. On any other day, he only had to reach out for his clothes without even thinking, and they'd be there, just the piece he wanted. Shirt, trousers, stockings, shoes. Always there in his hand when he reached. But on Sunday morning, it was like the clothes ran away from his hand. He'd go for his shirt and come back with his pants. He'd reach for a sock and come up with a shoe, time after time. It was like as if the clothes didn't want to get put on his body any more than he wanted them there.

So when Mama banged open the door, it wasn't altogether Alvin's fault that he didn't even have his pants on yet.

"You've missed breakfast! You're still half-naked! If you think I'm going to make the whole family parade into church late on account of you, you've got—"

"Another think coming," said Alvin.

It wasn't *his* fault that she always said the same thing. But she got mad at him as if he should have pretended to be *surprised* to hear her say it for the ninetieth time since summer. Oh, she was all set to give him a licking, all right, or call for Pa to do it even worse, when there was Taleswapper, come to save him.

"Goody Faith," said Taleswapper, "I'd be glad to see to it he comes to church, if you want to go on ahead with the others."

The minute Taleswapper spoke, Mama whirled around and tried to hide how mad she'd been. Alvin right away started doing a calming on her—with his right hand, where she couldn't see it, since if she saw him doing a spell on her, she'd break his arm, and that was one threat Alvin Junior truly believed. A calming didn't work so well without touching, but since she was trying so hard to *look* calm in front of Taleswapper, it worked all right.

"I hate to put you to any trouble," said Mama.

"No trouble, Goody Faith," said Taleswapper. "I do little enough to repay your kindness to me."

"Little enough!" The fretfulness was almost gone from Mama's voice now. "Why, my husband says you do the work of two grown men. And when you tell stories to the little ones I get more peace and quiet in this house than I've had since—since *ever*." She turned back to Alvin, but now her anger was more an act than real. "Will you do what Taleswapper tells you, and come to church right quick?"

"Yes, Mama," said Alvin Junior. "Quick as I can."

"All right then. Thank you kindly, Taleswapper. If you can get that boy to obey, that's more than anybody else has managed since he learned to talk."

"He's a real brat," said Mary, from the hallway outside.

"Shut your mouth, Mary," Mama said, "or I'll stuff your lower lip up your nose and tack it there to *keep* it shut."

Alvin sighed in relief. When Mama made impossible threats it meant she wasn't all that angry anymore. Mary put her nose in the air and flounced down the hall, but Alvin didn't even bother with it. He just grinned at Taleswapper, and Taleswapper grinned at him.

"Having trouble getting dressed for church, lad?" asked Taleswapper.

"I'd rather dress myself in lard and walk through a herd of hungry bears," said Alvin Junior.

"More people live through church than survive encounters with bears."

"Not by much, though."

Soon enough he got dressed. But he was able to talk Taleswapper into taking the shortcut, which meant walking through the woods up over the hill behind the house, instead of going around by way of the road. Since it was right cold outside, and hadn't rained in a while, and wasn't about to snow yet, there'd be no mud and Mama'd probably not even guess. And what Mama didn't know wouldn't hurt him.

"I noticed," said Taleswapper as they climbed up the leaf-covered slope, "that your father didn't go with your mother and Cally and the girls."

"He doesn't go to that church," said Alvin. "He says Reverend Thrower is a jackass. Course, he don't say that where Mama can hear."

"I suppose not," said Taleswapper.

They stood at the top of the hill, looking down across open meadowland toward the church. The church's own hill hid the town of Vigor Church from view. The frost was just beginning to melt off the brown autumn grass, so that the church looked to be the whitest thing in a world of whiteness, and the sun flashed on it like it was another sun. Alvin could see wagons still pulling into place, and horses being tied to the posts on the meadow. If they hurried right now, they'd probably be in their places before Reverend Thrower started up the hymn.

But Taleswapper didn't start down the hill. He just set himself on a stump and started to recite a poem. Alvin listened tight, because Taleswapper's poems often had a real bite to them.

> *"I went to the Garden of Love,*
> *And saw what I never had seen:*
> *A chapel was built in the midst,*
> *Where I used to play on the green.*
>
> *And the gates of this chapel were shut,*
> *And 'Thou shalt not' writ over the door,*
> *So I turned to the Garden of Love,*
> *That so many sweet flowers bore,*
>
> *And I saw it was filled with graves,*
> *And tombstones where flowers should be:*
> *And priests in black gowns were walking their rounds,*
> *And binding with briars my joys and desires."*

Oh, Taleswapper had a knack, he did, for as he recited, the very world changed before Alvin's eyes. The meadows and trees looked like the loudest shout of spring, vivid yellow-green with ten thousand blossoms, and the white of the chapel in the midst of it was no longer gleaming, but instead the dusty, chalky white of old bones. "Binding with briars my joys and desires," Alvin repeated. "You ain't got much use for religion."

"I breathe religion with my every breath," said the Taleswapper. "I long for visions, I search for the traces of God's hand. But in this world I see more traces of the other. A trail of glistening slime that burns me when I touch it. God is a bit standoffish these days, Al Junior, but Satan has no fear of getting down in the muck with mankind."

"Thrower says his church is the house of God."

Taleswapper, he just sat there and said nothing for the longest time.

Finally Alvin asked him right out: "Have you seen devil traces in that church?"

In the days that Taleswapper had been with them, Alvin had come to know that Taleswapper never exactly lied. But when he didn't want to get pinned down with the true answer, he'd say a poem. He said one now.

> *"O Rose, thou art sick.*
> *The invisible worm*
> *That flies in the night*
> *In the howling storm*
>
> *Has found out thy bed*
> *Of crimson joy,*
> *And his dark secret love*
> *Does thy life destroy."*

Alvin was impatient with such twisting answers. "If I want to hear something I don't understand, I can read Isaiah."

"Music to my ears, my lad, to compare me to the greatest of prophets."

"He ain't much of a prophet if nobody can understand a thing he wrote."

"Or perhaps he meant us all to become prophets."

"I don't hold with prophets," said Alvin. "Near as I can tell, they end up just as dead as the next man." It was something he had heard his father say.

"Everybody ends up dead," said Taleswapper. "But some who are dead live on in their words."

"Words never stay straight," said Alvin. "Now, when I *make* a thing, then it's the thing I made. Like when I make a basket. It's a basket. When it gets tore, then it's a tored-up basket. But when I say words, they can get all twisted up. Thrower can take those same very words I said and bend them back and make them mean just contrary to what I said."

"Think of it another way, Alvin. When you make one basket, it can never be more than one basket. But when you say words, they can be repeated over and over, and fill men's hearts a thousand miles from where you first spoke them. Words can magnify, but things are never more than what they are."

Alvin tried to picture that, and with Taleswapper saying it, the picture came easy to his mind. Words as invisible as air, coming out of Taleswapper's mouth and spreading from person to person. Growing larger all the time, but still invisible.

Then, suddenly, the vision changed. He saw the words coming from the preacher's mouth, like a trembling in the air, spreading out, seeping into everything—and suddenly it became his nightmare, the terrible dream that came on him, waking or sleeping, and spiked his heart to his spine till he like to died. The world filling up with an invisible trembling *nothing* that seeped into everything and shook it apart. Alvin could see it, rolling toward him like a huge ball, growing all the time. He knew from all the nightmares before that even if he clenched his fists it would thin itself out and seep between his fingers, and even when he closed his mouth and his eyes it would press on his face and ooze into his nose and ears and—

Taleswapper shook him. Shook him hard. Alvin opened his eyes. The trembling air retreated back to the edges of his sight. That's where Alvin saw it most of the time, waiting just barely out of sight, wary as a weasel, ready to flit away if he turned his head.

"What's wrong with you, lad?" asked Taleswapper. His face looked afraid.

"Nothing," said Alvin.

"Don't tell me nothing," said Taleswapper. "All of a sudden I saw a fear come over you, as if you were seeing a terrible vision."

"It wasn't a vision," said Alvin. "I had a vision once, and I know."

"Oh?" said Taleswapper. "What vision was that?"

"A Shining Man," said Alvin. "I never told nobody about it, and I don't reckon to start now."

Taleswapper didn't press him. "What you saw now, if it wasn't a vision—well, what was it?"

"It was nothing." It was a true answer, but he also knew it was no answer at all. But he didn't *want* to answer. Whenever he told people, they just scoffed at him for being such a baby about nothing.

But Taleswapper wouldn't let him slough off his question. "I've been longing for a true vision all my life, Al Junior, and you saw one, here in broad daylight, with your eyes wide open, you saw something so terrible it made you stop breathing, now tell me what it was."

"I told you! It was nothing!" Then, quieter: "It's *nothing*, but I can see it. Like the air gets wobbly wherever it goes."

"It's nothing, but not invisible?"

"It gets into everything. It gets into all the smallest cracks and shakes everything apart. Just shivers and shivers until there's nothing left but dust, and then it shivers the dust, and I try to keep it out, but it gets bigger and bigger, it rolls over everything, till it like to fills the whole sky and the whole earth." Alvin couldn't help himself. He was shaking with cold, even though he was bundled up thick as a bear.

"How many times have you seen this before?"

"Ever since I can remember. Just now and then it'll come on me. Most times I just think about other things and it stays back."

"Where?"

"Back. Out of sight." Alvin knelt down and then sat down, exhausted. Sat right in the damp grass with his Sunday pants, but he didn't hardly notice. "When you talked about words spreading and spreading, it made me see it again."

"A dream that comes again and again is trying to tell you the truth," said Taleswapper.

The old man was so plainly eager about the whole thing that Alvin wondered if he really understood how frightening it was. "This ain't one of your stories, Taleswapper."

"It will be," said Taleswapper, "as soon as I understand it."

Taleswapper sat beside him and thought in silence for the longest time. Alvin just sat there, twisting grass in his fingers. After a while he got impatient. "Maybe you can't understand everything," he said. "Maybe it's just a craziness in me. Maybe I get lunatic spells."

"Here," said Taleswapper, taking no notice that Alvin had even spoke. "I've thought of a meaning. Let me say it, and see if we believe it."

Alvin didn't like being ignored. "Or maybe *you* get lunatic spells, you ever think of that, Taleswapper?"

Taleswapper brushed aside Alvin's doubt. "All the universe is just a dream in God's mind, and as long as he's asleep, he believes in it, and things stay real. What you see is God waking up, gradually waking up, and his wakefulness sweeps through the dream, undoes the universe, until finally he sits up, rubs his eyes, and says, 'My, what a dream, I wish I could remember what it was,' and in that moment we'll all be gone." He looked eagerly at Alvin. "How was that?"

"If you believe that, Taleswapper, then you're a blamed fool, just like Armor-of-God says."

"Oh, he says that, does he?" Taleswapper suddenly snaked out his hand and took Alvin by the wrist. Alvin was so surprised he dropped what he was holding. "No! Pick it up! Look what you were doing!"

"I was just fiddling, for pete's sake."

Taleswapper reached down and picked up what Alvin had dropped. It was a tiny basket, not an inch across, made from autumn grasses. "You made this, just now."

"I reckon so," said Alvin.

"Why did you make it?"

"Just made it."

"You weren't even thinking about it?"

"It ain't much of a basket, you know. I used to make them for Cally. He called them bug baskets when he was little. They just fall apart pretty soon."

"You saw a vision of *nothing*, and then you had to make *something*."

Alvin looked at the basket. "Reckon so."

"Do you always do that?"

Alvin thought back to other times he'd seen the shivering air. "I'm always making things," he said. "Don't mean much."

"But you don't feel right again until you've made something. After you see the vision of nothing, you aren't at peace until you put something together."

"Maybe I've just got to work it off."

"Not just *work*, though, is it, lad? Chopping wood doesn't do the job for you. Gathering eggs, toting water, cutting hay, that doesn't ease you."

Now Alvin began to see the pattern Taleswapper had found. It was true, near as he could remember. He'd wake up after such a dream at night, and couldn't stop fidgeting until he'd done some weaving or built a haystack or done up a doll out of corn shucks for one of the nieces. Same thing when the vision came on him in the day—he wasn't no good at whatever chore he was doing, until he built something that hadn't been there before, even if it was nothing more than a pile of rocks or part of a stone wall.

"It's true, isn't it? You do that every time, don't you?"

"Mostly."

"Then let me tell you the name of the nothing. It's the Unmaker."

"Never heard of it," said Alvin.

"Neither did I, till now. That's because it likes to keep itself secret. It's the enemy of everything that exists. All it wants is to break everything into pieces, and break those pieces into pieces, until there's nothing left at all."

"If you break something into pieces, and break the pieces into pieces, you don't get *nothing*," said Alvin. "You just get lots of little pieces."

"Shut up and listen to the story," said Taleswapper.

Alvin was used to him saying that. Taleswapper said it to Alvin Junior more often than to anybody else, even the nephews.

"I'm not talking about good and evil," said Taleswapper. "Even the devil himself can't afford to break everything down, can he, or he'd cease to be, just like everything else. The most evil creatures don't desire the destruction of everything—they only desire to exploit it for themselves."

Alvin had never heard the word *exploit* before, but it sounded nasty.

"So in the great war between the Unmaker and everything else, God and the devil should be on the same side. But the devil, he doesn't know it, and so he serves the Unmaker as often as not."

"You mean the devil's out to beat himself?"

"My story isn't about the devil," said Taleswapper. He was steady as rain when a story was coming out of him. "In the great war against the Unmaker of your vision, all the men and women of the world should be allies. But the great enemy remains invisible, so that no one guesses that they unwittingly serve him. They don't realize that war is the Unmaker's ally, because it tears down everything it touches. They don't understand that fire, murder, crime, cupidity, and concupiscence break apart the fragile bonds that make human beings into nations, cities, families, friends, and souls."

"You must be a prophet right enough," said Alvin Junior, "cause I can't understand a thing you said."

"A prophet," murmured Taleswapper, "but it was your eyes that saw. Now I know the agony of Aaron: to speak the words of truth, yet never have the vision for himself."

"You're making a big lot out of my nightmares."

Taleswapper was silent, sitting on the ground, his elbows on his knees, his chin propped all dismal on his palms. Alvin tried to figure out what the man was talking about. It was a sure thing that what he saw in his bad dreams wasn't a thing of any kind, so it must be poetical to talk about the Unmaker like a person. Maybe it was true, though, maybe the Unmaker wasn't just something he imagined up in his brain, maybe it was real, and Al Junior was the only person who could see it. Maybe the whole world was in terrible danger, and it was Alvin's job to fight it off, to beat it back, to keep the thing at bay. It was sure enough that when the dream was on him, Alvin couldn't bear it, wanted to drive it away. But he never could figure out how.

"Sposing I believe you," said Alvin. "Sposing there's such a thing as the Unmaker. There ain't a blame thing I can do."

A slow smile crept over Taleswapper's face. He tipped himself to one side, to free up his hand, which slowly reached down to the ground and picked up the little bug basket where it lay in the grass. "Does that look like a blamed thing?"

"That's just a bunch of grass."

"It *was* a bunch of grass," said Taleswapper. "And if you tore it up it'd be a bunch of grass again. But now, right now, it's something more than that."

"A little bug basket is all."

"Something that you made."

"Well, it's a sure thing grass don't grow that way."

"And when you made it, you beat back the Unmaker."

"Not by much," said Alvin.

"No," said Taleswapper. "But by the making of one bug basket. By that much, you beat him back."

It came together in Alvin's mind. The whole story that the Taleswapper was trying to tell. Alvin knew all kinds of opposites in the world: good and evil, light and dark, free and slave, love and hate. But deeper than all those opposites was making and unmaking. So deep that hardly anybody noticed that it was the most important opposite of all. But *he* noticed, and so that made the Unmaker his enemy. That's why the Unmaker came after him in his sleep. After all, Alvin had his knack. His knack for setting things in order, putting things in the shape they ought to be in.

"I think my *real* vision was about the same thing," said Alvin.

"You don't have to tell me about the Shining Man," said Taleswapper. "I never mean to pry."

"You mean you just pry by accident?" said Alvin.

That was the kind of remark that got him a slap across the face at home, but Taleswapper only laughed.

"I did something evil and I didn't even know it," said Alvin. "The Shining Man came and stood by the foot of my bed, and first he showed me a vision of what I done, so I knowed it was bad. I tell you I cried, to know I was so wicked. But then he showed me what my knack was for, and now I see it's the same thing you're talking about. I saw a stone that I pulled out of a mountain, and it was round as a ball, and when I looked close I saw it was the whole world, with forests and animals and oceans and fish and all on it. That's what my knack is for, to try to put things in order."

Taleswapper's eyes were gleaming. "The Shining Man showed you such a vision," he said. "Such a vision as I'd give my life to see."

"Only cause I'd used my knack to cause harm to others, just for my own pleasure," said Alvin. "I made a promise then, my most solemn vow, that I'd never use my knack for my own good. Only for others."

"A good promise," said Taleswapper. "I wish all men and women in the world would take such an oath and keep it."

"Anyway, that's how I know that the—the Unmaker, it isn't a vision. The Shining Man wasn't even a vision. What he *showed* me, *that* was a vision, but him standing there, he was *real*."

"And the Unmaker?"

"Real, too. I don't just see it in my head, it's *there*."

Taleswapper nodded, his eyes never leaving Alvin's face.

"I've got to make things," said Alvin. "Faster than he can tear them down."

"Nobody can make things fast enough for that," said Taleswapper. "If all the men in all the world made all the earth into a million million million million bricks, and built a wall all the days of their lives, the wall would crumble faster than they could build it. Sections of the wall would fall apart even before they built them."

"Now that's silly," said Alvin. "A wall can't fall down before you build it up."

"If they keep at it long enough, the bricks will crumble into dust when they pick them up, their own hands will rot and slough like slime from their bones, until brick and flesh and bone alike all break down into the same indistinguishable dust. Then the Unmaker will sneeze, and the dust will be infinitely dispersed so that it can never come together again. The universe will be cold, still, silent, dark, and at last the Unmaker will be at rest."

Alvin tried to make sense out of what Taleswapper was saying. It was the same thing he did whenever Thrower talked about religion in school, so Alvin thought of it as kind of a dangerous thing to do. But he couldn't stop himself from doing it, and from asking his questions, even if they made people mad. "If things are breaking down faster than they're getting made, then how come anything's still around? Why hasn't the Unmaker already won? What are we doing here?"

Taleswapper wasn't Reverend Thrower. Alvin's question didn't make him angry. He just knit his brow and shook his head. "I don't know. You're right. We *can't* be here. Our existence is impossible."

"Well we *are* here, in case you didn't notice," said Alvin. "What kind of stupid tale is that, when we just have to look at each other to know it isn't true?"

"It has problems, I admit."

"I thought you only told stories you believe."

"I believed it while I was telling it."

Taleswapper looked so mournful that Alvin reached out and laid his hand on the man's shoulder, though his coat was so thick and Alvin's hand so small that he wasn't altogether sure Taleswapper felt his touch. "I believed it, too. Parts of it. For a while."

"Then there *is* truth in it. Maybe not much, but some." Taleswapper looked relieved.

But Alvin couldn't leave well enough alone. "Just because you believe it doesn't make it so."

Taleswapper's eyes went wide. Now I've done it, thought Alvin. Now I've made him mad, just like I make Thrower mad. I do it to everbody.

So he wasn't surprised when Taleswapper reached out both arms toward him, took Alvin's face between his hands, and spoke with such force as to drive the words deep into Alvin's forehead. "Everything possible to be believed is an image of truth."

And the words *did* pierce him, and he understood them, though he could not have put in words what it was he understood. Everything possible to be believed is an image of truth. If it feels true to me, then there is something true in it, even if it isn't all true. And if I study it out in my mind, then maybe I can find what parts of it are true, and what parts are false, and—

And Alvin realized something else. That all his arguments with Thrower came down to this: that if something just plain didn't make sense to Alvin, he didn't believe it, and no amount of quoting from the Bible would convince him. Now Taleswapper was telling him that he was *right* to refuse to believe things that made no sense. "Taleswapper, does that mean that what I *don't* believe *can't* be true?"

Taleswapper raised his eyebrows and came back with another proverb. "Truth can never be told so as to be understood, and not be believed."

Alvin was fed up with proverbs. "For once would you tell me straight!"

"The proverb *is* the straight truth, lad. I refuse to twist it up to fit a confused mind."

"Well, if my mind's confused, it's all your fault. All your talk about bricks crumbling before the wall is built—"

"Didn't you believe that?"

"Maybe I did. I reckon if I set out to weave all the grass of this meadow into bug baskets, before I got to the far end of the meadow the grass would all have died and rotted to nothing. I reckon if I set out to turn all the trees from here to Noisy River into barns, the trees'd all be dead and fell before I ever got to the last of them. Can't build a house out of rotted logs."

"I was going to say, 'Men cannot build permanent things out of impermanent pieces.' That is the law. But the way you said it was the proverb of the law: 'You can't build a house out of rotted logs.' "

"I said a proverb?"

"And when we get back to the house, I'll write it in my book."

"In the sealed part?" asked Alvin. Then he remembered that he had only seen that book by peeking through a crack in his floor late at night when Taleswapper was writing by candlelight in the room below him.

Taleswapper looked at him sharp. "I hope you never tried to conjure open that seal."

Alvin was offended. He might peek through a crack, but he'd never *sneak*. "Just knowing you don't want me to read that part is better than any old seal, and if you don't know that, you ain't my friend. I don't pry into your secrets."

"My secrets?" Taleswapper laughed. "I seal that back part because that's where my own writings go, and I simply don't want anyone else writing in that part of the book."

"Do other people write in the front part?"

"They do."

"Well, what do they write? Can I write there?"

"They write one sentence about the most important thing they ever did or ever saw with their own eyes. That one sentence is all I need from then on to remind me of their story. So when I visit in another city, in another house, I can open the book, read the sentence, and tell the story."

Alvin thought of a remarkable possibility. Taleswapper had lived with Ben Franklin, hadn't he? "Did Ben Franklin write in your book?"

"He wrote the very first sentence."

"He wrote down the most important thing he ever did?"

"That he did."

"Well, what *was* it?"

Taleswapper stood up. "Come back to the house with me, lad, and I'll show you. And on the way I'll tell you the story to explain what he wrote."

Alvin sprang up spry, and took the old man by his heavy sleeve, and fairly dragged him toward the path back down to the house. "Come on, then!" Alvin didn't know if Taleswapper had decided not to go on to church, or if he plumb forgot that's where they were supposed to go— whatever the reason, Alvin was happy enough with the result. A Sunday with no church at all was a Sunday worth being alive. Add to that Taleswapper's stories and Maker Ben's own writing in a book, and it was well nigh to being a perfect day.

"There's no hurry, lad. I won't die before noon, nor will you, and stories take some time to tell."

"Was it something he made?" asked Alvin. "The most important thing?"

"As a matter of fact, it was."

"I knew it! The two-glass spectacles? The stove?"

"People used to say to him all the time, Ben, you're a true Maker. But he always denied it. Just like he denied he was a wizard. I've got no knack for hidden powers, he said. I just take pieces of things and put them together in a better way. There were stoves before I made my stove. There were spectacles before I made my spectacles. I never really *made* anything in my life, in the way a true Maker would do it. I give you two-glass spectacles, but a *Maker* would give you new eyes.''

''He figured he never made *anything*?''

''I asked him that one day. The very day that I was starting out with my book. I said to him, Ben, what's the most important thing you ever made? And he started in on what I just told you, about how he never really made anything, and I said to him, Ben, you don't believe that, and I don't believe that. And he said, Bill, you found me out. There's one thing I made, and it's the most important thing I ever did, and it's the most important thing I ever saw.''

Taleswapper fell silent, just shambling down the slope through leaves that whispered loud underfoot.

''Well, what was it?''

''Don't you want to wait till you get home and read it for yourself?''

Alvin got real mad then, madder than he meant to. ''I hate it when people know something and they won't say!''

''No need to get your dander up, lad. I'll tell you. What he wrote was this: The only thing I ever truly made was Americans.''

''That don't make sense. Americans are *born*.''

''Well, now, that's not so, Alvin. *Babies* are born. In England the same as in America. So it isn't being born that makes them American.''

Alvin thought about that for a second. ''It's being born *in* America.''

''Well, that's true enough. But along about fifty years ago, a baby born in Philadelphia was never called an American baby. It was a Pennsylvanian baby. And babies born in New Amsterdam were Knickerbockers, and babies born in Boston were Yankees, and babies born in Charleston were Jacobians or Cavaliers or some such name.''

''They still are,'' Alvin pointed out.

''They are indeed, lad, but they're something else besides. All those names, Old Ben figured, those names divided us up into Virginians and Orangemen and Rhode Islanders, into Whites and Reds and Blacks, into Quakers and Papists and Puritans and Presbyterians, into Dutch, Swedish, French, and English. Old Ben saw how a Virginian could never quite trust a man from Netticut, and how a White man could never quite trust a Red, because they were *different*. And he said to himself, If we've got all these names to hold us apart, why not a name to bind us together? He toyed with a lot of names that already were used. Colonials, for instance. But he didn't like calling us all Colonials because that made us always turn our eyes back to Europe, and besides, the Reds aren't Colonials, are they! Nor are the Blacks, since they came as slaves. Do you see the problem?''

"He wanted a name we could all share the same," said Alvin.

"Just right. There was one thing we all had in common. We all lived on the same continent. North America. So he thought of calling us North Americans. But that was too long. So—"

"Americans."

"That's a name that belongs to a fisherman living on the rugged coast of West Anglia as much as to a baron ruling his slavehold in the southwest part of Dryden. It belongs as much to the Mohawk chief in Irrakwa as to the Knickerbocker shopkeeper in New Amsterdam. Old Ben knew that if people could once start thinking of themselves as Americans, we'd become a nation. Not just a piece of some tired old European country, but a single new nation here in a new land. So he started using that word in everything he wrote. Poor Richard's Almanac was full of talk about Americans this and Americans that. And Old Ben wrote letters to everybody, saying things like, Conflict over land claims is a problem for Americans to solve together. Europeans can't possibly understand what Americans need to survive. Why should Americans die for European wars? Why should Americans be bound by European precedents in our courts of law? Inside of five years, there was hardly a person from New England to Jacobia who didn't think of himself as being, at least partly, an American."

"It was just a name."

"But it is the name by which we call ourselves. And it includes everyone else on this continent who's willing to accept the name. Old Ben worked hard to make sure that name included as many people as possible. Without ever holding any public office except postmaster, he single-handedly turned a name into a nation. With the King ruling over the Cavaliers in the south, and the Lord Protector's men ruling over New England in the north, he saw nothing but chaos and war ahead, with Pennsylvania smack in the middle. He wanted to forestall that war, and he used the name 'American' to fend it off. He made the New Englanders fear to offend Pennsylvania, and made the Cavaliers bend over backward trying to woo Pennsylvanian support. He was the one who agitated for an American Congress to establish trade policies and uniform land law.

"And finally," Taleswapper continued, "just before he invited me over from England, he wrote the American Compact and got the seven original colonies to sign it. It wasn't easy, you know—even the number of states was the result of a great deal of struggle. The Dutch could see that most of the immigrants to America were English and Irish and Scotch, and they didn't want to be swallowed up—so Old Ben allowed them to divide New Netherland into three colonies so they'd have more votes in the Congress. With Suskwahenny split off from the land claimed by New Sweden and Pennsylvania, another squabble was put to rest.''

''That's only six states,'' said Alvin.

''Old Ben refused to allow anyone to sign the Compact unless the Irrakwa were included as the seventh state, with firm borders, with Reds governing themselves. There were plenty of people who wanted a White man's nation, but Old Ben wouldn't hear of it. The only way to have peace, he said, was for all Americans to join together as equals. That's why his Compact doesn't allow slavery or even bonding. That's why his Compact doesn't allow any religion to have authority over any other. That's why his Compact doesn't let the government close down a press or silence a speech. White, Black, and Red; Papist, Puritan, and Presbyterian; rich man, poor man, beggarman, thief—we all live under the same laws. One nation, created out of a single word.''

''American.''

''Now do you see why he calls it his greatest deed?''

''How come the Compact itself ain't more important?''

''The Compact was just the words. The name 'American' was the idea that made the words.''

''It still doesn't include the Yankees and the Cavaliers, and it didn't stop war, neither, cause the Appalachee folk are still fighting against the King.''

''But it *does* include all those people, Alvin. Remember the story of George Washington in Shenandoah? He was Lord Potomac in those days, leading King Robert's largest army against that poor ragtag band that was all Ben Arnold had left. It was plain to see that in the morning, Lord Potomac's Cavaliers would overrun that little fort and seal the doom of Tom Jefferson's free-mountain rebellion. But Lord Potomac had fought beside those mountain men in the wars against the French. And Tom Jefferson had been his friend in days gone by. In his heart he could not bear to think of the morrow's battle. Who was King Robert, that so much blood should be shed for him? All these rebels wanted was to own their land, and not have the King set barons over them, to tax them dry and turn them into slaves as surely as any Black in the Crown Colonies. He didn't sleep at all that night.''

''He was praying,'' said Alvin.

''That's the way Thrower tells it,'' Taleswapper said sharply. ''But no one knows. And when he spoke to the troops the next morning, he didn't say a word about *prayer*. But he did speak about the word Ben Franklin made. He wrote a letter to the King, resigning from his command and rejecting his lands and titles. He didn't sign it 'Lord Potomac,' he signed it 'George Washington.' Then he rose up in the morning and stood before the blue-coat soldiers of the King and told them what he had done, and told them that they were free to choose, all of them, whether to obey their officers and go into battle, or march instead in defense of Tom Jefferson's great Declaration of Freedom. He said, 'The choice is yours, but as for me—' ''

Alvin knew the words, as did every man, woman, and child on the continent. Now the words meant all the more to him, and he shouted them out: '' 'My American sword will never shed a drop of American blood!' ''

''And then, when most of his army had gone and joined the Appa-lachee rebels, with their guns and their powder, their wagons and their supplies, he ordered the senior officer of the men loyal to the King to arrest him. 'I broke my oath to the King,' he said. 'It was for the sake of a higher good, but still I broke my oath, and I will pay the price for my treason.' He paid, yes sir, paid with a blade through his neck. But how many people outside the court of the King think it was really treason?''

''Not a one,'' said Alvin.

''And has the King been able to fight a single battle against the Appalachees since that day?''

''Not a one.''

''Not a man on that battlefield in Shenandoah was a citizen of the United States. Not a man of them lived under the American Compact. And yet when George Washington spoke of American swords and American blood, they understood the name to mean themselves. Now tell me, Alvin Junior, was old Ben wrong to say that the greatest thing he ever made was a single word?''

Alvin would have answered, but right then they stepped up onto the porch of the house, and before they could get to the door, it swung open, and Ma stood there looking down at him. From the look on her face, Alvin knew that he was in trouble this time, and he knew why.

''I meant to go to church, Ma!''

''Lots of dead people meant to go to heaven,'' she answered, ''and they didn't get there, neither.''

''It was my fault, Goody Faith,'' said Taleswapper.

''It surely was not, Taleswapper,'' she said.

''We got to talking, Goody Faith, and I'm afraid I distracted the boy.''

''The boy was born distracted,'' said Ma, never taking her eyes from Alvin's face. ''He takes after his father. If you don't bridle and saddle him and ride him to church, he never gets there, and if you don't nail his feet to the floor of the church he's out that door in a minute. A ten-year-old boy who hates the Lord is enough to make his mother wish he'd never been born.''

The words struck Alvin Junior to the heart.

''That's a terrible thing to wish,'' said Taleswapper. His voice was real quiet, and Ma finally lifted her gaze to the old man's face.

''I *don't* wish it,'' she finally said.

''I'm sorry, Mama,'' said Alvin Junior.

''Come inside,'' she said. ''I left church to come and find you, and now there's not time to get back before the sermon ends.''

''We talked about a lot of things, Mama,'' Alvin said. ''About my dreams, and about Ben Franklin, and—''

''The only story I want to hear from you,'' said Ma, ''is the sound of hymn singing. If you won't go to the church, then you'll sit in the kitchen with me and sing me hymns while I fix the dinner.''

So Alvin didn't get to see Old Ben's sentence in Taleswapper's book, not for hours. Ma kept him singing and working till dinnertime, and after dinner Pa and the big boys and Taleswapper sat around planning tomorrow's expedition to bring a millstone down from the granite mountain.

''I'm doing it for you,'' Pa said to Taleswapper, ''so you better come along.''

''I never asked you to bring a millstone.''

''Not a day since you've been here that you haven't said something about what a shame it is that such a fine mill gets used as nothing but a haybarn, when people hereabouts need good flour.''

''I only said it the once, that I remember.''

''Well, maybe so,'' said Pa, ''but every time I see you, I think about that millstone.''

''That's because you keep wishing the millstone had been there when you threw me.''

''He don't wish that!'' shouted Cally. ''Cause then you'd be dead!'' Taleswapper just grinned, and Papa grinned back. And they went on talking about this and that. Then the wives brought the nephews and nieces over for Sunday supper, and they made Taleswapper sing them the laughing song so many times that Alvin thought he'd scream if he heard another chorus of ''Ha, Ha, Hee.''

It wasn't till after supper, after the nephews and nieces were all gone, that Taleswapper brought out his book.

''I wondered if you'd ever open that book,'' Pa said.

''Just waiting for the right time.'' Then Taleswapper explained about how people wrote down their most important deed.

''I hope you don't expect *me* to write in there,'' Pa said.

"Oh, I wouldn't let you write in it, not yet. You haven't even told me the story of your most important deed." Taleswapper's voice got even softer. "Maybe you didn't actually *do* your most important deed."

Pa looked just a little angry then, or maybe a little afraid. Whichever it was, he got up and came over. "Show me what's in that book, that other people thought was so all-fired important."

"Oh," said Taleswapper. "Can you read?"

"I'll have you know I got a Yankee education in Massachusetts before I ever got married and set up as a miller in West Hampshire, and *long* before I ever came out here. It may not amount to much compared to a *London* education like you got, Taleswapper, but you don't know how to write a word I can't read, lessen it's Latin."

Taleswapper didn't answer. He just opened the book. Pa read the first sentence. "The only thing I ever truly made was Americans." Pa looked up at Taleswapper. "Who wrote *that*?"

"Old Ben Franklin."

"The way I heard it the only American he ever made was illegitimate."

"Maybe Al Junior will explain it to you later," said Taleswapper.

While they said this, Alvin wormed his way in front of them, to stare at Old Ben's handwriting. It looked no different from other men's writing. Alvin felt a little disappointed, though he couldn't have said what he expected. Should the letters be made of gold? Of course not. There was no reason why a great man's words should look any different on a page than the words of a fool.

Still, he couldn't rid himself of frustration that the words were so plain. He reached out and turned the page, turned many pages, riffling them with his fingers. The words were all the same. Grey ink on yellowing paper.

A flash of light came from the book, blinding him for a moment.

"Don't play with the pages like that," said Papa. "You'll tear one."

Alvin turned around to look at Taleswapper. "What's the page with light on it?" he asked. "What does it say *there*?"

"Light?" asked Taleswapper.

Then Alvin knew that he alone had seen it.

"Find the page yourself," said Taleswapper.

"He'll just tear it," said Papa.

"He'll be careful," said Taleswapper.

But Papa sounded angry. "I said stand away from that book, Alvin Junior."

Alvin started to obey, but felt Taleswapper's hand on his shoulder. Taleswapper's voice was quiet, and Alvin felt the old man's fingers moving in a sign of warding. "The boy saw something in the book," said Taleswapper, "and I want him to find it again for me."

And, to Alvin's surprise, Papa backed down. "If you don't mind getting your book ripped up by that careless lazy boy," he murmured, then fell silent.

Alvin turned to the book and carefully thumbed the pages, one at a time. Finally one fell into place, and from it came a light, which at first dazzled him, but gradually subsided until it came only from a single sentence, whose letters were on fire.

"Do you see them burning?" asked Alvin.

"No," said Taleswapper. "But I smell the smoke of it. Touch the words that burn for you."

Alvin reached out and gingerly touched the beginning of the sentence. The flame, to his surprise, was not hot, though it did warm him. It warmed him through to the bone. He shuddered as the last cold of autumn fled from his body. He smiled, he was so bright inside. But almost as soon as he touched it, the flame collapsed, cooled, was gone.

"What does it say?" asked Mama. She was standing now, across the table from them. She wasn't such a good reader, and the words were upside down to her.

Taleswapper read. "A Maker is born."

"There hasn't been a Maker," said Mama, "since the one who changed the water into wine."

"Maybe not, but that's what she wrote," said Taleswapper.

"Who wrote?" demanded Mama.

"A slip of a girl. About five years ago."

"What was the story that went with her sentence?" asked Alvin Junior.

Taleswapper shook his head.

"You said you never let people write unless you knew their story."

"She wrote it when I wasn't looking," said Taleswapper. "I didn't see it till the next place I stopped."

"Then how did you know it was her?" asked Alvin.

"It was her," he answered. "She was the only one there who could have opened the hex I kept on the book in those days."

"So you don't know what it means? You can't even tell me why I saw those letters burning?"

Taleswapper shook his head. "She was an innkeeper's daughter, if I remember rightly. She spoke very little, and when she did, what she said was always strictly truthful. Never a lie, even to be kind. She was considered to be something of a shrew. But as the proverb says, If you always speak your mind, the evil man will avoid you. Or something like that.''

"Her name?'' asked Mama. Alvin looked up in surprise. Mama hadn't seen the glowing letters, so why did she look so powerful eager to know about who wrote them?

"Sorry,'' said Taleswapper. "I don't remember her name right now. And if I remembered her name, I wouldn't tell it, nor will I tell whether I know the place where she lived. I don't want people seeking her out, troubling her for answers that she may not want to give. But I will say this. She was a torch, and saw with true eyes. So if she wrote that a Maker was born, I believe it, and that's why I let her words stay in the book.''

"I want to know her story someday,'' said Alvin "I want to know why the letters were so bright.''

He looked up and saw Mama and Taleswapper looking steadily into each other's eyes.

And then, around the fringes of his own vision, where he could almost but not quite see it, he sensed the Unmaker, trembling, invisible, waiting to shiver the world apart. Without even thinking about it, Alvin pulled the front of his shirt out of his pants and knotted the corners together. The Unmaker wavered, then retreated out of sight.

11

Millstone

Taleswapper woke up to somebody shaking him. Still full dark outside, but it was time to be moving. He sat, flexed himself a little, and took some pleasure in how few knots and pains he had these days, sleeping on a soft bed. I could get used to this, he thought. I could enjoy living here.

The bacon was so fat he could hear it sizzling clear from the kitchen. He was just about to pull his boots on when Mary knocked at the door. "I'm presentable, more or less," he said.

She came in, holding out two pair of long thick stockings. "I knotted them myself," she said.

"I couldn't buy socks this thick in Philadelphia."

"Winter gets right cold here in the Wobbish country, and—" She didn't finish. Got too shy, ducked her head, and scampered out of the room.

Taleswapper pulled on the stockings, and his boots over them, and grinned. He didn't feel bad about accepting a few things like this. He worked as hard as anybody, and he'd done a lot to help ready this farm for winter. He was a good roof man—he liked climbing and didn't get dizzy. So his own hands had made sure the house and barns and coops and sheds all were tight and dry.

And, without anybody ever deciding to do it, he had prepared the millhouse to receive a millstone. He had personally loaded all the hay from the mill floor, five wagons full. The twins, who really hadn't got their two farms going yet, since they married only that summer, did the unloading up in the big barn. It was all done without Miller himself ever touching a pitchfork. Taleswapper saw to that, without making a fuss over it, and Miller never insisted.

Other things, though, weren't gong so well. Ta-Kumsaw and his Shaw-Nee Reds were driving off so many folks from down Carthage way that everybody had the jitters. It was fine for the Prophet to have his big town of thousands of Reds across the river, all talking about how they'd never again raise their hands in war for any reason. But there were a lot of Reds who felt the way Ta-Kumsaw did, that the White man ought to be forced to the shores of the Atlantic and floated back to Europe, with or without boats. There was war talk, and word was that Bill Harrison down in Carthage was only too happy to fan that particular flame, not to mention the French in Detroit, always urging the Reds to attack the American settlers in land the French claimed was part of Canada.

Folks in the town of Vigor Church talked about this all the time, but Taleswapper knew that Miller didn't take it all that seriously. He thought of Reds as country clowns that wanted nothing more than to guzzle such whisky as they could find. Taleswapper had seen that attitude before, but only in New England. Yankees never seemed to realize that New England Reds with any gumption had long since moved to the state of Irrakwa. It would surely open Yankee eyes to see that the Irrakwa were working heavily with steam engines brought straight from England, and up in the Finger Lakes country a White named Eli Whitney was helping them make a factory that could turn out guns about twenty times faster than it had ever been done before. Someday those Yankees were going to wake up and find out that the Reds weren't all likker-mad, and some White folks were going to have to scramble fast to catch up.

In the meantime, though, Miller didn't take the war talk very seriously. "Everybody knows there's Reds in the woods. Can't stop them from skulking around, but I haven't missed any chickens so it's no problem yet."

"More bacon?" asked Miller. He shoved the bacon board across the table toward Taleswapper.

"I'm not used to eating so much in the morning," said Taleswapper. "Since I've been here I've had more food at every meal than I used to eat in a whole day."

"Put some meat on your bones," said Faith. She slapped down a couple of hot scones with honey smeared on them.

"I can't eat another bite," protested Taleswapper.

The scones slid right off Taleswapper's plate. "Got em," said Al Junior.

"Don't reach across the table like that," said Miller. "And you can't eat both those scones."

Al Junior proved his father wrong in an alarmingly short time. Then they washed the honey off their hands, put on their gloves, and went out to the wagon. The first light was just showing in the east as David and Calm, who lived townward from the farm, rode up. Al Junior climbed in the back of the wagon, along with all the tools and ropes and tents and supplies—it would be a few days before they came back.

"So—do we wait for the twins and Measure?" asked Taleswapper.

Miller swung up onto the wagon seat. "Measure's on ahead, felling trees for the sledge. And Wastenot and Wantnot are staying back here, riding circuit from house to house." He grinned. "Can't leave the womenfolk unprotected, with all the talk of wild Reds prowling around, can we?"

Taleswapper grinned back. Good to know that Miller wasn't as complacent as he seemed.

It was a good long way up to the quarry. On the road they passed the ruins of a wagon with a split millstone right in the middle of it. "That was our first try," said Miller. "But an axle dried out and jammed up coming down this steep hill, and the whole wagon fell in under the weight of the stone."

They came near a good-sized stream, and Miller told about how they had tried to float two millstones down on a raft, but both times the raft just up and sank. "We've had bad luck," said Miller, but from the set of his face he seemed to take it personally, as if someone had set out to make things fail.

"That's why we're using a sledge and rollers this time," said Al Junior, leaning over the back of the seat. "Nothing can fall off, nothing can break, and even if it does, it's all just logs, and we got no shortage of replacements."

"As long as it don't rain," said Miller. "Nor snow."

"Sky looks clear enough," said Taleswapper.

"Sky's a liar," said Miller. "When it comes to anything I want to do, water always gets in my way."

They got to the quarry when the sun was full up, but still far from noon. Of course, the trip back would be much longer. Measure had already felled six stout young trees and about twenty small ones. David and Calm set right to work, stripping off branches and rounding them smooth as possible. To Taleswapper's surprise, it was Al Junior who picked up the sack of stonecutting tools and headed up into the rocks.

"Where are you going?" asked Taleswapper.

"Oh, I've got to find a good place for cutting," said Al Junior.

"He's got an eye for stone," said Miller. But he wasn't saying all he knew.

"And when you find the stone, what'll you do then?" asked Taleswapper.

"Why, I'll cut it." Alvin sauntered on up the path with all the arrogance of a boy who knows he's about to do a man's job.

"Got a good hand for stone, too," said Miller.

"He's only ten years old," said Taleswapper.

"He cut the first stone when he was six," said Miller.

"Are you saying it's a knack?"

"I ain't saying nothing."

"Will you say this, Al Miller? Tell me if by chance you are a seventh son."

"Why do you ask?"

"It's said, by those who know such things, that a seventh son of a seventh son is born with the knowledge of how things look under the surface. That's why they make such good dowsers."

"Is that what they say?"

Measure walked up, faced his father, put his hands on his hips, and looked plain exasperated. "Pa, what harm is there in telling him? Everybody in the whole country roundabout here knows it."

"Maybe I think Taleswapper here knows more than I want him to know already."

"That's a right ungracious thing to say, Pa, to a man who's proved himself a friend twice over."

"He doesn't have to tell me anything he doesn't want me to know," said Taleswapper.

"Then *I'll* tell you," said Measure. "Pa is a seventh son, all right."

"And so is Al Junior," said Taleswapper. "Am I right? You've never mentioned it, but I'd guess that when a man gives his own name to a son other than his firstborn, it's bound to be his seventh born."

"Our oldest brother Vigor died in the Hatrack River only a few minutes after Al Junior was born," said Measure.

"Hatrack," said Taleswapper.

"Do you know the place?" asked Measure.

"I know *every* place. But for some reason that name makes me think I should have remembered it before now, and I can't think why. Seventh son of a seventh son. Does he conjure the millstone out of the rock?"

"We don't talk about it like that," said Measure.

"He cuts," said Miller. "Just like any stonecutter."

"He's a *big* boy, but he's still just a boy," said Taleswapper.

"Let's just say," said Measure, "that when *he* cuts the stone it's a mite softer than when *I* cut it."

"I'd appreciate it," said Miller, "if you'd stay down here and help with the rounding and notching. We need a nice tight sledge and some smooth true rollers.'' What he didn't say, but Taleswapper heard just as plain as day, was, Stay down here and don't ask too many questions about Al Junior.

So Taleswapper worked with David and Measure and Calm all morning and well into the afternoon, all the time hearing a steady chinking sound of iron on stone. Alvin Junior's stonecutting set the rhythm for all their work, though no one commented on it.

Taleswapper wasn't the sort of man who could work in silence, though. Since the others weren't too conversational at first, he told stories the whole time. And since they were grown men instead of children, he told stories that weren't all adventure and heroics and tragic death.

Most of the afternoon, in fact, he devoted to the saga of John Adams: How his house was burnt down by a Boston mob after he won the acquittal of ten women accused of witchcraft. How Alex Hamilton invited him to Manhattan Island, where the two of them set up a law practice together. How in ten years they managed to maneuver the Dutch government to allow unlimited immigration of non-Dutch-speaking people, until English, Scotch, Welsh, and Irish were a majority in New Amsterdam and New Orange, and a large minority in New Holland. How they got English declared a second official language in 1780, just in time for the Dutch colonies to become three of the seven original states under the American Compact.

"I'll bet the Dutchmen hated those boys, by the time they were through," said David.

"They were better politicians than *that*," said Taleswapper. "Why, both of them learned to speak Dutch better than most Dutchmen, and had their children grow up speaking Dutch in Dutch schools. They were so dadgum Dutch, boys, that when Alex Hamilton ran for governor of New Amsterdam and John Adams ran for president of the United States, they both did better in the Dutch parts of New Netherland than they did among the Scotch and Irish."

"Reckon if I run for mayor, I could get those Swedes and Dutchmen downriver to vote for me?" said David.

"*I* wouldn't even vote for you," said Calm.

"*I* would," said Measure. "And I hope someday you *do* run for mayor."

"He can't run for mayor," said Calm. "This ain't even a proper town."

"It will be," said Taleswapper. "I've seen it before. Once you get this mill working, it won't be long before three hundred people dwell between your mill and Vigor Church."

"You think so?"

"Right now people come in to Armor's store maybe three or four times a year," said Taleswapper. "But when they can get flour, they'll come in much more often. They'll prefer your mill to any other around here for some time, too, since you've got a smooth road and good bridges."

"If the mill makes money," Measure said, "Pa's sure to send for a Buhr Stone from France. We had one back in West Hampshire, before the flood broke up the mill. And a Buhr Stone means fine white flour."

"And white flour means good business," said David. "We older ones, we remember." He smiled wistfully. "We were almost rich there, once."

"So," said Taleswapper. "With all that traffic here, it won't be just a store and a church and a mill. There's good white clay down on the Wobbish. Some potter's bound to go into business, making redware and stoneware for the whole territory."

"Sure wish they'd hurry with *that*," said Calm. "My wife is sick unto death, she says, of having to serve food on tin plates."

"That's how towns grow," said Taleswapper. "A good store, a church, then a mill, then a pottery. Bricks, too, for that matter. And when there's a town—"

"David can be mayor," said Measure.

"Not me," said David. "All that politics business is too much. It's Armor wants that, not me."

"Armor wants to be king," said Calm.

"That's not kind," said David.

"But it's true," said Calm. "He'd try to be God, if he thought the job was open."

Measure explained to Taleswapper. "Calm and Armor don't get along."

"It ain't much of a husband that calls his wife a witch," said Calm bitterly.

"Why would he call her that?" asked Taleswapper.

"It's sure he doesn't call her that *now*," said Measure. "She promised him to give them up. All her knacks in the kitchen. It's a shame to make a woman run a household with just her own two hands."

"That's enough," David said. Taleswapper caught just a corner of his warning look.

Obviously they didn't trust Taleswapper enough to let him in on the truth. So Taleswapper let them know that the secret was already in his possession. "It seems to me that she uses more than Armor guesses," said Taleswapper. "There's a clever hex out of baskets on the front porch. And she used a calming on him before my eyes, the day I arrived in town.''

Work stopped then, for just a moment. Nobody looked at him, but for a second they did nothing. Just took in the fact that Taleswapper knew Eleanor's secret and hadn't told about it to outsiders. Or to Armor-of-God Weaver. Still, it was one thing for him to know, and something else for them to confirm it. So they said nothing, just resumed notching and binding the sledge.

Taleswapper broke the silence by returning to the main topic. ''It's just a matter of time before these western lands have enough people in them to call themselves states, and petition to join the American Compact. When that happens, there'll be need for honest men to hold office.''

''You won't find no Hamilton or Adams or Jefferson out here in the wild country,'' said David.

''Maybe not,'' said Taleswapper. ''But if you local boys don't set up your own government, you can bet there'll be plenty of city men willing to do it for you. That's how Aaron Burr got to be governor of Suskwahenny, before Daniel Boone shot him dead in ninety-nine.''

''You make it sound like murder,'' said Measure. ''It was a fair duel.''

''To my way of thinking,'' said Taleswapper, ''a duel is just two murderers who agree to take turns trying to kill each other.''

''Not when one of them is an old country boy in buckskin and the other is a lying cheating city man,'' said Measure.

''I don't want no Aaron Burr trying to be governor over the Wobbish country,'' said David. ''And that's what kind of man Bill Harrison is, down there in Carthage City. I'd vote for Armor before I'd vote for him.''

''And I'd vote for you before I'd vote for Armor,'' said Taleswapper.

David grunted. He continued weaving rope around the notches of the sledge logs, binding them together. Taleswapper was doing the same thing on the other side. When he got to the knotting place, Taleswapper started to tie the two ends of the rope together.

''Wait on that,'' said Measure. ''I'll go fetch Al Junior.'' Measure took off at a jog up the slope to the quarry.

Taleswapper dropped the ends of the rope. ''Alvin Junior ties the knots? I would have thought grown men like you could tie them tighter.''

David grinned. ''He's got a knack.''

''Don't any of you have knacks?'' asked Taleswapper.

''A few.''

"David's got a knack with the ladies," said Calm.

"Calm's got dancing feet at a hoedown. Ain't nobody fiddles like him, neither," said David. "It ain't on tune all the time, but he keeps that bow busy."

"Measure's a true shot," said Calm. "He's got an eye for things too far off for most folks to see."

"We got our knacks," said David. "The twins have a way of knowing when trouble's brewing, and getting there just about in time."

"And Pa, he fits things together. We have him do all the wood joints when we're building furniture."

"The womenfolk got women's knacks."

"But," said Calm, "there ain't nobody like Al Junior."

David nodded gravely. "Thing is, Taleswapper, he don't seem to know about it. I mean, he's always kind of surprised when things turn out good. He's right proud when we give him a job to do. I never seen him lord it over nobody because he's got more of a knack than they do."

"He's a good boy," said Calm.

"Kind of clumsy," said David.

"Not *clumsy*," said Calm. "Most times it isn't his *fault*."

"Let's just say that accidents happen more common around him."

"I wouldn't say jinx or nothing," said Calm.

"No, I wouldn't say jinx."

Taleswapper noted that in fact they both had said it. But he didn't comment on their indiscretion. After all, it was the third voice that made bad luck true. His silence was the best cure for their carelessness. And the other two caught on quickly enough. They, too, held their silence.

After a while, Measure came down the hill with Alvin Junior. Taleswapper dared not be the third voice, since he had taken part in the conversation before. And it would be even worse if Alvin himself spoke next, since he was the one who had been linked with a jinx. So Taleswapper kept his eye on Measure, and raised his eyebrows, to show Measure that he was expected to speak.

Measure answered the question that he thought Taleswapper was asking. "Oh, Pa's staying up by the rock. To watch."

Taleswapper could hear David and Calm breathe a sigh of relief. The third voice didn't have jinx in his mind, so Alvin Junior was safe.

Now Taleswapper was free to wonder *why* Miller felt he had to keep watch at the quarry. "What could happen to a rock? I've never heard of Reds stealing rocks."

Measure winked. "Powerful strange things happen sometimes, specially with millstones."

Alvin was joking with David and Calm now, as he tied the knots. He worked hard to get them as tight as he could, but Taleswapper saw that it wasn't in the knot itself that his knack was revealed. As Al Junior pulled the ropes tight, they seemed to twist and bite into the wood in all the notches, drawing the whole sledge tighter together. It was subtle, and if Taleswapper hadn't been watching for it, he wouldn't have seen. But it was real. What Al Junior bound was bound tight.

"That's tight enough to be a raft," said Al Junior, standing back to admire.

"Well, it's floating on solid earth this time," said Measure. "Pa says he won't even piss into water no more."

Since the sun was low in the west, they set to laying the fire. Work had kept them warm today, but tonight they'd need the fire to back off the animals and keep the autumn cold at bay.

Miller didn't come down, even at supper, and when Calm got up to carry food up the hill to his father, Taleswapper offered to come along.

"I don't know," said Calm. "You don't need to."

"I want to."

"Pa—he don't like lots of people gathered at the rock face, time like this." Calm looked a little sheepish. "He's a miller, and it's his stone getting cut there."

"I'm not a lot of people," said Taleswapper. Calm didn't say anything more. Taleswapper followed him up among the rocks.

On the way, they passed the sites of two early stonecuttings. The scraps of cut stone had been used to make a smooth ramp from the cliff face to ground level. The cuts were almost perfectly round. Taleswapper had seen plenty of stone cut before, and he'd never seen one cut this way—perfectly round, right in the cliff. Most times it was a whole slab they cut, then rounded it on the ground. There were several good reasons for doing it that way, but the best of all was that there was no way to cut the back of the stone unless you took a whole slab. Calm didn't slow down for him, so Taleswapper didn't have a chance to look closely, but as near as he could tell there was no possible way that the stonecutter in *this* quarry could have cut the back of the stone.

It looked just the same at the new site, too. Miller was raking chipped rock into a level ramp in front of the millstone. Taleswapper stood back and, in the last specks of daylight, studied the cliff. In a single day, working alone, Al Junior had smoothed the front of the millstone and chipped away the whole circumference. The stone was practically polished, still attached to the cliff face. Not only that, but the center hole had been cut to take the main shaft of the mill machinery. It was fully cut. And there was no way in the world that anybody could get a chisel in position to cut away the back.

"That's some knack the boy has," said Taleswapper.

Miller grunted assent.

"Hear you plan to spend the night up here," said Taleswapper.

"Heard right."

"Mind company?" asked Taleswapper.

Calm rolled his eyes.

But after a little bit, Miller shrugged. "Suit yourself."

Calm looked at Taleswapper with wide eyes and raised eyebrows, as if to say, Miracles never cease.

When Calm had set down Miller's supper, he left. Miller set aside the rake. "You et yet?"

"I'll gather wood for tonight's fire," said Taleswapper. "While there's still light. You eat."

"Watch out for snakes," said Miller. "They're mostly shut in for the winter now, but you never know."

Taleswapper watched out for snakes, but he never saw any. And soon they had a good fire, laid with a heavy log that would burn all night.

They lay there in the firelight, wrapped in their blankets. It occurred to Taleswapper that Miller might have found softer ground a few yards away from the quarry. But apparently it was more important to keep the millstone in plain sight.

Taleswapper began talking. Quietly, but steadily, he talked about how hard it must be for fathers, to watch their sons grow, so full of hope for the boys, but never knowing when death would come and take the child away. It was the right thing to talk about, because soon it was Alvin Miller doing the talking. He told the story of how his oldest boy Vigor died in the Hatrack River, only a few minutes after Alvin Junior was born. And from there, he turned to the dozens of ways that Al Junior had almost died. "Always water," Miller said at the end. "Nobody believes me, but it's so. Always water."

"The question is," said Taleswapper, "is the water evil, trying to destroy a good boy? Or is it good, trying to destroy an evil power?"

It was a question that might have made some men angry, but Taleswapper had given up trying to guess when Miller's temper would flare. This time it didn't. "I've wondered that myself," said Miller. "I've watched him close, Taleswapper. Of course, he has a knack for making people love him. Even his sisters. He's tormented them unmerciful since he was old enough to spit in their food. Yet there's not a one of them who doesn't find a way to make him something special, and not just at

Christmas. They'll sew his socks shut or smear soot on the privy bench or needle up his nightshirt, but they'd also die for him.''

"I've found," said Taleswapper, "that some people have a knack for winning love without ever earning it."

"I feared that, too," said Miller. "But the boy doesn't know he has that knack. He doesn't trick people into doing what he wants. He lets me punish him when he does wrong. And he could stop me, if he wanted."

"How?"

"Because he knows that sometimes when I see him, I see my boy Vigor, my firstborn, and then I can't do him any harm, even harm that's for his own good."

Maybe that reason was partly true, Taleswapper thought. But it certainly wasn't the whole truth.

A bit later, after Taleswapper stirred the fire to make sure the log caught well, Miller told the story that Taleswapper had come for.

"I've got a story," he said, "that might belong in your book."

"Give it a try," said Taleswapper.

"Didn't happen to me, though."

"Has to be something you saw yourself," said Taleswapper. "I hear the craziest stories that somebody heard happened to a friend of a friend."

"Oh, I saw this happen. It's been going on for years now, and I've had some discussions with the fellow. It's one of the Swedes downriver, speaks English good as I do. We helped him put up his cabin and his barn when he first come here, the year after us. And I watched him a little bit even then. See, he has a boy, a blond Swede boy, you know how they get."

"Hair almost white?"

"Like frost in the first morning sun, white like that, and shiny. A beautiful boy."

"I can see him in my mind," said Taleswapper.

"And that boy, his papa loved him. Better than his life. You know that Bible story, about that papa who gave his boy a coat of many colors?"

"I've heard tell of it."

"He loved his boy like that. But I saw them two walking alongside the river, and the father all of a sudden lurched kind of, just bumped his boy, and sent the lad tumbling down into the Wobbish. Now, it happened that the boy caught onto a log and his father and I helped pull him in, but it was a scary thing to see that the father might have killed his own best-loved child. It wouldn't've been a-purpose, mind you, but that wouldn't make the boy any less dead, or the father any less blameful.''

"I can see the father might never get over such a thing."

"Well, of course *not*. Yet not long after that, I seen him a few more times. Chopping wood, and he swung that axe wild, and if the boy hadn't slipped and fell right at that very second, that axe would've bit into the boy's head, and I never seen nobody live after something like that."

"Nor I."

"And I tried to imagine what must be happening. What that father must be thinking. So I went to him one day, and I said, 'Nels, you ought to be more careful round that boy. You're likely to take that boy's head off someday, if you keep swinging that axe so free.'

"And Nels, he says to me, 'Mr. Miller, that wasn't no accident.' Well, you could've blowed me down with a baby's burp. What does he mean, no accident? And he says to me, 'You don't know how bad it is. I think maybe a witch cursed me, or the devil takes me, but I'm just working there, thinking how much I love the boy, and suddenly I have this wish to kill him. It came on me first when he was just a baby, and I stood at the top of the stairs, holding him, and it was like a voice inside my head, it said, "Throw him down," and I wanted to do it, even though I also knew it would be the most terrible thing in the world. I was hungry to throw him off, like a boy gets when he wants to smash a bug with a stone. I *wanted* to see his head break open on the floor.

" 'Well, I just fought off that feeling, just swallowed it back and held that boy so tight I like to smothered him. Finally when I got him back into his cradle, I knew that from then on I wasn't going to carry him up those stairs no more.

" 'But I couldn't just leave him alone, could I? He was my boy, and he grew up so bright and good and beautiful that I had to love him. If I stayed away, he cried cause his papa didn't play with him. But if I stayed with him, then those feelings came back, again and again. Not every day, but many a day, sometimes so fast that I did it afore I even knew what I was doing. Like the day I bumped him into the river, I just took a wrong step and tripped, but I knew even as I took that step that it was a wrong step, and that I'd trip, and that I'd bump him, I *knew* it, but I didn't have time to stop myself. And someday I know that I won't be able to stop myself, I won't mean to do it, but someday when that boy is under my hand, I'll kill him.' ''

Taleswapper could see Miller's arm move, as if to wipe tears away from his cheek.

"Ain't that the strangest thing?" Miller asked. "A man having that kind of feeling for his own son."

"Does that fellow have any other sons?"

"A few. Why?"

"I just wondered if he ever felt a desire to kill them."

"Never, not a speck. I asked him that, matter of fact. I asked him, and he said not a speck."

"Well, Mr. Miller, what did you tell him?"

Miller breathed in and out a few times. "I didn't know what to tell him. Some things are just too big for a man like me to understand. I mean, the way that water is out to kill my boy Alvin. And then this Swede fellow with his son. Maybe there's some children that wasn't meant to grow up. Do you think so, Taleswapper?"

"I think there are some children that are so important, that someone—some force in the world—may want them dead. But there are always other forces, maybe stronger forces, that want them alive."

"Then why don't those forces show theirselves, Taleswapper? Why don't some power from heaven come and say—come to that poor Swedish man and say, 'Don't you fear no more, your boy is safe, even from you!' "

"Maybe those forces don't speak out loud in words. Maybe those forces just show you what they're doing."

"The only force that shows itself in this world is the one that kills."

"I don't know about that Swedish boy," said Taleswapper, "but I'd guess thàt there's a powerful protection on *your* son. From what you said, it's a miracle he isn't dead ten times over."

"That's the truth."

"I think he's being watched over."

"Not well enough."

"The water never got him, did it?"

"It came so close, Taleswapper."

"And as for that Swedish boy, I *know* he's got somebody watching over him."

"Who?" asked Miller.

"Why, his own father."

"His father is the enemy," said Miller.

"I don't think so," said Taleswapper. "Do you know how many fathers kill their sons by accident? They're out hunting, and a shot goes wrong. Or a wagon crushes the boy, or he takes a fall. Happens all the time. Maybe those fathers just didn't *see* what was happening. But this Swedish man is sharp, he sees what's happening, and he watches himself, catches himself in time."

Miller sounded a little more hopeful. "You make it sound like maybe the father ain't all bad."

"If he were all bad, Mr. Miller, that boy would be dead and buried long ago."

"Maybe. Maybe."

Miller thought for a while more. So long, in fact, that Taleswapper dozed a little. He snapped awake with Miller already talking.

"—and it's just getting worse, not better. Harder to fight off those feelings. Not all that long ago, he was standing up in a loft in the—in his barn—and he was pitching down hay. And there below him was his boy, and all it would take is to let fly with the pitchfork, easiest thing in the world, he could say the pitchfork slipped and no one would ever know. Just let it fly, and stick that boy right through. And he was going to do it. Do you understand me? It was so hard to fight off those feelings, harder than ever before, and he just *gave up*. Just decided to have it done with, to give in. And in that very moment, why, a stranger appeared in the doorway, and shouted, 'No,' and I set down the pitchfork—that's what he said, 'I set down the pitchfork, but I was shaking so bad I could hardly walk, knowing that the stranger saw me with murder in my heart, he must think I'm the most terrible man in the world to think of killing my own boy, he can't even guess how hard I've struggled all those years before—' "

"Maybe that stranger knew something about the powers that can work inside a man's heart," said Taleswapper.

"Do you think so?"

"Oh, I can't be sure, but maybe that stranger also saw how much that father loved the boy. Maybe the stranger was confused for a long time, but finally began to realize that the child was extraordinary, with powerful enemies. And then maybe he came to understand that no matter how many enemies the boy had, his father wasn't one of them. Wasn't an enemy. And he wanted to say something to that father."

"What did he want to say?" Miller brushed his eyes with his sleeve again. "What do you think that stranger might want to say?"

"Maybe he wanted to say, 'You've done all you can do, and now it's too strong for you. Now you ought to send that boy away. To relatives back east, maybe, or as a prentice in some town.' That might be a hard thing for the father to do, since he loves the boy so much, but he'll do it because he knows that real love is to take the boy out of danger."

"Yes," said Miller.

"For that matter," said Taleswapper, "maybe you ought to do something like that with your own boy, Alvin."

"Maybe," said Miller.

"He's in some danger from the water around here, wouldn't you say? Somebody's protecting him, or some*thing*. But maybe if Alvin weren't living here—"

"Then some of the dangers would go away," said Miller.

"Think about it," said Taleswapper.

"It's a terrible thing," said Miller, "to send your boy away to live with strangers."

"It's a worse thing, though, to put him in the ground."

"Yes," said Miller. "That's the worst thing in the world. To put your child in the ground."

They didn't talk any more, and after a while they both slept.

The morning was cold, with a heavy frost, but Miller wouldn't even let Al Junior come up to the rock until the sun burned it away. Instead they all spent the morning preparing the ground from the cliff face to the sledge, so they could roll the stone down the mountain.

By now, Taleswapper was sure that Al Junior used a hidden power to get the millstone away from the cliff face, even if he didn't realize it himself. Taleswapper was curious. He wanted to see just how powerful this power was, so he could understand more about its nature. And since Al Junior didn't realize what he was doing, Taleswapper's experiment had to be subtle, too. "How do you dress your stone?" asked Taleswapper.

Miller shrugged. "Buhr Stone is what I used before. They all come with sickle dress."

"Can you show me?" asked Taleswapper.

Using a corner of the rake, Miller drew a circle in the frost. Then he drew a series of arcs, radiating from the center of the circle out to the edges. Between each pair of arcs he drew a shorter arc, which began at the edge but never came closer than two-thirds of the way toward the center. "Like that," said Miller.

"Most millstones in Pennsylvania and Suskwahenny are quarter dress," said Taleswapper. "You know that cut?"

"Show me."

So Taleswapper drew another circle. It didn't show up as well, since the frost was burning off now, but it was good enough. He drew straight lines instead of curved ones from the center to the edge, and the shorter lines branched directly from the long ones and ran straight to the edge. "Some millers like this better, because you can keep it sharp longer. Since all the lines are straight, you get a nice even draw when you're tooling the stone."

"I can see that," said Miller. "I don't know, though. I'm used to those curvy lines."

"Well, suit yourself," said Taleswapper. "I've never been a miller, so I don't know. I just tell stories about what I've seen."

"Oh, I don't mind you showing me," said Miller. "Don't mind a bit."

Al Junior stood there, studying both circles.

"I think if we once get this stone home," said Miller, "I'll try that quarter dress on it. Looks to me like it might be easier to keep up a clean grind."

Finally the ground was dry, and Al Junior walked to the cliff face. The other boys were all down below, breaking camp or bringing the horses up to the quarry. Only Miller and Taleswapper watched as Al Junior finally carried his hammer to the cliff face. He had a little more cutting to do, to get the circle to its full depth all around.

To Taleswapper's surprise, when Al Junior set the chisel in place and gave a whang with the hammer, a whole section of stone, some six inches long, split away from the cliff face and crumbled to the ground.

"Why, that stone's as soft as coal," said Taleswapper. "What kind of millstone can it make, if it's as weak as that?"

Miller grinned and shook his head.

Al Junior stepped away from the stone. "Oh, Taleswapper, it's *hard* stone, unless you know just the right place to crack it. Give it a try, you'll see."

He held out the chisel and hammer. Taleswapper took them and approached the rock. Carefully he laid the chisel onto the stone, a slight angle away from perpendicular. Then, after a few trial taps, he laid on a blow with the hammer.

The chisel practically jumped out of his left hand, and the shock of impact was so great that he dropped the hammer. "Sorry," he said, "I've done this before, but I must have lost the skill—"

"Oh, it's just the stone," said Al Junior. "It's kind of temperamental. It only likes to give in certain directions."

Taleswapper inspected the place where he had tried to cut. He couldn't find the spot. His mighty blow had left no mark at all.

Al Junior picked up the tools and laid the chisel against the stone. It looked to Taleswapper as though he put it in exactly the same place. But Al acted as though he had placed it quite differently. "See, it's getting just the angle on it. Like this."

He whanged with the hammer, the iron rang out, there was a cracking of stone, and once again crumbled stone pattered on the ground.

"I can see why you have him do all the cutting," Taleswapper said.

"Seems like the best way," said Miller.

In only a few minutes, the stone was fully rounded. Taleswapper said nothing, just watched to see what Al would do.

He set down his tools, walked to the millstone, and embraced it. His right hand curled around the lip of it. His left hand probed back into the cut on the other side. Alvin's cheek pressed against the stone. His eyes were closed. It looked for all the world as though he were listening to the rock.

He began to hum softly. A mindless little tune. He moved his hands. Shifted his position. Listened with the other ear.

"Well," Alvin said, "I can't hardly believe it."

"Believe what?" asked his father.

"Those last few cuts must have set up a real shiver in the rock. The back is already split right off."

"You mean that millstone is standing free?" asked Taleswapper.

"I think we can rock it forward now," said Alvin. "It takes a little rope work, but we'll get it out of there without too much trouble."

The brothers arrived with the ropes and horses. Alvin passed a rope back behind the stone. Even though not a single cut had been made against the back, the rope dropped easily into place. Then another rope, and another, and soon they were all tugging, first left, then right, as they slowly walked the heavy stone out of its bed in the cliff face.

"If I hadn't seen it," murmured Taleswapper.

"But you did," said Miller.

It was only a few inches clear when they changed the ropes, passing four lines through the center hole and hitching them to a team of horses uphill of the stone. "It'll roll on downhill just fine," Miller explained to Taleswapper. "The horses are there as a drag, pulling against it."

"It looks heavy."

"Just don't lie down in front of it," said Miller.

They started it rolling, very gently. Miller took hold of Alvin's shoulder and kept the boy well back from the stone—and uphill of it, too. Taleswapper helped with the horses, so he didn't get a good look at the back surface of the stone until it was down on level ground by the sledge.

It was smooth as a baby's backside. Flat as ice in a basin. Except that it was scored in a quarter dress pattern, straight lines radiating from the lip of the center hole to the edge of the stone.

Alvin came up to stand beside him. "Did I do it right?" he asked.

"Yes," said Taleswapper.

"It was the luckiest thing," said the boy. "I could just feel that stone ready to split right along those lines. It just wanted to split, easy as you please.''

Taleswapper reached out and drew his finger gently along the edge of a dress cut. It stung. He brought his finger to his mouth, sucked, and tasted blood.

"Stone holds a nice sharp edge, don't it?'' said Measure. He sounded as if this sort of thing happened every day. But Taleswapper could see the awe in his eyes.

"Good cut,'' said Calm.

"Best one yet,'' said David.

Then, with horses bracing against a rapid fall, they gently tipped it to lie on the sledge, dress side up.

"Will you do me a favor, Taleswapper?'' asked Miller.

"If I can.''

"Take Alvin back home with you now. His work's done.''

"No, Papa!'' Alvin shouted. He ran over to his father. "You can't make me go home *now*.''

"Don't need no ten-year-old boys underfoot while we're manhandling a stone that size,'' said his father.

"But I've got to watch the stone, to make sure it don't split or chip, Pa!''

The older sons looked at their father, waiting. Taleswapper wondered what they hoped for. They were too old now, surely, to resent their father's particular love for his seventh son. They also must hope to keep the boy safe from harm. Yet it meant much to all of them that the stone arrive safely, unbroken, to begin its service in the mill. There could be no doubt that young Alvin had the power to keep it whole.

"You can ride with us till sundown,'' Miller finally said. "By then we'll be close enough to home that you and Taleswapper can head back and spend the night in beds.''

"Fine with me,'' said Taleswapper.

Alvin Junior plainly wasn't satisfied, but he didn't answer back.

They got the sledge under way before noon. Two horses in front and two behind, for stopping, were hitched to the stone itself. The stone rested on the wooden raft of the sledge, and the sledge rode atop seven or eight of the small rollers at a time. The sledge moved forward, passing over new rollers waiting in front. As the rollers emerged from the back, one of the boys immediately yanked the roller out from under the ropes hitched to the trailing team, raced to the front, and laid it in place directly behind the lead them. It meant that each man ran about five miles for every mile the stone traveled.

Taleswapper tried to take his turn, but David, Calm, and Measure wouldn't hear of it. He ended up tending the trailing team, with Alvin perched atop one of the horses. Miller drove the leading team, walking backward half the time to make sure he wasn't going too fast for the boys to keep up.

Hour after hour they went on. Miller offered to let them stop and rest, but they seemed not to tire, and Taleswapper was amazed to see how the rollers held up. Not a one split on a rock or from the sheer weight of the stone. They got scuffed and dented, but that was about all.

And as the sun sank to about two fingers above the horizon, awash in the ruddy clouds of the western sky, Taleswapper recognized the meadow opening up before them. They had made the whole journey in a single afternoon.

"I think I got the strongest brothers in the whole world." Alvin murmured.

I have no doubt of it, Taleswapper said silently. You who can cut a stone from the mountain without hands, because you "find" the right fractures in the rock, it's no surprise that your brothers find in themselves exactly as much strength as you believe they have. Taleswapper tried again, as he had tried so many times before, to puzzle out the nature of the hidden powers. Surely there was some natural law that governed their use—Old Ben had always said so. And yet here was this boy who, by mere belief and desire, could cut stone like butter and give strength to his brothers. There was a theory that the hidden power came from friendship with a particular element, but which was it that could do all that Alvin did? Earth? Air? Fire? Certainly not water, for Taleswapper knew that Miller's stories were all true. Why was it that Alvin Junior could wish for something, and the earth itself would bend to his will, while others could long for things and never cause so much as a breeze to blow?

They needed lanterns inside the millhouse by the time they rolled the stone through the doors. "Might as well lay it in place tonight," said Miller. Taleswapper imagined the fears that ran through Miller's mind. If he left the stone upright, it would surely roll in the morning and crush a particular child as he innocently carried water up to the house. Since the stone had miraculously come down from the mountain in a single day, it would be foolish to leave it anywhere but in its proper place, on the foundation of rammed earth and stone in the millhouse.

They brought a team inside and hitched it to the stone, as they had when they lowered it on the sledge back by the quarry. The team would pull against the weight of the stone as they levered it downward onto the foundation.

At the moment, though, the stone was resting on built-up earth just outside the circle of foundation stones. Measure and Calm were working their lever poles under the outside edge of the stone, ready to pry it up and make it fall into place. The stone rocked a little as they worked. David was holding the horses, since it would be a disaster if they pulled too soon and rocked the stone over the wrong way, to lie on its dress face in the plain dirt.

Taleswapper stood aside, watching as Miller directed his sons with useless calls of "Careful there" and "Steady now." Alvin had been beside him ever since they brought the millstone inside. One of the horses got jumpy. Miller reacted at once. "Calm, go help your brother with the horses!" Miller also took a step that way.

At that moment, Taleswapper realized that Alvin was *not* beside him, after all. He was carrying a broom, walking briskly toward the millstone. Perhaps he had seen some loose stones lying on the foundation; he had to sweep them away, didn't he? The horses backed up; the lines went slack. Taleswapper realized, just as Alvin got behind the stone, that with ropes so slack there'd be nothing to keep the stone from falling all the way over, if it should fall at just this moment.

Surely it would not fall, in a reasonable world. But Taleswapper knew by now that it was *not* a reasonable world at all. Alvin Junior had a powerful, invisible enemy, and it would not miss such a chance as this.

Taleswapper bounded forward. Just as he came level with the stone, he felt a lurching in the earth under his feet, a collapse of the firm dirt. Not much, just a few inches, but it was enough to let the inside lip of the millstone fall that much, which rocked the top of the great wheel more than two feet, and so quickly that the momentum could not be stopped. The millstone would fall all the way down, right into its proper place on the foundation, with Alvin Junior underneath, ground like grain under the stone.

With a shout, Taleswapper caught hold of Alvin's arm and yanked him back, away from the stone. Only then did Alvin see the great stone falling upon him. Taleswapper had enough force in his movement to carry the boy several feet back, but it was not quite enough. The boy's legs still lay in the stone's shadow. It was falling fast now, too fast for Taleswapper to respond, to do anything but watch it crush Alvin's legs. He knew that such an injury was the same as death, except that it would take longer. He had failed.

In that moment, though, as he watched the stone in its murderous fall, he saw a crack appear in the stone and, in less than an instant, it became a clean split right through the stone. The two halves leapt apart from each other, each with such a movement that it would fall beside Alvin's legs, not touching him.

No sooner had Taleswapper seen lantern light through the middle of the stone than Alvin himself cried, ''No!''

To anyone else, it would seem the boy was shouting at the fall of the stone, at his impending death. But to Taleswapper, lying on the ground beside the boy, with the light of the lantern dazzling through the split in the millstone, the cry meant something else altogether. Heedless of his own danger, as children usually are, Alvin was crying out against the breaking of the millstone. After all his work, and the labors in bringing the stone home, he could not bear to see it breaking.

And because he could not bear it, it did not happen. The halves of the stone jumped back together like a needle jumping at a magnet, and the stone fell in one piece.

The shadow of the stone had exaggerated its footprint on the ground. It did not crush both Alvin's legs. His left leg, in fact, was completely clear of the stone, tucked up under him as it was. The right leg, however, lay so that the rim of the stone overlapped his shin by two inches at the widest point. Since Alvin was still pulling his legs away, the blow from the stone pushed it further in the direction it was already going. It peeled off all the skin and muscle, right down to the bone, but it did not catch the leg directly when it came to rest. The leg might not even have broken, had the broom not been lying crosswise under it. The stone drove Alvin's leg downward against the broom handle, just hard enough to snap both bones of the lower leg clean in half. The sharp edges of the bone broke the skin and came to rest like two sides of a vise, gripping the broom handle. But the leg was not under the millstone, and the bones were broken cleanly, not ground to dust under the rock.

The air was filled with the crash of stone on stone, the great-throated shouts of men surprised by grief, and above all the piercing cry of agony from one boy who was never so young and frail as now.

By the time anyone else could get there, Taleswapper had seen that both Alvin's legs were free of the stone. Alvin tried to sit up and look at his injury. Either the sight or the pain of it was too much for him, and he fainted. Alvin's father reached him then; he had not been nearest, but he had moved faster than Alvin's brothers. Taleswapper tried to reassure him, for with the bones gripping the broom handle, the leg did not look broken. Miller lifted his son, but the leg would not come, and even unconscious the pain wrung a cruel moan from the boy. It was Measure who steeled himself to pull on the leg and free it from the broom handle.

David already held a lantern, and as Miller carried the boy, David ran alongside, lighting the way. Measure and Calm would have followed, but Taleswapper called to them. "The womenfolk are there, and David, and your father," he said. "Someone needs to see to all this."

"You're right," said Calm. "Father won't be eager to come down here soon."

The young men used levers to raise the stone enough that Taleswapper could pull out the broom handle and the ropes that were still tied to the horses. The three of them cleared all the equipment out of the millhouse, then stabled the horses and put away the tools and supplies. Only then did Taleswapper return to the house to find that Alvin Junior was sleeping in Taleswapper's bed.

"I hope you don't mind," said Anne anxiously.

"Of course not," said Taleswapper.

The other girls and Cally were clearing away the supper dishes. In the room that had been Taleswapper's, Faith and Miller, both ashen and tight-lipped, sat beside the bed, where Alvin lay with his leg splinted and bandaged.

David stood near the door. "It was a clean break," he whispered to Taleswapper. "But the cuts in the skin—we fear infection. He lost all the skin off the front of his shin. I don't know if bare bone like that can ever heal."

"Did you put the skin back?" asked Taleswapper.

"Such as was left, we pressed into place, and Mother sewed it there."

"That was well done," said Taleswapper.

Faith lifted her head. "Do you know aught of physicking, then, Taleswapper?"

"Such as a man learns after years trying to do what he can among those who know as little as he."

"How could this happen?" Miller said. "Why now, after so many other times that did him no injury?" He looked up at Taleswapper. "I had come to think the boy had a protector."

"He has."

"Then the protector failed him."

"It did not fail," said Taleswapper. "For a moment, as the stone fell, I saw it split, wide enough that it wouldn't have touched him."

"Like the ridgebeam," whispered Faith.

"I thought I saw it too, Father," said David. "But when it came down whole, I decided I must have seen what I wished for, and not what was."

"There's no split in it now," said Miller.

"No," said Taleswapper. "Because Alvin Junior refused to let it split."

"Are you saying he knit it back together? So it would strike him and wreck his leg?"

"I'm saying he had no thought of his leg," said Taleswapper. "Only of the stone."

"Oh, my boy, my good boy," murmured his mother, gently caressing the arm that extended thoughtlessly toward her. As she moved his fingers, they limply bent as she pushed them, then sprang back.

"Is it possible?" asked David. "That the stone split and was made whole again, as quickly as that?"

"It must be," said Taleswapper, "because it happened."

Faith moved her son's fingers again, but this time they did not spring back. They extended even further, then flexed into a fist, then extended flat again.

"He's awake," said his father.

"I'll fetch some rum for the boy," said David. "To slack the pain. Armor'll have some in his store."

"No," murmured Alvin.

"The boy says no," said Taleswapper.

"What does he know, in pain as he is?"

"He has to keep his wits about him, if he can," said Taleswapper. He knelt by the bed, just to the right of Faith, so he was even nearer to the boy's face. "Alvin, do you hear me?"

Alvin groaned. It must have meant yes.

"Then listen to me. Your leg is very badly hurt. The bones are broken, but they've been set in place—they'll heal well enough. But the skin was torn away, and even though your mother has sewn it back in place, there's a good chance the skin will die and take gangrene, and kill you. Most surgeons would cut off your leg to save your life."

Alvin tossed his head back and forth, trying to shout. It came out as a moan: "No, no, no."

"You're making things worse!" Faith said angrily.

Taleswapper looked at the father for permission to go on.

"Don't torment the boy," said Miller.

"There's a proverb," said Taleswapper. "The apple tree never asks the beech how he shall grow, nor the lion the horse, how he shall take his prey."

"What does that mean?" asked Faith.

"It means that I have no business trying to teach *him* how to use powers that I can't begin to understand. But since he doesn't know how to do it himself, I'll have to try, won't I?"

Miller pondered a moment. "Go ahead, Taleswapper. Better for him to know how bad it is, whether he can heal himself or not."

Taleswapper held the boy's hand gently between his own. "Alvin, you want to keep your leg, don't you? Then you have to think of it the way you thought of the stone. You have to think of the skin of your leg, growing back, attaching to the bone as it should. You have to study it out. You'll have plenty of time for it, lying here. Don't think about the pain, think about the leg as it should be, whole and strong again."

Alvin lay there, squinting his eyes closed against the pain.

"Are you doing that, Alvin? Can you try?"

"No," said Alvin.

"You have to fight against the pain, so you can use your own knack to make things right."

"I never will," said Alvin.

"Why not!" cried Faith.

"The Shining Man," said Alvin. "I promised him."

Taleswapper remembered Alvin's oath to the Shining Man, and his heart sank.

"What's the Shining Man?" asked Miller.

"A—visitation he had, when he was little," said Taleswapper.

"How come we never heard of this afore now?" Miller asked.

"It was the night the ridgebeam split," said Taleswapper. "Alvin promised the Shining Man that he'd never use his power for his own benefit."

"But Alvin," said Faith. "This isn't to make you rich or nothing, this is to save your *life*."

The boy only winced against the pain and shook his head.

"Will you leave me with him?" said Taleswapper. "Just for a few minutes, so I can talk to him?"

Miller was rushing Faith out the door of the room before Taleswapper even finished his sentence.

"Alvin," said Taleswapper. "You must listen to me, listen carefully. You know I won't lie to you. An oath is a terrible thing, and I'd never counsel a man to break his word, even to save his own life. So I won't tell you to use your power for your own good. Do you hear me?"

Alvin nodded.

"Just think, though. Think of the Unmaker going through the world. Nobody sees him as he does his work, as he tears down and destroys things. Nobody but one solitary boy. Who is that boy, Alvin?"

Alvin's lips formed the word, though no sound came out. Me.

"And that boy has been given a power that he can't even begin to understand. The power to build against the enemy's unbuilding. And more than that, Alvin, the *desire* to build as well. A boy who answers every glimpse of the Unmaker with a bit of making. Now, tell me, Alvin, those who help the Unmaker, are they the friend or the enemy of mankind?''

Enemy, said Alvin's lips.

"So if you help the Unmaker destroy his most dangerous foe, you're an enemy of mankind, aren't you?''

Anguish wrung sound from the boy. ''You're twisting it,'' he said.

''I'm straightening it,'' said Taleswapper. ''Your oath was never to use your power for your own benefit. But if you die, only the Unmaker benefits, and if you live, if that leg is healed, then that's for the good of all mankind. No, Alvin, it's for the good of the world and all that's in it.''

Alvin whimpered, more against the pain in his mind than the pain in his body.

''But your oath was clear, wasn't it? Never to your own benefit. So why not satisfy one oath with another, Alvin? Take an oath now, that you will devote your whole *life* to building up against the Unmaker. If you keep *that* oath—and you will, Alvin, you're a boy who keeps his word—if you keep that oath, then saving your own life is truly for the benefit of others, and not for your private good at all.''

Taleswapper waited, waited, until at last Alvin nodded slightly.

''Do you take an oath, Alvin Junior, that you will live your life to defeat the Unmaker, to make things whole and good and right?''

''Yes,'' whispered the boy.

''Then I tell you, by the terms of your own promise, you must heal yourself.''

Alvin gripped Taleswapper's arm. ''How,'' he whispered.

''That I don't know, boy,'' said Taleswapper. ''How to use your power, you have to find that out inside yourself. I can only tell you that you must try, or the enemy has his victory, and I'll have to end your tale with your body being lowered into a grave.''

To Taleswapper's surprise, Alvin smiled. Then Taleswapper understood the joke. His tale would end with the grave no matter what he did today. ''Right enough, boy,'' said Taleswapper. ''But I'd rather have a few more pages about you before I put finis to the Book of Alvin.''

''I'll try,'' whispered Alvin.

If he tried, then surely he would succeed. Alvin's protector had not brought him this far only to let him die. Taleswapper had no doubt that Alvin had the power to heal himself, if he could only figure out the way. His own body was far more complicated than the stone. But if he was to live, he had to learn the pathways of his own flesh, bind the fissures in the bones.

They made a bed for Taleswapper out in the great room. He offered to sleep on the floor beside Alvin's bed, but Miller shook his head and answered, "That's my place."

Taleswapper found it hard to sleep, though. It was the middle of the night when he finally gave up, lit a lantern with a match from the fire, bundled on his coat, and went outside.

The wind was brisk. There was a storm coming, and from the smell in the air, it would be snow. The animals were restless in the big barn. It occurred to Taleswapper that he might not be alone outside tonight. There might be Reds in the shadows, or even wandering among the buildings of the farm, watching him. He shuddered once, then shrugged off the fear. It was too cold a night. Even the most bloodthirsty, White-hating Choc-Taws or Cree-Eks spying from the south were too smart to be outside with such a storm coming.

Soon the snow would fall, the first of the season, but it would be no slight trace. It would snow all day tomorrow, Taleswapper could feel it, for the air behind the storm would be even colder than this, cold enough for the snow to be fluffy and dry, the kind of snow that piled deeper and deeper, hour after hour. If Alvin had not hurried them home with the millstone in a single day, they would have been trying to sledge the stone home in the midst of the snowfall. It would have become slippery. Something even worse might have happened.

Taleswapper found himself in the millhouse, looking at the stone. It was so solid-looking, it was hard to imagine anyone ever moving it. He touched the face of it again, being careful not to cut himself. His fingers brushed over the shallow dress cuts, where flour would collect when the great waterwheel turned the shaft and made the grindstone roll around and around atop the millstone, as steadily as the Earth rolled around and around the sun, year after year, turning time into dust as surely as the mill turned grain into flour.

He glanced down, to the place where the earth had given way slightly under the millstone, tipping it and nearly killing the boy. The bottom of the depression glistened in the lantern light. Taleswapper knelt and dipped his finger into a half-inch of water. It must have collected there, weakening the ground, carrying away the soil. Not so that it would ever be visibly moist. Just enough that when great weight was placed on it, it would give way.

Ah, Unmaker, thought Taleswapper, show yourself to me, and I'll build such a building that you'll be trussed up and held captive forever. But try as he might, he could not make his eyes see the trembling air that had shown itself to Alvin Miller's seventh son. Finally Taleswapper took up the lantern and left the millhouse. The first flakes were falling. The wind had almost died. The snow came faster and faster, dancing in the light of his lantern. By the time he reached the house, the ground was grey with snow, the forest invisible in the distance. He went inside the house, lay down on the floor without removing even his boots, and fell asleep.

12

Book

They kept a three-log fire, night and day, so the stones of the wall seemed to glow with heat, and the air in his room was dry. Alvin lay unmoving on his bed, his right leg heavy with splints and bandages, pressing into the bed like an anchor, the rest of his body afloat, adrift, pitching and rolling and yawing. He was dizzy, and a little sick.

But he hardly noticed the weight of his leg, or the dizziness. The pain was his enemy, throbs and stabs of it taking his mind away from the task that Taleswapper had set him: to heal himself.

Yet the pain was his friend, too. It built a wall around him so he scarce knew he was in a house, in a room, on a bed. The outside world could burn up and turn to ash and he'd never notice it. It was the world inside that he was exploring now.

Taleswapper didn't know half what he was talking about. It wasn't a matter of making pictures in his mind. His leg wouldn't get better from just pretending it was all healed up. But Taleswapper still had the right idea. If Alvin could feel his way through the rock, could find the weak and strong places and teach them where to break and where to hold firm, why couldn't he do it with skin and bone?

Trouble was, skin and bone was all mixed up. The rock was pretty much the same thing through and through, but the skin changed with every layer, and it wasn't no easy trick figuring where everything went. He lay there with his eyes closed, looking into his own flesh for the first time. At first he tried following the pain, but that didn't get nowhere, just led him to where everything was mashed and cut and messed up so he couldn't tell up from down. After a long while he tried a different tack. He listened to his heart beating. At first the pain kept tearing him away, but after a while he closed in on that sound. If there was noise in the world outside he didn't know about it, because the pain shut all that out. And the rhythm of the heartbeat, that shut out the pain, or mostly, anyway.

He followed the tracks of his blood, the big strong stream, the little streams. Sometimes he got lost. Sometimes a stab from his leg just broke in and demanded to be heard. But by and by he found his way to healthy skin and bone in the other leg. The blood wasn't half so strong there, but it led him where he wanted to go. He found all the layers, like the skin of an onion. He learned their order, saw how the muscle was tied together, how the tiny veins linked up, how the skin stretched taut and bonded tight.

Only then did he find his way to the bad leg. The patch of skin Mama sewed on was pretty much dead, just turning to rot. Alvin Junior knew what it needed, though, if any part of it was to live. He found the mashed-off ends of the arteries around the wound, and began to urge them to grow, just the way he made cracks travel through stone. The stone was easy, compared to this—to make a crack, it just had to let go, that's all. The living flesh was slower to do what he wanted, and pretty soon he gave up on all but the strongest artery.

He began to see how it was using bits and pieces of this and that to build with. A lot was happening that was far too small and fast and complicated for Alvin to get hold of with his mind. But he could get his body to free up what the artery needed in order to grow. He could send it where it was needed, and after a while the artery linked up with the rotted tissue. It took some doing, but he finally found the end of a shriveled artery and linked them up, and sent the blood flowing into the sewn-on patch.

Too soon, too fast. He felt the heat on his leg from blood pouring out of the dead flesh at a dozen points; it couldn't hold in all the blood he sent. Slow, slow, slow. He followed the blood, now seeping instead of pumping, and again linked up blood vessels, arteries to veins, trying to match it, as best he could, to the other leg.

Finally it was done, or well enough. The normal flow of blood could be contained. Many parts of the patch of skin came back to life as the blood returned. Other parts stayed dead. Alvin kept going around and around with the blood, stripping away the dead parts, breaking them up into bits and pieces too small for him to recognize. But the living parts recognized them well enough, took them up, put them to work. Wherever Alvin explored, he made the flesh grow.

Until he was so weary in his mind from thinking so small and working so hard that he fell asleep in spite of himself.

"I don't want to wake him."

"No way to change the bandage without touching it, Faith."

"All right, then—oh, be careful, Alvin! No, let me!"

"I've done this before—"

"On cows, Alvin, not on little boys!"

Alvin Junior felt pressure on his leg. Something pulling at the skin there. The pain wasn't as bad as yesterday. But he was still too tired even to open his eyes. Even to make a sound to let them know he was awake, he could hear them.

"Good laws, Faith, he must have bled something awful in the night."

"Mama, Mary says I have to—"

"Hush up and get on out of here, Cally! Can't you see your ma's worried about—"

"No need to yell at the boy, Alvin. He's only seven."

"Seven's old enough to keep his mouth shut and leave grown-ups alone when we've got things to—look at that."

"I can hardly believe it."

"I thought to see pus coming out like cream from a cow's tit."

"Clean as can be."

"And skin growing back, will you look at that? Your sewing must've took."

"I hardly dared to hope that skin would live."

"Can't even see no bone under there."

"The Lord is blessing us. I prayed all night, Alvin, and look what God has done."

"Well, you should've prayed harder, then, and got it healed up tight. I need this boy for chores."

"Don't you get blasfemious with me, Alvin Miller."

"It just gripes me hollow, the way God always sneaks in to take the credit. Maybe Alvin's just a good healer, you ever think of that?"

"Look, your nastiness is waking the boy."

"See if he wants a drink of water."

"He's getting one whether he wants it or not."

Alvin wanted it badly. His body was dry, not just his mouth; it needed to make back what it lost in blood. So he swallowed as much as he could, from a tin cup held to his mouth. A lot of it spilled around his face and neck but he didn't hardly notice that. It was the water that trickled into his belly that mattered. He lay back and tried to find out from the inside how his wound was doing. But it was too hard to get back there, too hard to concentrate. He dropped off before he was half-way there.

He woke again, and thought it must be night again, or maybe the curtains were drawn. He couldn't find out cause it was too hard to open his eyes, and the pain was back, fierce again, and something maybe even worse: the wound was a-tickling till he could hardly keep himself from reaching down to scratch. After a while, though, he was able to find the wound and once again help the layers to grow. By the time he slept, there was a thin, complete layer of skin over the whole wound. Underneath, the body was still working to renew the ravaged muscles and knit the broken bones. But there'd be no more loss of blood, no more open wound to get infected.

"Look at this, Taleswapper. You ever seen the like of this?"

"Skin like a newborn baby."

"Maybe I'm crazy, but except for the splint I can't see no reason to leave this leg bound up no more."

"Not a sign of a wound. No, you're right, there's no need for a bandage now."

"Maybe my wife is right, Taleswapper. Maybe God just rared back and passed a miracle on my boy."

"Can't prove anything. When the boy wakes up, maybe he'll know something about it."

"Not a chance of that. He hasn't even opened his eyes this whole time."

"One thing's certain, Mr. Miller. The boy isn't about to die. That's more than I could have guessed yesterday."

"I was set to build him a box to hold him underground, that I was. I didn't see no chance him living. Will you look at how healthy he is? I want to know what's protecting him, or who."

"Whatever is protecting him, Mr. Miller, the boy is stronger. That's something to think about. His protector split that stone, but Al Junior put it back together and not a thing his protector could do about it."

"Reckon he even knew what he was doing?"

"He must have some notion of his powers. He knew what he could do with the stone."

"I never heard of a knack like this, to tell you straight. I told Faith what he did with that stone, dressing it on the backside without ever laying on a tool, and she starts reading from the Book of Daniel and crying about fulfilment of the prophecy. Wanted to rush in here and warn the boy about clay feet. Don't that beat all? Religion makes them crazy. Not a woman I ever met wasn't crazy with religion."

The door opened.

"Get out of here! Are you so dumb I have to tell you twenty times, Cally? Where's his mother, can't she keep one seven-year-old boy away from—"

"Be easy on the lad, Miller. He's gone now, anyway."

"I don't know what's wrong with him. As soon as Al Junior is down, I see Cally's face wherever I look. Like an undertaker hoping for a fee."

"Maybe it's strange to him. To have Alvin hurt."

"As many times as Alvin's been an inch from death—"

"But never injured."

A long silence.

"Taleswapper."

"Yes, Mr. Miller?"

"You've been a good friend to us here, sometimes in spite of ourselfs. But I reckon you're still a walking man."

"That I am, Mr. Miller."

"What I'm saying is, not to rush you off, but if you go anytime soon, and you happen to be heading generally eastward, do you think you could carry a letter for me?"

"I'd be glad to. And no fee, to sender or receiver."

"That's right kind of you. I been thinking on what you said. About a boy needing to be sent far off from certain dangers. And I thought, in all the world where's there some folks I can trust to look after the boy? We got no kin worth speaking of back in New England—I don't want the boy raised Puritan on the brink of hell anyway."

"I'm relieved to hear that, Mr. Miller, because I have no great longing to see New England again myself."

"If you just follow back on the road we made coming west, sooner or later you come along to a place on the Hatrack River, some thirty miles north of the Hio, not all that far downriver from Fort Dekane. There's a roadhouse there, or leastwise there was, with a graveyard out back where a stone says 'Vigor he died to save his kin.' "

"You want me to take the boy?"

"No, no, I'll not send him now that the snow's come. Water—"

"I understand."

"There's a blacksmith there, and I thought he might want a prentice. Alvin's young, but he's big for his age, and I reckon he'll be a bargain for the smith."

"Prentice?"

"Well, I sure won't make him a bond slave, now, will I? And I got no money to send him off to school."

"I'll take the letter. But I hope I can stay till the boy is awake, so I can say good-bye."

"I wasn't going to send you out tonight, was I? Nor tomorrow, with new snow deep enough to smother bunnies."

"I didn't know if you had noticed the weather."

"I always notice when there's water underfoot." He laughed wryly, and they left the room.

Alvin Junior lay there, trying to figure why Pa wanted to send him away. Hadn't he done right all his life, as best he could? Hadn't he tried to help all he knew how? Didn't he go to Reverend Thrower's school, even though the preacher was out to make him mad or stupid? Most of all, didn't he finally get a perfect stone down from the mountain, holding it together all the time, teaching it the way to go, and at the very end risking his leg just so the stone wouldn't split? And now they were going to send him away.

Prentice! To a blacksmith! In his whole life he never even saw a blacksmith up to now. They had to ride three days to the nearest smithy, and Pa never let him go along. In his whole life he never even been ten mile from home one way or any other.

In fact, the more he thought about it the madder he got. Hadn't he been begging Mama and Papa just to let him go out walking in the woods alone, and they wouldn't let him. Had to have somebody with him all the time, like he was a captive or a slave about to run off. If he was five minutes late getting somewhere, they came to look for him. He never got to go on long trips—the longest one ever was to the quarry a few times. And now, after they kept him penned up like a Christmas goose all his life, they were set to send him off to the end of the whole earth.

It was so blame unfair that tears come to his eyes and squeezed out and tickled down his cheeks right into his ears, which felt so silly it made him laugh.

"What you laughing at?" asked Cally.

Alvin hadn't heard him come in.

"Are you all better now? It ain't bleeding nowhere, Al."

Cally touched his cheek.

"You crying cause it hurts so bad?"

Alvin probably could have spoke to him, but it seemed like too much work to open up his mouth and push words out, so he kind of shook his head, slow and gentle.

"You going to die, Alvin?" asked Cally.

He shook his head again.

"Oh," said Cally.

He sounded so disappointed that it made Alvin a little mad. Mad enough to get his mouth working after all. "Sorry," he croaked.

"Well it ain't fair, anyhow," said Cally. "I didn't want you dead, but they all said you was going to die. And I got to thinking what it'd be like if *I* was the one they all took care of. All the time, everybody watching out for you, and when I say one little thing they just say, Get out of here, Cally, Just shut up, Cally. Nobody asked you, Cally, Ain't you spose to be in bed, Cally? They don't care what I do. Except when I start hitting *you*, then they all say, Don't get in fights, Cally.''

"You wrestle real good for a field mouse." At least that was what Alvin meant to say, but he didn't know for sure if his lips even moved.

"You know what I did one time when I was six? I went out and got myself lost in the woods. I just walked and walked. Sometimes I closed my eyes and spun around a few times so I'd sure not know where I was. I must have been lost half the day. Did one soul come looking for me? I finally had to turn around and find my own way home. Nobody said, Where you been all day, Cally? Mama just said, Your hands are dirty as the back end of a sick horse, go wash yourself.''

Alvin laughed again, near silently, his chest heaving.

"It's funny for *you*. Everybody looks after *you*.''

Alvin worked hard to make a sound this time. "You want me gone?''

Cally waited a long time to answer. "No. Who'd play with me then? Just the dumb old cousins. There ain't a good wrassler in the bunch of them.''

"I'm going," whispered Alvin.

"No you ain't. You're the seventh son and they'll never let you go.''

"Going.''

"Course the way I count up it's *me* that's number seven. David, Calm, Measure, Wastenot, Wantnot, Alvin Junior that's you, and then me, that's seven.''

"Vigor.''

"He's dead. He's been dead a long time. Somebody ought to tell that to Ma and Pa.''

Alvin lay there, near wore out from the few things he said. Cally didn't say anything much after that. Just sat there, still as could be. Holding Alvin's hand real tight. Pretty soon Alvin started drifting, so he wasn't sure altogether whether Cally really spoke or it was in a dream. But he heard Cally say, "I don't never wish you dead, Alvin.'' And then he might have said, "I wish I was you.'' But anyway Alvin drifted off to sleep, and when he woke up again there was nobody with him and the house was still except for nightsounds, the wind rattling the shutters, the timbers popping as they shrunk from the cold, the log snapping in the hearth.

One more time Alvin went inside himself and worked his way down to the wound. Only this time he didn't have much to do with the skin and muscle. It was the bones he worked on now. It surprised him how lacy it was, pocked with little hollows all over, not solid straight through like the millstone was. But he learned the way of it soon enough, and it was easy after a while to knit the bones up tight.

Still, there was something wrong with that bone. Something in his bad leg just wouldn't get exactly like the good leg. But it was so small he couldn't see it clear. Just knew that whatever it was, it made the bone sick inside, just a little patch of sickness, but he couldn't figure how to make it better. Like trying to pick up snowflakes off the ground, whenever he thought he had ahold of something, it turned out to be nothing, or maybe just too small to see.

Maybe, though, it would just go away. Maybe if everything else got better, that sick place on his bone would get better by itself.

Eleanor was late getting back from her mother's house. Armor believed that a wife should have strong ties with her family, but coming home at dusk was too dangerous.

"There's talk of wild Reds up from the south," said Armor-of-God. "And you traipsing about after dark."

"I hurried home," she said. "I know the way in the dark."

"It's not a question of knowing the way," he said sternly. "The French are giving guns as bounty on White scalps now. It won't tempt the Prophet's people, but there's many a Choc-Taw who'd be glad to come up to Fort Detroit, gathering scalps along the way."

"Alvin isn't going to die," said Eleanor.

Armor hated it when she turned the subject like that. But it was such news that he couldn't very well not ask after it. "They decide to take off the leg, then?"

"I saw the leg. It's getting better. And Alvin Junior was awake late this afternoon. I talked to him awhile."

"I'm glad he was awake, Elly, I truly am, but I hope you don't expect the leg to get better. A big wound like that may look to be healing for a while, but the rot'll set in pretty soon."

"I don't think so this time," she said. "You want supper?"

"I must have gnawed down two loaves just pacing back and forth wondering whether you were even coming home."

"It isn't good for a man to get a belly."

"Well, I got one, and it calls out for food just like any other man's."

"Mama gave me a cheese to bring home." She set it out on the table.

Armor had his doubts. He figured half the reason Faith Miller's cheeses turned out so good was because she *did* things to the milk. At the same time, there wasn't no better cheese on the banks of the Wobbish, nor up Tippy-Canoe Creek neither.

It put him out of sorts when he caught himself compromising with witchery. And being out of sorts, he wasn't about to let anything lie, even though he knew Elly plain didn't want to talk about it. "Why don't you think the leg will rot?"

"It's just getting better so fast," she said.

"How much better?"

"Oh, pert near fixed."

"How near?"

She turned around, rolled her eyes, and turned back away from him. She started cutting up an apple to eat with the cheese.

"I said *how* near, Elly? How near fixed?"

"Fixed."

"Two days after a millstone rips off the front half of his leg, and it's fixed?"

"Only two days?" she said. "Seems like a week to me."

"Calendar says it's two days," said Armor. "Which means there's been witchery up there."

"As I read the gospels, the one that healed people wasn't no witch."

"Who did it? Don't tell me your pa or ma suddenly figured out something as strong as that. Did they conjure up a devil?"

She turned around, the knife in her hands still poised for cutting. There was a flash in her eyes. "Pa may be no kind of church man, but the devil never set foot in our house."

That wasn't what Reverend Thrower said, but Armor knew better than to bring *him* into the conversation. "It's that beggar, then."

"He works for his room and board. Hard as anyone."

"They say he knew that old wizard Ben Franklin. And that atheist from Appalachee, Tom Jefferson."

"He tells good stories. And he didn't heal the boy neither."

"Well, *somebody* did."

"Maybe he just healed up himself. Anyway, the leg's still *broke*. So it ain't a miracle or nothing. He's just a fast healer."

"Well maybe he's a fast healer cause the devil takes care of his own."

From the look in her eye when she turned around, Armor kind of wished he hadn't said it. But dad-gum it, Reverend Thrower as much as said the boy was as bad as the Beast of the Apocalypse.

But beast or boy, he was Elly's brother, and whereas she might be as quiet as you please most of the time, when she got her dander up she could be a terror.

"Take that back," she said.

"Now, that's about as silly a thing as I ever heard. How can I take back what I said?"

"By saying you know it ain't so."

"I don't know it is and I don't know it ain't. I said maybe, and if a man can't say his maybes to his wife then he might as well be dead."

"I reckon that's about true," she said. "And if you don't take that back you'll wish you was dead!" And she started coming after him with two chunks of apple, one in each hand.

Now, most times she came for him like that, even if she was really mad, if he let her chase him around the house awhile she usually ended up laughing. But not this time. She mushed one apple in his hair and threw the other one at him, and then just sat down in the upstairs bedroom, crying her eyes out.

She wasn't one to cry, so Armor figured this had got right out of hand.

"I take it back, Elly," he said. "He's a good boy, I know that."

"Oh, I don't care what you think," she said. "You don't know a thing about it anyway."

There weren't many husbands who'd let their wife say such a thing without slapping her upside the head. Armor wished sometimes that Elly'd appreciate how him being a Christian worked to her advantage.

"I know a thing or two," he said.

"They're going to send him off," she said. "Once spring comes, they're going to prentice him out. He's none too happy about it, I can tell, but he don't argue none, he just lies there in his bed, talking real quiet, but looking at me and everybody else like he was saying goodbye all the time."

"What are they wanting to send him off for?"

"I told you, to prentice him."

"The way they baby that boy, I can't hardly believe they'd let him out of their sight."

"They ain't talking about nothing close by, neither. Clear back at the east end of Hio Territory, near Fort Dekane. Why, that's halfway to the ocean."

"You know, it just makes sense, when you think about it."

"It does?"

"With Red trouble starting up, they want him plumb gone. The others can all stick around to get an arrow in their face, but not Alvin Junior."

She looked at him with withering contempt. "Sometimes you're so suspicious you make me want to puke, Armor-of-God."

"It ain't suspicion to say what's really happening."

"You can't tell real from a rutabaga."

"You going to wash this apple out of my hair, or do I have to make you lick it out?"

"I expect I'll have to do something, or you'll rub it all over the bed linen."

Taleswapper felt almost like a thief, to take so much with him as he left. Two pair of thick stockings. A new blanket. An elkhide cloak. Jerky and cheese. A good whetstone.

And things they couldn't even know they gave him. A rested body, free of aches and bruises. A jaunty step. Kind faces fresh in his mind. And stories. Stories jotted in the sealed-up part of the book, the ones he wrote down himself. And true stories painfully inscribed by their own hands.

Still, he gave them fair return, or tried to. Roofs patched for winter, other jobs here and there. More important, they'd seen a book with Ben Franklin's own handwriting in it, with sentences from Tom Jefferson, Ben Arnold, Pat Henry, John Adams, Alex Hamilton—even Aaron Burr, from before the duel, and Daniel Boone, from after. Before Taleswapper came they were part of their family, and part of the Wobbish country, and that's all. Now they belonged to much larger stories. The War of Appalachee Independence. The American Compact. They saw their own trek through the wilderness as one thread among many, and felt the strength of the whole tapestry woven from those threads. Not a tapestry, really. A rug. A good, thick, solid rug that generations of Americans after them could tread on. There was a poem in that; he'd work that into a poem sometime.

He left them a few other things, too. A beloved son he pulled from under a falling millstone. A father who now had the strength to send away his son before he killed him. A name for a young man's night-mare, so he could understand that his enemy was real. A whispered encouragement for a broken child to heal himself.

And a single drawing, burnt into a fine slab of oakwood with the tip of a hot knife. He'd rather have worked with wax and acid on metal, but there was neither to be had in this place. So he burnt lines into the wood, making of it what he could. A picture of a young man caught in a strong river, bound up in the roots of a floating tree, gasping for breath, his eyes facing death fearlessly. It would have earned nothing but scorn at the Lord Protector's Academy of Art, being so plain. But Goody Faith cried out when she saw it, and hugged it to her, dropping her tears over it like the last drips from the eaves after a rainstorm. And Father Alvin, when he saw it, nodded and said, "That's your vision, Taleswapper. You got his face perfect, and you never even saw him. That's Vigor. That's my boy." Then he cried, too.

They set it right up on the mantel. It might not be great art, thought

Taleswapper, but it was true, and it meant more to these folks than any portrait could mean to some fat old lord or parliamentarian in London or Camelot or Paris or Vienna.

"It's fair morning now," said Goody Faith. "You've got long to go before dark."

"You can't blame me for being reluctant to leave. Though I'm glad you trusted me with this errand, and I won't fail you." He patted his pocket, wherein lay the letter to the blacksmith of Hatrack River.

"You can't go without you say good-bye to the boy," said Miller. He'd put it off as long as it could be delayed. He nodded once, then eased himself from the comfortable chair by the fire and went on into the room where he'd slept the best nights of his life. It was good to see Alvin Junior's eyes wide open, his face lively, no longer slack the way it was for a while, or winced up with pain. But the pain was still there, Taleswapper knew.

"You going?" asked the boy.

"I'm gone, except for saying good-bye to you."

Alvin looked a little angry. "So you ain't even going to let me write in your book?"

"Not everybody does, you know."

"Pa did. And Mama."

"And Cally, too."

"I bet that looks good," said Alvin. "He writes like a, like a—"

"Like a seven-year-old." It was a rebuke, but Alvin had no intention of squirming.

"Why not me, then? Why Cally and not me?"

"Because I only let people write the most important thing they ever did or ever saw with their own eyes. What would *you* write?"

"I don't know. Maybe about the millstone."

Taleswapper made a face.

"Then maybe my vision. That's important, you said so yourself."

"And that got written up somewhere else, Alvin."

"I want to write in the book," he said. "I want my sentence in there along with Maker Ben's."

"Not yet," said Taleswapper.

"When!"

"When you've whipped that old Unmaker, lad. That's when I'll let you write in this book."

"What if I don't ever whip him?"

"Then this book won't amount to much, anyway."

Tears sprang to Alvin's eyes. "What if I die?"

Taleswapper felt a thrill of fear. "How's the leg?"

The boy shrugged. He blinked back the tears. They were gone.

"That's no answer, lad."

"It won't stop hurting."

"It'll be that way till the bone knits."

Alvin Junior smiled wanly. "Bone's all knit."

"Then why don't you walk?"

"It pains me, Taleswapper. It never goes away. It's got a bad place on the bone, and I ain't figured out yet how to make it right."

"You'll find a way."

"I ain't found it yet."

"An old trapper once said to me, 'It don't matter if you start at the bung or the breastbone, any old way you get the skin off a panther is a good way.' "

"Is that a proverb?"

"It's close. You'll find a way, even if it isn't what you expect."

"Nothing's what I expect," said Alvin. "Nothing turns out like anything I figured."

"You're ten years old, lad. Weary of the world already?"

Alvin kept rubbing folds of the blanket between his thumb and fingers. "Taleswapper, I'm dying."

Taleswapper studied his face, trying to see death there. It wasn't. "I don't think so."

"The bad place on my leg. It's growing. Slow, maybe, but it's growing. It's invisible, and it's eating away at the hard places of the bone, and after a while it'll go faster and faster and—"

"And Unmake you."

Alvin started to cry for real this time, and his hands were shaking. "I'm scared to die, Taleswapper, but it got inside me and I can't get it out."

Taleswapper laid a hand on his, to still the trembling. "You'll find a way. You've got too much work to do in this world, to die now."

Alvin rolled his eyes. "That's about as dumb a thing as I've heard this year. Just because somebody's got things to do don't mean he won't die."

"But it does mean he won't die *willingly*."

"I ain't willing."

"That's why you'll find a way to live."

Alvin was silent for a few seconds. "I've been thinking. About if I do live, what I'll do. Like what I done to make my leg get mostly better. I can do that for other folks, I bet. I can lay hands on them and feel the way it is inside, and fix it up. Wouldn't that be good?"

"They'd love you for it, all the folks you healed."

"I reckon the first time was the hardest, and I wasn't partickler strong when I done it. I bet I can do it faster on other people."

"Maybe so. But even if you heal a hundred sick people every day, and move on to the next place and heal a hundred more, there'll be ten thousand people die behind you, and ten thousand more ahead of you, and by the time you die, even the ones you healed will almost all be dead."

Alvin turned his face away. "If I know how to fix them, then I got to fix them, Taleswapper."

"Those you can, you must," said Taleswapper. "But not as your life's work. Bricks in the wall, Alvin, that's all they'll ever be. You can never catch up by repairing the crumbling bricks. Heal those who chance to fall under your hand, but your life's work is deeper than that."

"I know how to heal people. But I don't know how to beat down the Un—the Unmaker. I don't even know what it is."

"As long as you're the only one that can see him, though, you're also the only one who has a hope of beating him."

"Maybe."

Another long silence. Taleswapper knew it was time to go.

"Wait."

"I've got to leave now."

Alvin caught at his sleeve. "Not yet."

"Pretty soon."

"At least—at least let me read what the others wrote."

Taleswapper reached into his bag and pulled out the book pouch. "I can't promise I'll explain what they mean," he said, sliding the book out of its waterproof cover.

Alvin quickly found the last, newest writings.

In his mother's hand: "Vigor he push a log and he don die til the boy is bornd."

In David's hand: "A mil ston splits in two then it suks bak not a crak."

In Cally's hand: "A sevent sunn."

Alvin looked up. "He ain't talking about me, you know."

"I know," said Taleswapper.

Alvin looked back at the book. In his father's hand: "He don't kil a boy cus a stranjer com in time."

"What's Pa talking about?" asked Alvin.

Taleswapper took the book from his hands and closed it. "Find a way to heal your leg," he said. "There's a lot more souls than you who need it to be strong. It's not for yourself, remember?"

He bent over and kissed the boy on the forehead. Alvin reached up and held him with both arms, hanging on him so that he couldn't stand up without lifting the boy clear out of bed. After a while, Taleswapper had to reach up and pull the boy's arms away. His cheek was wet with Alvin's tears. He didn't wipe them away. He let the breeze dry them as he trudged along the cold dry path, with fields of half-melted snow stretching left and right.

He paused a moment on the second covered bridge. Just long enough to wonder if he'd ever come back here, or see them again. Or get Alvin Junior's sentence for his book. If he were a prophet, he'd know. But he hadn't the faintest idea.

He walked on, setting his feet toward morning.

13

Surgery

The Visitor sat comfortably upon the altar, leaning casually on his left arm, so that his body had a jaunty tilt. Reverend Thrower had seen just such an informal pose taken by a dandy from Camelot, a rakehell who clearly despised everything that the Puritan churches of England and Scotland stood for. It made Thrower more than a little uncomfortable to see the Visitor in such an irreverent pose.

"Why?" asked the Visitor. "Just because the only way you can maintain control over your bodily passions is to sit straight in your chair, knees together, hands delicately arranged in your lap, fingers tightly interwined, does not mean that I am required to do the same."

Thrower was embarrassed. "It isn't fair to chastise me for my thoughts."

"It is, when your thoughts chastise me for my actions. Beware of hubris, my friend. Do not fancy yourself so righteous that *you* can judge the acts of angels."

It was the first time the Visitor had ever called himself an angel.

"I did not call myself *anything*," said the Visitor. "You must learn to control your thoughts, Thrower. You leap to conclusions far too easily."

"Why have you come to me?"

"It's a matter of the maker of this altar," said the Visitor. He patted one of the crosses Alvin Junior had burnt into the wood.

"I've done my best, but the boy is unteachable. He doubts everything, and contests each point of theology as if it were required to meet the same tests of logic and consistency that prevail in the world of science."

"In other words, he expects your doctrines to make sense."

"He is unwilling to accept the idea that some things remain mysteries, comprehensible only to the mind of God. Ambiguity makes him saucy, and paradox causes open rebellion.''

''An obnoxious child.''

''The worst I have ever seen,'' said Thrower.

The Visitor's eyes flashed. Thrower felt a stab in his heart.

''I've tried,'' said Thrower. ''I've tried to turn him to serve the Lord. But the influence of his father—''

''It is a weak man who blames his failures on the strength of others,'' said the Visitor.

''I haven't failed yet!'' said Thrower. ''You told me I had until the boy was fourteen—''

''No. I told you *I* had until the boy was fourteen. *You* only have him as long as he lives here.''

''I've heard nothing about the Millers moving. They just got their millstone in place, they're going to start grinding in the spring, they wouldn't leave without—''

The Visitor stood up from the altar. ''Let me put a case to you, Reverend Thrower. Purely hypothetical. Let us suppose you were in the same room with the worst enemy of all that I stand for. Let us suppose that he were ill, and lay helpless in his bed. If he recovered, he would be removed from your reach, and would thus go on to destroy all that you and I love in this world. But if he died, our great cause would be safe. Now suppose that someone put a knife into your hand, and begged you to perform a delicate surgery upon the boy. And suppose that if you were to slip, just the tiniest bit, your knife could cut a great artery. And suppose that if you simply delayed, his lifeblood would flow out so quickly that in moments he would die. In that case, Reverend Thrower, what would be your duty?''

Thrower was aghast. All his life he had prepared to teach, persuade, exhort, expound. Never to perform a bloody-handed act like the one the Visitor suggested. ''I'm not suited for such things,'' he said.

''Are you suited for the kingdom of God?'' asked the Visitor.

''But the Lord said Thou shalt not kill.''

''Oh? Is that what he said to Joshua, when he sent him into the promised land? Is that what he said to Saul, when he sent him against the Amalekites?''

Thrower thought of those dark passages in the Old Testament, and trembled with fear at the thought of taking part in such things himself.

But the Visitor did not relent. ''The high priest Samuel commanded King Saul to kill all the Amalekites, every man and woman, every *child*. But Saul hadn't the stomach for it. He saved the king of the Amalekites and brought him back alive. For that crime of disobedience, what did the Lord do?''

"Chose David to be king in his place," murmured Thrower.

The Visitor stood close to Thrower, his eyes wounding him with their fire. "And then Samuel, the high priest, the *gentle* servant of God, what did he do?''

"He called for Agag the kind of the Amalekites to be brought before him.''

The Visitor would not relent. "And what did Samuel *do?*''

"Killed him," whispered Thrower.

"What does the scripture say that he did!" roared the Visitor. The walls of the meetinghouse shook, the glass of the windows rattled.

Thrower wept in fear, but he spoke the words that the Visitor demanded: "Samuel hacked Agag in pieces—in the presence of the Lord.''

Now the only sound in the church was Thrower's own ragged breath as he tried to control his hysterical weeping. The Visitor smiled at him, his eyes filled with love and forgiveness. Then he was gone.

Thrower sank to his knees before the altar and prayed. O Father, I would die for Thee, but do not ask me to kill. Take away this cup from my lips, I am too weak, I am unworthy, do not lay this burden upon my shoulders.

His tears fell on the altar. He heard a sizzling sound and jumped back from the altar, startled. His tears skittered along the surface of the altar like water on a hot skillet, until finally they were consumed.

The Lord has rejected me, he thought. I pledged to serve Him however He required, and now, when He asks something difficult, when He commands me to be as strong as the great prophets of old, I discover myself to be a broken vessel in the hands of the Lord. I cannot contain the destiny He wanted to pour into me.

The door of the church opened, letting in a wave of freezing air that rushed along the floor and sent a chill through the minister's flesh. He looked up, fearing that it was an angel sent to punish him.

It was no angel, though. Merely Armor-of-God Weaver.

"I didn't mean to interrupt you in prayer," said Armor.

"Come in," said Thrower. "Close the door. What can I do for you?''

"Not for me," said Armor.

"Come here. Sit down. Tell me.''

Thrower hoped that perhaps it was a sign from God that Armor had come just now. A member of the congregation, coming to him for help, right after he prayed—surely the Lord was letting him know that he was accepted after all.

"It's my wife's brother," said Armor. "The boy, Alvin Junior."

Thrower felt a thrill of dread run through him, freezing him to the bone. "I know him. What about him?"

"You know he got his leg mashed."

"I heard of it."

"You didn't happen to go visit and see him afore it healed up?"

"I've been given to believe that I'm not welcome in that house."

"Well, let me tell you, it was bad. A whole patch of skin tore off. Bones broke. But two days later, it was healed right up. Couldn't even see no scar. Three days later he was *walking*."

"It must not have been as bad as you thought."

"I'm telling you, that leg was *broke* and the wound was *bad*. The whole family figured the boy was bound to die. They asked me about buying nails for a coffin. And they looked so bad from grieving that I wasn't sure but what we'd bury the boy's ma and pa, too."

"Then it can't be as fully healed as you say."

"Well, it ain't *fully* healed, and that's why I come to you. I know you don't believe in such things, but I tell you they witched the boy's leg to heal somehow. Elly says the boy did the witching himself. He was even walking on the leg for a few days, no splint even. But the pain never let up, and now he says there's a sick place on his bone. He's got a fever, too."

"There's a perfectly natural explanation for everything," said Thrower.

"Well, be that as you like, the way I see it the boy invited the devil with his witchery, and now the devil's eating him alive inside. And seeing how you're an ordained minister of God, I thought maybe you could cast out that devil in the name of the Lord Jesus."

Superstitions and sorceries were nonsense, of course, but when Armor brought up the possibility of a devil being in the boy, it made sense, it fit with what he knew from the Visitor. Maybe the Lord wanted him to exorcise the child, to purge the evil from him, not to kill the boy at all. It was a chance for him to redeem himself from his failure of will a few minutes before.

"I'll go," he said. He reached for his heavy cloak and whipped it around his shoulders.

"I better warn you, nobody up at their house asked me to bring you."

"I'm prepared to deal with the anger of the unfaithful," said Thrower. "It's the victim of deviltry that concerns me, not his foolish and superstitious family."

*　　*　　*

Alvin lay on his bed, burning with the heat of his fever. Now, in the daylight, they kept his shutters closed, so the light wouldn't hurt his eyes. At night, though, he made them open things up, let some of the cold air in. He would breathe it in relief. During the few days when he could walk, he had seen the snow covering the meadow. Now he tried to imagine himself lying under that blanket of snow. Relief from the fire burning through his body.

He just couldn't see small enough inside himself. What he did with the bone, with the strands of muscle and layers of skin, it was harder than ever it was to find the cracks in the quarry stone. But he could feel his way through the labyrinth of his body, find the large wounds, help them to close. Most of what went on, though, was too small and fast for him to comprehend. He could see the result, but he couldn't see the pieces, couldn't make out how it happened.

That's how it was with the bad place in his bone. Just a patch of it that was weakening, rotting away. He could feel the difference between the bad place and the good healthy bone, he could find the borders of the sickness. But he couldn't actually see what was happening. He couldn't undo it. He was going to die.

He wasn't alone in the room, he knew. Someone always sat at his bedside. He would open his eyes and see Mama, or Papa, or one of the girls. Sometimes even one of the brothers, even though it meant he had left his wife and his chores. It was a comfort to Alvin, but it was also a burden. He kept thinking he ought to hurry up and die so they could all get back to their regular lives.

This afternoon it was Measure sitting there. Alvin said howdy to him when he first came, but there wasn't much to talk about. Howdy do? I'm dying, thanks, and you? Kind of hard to keep chatting. Measure talked about how he and the twins had tried to cut a grindstone. They chose a softer stone than what Alvin worked with, and still they had a devil of a time cutting. "We finally gave right up," said Measure. "It's just going to have to wait till you can go up the mountain and get us a stone yourself."

Alvin didn't answer that, and they neither one said a word since then. Alvin just lay there, sweating, feeling the rot in his bone as it slowly, steadily grew. Measure sat there, lightly holding his hand.

Measure started to whistle.

The sound of it startled Alvin. He'd been so caught up inside himself that the music seemed to come from a great distance, and he had to travel some distance to discover where it was coming from.

"Measure," he cried; but the sound of his voice was a whisper.

The whistling stopped. "Sorry," said Measure. "Does it bother you?"

"No," said Alvin.

Measure started in whistling again. It was a strange tune, one that Alvin didn't recollect he ever heard before. In fact it didn't sound like any kind of tune at all. It never did repeat itself, just went on with new patterns all the time, like as if Measure was making it up on the way. As Alvin lay there and listened, the melody seemed like it was a map, winding through a wilderness, and he started to follow it. Not that he *saw* anything, the way he would following a real map. It just seemed always to show him the center of things, and everything he thought about, he thought about as if he was standing in that place. Almost like he could see all the thinking he had done before, trying to figure out a way to fix the bad place on his bone, only now he was looking from a ways off, maybe higher up a mountain or in a clearing, somewhere that he could see *more*.

Now he thought of something he never thought of before. When his leg was first broke, with the skin all tore up, everybody could see how bad off he was, but nobody could help him, only himself. He had to fix it all from inside. Now, though, nobody else could see the wound that was killing him. And even though *he* could see it, he couldn't do a blame thing to make it better.

So maybe this time, somebody else could fix him up. Not using any kind of hidden power at all. Just plain old bloody-handed surgery.

"Measure," he whispered.

"I'm here," said Measure.

"I know a way to fix my leg," he said.

Measure leaned in close. Alvin didn't open his eyes, but he could feel his brother's breath on his cheek.

"The bad place on my bone, it's growing, but it ain't spread all over yet," Alvin said. "I can't make it better, but I reckon if somebody cut off that part of my bone and took it right out of my leg, I could heal it up the rest of the way."

"Cut it out?"

"Pa's bone saw that he uses when he's cutting up meat, that'd do the trick I think."

"But there ain't a surgeon in three hundred mile."

"Then I reckon somebody better learn how real quick, or I'm dead."

Measure was breathing quicker now. "You think cutting your bone would save your life?"

"It's the best I can think of."

"It might mess up your leg real bad," said Measure.

"If I'm dead, I won't care. And if I live, it'll be worth a messed-up leg."

"I'm going to fetch Pa." Measure scuffed back his chair and thumped out of the room.

Thrower let Armor lead the way onto the Millers' porch. They couldn't very well turn away their daughter's husband. His concern was unfounded, however. It was Goody Faith who opened the door, not her pagan husband.

"Why, Reverend Thrower, if you ain't being too kind to us, stopping up here," she said. The cheerfulness of her voice was a lie, though, if her haggard face was telling the truth. There hadn't been much good sleep in this house lately.

"I brought him along, Mother Faith," said Armor. "He come only cause I asked him."

"The pastor of our church is welcome in my home whenever it pleases him to come by," said Faith.

She ushered them into the great room. A group of girls making quilt squares looked up at him from their chairs near the hearth. The little boy, Cally, was doing his letters on a board, writing with charcoal from the fire.

"I'm glad to see you doing your letters," said Thrower.

Cally just looked at him. There was a hint of hostility in his eyes. Apparently the boy resented having his teacher look at his work here at home, which he had supposed was a sanctuary.

"You're doing them well," said Thrower, trying to put the boy at ease. Cally said nothing, just looked down again at his makeshift slate and kept on scrawling out words.

Armor brought up their business right away. "Mother Faith, we come cause of Alvin. You know how I feel about witchery, but I never before said a word against what you folks do in your house. I always reckoned that was your business and none of mine. But that boy is paying the price for the evil ways that you've let go on here. He witched his leg, and now there's a devil in him, killing him off, and I brought Reverend Thrower here to wring that devil on out of him."

Goody Faith looked puzzled. "There ain't no devil in this house."

Ah, poor woman, said Thrower silently. If you only knew how long a devil has dwelt here. "It is possible to become so accustomed to the presence of a devil as not to recognize that it is present."

A door by the stairs opened up, and Mr. Miller stepped backward through the doorway. "Not me," he said, talking to whoever was in that room. "I'll not lay a knife to the boy."

Cally jumped up at the sound of his father's voice and ran to him. "Armor brung old Thrower here, Papa, to kill the devil."

Mr. Miller turned around, his face twisted with unidentified emotion, and looked at the visitors as if he hardly recognized them.

"I've got good strong hexes on this house," said Goody Faith.

"Those hexes are a summons for the devil," said Armor. "You think they protect your house, but they drive away the Lord."

"No devil ever came in here," she insisted.

"Not by itself," said Armor. "You called it in with all your conjuring. You forced the Holy Spirit to leave your house by your witchery and idolatry, and having swept goodness from your home, the devils naturally come right in. They always come in, where they see a fair chance to do mischief."

Thrower became a little concerned that Armor was saying too much about things he didn't really understand. It would have been better had he simply asked if Thrower could pray for the boy at Alvin's bedside. Now Armor was drawing battle lines that should never have been drawn.

And whatever was going on in Mr. Miller's head right now, it was plain to see that this wasn't the best of times to provoke the man. He slowly walked toward Armor. "You telling me that what comes into a man's house to do mischief is the devil?"

"I bear you my witness as one who loves the Lord Jesus," Armor began, but before he could get any further into his testimony, Miller had him by the shoulder of his coat and the waist of his pants, and he turned him right toward the door.

"Somebody better open this door!" roared Miller. "Or there's going to be a powerful big hole right in the middle of it!"

"What do you think you're doing, Alvin Miller!" shouted his wife.

"Casting out devils!" cried Miller. Cally had swung the door open by then, and Miller walked his son-in-law to the edge of the porch and sent him flying. Armor's cry of outrage ended up muffled by the snow on the ground, and there wasn't much chance to hear his yelling after that because Miller closed and barred the door.

"Ain't you a big man," said Goody Faith, "throwing out your own daughter's husband."

"I didn't do but what he said the Lord wanted done," said Miller. Then he turned his gaze upon the pastor.

"Armor didn't speak for me," said Thrower mildly.

"If you lay a hand on a man of the cloth," said Goody Faith, "you'll sleep in a cold bed for the rest of your life."

"Wouldn't think of touching the man," said Miller. "But the way I figure it, I stay out of his place, and he ought to stay out of mine."

"You may not believe in the power of prayer," said Thrower.

"I reckon it depends on who's doing the praying, and who's doing the listening," said Miller.

"Even so," said Thrower, "your wife believes in the religion of Jesus Christ, in the which I have been called and ordained a minister. It is her belief, and my belief, that for me to pray at the boy's bedside might be efficacious in his cure."

"If you use words like that in your praying," said Miller, "it's a wonder the Lord even knows what you're talking about."

"Though you don't believe such prayer will help," Thrower went on, "it certainly can't hurt, can it?"

Miller looked from Thrower to his wife and back again. Thrower had no doubt that if Faith had not been there, he would have been eating snow alongside Armor-of-God. But Faith *was* there and had already uttered the threat of Lysistrata. A man does not have fourteen children if his wife's bed holds no attraction to him. Miller gave in. "Go on in," he said. "But don't pester the boy too long."

Thrower nodded graciously. "No more than a few hours," he said.

"Minutes!" Miller insisted. But Thrower was already headed for the door by the stairs, and Miller made no move to stop him. He could have hours with the boy, if he wanted to. He closed the door behind him. No sense in letting any of the pagans interfere with this.

"Alvin," he said.

The boy was stretched out under a blanket, his forehead beaded with sweat. His eyes were closed. After a while, though, he opened his mouth a little. "Reverend Thrower," he whispered.

"The very same," said Thrower. "Alvin, I've come to pray for you, so the Lord will free your body of the devil that is making you sick."

Again a pause, as if it took a while for Thrower's words to reach Alvin and just as long again for his answer to return. "Ain't no devil," he said.

"One can hardly expect a child to be well-versed in matters of religion," said Thrower. "But I must tell you that healing comes only to those who have the faith to be healed." He then devoted several minutes to recounting the story of the centurion's daughter and the tale of the woman who had an issue of blood and merely touched the Savior's robe. "You recall what he said to her. Thy faith hath made thee whole, he said. So it is, Alvin Miller, that your faith must be strong before the Lord can make you whole."

The boy didn't answer. Since Thrower had used his considerable eloquence in the telling of both stories, it offended him a bit that the boy might have fallen asleep. He reached out a long finger and poked Alvin's shoulder.

Alvin flinched away. "I heard you," he muttered.

It wasn't good that the boy could still be sullen, after hearing the light-giving word of the Lord. "Well?" asked Thrower. "Do you believe?"

"In what," murmured the boy.

"In the gospel! In the God who would heal you, if you only soften your heart!"

"Believe," he whispered. "In God."

That should have been enough. But Thrower knew too much of the history of religion not to press for more detail. It was not enough to confess faith in a deity. There were so many deities, and all but one was false. "*Which* God do you believe in, Al Junior?"

"God," said the boy.

"Even the heathen Moor prays toward the black stone of Mecca and calls it God! Do you believe in the true God, and do you believe in Him correctly? No, I understand, you're too weak and fevered to explain your faith. I will help you, young Alvin. I'll ask you questions, and you tell me, yes or no, whether you believe."

Alvin lay still, waiting.

"Alvin Miller, do you believe in a God without body, parts, or passions? The great Uncreated Creator, Whose center is everywhere, yet Whose circumference can never be found?"

The boy seemed to ponder this for a while before he spoke. "That don't make a bit of sense to me," he said.

"He isn't supposed to make sense to the carnal mind," Thrower said. "I merely ask if you *believe* in the One who sits atop the Topless Throne; the self-existing Being who is so large He fills the universe, yet so penetrating that He lives in your heart."

"How can he sit on the top of something that ain't got no top?" the boy asked. "How can something that big fit inside my heart?"

The boy was obviously too uneducated and simple-minded to grasp sophisticated theological paradox. Still, it was more than a life or even a soul at stake here—it was all the souls that the Visitor had said this boy would ruin if he could not be converted to the true faith. "That's the beauty of it," said Thrower, letting emotion fill his voice. "God is beyond our comprehension; yet in His infinite love He condescends to save us, despite our ignorance and foolishness."

"Ain't love a passion?" asked the boy.

"If you have trouble with the idea of God," said Thrower, "then let me pose another question, which may be more to the point. Do you believe in the bottomless pit of hell, where the wicked writhe in flames, yet are never burned up? Do you believe in Satan, the enemy of God, who wishes to steal your soul and take you captive into his kingdom, to torment you through all eternity?"

The boy seemed to perk up a little, turning his head toward Thrower, though he still didn't open his eyes. "I might believe in something like that," he said.

Ah, yes, thought Thrower. The boy *has* had some experience with the devil. "Have you seen him, child?"

"What's *your* devil look like?" whispered the boy.

"He is not *my* devil," said Thrower. "And if you had listened in services, you would have known, for I have described him many times. Where a man has hair on his head, the devil has the horns of a bull. Where a man has hands, the devil has the claws of a bear. He has the hooves of a goat, and his voice is the roar of a ravening lion."

To Thrower's amazement, the boy smiled, and his chest bounced silently with laughter. "And you call *us* superstitious," he said.

Thrower would never have believed how firm a grip the devil could have on a child's soul, had he not seen the boy laugh with pleasure at the description of the monster Lucifer. That laughter must be stopped! It was an offense against God!

Thrower slapped his Bible down on the boy's chest, causing Alvin to wheeze out his breath. Then, with his hand pressing on the book, Thrower felt himself fill up with inspired words, and he cried out with more passion than he had ever felt before in his life: "Satan, in the name of the Lord I rebuke you! I command you to depart from this boy, from this room, from this house forever! Never again seek to possess a soul in this place, or the power of God will wreak destruction unto the uttermost bounds of hell!"

Then silence. Except for the boy's breathing, which seemed labored. There was such peace in the room, such exhausted righteousness in Thrower's own heart, that he felt convinced the devil had heeded his peroration and retreated forthwith.

"Reverend Thrower," said the boy.

"Yes, my son?"

"Can you take that Bible off my chest now? I reckon if there was any devils here, they're all gone now."

Then the boy began to laugh again, causing the Bible to jump up and down under Thrower's hand.

In that moment Thrower's exultation turned to bitter disappointment. Indeed, the fact that the boy could laugh so devilishly with the Bible itself resting on his body was proof that no power could purge him of evil. The Visitor had been right. Thrower should never have refused the mighty work that the Visitor had called him to do. It had been in his power to be the slayer of the Beast of the Apocalypse, and he had been too weak, too sentimental to accept the divine calling. I could have been a Samuel, hewing to death the enemy of God. Instead I am a Saul, a weakling, who cannot kill what the Lord commands must die. Now I will see this boy rise up with the power of Satan in him, and I will know that he thrives only because I was weak.

Now the room was stifling hot, choking him. He had not realized until now how his clothing sogged with sweat. It was hard to breathe. But what should he expect? The hot breath of hell was in this room. Gasping, he took the Bible, held it out between him and the satanic child who lay giggling feverishly under the blanket, and fled.

In the great room he stopped, breathing heavily. He had interrupted a conversation, but he scarcely took notice of it. What did the conversations of these benighted people amount to, compared to what he had just experienced? I have stood in the presence of Satan's minion, masquing it as a young boy; but his mockery revealed him to me. I should have known what the boy was years ago, when I felt his head and found it to be so perfectly balanced. Only a counterfeit would be so perfect. The child was never *real*. Ah, that I had the strength of the great prophets of old, so I could confound the enemy and bear the trophy back to my Lord!

Someone was tugging at his sleeve. "Are you well, Reverend?" It was Goody Faith, but Reverend Thrower did not think to answer her. Her tugging pulled him around, though, so he faced the fireplace. There on the mantel he saw a carven image, and in his distracted state he could not at once determine what it was. It seemed to be the face of a soul in torment, surrounded by writhing tendrils. Flames, that's what they are, he thought, and that is a soul drowning in brimstone, burning in hellfire. The image was a torment to him, and yet it was also satisfying, for its presence in this house signified how closely bound this family was to hell. He stood in the midst of his enemies. A phrase from the Psalmist came to his mind: Bulls of Bashan stare upon me, and I can tell all my bones. My God, my God, why hast Thou forsaken me?

"Here," said Goody Faith. "Sit down."

"Is the boy all right?" demanded Miller.

"The boy?" asked Thrower. Words could hardly come to his mouth. The boy is a fiend from Sheol, and you ask how he is? "As well as can be expected," said Thrower.

They turned away from him then, back to their conversation. Gradually he came to understand what they were discussing. It seemed that

Alvin wanted someone to cut away the diseased portion of his bone. Measure had even brought a fine-toothed bone saw from the butchery shed. The argument was between Faith and Measure, because Faith didn't want anyone cutting her son, and between Miller and the other two, because Miller refused to do it, and Faith would only consent if Alvin's father did the cutting.

"If you think it ought to be done," said Faith, "then I don't see how you'd be willing to have anyone but yourself cut into him."

"Not me," said Miller.

It struck Thrower that the man was afraid. Afraid to lay the knife against his own son's flesh.

"He asked for you, Pa. He said he'd draw the marks for cutting, right on his own leg. You just cut a flap of skin and peel it back, and right under it there's the bone, and you just cut a wedge in the bone that takes out the whole bad place."

"I'm not the fainting kind," said Faith, "but my head is getting light."

"If Al Junior says it's got to be done, then do it!" said Miller. "But not me!"

Then, like a rush of light into a dark room, Reverend Thrower saw his redemption. The Lord was clearly offering him exactly the opportunity that the Visitor had prophesied. A chance to hold a knife in his hand, to cut into the boy's leg, and *accidently* sever the artery and spill the blood until the life was gone. What he had shrunk to do in the church, thinking of Alvin as a mere boy, he would do gladly, now that he had seen the evil that disguised itself in child-shape.

"I'm here," he said.

They looked at him.

"I'm no surgeon," he said, "but I have some knowledge of anatomy. I *am* a scientist."

"Head bumps," said Miller.

"You ever butchered cattle or pigs?" asked Measure.

"Measure!" said his mother, horrified. "Your brother is not a beast."

"I just wanted to know if he was going to throw up when he saw blood."

"I've seen blood," said Thrower. "And I have no fear, when the cutting is for salvation."

"Oh, Reverend Thrower, it's too much to ask of you," said Goody Faith.

"Now I see that perhaps it *was* inspiration that brought me up here today, after so long being away from this house."

"It was my pebble-headed son-in-law brought you here," said Miller.

"Well," said Thrower, "it was just a thought. I can see that you don't want me to do it, and I can't say that I blame you. Even if it means saving your son's life, it's still a dangerous thing to let a stranger cut into your own child's body."

"You're no stranger," insisted Faith.

"What if something went wrong? I might slip. His previous injury might have changed the path of certain blood vessels. I might cut an artery, and he could bleed to death in moments. Then I'd have the blood of your child on my hands."

"Reverend Thrower," said Faith, "we can't blame you for chance. All we can do is try."

"It's sure that if we don't do something he'll die," said Measure. "He says we got to cut right away, before the bad place spreads too far."

"Perhaps one of your older sons," said Thrower.

"We got no time to fetch them!" cried Faith. "Oh, Alvin, he's the boy you chose to have your name. Are you set to let him die, just cause you can't abide the preacher here?"

Miller shook his head miserably. "Do it, then."

"He'd rather *you* did, Pa," said Measure.

"No!" said Miller vehemently. "Better anyone than me. Better even him than me."

Thrower saw disappointment, even contempt, on Measure's face. He stood and walked to where Measure sat, holding a knife and the bone saw in his hands. "Young man," he said, "do not ajudge any man to be a coward. You cannot guess what reasons he hides in his heart."

Thrower turned to Miller and saw a look of surprise and gratitude on the man's face. "Give him them cutting tools," Miller said.

Measure held out the knife and the bone saw. Thrower pulled out a handkerchief, and had Measure lay the implements carefully within it.

It had been so easy to do. In just a few moments he had them all asking him to take the knife, absolving him in advance of any accident that might happen. He had even won the first scrap of friendship from Alvin Miller. Ah, I have deceived you all, he thought triumphantly. I am a match for your master the devil. I have deceived the great deceiver, and will send his corrupt progeny back to hell within the hour.

"Who will hold the boy?" asked Thrower. "Even with wine in him, the pain will make him jump if he isn't held down."

"I'll hold him," said Measure.

"He won't take no wine," said Faith. "He says he has to have his head clear."

"He's a ten-year-old boy," said Thrower. "If you insist that he drink it, he's bound to obey you."

Faith shook her head. "He knows what's best. He bears up right smart under pain. You never seen the like."

I imagine not, said Thrower silently. The devil within the boy no doubt revels in the pain, and doesn't want the wine to dim the ecstasy. "Very well, then," he said. "There's no reason to delay further." He led the way into the bedroom and boldly pulled the blanket off Alvin's body. The boy immediately began trembling in the sudden cold, though he continued sweating from the fever. "You say that he has marked the place to cut?"

"Al," said Measure. "Reverend Thrower here is going to do the cutting."

"Papa," said Alvin.

"It's no use asking him," said Measure. "He just plain won't."

"Are you sure you won't have some wine?" asked Faith.

Alvin started to cry. "No," he said. "I'll be all right if Pa holds me."

"That does it," said Faith. "He may not do the cutting, but he'll be here with the boy or he'll be stuffed up the chimney, one or the other." She stormed out of the room.

"You said the boy would mark the place," Thrower said.

"Here, Al, let me set you up here. I got some charcoal, and you mark right on your leg here just exactly where you want that flap of skin took up."

Alvin moaned as Measure lifted him to a sitting position, but his hand was steady as he marked a large rectangle on his shin. "Cut it from the bottom, and leave the top attached," he said. His voice was thick and slow, each word an effort. "Measure, you hold that flap back out of the way while he cuts."

"Ma'll have to do that," said Measure. "I got to hold you down so you don't jump."

"I won't jump," said Alvin. "If Pa's holding me."

Miller came slowly into the room, his wife right behind. "I'll be holding you," he said. He took Measure's place, sitting behind the boy with his arms wrapped clear around him. "I'm holding you," he said again.

"Very well, then," said Thrower. He stood there, waiting for the next step.

He waited for a good little while.

"Ain't you forgetting something, Reverend?" asked Measure.

"What?" asked Thrower.

"The knife and the saw," he said.

Thrower looked at his handkerchief, wadded in his left hand. Empty. "Why, they were right here."

"You set them down on the table on the way in," said Measure.

"I'll fetch them," said Goody Faith. She hurried out of the room.

They waited and waited and waited. Finally Measure got up. "I can't guess what's keeping her."

Thrower followed him out of the room. They found Goody Faith in the great room, piecing together quilt squares with the girls.

"Ma," said Measure. "What about the saw and the knife?"

"Good laws," said Faith, "I can't imagine what's got into me. I clean forgot why I come out here." She picked up the knife and saw and marched back to the room. Measure shrugged at Thrower and followed her. Now, thought Thrower. Now I'll do all that the Lord ever expected of me. The Visitor will see that I am a true friend to my Savior, and my place in heaven will be assured. Not like this poor, miserable sinner caught up in the flames of hell.

"Reverend," said Measure. "What are you doing?"

"This drawing," said Thrower.

"What about it?"

Thrower looked closely at the drawing over the hearth. It wasn't a soul in hell at all. It was a depiction of the family's oldest boy, Vigor, drowning. He had heard the story at least a dozen times. But why was he standing here looking at it, when he had a great and terrible mission to perform in the other room?

"Are you all right?"

"Perfectly all right," said Thrower. "I just needed a moment of silent prayer and meditation before I undertook this task."

He strode boldly into the room and sat down on the chair beside the bed where Satan's child lay trembling, waiting for the knife. Thrower looked around for his tools of holy murder. They were nowhere in sight. "Where is the knife?" he asked.

Faith looked at Measure. "Didn't you bring them back in with you?" she asked.

"You're the one brought them in here," said Measure.

"But when you went back out to get the preacher, you took them," she said.

"Did I?" Measure looked confused. "I must have set them down out there." He got up and left the room.

Thrower began to realize that something strange was going on here, though he couldn't quite put his finger on it. He walked to the door and waited for Measure to return.

Cally was standing there, holding his slate, looking up at the minister. "You going to kill my brother?" he asked.

"Don't even think of such a thing," Thrower answered.

Measure looked sheepish as he handed the implements to Thrower. "I can't believe I just set them on the mantel like that." Then the young man pushed past Thrower into the room.

A moment later, Thrower followed him into Alvin's room and took his place beside the exposed leg, with the box drawn in black.

"Well where'd you put them?" asked Faith.

Thrower realized that he didn't have the knife or the saw. He was completely confused. Measure handed them to him just outside the door. How could he have lost them?

Cally stood in the doorway. "Why'd you give me these?" he asked. He was, in fact, holding both blades.

"That's a good question," said Measure, eyeing the pastor with a frown. "Why'd you give them to Cally?"

"I didn't," said Thrower. "*You* must have given them to him."

"I put them right in your hands," said Measure.

"The preacher give them to me," said Cally.

"Well, bring them here," said his mother.

Cally obediently started into the room, brandishing the blades like trophies of war. Like the attack of a great army. Ah, yes, a great army, like the army of the Israelites that Joshua led into the promised land. This is how they held their weapons, high above their heads, as they marched around and around the city of Jericho. Marched and marched. Marched and marched. And on the seventh day they stopped and blew their trumpets and gave a great shout, and *down* came the walls, and they held their swords and knives high over their heads and charged into the city, hacking men, women, and children, all the enemies of God, so the promised land would be purged of their filthiness and be ready to receive the people of the Lord. They were spattered in blood by the end of the day, and Joshua stood in their midst, the great prophet of God, holding a bloody sword above his head, and he shouted. What did he shout?

I can't remember what he shouted. If I could only remember what he shouted, I'd understand why I'm standing here on the road, surrounded by snow-covered trees.

Reverend Thrower looked at his hands, and looked at the trees. He had somehow walked half a mile away from the Millers' house. He wasn't even wearing his heavy cloak.

Then the truth came clear. He hadn't fooled the devil at all. Satan had transported him here, in the twinkling of an eye, rather than let him kill the Beast. Thrower had failed in his one opportunity for greatness. He leaned against a cold black trunk and cried bitterly.

Cally walked into the room, holding the blades above his head. Measure was all set to get a grip on the leg, when all of a sudden old Thrower stood right up and walked out of the room just as quick as if he was trotting to the privy.

"Reverend Thrower," cried Ma. "Where are you going?"

But Measure understood now. "Let him go, Ma," he said.

They heard the front door of the house open, and the minister's heavy steps on the porch.

"Go shut the front door, Cally," said Measure.

For once Cally obeyed without a speck of backsass. Ma looked at Measure, then at Pa, then at Measure again. "I don't understand why he left like that," she said.

Measure gave her a little half-smile and looked at Pa. "*You* know, don't you, Pa?"

"Maybe," he said.

Measure explained to his mother. "Them knives and that preacher, they can't be in this room with Al Junior at the same time."

"But why not!" she said. "He was going to do the surgery!"

"Well, he sure ain't going to do it now," said Measure.

The knife and the bone saw lay on the blanket.

"Pa," said Measure.

"Not me," said Pa.

"Ma," said Measure.

"I can't," Faith said.

"Well then," said Measure, "I reckon I just turned surgeon." He looked at Alvin.

The boy's face had a deathly pallor to it that was even worse than the ruddiness of the fever. But he managed a sort of smile, and whispered, "Reckon so."

"Ma, you're going to have to hold back that flap of skin."

She nodded.

Measure picked up the knife and brought the blade to rest against the bottom line.

"Measure," Al Junior whispered.

"Yes, Alvin?" Measure asked.

"I can stand the pain and hold right still, iffen you whistle."

"I can't keep no tune, if I'm trying to cut straight at the same time," said Measure.

"Don't want no tune," said Alvin.

Measure looked into the boy's eyes and had no choice but to do as he asked. It was Al's leg, after all, and if he wanted a whistling surgeon, he'd get one. Measure took a deep breath and started in whistling, no kind of tune at all, just notes. He put the knife on the black line again and began to cut. Shallow at first, cause he heard Al take a gasp of air.

"Keep whistling," Alvin whispered. "Right to the bone."

Measure whistled again, and this time he cut fast and deep. Right to the bone in the middle of the line. A deep slit up both sides. Then he worked the knife under the two corners and peeled the skin and muscle right back. At first it bled more than a little bit, but almost right away the bleeding stopped. Measure figured it must be something Alvin did inside himself, to stop the bleeding like that.

"Faith," said Pa.

Ma reached over and laid her hand on the bloody flap of skin. Al reached out a trembling hand and traced a wedge on the red-streaked bone of his own leg. Measure laid down the knife and picked up the saw. It made an awful, squeaky sound as he cut. But Measure just whistled and sawed, sawed and whistled. And pretty soon he had a wedge of bone in his hand. It didn't look no different from the rest of the bone.

"You sure that was the right place?" he asked.

Al nodded slowly.

"Did I get it all?" Measure asked.

Al sat for a few moments, then nodded again.

"You want Ma to sew this back up?" Measure asked.

Al didn't say a thing.

"He fainted," said Pa.

The blood started to flow again, just a little, seeping into the wound. Ma had a needle and thread on the pincushion she wore around her neck. In no time she had that flap of skin right back down, and she was stitching away at it, making a fine tight seam.

"You just keep on whistling, Measure," she said.

So he kept right on whistling and she kept right on sewing, till they had the wound all bandaged up and Alvin was laying back sleeping like a baby. They all three stood up to go. Pa laid a hand on the boy's forehead, as gentle as you please.

"I think his fever's gone," he said.

Measure's tune got downright jaunty as they slipped on out the door.

14

Chastisement

As soon as Elly saw him, she was sweet as could be, brushing snow off him, helping with his cloak, and never so much as whispering a question of how it happened.

Didn't make no difference how kindly she might be. He was shamed afore his own wife, cause sooner or later she'd hear the tale from one of those children. Soon enough the tale would be all up and down the Wobbish. How Armor-of-God Weaver, storekeeper for the western country, future governor, got throwed right off a porch into the snow by his old father-in-law. They'd be laughing behind their hands, all right. They'd laugh him up and down. Never to his face, of course, cause there was hardly a soul between Lake Canada and the Noisy River who didn't owe him money or need his maps to prove their claims. Come the time when the Wobbish country was made a state, they'd tell that story at every polling place. They might like a man they laughed at, but they wouldn't respect him, and they wouldn't vote for him.

It was the death of his plans he was facing, and his wife just had too much of that Miller family look about her. She was pretty enough, for a frontier woman, but he didn't care about pretty right now. He didn't care about sweet nights and gentle mornings. He didn't care about her working alongside him in the store. All he cared about was shame and rage.

"Don't do that."

"You got to get that wet shirt off. How'd you get snow clear down your shirt?"

"I said get your hands off me!"

She stepped back, surprised. "I was just—"

"I know what you 'was just.' Poor little Armor, you just pat him like a little boy and he'll feel better."

"You could catch your death—"

"Tell that to your pa! If I cough my guts out, you tell him what it means to throw a man in the snow!"

"Oh no!" she cried. "I can't believe Papa would—"

"See? You don't even believe your own husband."

"I *do* believe you, it just ain't like Pa—"

"No ma'am, it's like the devil himself, that's what it's like! That's what fills that house of yours up there! The spirit of evil! And when a body tries to speak the words of God in that house, they throw him right out in the snow!"

"What were you doing up at the house?"

"Trying to save your brother's life. He's no doubt dead by now."

"How could *you* save him?"

Maybe she didn't mean to sound so contemptuous. It didn't matter. He knew what she meant. That him having no hidden power, there wasn't a thing he could do to help anybody. After years of being married, she still put her faith in witchery, just like her kin. He hadn't changed her a bit. "You're just the same," he said. "Evil's in you so deep that I can't *pray* it out of you, and I can't *preach* it out of you, and I can't *love* it out of you, and I can't *yell* it out of you!" When he said "pray," he shoved her a little, just to make his point. When he said "preach," he shoved her harder, and she stumbled back. When he said "love," he took her by the shoulders and gave her such a shake her hair broke right out of the bun she'd made of it, and fluttered around her head. When he said "yell," he knocked her back so far she stumbled down on the floor.

Seeing her falling, even before she hit the floor, he felt such a shame go through him, even worse than when her father threw him in the snow. A strong man makes me feel weak, so I go home and shove around my wife, what a big man that makes me. Here I been a Christian who never hit or hurt a man or woman, and I knock my own wife, flesh of my flesh, right down on the floor.

That was his thinking, and he was about to throw himself on his knees and bawl like a baby and beg forgiveness. He would've done it, too, except that when she saw the look on his face, all twisted up with shame and rage, she didn't know that he was angry at himself, she just knew that he was hurting her, and so she did what come natural to a woman who grew up like she did. She moved her fingers to make a fending, and whispered a word to hold him back.

He couldn't fall on his knees before her. He couldn't take one step toward her. He couldn't even *think* of taking a step toward her. Her fending was so strong he staggered back, he headed for the door, he opened it and ran outside in just his shirt. Everything he'd been afraid of came true today. He probably lost his future in politics, but that was nothing compared to this: his own wife did witchery in his own home, and she did it against *him*, and he had no defense against it. She was a witch. She was a witch. And his house was unclean.

It was cold. He had no coat, not even his waistcoat. His shirt was already wet, and now it clung to him and froze him to the bone. He had to get indoors, but he couldn't bear to knock on anybody's door. There was only one place he could go. Up the hill to the church. Thrower had firewood there, so he'd be warm. And in the church he could pray and try to understand why the Lord didn't help him. Haven't I served you, Lord?

Reverend Thrower opened the door of the church and walked slowly, fearfully inside. He could not bear to face the Visitor, knowing how he had failed. For it had been his own failure, he knew that now. Satan should have had no power over him, to drive him from the house that way. An ordained minister, acting as the emissary of the Lord, following instructions given to him by an angel—Satan should not have been able to thrust him out of the house like that, before he even knew what was happening.

He stripped off his cloak, and his topcoat as well. The church was hot. The fire in the stove must have burned longer than he expected. Or maybe he felt the heat of shame.

It could not be that Satan was stronger than the Lord. The only possible explanation was that Thrower himself was too weak. It was his own faith that faltered.

Thrower knelt at the altar and cried out the name of the Lord. "Forgive thou my unbelief!" he cried. "I held the knife, but Satan stood against me, and I had no strength!" He recited a litany of self-excoriation, he rehearsed all his failures of the day, until at last he was exhausted.

Only then, with his eyes sore from crying, his voice feeble and hoarse, did he realize the moment when his faith was undermined. It was when he stood in Alvin's room, asking the boy to confess his faith, and the boy scoffed at the mysteries of God. "How can he be on top of something that ain't got no top?" Even though Thrower had rejected the questions as the result of ignorance and evil, the question had nevertheless pierced his heart and penetrated to the core of his belief. Certainties that had sustained him most of his life were suddenly split through by the questions of an ignorant boy. "He stole my faith," said Thrower. "I went into his room a man of God, and came out as a doubter."

"Indeed," said a voice behind him. A voice he knew.

A voice that now, in his moment of failure, he both feared and longed for. Oh, forgive me, comfort me, my Visitor, my friend! Yet do not fail also to chastise me with the terrible wrath of a jealous God.

"Chastise you?" asked the Visitor. "How could I chastise you, such a glorious specimen of humanity?"

"I am not glorious," said Thrower miserably.

"You're barely human, for that matter," said the Visitor. "In whose image were *you* made? I sent you to bring my word into that house, and instead they have nearly converted *you*. What do I call you now? A heretic? Or merely a skeptic?"

"A Christian!" cried Thrower. "Forgive me and call me once again a Christian."

"You had the knife in your hand, but you set it down."

"I didn't mean to!"

"Weak, weak, weak, weak, weak . . ." Each time the Visitor repeated the word, he stretched it longer and longer, until each repetition became a song in itself. As he sang, he began to walk around the church. He did not run, but he walked quickly, far faster than any man could walk. "Weak, weak . . ." He was moving so fast that Thrower had to turn constantly just to keep him in sight. The Visitor was no longer walking on the floor. He was skittering along the walls, as smooth and fast in his motion as a cockroach, then even faster, until he became a blur, and Thrower could not keep up with him by turning. Thrower leaned on the altar, facing the empty pews, watching the Visitor race by again and again and again.

Gradually Thrower realized that the Visitor had changed shape, that he had stretched himself, like a long slender beast, a lizard, an alligator, bright-scaled and shining, longer and longer, until finally the Visitor's body was so long that it circled the room, a vast worm that gripped its own tail between its teeth.

And in his mind Thrower realized how very small and worthless he was, compared to this glorious being that sparkled with a thousand different colors, that glowed with inner fire, that breathed in darkness and exhaled light. I worship thee! he shouted inside himself. Thou art all that I desire! Kiss me with your love, so I may taste your glory!

Suddenly the Visitor stopped, and the great jaws came toward him. Not to devour, for Thrower knew he was unworthy even to be consumed. He saw now the terrible predicament of man: he saw that he dangled over the pit of hell like a spider on a slender thread, and the only reason God did not let him fall was because he was not even worthy of destruction. God did not hate him. He was so vile that God disdained him.

Thrower looked into the Visitor's eyes and despaired. For there was neither love, nor forgiveness, nor anger, nor contempt. The eyes were utterly empty. The scales dazzled, scattering the light of an inner fire. But that fire did not shine through the eyes. They were not even black. They simply were not there at all, a terrible emptiness that trembled, that would not hold still, and Thrower knew that this was his own reflection, that he was nothing, that for him to continue to exist was a cruel waste of precious space, that the only choice left to him was to be annihilated, uncreated, to restore the world to the greater glory it would have had if Philadelphia Thrower had never been born.

It was Thrower's praying that woke Armor up. He was curled up by the Franklin stove. Maybe he stoked that stove a mite too hot, but that's what it took to beat back the cold. Why, by the time he got to the church his shirt was solid ice. He'd get more charcoal to pay back the parson.

Armor meant to speak right up and let Thrower know he was there, but when he heard the words that Thrower was praying, he couldn't find no words to say. Thrower was talking about knives and arteries, and how he should've cut up the enemies of God. After a minute it came clear: Thrower hadn't gone up there to save that boy, he'd gone up to kill him! What's wrong around here, thought Armor, when a Christian man beats his wife, and a Christian wife witches her husband, and a Christian minister plots murder and prays for forgiveness cause he failed to commit the crime!

All of a sudden, though, Thrower stopped praying. He was so hoarse and his face so red that Armor thought he might have had the apoplexy. But no. Thrower lifted his head like he was listening to somebody. Armor listened, too, and he could hear something, like people talking in a windstorm, so you couldn't never hear what they were saying.

I know what this is, thought Armor. Reverend Thrower's having himself a vision.

Sure enough, Thrower talked, and the faint voice answered, and pretty soon Thrower started turning around and around, faster and faster, like he was watching something on the walls. Armor tried to see what it was he was watching, but he couldn't never make it out. It was like a shadow passing across the sun—you couldn't see it coming and you couldn't see it go, but for a second it was darker and colder. That's what Armor saw.

Then it stopped. Armor saw a shimmering in the air, a dazzle here and there like when a pane of glass catches the sunlight. Was Thrower seeing the glory of God, like Moses saw? Not likely, looking at the parson's face. Armor never did see such a face as that before. Like a man's face might look if he had to watch his own baby being killed.

The shimmering and dazzle went away. The church was quiet. Armor wanted to run to Thrower and ask him, What did you see! What was your vision! Was it a prophecy?

But Thrower didn't look much like he wanted to answer questions. That look of wishing to die was still on his face. The preacher walked real slow away from the altar. He wandered around among the pews, bumping into them sometimes, not watching or caring where his body went. Finally he ended up by the window, facing the glass, but Armor knew he didn't see nothing, he was just standing there, his eyes wide open, looking like death.

Reverend Thrower lifted up his right hand, the fingers spread, and he laid his palm on a pane of glass. He pressed. He pressed and pushed so hard that Armor could see the glass bowing outward. "Stop it!" shouted Armor. "You'll cut yourself!"

Thrower didn't even make a sign that he heard. Just kept pressing. Armor started walking toward him. Got to make that man stop before he breaks the glass and cuts up his arm.

With a crash the glass shattered. Thrower's arm went right through, up to the shoulder. The preacher smiled. He pulled his arm partway back into the church. Then he began to slide his arm around the frame, jamming it right into the shards of glass that hung there in the putty.

Armor tried to pull Thrower away from the window, but the man had a strength on him like Armor never seen before. Finally Armor had to take a run at him and knock him right down to the floor. Blood was spattered everywhere Armor grabbed at Thrower's arm, which was dripping all over with blood. Thrower tried to roll away from him. Armor didn't have no choice. For the first time since he became a Christian man he made his hand into a fist and popped Thrower right on the chin. It slammed the preacher's head back into the floor and knocked him silly.

Got to stop the bleeding, Armor thought. But first he had to get the glass out. Some of the big pieces were only stuck in a little way, and he could brush them right off. But other pieces, some of the little pieces, were in deep, only a bit of their top showing, and that was slimy with blood so he couldn't get much of a grip on it. Finally, though, he got all the glass he could find. Lucky enough there wasn't a single cut a-pumping blood, which told Armor that the big veins hadn't been cut. He stripped off his shirt, which left him naked to the waist with that cold draft coming in from the broken window, but he didn't hardly notice. He just ripped up the shirt and made bandages. He bound up the wounds and stopped the bleeding. Then he sat there and waited for Thrower to wake up.

Thrower was surprised to find he wasn't dead. He was lying on his back on a hard floor, covered up with heavy cloth. His head hurt. His arm hurt worse. He remembered trying to cut up that arm, and he knew he ought to try again, but he just couldn't work up the same wish for death that he had felt before. Even remembering the Visitor in the form of a great lizard, even remembering those empty eyes, Thrower just couldn't remember how it felt. He only knew that it was the worst feeling in the world.

His arm was bandaged tight. Who had bandaged him?

He heard the sloshing of water. Then the flopping sound of wet rags slapping against wood. In the winter twilight coming through the window, he could make out somebody washing the wall. One of the window panes was covered over with a piece of wood.

"Who is it?" asked Thrower. "Who are you?"

"Just me."

"Armor-of-God."

"Washing down the walls. This is a church, not a butcher shed."

Of course there'd be blood all over. "Sorry," said Thrower.

"I don't mind cleaning up," said Armor. "I think I got all the glass out of your arm."

"You're naked," said Thrower.

"Your arm is wearing my shirt."

"You must be cold."

"Maybe I was, but I got the window covered and the stove het up. You're the one with a face so white you look like you been dead a week."

Thrower tried to sit up, but he couldn't. He was too weak; his arm hurt too bad.

Armor pushed him back down. "Now, you just lay back, Reverend Thrower. You just lay back. You been through a lot."

"Yes."

"I hope you don't mind, but I was here in the church when you come in. I was asleep by the stove—my wife threw me out of the house. I been thrown out twice today." He laughed, but there was no mirth in it. "So I saw you."

"Saw?"

"You were having a vision, weren't you?"

"Did you see him?"

"I didn't see much. I mostly saw *you*, but there was a few glimpses, if you know what I mean. Running around the walls."

"You saw," said Thrower. "Oh, Armor, it was terrible, it was beautiful."

"Did you see God?"

"See *God?* God has no body to be seen, Armor. No, I saw an angel, an angel of chastisement. Surely this was what Pharaoh saw, the angel of death that came through the cities of Egypt and took the firstborn."

"Oh," said Armor, sounding puzzled. "Was I spose to let you die, then?"

"If I were supposed to die, you could not have saved me," said Thrower. "Because you saved me, because you were here at the moment of my despair, it is a sure sign that I am meant to live. I was chastised, but not destroyed. Armor-of-God, I have another chance."

Armor nodded, but Thrower could see that he was worried about something. "What is it?" Thrower asked. "What is it that you want to ask me?"

Armor's eyes widened. "Can you hear what I'm thinking?"

"If I could, I wouldn't have to ask you."

Armor smiled. "Reckon not."

"I'll tell you what you want to know, if I can."

"I heard you praying," said Armor. He waited, as if that were the question.

Since Thrower didn't know what the question was, he wasn't sure what to answer. "I was in despair, because I failed the Lord. I was given a mission to perform, but at the crucial moment my heart was filled with doubt." With his good hand he reached out and clutched at Armor. All he could touch was the cloth of Armor's trousers, where he knelt beside him. "Armor-of-God," he said, "never let doubt enter your heart. Never question what you know is true. It's the doorway to let Satan have power over you."

But that wasn't the answer to Armor's question.

"Ask me what you want to ask me," said Thrower. "I'll tell you the truth, if I can."

"You prayed about killing," said Armor.

Thrower had not thought to tell anyone about the burden the Lord had placed upon him. Yet if the Lord had wanted the secret kept from

Armor, He would not have allowed the man to be there in the church
to overhear. "I believe," said Thrower, "that it was the Lord God that
brought you to me. I am weak, Armor, and I failed at what the Lord
required. But now I see that you, a man of faith, have been given to
me as a friend and helper."

"What did the Lord require?" asked Armor.

"Not murder, my brother. The Lord never asked me to kill a man. It
was a devil I was sent to kill. A devil in man-shape. Living in that
house."

Armor pursed his lips, deep in thought. "The boy ain't just possessed,
is that what you're saying? It ain't something you can cast right out?"

"I tried, but he laughed at the Holy Book and mocked my words of
exorcism. He is not possessed, Armor-of-God. He is the devil's own
kin."

Armor shook his head. "My wife ain't a devil, and she's his own
sister."

"She has given up witchcraft, and so she has been made pure," said
Thrower.

Armor gave one bitter laugh. "I thought so."

Thrower understood, now, why Armor had taken refuge in the church,
in the house of God: His own house had been polluted.

"Armor-of-God, will you help me purge this country, this town, that
house, that *family*, of the evil influence that has corrupted them?"

"Will it save my wife?" asked Armor. "Will it end her love of
witchery?"

"It may," said Thrower. "Perhaps the Lord has brought us together
so we can purify both our houses."

"Whatever it takes," said Armor. "I'm with you against the devil."

15

Promises

The blacksmith listened as Taleswapper read the letter from beginning to end.

"Do you remember the family?" asked Taleswapper.

"I do," said Makepeace Smith. "The graveyard almost began with their oldest boy. I pulled his body from the river with my own hands."

"Well then, will you take him as your prentice?"

A youth, perhaps sixteen years old, walked into the forge carrying a bucket of snow. He glanced at the visitor, ducked his head, and walked to the cooling barrel that stood near the hearth.

"You see I have a prentice," said the smith.

"He looks like a big one," said Taleswapper.

"Getting on," the smith agreed. "Ain't that right, Bosey? You ready to go on your own?"

Bosey smiled a bit, stifled it, nodded. "Yes, sir," he said.

"I'm not an easy master," said the smith.

"Alvin's a good-hearted boy. He'll work hard for you."

"But will he obey me? I like to be obeyed."

Taleswapper looked again at Bosey. He was busy scooping snow into the barrel.

"I said he's a good-hearted boy," said Taleswapper. "He'll obey you if you're fair with him."

The smith met his gaze. "I give honest measure. I don't beat the boys I take on. Have I ever laid hand on you, Bosey?"

"Never, sir."

"You see, Taleswapper, a prentice can obey out of fear, and he can obey out of greed. But if I'm a good master, he'll obey me cause he knows that's how he'll learn."

Taleswapper grinned at the smith. "There's no fee," said Taleswapper. "The boy will earn it out. And he gets his schooling."

"No need for a smith to have letters, as I should know."

"Won't be long before Hio's part of the United States," said Taleswapper. "The boy's got to vote, I think, and read the newspapers. A man who can't read only knows what other folks tell him."

Makepeace Smith looked at Taleswapper with a grin half-hid on his face. "That so? And ain't it you telling me? So don't I only know this cause other folks, namely you, is telling me so?"

Taleswapper laughed and nodded. The smith had shot the head clean off the turkey with that one. "I make my way in the world telling tales," said Taleswapper, "so I know you can get much with just the sound of a man's voice. He already reads above his years, so it won't do him harm to miss a bit of school. But his ma is set on him having letters and ciphering like a scholar. So just promise me you won't stand between him and schooling, if he wants it, and we'll leave it at that."

"Got my word on that," said Makepeace Smith. "And you don't have to write it down. A man who keeps his word doesn't have to read and write. But a man who has to write down his promises, you got to watch him all morning. I know that for a fact. We got lawyers in Hatrack these days."

"The curse of civilized man," said Taleswapper. "When a man can't get folks to believe his lies anymore, then he hires him a professional to lie in his place."

They laughed together over that one, setting there on two stout stumps just inside the door of the forge, the fire smoldering in its brick chimney place behind them, the sun shining on half-melted snow outside. A redbird flew across the grassy, trampled, dunged-up ground in front of the forge. It dazzled Taleswapper's eyes for a moment, it was such a startlement against the whites and greys and browns of late winter.

In that moment of amazement at the redbird's flight, Taleswapper knew for certain, though he couldn't say why, that it would be a while yet before the Unmaker let young Alvin come to this place. And when he came he'd be like a redbird out of season, to dazzle folks all hereabouts, them thinking he was just as natural as a bird flying, not knowing what a miracle it was every minute that the bird stayed in the air.

Taleswapper shook himself, and the moment's clear vision passed. "Then it's done, and I'll write to them to send the boy."

"I'll look for him the first of April. No later!"

"Unless you expect the boy to control the weather, you'd best be flexible about the date."

The smith grumbled and waved him away. All in all, a successful meeting. Taleswapper left feeling good—he had discharged his duty. It'd be easy to send a letter with a westbound wagon—several groups passed through the town of Hatrack every week.

Though it had been a long time since he passed through this place, he still knew the way from the forge to the inn. It was a well-traveled road, and not a long one. The inn was much larger now than it had been, and there were several shops a bit farther up the road. An outfitter, a saddler, a cobbler. The kind of service traveling folk could use.

He hardly set foot on the porch when the door opened and Old Peg Guester came out, her arms spread wide to embrace him. "Ah, Taleswapper, you've been away too long, come in, come in!"

"It's good to see you again, Peg," he said.

Horace Guester growled at him from behind the bar in the common room, where he was serving several thirsty visitors. "What I don't need here is another teetotaling man!"

"Good news, then, Horace," Taleswapper answered cheerfully. "I gave up tea as well."

"What do you drink, *water*?"

"Water and the blood of greasy old men," said Taleswapper.

Horace gestured to his wife. "You keep that man away from me, Old Peg, you hear?"

Old Peg helped him strip off a few layers of clothing. "Look at you," said Old Peg, sizing him up. "There ain't enough meat on you to make a stew."

"The bears and panthers pass me by in the night, looking for richer fare," said Taleswapper.

"Come in and tell me stories while I fix up a mess of supper for the company."

There was talk and chatter, especially once Oldpappy came in to help. He was getting feeble now, but he still had a hand in the kitchen, which was all to the benefit of those who ate here; Old Peg meant well and worked hard, but some folks had the knack and some folks didn't. But it wasn't food that Taleswapper came for, nor conversation either, and after a while he realized he'd have to bring it up himself. "Where's your daughter?"

To his surprise, Old Peg stiffened, and her voice went cold and hard. "She ain't so little no more. She's got a mind of her own, she's the first to tell you."

And you don't much like it, thought Taleswapper. But his business with the daughter was more important than any family squabbles. "Is she still a—"

"A torch? Oh, yes, she does her duty, but it's no pleasure for folks to come for her. Snippy and cold, that's what she is. It's got her a name for being sharp-tongued." For a moment Old Peg's face softened. "She used to be such a soft-hearted child."

"I've never seen a soft heart turn hard," said Taleswapper. "At least not without good reason."

"Well, whatever her reason, she's one whose heart has crusted up like a waterbucket on a winter's night."

Taleswapper held his tongue and didn't sermonize, didn't talk about how if you chip the ice it'll freeze up again right away, but if you take it inside, it'll warm up fresh as you please. No use stepping in the middle of a family squabble. Taleswapper knew enough of the way people lived that he took this particular quarrel as a natural event, like cold winds and short days in autumn, like thunder after lightning. Most parents didn't have much use for a half-grown child.

"I have a matter to discuss with her," said Taleswapper. "I'll take the risk of having my head bitten off."

He found her in Dr. Whitley Physicker's office, working on his accounts. "I didn't know you were a bookkeeper," he said.

"I didn't know you held much with physicking," she answered. "Or did you just come to see the miracle of a girl who does sums and ciphers?"

Oh, yes, she was as sharp as could be. Taleswapper could see how a wit like that might discommode a few folks who expected a young woman to cast down her eyes and speak softly, glancing upward only now and then under heavy-lidded eyes. There was none of that young ladyness about Peggy. She looked Taleswapper in the face, plain as could be.

"I didn't come to be healed," said Taleswapper. "Or to have my future told. Or even to have my accounts added up."

And there it was. The moment a man answered her right back instead of getting his dander up, why, she flashed a smile fit to charm the warts off a toad. "I don't recollect you having much to add or subtract anyhow," she said. "Naught plus naught is naught, I think."

"You've got it wrong, Peggy," said Taleswapper. "I own this whole world, and folks haven't been keeping up too well on the payments."

She smiled again, and set aside the doctor's account book. "I keep his records for him, once a month, and he brings me things to read from Dekane." She talked about the things she read, and Taleswapper began to see that her heart yearned for places far beyond Hatrack River. He also saw other things—that she, being a torch, knew the folks around here too well, and thought that in faraway places she'd find people with jewel-like souls that would never disappoint a girl who could see clean into their heart.

She's young, that's all. Give her time, and she'll learn to love such goodness as she finds, and forgive the rest.

After a while the doctor came in, and they chatted a bit, and it was well into the afternoon by the time Taleswapper was alone with Peggy again and could ask her what he came to ask.

"How far off can you see, Peggy?"

He could almost see wariness fall across her face like a thick velvet curtain. "I don't reckon you're asking me whether I need spectacles," she said.

"I just wonder about a girl who once wrote in my book, A Maker is born. I wonder if she still keeps an eye on that Maker, now and then, so she can see how he fares."

She looked away from him, gazing at the high window above where the curtain gave privacy. The sun was low and the sky outside was grey, but her face was full of light, Taleswapper saw that right enough. Sometimes you didn't have to be a torch to know full well what was in a person's heart.

"I wonder if that torch saw a ridgebeam falling on him one time," said Taleswapper.

"I wonder," she said.

"Or a millstone."

"Could be."

"And I wonder if somehow she didn't have some way to split that ridgebeam clean in twain, and crack that millstone so a certain old Taleswapper could see lantern light right through the middle of that stone."

Tears glistened in her eyes, not like she was about to cry, but like she was looking into the sun straight on, and it made her water up. "A scrap of his birth caul, rubbed into dust, and a body can use the boy's own power to work a few clumsy makings," she said softly.

"But now he knows something of his own knack, and he undid what you did for him."

She nodded.

"Must be lonely, watching out for him from so far away," said Taleswapper.

She shook her head. "Not to me. I got folks all around me, all the time." She looked at Taleswapper and smiled wanly. "It's almost a relief to spend time with that one boy who doesn't want a thing from me, because he doesn't even know that I exist."

"I know, though," said Taleswapper. "And I don't want a thing from you, either."

She smiled. "You old fraud," she said.

"All right, I *do* want something from you, but not something for myself. I've met that boy, and even if I can't see into his heart the way you can, I think I know him. I think I know what he might be, what he might do, and I want you to know that if you ever need my help for anything, just send me word, just tell me what to do, and if it's in my power I'll do it."

She didn't answer, nor did she look at him.

"So far you didn't need help," said Taleswapper, "but now he has a mind of his own, and you can't always do for him the things he'll need. The dangers won't come just from things that fall on him or hurt him in the flesh. He's in as much danger from what he decides to do himself. I'm just telling you that if you see such danger and you need me to help, I'll come no matter what."

"That's a comfort," she said. That was honest enough, Taleswapper knew; but she was feeling more than she said, he knew that too.

"And I wanted to tell you he was coming here, first of April, to prentice with the smith."

"I know he's coming," she said, "but it won't be the first of April."

"Oh?"

"Or even this year at all."

Fear for the boy stabbed at Taleswapper's heart. "I guess I did come to hear the future after all. What's in store for him? What's to come?"

"All kinds of things might happen," she said, "and I'd be a fool to guess which one. I see it open like a thousand roads before him, all the time. But there's precious few of those roads that bring him here by April, and a whole lot more that leave him dead with a Red man's hatchet in his head."

Taleswapper leaned across the doctor's writing table and rested his hand on hers. "Will he live?"

"As long as I have breath in my body," she said.

"Or I in mine," he answered.

They sat in silence for a moment, hand on hand, eye to eye, until she burst into laughter and looked away.

"Usually when folks laugh I get the joke," said Taleswapper.

"I was just thinking we're a poor excuse for a conspiracy, the two of us, against the enemies that boy will face."

"True," said Taleswapper, "but then, our cause is good, and so all nature will conspire with us, don't you think?"

"And God, too," she added firmly.

"I can't say about that," said Taleswapper. "The preachers and priests seem to have him so fenced up with doctrine that the poor old Father hardly has room to act anymore. Now that they've got the Bible safely interpreted, the last thing they ever want is for him to speak another word, or show his hand of power in this world."

"I saw his hand of power in the birth of a seventh son of a seventh son, some years back," she said. "Call it nature if you want to, since you've got all kinds of learning from philosophers and wizards. I just know that he's tied as tight to my life as if we was born from the same womb."

Taleswapper didn't plan his next question, it just came unthought of from his lips. "Are you glad of it?"

She looked at him with terrible sadness in her eyes. "Not often," she said. She looked so weary then that Taleswapper couldn't help himself, he walked around the table and stood beside her chair and held her tight like a father holds his daughter, held her for a good long while. If she was crying or just holding on, he couldn't say. They spoke not a word. Finally she let go of him and turned back to the account book. He left without breaking the silence.

Taleswapper wandered on over to the inn to take his supper. There were tales to tell and chores to do in order to earn his keep. Yet all the stories seemed to pale beside the one story that he could *not* tell, the one story whose end he didn't know.

On the meadow around the millhouse were a half dozen farm wagons, watched over by farmers who had come a good long way to get high-quality flour. No more would their wives sweat over a mortar and pestle to make coarse meal for hard and lumpy bread. The mill was in business, and everyone for miles around would bring their grain to the town of Vigor Church.

The water poured through the millrace, and the great wheel turned. Inside the millhouse, the force of the wheel was carried by interlocking gears, to make the grindstone roll around and around, riding on the face of a quarter dress millstone.

The miller poured out the wheat upon the stone. The grindstone passed over it, crushing it to flour. The miller swept it smooth for a second pass, then brushed it off into a basket held by his son, a ten-year-old boy. His son poured the flour into a sieve, and shook the good flour into a cloth sack. He emptied what stayed in the sieve into a silage barrel. Then he returned to his father's side for the next basket of wheat.

Their thoughts were remarkably alike, as they worked silently together. This is what I want to do forever, each one thought. Rise in the morning, come to the mill, and work all day with him beside me. Never mind that the wish was impossible. Never mind that they might never see each other again, once the boy left for his apprenticeship back in the place of his birth. That only added to the sweetness of the moment, which would soon become a memory, would soon become a dream.

RED PROPHET

In memory of my grandfather, Orson Rega Card (1891–1984),
whose life was saved by Indians of the Blood tribe
when he was a child on the Canadian frontier

.

AUTHOR'S NOTE

This story takes place in an America whose history is often similar to, but often quite different from our own. You should not assume that the portrayal in this book of a person who shares a name with a figure from American history is an accurate portrayal of that historical figure. In particular, you should be aware that William Henry Harrison, famed in our own history for having the briefest presidency and for his unforgettable election slogan "Tippecanoe and Tyler too," was a somewhat nicer person than his counterpart in this book.

My thanks to Carol Breakstone for American Indian lore; to Beth Meacham for Octagon Mound and Flint Ridge; to Wayne Williams for heroic patience; and to my great-great-grandfather Joseph for the stories behind the story in this book.

As always with my work, Kristine A. Card has influenced and improved every page in this book.

CONTENTS

1

Hooch

Not many flatboats were getting down the Hio these days, not with pioneers aboard, anyway, not with families and tools and furniture and seed and a few shoats to start a pig herd. It took only a couple of fire arrows and pretty soon some tribe of Reds would have themselves a string of half-charred scalps to sell to the French in Detroit.

But Hooch Palmer had no such trouble. The Reds all knew the look of *his* flatboat, stacked high with kegs. Most of those kegs sloshed with whisky, which was about the only musical sound them Reds understood. But in the middle of the vast heap of cooperage there was one keg that didn't slosh. It was filled with gunpowder, and it had a fuse attached.

How did he use that gunpowder? They'd be floating along with the current, poling on round a bend, and all of a sudden there'd be a half-dozen canoes filled with painted-up Reds of the Kicky-Poo persuasion. Or they'd see a fire burning near shore, and some Shaw-Nee devils dancing around with arrows ready to set alight.

For most folks that meant it was time to pray, fight, and die. Not Hooch, though. He'd stand right up in the middle of that flatboat, a torch in one hand and the fuse in the other, and shout, "Blow up whisky! Blow up whisky!"

Well, most Reds didn't talk much English, but they sure knew what "blow up" and "whisky" meant. And instead of arrows flying or canoes overtaking them, pretty soon them canoes passed by him on the far side of the river. Some Red yelled, "Carthage City!" and Hooch hollered back, "That's right!" and the canoes just zipped on down the Hio, heading for where that likker would soon be sold.

The poleboys, of course, it was their first trip downriver, and they didn't know all that Hooch Palmer knew, so they about filled their

trousers first time they saw them Reds with fire arrows. And when they
saw Hooch holding his torch by that fuse, they like to jumped right in
the river. Hooch just laughed and laughed. "You boys don't know about
Reds and likker," he said. "They won't do nothing that might cause a
single drop from these kegs to spill into the Hio. They'd kill their own
mother and not think twice, if she stood between them and a keg, but
they won't touch *us* as long as I got the gunpowder ready to blow if
they lay one hand on me."

Privately the poleboys might wonder if Hooch really would blow the
whole raft, crew and all, but the fact is Hooch *would*. He wasn't much
of a thinker, nor did he spend much time brooding about death and the
hereafter or such philosophical questions, but this much he had decided:
when he died, he supposed he wouldn't die alone. He also supposed
that if somebody killed him, they'd get no profit from the deed, none
at all. Specially not some half-drunk weak-sister cowardly Red with a
scalping knife.

The best secret of all was, Hooch wouldn't need no torch and he
wouldn't need no fuse, neither. Why, that fuse didn't even go right into
the gunpowder keg, if the truth be known—Hooch didn't want a chance
of that powder going off by accident. No, if Hooch ever needed to blow
up his flatboat, he could just set down and think about it for a while.
And pretty soon that powder would start to hotten up right smart, and
maybe a little smoke would come off it, and then pow! it goes off.

That's right. Old Hooch was a spark. Oh, there's some folks says
there's no such thing as a spark, and for proof they say, "Have you
ever *met* a spark, or knowed anybody who did?" but that's no proof at
all. Cause if you happen to be a spark, you don't go around telling
everybody, do you? It's not as if anybody's hoping to hire your services—it's too easy to use flint and steel, or even them alchemical
matches. No, the only value there is to being a spark is if you want to
start a fire from a distance, and the only time you want to do that is if
it's a *bad* fire, meant to hurt somebody, burn down a building, blow
something up. And if you hire out *that* kind of service, you don't exactly
put up a sign that says Spark For Hire.

Worst of it is that if word once gets around that you're a spark, every
little fire gets blamed on you. Somebody's boy lights up a pipe out in
the barn, and the barn burns down—does that boy ever say, "Yep, Pa,
it was me all right." No sir, that boy says, "Must've been some spark
set that fire, Pa!" and then they go looking for *you*, the neighborhood
scapegoat. No, Hooch was no fool. He didn't ever tell nobody about
how he could get things het up and flaming.

There was another reason Hooch didn't use his sparking ability too much. It was a reason so secret that Hooch didn't rightly know it himself. Thing was, fire scared him. Scared him deep. The way some folks is scared of water, and so they go to sea; and some folks is scared of death, and so they take up gravedigging; and some folks is scared of God, and so they set to preaching. Well Hooch feared the fire like he feared no other thing, and so he was always drawn to it, with that sick feeling in his stomach; but when it was time for him to lay a fire himself, why, he'd back off, he'd delay, he'd think of reasons why he shouldn't do it at all. Hooch had a knack, but he was powerful reluctant to make much use of it.

But he would have done it. He would have blown up that powder and himself and his poleboys and all his likker, before he'd let a Red take it by murder. Hooch might have his bad fear of fire, but he'd overcome it right quick if he got mad enough.

Good thing, then, that the Reds loved likker so much they didn't want to risk spilling a drop. No canoe came too close, no arrow whizzed in to thud and twang against a keg, and Hooch and his kegs and casks and firkins and barrels all slipped along the top of the water peaceful as you please, clear to Carthage City, which was Governor Harrison's highfalutin name for a stockade with a hundred soldiers right smack where the Little My-Ammy River met the Hio. But Bill Harrison was the kind of man who gave the name first, then worked hard to make the place live up to the name. And sure enough, there was about fifty chimney fires outside the stockade this time, which meant Carthage City was almost up to being a village.

He could hear them yelling before he hove into view of the wharf—there must be Reds who spent half their life just setting on the riverbank waiting for the likker boat to come in. And Hooch knew they were specially eager this time, seeing as how some money changed hands back in Fort Dekane, so the other likker dealers got held up this way and that until old Carthage City must be dry as the inside of a bull's tit. Now here comes Hooch with his flatboat loaded up heavier than they ever saw, and he'd get a price this time, that's for sure.

Bill Harrison might be vain as a partridge, taking on airs and calling himself governor when nobody elected him and nobody appointed him but his own self, but he knew his business. He had those boys of his in smart-looking uniforms, lined up at the wharf just as neat as you please, their muskets loaded and ready to shoot down the first Red who so much as took a step toward the shore. It was no formality, neither—them Reds looked mighty eager, Hooch could see. Not jumping up and down like children, of course, but just standing there, just standing and watching, right out in the open, not caring who saw them, half-naked the way they mostly were in summertime. Standing there all *humble*, all ready to bow and scrape, to beg and plead, to say, Please Mr. Hooch one keg for thirty deerskins, oh that would sound sweet, oh indeed it would; Please Mr. Hooch one tin cup of likker for these ten muskrat hides. "Whee-haw!" cried Hooch. The poleboys looked at him like he was crazy, cause they didn't know, they never saw how these Reds used to look, back before Governor Harrison set up shop here, the way they never deigned to look at a White man, the way you had to crawl into their wicky-ups and choke half to death on smoke and steam and sit there making signs and talking their jub-jub until you got permission to trade. Used to be the Reds would be standing there with bows and spears, and you'd be scared to death they'd decide your scalp was worth more than your trade goods.

Not anymore. Now they didn't have a single weapon among them. Now their tongues just hung out waiting for likker. And they'd drink and drink and drink and drink and drink and *whee-haw!* They'd drop down dead before they'd ever stop drinking, which was the best thing of all, best thing of all. Only good Red's a dead Red, Hooch always said, and the way he and Bill Harrison had things going now, they had them Reds dying of likker at a good clip, and paying for the privilege along the way.

So Hooch was about as happy a man as you ever saw when they tied up at the Carthage City Wharf. The sergeant even saluted him, if you could believe it! A far cry from the way U.S. Marshalls treated him back in Suskwahenny, acting like he was scum they just scraped off the privy seat. Out here in this new country, free-spirited men like Hooch were treated most like gentlemen, and that suited Hooch just fine. Let them pioneers with their tough ugly wives and wiry little brats go hack down trees and cut up the dirt and raise corn and hogs just to live. Not Hooch. He'd come in after, after the fields were all nice and neat looking and the houses were all in fine rows on squared-off streets, and then he'd take his money and buy him the biggest house in town, and the banker would step off the sidewalk into the mud to make way for him, and the mayor would call him sir—if he didn't decide to be mayor himself by then.

This was the message of the sergeant's salute, telling his future for him, when he stepped ashore.

"We'll unload here, Mr. Hooch," said the sergeant.

"I've got a bill of lading," said Hooch, "so let's have no privateering by your boys. Though I'd allow as how there's probably one keg of good rye whisky that somehow didn't exactly get counted on here. I'd bet that one keg wouldn't be missed."

"We'll be as careful as you please, sir," said the sergeant, but he had a grin so wide it showed his hind teeth, and Hooch knew he'd find a way to keep a good half of that extra keg for himself. If he was stupid, he'd sell his half-keg bit by bit to the Reds. You don't get rich off a half keg of whisky. No, if that sergeant was smart, he'd *share* that half keg, shot by shot, with the officers that seemed most likely to give him advancement, and if he kept that up, someday that sergeant wouldn't be out greeting flatboats, no sir, he'd be sitting in officers' quarters with a pretty wife in his bedroom and a good steel sword at his hip.

Not that Hooch would ever tell this to the sergeant. The way Hooch figured, if a man had to be told, he didn't have brains enough to do the job anyway. And if he had the brains to bring it off, he didn't need no flatboat likker dealer telling him what to do.

"Governor Harrison wants to see you," said the sergeant.

"And I want to see *him*," said Hooch. "But I need a bath and a shave and clean clothes first."

"Governor says for you to stay in the old mansion."

"*Old* one?" said Hooch. Harrison had built the official mansion only four years before. Hooch could think of only one reason why Bill might have upped and built another so soon. "Well, now, has Governor Bill gone and got hisself a new wife?"

"He has," said the sergeant. "Pretty as you please, and only fifteen years old, if you like that! She's from Manhattan, though, so she don't talk much English or anyway it don't *sound* like English when she does."

That was all right with Hooch. He talked Dutch real good, almost as good as he talked English and a lot better than he talked Shaw-Nee. He'd make friends with Bill Harrison's wife in no time. He even toyed with the idea of—but no, no, it wasn't no good to mess with another man's woman. Hooch had the desire often enough, but he knew things got way too complicated once you set foot on that road. Besides, he didn't really need no White woman, not with all these thirsty squaws around.

Would Bill Harrison bring his children out here, now he had a second wife? Hooch wasn't too sure how old them boys would be now, but old enough they might relish the frontier life. Still, Hooch had a vague feeling that the boys'd be a lot better off staying in Philadelphia with their aunt. Not because they shouldn't be out in wild country, but because they shouldn't be near their father. Hooch liked Bill Harrison just fine, but he wouldn't pick him as the ideal guardian for children—even for Bill's own.

Hooch stopped at the gate of the stockade. Now, there was a nice touch. Right along with the standard hexes and tokens that were supposed to ward off enemies and fire and other such things, Governor Bill had put up a sign, the width of the gate. In big letters it said

CARTHAGE CITY

and in smaller letters it said

CAPITAL OF THE STATE OF WOBBISH

which was just the sort of thing old Bill would think of. In a way, he expected that sign was more powerful than any of the hexes. As a spark, for instance, Hooch knew that the hex against fire wouldn't stop him, it'd just make it *harder* to start a fire up right near the hex. If he got a good blaze going somewhere else, that hex would burn up just like anything else. But that sign, naming Wobbish a state and Carthage its capital, why, that might actually have some power in it, power over the way folks thought. If you say a thing often enough, people come to expect it to be true, and pretty soon it *becomes* true. Oh, not something like "The moon is going to stop in its tracks and go backward tonight," cause for that to work the moon'd have to hear your words. But if you say things like "That girl's easy" or "That man's a thief," it doesn't much matter whether the person you're talking about believes you or not—everybody *else* comes to believe it, and treats them like it was true. So Hooch figured that if Harrison got enough people to see a sign that named Carthage as the capital of the state of Wobbish, someday it'd plumb come to be.

Fact is, though, Hooch didn't much care whether it was Harrison who got to be governor and put his capital in Carthage City, or whether it was that teetotaling self-righteous prig Armor-of-God Weaver up north, where Tippy-Canoe Creek flowed into the Wobbish River, who got to be governor and make Vigor Church the capital. Let those two fight it out; whoever won, Hooch intended to be a rich man and do as he liked. Either that or see the whole place go up in flames. If Hooch ever got completely beat down and broken, he'd make sure nobody else profited. When a spark had no hope left, he could still get even, which is about all the good Hooch figured he got out of being a spark.

Well, of course, as a spark he made sure his bath-water was always hot, so it wasn't a total loss. Sure was a nice change, getting off the river and back into civilized life. The clothes laid out for him were clean, and it felt good to get that prickly beard off his face. Not to mention the fact that the squaw who bathed him was real eager to get an extra dose of likker, and if Harrison hadn't sent a soldier knocking on his door telling him to hurry it up, Hooch might have collected the first installment of her trade goods. Instead, though, he dried and dressed.

She looked real concerned when he started for the door. "You be back?" she asked.

"Look here, of course I will," he said. "And I'll have a keg with me."

"Before dark though," she said.

"Well maybe yes and maybe no," he answered. "Who cares?"

"After dark, all Reds like me, outside fort."

"Is that so," murmured Hooch. "Well, I'll try to be back before dark. And if I don't, I'll remember you. May forget your face, but I won't forget your hands, hey? That was a real nice bath."

She smiled, but it was a grotesque imitation of a real smile. Hooch just couldn't figure out why the Reds didn't die out years ago, their women were so ugly. But if you kind of closed your eyes, a squaw would do well enough until you could get back to real women.

It wasn't just a new mansion Harrison had built—he had added a whole new section of stockade, so the fort was about twice the size it used to be. And a good solid parapet ran the whole length of the stockade. Harrison was ready for war. That made Hooch pretty uneasy. The likker trade didn't thrive too good in wartime. The kind of Reds who fought battles weren't the kind of Reds who drank likker. Hooch saw so much of the latter kind that he pretty much forgot the former kind existed. There was even a cannon. No, two cannons. This didn't look good at all.

Harrison's office wasn't in the mansion, though. It was in another building entirely, a new headquarters building, and Harrison's office was in the southwest corner, with lots of light. Hooch noticed that besides the normal complement of soldiers on guard and officers doing paperwork, there were several Reds sprawling or sitting in the headquarters building. Harrison's tame Reds, of course—he always kept a few around.

But there were more tame Reds than usual, and the only one Hooch recognized was Lolla-Wossiky, a one-eyed Shaw-Nee who was always about the drunkest Red who wasn't dead yet. Even the other Reds made fun of him, he was so bad, a real lickspittle.

What made it even funnier was the fact that Harrison himself was the man who shot Lolla-Wossiky's father, some fifteen years ago, when Lolla-Wossiky was just a little tyke, standing right there watching. Harrison even told the story sometimes right in front of Lolla-Wossiky, and the one-eyed drunk just nodded and laughed and grinned and acted like he had no brains at all, no human dignity, just about the lowest, crawliest Red that Hooch ever seen. He didn't even care about revenge for his dead papa, just so long as he got his likker. No, Hooch wasn't a bit surprised to see that Lolla-Wossiky was lying right on the floor outside Harrison's office, so every time the door opened, it bumped him right in the butt. Incredibly, even now, when there hadn't been new likker in Carthage City in four months, Lolla-Wossiky was pickled. He saw Hooch come in, sat up on one elbow, waved an arm in greeting, and then rocked back onto the floor without a sound. The handkerchief he kept tied over his missing eye was out of place, so the empty socket with the sucked-in eyelids was plainly visible. Hooch felt like that empty eye was looking at him. He didn't like that feeling. He didn't like Lolla-Wossiky. Harrison was the kind of man who liked having such squalid creatures around—made him feel real good about himself, by contrast, Hooch figured—but Hooch didn't like seeing such miserable specimens of humanity. Why hadn't Lolla-Wossiky died yet?

Just as he was about to open Harrison's door, Hooch looked up from the drunken one-eyed Red into the eyes of another man, and here's the funny thing: He thought for a second it was Lolla-Wossiky again, they looked so much alike. Only it was Lolla-Wossiky with both eyes, and not drunk at all, no sir. This Red must be six feet from sole to scalp, leaning against the wall, his head shaved except his scalplock, his clothing clean. He stood *straight*, like a soldier at attention, and he didn't so much as look at Hooch. His eyes stared straight into space. Yet Hooch knew that this boy saw *everything*, even though he focused on nothing. It had been a long time since Hooch saw a Red who looked like that, all cold and in control of things.

Dangerous, dangerous, is Harrison getting careless, to let a Red into his own headquarters with eyes like those? With a bearing like a king, and arms so strong he looks like he could pull a bow made from the trunk of a six-year-old oak? Lolla-Wossiky was so contemptible it made Hooch sick. But this Red who looked like Lolla-Wossiky, he was the opposite. And instead of making Hooch sick, he made Hooch mad, to be so proud and defiant as if he thought he was as good a man as any White. No, better. That's how he looked—like he thought he was *better*.

Then he realized he was just standing there, his hand on the latch pull, staring at the Red. Hadn't moved in how long? That was no good, to let folks see how this Red made him uncomfortable. He pulled the door open and stepped inside.

But he didn't talk about that Red, no sir, that wouldn't do at all. It wouldn't do to let Harrison know how much that one proud Shaw-Nee bothered him, made him angry. Because there sat Governor Bill behind a big old table, like God on his throne, and Hooch realized things had changed around here. It wasn't just the fort that had got bigger—so had Bill Harrison's vanity. And if Hooch was going to make the profit he expected to on this trip, he'd have to make sure Governor Bill came down a peg or two, so they could deal as equals instead of dealing as a tradesman and a governor.

"Noticed your cannon," said Hooch, not bothering even to say howdy. "What's the artillery *for*, French from Detroit, Spanish from Florida, or Reds?"

"No matter who's buying the scalps, it's always Reds, one way or another," said Harrison. "Now sit down, relax, Hooch. When my door is closed there's no ceremony between us." Oh, yes, Governor Bill liked to play his games, just like a politician. Make a man feel like you're doing him a favor just to let him sit in your presence, flatter him by making him feel like a real *chum* before you pick his pocket. Well, thought Hooch, I have some games of my own to play, and we'll see who comes out on top.

Hooch sat down and put his feet up on Governor Bill's desk. He took out a pinch of tobacco and tucked it into his cheek. He could see Bill flinch a little. It was a sure sign that his wife had broke him of some manly habits. "Care for a pinch?" asked Hooch.

It took a minute before Harrison allowed as how he wouldn't mind a bit of it. "I mostly swore off this stuff," he said ruefully.

So Harrison still missed his bachelor ways. Well, that was good news to Hooch. Gave him a handle to get the Gov off balance. "Hear you got yourself a white bedwarmer from Manhattan," said Hooch.

It worked: Harrison's face flushed. "I married a *lady* from New Amsterdam," he said. His voice was quiet and cold. Didn't bother Hooch a bit—that's just what he wanted.

"A *wife!*" said Hooch. "Well, I'll be! I beg your pardon, Governor, that wasn't what I heard, you'll have to forgive me, I was only going by what the—what the rumors said."

"Rumors?" asked Harrison

"Oh, no, you just never mind. You know how soldiers talk. I'm ashamed I listened to them in the first place. Why, you've kept the memory of your first wife sacred all these years, and if I was any kind of friend of yours, I would've known any woman you took into your house would be a lady, and a properly married wife."

"What I want to know," said Harrison, "is who told you she was anything *else?*"

"Now, Bill, it was just loose soldiers' talk; I don't want any man to get in trouble because he can't keep his tongue. A likker shipment just came in, for heaven's sake, Bill! You won't hold it against them, what they said with their minds on whisky. No, you just take a pinch of this tobacky and remember that your boys all like you fine.''

Harrison took a good-sized chaw from the offered tobacco pouch and tucked it into his cheek. ''Oh, I know, Hooch, they don't bother me.'' But Hooch knew that it *did* bother him, that Harrison was so angry he couldn't spit straight, which he proved by missing the spittoon. A spittoon, Hooch noticed, which had been sparkling clean. Didn't *anybody* spit around here anymore, except Hooch?

''You're getting civilized,'' said Hooch. ''Next thing you know you'll have lace curtains.''

''Oh, I do,'' said Harrison. ''In my house.''

''And little china chamber pots?''

''Hooch, you got a mind like a snake and a mouth like a hog.''

''That's why you love me, Bill—cause you got a mind like a hog and a mouth like a snake.''

''Keep that in mind,'' said Harrison. ''You just keep that in mind, how I might bite, and bite deep, and bite with poison in it. You keep that in mind before you try to play your diddly games with me.''

''Diddly games!'' cried Hooch. ''What do you mean, Bill Harrison! What do you accuse me of!''

''I accuse you of arranging for us to have no likker at all for four long months of springtime, till I had to hang three Reds for breaking into military stores, and even my soldiers ran out!''

''Me! I brought this load here as fast as I could!''

Harrison just smiled.

Hooch kept his look of pained outrage—it was one of his best expressions, and besides it was even partly true. If even one of the other whisky traders had half a head on him, he'd have found a way downriver despite Hooch's efforts. It wasn't *Hooch's* fault if he just happened to be the sneakiest, most malicious, lowdown, competent skunk in a business that wasn't none too clean and none too bright to start with.

Hooch's look of injured innocence lasted longer than Harrison's smile, which was about what Hooch figured would happen.

''Look here, Hooch,'' said Harrison.

''Maybe you better start calling me Mr. Ulysses Palmer,'' said Hooch. ''Only my *friends* call me Hooch.''

But Harrison did not take the bait. He did not start to make protests of his undying friendship. ''Look here, *Mr.* Palmer,'' said Harrison, ''you know and I know that this hasn't got a thing to do with friendship. You want to be rich, and I want to be governor of a real state. I need your likker to be governor, and you need my protection to be rich. But this time you pushed too far. You understand me? You can have a monopoly for all I care, but if I don't get a steady supply of whisky from you, I'll get it from someone else.''

''Now Governor Harrison, I can understand you might've started fretting along in there sometime, and I can make it right with you. What if you had six kegs of the best whisky all on your own—''

But Harrison wasn't in the mood to be bribed, either. ''What you forget, Mr. Palmer, is that I can have *all* this whisky, if I want it.''

Well, if Harrison could be blunt, so could Hooch, though he made it a practice to say things like this with a smile. ''Mr. Governor, you can take all my whisky *once*. But then what trader will want to deal with you?''

Harrison laughed and laughed. ''Any trader at all, Hooch Palmer, and you know it!''

Hooch knew when he'd been beat. He joined right in with the laughing.

Somebody knocked on the door. ''Come in,'' said Harrison. At the same time he waved Hooch to stay in his chair. A soldier stepped in, saluted, and said, ''Mr. Andrew Jackson here to see you, sir. From the Tennizy country, he says.''

''Days before I looked for him,'' said Harrison. ''But I'm delighted, couldn't be more pleased, show him in, show him in.''

Andrew Jackson. Had to be that lawyer fellow they called Mr. Hickory. Back in the days when Hooch was working the Tennizy country, Hickory Jackson was a real country boy—killed a man in a duel, put his fists into a few faces now and then, had a name for keeping his word, and the story was that he wasn't exactly completely married to his wife, who might well have another husband in her past who wasn't even dead. That was the difference between Hickory and Hooch— Hooch would've made sure the husband was dead and buried long since. So Hooch was a little surprised that this Jackson was big enough now to have business that would take him clear from Tennizy up to Carthage City.

But that was nothing to his surprise when Jackson stepped through the door, ramrod straight with eyes like fire. He strode across the room and offered his hand to Governor Harrison. Called him *Mr.* Harrison, though. Which meant he was either a fool, or he didn't figure he needed Harrison as much as Harrison needed *him.*

''You got too many Reds around here,'' said Jackson. ''That one-eyed drunk by the door is enough to make a body puke.''

"Well," said Harrison, "I think of him as kind of a pet. My own pet Red."

"Lolla-Wossiky," said Hooch helpfully. Well, not really helpfully. He just didn't like how Jackson hadn't noticed him, and Harrison hadn't bothered to introduce him.

Jackson turned to look at him. "What did you say?"

"Lolla-Wossiky," said Hooch.

"The one-eyed Red's name," said Harrison.

Jackson eyed Hooch coldly. "The only time I need to know the name of a horse," he said, "is when I plan to ride it."

"My name's Hooch Palmer," said Hooch. He offered his hand.

Jackson didn't take it. "Your name is Ulysses Brock," said Jackson, "and you owe more than ten pounds in unpaid debts back in Nashville. Now that Appalachee has adopted U.S. currency, that means you owe two hundred and twenty dollars in gold. I bought those debts and it happens that I have the papers with me, since I heard you were trading whisky up in these parts, and so I think I'll place you under arrest."

It never occurred to Hooch that Jackson would have that kind of memory, or be such a skunk as to buy a man's paper, especially seven-year-old paper, which by now should be pretty much forgot. But sure enough, Jackson took a warrant out of his coat pocket and laid it on Governor Harrison's desk.

"Since I appreciate your already having this man in custody when I arrived," said Jackson, "I am glad to tell you that under Appalachee law the apprehending officer is entitled to ten percent of the funds collected."

Harrison leaned back in his chair and grinned at Hooch. "Well, Hooch, maybe you better set down and let's all get better acquainted. Or I guess maybe we don't have to, since Mr. Jackson here seems to know you better than I did."

"Oh, I know Ulysses Brock all right," said Jackson. "He's just the sort of skunk we had to get rid of in Tennizy before we could lay claim to being civilized. And I expect you'll be rid of his sort soon enough here, too, as you get the Wobbish country ready to apply for admission to the United States."

"You take a lot for granted," said Harrison. "We might try to go it alone out here, you know."

"If Appalachee couldn't make a go of it alone, with Tom Jefferson as President, you won't do any better here, I reckon."

"Well maybe," said Harrison, "just maybe we've got to do something that Tom Jefferson didn't have the guts to do. And maybe we've got a need for men like Hooch here."

"What you have need for is soldiers," said Jackson. "Not rummers."

Harrison shook his head. "You're a man who forces me to come to the point, Mr. Jackson, and I can calculate right enough why the folks in Tennizy sent you on up here to meet with me. So I'll come to the point. We've got the same trouble up here that you've got down there, and that trouble can be summed up in one word: Reds."

"Which is why I'm perplexed that you let drunken Reds sit around here in your own headquarters. They all belong west of the Mizzipy, and that's as plain as day. We won't have peace and we won't have civilization until that's done. And since Appalachee and the U.S. alike are convinced that Reds can be treated like human beings, we've got to solve our Red problem *before* we join the Union. It's as simple as that."

"Well, you see?" said Harrison. "We already agree completely."

"Then why is it that you keep your headquarters as full of Reds as Independence Street in Washington City? They have Cherriky men acting as clerks and even holding government offices in Appalachee, right in the capital, jobs that White men ought to have, and then I come here and find you keep Reds around you, too."

"Cool down, Mr. Jackson, cool right down. Don't the King keep his Blacks there in his palace in Virginia?"

"His Blacks are slaves. Everybody knows you can't make slaves out of Reds. They aren't intelligent enough to be properly trained."

"Well, you just set yourself there in that chair, Mr. Jackson, and I'll make my point the best way I know how, by showing you two prime Shaw-Nee specimens. Just set down."

Jackson picked up the chair and moved it to the opposite side of the room from Hooch. It made something gnaw in Hooch's gut, the way Jackson acted. Men like Jackson were so upright and honest-seeming, but Hooch knew that there wasn't no such thing as a good man, just a man who wasn't bought yet, or wasn't in deep enough trouble, or didn't have the guts to reach out and take what he wanted. That's all that virtue ever boiled down to, so far as Hooch ever saw in his life. But here was Jackson, putting on airs and calling for Bill Harrison to arrest him! Think of that, a stranger from Tennizy country coming up here and waving around a warrant from an Appalachee judge, of all things, which didn't have no more force in Wobbish country than if it was written by the King of Ethiopia. Well, Mr. Jackson, it's a long way home from here, and we'll just see if you don't have some kind of accident along the way.

No, no, no, Hooch told himself silently. Getting even don't amount to nothing in this world. Getting even only gets you behind. The best revenge is to get rich enough to make them all call you sir, that's how you get even with these boys. No bushwhacking. If you ever get a name for bushwhacking, that's the end of you, Hooch Palmer.

So Hooch sat there and smiled, as Harrison called for his aide. "Why don't you invite Lolla-Wossiky in here? And while you're at it, tell his brother he can come in, too."

Lolla-Wossiky's brother—had to be the defiant Red who was standing up against the wall. Funny, how two peas from the same pod could grow up so different.

Lolla-Wossiky came in fawning, smiling, looking quickly from one White face to the next, wondering what they wanted, how he could make them happy enough to reward him with whisky. It was written all over him, how thirsty he was, even though he was already so drunk he didn't walk straight. Or had he already drunk so much likker that he couldn't walk straight even when he was sober? Hooch wondered—but soon enough he knew the answer. Harrison reached into the bureau behind him and took out a jug and a cup. Lolla-Wossiky watched the brown liquid splash into the cup, his one eye so intense it was like he could taste the likker by vision alone. But he didn't take even a single step toward the cup. Harrison reached out and set the cup on the table near the Red, but still the man stood there, smiling, looking now at the cup, now at Harrison, waiting, waiting.

Harrison turned to Jackson and smiled. "Lolla-Wossiky is just about the most civilized Red in the whole Wobbish country, Mr. Jackson. He never takes things that don't belong to him. He never speaks except when spoken to. He obeys and does whatever I tell him. And all he ever asks in return is just a cup of liquid. Doesn't even have to be good likker. Corn whisky or bad Spanish rum are just fine with him, isn't that right, Lolla-Wossiky?"

"Very so right, Mr. Excellency," said Lolla-Wossiky. His speech was surprisingly clear, for a Red. Especially a drunken Red.

Hooch saw Jackson study the one-eyed Red with disgust. Then the Tennizy lawyer's gaze shifted to the door, where the tall, strong, defiant Red was standing. Hooch enjoyed watching Jackson's face. From disgust, his expression plainly changed to anger. Anger and, yes, fear. Oh, yes, you aren't fearless, Mr. Jackson. You know what Lolla-Wossiky's brother is. He's your enemy, and my enemy, the enemy of every White man who ever wants to have this land, because sometime this uppity Red is going to put his tommy-hawk in your head and peel off your scalp real slow, and he won't sell it to no Frenchman, neither, Mr. Jackson, he'll keep it and give it to his children, and say to them, "This is the only good White man. This is the only White man who doesn't break his word. This is what you do to White men." Hooch knew it,

Harrison knew it, and Jackson knew it. That young buck by the door was death. That young buck was White men forced to live east of the mountains, all crammed into the old towns with all their lawyers and professors and high-toned people who never gave you room to breathe. People like Jackson himself, in fact. Hooch gave one snort of laughter at that idea. Jackson was exactly the sort of man that folks moved west to get away from. How far west will I have to go before the lawyers lose the trail and get left behind?

"I see you've noticed Ta-Kumsaw. Lolla-Wossiky's older brother, and my very, very dear friend. Why, I've known that lad since before his father died. Look what a strong buck he's grown into!"

If Ta-Kumsaw noticed how he was being ridiculed, he showed no sign of it. He looked at no person in the room. Instead he looked out the window on the wall behind the governor. Didn't fool Hooch, though. Hooch knew what he was watching, and had a pretty good idea what Ta-Kumsaw was feeling, too. These Reds, they took family real serious. Ta-Kumsaw was secretly watching his brother, and if Lolla-Wossiky was too likkered up to feel any shame, that just meant Ta-Kumsaw would feel it all the more.

"Ta-Kumsaw," said Harrison. "You see I've poured a drink for you. Come, sit down and drink, and we can talk."

At Harrison's words, Lolla-Wossiky went rigid. Was it possible that the drink wasn't for him, after all? But Ta-Kumsaw did not twitch, did not show any sign that he heard.

"You see?" said Harrison to Jackson. "Ta-Kumsaw isn't even civilized enough to sit down and have a convivial drink with friends. But his younger brother is civilized, isn't he? Aren't you, Lolly? I'm sorry I don't have a chair for you, my friend, but you can sit on the floor under my table here, sit right at my feet, and drink this rum."

"You are remarkable kind," said Lolla-Wossiky in that clear, precise speech of his. To Hooch's surprise, the one-eyed Red did not scramble for the cup. Instead he walked carefully, each step a labor of precision, and took the cup between only slightly trembling hands. Then he knelt down before Harrison's table and, still balancing the cup, sank into a seated position, his legs crossed.

But he was still out in front of the table, not under it, and Harrison pointed this out to him. "I'd like you to sit under my table," said the governor. "I'd regard it as a great courtesy to me if you would."

So Lolla-Wossiky bent his head almost down into his lap and waddled on his buttocks until he was under the table. It was very hard for him to drink in that position, since he couldn't lift his head straight up, let alone tip it back to drain the cup. But he managed anyway, drinking carefully, rocking from one side to the other.

All this time, Ta-Kumsaw said nary a word. Didn't even show that he saw how his brother was being humiliated. Oh, thought Hooch, oh, the fire that burns in that boy's heart. Harrison's taking a real risk here. Besides, if he's Lolla-Wossiky's brother, he must know Harrison shot his daddy during the Red uprisings back in the nineties sometime, when General Wayne was fighting the French. A man doesn't forget that kind of thing, especially a Red man, and here Harrison was testing him, testing him right to the limit.

"Now that everybody's comfortable," said Harrison, "why don't you set down and tell us what you came for, Ta-Kumsaw."

Ta-Kumsaw didn't sit. Didn't close the door, didn't take a step farther into the room. "I speaking for Shaw-Nee, Caska-Skeeaw, Pee Orawa, Winny-Baygo."

"Now, Ta-Kumsaw, you know that you don't even speak for all the Shaw-Nee, and you sure don't speak for the others."

"All tribes who sign General Wayne's treaty." Ta-Kumsaw went on as if Harrison hadn't said a thing. "Treaty says Whites don't sell whisky to Reds."

"That's right," said Harrison. "And we're keeping that treaty."

Ta-Kumsaw didn't look at Hooch, but he lifted his hand and pointed at him. Hooch felt the gesture as if Ta-Kumsaw had actually touched him with that finger. It didn't make him mad this time, it plain scared him. He heard that some Reds had a come-hither so strong that didn't no hex protect you, so they could lure you off into the woods alone and slice you to bits with their knives, just to hear you scream. That's what Hooch thought of, when he felt Ta-Kumsaw point to him with hatred.

"Why are you pointing at my old friend Hooch Palmer?" asked Harrison.

"Oh, I reckon nobody likes me today," Hooch said. He laughed, but it didn't dispel his fear after all.

"He bring his flatboat of whisky," said Ta-Kumsaw.

"Well, he brought a lot of things," said Harrison. "But if he brought whisky, it'll be delivered to the sutler here in the fort and not a drop of it will be sold to the Reds, you can be sure. We uphold that treaty, Ta-Kumsaw, even though you Reds aren't keeping it too good lately. It's got so flatboats can't travel alone down the Hio no more, my friend, and if things don't let up, I reckon the army's going to have to take some action."

"Burn a village?" asked Ta-Kumsaw. "Shoot down our babies? Our old people? Our women?"

"Where do you get these ideas?" said Harrison. He sounded down-right offended, even though Hooch knew right well that Ta-Kumsaw was describing the typical army operation.

Hooch spoke right up, in fact. "You Reds burn out helpless farmers in their cabins and pioneers on their flatboats, don't you? So why do you figure your villages should be any safer, you tell me that!"

Ta-Kumsaw still didn't look at him. "English law says, Kill the man who steals your land, you are not bad. Kill a man to steal his land, and you are very bad. When we kill White farmers, we are not bad. When you kill Red people who live here a thousand years, you are very bad. Treaty says, stay all east of My-Ammy River, but they don't stay, and you help them."

"Mr. Palmer here spoke out of turn," said Harrison. "No matter what you savages do to our people—torturing the men, raping the women, carrying off the children to be slaves—we don't make war on the helpless. We are civilized, and so we behave in a civilized manner."

"This man will sell his whisky to Red men. Make them lie in dirt like worms. He will give his whisky to Red women. Make them weak like bleeding deer, do all things he says."

"If he does, we will arrest him," said Harrison. "We will try him and punish him for breaking the law."

"If he does, you *not* will arrest him." said Ta-Kumsaw. "You will share pelts with him. You will keep him safe."

"Don't call me a liar," said Harrison.

"Don't lie," said Ta-Kumsaw.

"If you go around talking to White men like this, Ta-Kumsaw, old boy, one of them's going to get real mad at you and blast your head off."

"Then I know you will arrest him. I know you will try him and punish him for breaking the law." Ta-Kumsaw said it without cracking a smile, but Hooch had traded with the Reds enough to know their kind of joke.

Harrison nodded gravely. It occurred to Hooch that Harrison might not realize it was a joke. He might think Ta-Kumsaw actually believed it. But no, Harrison knew he and Ta-Kumsaw was lying to each other; and it came into Hooch's mind that when both parties are lying and they both know the other party's lying, it comes powerful close to being the same as telling the truth.

What was really hilarious was that Jackson actually *did* believe all this stuff. "That's right," said the Tennizy lawyer. "Rule of law is what separates civilized men from savages. Red men just aren't advanced enough yet, and if you aren't willing to be subject to White man's law, you'll just have to make way."

For the first time, Ta-Kumsaw looked one of them in the eye. He stared coldly at Jackson and said, "These men are liars. They know what is true, but they say it is not true. You are not a liar. You believe what you say."

Jackson nodded gravely. He looked so vain and upright and godly that Hooch couldn't resist it, he hottened up the chair under Jackson just a little, just enough that Jackson had to wiggle his butt. That took off a few layers of dignity. But Jackson still kept his airs. "I believe what I say because I tell the truth."

"You say what you believe. But still it is not true. What is your name?"

"Andrew Jackson."

Ta-Kumsaw nodded. "Hickory."

Jackson looked downright surprised and pleased that Ta-Kumsaw had heard of him. "Some folks call me that." Hooch hottened up his chair a little more.

"Blue Jacket says, Hickory is a good man."

Jackson still had no idea why his chair was so uncomfortable, but it was too much for him. He popped right up, stepped away from the chair, kind of shaking his legs with each step to cool himself off. But still he kept talking with all the dignity in the world. "I'm glad Blue Jacket feels that way. He's chief of the Shaw-Nee down in Tennizy country, isn't he?"

"Sometimes," said Ta-Kumsaw.

"What do you mean sometimes?" said Harrison. "Either he's a chief or he isn't."

"When he talks straight, he is chief," said Ta-Kumsaw.

"Well, I'm glad to know he trusts me," said Jackson. But his smile was a little wan, because Hooch was busy hotting up the floor under his feet, and unless old Hickory could fly, he wasn't going to be able to get away from *that*. Hooch didn't plan to torment him long. Just until he saw Jackson take a couple of little hops, and then try to explain why he was dancing right there in front of a young Shaw-Nee warrior and Governor William Henry Harrison.

Hooch's little game got spoiled, though, cause at that very moment, Lolla-Wossiky toppled forward and rolled out from under the table. He had an idiotic grin on his face, and his eyes were closed. "Blue Jacket!" he cried. Hooch took note that drink had finally slurred his speech. "Hickory!" shouted the one-eyed Red.

"You are my enemy," said Ta-Kumsaw, ignoring his brother.

"You're wrong," said Harrison. "I'm your friend. Your enemy is up north of here, in the town of Vigor Church. Your enemy is that renegade Armor-of-God Weaver.''

"Armor-of-God Weaver sells no whisky to Reds.''

"Neither do I,'' said Harrison. "But he's the one making maps of all the country west of the Wobbish. So he can parcel it up and sell it after he's killed all the Reds.''

Ta-Kumsaw paid no attention to Harrison's attempt to turn him against his rival to the north. "I come to warn you,'' said Ta-Kumsaw.

"Warn me?'' said Harrison. "You, a Shaw-Nee who doesn't speak for anybody, you *warn* me, right here in my stockade, with a hundred soldiers ready to shoot you down if I say the word?''

"Keep the treaty,'' said Ta-Kumsaw.

"We *do* keep the treaty! It's you who always break the treaties!''

"Keep the treaty,'' said Ta-Kumsaw.

"Or what?'' asked Jackson.

"Or every Red west of the mountains will come together and cut you to pieces.''

Harrison leaned back his head and laughed and laughed. Ta-Kumsaw showed no expression.

"*Every* Red, Ta-Kumsaw?'' asked Harrison. "You mean, even Lolly here? Even my pet Shaw-Nee, my tame Red, even *him*?''

For the first time Ta-Kumsaw looked at his brother, who lay snoring on the floor. "The sun comes up every day, White man. But is it tame? Rain falls down every time. But is it tame?''

"Excuse me, Ta-Kumsaw, but this one-eyed drunk here is as tame as my horse.''

"Oh yes,'' said Ta-Kumsaw. "Put on the saddle. Put on the bridle. Get on and ride. See where this tame Red goes. Not where you want.''

"Exactly where I want,'' said Harrison. "Keep that in mind. Your brother is always within my reach. And if you ever get out of line, boy, I'll arrest him as your conspirator and hang him high.''

Ta-Kumsaw smiled thinly. "You think so. Lolla-Wossiky thinks so. But he will learn to see with his other eye before you ever lay a hand on him.''

Then Ta-Kumsaw turned around and left the room. Quietly, smoothly, not stalking, not angry, not even closing the door behind him. He moved with grace, like an animal, like a very dangerous animal. Hooch saw a cougar once, years ago, when he was alone in the mountains. That's what Ta-Kumsaw was. A killer cat.

Harrison's aide closed the door.

Harrison turned to Jackson and smiled. "You see?'' he said.

"What am I supposed to see, Mr. Harrison?''

"Do I have to spell it out for you, Mr. Jackson?"

"I'm a lawyer. I like things spelled out. If you can spell."

"I can't even *read*," said Hooch cheerfully.

"You also can't keep your mouth shut," said Harrison. "I'll spell it out for you, Jackson. You and your Tennizy boys, you talk about moving the Reds west of the Mizzipy. Now let's say we do that. What are you going to do, keep soldiers all the way up and down the river, watching all day and all night? They'll be back across this river whenever they want, raiding, robbing, torturing, killing."

"I'm not a fool," said Jackson. "It will take a great bloody war, but when we get them across the river, they'll be broken. And men like that Ta-Kumsaw—they'll be dead or discredited."

"You think so? Well, during that great bloody war you talk about, a lot of White boys will die, and White women and children, too. But I have a better idea. These Reds suck down likker like a calf sucks down milk from his mama's tit. Two years ago there was a thousand Pee-Ankashaw living east of the My-Ammy River. Then they started getting likkered up. They stopped working, they stopped eating, they got so weak that the first little sickness came through here, it wiped them out. Just wiped them out. If there's a Pee-Ankashaw left alive here, I don't know about it. Same thing happened up north, to the Chippy-Wa, only it was French traders done it to them. And the best thing about likker is, it kills off the Reds and not a White man dies."

Jackson rose slowly to his feet. "I reckon I'll have to take three baths when I get home," he said, "and even then I still won't feel clean."

Hooch was delighted to see that Harrison was really mad. He rose to his feet and shouted at Jackson so loud that Hooch could feel his chair shake. "Don't get high and mighty with me, you hypocrite! You want them all dead, just like I do! There's no difference between us."

Jackson stopped at the door and eyed the governor with disgust. "The assassin, Mr. Harrison, the *poisoner*, he can't see the difference between himself and a soldier. But the soldier can."

Unlike Ta-Kumsaw, Jackson was not above slamming the door.

Harrison sank back down onto his chair. "Hooch, I've got to say, I don't much like that fellow."

"Never mind," said Hooch. "He's with you."

Harrison smiled slowly. "I know. When it comes to war, we'll all be together. Except for maybe that Redkisser up in Vigor Church."

"Even him," said Hooch. "Once a war starts, the Reds won't be able to tell one White man from another. Then his people will start dying just like ours. Then Armor-of-God Weaver will fight."

"Yeah, well, if Jackson and Weaver would likker up their Reds the way we're doing ours, there wouldn't have to *be* a war."

Hooch aimed a mouthful at the spittoon and didn't miss by much. "That Red, that Ta-Kumsaw."

"What about him?" asked Harrison.

"He worries me."

"Not me," said Harrison. "I've got his brother here passed out on my floor. Ta-Kumsaw won't do nothing."

"When he pointed at me, I felt his finger touch me from across the room. I think he's maybe got a come-hither. Or a far-touch. I think he's dangerous."

"You don't believe in all that hexery, do you, Hooch? You're such an educated man, I thought you were above that kind of superstition."

"I'm not and neither are you, Bill Harrison. You had a doodlebug tell you where firm ground was so you could build this stockade, and when your first wife had her babies, you had a torch in to see how the baby was laying in the womb."

"I warn you," said Harrison, "to make no more comment about my wife."

"Which one, now, Bill? The hot or the cold?"

Harrison swore a good long string of oaths at that. Oh, Hooch was delighted, Hooch was pleased. He had such knack for hotting things up, yes sir, and it was more fun hotting up a man's temper, because there wasn't no *flame* then, just a lot of steam, a lot of hot air.

Well, Hooch let old Bill Harrison jaw on for a while. Then he smiled and raised his hands like he was surrendering. "Now, you know I didn't mean no harm, Bill. I just didn't know as how you got so prissy these days. I figured we both know where babies grow, how they got in there, and how they come out, and your women don't do it any different than mine. And when she's lying there screaming, you know you've got a midwife there who knows how to cast a sleep on her, or do a pain-away, and when the baby's slow to come you've got a torch telling where it lays. And so you listen to me, Bill Harrison. That Ta-Kumsaw, he's got some kind of knack in him, some kind of power. He's more than he seems."

"Is he now, Hooch? Well maybe he is and maybe he ain't. But he said Lolla-Wossiky would see with his other eye before I laid a hand on him, and it won't be long before I prove that he's no prophet."

"Speaking of old one-eye, here, he's starting to fart something dreadful."

Harrison called for his aide. "Send in Corporal Withers and four soldiers, at once."

Hooch admired the way Harrison kept military discipline. It wasn't thirty seconds before the soldiers were there, Corporal Withers saluting and saying, "Yes, sir, General Harrison."

"Have three of your men carry this animal out to the stable for me."

Corporal Withers obeyed instantly, pausing only to say, "Yes sir, General Harrison."

General Harrison. Hooch smiled. He knew that Harrison's only commission was as a colonel under General Wayne during the last French war, and he didn't amount to much even then. General. Governor. What a pompous—

But Harrison was talking to Withers again, and looking at Hooch as he did so. "And now you and Private Dickey will kindly arrest Mr. Palmer here and lock him up."

"Arrest me!" shouted Hooch. "What are you talking about!"

"He carries several weapons, so you'll have to search him thoroughly," said Harrison. "I suggest stripping him here before you take him to the lock-up, and leave him stripped. Don't want this slippery old boy to get away."

"What are you arresting me for!"

"Why, we have a warrant for your arrest for unpaid debts," said Harrison. "And you've also been accused of selling whisky to Reds. We'll naturally have to seize all your assets—those suspicious-looking kegs my boys've been hauling into the stockade all day—and sell them to make good the debt. If we can sell them for enough, and we can clear you of those ugly charges of likkering up the Reds, why, we'll let you go."

Then Harrison walked on out of his office. Hooch cussed and spit and made remarks about Harrison's wife and mother, but Private Dickey was holding real tight to a musket, and that musket had a bayonet attached to the business end; so Hooch submitted to the stripping and the search. It got worse, though, and he cussed again when Withers marched him right across the stockade, stark naked, and didn't give him so much as a blanket when he locked him into a storage room. A storage room filled with empty kegs from the *last* shipment of likker.

He sat in that lock-up room for two days before his trial, and for the first while there was murder in his heart. He had a lot of ideas for revenge, you can bet. He thought of setting fire to the lace curtains in Harrison's house, or burning the shed where the whisky was kept, starting all kinds of fire. Cause what good is it to be a spark if you can't use it to get even with folks who pretend to be your friends and then lock you into jail?

But he didn't start no fires, because Hooch was no fool. Partly, he knew that if a fire once got started anywhere in the stockade, there was a good chance it'd spread from one end to the other inside half an hour. And there was a good chance that while everybody's rushing around to save their wives and children and gunpowder and likker, they might not remember about one whisky trader locked up in a storage room. Hooch didn't hanker to die in a fire of his own setting—that wasn't no kind of vengeance. Time enough to start fires when he had a noose around his neck someday, but he wasn't going to risk burning to death just to get even over something like this.

But the main reason he didn't start a fire wasn't fear, it was plain business sense. Harrison was doing this to show Hooch that he didn't like the way Hooch delayed shipments of likker to jack up the price. Harrison was showing him that he had real power, and all Hooch had was money. Well, let Harrison play at being a powerful man. Hooch knew some things, too. He knew that someday the Wobbish country would petition the U.S. Congress in Philadelphia to become a state. And when it did, a certain William Henry Harrison would have his little heart set on being governor. And Hooch had seen enough elections back in Suskwahenny and Pennsylvania and Appalachee to know that you can't get votes without silver dollars to pass around. Hooch would have those silver dollars. And when the time came, he might pass around those silver dollars to Harrison voters; and then again he might not. He just might not. He might help another man sit in the governor's mansion, someday when Carthage was a real city and Wobbish was a real state, and then Harrison would have to sit there the rest of his life and remember what it was like to be able to lock people up, and he would grind his teeth in anger at how men like Hooch took all that away from him.

That's how Hooch kept himself entertained, sitting in that lock-up room for two long days and nights.

Then they hauled him out and brought him into court—unshaven, dirty, his hair wild, and his clothes all wrinkled up. General Harrison was the judge, the jury was all in uniform, and the defense attorney was—Andrew Jackson! It was plain Governor Bill was trying to make Hooch get mad and start in ranting, but Hooch wasn't born yesterday. He knew that whatever Harrison had in mind, it wouldn't do no good to yell about it. Just sit tight and put up with it.

It took only a few minutes.

Hooch listened with a straight face as a young lieutenant testified that all Hooch's whisky had been sold to the sutler at exactly the price it sold for last time. According to the legal papers, Hooch didn't make a penny more from having kept them waiting four months between shipments. Well, thought Hooch, that's fair enough, Harrison's letting me know how he wants things run. So he didn't say a word. Harrison looked as merry as you please, behind his magisterial solemnity. Enjoy yourself, thought Hooch. You can't make me mad.

But he *could*, after all. They took 220 dollars right off the top and handed it over to Andrew Jackson right there in court. Counted out eleven gold twenty-dollar coins. That caused Hooch physical pain, to see that fiery metal dropping into Jackson's hands. He couldn't keep his silence then. But he did manage to keep his voice low and mild-sounding. "It don't seem regular to me," he said, "to have the plaintiff acting as defense attorney."

"Oh, he's not your defense attorney on the debt charges," said His Honor Judge Harrison. "He's just your defense attorney on the likker charges." Then Harrison grinned and gaveled that matter closed.

The likker business didn't take much longer. Jackson carefully presented all the same invoices and receipts to prove that every keg of whisky was sold to the sutler of Carthage Fort, and not a speck of it to any Reds. "Though I will say," said Jackson, "that the amount of whisky represented by these receipts seems like enough for three years for an army ten times this size."

"We've got a bunch of hard-drinking soldiers," said Judge Harrison. "And I reckon that likker won't last six months. But not a drop to the Reds, Mr. Jackson, you may be sure!"

Then he dismissed all charges against Hooch Palmer, alias Ulysses Brock. "But let this be a lesson to you, Mr. Palmer," said Harrison in his best judicial voice. "Justice on the frontier is swift and sure. See to it you pay your debts. And avoid even the appearance of evil."

"Sure enough," said Hooch cheerfully. Harrison had rolled him over good, but everything had worked out fine. Oh, the 220 dollars bothered him, and so did the two days in jail, but Harrison didn't mean for Hooch to suffer much. Because what Jackson didn't know, and no one else saw fit to mention, was that Hooch Palmer happened to have the contract as sutler for the U.S. Army in Wobbish Territory. All those documents that proved he hadn't sold the likker to the Reds *really* showed that he sold the likker to himself—and at a profit, too. Now Jackson would head on home and Hooch would settle down in the sutler's store, selling likker to the Reds at extortionate prices, splitting the profits with Governor Bill and watching the Reds die like flies. Harrison had played his little joke on Hooch, right enough, but he'd played an even bigger one on old Hickory.

Hooch made sure to be at the wharf when they ferried Jackson back across the Hio. Jackson had brought along two big old mountain boys with rifles, no less. Hooch took note that one of them looked to be half Red himself, probably a Cherriky half-breed—there was lots of that kind of thing in Appalachee, White men actually *marrying* squaws like as if they was real women. And both those rifles had "Eli Whitney" stamped on the barrel, which meant they was made in the state of Irrakwa, where this Whitney fellow set up shop making guns so fast he made the price drop; and the story was that all his workmen was *women*, Irrakwa *squaws*, if you can believe it. Jackson could talk all he wanted about pushing the Reds west of the Mizzipy, but it was already too late. Ben Franklin did it, by letting the Irrakwa have their own state up north, and Tom Jefferson made it worse by letting the Cherriky be full voting citizens in Appalachee when they fought their revolution against the King. Treat them Reds like citizens and they start to figure they got the same rights as a White man. There was no way to have an orderly society if *that* sort of thing caught on. Why, next thing you know them Blacks'd start trying to get out of being slaves, and first thing you know you'd sit down at the bar in a saloon and you'd look to your left and there'd be a *Red*, and you'd look to your right and there'd be a *Black*, and that was just plain against nature.

There went Jackson, thinking he was going to save the White man from the Red, when he was traveling with a half-breed and toting Red-made rifles. Worst of all, Jackson had eleven gold coins in his saddle pouch, coins that properly belonged to Hooch Palmer. It made Hooch so mad he couldn't think straight.

So Hooch hotted up that saddle pouch, right where the metal pin held it onto the saddle. He could feel it from here, the leather charring, turning ash-black and stiff around that pin. Pretty soon, as the horse walked along, that bag would drop right off. But since they was likely to notice it, Hooch figured he wouldn't stop with the pouch. He hotted up a whole lot of other places on that saddle, and on the other men's saddles, too. When they reached the other shore they mounted up and rode off, but Hooch knew they'd be riding bareback before they got back to Nashville. He most sincerely hoped that Jackson's saddle would break in such a way and at such a time that old Hickory would land on his butt or maybe even break his arm. Just thinking about the prospect made Hooch pretty cheerful. Every now and then it was kind of fun to be a spark. Take some pompous holy-faced lawyer down a peg.

Truth is, an honest man like Andrew Jackson just wasn't no match for a couple of scoundrels like Bill Harrison and Hooch Palmer. It was just a crying shame that the army didn't give no medals to soldiers who likkered their enemies to death instead of shooting them. Cause if they did, Harrison and Palmer would both be heroes, Hooch knew that for sure.

As it was, Hooch reckoned Harrison would find a way to make himself a hero out of all this anyway, while Hooch would end up with nothing but money. Well, that's how it goes, thought Hooch. Some people get the fame, and some people get the money. But I don't mind, as long as I'm not one of the people who end up with nothing at all. I sure never want to be one of them. And if I am, they're sure going to be sorry.

2

Ta-Kumsaw

While Hooch was watching Jackson cross the river, Ta-Kumsaw watched the White whisky trader and knew what he did. So did any other Red man who cared to watch—sober Red man, anyway. White man does a lot of things Red man don't understand, but when he fiddle with fire, water, earth, and air, he can't hide it from a Red man.

Ta-Kumsaw didn't *see* the saddle leather burn on Jackson's horse. He didn't feel the heat. What he saw was like a stirring, a tiny whirlwind, sucking his attention out across the water. A twisting in the smoothness of the land. Most Red men couldn't feel such things as keen as Ta-Kumsaw. Ta-Kumsaw's little brother, Lolla-Wossiky, was the only one Ta-Kumsaw ever knew who felt it more. Very much more. He knew all those whirlpools, those eddies in the stream. Ta-Kumsaw remembered their father, Pucky-Shinwa, he spoke of Lolla-Wossiky, that he would be shaman, and Ta-Kumsaw would be war-leader.

That was before Lying-Mouth Harrison shot Pucky-Shinwa right before Lolla-Wossiky's eyes. Ta-Kumsaw was off hunting that day, four-hands walk to the north, but he felt the murder like a gun fired right behind him. When a White man laid a hex or a curse or cast a doodlebug, it felt to Ta-Kumsaw like an itch under his skin, but when a White man killed, it was like a knife stabbing.

He was with another brother, Methowa-Tasky, and he called to him. "Did you feel it?"

Methowa-Tasky's eyes went wide. He had not. But even then, even at that age—not yet thirteen—Ta-Kumsaw had no doubt of himself. He felt it. It was true. A murder had been done, and he must go to the dying man.

He led the way, running through the forest. Like all Red men in the old days, his harmony with the woodland was complete. He did not have to think about where he placed his feet; he knew that the twigs under his feet would soften and bend, the leaves would moisten and not rustle, the branches he brushed aside would go back quick to their right place and leave no sign he passed. Some White men prided themselves that they could move as quiet as a Red, and in truth some of them could—but they did it by moving slow, careful, watching the ground, stepping around bushes. They never knew how little thought a Red man took for making no sound, for leaving no trace.

What Ta-Kumsaw thought of was not his steps, not himself at all. It was the green life of the woodland all around him, and in the heart of it, before his face, the black whirlpool sucking him downward, stronger, faster, toward the place where the living green was torn open like a wound to let a murder through. Long before they got there, even Methowa-Tasky could feel it. There on the ground lies their father, a bullet through his face. And by him, silent and unseeing, stands Lolla-Wossiky, ten years old.

Ta-Kumsaw carried his father's body home across his shoulders, like a deer. Methowa-Tasky led Lolla-Wossiky by the hand, for otherwise the boy would not move. Mother greeted them with great wails of grief, for she also felt the death, but did not know it was her own husband until her sons brought him back. Mother tied her husband's corpse to Ta-Kumsaw's back; then Ta-Kumsaw climbed the tallest tree, untied his father's corpse from his back, and bound it to the highest branch he could reach.

It would have been very bad if he had climbed beyond his strength, and his father's body had fallen from his grasp. But Ta-Kumsaw did not climb beyond his strength. He tied his father to a branch so high the sun touched his father's face all day. The birds and insects would eat of him; the sun and air would dry him; the rain would wash the last of him downward to the earth. This was how Ta-Kumsaw gave his father back to the land.

But what could they do with Lolla-Wossiky? He said nothing, he wouldn't eat unless someone fed him, and if you didn't take his hand and lead him, he would stay in one place forever. Mother was frightened at what had happened to her son. Mother loved Ta-Kumsaw very much, more than any other mother in the tribe loved any other son; but even so, she loved Lolla-Wossiky more. Many times she told them all how baby Lolla-Wossiky cried the first time the air grew bitter cold each winter. She could never get him to stop, no matter how she covered him with bearskins and buffalo robes. Then one winter he was old enough to talk, and he told her why he cried. "All the bees are dying," he said.

That was Lolla-Wossiky, the only Shaw-Nee who ever felt the death of bees.

That was the boy standing beside his father when Colonel Bill Harrison shot him dead. If Ta-Kumsaw felt that murder like a knife wound, half a day's journey away, what did Lolla-Wossiky feel, standing so close, and already so sensitive? If he cried for the death of bees in winter, what did he feel when a White man murdered his father before his eyes?

After a few years, Lolla-Wossiky finally began to speak again, but the fire was gone from his eyes, and he was careless. He put his own eye out by accident, because he tripped and fell on the short jagged stump of a broken bush. Tripped and fell! What Red man ever did that? It was like Lolla-Wossiky lost all feeling for the land; he was dull as a White man.

Or maybe, Ta-Kumsaw thought, maybe the sound of that ancient gunshot still rings in his head so loud he can't hear anything else now; maybe that old pain is still so sharp that he can't feel the tickling of the living world. Pain all the time till the first taste of whisky showed Lolla-Wossiky how to take away the sharp edge of it.

That was why Ta-Kumsaw never beat Lolla-Wossiky for likkering, though he would beat any other Shaw-Nee, even his brothers, even an old man, if he found him with the White man's poison in his hand.

But the White man never guessed at what the Red man saw and heard and felt. The White man brought death and emptiness to this place. The White man cut down wise old trees with much to tell; young saplings with many lifetimes of life ahead; and the White man never asked, Will you be glad to make a lodgehouse for me and my tribe? Hack and cut and chop and burn, that was the White man's way. Take from the forest, take from the land, take from the river, but put nothing back. The White man killed animals he didn't need, animals that did him no harm; yet if a bear woke hungry in the winter and took so much as a single young pig, the White man hunted him down and killed him in revenge. He never felt the balance of the land at all.

No wonder the land hated the White man! No wonder all the natural things of the land rebelled against his step: crackling underfoot, bending the wrong way, shouting out to the Red man. Here was where the enemy stood! Here came the intruder, through these bushes, up this hill! The White man joked that Reds could even track a man on water, then laughed as if it wasn't true. But it *was* true, for when a White man passed along a river or a lake, it bubbled and foamed and rippled loud for hours after he had passed.

Now Hooch Palmer, poison-seller, sly killer, now he stands making his silly fire on another White man's saddles, thinking no one knows. These White men with their weak little knacks. These White men with their hexes and their wardings. Didn't they know their hexes only fended off *unnatural* things? If a thief comes, knowing he does wrong, then a good strong fending hex makes his fear grow till he cries out and runs away. But the Red man never is a thief. The Red man belongs wherever he is in this land. To him the hex is just a cold place, a stirring in the air, and nothing more. To him a knack is like a fly, buzz buzz buzz. Far above this fly, the power of the living land is a hundred hawks, watching, circling.

Ta-Kumsaw watched Hooch turn away, return to the fort. Soon Hooch sells his poison in earnest. Most of the Red men gathered here will be drunk. Ta-Kumsaw will stay, keeping watch. He does not have to speak to anyone. They only see him, and those with any pride left will turn away without likkering. Ta-Kumsaw is not a chief yet. But Ta-Kumsaw is not to be ignored. Ta-Kumsaw is the pride of the Shaw-Nee. All other Red men of every tribe must measure themselves against him. Whisky-Reds are very small inside when they see this tall strong Red man.

He walked to the place where Hooch had stood, and let his calm replace the twisting Hooch put there. Soon the buzzing, furious insects quieted. The smell of the likkery man settled. Again the water lapped the shore with accidental song.

How easy to heal the land after the White man passes. If all the White men left today, by tomorrow the land would be at rest, and in a year it would not show any sign the White man ever came. Even the ruins of the White man's buildings would be part of the land again, making homes for small animals, crumbling in the grip of the hungering vines. White man's metal would be rust; White man's stone work would be low hills and small caves; White man's murders would be wistful, beautiful notes in the song of the redbird—for the redbird remembered everything, turning it into goodness when it could.

All day Ta-Kumsaw stood outside the fort, watching Red men go in to buy their poison. Men and women from every tribe—Wee-Aw and Kicky-Poo, Potty-Wottamee and Chippy-Wa, Winny-Baygo and Pee-Orawa—they went in carrying pelts or baskets and came out with no more than cups or jugs of likker, and sometimes with nothing more than what they already had in their bellies. Ta-Kumsaw said nothing, but he could feel how the Reds who drank this poison were cut off from the land. They did not twist the green of life the way the White man did; rather it was as if they did not exist at all. The Red man who drank whisky was already dead, as far as the land knew. No, not even dead, for they give nothing back to the land at all. I stand here to watch them be ghosts, thought Ta-Kumsaw, not dead and not alive. He said this only inside his head, but the land felt his grief, and the breeze answered him by weeping through the leaves.

Come dusk, a redbird walks on the dirt in front of Ta-Kumsaw.

Tell me a story, says the redbird in its silent way, its eyes cocked upward at the silent Red man.

You know my story before I tell it, says Ta-Kumsaw silently. You feel my tears before I shed them. You taste my blood before it is spilled.

Why do you grieve for Red men who are not of the Shaw-Nee?

Before the White man came, says Ta-Kumsaw silently, we did not see that all Red men were alike, brothers of the land, because we thought all creatures were this way; so we quarreled with other Red men the way the bear quarrels with the cougar, the way the muskrat scolds the beaver. Then the White man came, and I saw that all Red men are like twins compared to the White man.

What is the White man? What does he do?

The White man is like a human being, but he crushes all other living things under his feet.

Then why, O Ta-Kumsaw, when I look into your heart, why is it that you do not wish to hurt the White man, that you do not wish to kill the White man?

The White man doesn't know the evil that he does. The White man doesn't feel the peace of the land, so how can he tell the little deaths he makes? I can't blame the White man. But I can't let him stay. So when I make him leave this land, I won't hate him.

If you are free of hate, O Ta-Kumsaw, you will surely drive the White man out.

I'll cause him no more pain than it takes to make him go away.

The redbird nods. Once, twice, three times, four. It flutters up to a branch as high as Ta-Kumsaw's head. It sings a new song. In this song Ta-kumsaw hears no words; but he hears his own story being told. From now on, his story is in the song of every redbird in the land, for what one redbird knows, all remember.

Whoever watched Ta-Kumsaw all that time had no idea of what he said and saw and heard. Ta-Kumsaw's face showed nothing. He stood where he had been standing; a redbird landed near him, stayed awhile, sang, and went away.

Yet this moment turned Ta-Kumsaw's life; he knew it right away. Until this day he had been a young man. His strength and calm and courage were admired, but he spoke only as any Shaw-Nee could speak, and having spoken, he then kept still and older men decided. Now he would decide for himself, like a true chief, like a war chief. Not a chief of the Shaw-Nee, or even a chief of the Red men of this north country, but rather the chief of all Red tribes in the war against the White man. He knew for many years that such a war must come; but until this moment he had thought that it would be another man, a chief like Corn-stalk, Blackfish, or even a Cree-Ek or Chok-Taw from the south. But the redbird came to *him*, Ta-Kumsaw, and put him in the song. Now wherever Ta-Kumsaw went throughout the land that knew the redbird song, his name would be well known to the wisest Red men. He was war chief of all Red men who loved the land; the land had chosen him.

As he stood there near the bank of the Hio, he felt like he was the face of the land. The fire of the sun, the breath of the air, the strength of the earth, the speed of the water, all reached into him and looked out on the world through his eyes. I am the land; I am the hands and feet and mouth and voice of the land as it struggles to rid itself of the White man.

These were his thoughts.

He stood there until it was fully dark. The other Red men had returned to their lodges or their cabins to sleep—or to lie drunken and as good as dead till morning. Ta-Kumsaw came out of his red-bird trance and heard laughter from the Red village, laughter and singing from the White soldiers inside the fort.

Ta-Kumsaw walked away from the place where he had stood so many hours. His legs were stiff, but he did not stagger; he forced his legs to move smoothly, and the ground yielded gently under his feet. The White man had to wear rough heavy boots to walk far in this land, because the dirt scuffed and tore at his feet; the Red man could wear the same moccasins for years, because the land was gentle and welcomed his step. As he moved, Ta-Kumsaw felt soil, wind, river, and lightning all moving with him; the land within him, all things living, and he the hands and feet and face of the land.

There was a shout inside the fort. And more shouts:

"Thief! Thief!"

"Stop him!"

"He's got a keg!"

Curses, howls. Then the worst sound: a gunshot. Ta-Kumsaw waited for the sting of death. It didn't come.

A shadowy man rose above the parapet. Whatever man it was, he balanced a keg on his shoulders. For a moment he teetered on the very peak of the stockade poles, then jumped down. Ta-Kumsaw knew it was a Red man because he could jump from three man-heights, holding a heavy keg, and make almost no sound upon landing.

On purpose maybe, or maybe not, the fleeing thief ran straight to Ta-

Kumsaw and stopped before him. Ta-Kumsaw looked down. By starlight he knew the man.

"Lolla-Wossiky," he said.

"Got a keg," said Lolla-Wossiky.

"I should break that keg," said Ta-Kumsaw.

Lolla-Wossiky cocked his head like the redbird and regarded his brother. "Then I'd have to take another."

The White men chasing Lolla-Wossiky came to the gate, clamoring for the guard to open it. I have to remember this, thought Ta-Kumsaw. This is a way to get them to open the gate for me. Even as he thought that, however, he also put his arm around his brother, keg and all. Ta-Kumsaw felt the green land like a second heartbeat, strong within him, and as he held his brother, the same power of the land flowed into Lolla-Wossiky. Ta-Kumsaw heard him gasp.

The Whites ran out of the fort. Even though Ta-Kumsaw and Lolla-Wossiky stood in the open, in plain sight, the White soldiers did not see them. Or no, they *saw;* they simply did not notice the two Shaw-Nee. They ran past, shouting and firing randomly into the woods. They gathered near the brothers, so close they could have lifted an arm and touched them. But they did not lift their arms; they did not touch the Red men.

After a while the Whites gave up the search and returned to the fort, cursing and muttering.

"It was that one-eye Red."

"The Shaw-Nee drunk."

"Lolla-Wossiky."

"If I find him, I'll kill him."

"Hang the thieving devil."

They said these things, and there was Lolla-Wossiky, not a stone's throw from them, holding the keg on his shoulder.

When the last White man was inside the fort, Lolla-Wossiky giggled.

"You laugh with the White man's poison on your shoulders," said Ta-Kumsaw.

"I laugh with my brother's arm across my back," answered Lolla Wossiky.

"Leave that whisky, Brother, and come with me," said Ta-Kumsaw. "The redbird heard my story, and remembers me in her song."

"Then I will listen to that song and be glad all my life," said Lolla-Wossiky.

"The land is with me, Brother. I'm the face of the land, the land is my breath and blood."

"Then I will hear your heartbeat in the pulse of the wind," said Lolla-Wossiky.

"I will drive the White man back into the sea," said Ta-Kumsaw.

In answer, Lolla-Wossiky began to weep; not drunken weeping, but the dry, heavy sobs of a man burdened down with grief. Ta-Kumsaw tried to tighten his embrace, but his brother pushed him away and staggered off, still carrying the keg, into the darkness and the trees.

Ta-Kumsaw did not follow him. He knew why his brother was grieving: because the land had filled Ta-Kumsaw with power, power enough to stand among the drunken Whites and seem as invisible as a tree. And Lolla-Wossiky knew that by rights whatever power Ta-Kumsaw had, Lolla-Wossiky should have had ten times that power. But the White man had stolen it from Lolla-Wossiky with murders and likker, until Lolla-Wossiky wasn't man enough to have the redbird learn his song or the land fill up his heart.

Never mind, never mind, never mind.

The land has chosen me to be its voice, and so I must begin to speak. I will no longer stay here, trying to shame the wretched drunks who have already been killed by their thirst for the White man's poison. I will give no more warnings to White liars. I will go to the Reds who are still alive, still men, and gather them together. As one great people we will drive the White man back across the sea.

3

De Maurepas

Frederic, the young Comte de Maurepas, and Gilbert, the aging Marquis de La Fayette, stood together at the railing of the canal barge, looking out across Lake Irrakwa. The sail of the *Marie-Philippe* was plainly visible now; they had been watching for hours as it came closer across this least and lowest of the Great Lakes.

Frederic could not remember when he had last been so humiliated on behalf of his nation. Perhaps the time when Cardinal What's-his-name had tried to bribe Queen Marie-Antoinette. Oh but of course Frederic had only been a boy, then, a mere twenty-five years old, callow and young, without experience of the world. He had thought that no greater humiliation could come to France than to have it known that a cardinal would actually believe that the Queen could be bribed with a diamond necklace. Or bribed at all, for that matter. Now, of course, he understood that the real humiliation was that a French cardinal would be so stupid as to suppose that bribing the Queen was worth doing; the most she could do was influence the King, and since old King Louis never influenced anybody, there you were.

Personal humiliation was painful. Humiliation of one's family was much worse. Humiliation of one's social standing was agony to bear. But humiliation of one's nation was the most excruciating of human miseries.

Now here he stood on a miserable canal barge, an *American* canal barge, tied at the verge of an *American* canal, waiting to greet a French general. Why wasn't it a French canal? Why hadn't the French been the first to engineer those clever locks and build a canal around the Canadian side of the falls?

"Don't fume, my dear Frederic," murmured La Fayette.

"I'm not fuming, my dear Gilbert."

"Snorting, then. You keep snorting."

"Sniffing. I have a cold." Canada certainly was a repository for the dregs of French society, Frederic thought for the thousandth time. Even the nobility that ended up here was embarrassing. This Marquis de La Fayette, a member of the—no, a *founder* of the Club of the Feuillants, which was almost the same as saying he was a declared traitor to King Charles. Democratic twaddle. Might as well be a Jacobin like that terrorist Robespierre. Of course they exiled La Fayette to Canada, where he could do little harm. Little harm, that is, except to humiliate France in this unseemly manner—

"Our new general has brought several staff officers with him," said La Fayette, "and all their luggage. It makes no sense to disembark and make the miserable portage in wagons and carriages, when it can all be carried by water. It will give us a chance to become acquainted."

Since La Fayette, in his normal crude way (disgrace to the aristocracy!), insisted on being blunt about the matter at hand, Frederic would have to stoop to his level and speak just as plainly. "A French general should not have to travel on foreign soil to reach his posting!"

"But my dear Frederic, he'll never set foot on American soil, now, will he! Just boat to boat, on water all the way."

La Fayette's simper was maddening. To make light of this smudge on the honor of France. Why, oh, why couldn't Frederic's father have remained in favor with the king just a little longer, so Frederic could have stayed in France long enough to win promotion to some elegant posting, like Lord of the Italian March or something—did they have such a posting?—anyway, somewhere with decent food and music and dancing and theatre—ah, Moliere! In Europe, where he could face a civilized enemy like the Austrians or the Prussians or even—though it stretched the meaning of the word *civilized*—the English. Instead here he was, trapped forever—unless Father wormed his way back into the King's favor—facing a constant ragtag invasion of miserable uneducated Englishmen, the worst, the utter dregs of English society, not to mention the Dutch and Swedes and Germans—oh, it did not bear thinking about. And even worse were the allies! Tribes of Reds who weren't even heretics, let alone Christians—they were *heathen*, and half the military operation in Detroit consisted of buying those hideous bloody trophies—

"Why, my dear Frederic, you really are taking a chill," said La Fayette.

"Not a bit."

"You shivered."

"I *shuddered.*"

"You must stop pouting and make the best of this. The Irrakwa have been very cooperative. They provided us with the governor's own barge, free of charge, as a gesture of goodwill."

"The governor! The *governor?* You mean that fat hideous red-skinned heathen *woman?*"

"She can't help her red skin, and she isn't heathen. In fact she's a Baptist, which is almost like being Christian, only louder."

"Who can keep track of these English heresies?"

"I think there's something quite elegant about it. A woman as governor of the state of Irrakwa, and a Red at that, accepted as the equal of the governors of Suskwahenny, Pennsylvania, New Amsterdam, New Sweden, New Orange, New Holland—"

"I think sometimes you prefer those nasty little United States to your own native land."

"I am a Frenchman to the heart," said La Fayette mildly. "But I admire the American spirit of egalitarianism."

Egalitarianism again. The Marquis de La Fayette was like a piano-forte that had but a single key. "You forget that our enemy in Detroit is American."

"*You* forget that our enemy is the horde of illegal squatters, no matter what nation they come from, who have settled in the Red Reserve."

"That's a quibble. They're all Americans. They all pass through New Amsterdam or Philadelphia on their way west. So you encourage them here in the east—they all know how much you admire their anti-monarchist philosophy—and then I have to pay for their scalps when the Reds massacre them out west."

"Now, now, Frederic. Even in humor, you mustn't accuse me of being anti-monarchist. M. Guillotin's clever meat-slicing machine awaits anyone convicted of *that.*"

"Oh, do be serious, Gilbert. They'd never use it against a marquis. They don't cut off the heads of aristocrats who propound these insane democratic ideas. They just send them to Quebec." Frederic smiled—he couldn't resist driving home the nail. "The ones they really despise, they send to Niagara."

"Then what in the world did *you* do—to get sent to Detroit?" murmured La Fayette.

More humiliation. Would it never end?

The *Marie-Philippe* was near enough for them to see individual sailors and hear them shouting as the ship made its final tack into Port Irrakwa. The lowest of the Great Lakes, Irrakwa was the only one that could be visited by oceangoing vessels—the Niagara Falls saw to that.

In the last three years, since the Irrakwa finished their canal, almost all the shipping that needed to be transported past the falls into Lake Canada came to the American shore and was taken up the Niagara Canal. The French portage towns were dying; an embarrassing number of Frenchmen had moved across the lake to live on the American side, where the Irrakwa were only too happy to put them to work. And the Marquis de La Fayette, supposedly the supreme governor of all Canada south and west of Quebec, didn't seem to mind at all. If Frederic's father ever got back into King Charles's good graces, Frederic would see to it that La Fayette was the first aristocrat to feel the Guillotin knife. What he had done here in Canada was plain treason.

As if he could read Frederic's mind, La Fayette patted his shoulder and said, "Very soon, now, just be patient." For a moment Frederic thought, insanely, that La Fayette was calmly prophesying his own execution for treason.

But La Fayette was merely talking about the fact that at last the *Marie-Philippe* was near enough to heave a line to the wharf. The Irrakwa stevedores caught the line and affixed it to the windlass, and then chanted in their unspeakable language as they towed the ship close in. As soon as it was in place, they began unloading cargo on the one side, and passengers on the other.

"Isn't that ingenious, how they speed the transfer of cargo," said La Fayette. "Unload it on those heavy cars, which sit on rails—rails, just like mining carts!—and then the horses tow it right up here, smooth and easy as you please. On rails you can carry a much heavier load than on regular wagons, you know. Stephenson explained it to me the last time I was here. It's because you don't have to steer." On and on he blathered. Sure enough, within moments he was talking again about Stephenson's steam engine, which La Fayette was convinced would replace the horse. He had built some in England or Scotland or somewhere, but now he was in America, and do you think La Fayette would invite Stephenson to build his steam wagons in Canada? Oh, no—La Fayette was quite content to let him build them for the Irrakwa, mumbling some idiotic excuse like: The Irrakwa are already using steam engines for their spinning wheels, and all the coal is on the American side—but Frederic de Maurepas knew the truth. La Fayette believed that the steam engine, pulling cars on railed roads, would make commerce and travel infinitely faster and cheaper—and he thought it would be better for the world if it were built within the borders of a *democracy*! Of course Frederic did not believe the engines would ever be as fast as horses, but that didn't matter—La Fayette *did* believe in them, and so the fact that he didn't bring them to Canada was pure treason.

He must have been forming the word with his lips. Either that or La Fayette could hear other men's thoughts—Frederic had heard rumors that La Fayette had a knack for that. Or perhaps La Fayette merely guessed. Or perhaps the devil told him—there's a thought! Anyway, La Fayette laughed aloud and said, "Frederic, if I had Stephenson build his railroad in Canada, you'd have me cashiered for wasting money on nonsense. As it is, if you made a report accusing me of treason for encouraging Stephenson to remain in Irrakwa, they'd call you home and lock you up in a padded room!"

"Treason? I accuse you?" said Frederic. "It's the farthest thought from my mind." Still, he crossed himself, on the off-chance that it was the devil who had told La Fayette. "Now, haven't we had enough of watching the stevedores loading cargo? I believe we have an officer to greet."

"Why are you so eager to meet him now?" asked La Fayette. "Yesterday you kept reminding me that he *is* a commoner. He even entered the service as a corporal, I think you said."

"He's a general now, and His Majesty has seen fit to send him to us." Frederic spoke with stiff propriety. Still La Fayette insisted on smiling with amusement. Someday, Gilbert, someday.

Several officers in full army dress uniform were milling about on the wharf, but none was of general rank. The hero of the battle of Madrid was obviously waiting to make a grand entrance. Or did he expect a Marquis and the son of a Comte to come and meet *him* in his cabin? Unthinkable.

And, in fact, he did not think it. The officers stepped back, and from their position by the railing of the canal barge de Maurepas and La Fayette could see him step off the *Marie-Phillippe* onto the wharf.

"Why, he's not a very large man, is he," said Frederic.

"They aren't very tall in the south of France."

"South of France!" said Frederic scornfully. "He's from Corsica, my dear Gilbert. That's hardly even French at all. More like Italian."

"He defeated the Spanish army in three weeks, while his superior officer was indisposed with dysentery," La Fayette reminded him.

"An act of subordination for which he should have been cashiered," said Frederic.

"Oh, I quite agree with you," said La Fayette. "Only, you see, he did win the war, and as long as King Charles was adding the crown of Spain to his collection of headgear, he thought it would be churlish to court-martial the soldier who won it for him."

"Discipline above all. Everybody must know his place and stay in it, or there will be chaos."

"No doubt. Well, they *did* punish him. They made him a general, but they sent him *here*. Didn't want him involved with the Italian campaign. His Majesty wouldn't mind being Doge of Venice, but this General Bonaparte might get carried away, capture the College of Cardinals, and make King Charles pope."

"Your sense of humor is a crime."

"Frederic, look at the man."

"I *am* looking at him."

"Then *don't* look at him. Look at everyone else. Look at his officers. Have you ever seen soldiers show so much love for their commander?"

Frederic reluctantly tore his gaze from the Corsican general and looked at the underlings who walked quietly behind. Not like courtiers—there was no sense of jockeying for position. It was like—it was like—Frederic couldn't find words for it—

"It's as if each man knows that Bonaparte loves him, and values him."

"A ridiculous system, if that's what his system is," said Frederic. "You cannot control your underlings if you don't keep them in constant fear of losing their position."

"Let's go meet him."

"Absurd! He must come to us!"

But La Fayette, as usual, did not hesitate between the word and the deed—he was already on the wharf, striding the last few yards to stand before Bonaparte and receive his salute. Frederic, however, knew his station in life, and knew Bonaparte's as well, and Bonaparte would have to come to *him*. They might make Bonaparte a general, but they could never make him a gentleman.

La Fayette was fawning, of course. "General Bonaparte, we're honored to have you here. I only regret that we cannot offer you the amenities of Paris—"

"My lord Governor," said Bonaparte—naturally getting the form of address all wrong, "I have never known the amenities of Paris. All my happiest moments have been in the field."

"And the happiest moments, too, for France, are when you are in the field. Come, meet General de Maurepas. He will be your superior officer in Detroit."

Frederic heard the slight pause before La Fayette said the word *superior*. Frederic knew when he was being ridiculed. I will remember every slight, Gilbert, and I will repay.

The Irrakwa were very efficient at transferring cargo; it wasn't an hour before the canal barge was under way. Naturally, La Fayette spent the first afternoon telling Bonaparte all about Stephenson's steam engine. Bonaparte made a show of being interested, asking all about the possibilities of troop transport, and how quickly track could be laid behind an advancing army, and how easily these railed roads might be disrupted by enemy action—but it was all so tedious and boring that Frederic could not imagine how Bonaparte kept it up. Of course an officer had to *pretend* to be interested in everything a Governor said, but Bonaparte was taking it to extremes.

Before too long the conversation obviously excluded Frederic, but he didn't mind. He let his thoughts wander, remembering that actress, What's-her-name, who did such an exquisite job of that part, whatever it was, or was she a ballerina? He remembered her legs, anyway, such graceful legs, but she refused to come to Canada with him, even though he assured her he loved her and promised to set her up in a house even nicer than the one he would build for his wife. If only she had come. Of course, she might have died of fever, the way his wife did. So perhaps it was all for the best. Was she still on the stage in Paris? Bonaparte would not know, of course, but one of his junior officers might have seen her. He would have to inquire.

They supped at Governor Rainbow's table, of course, since that was the only table on the canal boat. The governor had sent her regrets that she could not visit the distinguished French travelers, but she hoped her staff would make them comfortable. Frederic, supposing this meant an Irrakwa chef, had braced himself for another tedious Red meal of tough deer gristle—one could hardly call such fare *venison*—but instead the chef was, of all things, a Frenchman! A Huguenot, or rather the grandson of Huguenots, but he didn't hold grudges, so the food was superb. Who would have imagined good French food in a place like this—and not the spicy Acadian style, either.

Frederic did try to take a more active part in the conversation at supper, once he had finished off every scrap of food on the table. He tried his best to explain to Bonaparte the almost impossible military situation in the southwest. He counted off the problems one by one— the undisciplined Red allies, the unending flow of immigrants. "Worst of all is our own soldiers, though. They are a determinedly superstitious lot, as the lower classes always are. They see omens in everything. Some Dutch or German settler puts a hex on his door and you practically have to beat our soldiers to get them to go in."

Bonaparte sipped his coffee (barbaric fluid! but he seemed to relish it exactly as the Irrakwa did), then leaned back in his chair, regarding Frederic with his steady, piercing eyes. "Do you mean to say that you accompany foot soldiers in house-to-house searches?"

Bonaparte's condescending attitude was outrageous, but before Frederic could utter the withering retort that was just on the tip of his tongue, La Fayette laughed aloud. "Napoleon," he said, "my dear friend, that is the nature of our supposed enemy in this war. When the largest city in fifty miles consists of four houses and a smithy, you don't conduct house-to-house searches. Each house *is* the enemy fortress."

Napoleon's forehead wrinkled. "They don't concentrate their forces into armies?"

"They have never fielded an army, not since General Wayne put down Chief Pontiac years ago, and that was an English army. The U.S. has a few forts, but they're all along the Hio."

"Then why are those forts still standing?"

La Fayette chuckled again. "Haven't you read reports of how the English king fared in his war against the Appalachee rebels?"

"I was otherwise engaged," said Bonaparte.

"You needn't remind us you were fighting in Spain," said Frederic. "We would all have gladly been there, too."

"Would you?" murmured Bonaparte.

"Let me summarize," said La Fayette, "what happened to Lord Cornwallis's army when he led it from Virginia to try to reach the Appalachee capital of Franklin, on the upper Tennizy River."

"Let *me*," said Frederic. "Your summaries are usually longer than the original, Gilbert."

La Fayette looked annoyed at Frederic's interruption, after all, La Fayette was the one who had insisted they address each other as brother generals, by first names. If La Fayette wanted to be treated like a marquis, he should insist on protocol. "Go ahead," said La Fayette.

"Cornwallis went out in search of the Appalachee army. He never found it. Lots of empty cabins, which he burned—but they can build new ones in a day. And every day a half-dozen of his soldiers would be killed or wounded by musketry."

"Rifle fire," corrected La Fayette.

"Yes, well, these Americans prefer the rifled barrel," said Frederic.

"They can't volley properly, rifles are so slow to load," said Bonaparte.

"They don't volley at all, unless they outnumber you," said La Fayette.

"I'm telling it," said Frederic. "Cornwallis got to Franklin and realized that half his army was dead, injured, or protecting his supply lines. Benedict Arnold—the Appalachee general—had fortified the city. Earthworks, balustrades, trenches all up and down the hillsides. Lord Cornwallis tried to lay a siege, but the Cherriky moved so silently that the Cavalier pickets never heard them bringing in supplies during the night. Fiendish, the way those Appalachee Whites worked so closely with the Reds—made them citizens, right from the start, if you can imagine, and it certainly paid off for them this time. Appalachee troops also raided Cornwallis's supply lines so often that after less than a month it became quite clear that Cornwallis was the besieged, not the besieger. He ended up surrendering his entire army, and the English King had to grant Appalachee its independence.''

Bonaparte nodded gravely.

"Here's the cleverest thing," said La Fayette. "After he surrendered, Cornwallis was brought into Franklin City and discovered that all the families had been moved out long before he arrived. That's the thing about these Americans on the frontier. They can pick up and move anywhere. You can't pin them down.''

"But you can kill them," said Bonaparte.

"You have to catch them," said La Fayette.

"They have fields and farms," said Bonaparte.

"Well, yes, you could try to find every farm," said La Fayette. "But when you get there, if anyone's at home you'll to find it's a simple farm family. Not a soldier among them. There's no *army*. But the minute you leave, someone is shooting at you from the forest. It might be the same humble farmer, and it might not.''

"An interesting problem," said Bonaparte. "You never know your enemy. He never concentrates his forces.''

"Which is why we deal with the Reds," said Frederic. "We can't very well go about murdering innocent farm families ourselves, can we?''

"So you pay the Reds to kill them for you.''

"Yes. It works rather well," said Frederic, "and we have no plans to do anything different.''

"*Well?* It works *well?*" said Bonaparte scornfully. "Ten years ago there weren't five hundred American households west of the Appalachee Mountains. Now there's ten thousand households between the Appalachees and the My-Ammy, and more moving farther west all the time.''

La Fayette winked at Frederic. Frederic hated him when he did that. "Napoleon read our dispatches," La Fayette said cheerfully. "Memorized our estimates of American settlements in the Red Reserve.''

"The King wants this American intrusion into French territory stopped, and stopped at once," said Bonaparte.

"Oh he does?" asked La Fayette. "What an odd way he has of showing it.''

"Odd? He sent me," said Bonaparte. "That means he expects victory.''

"But you're a general," said La Fayette. "We already have generals."

"Besides," said Frederic, "you're not in command. *I'm* in command."

"The Marquis has the supreme military authority here," said Bonaparte.

Frederic understood completely: La Fayette also had the authority to put Bonaparte in command over Frederic, if he desired. He cast an anxious look toward La Fayette, who was complacently spreading goose-liver paste on his bread. La Fayette smiled benignly. "General Bonaparte is under *your* command, Frederic. That will not change. Ever. I hope that's clear, my dear Napoleon."

"Of course," said Napoleon. "I would not dream of changing that. You should know that the King is sending more than generals to Canada. Another thousand soldiers will be here in the spring."

"Yes, well, I'm impressed to learn that he's promised to send more troops again—haven't we heard a dozen such promises before, Frederic? I'm always reassured to hear another promise from the King." La Fayette took the last sip from his wineglass. "But the fact is, my dear Napoleon, we already have soldiers, too, who do nothing but sit in garrison at Fort Detroit and Fort Chicago, paying for scalps with bourbon. Such a waste of bourbon. The Reds drink it like water and it kills them."

"If we don't need generals and we don't need soldiers," asked Bonaparte condescendingly, "what *do* you think we need to win this war?"

Frederic couldn't decide if he hated Bonaparte for speaking so rudely to an aristocrat, or loved him for speaking so rudely to the detestable Marquis de La Fayette.

"To win? Ten thousand French settlers," said La Fayette. "Match the Americans man for man, wife for wife, child for child. Make it impossible to do business in that part of the country without speaking French. Overwhelm them with numbers."

"No one would come to live in such wild country," said Frederic, as he had said so many times before.

"Offer them free land and they'd come," said La Fayette.

"Riff-raff," said Frederic. "We hardly need more riff-raff."

Bonaparte studied La Fayette's face a moment in silence. "The commercial value of these lands is the fur trade," said Bonaparte quietly. "The King was very clear on that point. He wants no European settlement at all outside the forts."

"Then the King will lose this war," said La Fayette cheerfully, "no matter how many generals he sends. And with that, gentlemen, I think we have done with supper.''

La Fayette arose and left the table immediately.

Bonaparte turned to face Frederic, who was already standing up to leave. He reached out his hand and touched Frederic's wrist. "Stay, please," he said. Or no, actually he merely said, "Stay," but it felt to Frederic that he was saying *please*, that he really *wanted* Frederic to remain with him, that he loved and honored Frederic—

But he couldn't, no, he couldn't, he was a commoner, and Frederic had nothing to say to him—

"My lord de Maurepas," murmured the Corsican corporal. Or did he say merely "Maurepas," while Frederic simply imagined the rest? Whatever his words, his voice was rich with respect, with trust, with hope—

So Frederic stayed.

Bonaparte said almost nothing. Just normal pleasantries. We should work well together. We can serve the King properly. I will help you all I can.

But to Frederic, there was so much more than words. A promise of future honor, of returning to Paris covered with glory. Victory over the Americans, and above all putting La Fayette in his place, triumphing over the democratic traitorous marquis. He and this Bonaparte could do it, together. Patience for a few years, building up an army of Reds so large that it provokes the Americans to raise an army, too; then we can defeat that American army and go home. That's all it will take. It was almost a fever of hope and trust that filled Frederic's heart, until—

Until Bonaparte took his hand away from Frederic's wrist.

It was as if Bonaparte's hand had been his connection to a great source of life and warmth; with the touch removed, he grew cold, weary. But still there was Bonaparte's smile, and Frederic looked at him and remembered the feeling of promise he had had a moment before. How could he have ever thought working with Bonaparte would be anything but rewarding? The man knew his place, that was certain. Frederic would merely *use* Bonaparte's undeniable military talents, and together they would triumph and return to France in glory—

Bonaparte's smile faded, and again Frederic felt a vague sense of loss.

"Good evening," said Bonaparte. "I will see you in the morning, sir."

The Corsican left the room.

If Frederic could have seen his face, he might have recognized his own expression: it was identical to the look of love and devotion that all Bonaparte's junior officers had worn. But he could not see his face. That night he went to bed feeling more at peace, more confident, more hopeful and excited than he had felt in all his years in Canada. He even felt—what, what is this feeling, he wondered—ah yes. Intelligent. He even felt intelligent.

It was deep night, but the canalmen were hard at work, using their noisy steam engine to pump water into the lock. It was an engineering marvel, the steepest system of locks on any canal in the world. The rest of the world did not know it. Europe still thought of America as a land of savages. But the enterprising United States of America, inspired by the example of that old wizard Ben Franklin, was encouraging invention and industry. Rumor had it that a man named Fulton had a working steam-powered boat plying up and down the Hudson—a steamboat that King Charles had been offered, and refused to fund! Coal mines were plunging into the earth in Suskwahenny and Appalachee. And here in the state of Irrakwa, the Reds were out-doing the Whites at their own game, building canals, steam-powered cars to run on railed roads, steam-powered spinning wheels that spat out the cotton of the Crown Colonies and turned it into fine yarns that rivaled anything in Europe—at half the cost. It was just beginning, just starting out, but already more than half the boats that came up the St. Lawrence River were bound for Irrakwa, and not for Canada at all.

La Fayette stood at the rail until the lock was filled and the fires of the steam engine were allowed to die. Then the clop, clop, clop of the canal horses and the boat slid forward again through the water. La Fayette left the rail and walked quietly up the stairs to his room. By dawn, they would be at Port Buffalo. De Maurepas and Bonaparte would go west to Detroit. La Fayette would return to the Governor's mansion in Niagara. There he would sit, issuing orders and watching Parisian policies kill any future for the French in Canada. There was nothing La Fayette could do to keep the Americans, Red and White together, from surpassing Canada and leaving it behind. But he *could* do a few things to help change France into the kind of nation that could reach out to the future as boldly as America was doing.

In his own quarters, La Fayette lay on his bed, smiling. He could imagine what Bonaparte had done tonight, alone in the room with poor empty-headed Freddie. The young Comte de Maurepas was doubtless completely charmed. The same thing might well have happened to La Fayette, but he had been warned about what Bonaparte could do, about his knack for making people trust their lives to him. It was a good knack for a general to have, as long as he only used it on his soldiers, so they'd be willing to die for him. But Bonaparte used it on everybody, if he thought he could get away with it. So La Fayette's good friend Robespierre had sent him a certain jeweled amulet. The antidote to Bonaparte's charm. And a vial of powder, too—the final antidote to Bonaparte, if he could be controlled no other way.

Don't worry, Robespierre, my dear fellow, thought La Fayette. Bonaparte will live. He thinks he is manipulating Canada to serve his ends, but I will manipulate him to serve the ends of democracy. Bonaparte does not suspect it now, but when he returns to France he will be ready to take command of a revolutionary army, and use his knack to end the tyranny of the ruling class instead of using it to add meaningless crowns to King Charles's most unworthy head.

For La Fayette's knack was not to read other men's thoughts, as de Maurepas suspected, but it was nearly that. La Fayette knew upon meeting them what other men and women wanted most. And knowing that, everything else could be guessed at. La Fayette already knew Napoleon better than Napoleon knew himself. He knew that Napoleon Bonaparte wanted to rule the world. And maybe he'd achieve it. But for now, here in Canada, La Fayette would rule Napoleon Bonaparte. He fell asleep clutching the amulet that kept him safe.

4

Lolla-Wossiky

When Lolla-Wossiky left Ta-Kumsaw standing by the gate of Fort Carthage, he knew what his brother thought. Ta-Kumsaw thought he was going off with his keg to drink and drink and drink.

But Ta-Kumsaw didn't know. White Murderer Harrison didn't know. Nobody knew about Lolla-Wossiky. This keg would last him two months maybe. A little bit now, a little bit then. Careful, careful, never spill a drop, drink just *this* much, close it tight, make it last. Maybe even three months.

Always before he had to stay close to White Murderer Harrison's fort, to get the cups of dribbling likker from the dark brown jug. Now, though, he had plenty to make his journey, his great north journey to meet his dream beast.

Nobody knew that Lolla-Wossiky had a dream beast. White man didn't know cause White man had no dream beast, White man slept all the time and never woke up. Red man didn't know cause Red man saw Lolla-Wossiky and thought he was a likker Red, going to die, had no dream beast, never wake up.

Lolla-Wossiky knew though. Lolla-Wossiky knew that light up north, he saw it come five years back. He knew it was his dream beast calling, but he never could go. He started five, six, twelve times north, but then the likker would seep out of his blood and then the noise would come back, terrible black noise that hurt him so bad all the time. When the black noise came it was like a hundred tiny knives in his head, twisting, twisting, so he couldn't feel the land no more, couldn't even see his dream beast light, had to go back, find the likker, still the noise so he could *think*.

This last was the very worst time. No likker came for a long, long time, and for two months at the end even White Murderer Harrison didn't have much for him, maybe one cup in a week, never enough to last more than a few hours, maybe a day. Two long months of black noise all the time.

Black noise made it so Lolla-Wossiky couldn't walk right. Everything wiggles, ground bumps up and down, how can you walk when the land looks like water? So everybody thought Lolla-Wossiky was drunk, stagger like a whisky-Red, fall down all the time. Where does he get the likker? they all ask. Nobody has likker but Lolla-Wossiky still gets drunk, how does he do it? Not one person has eyes to see that Lolla-Wossiky isn't drunk at all. Don't they hear how he talks, clear talking, not drunk-talk? Don't they smell he got no likker-stink? Nobody guesses, nobody reckons, nobody calculates, nobody figures. They know Lolla-Wossiky always needs likker. Never nobody thinks maybe Lolla-Wossiky has pain so bad he hopes to die.

And when he closes his eye to stop the world from rippling like the river, they all think he's asleep and they say things. Oh, they say things they don't want no Red to hear. Lolla-Wossiky figured that out very quick and so when the black noise got so bad he wanted to go lie down on the bottom of the river to shut out the noise forever, instead he staggered to White Murderer Harrison's office and fell down on the floor by his door and listened. Black noise was very loud, but it wasn't ear noise, so he could still hear voices even with the roaring of the black noise in his head. He thought very hard to hear every word under the door. He knew all that White Murderer Harrison said to everybody.

Lolla-Wossiky never told anybody what he heard.

Lolla-Wossiky never told anybody anything true. They never believed him anyway. You're drunk, Lolla-Wossiky. Shame on you, Lolla-Wossiky. Even when he wasn't drunk, even when he hurt so bad he wanted to kill everything alive to make it go away, even then they said, Too bad to see even a Red get so awful drunk. And Ta-Kumsaw, standing there never saying anything or when he did, being so strong and right, when Lolla-Wossiky was so weak and wrong.

North north north went Lolla-Wossiky, chanting to himself. North a thousand steps before I take a little drink. North with the black noise so loud I don't know where north is, but still north because I don't dare to stop.

Very dark night. Black noise so bad the land says nothing to Lolla-Wossiky. Even the white light of the dream beast is far off and seems to come from everywhere at the same time. One eye sees night, other eye sees black noise. Have to stop. Have to stop.

Very carefully Lolla-Wossiky found a tree, put down the keg, sat down and leaned against the tree, keg between his legs. Very slowly because he couldn't see, he felt the keg all over to make sure of the bung. Tap tap tap with the tommy-hawk, tap, tap, tap till the bung was loose. Slowly he wiggled it out with his fingers. Then he leaned over and put his mouth over the bunghole, tight as a kiss, tight as a baby on the nipple, that's how tight; then up with the keg, very slow, very slow, not very high, there's the taste, there's the likker, one swallow, two swallows, three swallows, four.

Four is all. Four is the end. Four is the true number, the whole number, the square number. Four swallows.

He put the bung back into the keg and tapped it into place, tight. Already the likker is getting to his head. Already the black noise is fading, fading.

Into silence. Into beautiful green silence.

But the green also goes away, fading with the black. Every time it goes this way. The land sense, the green vision that every Red has, nobody ever saw it clearer than Lolla-Wossiky. But now when it comes, right behind it comes the black noise every time. And when the black noise goes, when the likker chases it off, right behind it goes away the green living silence every time.

Lolla-Wossiky is left like a White man then. Cut off from the land. Ground crunching underfoot. Branches snagging. Roots tripping. Animals running away.

Lolla-Wossiky hoped, hoped for years to find just the right amount of likker to drink, to still the black noise and still leave the green vision. Four swallows, that was as close as he ever came. It left the black noise just out of reach, just behind the nearest tree. But it also left the green where he could just touch it. Just reach it. So he could pretend to be a true Red instead of a whisky-Red, which was really a White.

Tonight, though, he had been without likker so long, two months except for a cup now and then, that four swallows was too strong for him. The green was gone with the black. But he didn't care, not today. Didn't care, had to sleep.

When he woke up in the morning, the black noise was just coming back. He wasn't sure whether the sun or the noise woke him, and he didn't care. Tap on the bung, four swallows, tap it closed. This time the land sensed stayed close by, he could feel it a little. Enough to find the rabbit in the hole.

Thick old stick. Cut it here, slice it, slice it, so splintery burrs of wood stuck out in every direction.

Lolla-Wossiky knelt down in front of the rabbit hole.

"I am very hungry," he whispered. "And I am not very strong. Will you give me meat?"

He strained to hear the answer, strained to know if it was right. But it was too far off, and rabbits were very quiet in their land-voice. Once, he remembered, he could hear all the voices, and from miles and miles away. Maybe if the black noise ever went away, he could hear again. But for now, he had no way of knowing if the rabbits gave consent or not.

So he didn't know if he had the right or not. Didn't know if he was taking like a Red man, just what the land offered, or stealing like a White man, murdering whatever it pleased him to kill. He had no choice. He thrust the stick into the burrow, twisting it. He felt it quiver, heard the squeal, and pulled it out, still twisting. Little rabbit, not a big one, just a little rabbit squirming to get away from the splinters, but Lolla-Wossiky was quick, just at the moment the rabbit was at the burrow mouth, ready to get free and run, Lolla-Wossiky had his hand there, held the rabbit by the head, lifted it quickly into the air and gave it a snap and a shake. It came down dead, little rabbit, and Lolla-Wossiky carried it away from the burrow, back to the keg, because it is very bad, it makes an empty place in the land, if you skin a baby animal where its kin can see or hear you.

He did not make a fire. Too dangerous, and there was no time to smoke the meat, not this close to White Murderer Harrison's fort. There wasn't much meat anyway; he ate it all, raw so it took chewing but the flavor was very strong and good. If you can't smoke meat, Red man knows, carry all you can in your belly. He tucked the hide into the waist of his loincloth, hoisted the keg over his shoulder, and started north. The white light was on ahead of him, dream beast calling, dream beast urging him on. I will wake you up, said the dream beast. I will end your dream.

White man heard about dream beasts. White man thought the Red man went out into the forest and had dreams. Stupid White man, never understood. All of life at first is a long sleep, a long dream. You fall asleep at the moment you are born, and never wake up, never wake up until finally one day the dream beast calls you. You go then, into the forest, sometimes only a few steps, sometimes to the edge of the world. You go until you meet the beast who calls you. The beast is not in a dream. The beast wakes you up from the dream. The beast shows you who you are, teaches you your place in the land. Then you go home awake, awake at last, and tell the shaman and your mother and your sisters who the dream beast was. A bear? A badger? A bird? A fish? A hawk or an eagle? A bee or a wasp? The shaman will tell you stories and help you choose your woke-up name. Your mother and sisters will name all your children, whether they have been born yet or not.

All of Lolla-Wossiky's brothers met their dream beasts long ago. Now his mother was dead, his two sisters were gone to live with another tribe. Who would name his children?

I know, said Lolla-Wossiky. I know. Lolla-Wossiky will never have children, this old one-eyed whisky-Red. But Lolla-Wossiky will find his dream beast. Lolla-Wossiky will wake up. Lolla-Wossiky will have his woke-up name.

Then Lolla-Wossiky will see if he should live or die. If the black noise goes on, and waking up teaches him nothing more than he knows now, Lolla-Wossiky will go sleep in the river and let it roll him to the sea, far away from the land and the black noise. But if waking up teaches him some reason to live on, black noise or not, then Lolla-Wossiky will live, many long years of drink and pain, pain and drink.

Lolla-Wossiky drank four swallows every morning, four swallows every night, and then went to sleep hoping that when the dream beast woke him up, he then could die.

One day he stood on the banks of a clearwater stream, with the black noise thick in his vision and loud in his ears. A great brown bear stood in the water. It slapped the face of the water and a fish flew into the air. The bear caught it in his teeth, chomped twice, and swallowed. It was not the eating that Lolla-Wossiky cared about. It was the bear's eyes.

The bear had one eye missing, just like Lolla-Wossiky. This made Lolla-Wossiky wonder if the bear could be his dream beast. But that could not be. The white light that called him was still north and somewhat west of this place. So this bear was not the dream beast, it was part of the dream.

Still, it might have a message for Lolla-Wossiky. This bear might be here because the land wanted to tell Lolla-Wossiky a story.

This is the first thing Lolla-Wossiky noticed: When the bear caught the fish in his jaws, he was looking with his single eye, seeing the glimmer of sunlight shining on the fish. Lolla-Wossiky knew about this, cause Lolla-Wossiky tilted his head to one side just like the bear.

This is the second thing Lolla-Wossiky noticed: When the bear looked into the water to see the fish swimming, so he could slap at it, he looked with the other eye, with the eye that wasn't there. Lolla-Wossiky didn't understand this. It was very strange.

This is the last thing Lolla-Wossiky noticed: As he watched the bear, his own good eye was closed. And when he opened his eye, the river was still there, the sunlight was still there, the fishes still danced into the air and then disappeared, but the bear was gone. Lolla-Wossiky could see the bear only if he closed his good eye.

Lolla-Wossiky drank two swallows from the keg, and the bear went away.

One day Lolla-Wossiky crossed a White man's road, and felt it like a river moving under his feet. The current of the road swept him along. He staggered with it, then caught the stride and jogged along, the keg on his shoulder. A Red man never walked on the White man's road—the dirt was packed too hard in dry weather, mud too deep in rain, and the wagon wheel ruts reached out like White man's hands to turn the Red man's ankle, trip him up, break him down. This time, though, the ground was soft like spring grass on a riverbank, as long as Lolla-Wossiky ran along the road the right direction. Not toward the light anymore, cause the light was soft around him, and he knew the dream beast was very very close.

The road three times went over water—two little streams and a big one—and each time there was a bridge, made of great heavy logs and sturdy planks, with a roof like a White man's house. Lolla-Wossiky stood on the first bridge a long time. He never heard of such a thing. Here he was standing in the place where water was supposed to be, and yet the bridge was so heavy and strong, the walls so thick, that he couldn't see or hear the water at all.

And the river hated it. Lolla-Wossiky could hear how angry it was, how it wanted to reach up and tear the bridge away. White man's ways, thought Lolla-Wossiky, White man has to conquer, tear things away from the land.

Yet standing on the bridge, he noticed something else. Even though the likker was mostly gone from his body, the black noise was quieter on the bridge. He could hear more of the green silence than he had in a long time. As if the black noise came partly from the river. How can that be? River got no anger against Red man. And no White-built thing can bring the Red man closer to the land. Yet that was what happened in this place. Lolla-Wossiky hurried on down the road; maybe when his dream beast woke him up, he'd understand this thing.

Road poured out into a place of meadows and a few White man's buildings. Lots of wagons. Horses posted and tied, grazing on the meadow grass. Sound of metal hammers ringing, chopping of axes in the wood, screech of saws going back and forth, all kinds of White-man forest-killing sounds. A White man's town.

But *not* a White man's town. Lolla-Wossiky stopped at the edge of the open land. Why is this White man's town different, what's missing that I expect to see?

The stockade. There was no stockade.

Where did the White men go to hide? Where did they lock up drunken Reds and White man thieves? Where did they hide their guns?

"Lift! Lift! Lift!" White man's voice ringing out loud as a bell in the thick air of a summer afternoon.

Up a grassy hill, maybe half a mile off, a strange wooden thing was rising up. Lolla-Wossiky couldn't see the men raising it cause the angle was wrong; they were all hid up behind the brow of the hill. But he could see a new-wood frame go up, poles at the high end to raise it into place.

"Side wall now! Lift! Lift! Lift!"

Now another frame rose up, slowly, slowly, sideways to the first. When both frames were standing straight, they met just so along one edge. For the first time Lolla-Wossiky saw men. White boys scrambled up the frames and raised their hammers and brought them down like tommy-hawks to beat the wood into submission. After they pounded for a while, they stood up, three of them, standing on the very top of the wall frames, their hammers raised up high like spears just pulled from the body of the wild buffalo. The poles that had pushed the walls in place were pulled away. The walls stood, holding each other in place. Lolla-Wossiky heard a cheer.

Then suddenly the White men all appeared on the brow of the hill. Did they see me? Will they come to make me go away or lock me up? No, they were just going down the hill to where their horses and their wagons stood. Lolla-Wossiky melted into the woods.

He drank four swallows from the keg, then climbed into a tree and settled the keg into a place where three thick branches split apart. Nice and tight, nice and safe. Leaves nice and thick; nobody see it from the ground, not even Red man.

Lolla-Wossiky took the long way round, but pretty soon there he was on the hill where the new walls stood. Lolla-Wossiky looked a long time, but he couldn't understand what this building was going to be. It was the new way of building, those frame walls, like White Murderer Harrison's new mansion, but it was very big. Bigger than anything Lolla-Wossiky ever saw White men build, taller than the stockade.

First the strange bridges, tight as houses. Now this strange building, tall as trees. Lolla-Wossiky walked out from the shelter of the forest onto the open meadow, rocking back and forth because the ground never stayed level when he had likker in him. When he reached the building, he stepped up onto the wooden floor. White man's floor, White man's walls, but it didn't feel like any White man building Lolla-Wossiky ever saw. Big open space inside. Walls very high. First time ever he saw White man build something that wasn't closed in and dark. In this place a Red man still maybe glad to be here.

"Who's that? Who are you?"

Lolla-Wossiky turned around so fast he almost fell. A tall White man stood at the edge of the building. The floor was up so high it met this man at the waist. He wasn't in buckskin like a hunter, or in uniform like a soldier. He was dressed like a farmer maybe, only he was clean. In fact Lolla-Wossiky never saw such a man in Carthage City.

"Who are you?" demanded the man again.

"Red man," said Lolla-Wossiky.

"It's getting on dusk, but it sure ain't night yet. I'd have to be blind not to know you're Red. But I know the Reds close by and you ain't from around here."

Lolla-Wossiky laughed. What White man ever knew one Red from another so well he could say who was from close by and who was from far away?

"You got a name, Red man?"

"Lolla-Wossiky."

"You're likkered, ain't you. I can smell it, and you don't walk too good."

"Very likkered. Whisky-Red."

"Who gave you that likker! You tell me! Where'd you get that likker?"

Lolla-Wossiky was confused. White man never asked him where he got his likker before. White man always knew. "From White Murderer Harrison," he said.

"Harrison's two hundred miles southeast of here. What did you call him?"

"Governor Bill Harrison."

"You called him White Murderer Harrison."

"This Red *very* drunk."

"I can see *that*. But you sure didn't get drunk at Fort Carthage and then walk all this way without sobering up. Now where'd you get that likker?"

"You going to lock me up?"

"Lock you—now where would I lock you up, tell me that? You really *are* from Fort Carthage, aren't you. Well, I'll tell you, Mr. Lolla-Wossiky, we got no place to lock up drunk Reds around here, cause around here Reds don't get drunk. And if they do, we find the White man who gave him likker and that White man gets a flogging. So you tell me right now where you got that likker.''

"My whisky,'' said Lolla-Wossiky.

"Maybe you better come with me.''

"Lock me up?''

"I told you, we don't—listen, you hungry?''

"Reckon so,'' said Lolla-Wossiky.

"You got a place to eat?''

"Eat wherever I am.''

"Well, tonight you come on down and eat at my house.''

Lolla-Wossiky didn't know what to say. Was this a White man joke? White man jokes were very hard to understand.

"Aren't you hungry?''

"Reckon so,'' said Lolla-Wossiky again.

"Well, come on, then!''

Another White man came up the hill. "Armor-of-God!'' he called. "Your good wife wondered where you were.''

"Just a minute, Reverend Thrower. I think maybe we got us company for supper.''

"Who is that? Why, Armor-of-God, I daresay that's a Red.''

"He says his name's Lolla-Wossiky. He's a Shaw-Nee. He's also drunk as a skunk.''

Lolla-Wossiky was very surprised. This White man knew he was a Shaw-Nee without asking. From his hair, plucked out except the tall strip down the middle? Other Reds did this. The fringe on his loincloth? White man never saw these things.

"A Shaw-Nee,'' said the new-come White man. "Aren't they a particularly savage tribe?''

"Well, now, I don't know, Reverend Thrower,'' said Armor-of-God. "What they are is a particularly *sober* tribe. By which I mean they don't get so likkered as some of these others. Some folks think that the only safe Red is a whisky-Red, so they see all these sober Shaw-Nee and they think that makes them dangerous.''

"This one seems not to have that problem.''

"I know. I tried to find out who gave him his whisky, and he won't tell me.''

Reverend Thrower addressed Lolla-Wossiky. "Don't you know that whisky is the devil's tool and the downfall of the Red man?''

"I don't think he talks English enough to know what you're talking about, Reverend.''

"Likker very bad for Red man,'' said Lolla-Wossiky.

"Well, maybe he *does* understand,'' said Armor-of-God, chuckling.

"Lolla-Wossiky, if you know how bad likker is, how come you stink of cheap whisky like an Irish barroom?"

"Likker very bad for Red man," said Lolla-Wossiky, "but Red man thirsty all the time."

"There's a simple scientific explanation for that," said Reverend Thrower. "Europeans have had alcoholic beverages for so long that they've built up a tolerance. Europeans who desperately hunger for alcohol tend to die younger, have fewer children, provide less well for those children they do have. The result is that most Europeans have a resistance to alcohol built into them. But you Reds have never built up that tolerance."

"Very damn right," said Lolla-Wossiky. "True-talking White man, how come White Murderer Harrison not kill you yet?"

"Well, now, will you listen to that," said Armor-of-God. "That's the second time he called Harrison a murderer."

"He also swore, which I do not appreciate."

"If he's from Carthage, he learned to talk English from a class of White man that thinks words like 'damn' are punctuation, if you catch my drift, Reverend. But listen, Lolla-Wossiky. This man here, he's Reverend Philadelphia Thrower, and he's a minister of the Lord Jesus Christ, so mind you don't use no bad language around him."

Lolla-Wossiky hadn't the faintest idea what a minister was—there was no such thing in Carthage City. The best he could think of was that a minister was like a governor, only nicer.

"Will you live in this very big house?"

"Live here?" asked Thrower. "Oh, no. This is the Lord's house."

"Who?"

"The Lord Jesus Christ."

Lolla-Wossiky had heard of Jesus Christ. White man called out that name all the time, mostly when they were angry or lying. "Very angry man," said Lolla-Wossiky. "He live here?"

"Jesus Christ is a loving and forgiving Lord," said Reverend Thrower. "He won't live here the way a White man lives in a house. But when good Christians want to worship—to sing hymns and pray and hear the word of the Lord—we'll come together in this place. It's a church, or it will be."

"Jesus Christ talks here?" Lolla-Wossiky thought it might be interesting to meet this very important White man face to face.

"Oh, no, not in person. I speak *for* him."

From below the hill came a woman's voice. "Armor! Armor Weaver!"

Armor-of-God came alert. "Supper's ready, and there she is calling out, she hates when she has to do that. Come on, Lolla-Wossiky. Drunk or not, if you want supper you can come and get it.''

''I hope you will,'' said Reverend Thrower. ''And when supper is done, I hope to be able to teach you the words of the Lord Jesus.''

''Very most first thing,'' said Lolla-Wossiky. ''You promise not to lock me up. I don't want lock-up, I got to find dream beast.''

''We won't lock you up. You can walk out of my house any time.'' Armor-of-God turned to Reverend Thrower. ''You can see what these Reds learn about White men from William Henry Harrison. Likker and lock-ups.''

''I am more moved by his pagan beliefs. A dream beast! Is this their idea of gods?''

''The dream beast isn't God, it's an animal they dream about that teaches them things,'' explained Armor. ''They always take a long journey till they have the dream and come home. That explains what he's doing two hundred miles from the main Shaw-Nee settlements on the lower My-Ammy.''

''Dream beast *real*,'' said Lolla-Wossiky.

''Right,'' said Armor-of-God. Lolla-Wossiky knew he was saying that only to avoid offending him.

''This poor creature is obviously in dire need of the gospel of Jesus,'' said Thrower.

''Looks to me like he's in more need of supper at the moment. Gospel is learned best on a full belly, wouldn't you say?''

Thrower chuckled. ''I don't think it says that anywhere in the Bible, Armor-of-God, but I dare say you're correct.''

Armor-of-God put his hands on his hips and asked Lolla-Wossiky again. ''You coming or not?''

''Reckon so,'' said Lolla-Wossiky.

Lolla-Wossiky's belly was full, but it was White man's food, soft and smooth and overcooked, and it grumbled inside him. Thrower went on and on with very strange words. The stories were good, but Thrower kept going on about original sin and redemption. One time when Lolla-Wossiky thought he understood, he said, ''What a silly god, he makes everybody born bad to go to burning hell. Why so mad? All his fault!'' But this made Thrower get very upset and talk longer and faster, so after that Lolla-Wossiky did not offer any of his thoughts.

The black noise came back louder and louder the more Thrower talked. Whisky wearing off? It was very quick for the likker to go out of him. And when Thrower left one time to go empty himself, the black noise got quieter. Very strange—Lolla-Wossiky never before noticed anybody making the black noise louder or softer by coming or going.

But maybe that was because he was here in the dream beast place. He knew this was the place because the white light was all around him when he looked, and he couldn't see where to go. Don't be surprised at bridges that make black noise soft and White minister who makes black noise loud. Don't be surprised at Armor-of-God with his land-face picture who feeds Red man and doesn't sell likker or even give likker.

While Thrower was outside, Armor-of-God showed Lolla-Wossiky the map. "This is a picture of the whole land around here. Up to the northwest, there's the big lake—the Kicky-Poo call it Fat Water. Right there, Fort Chicago—it's a French outpost."

"French. One cup of whisky for a White man scalp."

"That's the going rate, all right," said Armor-of-God. "But the Reds around here don't take scalps. They trade fair with me, and I trade fair with them, and we don't go shooting down Reds and they don't go killing White folks for the bounty. You understand me? You start getting thirsty, you think about this: There was a whisky-Red from the Wee-Aw tribe here some four year back, he killed him a little Danish boy out in the woods. Do you think it was White men tracked him down? Reckon not; you know a White man's got no hope to find no Red in these woods, specially not farmers and such like us. No, it was Shaw-Nee and Otty-Wa who found him two hours after the boy turned up missing. And do you think it was White men punished that whisky-Red? Reckon not; they set that Wee-Aw down and said, 'You want to show brave?' and when he said yes, they took six hours killing him."

"Very kind," said Lolla-Wossiky.

"*Kind?* I reckon not," said Armor-of-God.

"Red man kills White boy for whisky, I never let him show brave, he die—uh! Like that, quick like rattlesnake, no man him."

"I got to say you Reds think real strange," said Armor. "You mean it's a favor when you torture somebody to death?"

"Not *somebody.* Enemy. Catch enemy, he shows brave before he dies so then his spirit flies back to home. Tell his mother and sisters he died brave, they sing songs and scream for him. He doesn't show brave, then his spirit falls flat on the dirt and you step on him, grind him in, he never goes home, nobody remembers his name."

"It's a good thing Thrower's out at the privy right now, or I reckon he'd wet his pants over *that* doctrine." Armor squinted at Lolla-Wossiky. "You mean they *honored* that Wee-Aw who killed that little boy?"

"Very bad thing, killing little boy. But maybe Red man knows about whisky-Red, very thirsty, making crazy. Not like killing man to take his house or his woman or his land, like White man all the time."

"I got to say, the more I learn about you Reds, the more it kind of starts to make sense. I better read the Bible more every night before I turn Red myself."

Lolla-Wossiky laughed and laughed.

"What's so funny?"

"Many Red men turn White and then die. But never does a White man turn Red. I have to tell this story, everybody laugh."

"You Reds have a sense of humor like I just don't understand." Armor patted the map. "Here's us, right here just downriver from where the Tippy-Canoe flows into the Wobbish. All these dots, they're White man's farms. And these circles, they're Red villages. This one's Shaw-Nee, this one's Winny-Baygo, see how it goes?"

"White Murderer Harrison tells Reds that you make this land-face picture so you can find Red villages. Killing everybody, he says."

"Well, that's just the kind of lie I'd expect him to tell. So you heard about me afore you came up here, did you? Well, I hope you don't believe his lies."

"Oh, no. Nobody believes White Murderer Harrison."

"Good thing."

"Nobody believes any White man. All lies."

"Well, not me, you understand that? Not me. Harrison wants to be governor so bad that he'll tell any lie he can to get power and keep it."

"He says you want to be governor, too."

Armor paused at that. Looked at the map. Looked at the door to the kitchen, where his wife was washing up. "Well, I reckon he didn't lie about that. But my idea of what it means to be governor and his are two different things. I want to be governor so Red men and White men can live together in peace here, farming the land side by side, going to the same schools so someday there ain't no difference between Red and White. But Harrison, he wants to get rid of the Red man altogether."

If you make the Red man just like the White man, then he won't be Red no more. Harrison's way or Armor's way, you end up with no Red men at the end. Lolla-Wossiky thought of this, but he didn't say it. He knew that even though turning all the Red men White would be very bad, killing them all with likker the way Harrison planned, or killing them and driving them off the land the way Jackson planned, those were even worse. Harrison was a very bad man. Armor wanted to be a good man, he just didn't know how. Lolla-Wossiky understood this, so he didn't argue with Armor-of-God.

Armor went on showing him the map. "Down here's Fort Carthage, it's got a square, cause it's a town. I put a square for us, too, even though we're not rightly a town yet. We're calling it Vigor Church, on account of that church we're building."

"Church for building. Why Vigor?"

"Oh, the first folks settled here, the ones who cut the road and made the bridges, the Miller family. They live on up behind the church, way along the road there. My wife is their oldest girl, in fact. They named this place Vigor on account of their oldest son was named Vigor. He drowned in the Hatrack River clear back near Suskwahenny, on their way coming here. So they named the place after him."

"Your wife, very pretty," said Lolla-Wossiky.

It took Armor just a few seconds to answer that, he looked so surprised. And in the shop in back, where they ate the meal, his wife Eleanor must have been listening, cause she was suddenly standing there in the doorway.

"Nobody ever called me pretty," she said softly.

Lolla-Wossiky was baffled. Most White women had narrow faces, no cheekbones, sick-looking skin. Eleanor was darker, wide-faced, high cheekbones.

"I think you're pretty," said Armor. "I really do."

Lolla-Wossiky didn't believe him, and neither did Eleanor, though she smiled and went away from the door. He never had thought she was pretty, that was plain. And after a moment, Lolla-Wossiky understood why. She was pretty like a *Red* woman. So naturally White men who never saw straight thought her pretty was very ugly.

This also meant that Armor-of-God was married to a woman he thought was ugly. But he didn't shout at her or hit her, like a Red man with an ugly squaw. This was a good thing, Lolla-Wossiky decided.

"You very happy," said Lolla-Wossiky.

"That's because we're Christians," said Armor-of-God. "You'd be happy, too, if you was Christian."

"I won't never be happy," said Lolla-Wossiky. He meant to say, "Till I hear green silence again, till black noise goes away." But no use saying that to a White man, they didn't know that half the things going on in the world were plain invisible to them.

"Yes you will," said Thrower. He strode into the room with all kinds of energy, ready to tackle this heathen all over again. "You accept Jesus Christ as your savior, and you will have true happiness."

Now, that was a promise worth looking into. That was a good reason to talk about this Jesus Christ. Maybe Jesus Christ was Lolla-Wossiky's dream beast. Maybe he would make the black noise go away and make

Lolla-Wossiky happy again like he was before White Murderer Harrison blew up the world with black noise from his gun.

"Jesus Christ makes me wake up?" asked Lolla-Wossiky.

"Come follow me, he said, and I will make you fishers of men," answered Thrower.

"He waking me up? He making me happy?"

"Eternal joy, in the bosom of the Heavenly Father," said Thrower.

None of this made any sense, but Lolla-Wossiky decided to go ahead anyway on the chance that it would wake him up and *then* he'd understand what Thrower was talking about. Even though Thrower made the black noise louder, maybe he also had the cure for it.

So that night Lolla-Wossiky slept out in the woods, took his four swallows of whisky in the morning, and staggered on up to the church. Thrower was annoyed that Lolla-Wossiky was drunk, and Armor once again insisted on knowing who gave him likker. Since all the other men who were doing the church-raising were gathered around, Armor made a speech, with a whole bunch of threats in it. "If I find out who's likkering up these Reds, I swear I'll burn his house down and make him go live with Harrison down on the Hio. Up here we're Christian folk. Now I can't stop you from putting those hexes on your houses and making those spells and conjures, even though they show lack of faith in the Lord, but I *sure* can stop you from poisoning the folk that the Lord saw fit to put on this land. Do you understand me?"

All the White folk nodded and said yes and that's right and reckon so.

"Nobody here gave me whisky," said Lolla-Wossiky.

"Maybe he carried it with him in a cup!" said one of the men.

"Maybe he's got him a still in the woods!" said another.

They all laughed.

"Please be reverent," said Thrower. "This heathen is accepting the Lord Jesus Christ. He shall be covered with the water of baptism as was Jesus himself. Let this mark the beginning of a great missionary labor among the Red men of the American forest!"

Amen, murmured the men.

Well, the water was cold, and that's about all Lolla-Wossiky noticed, except that when Thrower sprinkled it on him the black noise just got louder. Jesus Christ didn't show up, so he wasn't the dream beast after all. Lolla-Wossiky was disappointed.

But Reverend Thrower wasn't. That was the strange thing about White men. They just seemed not to notice what went on around them. Here Thrower performed a baptism that didn't do a lick of good, and he went strutting around the rest of the day like he had just called a buffalo into a starving village in the dead of winter.

Armor-of-God was just as blind. At noon, when Eleanor brought dinner up the hill to the workmen, they let Lolla-Wossiky eat with them. "Can't turn away a Christian, can we?" said one. But none of them was too happy about sitting next to Lolla-Wossiky, probably because he stank of liquor and sweat and he staggered when he walked. It ended up that Armor-of-God sat with Lolla-Wossiky off a ways from the others, and they talked about this and that.

Till Lolla-Wossiky asked him, "Jesus Christ, he don't like hexes?"

"That's right. *He* is the way, and all this beseeching and suchlike is blasphemy."

Lolla-Wossiky nodded gravely. "Painted hex no good. Paint never was alive."

"Painted, carved, same thing."

"Wooden hex, a little strong. Tree used to be alive."

"Doesn't matter to me, wooden or painted, I won't have no hexes in my house. No conjures, no come-hithers, no fendings, no wardings, none of that stuff. A good Christian relies on prayer, and that's that. The Lord is my shepherd, I shall not want."

Lolla-Wossiky knew then that Armor-of-God was just as blind as Thrower. Because Armor-of-God's house was the strongest-hexed house Lolla-Wossiky ever saw. That was part of the reason Lolla-Wossiky was impressed with Armor, that his house was actually well protected, because he understood enough to make his hexes out of living things. Arrangements of living plants hanging on the porch, seeds with the life in them sitting in carefully placed jars, garlics, stains of berry juices, all so strongly placed that even with the likker in him to dull the black noise, Lolla-Wossiky could feel the pushing and pulling of the fendings and wardings and hexes.

Yet Armor-of-God didn't have the faintest idea that his house had any hexes at all. "My wife Eleanor, her folks always had hexes. Her little brother Al Junior, he's that six-year-old wrassling with the blond-headed Swedish boy there—see him? He's a real hex-carver, they say."

Lolla-Wossiky looked at the boy, but couldn't exactly see him. He saw the yellow-hair boy he was tussling with, but the other boy just couldn't come clear for him, he didn't know why.

Armor was still talking. "Don't that make you sick? That young, and already he's being turned away from Jesus. Anyway, it was real hard for Eleanor to give up those hexes and such. But she did it. Gave me her solemn oath, or we never would've got married."

At that moment Eleanor, the pretty wife that White men thought was ugly, came up to take away the dinner basket. She heard the last words that her husband said, but she gave no sign that it meant anything to her. Except that when she took Lolla-Wossiky's bowl from him, and looked him in the eye, he felt like she was asking him. Did you see those hexes?

Lolla-Wossiky smiled at her, his biggest smile, so she'd know he didn't have any plan to tell her husband.

She smiled back, hesitantly, untrustingly. "Did you like the food?" she asked him.

"Everything cooked too much," said Lolla-Wossiky. "Blood taste all gone."

Her eyes went wide. Armor only laughed and clapped Lolla-Wossiky on the shoulder. "Well, that's what it means to be civilized. You give up drinking blood, and that's a fact. I hope your baptism sets you on the right road—it's plain you've been a long time on the wrong one."

"I wondered," said Eleanor—and she stopped, glanced down at Lolla-Wossiky's loincloth, and then looked at her husband.

"Oh, yes, we talked about that last night. I've got some old trousers and a shirt I don't use anymore, and Eleanor's making me new ones anyway, so I thought, now that you're baptized, you really ought to start dressing like a Christian."

"Very hot day," said Lolla-Wossiky.

"Yes, well, Christians believe in modesty of dress, Lolla-Wossiky." Armor laughed and hit him on the shoulder again.

"I can bring the clothes up this afternoon," said Eleanor.

Lolla-Wossiky thought this was a very stupid idea. Red men always looked stupid dressed in White man's clothes. But he didn't want to argue with them because they were trying to be very friendly. And maybe the baptism would work after all, if he put on White man's clothes. Maybe then the black noise would go away.

So he didn't answer. He just looked at where the yellow-hair boy was running around in circles, shouting, "Alvin! Ally!" Lolla-Wossiky tried very hard to see the boy that he was chasing. He saw a foot touching the ground and raising dust, a hand moving through the air, but never quite saw the boy himself. Very strange thing.

Eleanor was waiting for him to answer. Lolla-Wossiky said nothing, since he was now watching the boy who wasn't there. Finally Armor-of-God laughed and said, "Bring the clothes up, Eleanor. We'll dress him like a Christian, all right, and maybe tomorrow he can lend a hand on building the church, start learning a Christian trade. Get a saw into his hand."

Lolla-Wossiky didn't actually hear that last, or he might have taken off into the woods right away. He had seen what happened to Red men who started using White man's tools. The way they got cut off from the land, bit by bit, every time they hefted that metal. Even guns. A Red man starts using guns for hunting, he's half White the first time he pulls the trigger; only thing a Red man can use a gun for is killing White men, that's what Ta-Kumsaw always said, and he was right. But Lolla-Wossiky didn't hear Armor talk about wanting Lolla-Wossiky to use a saw because he had just made the most remarkable discovery. When he closed his good eye, he could see that boy. Just like the one-eyed bear in the river. Open his eye, and there was the yellow-head boy chasing and shouting, but no Alvin Miller Junior. Close his eye, and there was nothing but the black noise and the traces of the green—and then, right in the middle, there was the boy, bright and shining with light as if he had the sun in his back pocket, laughing and playing with a voice like music.

And then he didn't see him at all.

Lolla-Wossiky opened his eye. There was Reverend Thrower. Armor and Eleanor were gone—all the men were back to work on the church. It was Thrower who made the boy disappear, that was plain enough. Or maybe not—because now, with Thrower standing by him, Lolla-Wossiky could see the boy with his good eye. Just like any other child.

"Lolla-Wossiky, it occurs to me that you really ought to have a Christian name. I've never baptized a Red before, and so I just thoughtlessly used your uncivilized nomenclature. You're supposed to take a new name, a Christian name. Not necessarily a saint's name—we're not Papists—but something to suggest your new commitment to Christ."

Lolla-Wossiky nodded. He knew he would need a new name, if the baptism turned out to work after all. Once he met his dream beast and went back home, he would get a name. He tried to explain this to Thrower, but the White minister didn't really understand. Finally, though, he grasped the idea that Lolla-Wossiky *wanted* a new name and meant to get one soon, so he was mollified.

"While we're both right here, by the way," said Thrower, "I wondered if I might examine your head. I am working on developing some orderly categorizations for the infant science of phrenology. It is the idea that particular talents and propensities in the human soul are reflected in or perhaps even caused by protuberances and depressions in the shape of the skull."

Lolla-Wossiky didn't have any idea what Thrower was talking about, so he nodded silently. This usually worked with White men who were talking nonsense, and Thrower was no exception. The end of it was that Thrower felt all over Lolla-Wossiky's head, stopping now and then to make sketches and notes on a piece of paper, muttering things like "Interesting," "Ha!" and "So much for *that* theory." When it was over, Thrower thanked him. "You've contributed greatly to the cause of science, Mr. Wossiky. You are living proof that a Red man does not necessarily have the bumps of savagery and cannibalism. Instead you have the normal array of knacks and lacks that any human has. Red men are not intrinsically different from White men, at least not in any simple, easily categorized way. In fact, you have every sign of being quite a remarkable speaker, with a profoundly developed sense of religion. It is no accident that you are the first Red man to accept the gospel in my ministry here in America. I must say that your phrenological pattern has many great similarities to my own. In short, my dear new-baptized Christian, I would not be surprised if you ended up being a missionary of the gospel yourself. Preaching to great multitudes of Red men and women and bringing them to an understanding of heaven. Contemplate that vision, Mr. Wossiky. If I am not mistaken, it is your future."

Lolla-Wossiky barely caught the gist of what Thrower said. Something about him being a preacher. Something about telling the future. Lolla-Wossiky tried to make sense of this, but it didn't work.

By nightfall, Lolla-Wossiky was dressed in White man's clothes, looking like a fool. His likker had worn off and he hadn't had a chance to dodge back into the woods and get his four swallows, so the black noise was getting very bad. Worse yet, it looked to be a rainy night, so he couldn't see with his eye, and with the black noise as bad as it was, his land sense couldn't lead him to his keg, either.

The result was that he was staggering worse than when he had likker in him, the ground heaved and tossed so much under his feet. He fell over trying to get out of his chair at Armor's supper table. Eleanor insisted that he had to spend the night there. "We can't have him sleep in the woods, not when it rains," she said, and as if to buttress her point there was a clap of thunder and rain started pelting the roof and walls. Eleanor made up a bed on the floor of the kitchen while Thrower and Armor went around the house closing shutters. Gratefully Lolla-Wossiky crawled to the bed, not even removing the stiff uncomfortable trousers and shirt, and lay down, his eye closed, trying to endure the stabbing in his head, the pain of the black noise like knives cutting out his brain slice by slice.

As usual, they thought he was asleep.

"He seems drunker than he did this morning," said Thrower.

"I know he never left the hill," said Armor. "There's not a chance he got a drink anywhere."

"I've heard it said that when a drunk becomes sober," said Thrower, "at first he acts more drunk than when he has alcohol in him."

"I hope that's all it is," said Armor.

"I daresay he was somewhat disappointed at the baptism today," said Thrower. "Of course it's impossible to understand what a savage is feeling, but—"

"I wouldn't call him a savage, Reverend Thrower," said Eleanor. "I think in his own way he's civilized."

"You might as well call a badger civilized, then," said Thrower. "In his own *way*, anyway."

"I mean to say," Eleanor said, her voice even quieter and meeker-sounding, but therefore carrying all the more weight, "that I saw him reading."

"Turning pages you mean," said Thrower. "He couldn't be *reading*."

"No. He read, and his lips formed the words," she said. "The signs on the wall in the front room, where we serve customers. He read the words."

"It's possible, you know," said Armor. "I know for a fact that the Irrakwa read just as good as any White men. I been there to do business often enough, and you can bet you have to read the fine print on the contracts they write up. Red men can learn to read, and that's a fact."

"But this one, this drunk—"

"Who knows what he can become, when the likker ain't in him?" said Eleanor.

Then they went away to the other room, and left the house for a while, walking Thrower home to the cabin he was staying in before the rain got so bad he had to stay the night.

Alone in the house, Lolla-Wossiky tried to make sense of things. Baptism alone hadn't wakened him from his dream. Nor had White man's clothes. Maybe going without likker for a night would do it, like Eleanor suggested, though it made him crazy with pain so he couldn't sleep.

Whatever happened, though, he knew that the dream beast was waiting somewhere near here. The white light was suffused all around him now; this was the waking place for Lolla-Wossiky. Maybe if he stayed away from the church hill today, maybe if he wandered in the woods around Vigor Church, then the dream beast could find him.

One thing was sure. He wasn't going to spend another night without whisky. Not when he had a keg out in a crotch of a tree that could take away the black noise and let him sleep.

* * *

Lolla-Wossiky walked everywhere in the woods. He saw many animals, but they all ran from him; he was so drunk or so bound up in the black noise that he never was part of the land, and they ran from him just as if he were White.

Discouraged, he began to drink more than four swallows, even though he knew he would run out of whisky too fast. He walked less and less in the forest, more and more along the White man's paths and roads, showing up at farmhouses in the middle of the day. The women sometimes screamed and ran away, carrying a baby and leading children off into the woods. Other women pointed guns at him and made him leave. Some of them fed him and talked about Jesus Christ. Finally Armor-of-God told him not to visit the farms when the men were away, working on the church.

So there was nothing left for Lolla-Wossiky to do. He knew he was close to the dream beast, but he couldn't find it. He couldn't walk in the forest because the animals ran from him and he stumbled and fell all the time, more and more, until he feared he might break a bone and die of starvation because he couldn't even call small animals to feed him. He couldn't visit the farms because the men were angry. So he lay on the commons, sleeping from drunkenness or trying to endure the pain of the black noise, one or the other.

Sometimes he worked up the energy to go up the hill and see the men working on the church. Whenever he got there, some man would call out, "Here comes the Red Christian!" and Lolla-Wossiky knew that there was malice and ridicule in the voices that said it and the voices that laughed.

He was not at the church the day the roof-beam fell. He was sleeping on the grass of the commons, near the porch of Armor's house, when he heard the crash. It startled him awake, and the black noise came back harsher than ever, even though he had drunk eight swallows that morning and ought to be drunk till noon. He lay there holding his head until men started coming down from the hill, cursing and muttering about the strange thing that happened.

"What happened?" Lolla-Wossiky asked. He had to know, because whatever it was, it had made the black noise worse than it had been in years. "Was a man killed?" He knew that a gunshot made the black noise in the first place. "Did White Murderer Harrison shoot somebody?"

At first they paid him no attention, because they thought he was drunk, of course. But finally someone told him what happened.

They had been laying the first ridgebeam in place, high on top of the building, when the central ridgepole shivered and tossed the ridgebeam up in the air. "Came down flat, just like God's own foot stepping on the earth, and wouldn't you know, there was that little Alvin Junior, Al Miller's boy, right under the beam. Well, we thought he was dead. The boy just stood there, the beam landed smack—you must have heard the noise, that's why it sounded like a gun to you—but you won't believe this. That ridgebeam split right in half, right in the very place where Alvin was standing, split right in two and landed on this side and that side of him, didn't touch a hair on his head."

"Something strange about that boy," said a man.

"He's got a guardian angel, that's what he's got," said another.

Alvin Junior. The boy he couldn't see with his eye open.

There was no one at the church when Lolla-Wossiky got there. The ridgebeam was also gone, everything swept out, no sign of the accident. But Lolla-Wossiky was not looking with his eye. He could feel it, almost as soon as he got within sight of the church. A whirlpool, not fast at the edges, but stronger and stronger the closer he came. A whirlwind of light, and the closer he got, the weaker the black noise became. Until he stood on the church floor, in the spot that he knew was where the boy was standing. How did he know? The black noise was quieter. Not gone, the pain not healed, but Lolla-Wossiky could feel the green land again, just a little, not like it used to be, but he could feel the small life under the floor, a squirrel in the meadow not far off, things he hadn't felt, drunk or sober, in all the years since the gun blew the black noise into his head.

Lolla-Wossiky turned around and around, seeing nothing but the walls of the church. Until he closed his eye. Then he saw the whirlwind, yes, white light spinning and spinning around him, and the black noise retreating. He was in the end of his own dream now, and he could see with his eye closed, see clearly. There was a shining path ahead of him, a road as bright as the noonday sky, dazzling like meadow snow on a clear day. He knew already, without opening his eye to see, where the path would lead. Up the hill, down the other side, up a higher hill, to a house not far from a stream, a house where lived a White boy who was only visible to Lolla-Wossiky with his eye closed.

His silent step had returned to him, now that the black noise had backed off a bit. He walked around the house, around and around. No one heard him. Inside laughter, shouting, screaming. Happy children, quarreling children. Stern voices of parents. Except for the language, it could be his village. His own sisters and brothers in the happy days before White Murderer Harrison took his father's life.

The White father, Alvin Miller, came out to the privy. Not long after, the boy himself came, running, as if he was afraid. He shouted at the privy door. With his eye open, Lolla-Wossiky only knew that someone was standing there, shouting. With his eye closed, he saw the boy clearly, radiant, and heard his voice like birdsong across a river, all music, even though what he said was silly, foolish, like a child.

"If you don't come out I'll do it right in front of the door so you'll step in it when you come out!"

Then silence, as the boy grew more worried, hitting himself on the top of his head with his own fist, as if to say, Stupid, stupid, stupid. Something changed in Al Junior's expression; Lolla-Wossiky opened his eye to see that the father had come out, was saying something.

The boy answered him, ashamed. The father corrected him. Lolla-Wossiky closed his eye.

"Yes sir," said the boy.

Again the father must be speaking, but with his eye closed Lolla-Wossiky did not hear the father.

"Sorry, Papa."

Then the father must have walked away, because little Alvin went into the privy. Muttering, so soft no one could hear. But Lolla-Wossiky heard. "Well, if you'd just build another outhouse I'd be fine."

Lolla-Wossiky laughed. Foolish boy, foolish father, like all boys, like all fathers.

The boy finished and went into the house.

Here I am, said Lolla-Wossiky silently. I followed the shining path, I came to this place, I saw silly White family things; now where is my dream beast?

And again he saw the white light gather, inside the house, following the boy up the stairs. For Lolla-Wossiky there were no walls. He saw the boy being very careful, as if he were watching for an enemy, for some attack. When he reached the bedroom he ducked inside, closed his door quickly behind him. Lolla-Wossiky saw him so clearly that he thought he could almost hear his thoughts; and then, because he thought it, and because this was near the end of his dream, almost to the time of waking, he *did* hear the boy's thoughts, or at least felt his feelings. It was his sisters he was afraid of. A silly quarrel, begun with teasing, but malicious now—he was afraid of their vengeance.

It came as he stripped off his clothes and pulled his nightshirt over his head. Stinging! Insects, thought the boy. Spiders, scorpions, tiny snakes! He pulled the nightshirt off, slapped himself, cried out from the pain, the surprise, the fear.

But Lolla-Wossiky could feel the land well enough to know there were no insects. Not on his body, not in the shirt. Though there were many living creatures there. Small life, little animals. Roaches, hundreds of them living in the walls and floors.

Not in *all* the walls and floors, though. Just in Alvin Junior's room. All gathered to his room.

Was it enmity? Roaches were too small for hate. They knew only three feelings, those little creatures. Fear, hunger, and the third sense, the land sense. The trust in how things ought to be. Did the boy feed them? No. They came to him for the other thing. Lolla-Wossiky could hardly believe it, but he felt it in the roaches and couldn't doubt. The boy had called them somehow. The boy had the land sense, at least enough to call these small creatures.

Call them why? Who wanted roaches? But he was only a boy. There didn't have to be sense in it. Just the discovery that the little life would come when you called it. Red boys learned this, but always with their father or a brother, always out on the first hunt. Kneel and speak silently to the life you need to take, and ask it if this is a good time, and if it is willing to die to make your life strong. Is it your time to die? asks the Red boy. And if the life consents, it will come.

This is what the boy did. Except it wasn't so simple. He didn't call the roaches to die for his need, because he had no need. No, he called them and kept them safe. He protected them. It was like a treaty. There were certain places the roaches didn't go. Into Alvin's bed. Into his little brother Calvin's cradle. Into Alvin's clothing, folded on the stool. And in return Alvin never killed them. They were safe in his room. It was a sanctuary, a reserve. A very silly thing, a child playing with things he didn't understand.

But the marvel of it was—this was a White boy, doing something beyond even a Red man's reach. When did the Red man ever say to the bear, come and live with me and I will keep you safe? When did the bear ever believe such a thing? No wonder the light was centered on this boy. This wasn't the foolish knack of the White man Hooch, or even the strong living hexes of the woman Eleanor. This wasn't the Red man's power to fit himself into the pattern of the land. No, Alvin didn't fit himself into anything. The land fit itself to him. If he wanted the roaches to live a certain way, to make a bargain, then that was how the land ordered itself. In this small place, for this time, with these tiny lives, Alvin Junior had commanded and the land obeyed.

Did the boy understand how miraculous this was?

No, no, he had no idea. How could he know? What White man could even understand it?

And now, because he didn't understand, Alvin Junior was destroying the delicate thing that he had done. The insects that had bitten him were metal pins that his sisters had poked into his nightshirt. Now he could hear them laughing behind their wall. Because he had been very frightened, now he was very angry. Get even, get back at them; Lolla-Wossiky could feel his childish rage. He only did one little thing to tease them, and they pay him back by scaring him, poking him a hundred times and making him bleed. Get even, give them such a scare—

Alvin Junior sat on the edge of the bed, angrily taking the pins out of his nightshirt, saving them—White men were so careful with all their useless metal tools, even such tiny ones as those. As he sat there he saw the roaches scurrying along the walls, running in and out of cracks in the floor, and he saw his vengeance.

Lolla-Wossiky felt him making the plan in his mind. Then Alvin knelt on the floor and explained it softly to the roaches. Because he was a child, and a White boy with no one to teach him, Alvin thought he had to say the words aloud, that the roaches somehow understood his language. But no—it was the order of things, the way he arranged the world in his mind.

And in his mind he lied to them. Hunger, he told them. And in the other room, food. He showed them food if they went under the wall into the sisters' room and climbed on the beds and the bodies there. Food if they hurried, food for all of them. It was a lie, and Lolla-Wossiky wanted to shout at him not to do this.

If a Red man knelt and called to prey that he didn't need, the prey would know his lie and wouldn't come. The lie itself would cut the Red man from the land, make him walk alone awhile. But this White boy could lie with such force and strength that the tiny minds of the roaches believed him. They scurried, a hundred, a thousand of them under the walls, into the other room.

Alvin Junior heard something, and he was delighted. But Lolla-Wossiky was angry. He opened his eye, so he didn't have to see Alvin Junior's glee at his revenge. Instead now he heard the sisters screaming as the roaches climbed all over them. And then the parents and brothers rushing into their room. And the stomping. The stomping, the smashing, the murders of the roaches. Lolla-Wossiky closed his eye and felt the deaths, each one a pinprick. It had been so long with the black noise masking all the deaths behind one vast memory of murder that Lolla-Wossiky had forgotten what the small pains felt like.

Like the death of bees.

Roaches, useless animals, eating up garbage, making filthy rustling noises in their dens, loathsome when they crawled on the skin; but part of the land, part of the life, part of the green silence, and their death was an evil noise, their useless murder because they believed in a lie.

This is why I came, Lolla-Wossiky realized. The land brought me here, knowing that this boy had such power, knowing that there was no one to teach him how to use it, no one to teach him to wait to feel the need of the land before changing it. No one to teach him how to be Red instead of White.

I didn't come for my own dream beast, but to be the dream beast for this boy.

The noise settled. The sisters, the brothers, the parents went back to sleep. Lolla-Wossiky pressed his fingers into the cracks between the logs, climbed carefully, his eye closed so that the land would guide him instead of trusting in himself. The boy's shutters were open, and Lolla-Wossiky thrust his elbows over the sill and hung there, looking in.

First with his eye open. He saw a bed, a stool with clothes neatly folded, and at the foot of the bed, a cradle. The window opened onto the space between the bed and the cradle. In the bed, a shape, boy-sized, unidentifiable.

Lolla-Wossiky closed his eye again. Alvin lay in the bed. Lolla-Wossiky felt the heat of the boy's excitement like a fever. He had been so afraid of being caught, so exhilarated at his victory, and now lay trembling, trying to breathe calmly, trying to stifle laughter.

His eye open again, Lolla-Wossiky scrambled up onto the sill and swung onto the floor. He expected Alvin to notice him, to cry out; but the shape of the boy lay still in the bed; there was no sound.

The boy couldn't see him when his eye was open, any more than he could see the boy. This was the end of the dream, after all, and Lolla-Wossiky was dream beast for the boy. It was Lolla-Wossiky's duty to give visions to the boy, not to be seen as himself, a whisky-Red with one eye missing.

What vision will I show him?

Lolla-Wossiky reached inside his white man's trousers to where he still wore his loincloth, and pulled his knife from its sheath. He held both his hands high, the one holding the knife. Then he closed his eye.

The boy still didn't see him; his eyes were closed. So Lolla-Wossiky gathered the white light he could feel around him, gathered it close to himself, so that he could feel himself shining brighter and brighter. The light came from his skin, so he tore open the breast of the White man's shirt he wore, then raised his hands again. Now, even through closed eyelids, the boy could see the brightness, and he opened his eye.

Lolla-Wossiky felt the boy's terror at the sight of the apparition he had become: a bright and shining Red man, one-eyed, with a sharp knife in his hand. But it wasn't fear Lolla-Wossiky wanted. No one should

fear his own dream beast. So he sent the light outward to the boy, to
include him, and with the light he sent calm, calm, don't be scared.

The boy relaxed a little, but still wriggled up in his bed, so he was
sitting up, leaning against the wall.

It was time to begin to wake the boy from his life of sleep. How did
Lolla-Wossiky know what to do? No man, Red or White, had ever been
another man's dream beast. Yet he knew without thinking what he ought
to do. What the boy needed to see and feel. Whatever came to Lolla-
Wossiky's mind that felt right to do, that was what he did.

Lolla-Wossiky took his shining knife and brought the blade against
his other palm—and cut. Sharp, hard, deep, so blood leapt from the
wound, rushed down his forearm to gather and pool in his sleeve.
Quickly it began to drip on the floor.

The pain came suddenly, a moment later; Lolla-Wossiky knew at
once how to take the pain and make it into a picture and put it into the
boy's mind. The picture of his sisters' room as a small weak creature
saw it. Rushing in, hungering, hungering, looking for the food, certain
that the food was there; on the soft body was the promise, climb the
body, find the food. But great hands slapped and brushed, and the small
creature was thrown onto the floor. The floor shook with giant footfalls,
a sudden shadow, the agony of death.

Again and again, each small life, hungering, trusting, and then betrayed, crushed, battered.

Many lived, but they cowered, they scurried, they fled. The sisters'
room, the room of death, yes, they fled from there. But better to stay
there and die than run into the other room, the room of lies. Not words,
there were no words in the small creature's life, there were no thoughts
that could be named as thoughts. But the fear of death in the one place
was not as strong as another kind of fear, the fear of a world gone crazy,
a place where anything could happen, where nothing could be trusted,
where nothing was certain. A terrible place.

Lolla-Wossiky ended the vision. The boy was pressing his hands
against his eyes, sobbing desperately. Lolla-Wossiky had never seen
anyone so tortured by remorse; the vision Lolla-Wossiky had given him
was stronger than any dream a man could imagine for himself. I am a
terrible dream beast, thought Lolla-Wossiky. He will wish I hadn't wakened him. In dread of his own strength, Lolla-Wossiky opened his eye.

At once the boy disappeared, and Lolla-Wossiky knew that the boy
would think that Lolla-Wossiky had also disappeared. What now? he
thought. Am I here to make this boy crazy? To give him a terrible thing,
as bad as the black noise was to me?

He could see from the shaking of the bed, the movement of the bedclothes, that the boy was still crying passionately. Lolla-Wossiky closed his eye, and again sent the light to the boy. Calm, calm.

The boy's weeping became a whimper, and he looked again at Lolla-Wossiky, who was still shining with a dazzling light.

Lolla-Wossiky didn't know what to do. While he was silent and uncertain, Alvin began to speak, to plead. "I'm sorry, I'll never do it again, I'll—"

Babbling on and on. Lolla-Wossiky pushed more light at him, to help him see better. It came to the boy almost as a question. What will you never do again?

Alvin couldn't answer, didn't know. What was it he actually did? Was it because he sent the roaches to die?

He looked at the Shining Man and saw an image of a Red kneeling before a deer, calling it to come and die; the deer came, trembling, afraid; the Red loosed his arrow and it stood quivering on the deer's flank; the deer's legs wobbled, and it fell. It wasn't the dying or the killing that was his sin, because dying and killing were a part of life.

Was it the power he had? The knack he had for making things go just where he wanted, to break just at the right place, or fit together so tight that they joined forever without any gluing or hammering. The knack he had for making things do what he wanted, arrange themselves in the right order. Was it that?

Again he looked at the Shining Man, and now he saw a vision of himself pressing his hands against a stone, and the stone melted like butter under his hands, came out in just the shape he wanted, smooth and whole, fell from the side of the mountain and rolled away, a perfect ball, a perfect sphere, growing and growing until it was a whole world, shaped just the way his hands had made it, with trees and grass springing up in its face, and animals running and leaping and flying and swimming and crawling and burrowing on and above and beneath the ball of stone that he had made. No, it wasn't a terrible power, it was a glorious one, if he only knew how to use it.

If it isn't the dying and it isn't the power, what did I do wrong?

This time the Shining Man didn't show him anything. This time Alvin didn't have the answer come to him in a vision. This time he studied it out in his mind. He felt like he couldn't understand, he was too stupid to understand, and then suddenly he knew.

It was because he did it for himself. It was because the roaches thought he was doing it for them, and really he was doing it for himself. Hurting the roaches, his sisters, everyone, making everyone suffer and all for what? Because Alvin Miller Junior was angry and wanted to get *even—*

Now he looked at the Shining Man and saw a fire leap from his single eye and strike him in the heart. "I'll never use it for myself again," murmured Alvin Junior, and when he said the words he felt as though his heart were on fire, it burned so hot inside. And then the Shining Man disappeared again.

Lolla-Wossiky stood panting, his head spinning. He felt weak, weary. He had no idea what the boy had been thinking. He only knew what visions to send him, and then at the end, no vision at all, just to stand there, that's all he was to do, stand there and stand there until, suddenly, he sent a strong pulse of fire at the boy and buried it in his heart.

And now what? Twice now he had closed his eye and appeared to the boy. Was he through? He knew that he was not.

For the third time Lolla-Wossiky closed his eye. Now he could see that the boy was much brighter than *he* was; that the light had passed from him into the child. And then he understood—he was the boy's dream beast, yes, but the boy was also his. Now it was time for him to wake up from his dream life.

He took three steps and knelt beside the bed, his face only a little way from the boy's small and frightened face, which now shone so brightly that Lolla-Wossiky could hardly see that it was a child and not a man who looked at him. What do I want from him? Why am I here? What can he give me, this powerful child?

"Make all things whole," Lolla-Wossiky whispered. He spoke, not in English, but in Shaw-Nee.

Did the boy understand? Alvin raised his small hand, reached out gently and touched Lolla-Wossiky's cheek, under the broken eye. Then he raised his finger until it touched the slack eyelid.

There was a cracking sound in the air, and a spark of light. The boy gasped and drew back his hand. Lolla-Wossiky didn't see him, though, because suddenly the boy was invisible. But Lolla-Wossiky had no care for what he saw, for what he *felt* was the most impossible thing of all:

Silence. Green silence. The black noise was utterly, completely gone. His land-sense had returned, and the ancient injury was healed.

Lolla-Wossiky knelt there, gasping for breath, as the land returned to him the way that it had been before. All these years had passed; he had forgotten how strong it was, to see in all directions, hear the breath of every animal, smell the scent of every plant. A man who has been dry and thirsty until he was at the point of death, and suddenly cold water pours down his throat so fast he can't swallow, can't breathe; it's what he longed for, but much too strong, much too sudden, can't contain it, can't endure it—

"It didn't work," the boy whispered. "I'm sorry."

Lolla-Wossiky opened his good eye, and now for the first time saw the boy as a natural man. Alvin was staring at his bad eye. Lolla-Wossiky wondered why; he reached up, touched his missing eye. The lid still hung over an empty socket. Then he understood. The boy thought that was what he was supposed to heal. No, no, don't be disappointed, child, you healed me from the *deep* injury; what do I care about this tiny wound? I never lost my sight; it was my land-sense that was gone, and you gave it back to me.

He meant to shout all this to the boy, cry out and sing for the joy of it. But it was all too strong for him. The words never came to his lips. He couldn't even send him visions now because both of them were now awake. The dream was over. They had each been dream beast for the other.

Lolla-Wossiky seized the boy with both hands, pulled him close, kissed him on the forehead, hard and strong, like a father to a son, like brothers, like true friends the day before they die. Then he ran to the window, swung out and dropped to the ground. The earth yielded to his feet as it did to other Red men, as it hadn't done for him in so many years; the grass rose up stronger where he stepped; the bushes parted for him, the leaves softened and yielded as he ran among the trees; and now he did cry out, shouted, sang, caring not at all who heard him. Animals didn't run from him, as they used to; now they came to hear his song; songbirds awoke to sing with him; a deer leapt from the wood and ran beside him through a meadow, and he rested his hand upon her flank.

He ran until he had no breath, and in all that time he met no enemy, he felt no pain; he was whole again, in every way that mattered. He stood on the bank of the Wobbish River, across from the mouth of the Tippy-Canoe, panting, laughing, gasping for air.

Only then did he realize that his hand was still dripping blood from where he had cut himself to give pain to the White boy. His pants and shirt were thick with it. White man's clothing! I never needed it. He stripped it off and flung it into the river.

A funny thing happened. The clothing didn't move. It sat on the surface of the water, not sinking, not sliding leftward with the current.

How could this be? Wasn't the dream over? Wasn't he fully awake yet?

Lolla-Wossiky closed his eye.

Immediately he saw a terrible thing and shouted in fear. As soon as he closed his eye, he saw the black noise again, a great sheet of it, hard and frozen. It was the river. It was the water. It was made of death.

He opened his eye, and it was water again, but still his clothing didn't move.

He closed his eye, and saw that where the clothing was, light sparkled on the surface of the black. It pooled, it shone, it dazzled. It was his own blood shining.

Now he could see that the black noise wasn't a thing. It was nothing. Emptiness. The place where the land ended, and emptiness began; it was the edge of the world. But where his own blood sparkled, it was like a bridge across nothingness. Lolla-Wossiky knelt, his eye still closed, and reached out with his cut and still-bleeding hand, touched the water.

It was solid, warm and solid. He smeared his blood across the surface, and it made a platform. He crawled out onto the platform. It was smooth and hard as ice, only warm, welcoming.

He opened his eye. It was a river again, except that under him it was solid. Wherever his blood had touched, the water was hard and smooth.

He crawled out to where the clothing was, slid it ahead of him. All the way out to the middle of the river he crawled, and beyond the middle, making a thin, glowing bridge of blood to the other side.

What he was doing was impossible. The boy had done much more than heal him. He had changed the order of things. It was frightening and wonderful. Lolla-Wossiky looked down into the water between his hands. His own one-eyed reflection looked back up at him. Then he closed his eye, and a whole new vision leapt to view.

He saw himself standing in a clearing, speaking to a hundred Red men, a thousand, from every tribe. He saw them build a city of lodges, a thousand, five thousand, ten thousand Reds, all of them strong and whole, free of the White man's likker, the White man's hate. In his vision they called him the Prophet, but he insisted that he was not that at all. He was only the door, the open door. Step through, he said, and be strong, one people, one land.

The door. Tenskwa-Tawa.

In his vision, his mother's face appeared, and she said that word to him. Tenskwa-Tawa. It is your name now, for the dreamer is awake.

And more, he saw much more that night, staring downward into the solid water of the Wobbish River, he saw so much that he could never tell it all; in that hour on the water he saw the whole history of the land, the life of every man and woman, White or Red or Black, who ever set foot on it. He saw the beginning and he saw the end. Great wars and petty cruelties, all the murderings of men, all the sins; but also all the goodness, all the beauty.

And above all, a vision of the Crystal City. The city made of water as solid and as clear as glass, water that would never melt, formed into crystal towers so high that they should have cast shadows seven miles across the land. But because they were so pure and clear they cast no shadow at all, the sunlight passed unblocked through every inch and yard and mile of it. Wherever a man or woman stood, they could look deep into the crystal and see all the visions that Lolla-Wossiky saw now. Perfect understanding, that was what they had, seeing with eyes of pure sunlight and speaking with the voice of lightning.

Lolla-Wossiky, who from now on would be named Tenskwa-Tawa, did not know if he would build the Crystal City, or live in it, or even see it before he died. It was enough to do the first things that he saw in the solid water of the Wobbish River. He looked and looked until his mind couldn't see more. Then he crawled across to the far shore, climbed onto the bank, and walked until he came to the meadow he had seen in the vision.

This was where he would call the Reds together, teach them what he saw in his vision, and help them to be, not the strongest, but strong; not the largest, but large; not the freest, but free.

A certain keg in the crotch of a certain tree. All summer it was hidden from view. But the rain still found it, and the heat of high summer, and the insects, and the teeth of salt-hungry squirrels. Wetting, drying, heating, cooling; no keg can last forever in such conditions. It split, just a little, but enough; the liquid inside seeped out, drop by drop; in a few hours the keg was empty.

It didn't matter. No one ever looked for it. No one ever missed it. No one mourned when it broke apart from ice in the winter, the fragments tumbling down the tree into the snow.

5

A Sign

When word started spreading about a one-eyed Red man who was called
the Prophet, Governor Bill Harrison laughed and said, "Why, that ain't
nobody but my old friend Lolla-Wossiky. When he runs out of that
likker keg he stole from me, he'll quit seeing visions."

After a little while, though, Governor Harrison took note of how
much store was set by the Prophet's words, and how the Reds spoke
his name as reverent as a true Christian says the name of Jesus, and it
got him somewhat alarmed. So he called together all the Reds around
Carthage City—it was nigh onto a whisky day, so there wasn't no shortage of audience for him—and he gave them a speech. And in that speech
he said one particular thing:

"If old Lolla-Wossiky is really a Prophet, then he ought to do us a
miracle, to show he's got more to him than just talk. You ought to make
him cut off a hand or a foot and then put it back—that'd prove he was
a prophet now, wouldn't it? Or better still, make him put out an eye
and then heal it back. What's that you say? You mean he *already* had
his eye put out? Well then he's ripe for a miracle, wouldn't you say? I
say that as long as he's only got one eye, he ain't no prophet!"

Word of that came to the Prophet while he was teaching in a meadow
that sloped gently down to the banks of the Tippy-Canoe, not a mile
above where it poured into the waters of the Wobbish. It was some
whisky-Reds brought that challenge, and they wasn't above mocking
the Prophet and saying, "We came to see you make your eye whole."

The Prophet looked at them with his one good eye, and he said,
"With this eye I see two Red men, weak and sick, slaves of likker, the
kind of men who would mock me with the words of the man who killed
my father." Then he closed his good eye, and he said, "With this eye

I see two children of the land, whole and strong and beautiful, who love wives and children, and do good to all creatures.'' Then he opened his eye again and said, ''Which eye is sick, and which eye sees true?'' And they said to him, ''Tenskwa-Tawa, you are a true prophet, and both your eyes are whole.''

''Go tell White Murderer Harrison that I have performed the sign he asked for. And tell him another sign that he didn't ask for. Tell him that one day a fire will start in his own house. No man's hand will set this fire. Only rain will put out this fire, and before the fire dies, it will cut off something he loves more than a hand or a foot or an eye, and he will not have the power to restore it, either.''

6

Powder Keg

Hooch was astounded. "You mean you *don't want* the whole shipment?"

"We ain't used up what you sold us last time, Hooch," said the quartermaster. "Four barrels, that's all we want. More than we need, to tell the truth."

"I come down the river from Dekane, loaded up with likker, not stopping to sell any at the towns along the way, I make that *sacrifice* and you tell me—"

"Now, Hooch, I reckon we all know what kind of sacrifice that was." The quartermaster smirked a little. "I think you'll still recover your costs, pretty much, and if you don't, well, it just means you ain't been careful with the profits you've made off us afore."

"Who else is selling to you?"

"Nobody," said the quartermaster.

"I been coming to Carthage City for nigh on seven years now, and the last four years I've had a monopoly—"

"And if you'll pay heed, you'll remember that in the old days it used to be Reds what bought most of your likker."

Hooch looked around, walked away from the quartermaster, stood on the moist grassy ground of the riverbank. His flatboat rocked lazily on the water. There wasn't a Red to be seen, not a one, and that was a fact. But it wasn't no conspiracy, Hooch knew that. Reds had been slacking off the last few times he came. Always there used to be a few drunks, though.

He turned and shouted at the quartermaster. "You telling me there ain't no whisky-Reds left!"

"Sure there's whisky-Reds. But we ain't run out of whisky yet. So they're all off somewhere lying around being drunk."

Hooch cussed a little. "I'm going to see the Gov about this."

"Not today you ain't," said the quartermaster. "He's got himself a right busy schedule."

Hooch grinned nastily. "Oh, his schedule ain't too busy for *me*."

"It sure is, Hooch. He said it real specific."

"I reckon he might *think* his schedule is too busy, boy, but I reckon it just ain't so."

"Suit yourself," said the quartermaster. "Want me to unload the four barrels I got here?"

"No I don't," he said. Then he shouted at his poleboys, most specially at that Mike Fink, cause he looked to be the most likely to do murder if need be. "Anybody tries to lay a hand on that whisky, I want to see four bullet holes in their body before we chuck him in the water!"

The poleboys laughed and waved, except Mike Fink, who just sort of screwed his face up a little tighter. That was one mean old boy. They said you could tell which men had ever tried to wrassle Mike Fink, cause they got no ears. They said, if you want to get away from Fink with one ear still on your head, you got to wait till he's chewing on your first ear and then shoot him twice to distract him while you get away. A real good riverboy. But it made Hooch a little nervy to think what Fink might do if Hooch didn't have a payroll for him. Bill Harrison was going to pay for this whole load of likker, or there'd be real trouble.

Walking into the stockade, Hooch noticed a few things. The sign was the same one Harrison put up four years ago; it was getting ratty-looking now, weathered up, but nobody changed it. Town wasn't growing either. Everything had lost that new look, and now it was plain shabby.

Not like the way things were going back in Hio Territory. What used to be little stockade towns like this were turning into real towns, with painted houses, even a few cobbled streets. Hio was booming, at least the eastern part of it, close on to Suskwahenny, and folks speculated on how it wasn't far from statehood.

But there wasn't no boom going on in Carthage City.

Hooch walked along the main street inside the stockade. Still plenty of soldiers, and they still looked to have pretty good discipline, had to give Governor Bill credit for that. But where there used to be whisky-Reds sprawled all over the place, now there was river-rat types, uglier-looking than Mike Fink, unshaved, with a whisky stink as bad as any likkered-up Red ever had. Four old buildings had been turned into saloons, too, and they were doing good business in the middle of the afternoon.

That's why, thought Hooch. That's the trouble. Carthage City's gone and turned into a river town, a saloon town. Nobody wants to live around here, with all these river rats. It's a whisky town.

But if it's a whisky town, Governor Bill ought to be buying whisky from me instead of this business about only wanting four barrels.

"You can wait if you want, Mr. Palmer, but the Governor won't see you today."

Hooch sat on the bench outside Harrison's office. He noticed that Harrison had switched offices with his adjutant. Gave up his nice big office in exchange for what? Smaller space, but—all interior walls. No windows. Now, that meant something. That meant Harrison didn't like having people look in on him. Maybe he was even afraid of getting himself killed.

Hooch sat there for two hours, watching soldiers come in and out. He tried not to get mad. Harrison did this now and then, making somebody sit around and wait so by the time they got in they was so upset they couldn't think straight. And sometimes he did it so a body'd get in a huff and go away. Or start to feeling small and unimportant, so Harrison could do some bullying. Hooch knew all this, so he tried to stay calm. But when it got on to evening, and the soldiers started changing shifts and going off duty, it was more than he could stand.

"What do you think you're doing?" he demanded of the corporal who sat at the front desk.

"Going off duty," said the corporal.

"But I'm still here," said Hooch.

"You can go off duty too, if you like," said the corporal.

That smart-mouthed answer was like a slap in the face. Time was these boys all tried to suck up to Hooch Palmer. Times were changing too fast. Hooch didn't like it at all. "I could buy your old mother and sell her at a profit," said Hooch.

That got to him. That corporal didn't look bored no more. But he didn't let himself haul off and take a swing, neither. Just stood there, more or less at attention, and said, "Mr. Palmer, you can wait here all night and wait here all day tomorrow, and you ain't going to get in to see His Excellency the Governor. And you just sitting here waiting all day is proof you're just too plain dumb to catch on to how things are."

So it was Hooch lost his temper and took a swing. Well, not a swing exactly. More like a kick, cause Hooch never did learn no rules about fighting like a gentleman. His idea of a duel was to wait behind a rock for his enemy to pass by, shoot him in the back, and run like hell. So that corporal got Hooch's big old boot in his knee, which bent his leg backward in a way it wasn't meant to go. That corporal screamed bloody murder, which he had a right to, and not just from the pain—after a kick like that, his leg would never be any good again. Hooch probably shouldn't've kicked him there, he knew, but that boy was so snooty. Practically begged for it.

Trouble was, the corporal wasn't exactly alone. First yelp he made, all of a sudden there was a sergeant and four soldiers, bayonets at the ready, popping right out of the Governor's office and looking mad as hornets. The sergeant ordered two of his boys to carry the corporal to the infirmary. The others put Hooch under arrest. But it wasn't gentlemanly like that last time, four years before. This time the butts of their muskets got bumped into Hooch's body in a few places, sort of accidentally, and Hooch had him some boot prints in various places on his clothes, can't say how they got there. He ended up locked in a jail cell—no storage room this time. They left him with his clothes and a lot of pain.

No doubt about it. Things had changed around here.

That night six other men were put in lock-up, three of them drunks, three for brawling. Not one was Red. Hooch listened to them talking. It's not like any of them was particularly bright, but Hooch couldn't believe that they didn't talk about beating up no Reds, or making fun with some of them or something. It was like Reds had practically disappeared from the vicinity.

Well, maybe that was true. Maybe the Reds had all took off, but wasn't that what Governor Harrison hoped for? With the Reds gone, why wasn't Carthage City prosperous, full of White settlers?

The only inkling Hooch got was something one of the brawlers said. "I reckon I'm broke till tax season." The others whooped and hollered a little. "I got to say I don't mind government service, but it sure ain't steady work."

Hooch knew better than to ask them what they meant. No need to call attention to himself. He sure didn't want word getting around about how he looked all beat up the night he spent in jail. That kind of idea starts spreading and pretty soon everybody thinks he can beat a body up, and Hooch didn't reckon to start all over as a common street brawler, not at his age.

In the morning the soldiers came for him. Different ones, and this time they wasn't so careless with their feet and their musket butts. They just marched Hooch on out of the jail and now, finally, he got to see Bill Harrison.

But not in his office. It was in his own Governor's mansion, in a cellar room. And the way they got there was peculiar. The soldiers—must have been a dozen of them—just marched along behind the house, when all of a sudden one of them dashed over, flung up the cellar door, and two others half dragged Hooch down the steps. Cellar door slammed shut almost before their heads were clear of it, and in all that time the soldiers just kept right on marching, as if nothing was happening. Hooch didn't like that at all. It meant that Harrison didn't want anybody to see that Hooch was with him. Which meant this meeting could get pretty ugly, cause Harrison could deny it ever happened. Oh, the *soldiers* knew, of course, but they all knew about a certain corporal who got his knee bent the wrong way last night; they weren't about to testify on Hooch Palmer's behalf.

Harrison was his old self, though, smiling and shaking Hooch by the hand and clapping him on the shoulder. "How are you, Hooch?"

"I been better, Gov. How's your wife? And that little boy of yours?"

"She's healthy as you could hope for, a refined lady like her being out here on the frontier. And my little boy, he's quite a soldier, we even stitched him up a little uniform, you should see him strutting on parade."

"It's talk like that makes me think I ought to take a wife someday."

"I heartily recommend it. Oh, here, Hooch, what am I thinking of? You set down, set down right there."

Hooch sat. "Thanks, Bill."

Harrison nodded, satisfied. "It's good to see you, it's been so long."

"Wisht I'd've seen you yesterday," said Hooch.

Harrison smiled ruefully. "Well, I get busy. Didn't my boys tell you I had a full-up schedule?"

"Schedule never used to be full for *me*, Bill."

"You know how it gets sometimes. Real busy, and what can I do about it?"

Hooch shook his head. "Now, Bill, we've lied to each other just about long enough, I think. What happened was part of a plan, and it wasn't *my* plan."

"What are you talking about, Hooch?"

"I'm saying maybe that corporal didn't want his leg broke, but I have a feeling his job was to get me swinging at him."

"His job was to see that nobody disturbed me unless they were on my schedule, Hooch. That's the only plan I know about." Harrison looked sad. "Hooch, I got to tell you, this is real ugly. Assaulting an officer of the U.S. Army."

"A corporal ain't no officer, Bill."

"I only wish I could ship you back to Suskwahenny for trial, Hooch. They got lawyers there, and juries, and so on. But the trial has to be *here*, and juries around here ain't too partial to folks who go around breaking corporals' knees."

"Suppose you stop the threats and tell me what you really want?"

"Want? I ain't asking for favors, Hooch. Just concerned about a friend of mine who's got himself in trouble with the law."

"It must be something real sickening or you'd bribe me to do it instead of trying to strong-arm me. It must be something that you think I wouldn't be willing to do unless you scare me to death, and I keep trying to imagine what *you* think is so bad that you think I wouldn't do it. It ain't much of a list, Bill."

Harrison shook his head. "Hooch, you got me wrong. Just plain wrong."

"This town is dying, Bill," said Hooch. "Things ain't working out like you planned. And I think it's cause you done some real dumb things. I think the Reds started going away—or maybe they all died off—and you made the stupid mistake of trying to make up for all that lost likker income by bringing in the scum of the earth, the worst kind of White man, the river rats who spent the night in jail with me. You've used them to collect taxes, right? Farmers don't like taxes. They specially don't like taxes when they're collected by scum like this."

Harrison poured himself three fingers of whisky in a tumbler and drank off half of it in a single gulp.

"So you been losing your whisky-Reds, and you been losing your White farmers, and all you got left is your soldiers, the river rats, and whatever money you can steal from the United States Army appropriation for peace-keeping in the west."

Harrison drank the rest of the whisky and belched.

"What that means is you've been unlucky and you've been stupid, and somehow you think you can make me get you out of it."

Harrison poured another three fingers into the glass. But instead of drinking it, he hauled off and threw it into Hooch's face. The whisky splashed in his eyes, the tumbler bounced off his forehead, and Hooch found himself rolling on the floor trying to dig the alcohol out of his eyes.

A while later, with a wet cloth pressed against his forehead, Hooch was sitting in the chair again, acting a lot more meek and reasonable. But that was because he knew Harrison had a flush and his own hand was just two pair. Get out of here alive and then just see what comes next, right?

"I wasn't stupid," Harrison said.

No, you're the smartest governor Carthage ever had. I'm surprised you ain't King. That's what Hooch *would've* said. But he was keeping his mouth shut.

"It was that Prophet. That Red up north. Building his Prophets-town right across the Wobbish from Vigor Church—you can't tell me that's just a coincidence. It's Armor-of-God, that's what it is, trying to take the state of Wobbish away from me. Using a *Red* to do it, too. I knew that a lot of Reds were going north, everybody knew that, but I still had me my whisky-Reds, them as hadn't died off. And with fewer Reds around here—especially the Shaw-Nee, when they left—well, I thought I'd get more White settlers. And you're wrong about my tax collectors. They didn't run the White settlers off. It was Ta-Kumsaw."

"I thought it was the Prophet."

"Don't get smart with me, Hooch, I don't have much patience these days."

Why didn't you warn me before you threw the glass? No, no, don't say nothing to make him mad. "Sorry, Bill."

"Ta-Kumsaw's been real smart. He doesn't kill White folks. He just shows up at their farms with fifty Shaw-Nee. Doesn't shoot anybody, but when you got fifty painted-up warriors all around your house, these White folks didn't exactly figure it was smart to start shooting. So the White farmers watched while the Shaw-Nee opened every gate, every stable, every coop. Let them animals go on out. Horses, pigs, milk cows, chickens. Just like Noah bringing beasts into the ark, the Shaw-Nee walk into the woods and the animals trot on right behind. Just like that. Never see them again."

"You can't tell me they never round up at least some of their stock."

"All gone. Never find even their tracks. Never even a feather from a chicken. That's what run the White farmers off, is knowing that any day, all their animals can disappear."

"Shaw-Nee eating them or something? Ain't no chicken smart enough to live long in the woods. It's just Christmastime for foxes, that's all it is."

"How should I know? White folks come to me, they say, Get our animals back, or kill Reds that took them. But my soldiers, my scouts, nobody can find where Ta-Kumsaw's people are. No villages at all! I tried raiding a Caska-Skeeaw village up the Little My-Ammy, but all that did was convince more Reds to leave, didn't even slow down what Ta-Kumsaw was doing."

Hooch could imagine what that raid on the Caska-Skeeaw village was like. Old men, women, children, their corpses shot up and half-burnt—Hooch knew how Harrison dealt with Reds.

"And then last month, here comes the Prophet. I knew he was coming—even the whisky-Reds couldn't talk about nothing else. Prophet's coming. Got to go see the Prophet. Well, I tried to find out where he was going to be, where he was going to give a speech, I even had some of my tame Reds try to find out for me, but no dice, Hooch. Not a clue. Nobody knew. Just one day the word went through the whole town, Prophet's here. Where? Just come on, Prophet's here. No one ever said where. I swear these Reds can talk without talking, if you know what I mean.''

''Bill, tell me you had spies there, or I'll start to thinking you lost your touch.''

''Spies? I went myself, how's that? And do you know how? Ta-Kumsaw sent me an invitation, if that don't beat all. No soldiers, no guns, just me.''

''And you *went*? He could've captured you and—''

''He gave me his word. Ta-Kumsaw may be a Red, but he keeps his word.''

Hooch thought that was kind of funny. Harrison, the man who prided himself on never keeping a promise to a Red man, but he still counted on Ta-Kumsaw keeping a promise to him. Well, he got back alive, didn't he? So Ta-Kumsaw was as good as his word.

''I went there. Must've been every Red in the whole My-Ammy country there. Must've been ten thousand. Squatting around in this old abandoned cornfield—there's plenty of them in these parts, you can bet, thanks to Ta-Kumsaw. If I'd had my two cannon there and a hundred soldiers, I could've ended the whole Red problem, then and there.''

''Too bad you didn't,'' said Hooch.

''Ta-Kumsaw wanted me to sit right up front, but I wouldn't. I hung back and I listened. The Prophet got up, stood on an old stump in the field, and he talked and talked and talked.''

''You understand any of it? I mean, you don't talk Shaw-Nee.''

''He was talking English, Hooch. Too many different tribes there, the only language they all knew was English. Oh, sometimes he talked in that Red gibberish, but there was plenty of English. Talking about the destiny of the Red man. Stay pure from White contamination. Live all together and fill up a part of the land so the White man will have his place and the Red man will have *his*. Build a city—a crystal city, he said, it sounded real pretty except these Reds can't even build a proper shed, I hate to think how they'd do at building a city out of glass! But most of all, he said, Don't drink likker. Not a drop. Give it up, stay away from it. Likker is the chain of the White man, the chain and the whip, the chain and the whip and the knife. First he'll catch you, then he'll whip you, then he'll kill you, likker will, and when the White man's killed you with his whisky, he'll come in and steal your land, destroy it, make it unfit, dead, useless.''

"Sounds like he made a real impression on you, Bill," said Hooch. "Sounds like you memorized the speech he gave."

"Memorized? He talked for three straight hours. Talked about visions of the past, visions of the future. Talked about—oh, Hooch, it was *crazy* stuff, but those Reds were drinking it up like, like—"

"Whisky."

"Like whisky except it was *instead* of whisky. They all went with him. Pretty near all of them, anyway. Only ones left are a few whisky-Reds that're bound to die soon. And of course my tame Reds, but that's different. And some wild Reds across the Hio."

"Went with him where?"

"Prophetstown! That's what kills me, Hooch. They all go up to Prophetstown, or thereabouts, right across the river from Vigor Church. And that's exactly where all the Whites are going! Well, not all to Vigor Church, but up into the lands where Armor-of-Hell Weaver has his maps. They're in cahoots, Hooch, I promise you that. Ta-Kumsaw, Armor-of-God Weaver, and the Prophet."

"Sounds like."

"The worst thing is I had that Prophet here in my own office must be a thousand times, I could have killed that boy and saved myself more trouble—but you never know, do you?"

"You know this Prophet?"

"You mean you *don't* know who it is?"

"I don't know that many Reds by name, Bill."

"How about if I tell you that he's only got one eye?"

"You ain't saying it's Lolla-Wossiky!"

"Reckon so."

"That one-eyed drunk?"

"God's own truth, Hooch. Calls himself Tenskwa-Tawa now. It means 'the open door' or something. I'd like to shut that door. I *should've* killed him when I had the chance. But I figured when he ran off—he ran off, you know, stole a keg and took off into the woods—"

"I was here that night, I helped chase him."

"Well when he didn't come back, I figured he probably drank himself to death off that keg. But there he is telling Reds how he used to have to drink all the time, but God sent him visions and he's never had another drink."

"Send me visions, I'd give up drinking, too."

Harrison took another swallow of whisky. From the jug, this time, since the tumbler was on the floor in the corner of the room. "You see my problem, Hooch."

"I see you got lots of problems, Bill, and I don't know how any of them has a thing to do with me, except you weren't joking when you had the quartermaster tell me you only wanted four barrels.''

"Oh, it's got more to do with you than that, count on it, Hooch. More than that. Because I ain't beat. The Prophet's took away all my whisky-Reds, and Ta-Kumsaw's got my White citizens scared, but I ain't quitting.''

"No, you're no quitter," said Hooch. You're a slimy sneaky snake of a man, but you're no quitter. Didn't *say* that, of course, cause Harrison was bound to take it wrong—but to Hooch, it was all praise. His kind of man.

"It's Ta-Kumsaw and the Prophet, simple as that. I got to kill them. No, no, I take it back. I got to *beat* them and kill them. I got to take them on and make them both look like fools and *then* kill them.''

"Good idea. I'll handle the betting on it.''

"I bet you would. Stand there taking bets. Well, I can't just take my soldiers up north to Vigor Church and wipe out Prophetstown, cause Armor-of-God would fight me every step of the way, probably get the army detachment at Fort Wayne to back him up. Probably get my commission stripped or something. So I've got to arrange things so the people in Vigor Church, all along the Wobbish, they all beg me to come up and get rid of them Reds.''

Now, at last, Hooch understood what this was all about. "You want a provocation.''

"That's my boy, Hooch. That's my boy. I want some Reds to go up north and make some real trouble, and *tell* everybody that Ta-Kumsaw and the Prophet told them to do it. Blame it all on them.''

Hooch nodded. "I see. It couldn't be just running off their cows or nothing like that. No, the only thing that'll get those people up north screaming for Red blood is something real ugly. Like capturing children and torturing them to death and then signing Ta-Kumsaw's name on them and leaving them where they'll be found. Something like that.''

"Well, I wouldn't go so far as to tell anybody to do something awful like *that*, Hooch. In fact I don't reckon I'd give them specific instructions at all. Just tell them to do something that'd rile up the Whites up north, and then spread the word that Ta-Kumsaw ordered it.''

"But you wouldn't be surprised if it turned out to be rape and torture.''

"I wouldn't want them to touch any White women, Hooch. That's out of line.''

"Oh, that's right, pure truth," said Hooch. "So it's definitely torturing children. *Boy* children.''

"Like I said, I wouldn't ever tell somebody to do a thing like that.''

Hooch nodded a little, his eyes closed. Harrison might not tell somebody to do it, but he sure wasn't telling him not to do it, either. "And of course it couldn't be any Reds from around here, could it, Bill, cause they're all gone, and your tame Reds are the most worthless scum that ever lived on the face of the earth."

"Pretty much, that's true."

"So you need Reds from south of the river. Reds who still haven't heard the Prophet's preaching, so they still want likker. Reds who still have brains enough to do the job right. Reds who have the blood thirst to kill children real slow. And you need my cargo as a bribe."

"Reckon so, Hooch."

"You got it, Bill. Dismiss charges against me, and you got all my likker free. Just give me enough money to pay off my poleboys so they don't knife me on the way home, I hope that ain't too much to ask."

"Now, Hooch, you know that ain't all I need."

"But Bill, that's all I'll do."

"I can't be the one to go ask them, Hooch. I can't be the one to go tell them Cree-Eks or Choc-Taws what I need done. It's got to be somebody else, somebody who if it gets found out I can say, I never told him to do that. He used his own whisky to do it, I didn't have any idea."

"Bill, I understand you, but you guessed right from the start. You actually found something so low that I won't be part of it."

Harrison glowered at him. "Assaulting an officer is a hanging offense in this fort, Hooch. Didn't I make that clear?"

"Bill, I've lied, cheated, and sometimes killed to get ahead in the world. But one thing I've never done is bribe somebody to go steal some mother's children and torture them to death. I honestly never did that, and I honestly never will."

Harrison studied Hooch's face and saw that it was true. "Well, don't that beat all. There's actually a sin so bad that Hooch Palmer won't do it, even if he dies because of it."

"You won't kill me, Bill."

"Oh yes I will, Hooch. There's two reasons I will. First, you gave me the wrong answer to my request. And second, you heard my request in the first place. You're a dead man, Hooch."

"Fine with me," said Hooch. "Make it a real scratchy rope, too. A good and tall gallows, with a twenty-foot drop. I want a hanging that folks'll remember for a long time."

"You'll get a tree limb and we'll raise the rope up slow, so you strangle instead of breaking your neck."

"Just so it's memorable," said Hooch.

Harrison called in some soldiers and had them take Hooch back to jail. This time they did a little kicking and poking, so Hooch had a whole new batch of bruises, and maybe a broken rib.

He also didn't have much time.

So he lay down real calm on the floor of the jail. The drunks were gone, but the three brawlers were still there, using all the cots; the floor was all that was available. Hooch didn't much care. He knew Harrison would give him an hour or two to think about it, then take him out and put the rope around his neck and kill him. He might pretend to give him one last chance, of course, but he wouldn't mean it, because now he wouldn't trust Hooch. Hooch had told him no, and so he'd never trust him to carry out the assignment if he let him go.

Well, Hooch planned to use the time wisely. He started out pretty simply. He closed his eyes and let some heat build up inside him. A spark. And then he sent that spark outside himself. It was like what doodlebugs said they did, sending out their bug to go searching underground and see what it could see. He set his spark to searching and pretty soon he found what he was looking for. Governor Bill's own house. His spark was too far away by now for him to find some particular spot in the house. And his aim couldn't be too tight. So instead he just pumped all his hate and rage and pain into the spark, built it hotter and hotter and hotter. He let himself go like he never done before in his life. And he kept pushing it and pushing it until he started hearing that most welcome sound.

"Fire! Fire!" The shouts came from outside, from far away, but more and more people took up the cry. Gunshots went off—distress signals.

The three brawlers heard it, too. One of them stepped on Hooch where he was lying on the floor, they were in such a hurry. Stood at the door, they did, rattling and shouting at the guard. "Let us out! Don't go trying to fight that fire without letting us out first! Don't let us die in here!"

Hooch hardly noticed the man stepping on him, he already hurt so bad. Instead he just lay there, using his spark again, only this time heating up the metal inside the lock of the jail door. Now his aim was tight and his spark could get much hotter.

The guard came in and put his key in the lock, turned it, opened the door. "You boys can come on out," he said. "Sergeant said so, we need you to help with the fire brigade."

Hooch struggled to his feet, but the guard straight-armed him and shoved him back into the cell. Hooch wasn't surprised. But he made the spark go hotter yet, so hot that now the iron of the lock melted inside. It even glowed red a little. The guard slammed the door shut and went to turn the key. By now it was so hot that it burned his hand. He cussed and went for his shirttail to try and grab the key, but Hooch kicked the door open, knocking the guard down. He stomped the guard in the face and kicked his head, which probably broke his neck, but Hooch didn't think of that as murder. He thought of it as justice, cause the guard had been all set to leave him locked in his cell to burn to death.

Hooch walked on out of the jail. Nobody paid him much attention. He couldn't see the mansion from here, but he could see the smoke rising. Sky was low and grey. Probably it'd rain before it burned the stockade. Hooch sure hoped not, though. Hoped the whole place burned to the ground. It was one thing to want to kill off Reds, that was fine with Hooch, he and Harrison saw eye to eye on that. Kill them with likker if you can, bullets if you can't. But you don't go killing White folks, you don't go hiring Reds to torture White babies. Maybe to Harrison it was all part of the same thing. Maybe to him it was like White soldiers having to die in a war with Reds, only the soldiers'd just be a little younger. All in a good cause, right? Maybe Harrison could think that way, but Hooch couldn't. It actually took him by surprise, to tell the truth. He was more like Andrew Jackson than he ever supposed. He had a line he wouldn't cross. He drew it in a different place than old Hickory did, but still, he had a line, and he'd die before he crossed it.

Of course he didn't reckon to die if he could help it. He couldn't go out the stockade gate, cause the bucket line to the river would go through there and he'd be seen. But it was easy enough to climb up to the parapet. The soldiers weren't exactly keeping a lookout. He clambered over the wall and dropped down outside the fort. Nobody saw him. He walked the ten yards into the woods, then made his way—slowly, cause his ribs hurt pretty bad and he was a little weak from so much sparking, it took something out of him—through the woods to the riverbank.

He came out of the woods on the far side of the open area around the wharf. There was his flatboat, still loaded up with all his kegs. And his poleboys standing around, watching the bucket brigade dipping into the river some thirty yards farther upstream. It didn't surprise Hooch a bit that his poleboys weren't over there helping with the buckets. They weren't exactly the public-spirited type.

Hooch walked out onto the wharf, beckoning for the poleboys to come join him. He jumped down to the flatboat; stumbled a little, from being weak and hurting. He turned around to tell his boys what was happening, why they had to push off, but they hadn't followed. They just stood there on the bank, looking at him. He beckoned again, but they didn't make a move to come.

Well, then, he'd go without them. He was even moving toward the rope, to cast off and pole himself away, when he realized that not all the poleboys were on shore. No, there was one missing. And he knew right where that missing boy would be. Right there on the flatboat, standing right behind him, reaching out his hands—

Mike Fink wasn't the knifing kind. Oh, he'd knife you if he had to, but he'd rather kill with his bare hands. He used to say something about killing with a knife, some comparison with whores and a broomstick. Anyway, that's why Hooch knew that it wouldn't be a knife. That it wouldn't be quick. Harrison must've known Hooch might get away, so he bought off Mike Fink, and now Fink would kill him sure.

Sure, but slow. And slow gave Hooch time. Time to make sure he didn't die alone.

So as the fingers closed around his throat and cinched tight, much tighter than Hooch ever imagined, clamping him so he thought his head would get wrung right off, he forced himself to make his spark go, to find that keg, that one place, he knew right where the place was on the flatboat, to hot up that keg, as hot as he could, hotter, hotter—

And he waited for the explosion, waited and waited, but it never came. It felt like Fink's fingers had pressed through the front of his throat clear to the spine, and he felt all his muscles just give way, he felt himself kicking, his lungs heaving to try to suck in air that just wouldn't come, but he kept his spark going till the last second, waiting for the gunpowder keg to blow.

Then he died.

Mike Fink hung on to him for another whole minute after he was dead, maybe just cause he liked the feel of a dead man dangling from his hands. Hard to tell with Mike Fink. Some folks said he was as nice a man as you could hope to find, when he was in the mood. Sure that's what Mike thought of himself. He *liked* to be nice and have friends and drink real sociable. But when it came to killing, well, he liked that too.

But you can't just hang on to a dead body forever. For one thing, somebody's going to start complaining about it or maybe puking. So he shoved Hooch's body off into the water.

"Smoke," said one of the poleboys, pointing.

Sure enough, there was smoke coming out of the middle of the pile of kegs.

"It's the gunpowder keg!" shouted one of them.

Well, the poleboys took off running to get away from the explosion, but Mike Fink just laughed and laughed. He walked over and started unloading kegs, hoisting them onto the wharf, unloading them until he got to the middle where there was a keg with a fuse coming out of it. He didn't pick *that* one up with his hands, though. He tipped it over with his heel, then kind of rolled it along till it was on the open area around the edge of the boat.

By now the poleboys had come back to see what was going on, since it looked pretty much like Mike Fink wasn't going to blow up after all. "Hatchet," Mike called out, and one of the boys tossed him the one he kept in a sheath at his belt. It took a few good whacks, but the top finally sprung off the keg, and a whole cloud of steam came up. The water inside was so hot it was still boiling.

"You mean it wasn't gunpowder after all?" asked of the boys. Not a bright one, but then not many rivermen was famous for brains.

"Oh, it was gunpowder when he set it down here," said Mike. "Back in Suskwahenny. But you don't think Mike Fink'd go all the way down the Hio River on the same flatboat with a keg of powder with a fuse coming out of it, do you?"

Then Mike jumped off the boat up onto the wharf and bellowed at the top of his voice, so loud that they heard him clear inside the fort, so loud that the bucket brigade stopped long enough to listen.

"My name is Mike Fink, boys, and I'm the meanest lowdown son of an alligator that ever bit off the head of a buffalo! I eat growed men's ears for breakfast and bears' ears for supper, and when I'm thirsty I can drink enough to stop Niagara from falling. When I piss folks get on flatboats and float downstream for fifty mile, and when I fart the Frenchmen catch the air in bottles and sell it for perfume. I'm Mike Fink, and this my flatboat, and if you miserable little pukes ever put that fire out, there's a free pint of whisky in it for every one of you!"

Then Mike Fink led the poleboys over and joined the bucket brigade, and they slowed the fire down until the rain came and put it out.

That night, with all the soldiers drinking and singing, Mike Fink was sitting up sober as you please, feeling pretty good about finally being in the likker business for himself. Only one of the poleboys was with him now, the youngest fellow, who kind of looked up to Fink. The boy was setting there playing with the fuse that used to go into a gunpowder keg.

"This fuse wasn't lit," said the poleboy.

"No, I reckon not," said Mike Fink.

"Well, how'd the water get to boiling then?"

"Reckon Hooch had a few tricks up his sleeve. Reckon Hooch had something to do with the fire in the fort."

"You knew that, didn't you?"

Fink shook his head. "Nope, just lucky. I'm just plain lucky. I just get a feeling about things, like I had a feeling about that gunpowder keg, and I just do what I feel like doing."

"You mean like a knack?"

In answer, Fink stood up and pulled down his trousers. There on his left buttock was a sprawl of a tattoo, six-sided and dangerous-looking.

"My mama had that poked on when I wasn't a month old. Said that'd keep me safe so I'd live out my whole natural life." He turned and showed the boy the other buttock. "And that one she said was to help me make my fortune. I didn't know how it'd work, and she died without telling me, but as near as I can tell it makes me lucky. Makes it so I just kind of know what I ought to do." He grinned. "Got me a flatboat now, and a cargo of whisky, don't I?"

"Is the Governor really going to give you a medal for killing Hooch?"

"Well, for catching him, anyhow, looks like."

"I don't guess the Gov looked too bothered that old Hooch was dead, though."

"Nope," said Fink. "No, I reckon not. No, me and the Gov, we're good friends now. He says he's got some things need doing, that only a man like me can do."

The poleboy looked at him with adoration in his eighteen-year-old eyes. "Can I help you? Can I come with you?"

"You ever been in a fight?"

"A lot of fights!"

"You ever bit off an ear?"

"No, but I gouged out a man's eye once."

"Eyes are easy. Eyes are soft."

"And I butted a man's head so he lost five teeth."

Fink considered that for a few seconds. Then he grinned and nodded. "Sure, you come along with me, boy. By the time I'm through, there ain't a man woman or child within a hundred mile of this river who won't know my name. Do you doubt that, boy?"

The boy didn't doubt it.

In the morning, Mike Fink and his crew pushed off for the south bank of the Hio, loaded with a wagon, some mules, and eight kegs of whisky. Bound to do a little trading with the Reds.

In the afternoon, Governor William Harrison buried the charred remains of his second wife and their little boy, who had the misfortune of being in the nursery together, dressing the boy in his little parade uniform, when the room burst into flames.

A fire in his own house, set by no hand, which cut off what he loved the most, and no power on earth could bring them back.

7

Captives

Alvin Junior never felt small except when he was setting on the back of a big old horse. Not to say he wasn't a good rider—he and horses got along pretty good, they never throwing him and he never whipping them. It's just that his legs stuck way out on both sides, and since he was riding with a saddle on this trip, the stirrup had to be hiked up so far they punched new holes in the leather so he could ride. Al was looking forward to the day he growed up to be man-size. Other folks might tell him he was right big for his age, but that didn't amount to nothing in Alvin's opinion. When your age is ten, big for your age ain't nothing like being big.

"I don't like it," said Faith Miller. "Don't like sending my boys off in the middle of all these Red troubles."

Mother always worried, but she had good cause. All his life Al was kind of clumsy, always having accidents. Things turned out fine in the end, but it was nip and tuck a lot of the time. Worst was a few months ago, when the new millstone fell on his leg and gave it a real ugly break. It looked like he was going to die, and he pretty much expected to himself. Would have, too. Surely would have. Even though he knew he had the power to heal himself.

Ever since the Shining Man came to him in his room that night when he was six, Al had never used his knack to help himself. Cutting stone for his father, that he could do, cause it would help everybody. He'd run his fingers on the stone, get the feel of it, find the hidden places in the stone where it could break, and then set it all in order, just make it go that way; and the stone would come out, just right, just the way he asked. But never for his own good.

Then with his leg broke and the skin tore up, everybody knowed he was bound to die. And Al never would've used his knack for fixing things to heal himself, never would've tried, except old Taleswapper was there. Taleswapper asked him, why don't you fix your leg yourself? And so Al told him what he never told a soul before, about the Shining Man. Taleswapper believed him, too, didn't think he was crazy or dreaming. He made Al think back, think real hard, and remember what the Shining Man said. And when Al remembered, it come to him that it was Al himself who said that about never doing it for himself. The Shining Man just said, "Make all things whole."

Make all things whole. Well, wasn't his leg part of "all things"? So he fixed it, best he could. There was a lot more to it than that, but all in all he used his own power, with the help of his family, to heal himself. That's why he was alive.

But during those days he looked death in the face and he wasn't as scared of it as he thought he'd be. Lying there with death seeping through his bone, he began to feel like his body was just a kind of lean-to, a shelter he lived in during bad weather till his house was built. Like them shanty cabins new folks built till they could get a log house set up proper. And if he died, it wouldn't be awful at all. Just different, and maybe better.

So when his ma went on and on about the Reds and how dangerous it was and how they might get killed, he didn't give no heed. Not because he thought that she was wrong, but because he didn't much care whether he died or not.

Well, no, that wasn't quite so. He had a lot of things to do, though he didn't know yet what they were, and so he'd be *annoyed* about dying. He sure didn't *plan* to die. It just didn't fill him up with fear like it did some folks.

Al's big brother Measure was trying to get Ma to ease off and not get herself all worked up. "We'll be all right, Mama," said Measure. "All the trouble's down south, and we'll be on good roads all the way."

"Folks disappear every week on those good roads," she said. "Those French up in Detroit are buying scalps, they don't never let up on that, don't matter one bit what Ta-Kumsaw and his savages are doing, it only takes one arrow to kill you—"

"Ma," said Measure. "If you're a-scared of Reds getting us, you ought to *want* us to go. I mean there's ten thousand Reds at *least* living in Prophetstown right across the river. It's the biggest city west of Philadelphia right now, and every one of them is a Red. We're getting *away* from Reds by going east—"

"That one-eyed Prophet don't worry me," she said. "He never talks about killing. I just think you shouldn't—"

"It don't matter what you think," said Pa.

Ma turned to face him. He'd been slopping the hogs out back, but now he has come around to say good-bye. "Don't you tell me it don't matter what I—"

"It don't matter what I think, neither," said Pa. "It don't matter what anybody thinks, and you know it."

"Then I don't see why the good Lord gave us brains, then, if that's how things are, Alvin Miller!"

"Al's going east to Hatrack River to be an apprentice blacksmith," said Pa. "I'll miss him, you'll miss him, everybody except maybe Reverend Thrower's going to miss the boy, but the papers are signed and Al Junior is going. So instead of jawing how you don't want them to go, kiss the boys good-bye and wave them off."

If Pa'd been milk she would've curdled him on the spot, she gave him such a look. "I'll kiss my boys, and I'll wave them off," she said. "I don't need you to tell me that. I don't need you to tell me anything."

"I reckon not," said Pa. "But I'll tell you anyway, and I reckon you'll return the favor, just like you always done." He reached up a hand to shake with Measure, saying good-bye like a man does. "You get him there safe and come right back," he told Measure.

"You know I will," said Measure.

"Your ma's right, it's dangerous every step of the way, so keep your eyes open. We named you right, you got such keen eyes, boy, so use them."

"I will, Pa."

Ma said her good-bye to Measure while Pa came on over to Al. He gave Al a good stinging slap on the leg and shook *his* hand, too, and that felt good, Pa treating him like a man, just like Measure. Maybe if Al wasn't sitting up on a horse, Pa would've roughed his hair like a little boy, but then maybe he wouldn't have, either, and it still felt grown-up, all the same.

"I ain't scared of the Reds," said Al. He spoke real soft, so Ma wouldn't hear. "But I sure wish I didn't have to go."

"I know it, Al," said Pa. "But you got to. For your own good."

Then Pa got that faraway sad look on his face, which Al Junior had seen before more than once, and never understood. Pa was a strange man. It took Al a long time to realize that, since for the longest time while Al was just little, Pa was Pa, and he didn't try to understand him.

Now Al was getting older, and he began to compare his father to the other men around. To Armor-of-God Weaver, for instance, the most important man in town, always talking about peace with the Red man, sharing the land with him, mapping out Red lands and White lands—

everybody listened to him with respect. Nobody listened to Pa that way, considering his words real serious, maybe arguing a little, but knowing that what he said was *important*. And Reverend Thrower, with his high-falutin educated way of talking, shouting from his pulpit about death and resurrection and the fires of hell and the rewards of heaven, everybody listened to *him*, too. It was different from the way they listened to Armor, cause it was always about religion and so it didn't have nothing to do with little stuff like farming and chores and how folks lived. But *respect*.

When Pa talked, other folks listened to him, all right, but they just scoffed sometimes. "Oh, Alvin Miller, you just go on, don't you!" Al noticed that, and it made him mad at first. But then he realized that when folks was in trouble and needed help, they didn't go to Reverend Thrower, no sir, and they didn't go to Armor-of-God, cause neither of them knew all that much about how to solve the kind of problems folks had from time to time. Thrower might tell them how to stay out of hell, but that wasn't till they was dead, and Armor might tell them how to keep peace with the Reds, but that was politics except when it was war. When they had a quarrel about a boundary line, or didn't know what to do about a boy that always sassed his ma no matter how many lickings he got, or when the weevils got their seed corn and they didn't have nothing to plant, they come to Al Miller. And he'd say his piece, just a few words usually, and they'd go off shaking their heads and saying, "Oh, Alvin Miller, you just go on, don't you!" But then they'd go ahead and settle that boundary line and build them a stone fence there; and they'd let their smart-mouth boy move on out of the house and take up as a hired man on a neighbor's farm; and come planting time a half-dozen folks'd come by with sacks of "spare" seed cause Al Miller mentioned they might be a little shy.

When Al Junior compared his pa to other men, he knew Pa was strange, knew Pa did things for reasons known only to himself. But he also knew that Pa could be trusted. Folks might give their respect to Armor-of-God and Reverend Philadelphia Thrower, but they *trusted* Al Miller.

So did Al Junior. Trusted his pa. Even though he didn't want to leave home, even though having been so close to death he felt like apprenticing and suchlike was a waste of time—what did it matter what his trade was, would there be smiths in heaven?—still he knew that if Pa said it was right for him to go, then Al would go. The way folks always knew that if Al Miller said, "Just do this and it'll work out," why, they should do the thing he said, and it'd work out like he said.

He had told Pa he didn't want to go; Pa had said, Go anyway, it's for your own good. That's all Alvin Junior needed to hear. He nodded his head and did what Pa said, not cause he had no spunk, not cause he was scared of his pa like other boys he knew. He just knew his pa well enough to trust his judgment. Simple as that.

"I'll miss you, Pa." And then he did a crazy fool thing, which if he stopped to think about it he never would've done. He reached down and tousled his *father's* hair. Even while he was doing it, he thought, Pa's going to slap me silly for treating him like a boy! Pa's eyebrows *did* go up, and he reached up and caught Al Junior's hand by the wrist. But then he got him a twinkle in his eye and laughed loud and said, "I reckon you can do that *once*, Son, and live."

Pa was still laughing when he stepped back to give Ma space to say her good-bye. She had tears running down her face, but she didn't have no last-minute list of *do*s and *don't*s for him, the way she had for Measure. She just kissed his hand and clung on to it, and looked him in the eye and said, "If I let you go today, I'll never see you with my natural eyes again, as long as I live."

"No, Ma, don't say that," he told her. "Nothing bad's going to happen to me."

"You just remember me," she said. "And you keep that amulet I gave you. You wear that all the time."

"What's it do?" he asked, taking it from his pocket again. "I don't know this kind."

"Never you mind, you just keep it close to you all the time."

"I will, Ma."

Measure walked his horse up beside Al Junior's. "We best be going now," he said. "We want to get to country we don't see every day before we bed down tonight."

"Don't you do that," said Pa sternly. "We arranged for you to stay with the Peachee family tonight. That's as far as you need to get in one day. Don't want you to spend a night in the open when you don't have to."

"All right, all right," said Measure, "but we at least ought to get there before supper."

"Go on then," said Ma. "Go on then, boys."

They only got a rod or so on the way before Pa came running out and caught Measure's horse by the bridle, and Al Junior's, too. "Boys, you remember! Cross rivers at the bridges. You hear me? Only at the bridges! There's bridges at every river on this road, between here and Hatrack River."

"I know, Pa," said Measure. "I helped build them all, you know."

"Use them! That's all I'm saying. And if it rains, you stop, you find a house and stop, you hear me? I don't want you out in the water."

They both pledged most solemnly not to get near anything wet. "Won't even stand downstream from the horses when they spurt," said Measure.

Pa shook a finger at him. "Don't you make light," he said.

Finally they got on their way, not looking back cause that was awful luck, and knowing that Ma and Pa went back into the house well before they was out of sight, cause it was calling for a long separation if you watched a long time when folks were leaving, and if you watched them clear out of sight it was a good chance somebody'd die before you ever saw them again. Ma took that real serious. Going inside quick like that was the last thing she'd be able to do to help protect her boys on their way.

Al and Measure stopped in a stretch of woods between Hatchs' and Bjornsons' farms, where the last storm knocked down a tree half onto the road. They could get by all right, being on horseback as they were, but you don't leave a thing like that for somebody else to find. Maybe somebody in a wagon, hurrying to make home before dark on a stormy night, maybe that's who'd come by next, and find the road blocked. So they stopped and ate the lunch Ma packed for them, and then set to work with their hatchets, cutting it free from the few taut strands of wood that clung to the ragged stump. They were wishing for a saw long before they were done, but you don't carry a saw with you on a three-hundred-mile trip on horseback. A change of clothes, a hatchet, a knife, a musket for hunting, powder and lead, a length of rope, a blanket, and a few odd tokens and amulets for wardings and fendings. Much more than that and you'd have to bring a wagon or a pack horse.

After the trunk was free, they tied both horses to it and pulled it out of the way. Hard work, sweaty work, cause the horses weren't used to pulling as a team and they bothered each other. Tree kept snagging up on them, too, and they had to keep rolling it and chopping away branches. Now, Al knew he could've used his knack to change the wood of that tree inside, to make it split apart in all the right places. But that wouldn't have been right, he knew. The Shining Man wouldn't've stood for that—it would've been pure selfishness, pure laziness, and no good to anybody. So he hacked and tugged and sweated right alongside Measure. And it wasn't so bad. It was *good* work, and when it was all done it was no more than an hour. It was time well spent.

They talked somewhat during the work, of course. Some of the conversation turned on the stories about Red massacres down south. Measure was pretty skeptical. "Oh, I hear those stories, but the bloody ones are all things somebody heard from somebody else about somebody else. The folks who actually lived down there and got run out, all they ever say is that Ta-Kumsaw come and run off their pigs and chickens, that's all. Not a one ever said nothing about no arrows flying or folks getting killed."

Al, being ten years old, was more inclined to believe the stories, the bloodier the better. "Maybe when they kill somebody, they kill the whole family so nobody talks about it."

"Now you think about it, Al. That don't make sense. Ta-Kumsaw wants all the White people out of there, don't he? So he wants them scared to death, so they pack up and move, don't he? So wouldn't he leave one alive to tell about it, if he was doing massacres? Wouldn't somebody've found some *bodies*, at least?"

"Well where do the stories come from, then?"

"Armor-of-God says Harrison's telling lies, to try to get people het up against the Reds."

"Well, he couldn't very well lie about them burning down his house and his stockade. People could plain *see* if it got burnt, couldn't they? And he couldn't very well lie about it killing his wife and his little boy, could he?"

"Well of course it *did* burn, Al. But maybe it wasn't fire arrows from Ta-Kumsaw started that fire. You ever think of that?"

"Governor Harrison isn't going to burn down his own house and kill his own family just so he can get people hot against the Reds," said Al. "That's plain dumb."

And they speculated on and on about Red troubles in the south part of the Wobbish country, because that was the most important topic of conversation around, and since nobody knowed anything accurate anyway, everybody's opinion was as good as anybody else's.

Seeing how they weren't more than a half mile from two different farms, in country they'd visited four or five times a year for ten years, it never even came to mind they ought to keep their eyes open for trouble. You just don't keep too wary that close to home, not even when you're talking about Red massacres and stories about murders and torture. Fact is, though, careful or not there wasn't much they could've done. Al was coiling ropes and Measure was cinching up the saddles when all of a sudden there was about a dozen Reds around them. One minute nobody but crickets and mice and a bird here and there, the next minute Reds all painted up.

It took a few seconds even at that for them to be afraid. There was a lot of Reds in Prophetstown, and they came pretty regular to trade at

Armor-of-God's store. So Alvin spoke before he even hardly looked at them. "Howdy," said Alvin.

They didn't howdy him back. They had paint all over their faces.

"These ain't no howdy Reds," said Measure softly. "They got muskets."

That made it sure these weren't no Prophetstown Reds. The Prophet taught his followers never to use White man's weapons. A true Red didn't need to hunt with a gun, because the land knew his need, and the game would come near enough to kill with a bow. Only reason for a Red to have a gun, said the Prophet, was to be a murderer, and murdering was for White men. That's what he said. So it was plain these weren't Reds that put much store in the Prophet.

Alvin was looking one right in the face. Al must've showed his fear, cause the Red got a glint in his eye and smiled a little. The Red reached out his hand.

"Give him the rope," said Measure.

"It's our rope," said Al. As soon as he said it he knew it didn't make no sense. Al handed both ropes to him.

The Red took the coils, gentle as you please. Then he tossed one over the White boys' heads, to another Red, and the whole bunch of them set to work, stripping off the boys' outer clothes and then tying their arms behind them so tight it was pulling on their shoulder joints something painful.

"Why do they want our clothes?" Al asked.

In answer, one of the Reds slapped him hard across the face. He must've liked the sound it made, because he slapped him again. The sting of it brought tears to Al's eyes, but he didn't cry out, partly cause he was so surprised, partly cause it made him mad and he didn't want to give them no satisfaction. Slapping was an idea that caught on real good with the other Reds, cause they started in slapping Measure, too, both of the boys, again and again, till they were half-dazed and their cheeks were bleeding inside and out.

One Red babbled something, and they gave him Al's shirt. He slashed at it with his knife, and then rubbed it on Al's bleeding face. Must not have got enough blood on it, because he took his knife and slashed right across Al's forehead. The blood just gushed out, and a second later the pain hit Al and for the first time he *did* cry out. It felt like he'd been laid open right to the bone, and the blood was running down in his eyes so he couldn't see. Measure yelled for them to leave Al alone, but there wasn't no chance of that. Everybody knew that once a Red started in to cutting on you, you were bound to end up dead.

Minute Al cried out and the blood started coming, them Reds started laughing and making little hooting sounds. This bunch was out for real trouble, and Al thought back to all the stories he heard. Most famous one was probably about Dan Boone, a Pennsylvania man who tried to settle in the Crown Colonies for a while. That was back when the Cherriky were against the White man, and one day Dan Boone's boy got kidnapped. Boone wasn't a half hour behind them Reds. It was like they were playing with him. They'd stop and cut off parts of the boy's skin, or poke out an eye, something to cause bad pain and make him scream. Boone heard his boy screaming, and followed, him and his neighbors, armed with their muskets and half-mad with rage. They'd reach the place where the boy'd been tortured, and the Reds were gone, not a trace of a track in the wood, and then there'd come another scream. Twenty miles they went that day, and finally at nightfall they found the boy hanging from three different trees. They say Boone never forgot that, he could never look a Red in the eye after that without thinking on that twenty-mile day.

Al had that twenty-mile day on his mind now, too, hearing them Reds laugh, feeling the pain, just the start of the pain, knowing that whatever these Reds were after, they wanted it to start with two dead White boys, and they wouldn't mind a little noise along the way. Keep still, he told himself. Keep still.

They rubbed his slashed-up shirt on his face, and Measure's hacked up clothes, too. While they were doing that, Al kept his mind on other things. Only time he ever tried to heal himself was that busted leg of his, and then he was lying down, resting, plenty of time to study it out, to find his way to all those small places where there was broken veins and heal them up, knit together the skin and bone. This time he was a-scared and getting pushed this way and that, not calm, not resting. But he still managed to find the biggest veins and arteries, make them close up. Last time they wiped his face on a shirt, his forehead didn't gush blood down to cover his eyes again. It was still bleeding, but just a trickle now, and Al tipped his head up so the blood would ooze on down his temples, and leave his eyes clear to see.

They hadn't cut Measure yet. He was looking at Al, and there was a sick look on Measure's face. Al knew his brother well enough to guess what he was thinking, about how Ma and Pa trusted Al into Measure's keeping, and now look how he let them down. That was crazy, to blame himself. They could've done what they were doing now at any cabin or house in the whole countryside, and weren't nobody could stop them. If Al and Measure hadn't been going off on a long trip, they might still have been on this very road at this very time anyhow. But Al couldn't say nothing like that to Measure, couldn't do much except to smile.

Smile and, as best he could, work on healing up his own wound. Making everything in his forehead go back to the way it was supposed to be. He kept at it, finding it easier and easier to do, while he watched what the Reds were doing.

They didn't talk much. They pretty much knew what to do. They got the blood-smeared clothes and tied them to the saddles. Then with a knife one of them carved the English letters for "Ta-Kumsaw" in one of the saddle seats, and "Prophet" in the other. For a second Al was surprised that he could write English, but then he saw him checking how he made the letters, comparing them to a paper he had folded up in the waistband of his loincloth. A paper.

Then, while two of them held each horse by the bridle, another Red jabbed the horse's flanks with a knife, little cuts, not all that deep, but enough to make them crazy with pain, kicking out, bucking, rearing up. The horses knocked down the Reds holding them and took off, ran away, heading—as the Reds knowed they would—on up the road toward home.

A message, that's what it was. These Reds wanted to be followed. They wanted a whole bunch of White folks to get their muskets and horses and follow. Like Daniel Boone in the story. Follow the sound of screaming. Go crazy from the sound of their children dying.

Well Alvin decided then and there that, live or die, he and Measure wouldn't let Reds make his parents hear what Daniel Boone heard. There wasn't a chance in the world of them getting away. Even if Al made the rope come apart—which he could do easy enough—there wasn't no way two White boys could outrun Reds in the forest. No, these Reds had them as long as they wanted. But Al knew ways to keep them from doing things to them. And it would be all right to do it, too, to use his knack, because it wouldn't just be for himself. It would be for his brother, and for his family, and in a funny way he knew it would be for the Reds, too, because if there was something real, if some White boys really did get tortured to death, then there'd be a war, there'd be a real knock-down-drag-out fight between Reds and Whites, and a lot of people on both sides would die. As long as he didn't kill anybody, then, it would be all right for Al to use his knack.

With the horses gone, the Reds tied thongs around Al's and Measure's necks. Then they pulled on the thongs to drag them along. Measure was a big man, taller than any of the Reds, so as they led him they made him bend over. It was hard for him to run, and the thong was real tight on him. Al was getting pulled along behind him, so he could see how Measure was being treated, could hear him choking a little. It was a simple thing for Al, though, to get inside that thong and stretch it out, stretch it and stretch it, so it was loose around Measure's neck, and long enough that Measure could run pretty much upright. It happened slow enough that the Reds didn't really notice it. But Al knew that they'd notice what he was doing soon enough.

Everybody knew that Reds didn't leave footprints. And when Reds took White captives, they usually carried them, slung by their arms and legs like dressed-out deer, so the clumsy White folks wouldn't leave no tracks. These Reds meant to be followed, then, cause they were letting Al and Measure leave tracks and traces every step they took.

But they didn't mean it to be *too* easy to find them. After they'd gone forever, it felt like—a couple of hours at least—they came to a brook and walked on upstream a ways, and then ran on another half mile or maybe a mile before they finally stopped in a clearing and built a fire.

No farms close by, but that didn't mean much. By now the horses were home with the bloody clothing and the wounds in the horses' flanks and those names carved into the saddles. By now every White man in the whole area was bringing his family in to Vigor Church, where a few men could protect them while the rest went out searching for the missing boys. By now Ma was pale with terror, Pa raging for the other men to hurry, hurry, not a minute to waste, got to find the boys, if you don't come now I'll go on alone! And the others saying, Calm down, calm down, can't do no good by yourself, we'll catch them, you bet. Nobody admitting what they all knew—that Al and Measure were as good as dead.

But Al didn't plan to be dead. No sir. He planned to be absolutely alive, him and Measure both.

The Reds built up the fire good and hot, and it sure wasn't no cook fire. Since the sun was shining bright and hard already, it made Al and Measure sweat something awful, even in their short summer underwear. They sweated even more when the Reds cut even that much off them, popping off the buttons down the front and slicing it right down the back, so they were naked right down to the ground they sat on.

It was about then that one of the Reds noticed Al's forehead. He took a big hank of underwear cloth and wiped at Al's face, rubbing pretty hard to get the dried blood off. Then he started jabbering at the others. They all gathered around to see. Then they checked Measure's forehead, too. Well, Al knew what they were looking for. And he knew they wouldn't find it. Cause he had healed up his own forehead without a scar, not a mark on his own face. And of course no mark on Measure, either, since he wasn't cut. That'd make them think a little.

But it wasn't healing that Al was depending on to save them. It was too hard, too slow—they could sure cut faster than Al could heal, and that was the truth. It was a lot faster for him to use that knack he had on things like stone and metal, which was all the same straight through; living flesh, on the other hand, was complicated with all kinds of little stuff that he had to get right in his head before he could change it and make it whole.

So when one of the Reds sat down in front of Measure, brandishing a knife, Al didn't wait for him to start cutting. He got that knife into his head, the steel of the blade—White man's knife, just like they were carrying White man's muskets. He found the edge of it, the point, and flattened it out, smoothed it, rounded it.

The Red laid that knife up against Measure's bare chest and tried to cut. Measure braced himself for the pain to start. But that knife made no more mark on Measure than if it was a spoon.

Al almost laughed to see that Red pull his knife away and look at it, try to see what was wrong. He ran the edge against his own finger, to test it; Al thought of making the blade razor sharp right then, but no, no, the rule was to use his knack to make things right, not to cause injury. The others gathered round to look at the knife. Some of them mocked the knife's owner, probably thinking he hadn't kept the edge sharp. But Al spent that time finding all the other steel edges that those Red men had and making them round and smooth. They couldn't've cut a pea pod in half with them knives when Al was through.

Sure enough, all the others pulled out their knives to try them, running the edges against Al or Measure first, and finally yelling and shouting and accusing each other, quarreling over whose fault it was, probably.

But they had a job to do, didn't they? They were supposed to torture these White boys and make them scream, or at least hack them up bad enough that when their folks found the bodies they'd thirst for revenge.

So one of the Reds took his old-fashioned stone-edged tommy-hawk and brandished it in front of Al's face, waving it around so he'd get good and scared. Al used the time to soften up the stone, weaken the wood, loosen the thongs that held it all together. By the time the Red got to lifting it up ready to do some real business, like smashing Al in the face with it, it crumbled apart in his hand. The wood was rotted clear through, the stone fell to the ground as gravel, and even the thong was split and frayed through. That Red man shouted and jumped back like as if he had a rattler a-biting at him.

Another one had a steel-blade hatchet, and he didn't waste no time waving it around, he just laid out Measure's hand on a rock and whacked it down, meaning to cut Measure's fingers off. This was easy stuff to Al, though. Hadn't he cut whole millstones, when the need was? So the hatchet struck and rang on the stone, and Measure gasped at the sight of it, sure it'd take his fingers clean off; but when the Red picked up the hatchet, there was Measure's hand just like before, not marked a bit, while the hatchet had finger-shaped depressions in the blade, like it was made of cool butter or wet cake-soap.

Them Reds, they howled, they looked at each other with fear in their eyes, fear and anger at the strange things going on. Alvin couldn't know it, being White, but the thing that made this worst of all for them was they couldn't feel it like they felt a White man's spells or charms or doodles. A White man put a hex, they felt it like a bump in their land-sense; a beseeching was a nasty stink; a warding was a buzz when they came close. But this that Alvin did, it didn't interrupt the land at all, their sense of how things ought to be didn't show them nothing different going on. It was like all the natural laws had changed on them, and suddenly steel was soft and flesh was hard, rock was brittle and leather weak as grass. They didn't look to Al or Measure as the cause of what was going on. It was some natural force doing it, as best they could figure.

All that Alvin saw was their fear and anger and confusion, which pleased him well enough. He wasn't cocky, though. He knew there was some things he didn't know how to handle. Water was the main one; if they took it in their heads to drown the boys, Al wouldn't know how to stop them, or save himself or Measure. He was only ten, and being bound by rules he didn't understand, he hadn't figured out what-all his knack was good for, or how it worked. Maybe there was things within his power that could be right spetackler, if he only knowed how, but the point was he didn't know, and so he only did the things that were within his reach.

This much was on his side—they didn't think of drowning. But they thought of fire. Most likely they were planning that from the start—folks told tales of finding torture victims in the Red wars back in New England, their blackened feet in the cooling ashes of a fire, where they had to watch their own toes char until the pain and bleeding and mad-ness of it killed them. Alvin saw them stoking up the fire, putting hot-burning branches on it to make it flare. He didn't know how to take the heat out of a fire, he'd never tried. So he thought as fast as he could, and while they were picking Measure up by his armpits and dragging him to the fire, Al got inside the firewood and broke it up, made it crumble into dust, so it burnt up fast, all at once, in a fire so fast it made a loud clap and a puff of bright hot light shot upward. It rose so fast that it made a wind blow in from all directions onto the place where the fire had been, and it made a whirlwind for a second or two, whipping around, sucking up the ashes and then puffing them out to drift down like dust.

Just like that, nothing left of the fire at all except dust settling fine as mist all over the clearing.

Oh, they howled, they jumped and danced and beat on their own shoulders and chests. And while they were carrying on like an Irish funeral, Al loosened the ropes on him and Measure, hoping against hope that they might even get away after all before their folks and neighbors found them and started in with shooting and killing and dying.

Measure felt the ropes loosening, of course, and looked sharp at Alvin; up to then he'd been almost as crazy with what was happening as the Reds. Of course, he knew right off that it was Alvin doing it, but it wasn't as if Alvin could explain what he was planning—it took Measure by surprise same as the others. Now, though, he looked at Alvin and nodded, starting to twist his arms out of the ropes. None of the Reds had noticed so far, and maybe they could get a running start, or maybe— just maybe—the Reds were so upset they wouldn't even try to follow.

Right then, though, everything changed. There was a hooting sound from the forest, and then it got picked up by what sounded like three hundred owls, all in a circle. Measure must have thought for a second that Al was causing *that* to happen, too, the way he looked at his little brother—but the Reds knew what it was, and stopped their carrying on right away. From the fear on their faces, though, Al figured it must be something good, maybe even something like rescue.

From the forest all around the clearing there stepped out dozens, then a hundred Reds. These were all carrying bows—not a musket among them—and the way they dressed and had their hair, Al reckoned them to be Shaw-Nee, and followers of the Prophet. It was about the last thing Al expected, truth to tell. It was White faces he wanted to see, not more Red ones.

One Red stepped out of the mass of the newcomers, a tall strong man with a face as hard and sharp as stone, it looked like. He fired off a couple of harsh-sounding words, and immediately their captors began babbling, jabbering, *pleading*. It was like a bunch of children, Al thought, doing something they knew they shouldn't ought to, and then their pa comes along and catches them at it. Having been caught in such mischief himself sometimes, he almost felt a little sympathy, till he remembered that what his captors had had in mind was cruel death for him and his brother. Just because they ended up without a scratch didn't mean them Reds weren't guilty of the bad intent.

Then one word stuck out of all the yammering—a name: Ta-Kumsaw. Al looked at Measure to see if he'd heard, and Measure was looking at

him, raising his eyebrows, asking the same thing. They both mouthed
the name at the same time. Ta-Kumsaw.

Did this mean Ta-Kumsaw was in charge of all this? Was he angry
at the captors because they failed at the torture, or because they'd captured White boys at all? There wasn't no explanation from the Reds,
that was sure. All that Al could know for sure was what they *did*. The
new-come Reds took all the muskets away from the gun-toters, and then
led them off into the woods. Only about a dozen Reds stayed with Al
and Measure. Among them was Ta-Kumsaw.

"They say you have fingers made of steel," said Ta-Kumsaw.

Measure looked at Al for him to answer, and Al couldn't think of
anything to say. He was sure reluctant about telling this Red what it
was he done. So it was Measure answered him after all, by raising his
hands and wiggling his fingers. "Just regular fingers near as I can tell,"
he said.

Ta-Kumsaw reached out and took him by the hand—a strong, hard
grip, it must have been, cause Measure tried to pull away and couldn't.
"Iron skin," said Ta-Kumsaw. "Can't cut with knife. Can't burn. Boys
made of stone."

He pulled Measure up to a standing position and, with his free hand,
slapped him hard on the upper part of the arm. "Stone boy, throw me
on the dirt!"

"I can't wrassle you," said Measure. "I don't want a fight with
nobody."

"Throw me!" commanded Ta-Kumsaw. And he adjusted his grip,
put out his foot, and waited until Measure put out his own foot to join
him. Facing off, man to man, the way the Reds did in their games. Only
this wasn't no game, not to these boys who'd been looking death in the
face and didn't have no guarantee that it still wasn't just around the
corner.

Al didn't know what he ought to do, but he was in a mood for doing
something, coming on the heels of all his changing of things. So it was
almost without a thought of the consequences that the very moment
Measure and Ta-Kumsaw started to push and pull on each other, Al
made the dirt come all loose under Ta-Kumsaw's feet, so his own pushing made him fall ass over elbow in the dirt.

The other Reds had been kind of laughing and joshing about the
wrassle, but when they saw the greatest chief of all the tribes, a man
whose name was known from Boston to New Orleans, when they saw
him smash on the ground like that they kind of left off laughing. Truth
to tell there wasn't a sound in that clearing. Ta-Kumsaw picked himself
up and looked at the dirt under his feet, scraping on it with his foot. It

was solid enough now, of course. But he stepped a few feet away, onto the grass, and held out his hand again.

This time Measure had a little more confidence, and reached out to take his hand—but at the last second, Ta-Kumsaw snatched his own hand away. He stood very still, not looking at Measure or Al or anybody, just looking into space, his face all hard and set. Then he turned to the other Reds and fired off a volley of words, spitting them out with all the Ss and Ks and Xs of Shaw-Nee talk. Al and the other children of Vigor Church used to imitate Red talk by saying things like "boxy talksy skock woxity" and laughing till their sides ached. But it didn't sound too funny the way Ta-Kumsaw said it, and when he was done Al and Measure found themselves getting pulled along by them thongs again. And when the rags of their underjohns fell down and started tripping them up, Ta-Kumsaw came back and tore them off the boys, ripping that fabric to shreds with his bare hands, his face all angry. Neither Al nor Measure felt like mentioning that they was left pretty near naked by this time, considering that the only wearing apparel left on them was the thong around their neck; it just didn't seem like a good time to complain. Where Ta-Kumsaw was taking them they had no idea, and since they also had no choice about going, there wasn't much point in asking, either.

Al and Measure never ran so long or so far in their lives. Hour after hour, mile after mile, never going too terrible fast, but never stopping, neither. Moving like this, a Red could travel faster on foot than a White usually could on horseback, unless he was making his nag run all the way. Which wasn't too good on the horse. And the horse had to stay on cleared roads. While Reds—Reds didn't even need a *path*.

Al noticed real quick that running through the woods was different for the Reds than it was for him and Measure. The only sound he heard was his and Measure's footfalls. Al being near the back, he could see how things went with Measure. The Red who was pulling Measure would push a branch with his body, and the branch would bend to make way. But the next second when Measure tried to push through, it would snatch at his skin and then break off. Reds would step on roots or twigs and there'd be no sound, nothing snagging their feet; Al would step on the same spot, and he'd trip up, stumble, the thong catching at his neck; or the twig would snap under his bare foot, or the rough bark of the root would tear at his skin. Al, on account of being just a boy, was used to walking around barefoot a good deal of the time, so the soles of his feet were somewhat toughened up. But Measure'd been in growed-man's boots for some years now, and Al could see that after maybe half a mile Measure was bleeding.

One thing he could do, Al reckoned, was help his brother's feet to heal up. He tried to start, to find his way into his brother's body the way he'd found his way into the stone and the steel and the wood. Running along like that, though, it was hard to concentrate. And living flesh was just too complicated.

Al wasn't the kind to give up. No, he just tried a different way. Since it was running that distracted him, he just quit thinking about running. Didn't look at the ground. Didn't try to step where the Red ahead of him stepped, just didn't think about it at all. Like trimming an oil lamp, he trimmed his own wick, as they say, letting his eyes focus on nothing, thinking about nothing, letting his body work like a pet animal that could be let to have its own head and go its own way.

He had no notion that he was doing what doodlebugs do, when they let their bug go out of their head and travel on its own. And anyway it wasn't the same, on account of there wasn't no doodlebug in the natural world who ever tried to doodle while he was running with a thong around his neck.

Now, though, he didn't have a speck of trouble getting into Measure's body, finding the sore places, the bleeding cuts on his feet, the ache in his legs, the pain in his side. Healing the feet, toughing them up, callusing them, that was easy enough. For the others, Al felt how Measure's body was craving for him to breathe more, deeper, faster; so Al got into his lungs and cleared them, opened them into the deepest places. Now when Measure sucked in air, his body got more of a use out of it, like it could wring out each rag of air to get the very last drop of good out of it. Al didn't even half understand what he was doing—but he knowed it worked, cause the pain in Measure's body began to ease, he didn't weary so much, he didn't gasp for breath.

As he returned to himself, Al noticed that in the whole time he was helping Measure, he didn't step on no twig that broke or get smacked by some snaggy branch flipping back from the Red in front of him. Now, though, he was getting poked and tripped and snapped as much as ever. He thought right off, it was happening just the same all along, only I didn't hardly notice cause I wasn't rightly paying attention to my own skin. But even as he decided that was true and even mostly believed it, he also realized that the sound of the world had changed. Now it was just breathing and pale-skinned feet thumping on the dirt or swishing through ancient dead leaves. A bird sound now and then, a fly buzzing. Nothing remarkable, except that Al could remember, just as plain as anything, that until he came back from fixing up Measure's body he could hear something else, a kind of music, a kind of—green music. Well, that didn't make no sense. There wasn't no way music could have a color to it, that was plain crazy. So Al put that out of his mind, just didn't think about it. Without thinking about it, though, he was still longing to hear it again. Hear it or see it or smell it, however it came into him, he wanted it back again.

And one more little thing. Until he went out of himself to help Measure, his own body wasn't doing all that well, neither; in fact he was near wore out. But now he was all right, his body was doing fine, he was breathing deep, his legs and arms felt like he could go on forever, sturdy in their motion as trees were in their stillness. Now maybe that was because in healing Measure, he also somehow healed himself—but he didn't rightly believe that, cause he always knew what he did and what he didn't do. No, to Al Junior's thinking, his body was doing better because of something else. And that something else, either it was part of the green music, or it caused the music, or they both were caused by the same thing. As near as Al could figure.

Running along like that, Al and Measure didn't have no chance to talk till getting on nightfall, when they came to a Red village on the curve of a dark deep river. Ta-Kumsaw led them right into the middle of the village and then walked off and left them. The river was just down the slope from them, maybe a hundred yards of grassy ground.

"Think we could make it down to the river without them catching us?" whispered Measure.

"No," said Al. "And anyways I can't swim. Pa never let me near the water."

Then all the Red women and children come out of the stick-and-mud huts they lived in and pointed at them two naked Whites, man and boy, and laughed and threw sods at them. At first Al and Measure tried to dodge, but it just made them laugh harder and run around and around throwing wet dirt from different angles, trying to catch them in the face or the crotch. Finally Measure just sat down on the grass, put his face to his knees, and let them throw all they wanted. Al did the same. Finally somebody barked a few words and the sod-throwing stopped. Al looked up in time to see Ta-Kumsaw walking away, and a couple of his fighting men come out to watch and make sure nothing else happened.

"That was the farthest I ever run in my whole life," said Measure.

"Me too," said Al.

"Right at the start there I thought I was like to die, I was so tired," said Measure. "Then I got my second wind. I didn't think I had it in me."

Al didn't say nothing.

"Or did you have something to do with that?"

"Maybe some," said Al.

"I never know what you can do, Alvin."

"Me neither," said Al, and it was the truth.

"When that hatchet come down on my fingers I thought that was the end of my working days."

"Just be glad they didn't try to drown us."

"You and water again," said Measure. "Well I'm glad you done what you done, Al. Though, I *will* say it might've worked out better if you hadn't made the chief slip like that when he was set to arm-wrassle me."

"Why not?" said Al. "I didn't want him to hurt you—"

"There's no way you should know it, Al, so don't blame yourself. But that kind of wrassling ain't to hurt a body, it's kind of a test. Of manliness and quickness and what all. If he beat me, but I put up a fair fight, then I'd have his respect, and if I beat him fair, why, there's respect in that, too. Armor told me about it. They do it all the time."

Alvin thought about this. "So when I made him fall, was that real bad?"

"I don't know. Depends on why they think it happened. Might be they'll think it means that God is on my side or something."

"Do they believe in God?"

"They've got a Prophet, don't they? Just like in the Bible. Anyway I just hope they don't think it means I'm a coward and a cheater. Things won't go so good for me then."

"Well I'll tell them it was me done it," said Al.

"Don't you dare," said Measure. "The only thing saved us was they didn't know it was you doing them changes on the knives and hatchets and such. If they knowed it was you, Al, they would've hacked your head open, mashed you flat and then done what they wanted with me. Only thing that saved you was they didn't know what was causing it."

Then they got to talking about how worried Pa and Ma would be, speculating on how Ma would be so mad, or maybe she'd be too worried to be angry at Pa, and there must be men out looking for them by now even if the horses never came home, cause when they didn't show up for supper at the Peachees they wouldn't waste a minute giving the warning.

"They'll be talking about war with the Reds," said Measure. "I know that much—there's plenty of folks from down Carthage way who hate Ta-Kumsaw already, from his running off their livestock earlier this year."

"But it was Ta-Kumsaw who saved us," said Al.

"Or that's how it looks, anyway. But I notice he didn't take us home, or even ask us where home *was*. And how did he happen to come along right at that very minute, if he wasn't part of it himself? No, Al, I don't know what's going on, but Ta-Kumsaw didn't save us, or if he did he saved us for his own reasons, and I don't know as how I trust him to do good for us. For one thing, I really ain't much for setting around naked in the middle of a Red village."

"Me neither. And I'm hungry."

It wasn't long, though, before Ta-Kumsaw himself came out with a pot of corn mash. It was almost funny, seeing that tall Red man, who carried himself like a king, toting a pot like one of the Red women. But after that first surprise, Al realized that when Ta-Kumsaw did it, pot-toting looked downright noble.

He set down the pot in front of Al and Measure, and then took a couple of strips of Red-weave cloth from around his neck. "Wrap up," he said, and handed each of them a strip. Neither one of them knowed the first thing about tying on a loincloth, beginning with the fact that Ta-Kumsaw was still holding the deerskin belts that were supposed to hold them on. Ta-Kumsaw laughed at how confused they were, and then made Al stand up. He dressed Al himself, and that showed Measure how it was done so he could cover himself, too. It wasn't like proper clothes, but it was sure better than being buck naked.

Then Ta-Kumsaw sat down on the grass, the pot between him and them, and showed them how to eat the mash—dipping in his hand, pulling out a tepid, jelly-thick glop of it and smacking it into his open mouth. Tasted so bland that Alvin like to gagged on it. Measure saw it, and said, "Eat." So Alvin ate, and once he got some swallowed he could feel how much his belly wanted more, even though it still took real persuasion to get his throat to take on the job of transportation.

When they had the pot cleaned right down to the bottom, Ta-Kumsaw set it aside. He looked at Measure for a while. "How did you make me fall down, White coward?" he said.

Al was all for speaking up right then, but Measure answered too quick and loud. "I ain't no coward, Chief Ta-Kumsaw, and if you wrassle me now it'll be fair and square."

Ta-Kumsaw smiled grimly. "So you can make me fall down with all these women and children watching?"

"It was me," said Alvin.

Ta-Kumsaw turned his head, slowly, the smile not leaving his face— but not so grim now, neither. "Very small boy," he said. "Very worthless child. You can make the ground loose under my feet?"

"I just got a knack," said Alvin. "I didn't know you weren't aiming to hurt him."

"I saw a hatchet," said Ta-Kumsaw. "Finger-marks like this." He waved his finger to show the kind of pattern Measure's fingers had left in the blade of the hatchet. "You did that?"

"It ain't right to cut a man's fingers off."

Ta-Kumsaw laughed out loud. "Very good!" Then he leaned in close. "White men's knacks, they make noise, very much noise. But you, what you do is so quiet nobody sees it."

Al didn't know what he was talking about.

In the silence, Measure spoke up bold as you please. "What you plan to do with us, Chief Ta-Kumsaw?"

"Tomorrow we run again," he said.

"Well why don't you think about letting us run toward home? There's got to be a hundred of our neighbors out now, mad as hornets. There's going to be a lot of trouble if you don't let us go home."

Ta-Kumsaw shook his head. "My brother wants you."

Measure looked at Alvin, then back at Ta-Kumsaw. "You mean the Prophet?"

"Tenskwa-Tawa," said Ta-Kumsaw.

Measure looked plain sick. "You mean after he built up his Prophetstown for four years, nobody causing him a lick of trouble, White man and Red man getting along real good, now he goes around taking Whites captive and torturing them and—"

Ta-Kumsaw clapped his hands once, loudly. Measure fell silent. "Chok-Taw took you! Chok-Taw tried to kill you! My people don't kill except to defend our land and our families from White thieves and murderers. And Tenskwa-Tawa's people, they don't kill at all."

That was the first Al ever heard of there being a split between Ta-Kumsaw's people and the Prophet's people.

"Then how'd you know where we were?" demanded Measure. "How'd you know how to find us?"

"Tenskwa-Tawa saw you," said Ta-Kumsaw. "Told me to hurry and get you, save you from the Chok-Taw, bring you to Mizogan."

Measure, who knew more about Armor-of-God's maps than Alvin did, recognized the name. "That's the big lake, where Fort Chicago is."

"We don't go to Fort Chicago," said Ta-Kumsaw. "We go to the holy place."

"A church?" asked Alvin.

Ta-Kumsaw laughed. "You White people, when you make a place holy you build walls so nothing of the land can get in. Your god is nothing and nowhere, so you build a church with nothing alive inside, a church that could be anywhere, it doesn't matter—nothing and nowhere."

"Well what *does* make a place holy?" asked Alvin.

"Because that's where the Red man talks to the land, and the land answers." Ta-Kumsaw grinned. "Sleep now. We will go when it's still dark."

"It's going to be mighty cool tonight," said Measure.

"Women will bring you blankets. Warriors don't need them. This is summer." Ta-Kumsaw walked a few steps away, then turned back to Alvin. "Weaw-Moxiky ran behind you, White boy. He saw what you did. Don't try to keep the secret from Tenskwa-Tawa. He will know when you lie." Then the chief was gone.

"What's he talking about?" asked Measure.

"I wisht I knew," said Al. "I'm going to have trouble telling the truth when I don't know what the truth *is*."

The blankets came soon enough. Al snuggled close to his big brother, for courage more than warmth. He and Measure whispered awhile, trying to puzzle things out. If Ta-Kumsaw wasn't in on this from the start, how come them Chok-Taw cut his and the Prophet's names into the saddle? And even if that was a lie, it was going to look real bad that Ta-Kumsaw finally did end up with the captives, and then up and took them to Lake Mizogan instead of just letting them go home. It was going to take some tall talking to keep this from turning into a war.

Finally, though, they fell silent, weary to the bone from all their running, not to mention their work moving the tree and the plain terror when the Chok-Taw was out to torture them. Measure started snoring lightly. And Alvin, he found himself drifting. In the very last moments before sleep, he heard that green music again, or saw it, or anyhow knew that it was there. But before he could even listen, he dozed off. Dozed off and slept real peaceful, what with the night breeze blowing cool off the river, the blanket and the warmth of Measure's body keeping him warm, the nightsounds of the animals, the cries of a hungry infant from a hut somewhere; all of it was part of the green music flowing through his head.

8

Red-Lover

They gathered in the clearing, some thirty White men, grim-faced and angry and tired from walking through the woods. The trail was easy enough to follow, but it seemed like the branches grabbed at them and the roots tripped them up—the forest was never kind to a White man. Then there was an hour lost when the trail reached a stream, and they had to go up and down the stream to find where the Reds took them boys out of the water and up onto land again. Old Alvin Miller like to went crazy when he saw they dragged the boys through water—it took his son Calm about ten minutes to get him quiet and able to go on. The man was just mad with fear.

"Shouldn't've sent him away, I never should've let him go," he kept saying.

And Calm kept saying, "Could've happened anywhere, don't blame yourself, we'll find them all right, they're still walking ain't they?" All kinds of talk, but mostly it was his voice that soothed Al Miller, it was his manner—some folks even said it was his knack, that his ma named him straight for what he could best do.

Now they were in the clearing, and trails led off about five different ways, and all of them plumb disappeared after a few steps. They found the boys' tore-up underwear a few steps into the woods heading northwest. Nobody figured they ought to show that to Al Miller, so by the time he got there—him bringing up the rear at that point, with Calm by his side—the underjohns were tucked away out of sight.

"We'll never track them from here," said Armor-of-God. "The boys aren't leaving no footprints now—which don't mean nothing, Mr. Miller, so don't you fret." Armor called his father-in-law *Mr. Miller* ever since Al threw him out of the house into the snow that time he came to say Al Junior was dying cause the family committed the sin of using hexes and beseechings. It just don't seem right to call a man *Pa* after he heaves you off his porch. "They might be toting the boys, or they might be stepping after them, kind of wiping out their prints. We all know if a Red don't want to leave a trail, there ain't no trail."

"We all know about Reds," said Al Miller. "And what they do to White boys when they—"

"So far all we know is they're trying to scare us," said Armor.

"Doing a good job so far," said one of the Swedes. "Scared mostly to death, my family and me."

"Besides, everybody knows Armor-of-God here is a Red-lover."

Armor looked around, trying to see who said that. "If by Red-lover you mean I think Reds are human beings just like Whites, then it's true. But if you mean I like Reds *better* than Whites, then you best work up some courage to step out here and say it to my face, so I can mash your face into the bark of a tree."

"No need to quarrel," said Reverend Thrower, panting. He wasn't much for exercise, was Thrower, so he only just now caught up with the rest of them. "The Lord God loves all his children, even the heathens. Armor-of-God is a good Christian. But we all know that if it ever comes to fighting between Christian and heathen, Armor-of-God will stand on the side of righteousness."

The crowd murmured their agreement. After all, they all liked Armor; he'd loaned most of them money or given them credit at his store, and never nagged them for payment—a good many of them might not have made it through their first few years in Wobbish country if it wasn't for Armor. Grateful or not, though, they all knew he treated Reds like they was almost White, which was a bit suspicious at a time like this.

"It's coming to fighting right now," said a man. "We don't have to track down these Reds. We got their names on the saddles, carved right in."

"Now just wait a minute!" said Armor-of-God. "You just think a minute! In all this time Prophetstown's been a-growing there across the Wobbish from Vigor Church, has any Red so much as stole a thing from you? Slapped one of your children? Snatched a pig? Done any single bad thing to any one of you?"

"I think stealing Al Miller's boys is a pretty bad thing!" said a man.

"I'm talking about the Reds in Prophetstown! You know they never done nothing wrong, you *know* that! And you know why, too. You know it's cause the Prophet tells them to live in peace, keep to their own land and do no harm to the White man."

"That ain't what Ta-Kumsaw says!"

"Well even if they *did* want to do some terrible crime against White
folks—which I ain't saying—is there any one of you thinks Ta-Kumsaw
or Tenskwa-Tawa is so blamed stupid he's going to sign his name?"

"They're proud of killing White folks!"

"If the Red man was smart, he'd be White!"

"See what I mean about Red-lovers?"

Armor-of-God knew these people, and he knew that most of them
were still with him. Even the grumblers weren't about to go off half-
cocked; they'd sit tight until the whole group decided on action. So let
them call him a Red-lover, that was fine, when men was scared and
mad they said things that later they repented of. As long as they waited.
As long as they didn't jump into war against the Reds.

Cause Armor had his suspicions about this whole thing. It was just
too easy, the way them horses was sent on home with names carved in
the saddle. It wasn't the way Reds did things, even the bad ones that
would kill you soon as look at you. Armor knew enough about Reds to
know they only tortured to give a man a chance to show brave, not to
terrorize people. (Or most Reds, anyway—there were stories about the
Irrakwa before they got civilized.) So whoever did this wasn't acting
like a natural Red. Armor was near convinced it was a hired-out job.
The French in Detroit had been trying to cause war between Reds and
American settlers for years—it might've been them. And it might have
been Bill Harrison. Oh yes, it might well have been that man, down
there like a spider in his fort on the Hio. Armor thought that was the
most likely thing. Course he wouldn't dare to say it out loud, cause
folks would think he was just jealous of Bill Harrison, which was true—
he *was* jealous. But he also knew that Harrison was a wicked man,
who'd do anything to make things go his way. Maybe even get some
wild Reds to come up and kill a few White boys near Prophetstown.
After all, it was Tenskwa-Tawa who got most of the Reds from Harrison's part of the country to lay off whisky and come to Prophetstown.
And it was Ta-Kumsaw who ran off half the White settlers down there.
It looked to Armor like Harrison was behind this, a lot more likely than
the French.

But he couldn't say none of this, cause there was no proof. He just
had to try to keep things calm, till some real evidence showed up.

Which might be right now. They'd brought along old Tack Sweeper,
wheezing his way with the best of them—it was remarkable how vig-
orous he was, for a man whose lungs sounded like a baby's rattle when
he breathed. Tack Sweeper had him a knack, which wasn't all that
reliable, he was the first to say. But sometimes it worked remarkable
well. What he did was stand around in a place for a while with his eyes

closed and sort of see the things that happened there in the past. Just quick little visions, a few faces. Like that time they was afraid maybe Jan de Vries killed hisself on purpose, or maybe was murdered, Tack was able to see how it was an accident when his gun went off in his own face, so they could bury him in the churchyard and not have to worry about hunting for no killer.

So the hope was Tack could tell them something about what happened in this clearing. He shooed them all back to the edges of the wood, so they'd be out of the way. Then he walked around in the middle, his eyes closed, moving slow. "You boys shouldn't have got so mad here," he said after a while. "All I can see is you all jawing." They laughed, kind of embarrassed. They should've knowed better than to mess up the memories of a place before Tack got there.

"It don't look good. I keep seeing them Red faces. Knife, all kind of knives getting slashed on folks' skin. A hatchet falling."

Al Miller moaned.

"It's all just a mess here, so much happened," said Tack. "I can't see right. No. No, I can—one man. A Red man, I know his face, I seen him—he's just standing there, just still as you please, I know that face."

"Who is it?" said Armor-of-God. But he knew, he had that sickening feeling of dread, oh he knew.

"Ta-Kumsaw," said Tack. He opened his eyes wide and looked at Armor, almost apologetic. "I wouldn't've believed it either, Armor," he said. "I always kind of thought Ta-Kumsaw was the bravest man I ever knew. But he was here, and he was in charge. I see him standing there, and telling people what to do. He stood right here. I can see him so clear cause there wasn't nobody else stood exactly in that place for so long. And he was mad. Ain't no mistake about it."

Armor believed it. They all did—they all knew Tack was a truthful man, and if he said he was sure, then he was sure. But there had to be some reason. "Maybe he come and saved the boys, did you think of that? Maybe he come and stopped some band of wild Reds from—"

"Red-lover!" somebody shouted.

"You know Ta-Kumsaw! He's no coward, and stealing them boys was a cowardly thing to do, you *know* that man!"

"Nobody ever knows a Red man."

"Ta-Kumsaw didn't take those boys!" insisted Armor-of-God. "I know it!"

Then everybody fell silent, cause old Al Miller was pushing his way forward, out to where Armor-of-God was standing. Faced down his son-in-law, he did, with a face like living hell he was so mad. "You don't know nothing, Armor-of-God Weaver. You are the most worthless scum ever formed on the top of a chamber pot. First you married my daughter and wouldn't let her work no hexes cause you were so cock-eyed sure it was the devil's work. Then you let all these Reds stay around here all the time. And when we thought of building a stockade you said, No, if we build a stockade that just gives them French something to attack and burn down, we'll be *friends* with the Reds and then they'll leave us alone, we'll *trade* with the Reds. Well look what it got us! Look what you done for us! Ain't we all glad we listened to you now! I don't think you're no Red-lover, Armor-of-God, I just think you're the blamedest fool ever to cross the Hio and come out west, and the only folks dumber than you is *us* if we listen to you for another minute!''

Then Al Miller turned to face the other men, who were looking at him with awe in their face like they just seen majesty for the first time in their lives. ''We done it Armor's way for ten years here. But I've done with that. I lost one boy in the Hatrack River on my way here, and this town is named for him. Now I lost two other boys. I only got me five sons left, but I tell you I'll put guns in their hands myself, and lead them all into the middle of Prophetstown and blast them Reds into hell, even if it means we all die! You hear me?''

They heard him, oh yes they did. They heard and shouted back. This was the word they wanted right now, the word of hate and anger and revenge, and nobody better to give it to them than Al Miller, who was normally a peaceable man, never picked a quarrel with nobody. Him being the father of the captured boys just made it all the stronger when he spoke.

''The way I see it,'' said Al Miller, ''Bill Harrison was right all along. Ain't no way the Red man and the White man can share this land. And I tell you something else. It ain't me that's leaving. There's too much blood of mine been shed here now for me to pack up and go away. I'm staying, either on this land or in it.''

Me too, said all them boys. That's the truth, Al Miller. We're staying.

''Thanks to Armor here, we got no stockade and we got no U.S. Army fort closer than Carthage City. If we fight right now, we might lose everything and everybody. So let's hold off the Reds as best we can and send for help. A dozen men down to Carthage City and beg Bill Harrison to send us up an army, and maybe bring his cannon if he can. My two boys are gone, and a thousand Reds for each of my sons won't be enough getting even for me!''

The dozen riders set on their way south first thing the next morning. They left from the commons, which was crowded with wagons as more and more families from outlying farms came in to town to put up with close-in friends and kinfolk. But Al Miller wasn't there to see them off. Yesterday his words set them all in motion, but that was all the leadership they'd get from him. He didn't want to be in charge. He just wanted his boys back.

In the church, Armor-of-God sat on the front pew, despondent. "We're making the most terrible mistake," he said to Reverend Thrower.

"That's what men do," said Thrower, "when they make their decisions without the help of the Lord."

"It wasn't Ta-Kumsaw, I know it. Nor the Prophet either."

"He's no Prophet, not of God, anyway," said Thrower.

"He's no killer, either," said Armor. "Maybe Tack was right, maybe somehow Ta-Kumsaw's got something to do with this. But I know one thing. Ta-Kumsaw's no killer. Even when he was a young man, during General Wayne's war, there was a bunch of Reds all set to burn a bunch of captives to death, the way they did in those days—Chippy-Wa, I think they were. And along comes Ta-Kumsaw, all by himself, just this one lone Shaw-Nee, and he makes them stop. We want the White man to respect us, to treat us as a nation, he says to them. White man won't respect us if we act like this! We got to be civilized. No scalps, no torture, no burning, no killing captives. That's what he says to them. He's stuck to that ever since. He kills in battle, yes, but in all his raids down south he didn't kill one soul, do you realize that? If Ta-Kumsaw's got them boys, then they're as safe as if their mama had them home in bed."

Thrower sighed. "I suppose you know these Reds better than I do."

"I know them better than anybody." He laughed bitterly. "So they call me a Red-lover and don't listen to a word I say. Now they're calling for that whisky-dealing tyrant from Carthage City to come up here and take over. No matter what he does he'll be a hero. They'll make him governor for real, then. Heck, they'll probably make him President, if Wobbish ever joins the U.S.A."

"I don't know this Harrison. He can't be the devil you make him out to be."

Armor laughed. "Sometimes, Reverend, I think you are as trusting as a little child."

"Which is how the Lord told us to be. Armor-of-God, be patient. All things will work out as the Lord intends."

Armor buried his face in his hands. "I sure hope so, Reverend. I sure do. But I keep thinking about Measure, as good a man as you can hope to find, and that boy Alvin, that sweet-faced boy, and how much store his papa sets by him, and—"

Thrower's face went grim. "Alvin Junior," he muttered. "Who would have imagined that the Lord would do his work through the hands of heathens?"

"What are you talking about?" asked Armor.

"Nothing, Armor, nothing. Just that everything about this may be exactly, *exactly* what the Lord intends."

Up the hill at the Miller house, Al still sat at the breakfast table. He didn't eat no supper the night before, and when he tried to eat breakfast he like to gagged on the food. Faith cleared it all away, and now she stood behind him, rubbing his shoulders. She never once said to him, I told you not to send them. But they both knew it. It hung between them like a sword, and neither dared reach out to the other for fear of it.

The silence broke when Wastenot came in, a rifle over his shoulder. He set it beside the front door, swung a chair between his legs, and sat and looked at his parents. "They're gone, down to fetch the army."

To his surprise, his father only lowered his head and rested it on his arms, which were crossed on the table.

Mother looked at him, her face haggard with worry and grief. "Since when did you learn how to use that thing?"

"Me and Wantnot been practicing," he said.

"And you're going to kill Reds with it?"

Wastenot was surprised at the loathing in her voice. "I sure hope so," he said.

"And when all the Reds are dead, and you pile all their bodies together, will Measure and Alvin somehow wriggle out of that pile and come on home to me?"

Wastenot shook his head.

"Last night some Red went home to his family, all proud because he killed him some White boys yesterday." Her voice caught when she said it, but she went on all the same, cause when Faith Miller had aught to say, it got said. "And maybe his wife or his mama patted him and kissed him and made him supper. But don't you ever walk through that door and tell me you killed a Red man. Cause you won't get no supper, boy, and you won't get no kiss, and you won't get no pat, and no word, and no home, and no mama, you hear me?"

He heard, all right, but he didn't like it. He stood up and walked back to the door and picked up the gun. "You think what you like, Mama," he said, "but this is a war, and I *am* going to kill me some Reds, and I'm going to come back home, and I'm going to own up to it proud as can be. And if that means you don't want to be my mama no more, then you might as well stop being my mama now, and not wait till I come back.'' He opened the door, but stopped before slamming it shut behind him. ''Cheer up, Mama. Maybe I won't come back at all.''

He never talked that way to his mother in his life, and he wasn't real sure that it felt good to do it now. But she was being crazy, not understanding that it was war now, that them Reds had declared it open season on White folks and so there wasn't no more choice about it.

What bothered him most, though, as he got on his horse and rode out to David's place, was that he couldn't exactly be sure but he thought, he just suspected anyway, that Papa was crying. If that didn't beat all. Yesterday Papa was so hot against the Reds, and now Mama talked against fighting, and Papa just sat there and cried. Maybe it was getting old that made Papa like that. But that wasn't Wastenot's business, not now. Maybe Papa and Mama didn't want to kill them as took their sons—but Wastenot knew what he was going to do to them as took his brothers. Their blood was his blood, and whoever shed his blood was going to shed some of their own, too, a gallon for every drop.

9

Lake Mizogan

In his whole life Alvin never saw so much water all in one place. He stood on the top of a sand dune, looking out over the lake. Measure stood beside him, a hand resting on Al's shoulder.

"Pa told me to keep you away from water," said Measure, "and now look where they bring you."

The wind was hot and hard, gusting sometimes and shooting sand around like tiny arrows. "Brought you, too," said Al.

"Look, there's a real storm coming."

Off in the southwest, the clouds got black and ugly. Not one of them summer-shower storms. Lightning crackled along the face of the clouds. The thunder came much later, muffled by distance. While Alvin was watching, he felt suddenly like he could see much wider, much farther than before, like he could see the twisting and churning in the clouds, feel the hot and cold of it, the icy air swooping down, the hot air shooting upward, all writhing in a vast circle of the sky.

"Tornado," said Al. "There's a tornado in that storm."

"I don't see one," said Measure.

"It's coming. Look how the air is spinning there. Look at that."

"I believe you, Al. But it's not like there's any place to hide around here."

"Look at all these people," said Alvin. "If it hits us here—"

"When did you learn how to tell the weather?" asked Measure. "You never done that before."

Al didn't have an answer to that. He never *had* felt a storm inside himself like this. It was like the green music he'd heard last night, all kinds of strange things happening now that he was captured by these

Reds. But he couldn't waste another minute trying to think about why he knew—it was enough that he knew it. "I've got to warn somebody."

Alvin took off down the dune, sliding so that each step was like leaping off the face of the hill, then landing on one foot and leaping again. He'd never run downhill so fast before. Measure chased after him, shouting, "They told us to stay up there till—" The wind gusted and whipped away his words. Now they were off the hill, the sand was even worse; the wind lifted big sheets of sand off the dunes, hurled it a ways, then let it fall. Al had to close his eyes, shield them with his hand, turn his face out of the wind—whatever it took to keep the sand from blinding him as he ran to the group of Reds gathered at the edge of the water.

Ta-Kumsaw was easy to spot, and not just cause he was so big. The other Reds left a space around him, and he stood there like a king. Al ran right up to him. "Tornado coming!" he yelled. "There's tornadoes in that cloud!"

Ta-Kumsaw leaned his head back and laughed; the wind was so loud Al barely heard him. Then Ta-Kumsaw reached over Al's head, to touch the shoulder of another Red standing there. "This is the boy!" shouted Ta-Kumsaw.

Al looked at the man Ta-Kumsaw touched. He didn't carry himself like a king at all—nothing like Ta-Kumsaw. He was stooped somewhat, and one eye was missing, the lid just hanging empty over nothing. He looked taut, his arms wiry rather than muscled, his legs downright scrawny. But as Al sat there looking up into his face, he knew him. There wasn't no mistake.

The wind died down for just a minute.

"Shining Man," said Al.

"Roach boy," said Tenskwa-Tawa, Lolla-Wossiky, the Prophet.

"You're real," said Al. Not a dream, not a vision. A real man who had stood there at the foot of his bed, vanishing and reappearing, his face shining like sunlight so it hurt to look at him. But it was the same man. "I didn't heal you!" said Al. "I'm sorry."

"Yes you did," said the Prophet.

Then Al remembered why he'd come running down the dune, busting into a conversation between the two greatest Reds in the whole world, these brothers whose names were known to every White man, woman, and child west of the Appalachee Mountains. "Tornadoes!" he said.

As if to answer him, the wind whipped up again, howling now. Al turned around, and what he'd seen and felt was coming true. There were four twisters forming, hanging down out of the storm like snakes hanging from trees, slithering lower toward the ground, their heads ready to strike. They were all four coming right toward them, but not touching the ground yet.

"Now!" shouted the Prophet.

Ta-Kumsaw handed his brother a flint-tipped arrow. The Prophet sat down in the sand and jammed the point of the arrow into the sole of his left foot, then his right foot. Blood oozed copiously from the wounds. Then he did the same to his hands, jabbing himself so deep in the palm that it was bleeding on the top side of his hands, too.

Almost without thinking, Al cried out and started to cast his mind into the Prophet's body, to heal the wounds.

"No!" cried the Prophet. "This is the power of the Red man—the blood of his body—the fire of the land!"

Then he turned and started walking out into Lake Mizogan.

No, not *into* the lake. *Onto* it. Alvin couldn't hardly believe it, but under the Prophet's bloody feet the water became smooth and flat as glass, and the Prophet was standing on it. His blood pooled on the surface, deep red. A few yards away, the water became loose and choppy, wind-whipped waves rushing toward the smooth place and then just flattening, calming, becoming smooth.

The Prophet kept walking, farther out onto the water, his bloody footprints marking the smooth path through the storm.

Al looked back at the tornadoes. They were close now, almost overhead. Al could feel them twisting inside *him*, as if he were part of the clouds, and these were the great raging emotions of his own soul.

Out on the water, the Prophet raised his hands and pointed at one of the twisters. Almost immediately, the other three twisters rose up, sucked back up into the clouds and disappeared. But the other came nearer, until it was directly over the Prophet, maybe a hundred feet up. It was near enough that around the edges of the Prophet's glassy smooth path, the water was leaping up, as if it wanted to dive upward into the clouds; the water started to circle, too, twisting around and around with the wind under the twister.

"Come!" shouted the Prophet.

Alvin couldn't hear him, but he saw his eyes—even from that far away—saw his lips move, and knew what the Prophet wanted. Alvin didn't hesitate. He stepped out onto the water.

By now, of course, Measure was caught up with him, and when Al started walking onto the warm, smooth glass of the Prophet's path, Measure shouted at him, grabbed at him. Before he could touch the boy, though, the Reds had him, pulled him back; he screamed at Alvin to come back, don't go, don't go onto the water—

Alvin heard him, and Alvin was as scared as he could be. But the

Shining Man was waiting for him under the mouth of the tornado, standing on the water. Inside himself Al felt such a longing, like Moses when he saw the burning bush—I have to stop and see this thing, said Moses, and that's what Alvin was saying, I have to go and see what this is. Because this wasn't the kind of thing that happened in the natural universe, and that was the truth. There wasn't no beseeching or hex or witchery he ever heard of that could call a tornado and turn a stormy lake into glass. Whatever this Red man was doing, it was the most important thing Al ever saw or ever was likely to see in his life.

And the Prophet loved him. That was one thing Al didn't have no doubt of. The Shining Man had stood once at the foot of his bed and taught him. Al remembered that the Shining Man cut himself then, too. Whatever the Prophet was doing, he used his own blood and pain to do it with. There was a real majesty to that. Under the circumstances, Al can't be much blamed for feeling kind of worshipful as he walked out onto the water.

Behind him, the path loosened up, dissolved, disappeared. He felt the waves licking at his heels. It scared him, but as long as he walked forward there wasn't no harm done to him. And finally he stood with the Prophet, who reached out and took Alvin's hands in his. "Stand with me," shouted the Prophet. "Stand here in the eye of the land, and see!"

Then the tornado sank quickly downward; the water leaped up, rising like a wall around them. They were in the very center of the tornado, getting sucked upward—

Until the Prophet reached out one bloody hand and touched the waterspout, and it, too, went smooth and hard as glass. No, not glass. It was as clear and clean as a drop of dew on a spiderweb. There wasn't no storm now. Just Al and the Shining Man, in the middle of a tower of crystal, bright and transparent.

Only instead of being like a window that showed what was happening outside, Al couldn't see the lake or the storm or the shore through the crystal wall. Instead he saw other things.

He saw a wagon caught in a flooding river, a tree floating down like a battering ram, and a young man leaping out onto the tree, rolling it over, turning if from the wagon. And then the man tangling in the roots of the tree, getting smashed against a boulder, then rolling and tumbling downstream, all the time struggling to live, to breathe just a while longer, keep breathing, keep breathing—

He saw a woman bearing a baby, and a little girl who stood nearby reached out and touched her belly. She shouted something, and the midwife reached in her hand and took the baby's head, pulled it out.

The mother tore and bled. The little girl reached under and pulled something off the baby's face; the baby cried. The man in the river heard that cry, somehow, knew that he had lived long enough, and so he died. Al didn't know what to make of it. Until he heard the Prophet whisper in his ear: "The first thing you see in here is the day you are born."

The baby was Alvin Junior; the man who died was his brother, Vigor. Who was the girl who took the birth caul off his face? Al never saw her before in his life.

"I will show you," said the Prophet. "This stays only a little while, and I have things to see for myself, but I will show you." He took Alvin by the hand and together they rose upward through the column of glass.

It didn't feel like flying, not like the soaring of a bird; it was as if there wasn't no up or down. The Prophet pulled him upward, but Al couldn't figure how the Prophet pulled *himself*. Didn't matter. There were so many things to see. Wherever he hung in the air, he could look in any direction and see something else through the wall of the tower. Until he realized that every moment of time, every human life must be visible through this tower wall. How could you find your way through here? How could you look for any one particular story in the hundreds, thousands, millions of moments of past time?

The Prophet stopped, hoisted the boy up until he could see what the Prophet was seeing, their cheeks pressed together, their breath mingling, the Prophet's heartbeat loud in Alvin's ear.

"Look," said the Prophet.

What Alvin saw was a city, shining in sunlight. Towers of ice, it looked like, or clear glass, because when the sun set behind the city its light didn't so much as dim, and the city cast no shadow on the meadowland around it. Inside that city there were people, like bright shadows moving here and there, going up and down the towers without stairs or wings. More important than what he saw, though, was what he felt, looking at that place. Not peace, no, there was nothing quiet about what he felt. It was excitement, his heart pumping fast as a horse in full gallop. The people there, they weren't perfect—they were sometimes angry, sometimes sad. But nobody was hungry, and nobody was ignorant, and nobody had to do something just because somebody else made them do it. "Where is that city!" whispered Alvin.

"I don't know," said the Prophet. "Every time I come here, I see it in a different shape. Sometimes these tall thin towers, sometimes big crystal mounds, sometimes just people living on a sea of crystal fire. I think this city was built many times in the past. I think it will be built again."

"Are you going to build it? Is that what Prophetstown is for?"

Tears came from the Prophet's eyes—spilling from his one good eye, oozing out of the slack lid of the other. "Red man can't build this place alone," he said. "We are part of the land, and this city is more than the land alone. The land is good and bad, life and death all together, the green silence."

Alvin thought of his sense of green music, but he didn't say nothing, cause the Prophet was saying things he wanted to hear, and Al was smart enough to know that sometimes it's better to listen than to talk.

"But this city," said the Prophet, "the crystal city is light without dark, clean without dirty, healthy without sick, strong without weak, plenty without hungry, drink without thirst, life without death."

"The people in that place, they aren't all happy," said Alvin. "They don't live forever."

"Ah," said the Prophet. "You don't see the same that I see."

"What I see is, they're building it." Al frowned. "At one end they're building it, and at the other end, it's falling down."

"Ah," said the Prophet. "The city I see will never fall."

"Well what's the difference? How come we don't see the same thing?"

"I don't know, Roach Boy. I never showed this to anybody. Now go back down, wait for me below. I have things to see before time starts again."

Just thinking about going down made Alvin start to sink, until he was clear to the bottom, on the shiny clear floor. Floor? It could have been the ceiling for all he knowed. There was light coming up from there just like it was shining through the other walls, and he saw pictures there, too.

He saw a huge cloud of dust spin faster and faster, but instead of spitting out dust it sucked it all in, and suddenly it started glowing, and then it caught fire, and it was the sun, just as plain as could be. Alvin knew somewhat about the planets, cause Thrower talked about them, so he wasn't surprised to see them glowing points of light that pretty soon got dim. And after a while instead of dust mixed with darkness, it was all either worlds or empty space, pretty much. He saw the Earth, so small, but then he came closer and he saw how big it was, spinning so fast, one face of the Earth lit up from sunlight, the other face dark. He stood in the sky, it seemed, looking down on the lit place, but he could see all that was going on. First bare rock, spouting volcanoes; then out of the ocean, plants spreading out, growing tall, ferns and trees. He saw fish leaping in the sea, crawly life on the shore where the tide came in, and then bugs and other small critters, hopping and nibbling on leaves and catching each other and eating each other up. Them animals kept getting bigger and bigger, so fast Alvin couldn't follow the changes, just the Earth spinning and him watching, huge monstrous creatures like he never heard of, with long snakey necks some of them, and teeth and jaws to tear down trees with a single bite, it looked like. And then they were gone, and there were elephants and antelopes and tigers and horses, all the life of the earth, getting more and more like what Alvin thought animals ought to look like. But nowhere in all this did he see a man. He found apes and hairy things that hit each other with rocks, things that walked on their hind legs but looked about as dumb as frogs.

And then he *did* see some folks, though he wasn't sure at first cause they were Black and he hadn't seen but one Black man in his life, a slave owned by a peddler from the Crown Colonies, who happened to come through Vigor Church maybe two years back. But they looked like human people, all right, Black or not, and they were pulling fruit down out of trees and berries off of bushes, feeding each other, a passel of pickaninnies following in their tracks. Two of the young ones got to fighting, and the big one killed the little one. The papa came back then, and kicked the one who did the killing, made him go away. Then he picked up the dead one and brought him back to the mama, both of them crying, and they laid that dead child down and covered him up with rocks. Then they gathered up their family and walked on, and after just a few steps they were eating again, and the tears stopped, and they went on, just went on. These are folks, that's sure, thought Alvin. This is just the way human people are.

The Earth kept turning, and by the time it come round again there was all kinds of folks, dark ones in the hot countries, light ones in the cold countries, with all shades in between. Except when America came under the light of the sun. In America folks was pretty much all the same kind, all Red, whether they lived north or south, hot or cold, wet or dry. And the land was at peace, compared to the other part of the world. It was strange for him to see, because when the big part of the land came by, with all its different races and nations, why, it changed with every sweep of the Earth, whole countries moved from one place to another, everything always shuffling around, and wars every minute, everywhere. The smaller land, America, it had some wars, too, but it was all slower, gentler. The people lived in a different rhythm. The land had its own heartbeat, its own life.

From time to time more people would come from the old world—fishermen, mostly. Off course, led astray by storms, running from enemies. They'd come, and for a time they'd live their old-world life in America, trying to build fast, and breed fast, and kill as much as they could. Like a sickness. But then they'd either join in with the Reds and disappear, or get killed off. None of them ever kept up their old-world ways.

Until now, thought Alvin. Now when we came, we were just too strong. Like getting a couple of colds maybe, and you begin to think you won't never get real sick, and then you get a dose of smallpox and you know that you were never truly sick before at all.

Alvin felt a hand on his shoulder.

"So there is where you looked," said the Prophet. "What did you see?"

"I think I saw the whole creation of the world," said Al. "Just like in the Bible. I think I saw—"

"I know what you saw. We all see this, all who have ever come to this place."

"I thought you said I was the first you brought."

"This place—there are many doors inside. Some walk in through fire. Some walk in through water. Some through being buried in the earth. Some by falling through the air. They come to this place and see. They go back and tell what they remember, as much of it as they understood, and tell it, as much as they have words to say, and others listen and remember, as much as they can understand. This is the seeing place."

"I don't want to leave," said Alvin.

"No, and neither does the other one."

"Who? Is there somebody else here?"

The Prophet shook his head. "Not his body. But I feel him in me, looking out of my eye." He tapped the cheekbone under his good eye. "Not this eye, the other."

"Can't you tell who it is?"

"White," he said. "It doesn't matter. Whoever it is did no harm. I think maybe—will do a good thing. Now we go."

"But I want to know all the stories in this place!"

The Prophet laughed. "You could live forever and not see all the stories. They change faster than a man can see."

"How will I ever come here again? I want to see everything, all of it!"

"I will never bring you back," said the Prophet.

"Why? Did I do something wrong?"

"Hush, Roach Boy. I will never bring you back, because I will never come here myself again. This is the last time. I have seen the end of all my dreams."

For the first time, Alvin realized how sad the Prophet looked. His face was haggard with grief.

"I saw you in this place. I saw that I had to bring you here. I saw you in the hands of the Chok-Taw. I sent my brother to get you, bring you back."

"Is it cause you brought me here that you can't never come here again yourself?"

"No. The land has chosen. The end will be soon." He smiled, but it was a ghastly smile. "Your preacher, Reverend Thrower, he said to me once—if your foot gets sick, cut it off. Right?"

"I don't remember that."

"I do," said the Prophet. "This part of the land, it is already sick. Cut it off, so the rest of the land can live."

"What do you mean?" Alvin conjured up pictures in his mind, about pieces of the land breaking off and falling into the sea.

"Red man will go west of the Mizzipy. White man will stay east. Red part of land will live. White part of land will be very dead, cut off. Full of smoke and metal, guns and death. Red men who stay in the east will turn White. And White men won't come west of the Mizzipy."

"There's already White men west of the Mizzipy. Trappers and traders, mostly, but a few farmers with their families."

"I know," said the Prophet. "But what I see here today—I know how to make the White man never come west again, and how to make the Red man never stay east."

"How're you going to do that?"

"If I tell," said the Prophet, "then it won't happen. Some things in this place, you can't tell, or it changes, and they go away."

"Is it the crystal city?" asked Alvin.

"No," said the Prophet. "It is the river of blood. It is the forest of iron."

"Show me!" demanded the boy. "Let me see what you saw!"

"No," said the Prophet. "You wouldn't keep the secret."

"Why wouldn't I? If I give my word I won't break it!"

"You could give your word all day, Roach Boy, but if you saw the vision you would cry out in fear and pain. And you would tell your brother. You would tell your family."

"Is something going to happen to them?"

"Not one of your family will die," said the Prophet. "All safe and healthy when this is over."

"Show me!"

"No," said the Prophet. "I will break the tower now, and you will remember what we did and said here. But the only way you'll ever come back and see these things is if you find the crystal city.''

The Prophet knelt down at the place where the wall met the floor. He pushed his bloody fingers into the wall and lifted. The wall rose up, dissolved, turned to wind. They were surrounded now by the scene they left so many hours before, it seemed. The water, the storm, the twister rising back up into the clouds above them. Lightning flashed all around them, and the rain came down, so fast it made the shore disappear. The rain that landed on the crystal place where they stood turned to crystal, too, became part of the floor under them.

The Prophet went to the edge nearest the shore, and stepped out onto the rough water. It went hard under his foot, but it still undulated slowly—it wasn't as firm as the platform. The Prophet reached back, took Alvin's hand, pulled him out onto the new path he was making on the surface of the lake. It wasn't near as smooth as before, and the farther they walked the rougher it got, the more it moved, the slicker it got so it was hard to go up and over the waves.

"We stayed too long!" cried the Prophet.

Alvin could feel the black water under the thin shell of crystal, roiling with hate. Nothingness out of an ancient nightmare, wanting to break through the crystal, get hold of Al, suck him down, drown him, tear him to pieces, to the tiniest pieces of all, and discard him into the darkness.

"It wasn't me!" shouted Alvin.

The Prophet turned around, picked him up, lifted him to his shoulders. The rain beat down on him, the wind tried to tear him from the Prophet's shoulders. Alvin clung tight to Tenskwa-Tawa's hair. He could feel that now the Prophet's feet were sinking down into the water more and more with every step. Behind them there wasn't a trace of a path, all of it gone, the waves rising higher and higher.

The Prophet stumbled, fell; Alvin fell too, forward, knowing he was going to drown—

And found himself sprawled on the wet sand of the beach, the water licking up around him, sucking sand out from under him, trying to pull him back out into the water. Then strong hands under his arms, pulling him away, up the beach, up toward the dunes.

"He's out there, the Prophet!" Alvin shouted. Or thought he shouted—his voice was just a whisper, and he hardly made a sound. It wouldn't have mattered, the wind being so loud. He opened his eyes and they were whipped full of sand and rain.

Then Measure's lips were against his ear, yelling to him. "The

Prophet's all right! Ta-Kumsaw pulled him out! I thought you were dead for sure, when that twister sucked you up! Are you all right?''

"I saw everything!'' Alvin cried. But he was so feeble now that he couldn't make a sound, and he gave it up, let his body go limp, and collapsed into exhausted sleep.

10

Gatlopp

Measure saw little of Alvin—too little. After the episode with the tornado on the lake, Measure would have thought Alvin would be awake to his danger here, eager to get away. Instead he seemed to care for nothing but to be with the Prophet, listening to his stories and the perverse poetic wisdom he dispensed.

Once when Alvin was actually with him long enough to set and talk, Measure asked him why he bothered. "Even when them Reds talk English I can't understand them. Talk about the land like it was a person, things about taking only the life that offers itself, the land dying east of the Mizzipy—it ain't dying here, Al, as any fool can see. And even if it's got smallpox, black death, and ten thousand hang-nails, there ain't no doctor knows how to cure it."

"Tenskwa-Tawa *does* know how," said Alvin.

"Then let him do it, and let's get on home."

"Another day, Measure."

"Ma and Pa'll be worried sick, they think we're dead!"

"Tenskwa-Tawa says the land is working out its own course."

"There you go again! Land is land, and it ain't got a thing to do with Pa getting a bunch of the boys together combing through the woods to find us!"

"Go on without me, then."

But Measure wasn't ready to do *that* yet. He didn't have no particular wish to face Ma if he came home without Alvin. "Oh, he was fine when I left him. Just playing around with tornadoes and walking on water with a one-eyed Red. Didn't want to come home just yet, you know how them ten-year-old boys are." No, Measure wasn't ripe to come home just now, not if he didn't have Alvin in tow. And it was sure he couldn't take Alvin against his will. The boy wouldn't even listen to talk of escape.

The worst of it was that while everybody liked Alvin just fine, jabbering to him in English and Shaw-Nee, not a soul there would so much as talk to Measure, except Ta-Kumsaw himself, and the Prophet, who talked all the time whether anybody was listening or not. It got powerful lonely, walking around all day. And not walking far, either. Nobody talked to him, but if he started heading away from the dunes toward the woods, somebody'd shoot off an arrow. It'd land with a thud in the sand right by him. They sure trusted their aim a lot better than Measure did. He kept thinking about arrows drifting a little this way or that and hitting them.

Escape *was* a silly idea, when Measure gave it serious thought. They'd track him down in no time. But what he couldn't figure was why they didn't want him to go. They weren't doing nothing with him. He was completely useless. And they swore they had no plans to kill him or even break him up a little.

Fourth day at the dunes, though, it finally came to a head. He went to Ta-Kumsaw and plain *demanded* that he be let go. Ta-Kumsaw looked annoyed, but that was pretty normal for him. This time, though, Measure didn't back down.

"Don't you know it's plain stupid for you to keep us here? It ain't like we disappeared without a trace, you know. Our horses must have been found by now with your name all over them."

That was the first time Measure realized that Ta-Kumsaw didn't have a notion about them horses. "My name isn't on horses."

"On their saddles, Chief. Don't you know? Them Chok-Taw who took us—if they weren't your own boys, which I ain't quite satisfied about either, if you want to know—they carved your name into the saddle on my horse and then jabbed the horse so it'd run. The Prophet's name was carved in Alvin's saddle. They must've gone home right away."

Ta-Kumsaw's face seemed to turn dark, his eyes flashing like lightning. If you want to see a sky-god, thought Measure, this is what he looks like. "All the Whites," said Ta-Kumsaw. "They'll think I stole you."

"You didn't know?" asked Measure. "Well if that don't beat all. I thought you Reds knew everything, the way you carry on. I even tried to mention it to some of your boys, but they just turn their backs on me. And all the time none of you knowed it."

"*I* didn't know," said Ta-Kumsaw. "But someone did." He stalked off, as best you can do that in loose sand; then he turned back around. "Come on, I want you!"

So Measure followed him to the bark-covered wigwam where the Prophet held Bible classes or whatever it was he did all day. Ta-Kumsaw wasn't shy about showing how angry he was. Didn't say a thing—just walked around the wigwam, kicking away the rocks that helped anchor it to the sand. Then he picked up one end of it and started lifting. "Needs two men for this," he said.

Measure squatted down next to him, got a grip, and counted to three. Then he heaved. Ta-Kumsaw didn't, so the wigwam only lifted about six inches and dropped back down.

Measure grunted from the exertion and glared at Ta-Kumsaw. "Why didn't you lift?"

"You only got to three," said Ta-Kumsaw.

"That's the count, Chief. One, two, three."

"You Whites are such fools. Every man knows four is the strong number."

Ta-Kumsaw counted to four. This time they lifted together, got it up, tipped it clean over. By now, of course, whoever was inside knew what was going on, but nobody shouted or nothing. And when the wigwam lay on its back like a stranded turtle, there sat the Prophet and Alvin and a few Reds, cross-legged on blankets on the sand, the one-eyed Red still talking away like as if nothing had happened at all.

Ta-Kumsaw started bellowing in Shaw-Nee, and the Prophet answered him, mildly at first, but louder and louder as time went on. It was quite a row, the sort of yelling that in Measure's experience always came to blows. But not with these two Reds. Just yelled for a half hour and then stood there, facing each other, breathing hard, saying nothing at all. The silence was only a few minutes, but it felt longer than the shouting.

"You understand any of this?" asked Measure.

"I just know that the Prophet said Ta-Kumsaw was coming today, and he'd be very angry."

"Well, if he knowed, why didn't he do something to change it?"

"Oh, he's real careful about that. He's got everything going just the way it needs to, for the land to be divided right between White and Red. If he goes and changes something because he knows what's going to happen, he might undo everything, mess it all up. So he knows what's going to happen, but he don't tell a soul who might change it."

"Well, what good does it do to know the future if you ain't going to do nothing about it?"

"Oh, he does things," said Alvin. "He just doesn't necessarily tell folks what he's doing. That's why he made the crystal tower when that storm came by. To make sure the vision was still the way it was supposed to be, to make sure things hadn't gotten themselves off the right path.''

"What's all *this* about? Why are they fighting?"

"You tell *me*, Measure. You're the one helped him turn over the wigwam."

"Beats me. I just told him about his and the Prophet's names being carved on our saddles."

"He knowed that," said Alvin.

"Well, he sure acted like he didn't hear of it before."

"I told the Prophet myself, the night after he took me into the tower."

"Didn't it come to your mind that maybe the Prophet didn't tell Ta-Kumsaw?"

"Why not?" asked Alvin. "Why wouldn't he tell it?"

Measure nodded wisely. "I have a feeling that's the very question Ta-Kumsaw's asking his brother about right now."

"It's crazy not to tell," said Alvin. "I figured Ta-Kumsaw must've sent somebody by now to tell our folks we were all right."

"You know what I think, Al? I think your Prophet's been playing us all for fools. I don't even have a guess as to why, but I think he's working out some plan, and part of that plan is keeping us from going home. And since that means all our family and neighbors and all are going to be up in arms about it, you can figure it out. The Prophet wants to get a real hot little shooting war going here."

"No!" said Alvin. "The Prophets says no man can kill another man who doesn't want to die, that it's as wrong to kill a White man as it is to kill a wolf or a bear that you don't want for food."

"Maybe he wants us for food. But he's going to *have* a war if we don't get home and tell our kin that we're safe."

That was right when Ta-Kumsaw and the Prophet fell silent. And it was Measure who broke the silence. "Think you boys are about set to let us go home?" he asked.

The Prophet immediately sank down into a cross-legged position, sitting on a blanket across from the two Whites. "Go home, Measure," said the Prophet.

"Not without Alvin."

"Yes without Alvin," said the Prophet. "If he stays in this part of the country, he will die."

"What are you talking about?"

"What I saw with my eyes!" said the Prophet. "The things to come.

If Alvin goes home now, he'll be dead in three days. But *you* go, Measure. Today in the afternoon is a very perfect time for you to go.''

"What are you going to do with Alvin? You think he's going to be any safer with *you*?''

"Not with *me*," said the Prophet. "With my brother.''

"This is all a stupid idea!'' shouted Ta-Kumsaw.

"My brother is going to make many visits. With the French at Detroit, with the Irrakwa, the Appalachee nation, with the Chok-Taw and the Cree-Ek, every kind of Red man, every kind of White who might stop a very bad war from happening.''

"If I talk to Reds, Tenskwa-Tawa, I'll talk to them about coming to fight with me and drive the White men back across the mountains, back into their ships, back into the sea!''

"Talk about whatever you want," said Tenskwa-Tawa. "But leave this afternoon, and take the White boy who walks like a Red man.''

"No," said Ta-Kumsaw.

Grief swept across Tenskwa-Tawa's face, and he moaned sharply. "Then all the land will die, not just a part. If you don't do what I say today, then White man will kill all the land, from one ocean to the other, from north to south, all the land dead! And Red men will die except a very few who will live on tiny pieces of ugly desert land, like prisons, live there all their lives, because you did not obey what I saw in my vision!''

"Ta-Kumsaw does not obey these mad visions! Ta-Kumsaw is the face of the land, the voice of the land! The redbird told me, and you know that, Lolla-Wossiky!''

The Prophet whispered. "Lolla-Wossiky is dead.''

"The voice of the land doesn't obey a one-eyed whisky-Red.''

The Prophet was stung to the heart, but he kept his face impassive. "You are the voice of the land's anger. You will stand in battle against a mighty army of Whites. I tell you this will happen before the first snow falls. If the White boy Alvin is not with you, then you will die in defeat.''

"And if he *is* with me?''

"Then you will live," said the Prophet.

"I'm glad to go," said Alvin. When Measure started to argue, Alvin touched his arm. "You can tell Ma and Pa I'm all right. But I *want* to go. The Prophet told me, I can learn more from Ta-Kumsaw than any other man in the whole world.''

"Then I'm going with you, too," said Measure. "I gave my word to Pa and Ma both.''

The Prophet looked coldly at Measure. "You will go back to your own people."

"Then Alvin comes with me."

"You are not the one who says," the Prophet retorted.

"And you are? Why, because your boys got all the arrows?"

Ta-Kumsaw reached out, touched Measure on the shoulder. "You are not a fool, Measure. Someone has to go back and tell your people that you and Alvin aren't dead."

"If I leave him behind, how do I *know* he ain't dead, tell me that?"

"You know," said Ta-Kumsaw, "because I say that while I live no Red man will hurt this boy."

"And while he's with you, nobody can hurt *you*, either, is that it? My little brother's a hostage, that's all—"

Measure could see that Ta-Kumsaw and Tenskwa-Tawa were both about as mad as they could be without killing him, and he knew he was so mad he was ready to break his hand on somebody's face. And it might've come to that, too, except Alvin stood up, all ten years and sixty inches of him, and took charge.

"Measure, you know better than anybody that I can take care of myself. You just tell Pa and Ma about what I did with them Chok-Taw, and they'll see that I'm fit. They were sending me off anyway, weren't they? To be a prentice to blacksmith. Well, I'm going to serve as prentice for a little while to Ta-Kumsaw, that's all. And everybody knows that except for maybe Tom Jefferson, Ta-Kumsaw is the greatest man in America. If I can somehow keep Ta-Kumsaw alive, then that's my duty. And if you can stop a war from happening by going home, then that's your duty. Don't you see?"

Measure *did* see, right enough, and he even agreed. But he also knew that he was going to have to face his parents. "There's a story in the Bible, about Joseph, the son of Jacob. He was his father's favorite son, but his brothers hated him and sold him into slavery, and then they took some of his clothes and soaked them in goat's blood and tore them up and came and told their father, Look, he got hisself et by lions. And his father tore his clothes and he just wouldn't stop grieving, not ever."

"But you're going to tell them I *ain't* dead."

"I'm going to tell them I saw you turn a hatchet head soft as butter, walk on the water, fly up into a tornado—that'll just make them feel all safe and warm, knowing you're tucked into such a common ordinary life with these here Reds."

Ta-Kumsaw interrupted. "You are a coward," he said. "You're afraid to tell the truth to your father and mother."

"I made an oath to them," said Measure.

"You're a coward. You take no risk. No danger. You want Alvin with you to keep you safe!"

That was just too much for Measure. He swung out with his right arm, aiming to connect with Ta-Kumsaw's smile. It didn't surprise him that Ta-Kumsaw blocked the blow—but it was kind of a shock that he caught Measure's wrist so easy, twisted it. Measure got even madder, punched at Ta-Kumsaw's stomach, and this time he *did* connect. But the chief's belly was about as soft as a stump, and he snagged Measure's other hand and held them both.

So Measure did what any good wrassler knows to do. He popped his knee up right between Ta-Kumsaw's legs.

Now, Measure had done that only twice before, and both times he did it, the other fellow got right down on the ground, writhing like a half-squished worm. Ta-Kumsaw just stood there, rigid, like he was soaking up the pain, getting madder and madder. Since he was still holding on to Measure's arms, Measure had a good notion that he was about to die, ripped right in half down the middle—that's how mad Ta-Kumsaw looked.

Ta-Kumsaw let go of Measure's arms.

Measure took his arms back, rubbed his wrists where the chief's fingermarks were white and sore. The chief looked angry, all right, but it was Alvin he was mad at. He turned and looked down at that boy like he was ready to peel off Alvin's skin and feed it to him raw.

"You did your filthy White man's tricks in me," he said.

"I didn't want neither of you getting hurt," said Alvin.

"You think I'm a coward like your brother? You think I'm afraid of pain?"

"Measure ain't no coward!"

"He threw me to the ground with White man's tricks."

Measure didn't like hearing that same accusation. "You know I didn't ask him to do that! I'll take you now, if you want! I'll fight you fair and square!"

"Strike a man with your knee?" said Ta-Kumsaw. "You don't know how to fight like a man."

"I'll face you any way you want," said Measure.

Ta-Kumsaw smiled. "Gatlopp, then."

By now a whole bunch of Reds had gathered round, and when they heard the word *gatlopp*, they started hooting and laughing.

There wasn't a White in America who hadn't heard stories about how Dan Boone ran the gatlopp and just kept on running, that first time he escaped from the Reds; but there was other stories, about Whites who got beat to death. Taleswapper told about it somewhat, the time he visited last year. It's like a jury trial, he said, where the Reds hit you hard or easy depending on how much they think you deserve to die. If they think you're a brave man, they'll strike you hard to test you with pain. But if they think you're a coward, they'll break your bones to you never get out of the gatlopp alive. The chief can't tell the gatlopp how hard to strike, or where. It's just about the most democratic and vicious system of justice ever seen.

"I see you're afraid of that," said Ta-Kumsaw.

"Of course I am," said Measure. "I'd be a fool not to, specially with your boys already thinking I'm a coward."

"I'll run the gatlopp before you," said Ta-Kumsaw. "I'll tell them to strike me as hard as they strike you."

"They won't do it," said Measure.

"They will if I ask them," said Ta-Kumsaw. He must have seen the disbelief on Measure's face, cause then he said, "And if they don't, I'll run the gatlopp again."

"And if they kill me, will you die?"

Ta-Kumsaw looked up and down Measure's body. Lean and strong, Measure knew he was, from chopping trees and firewood, toting pails, lifting hay, and hoisting grain bags in the mill. But he wasn't *tough*. His skin was burnt something awful from being near naked in the sun out here on the dunes, even though he tried to use a blanket to cover up. Strong but soft, that's what Ta-Kumsaw found when he studied Measure's body.

"The blow that would kill you," said Ta-Kumsaw, "it might bruise me."

"So you admit it ain't fair."

"Fair is when two men face the same pain. Courage is when two men face the same pain. You don't want fair, you want easy. You want safe. You're a coward. I knew you wouldn't do it."

"I'll do it," said Measure.

"And you!" cried Ta-Kumsaw, pointing at Alvin. "You touch nothing, you heal nothing, you cure nothing, you don't take away pain!"

Alvin didn't say a word, just looked at him. Measure knew that look. It was the expression Alvin got on his face whenever he had no intention of doing a thing you said.

"Al," said Measure. "You better promise me not to meddle."

Al just set his lips and didn't speak.

"You better promise me not to meddle, Alvin Junior, or I just won't go home."

Alvin promised. Ta-Kumsaw nodded and walked away, talking in Shaw-Nee to his boys. Measure felt sick with fear.

"Why are you afraid, White man?" asked the Prophet.

"Cause I'm not stupid," said Measure. "Only a stupid man wouldn't be scared to run the gatlopp."

The Prophet just laughed and walked off.

Alvin was sitting in the sand again, writing or drawing or something with his finger.

"You ain't mad at me, are you, Alvin? Cause I got to tell you, you can't be half as mad at *me* as I am at *you*. You got no duty to these Reds, but you sure got a duty to your ma and pa. Things being how they are, I can't make you do nothing, but I can tell you I'm ashamed of you for siding with them against me and your kin."

Al looked up, and there was tears in his eyes. "Maybe I *am* siding with my kin, did you think of that?"

"Well you sure got a funny way of doing it, seeing as how you'll keep Ma and Pa worried sick for months, no doubt."

"Don't you think about anything bigger than our family? Don't you think maybe the Prophet's working out a plan to save the lives of thousands of Reds and Whites?"

"That's where we're different," said Measure. "I don't believe there *is* anything bigger than our family."

Alvin was still writing as Measure walked away. It didn't even occur to Measure what Alvin wrote in the sand. He saw, but he didn't *look*, he didn't read it. Now, though, the words came to his mind. RUN AWAY NOW, that's what Al was writing. A message to him? Why didn't he say it with his mouth, then? Nothing made sense. The writing probably wasn't for him. And he *sure* wasn't going to run away and have Ta-Kumsaw and all them Reds sure he was a coward forever. What difference would it make if he ran away now? The Reds'd catch him in a minute, there in the woods, and then he'd run the gatlopp anyway, only it'd even be worse for him.

The warriors formed two lines in the sand. They were carrying heavy branches fallen or cut from trees. Measure watched as an old man took the beads from around Ta-Kumsaw's neck, then pulled off his loincloth. Ta-Kumsaw turned to Measure and grinned. "White man is naked when he has no clothes. Red man is never naked in his own land. The wind is my clothing, the fire of the sun, the dust of the earth, the water of rain. I wear all these. I am the voice and the face of the land!"

"Just get on with it," said Measure.

"I know someone who says a man like you has no poetry in his soul," said Ta-Kumsaw.

"And I know plenty of people who say that a man like you has no soul at all."

Ta-Kumsaw glared at him, barked a few words to his men, and then stepped between the lines.

He walked slowly, his chin high and arrogant. The first Red struck him a blow across his thighs, using the skinny end of a branch. Ta-Kumsaw snatched the branch out of his hands, turned it around, and made him strike again, this time in the chest, a harsh blow that drove the air out of Ta-Kumsaw's lungs. Measure could hear the grunting sound from where he stood.

The lines ran up the face of a dune, so that progress up the hill was slow. Ta-Kumsaw never paused as the blows came. His men were stern-faced, dutiful. They were helping him show courage, and so they gave him pain—but no damaging blows. His thighs and belly and shoulders took the worst of it. Nothing on his shins, nothing in his face. But that didn't mean he had it easy. Measure could see his shoulders, bloody from the rough bark of the branches. He imagined himself receiving every blow that fell, and knew that they'd strike him harder. I'm a royal fool, he said to himself. Here I am matching courage with the noblest man in America, as everybody knows.

Ta-Kumsaw reached the end, turned, faced Measure from the top of the dune. His body was dripping with blood, and he was smiling. "Come to me, brave White man," he called.

Measure didn't hesitate. He started toward the gatlopp. It was a voice from behind that stopped him. The Prophet, shouting in Shaw-Nee. The Reds looked at him. When he was finished, Ta-Kumsaw spat. Measure, not knowing what had been said, started forward again. When he got to the first Red, he expected at least as hard a blow as Ta-Kumsaw got. But there was nothing. He took another step. Nothing. Maybe to show their contempt they meant to hit him in the back, but he climbed higher and higher up the dune, and still there was not a blow, not a move.

He should have been relieved, he knew, but instead he was angry. They gave Ta-Kumsaw help in showing his courage, and now they were making Measure's passage through the gatlopp a walk of shame instead of honor. He whirled around and faced the Prophet, who stood at the bottom of the dune, his arm across Alvin's shoulders.

"What did you say to them?" Measure demanded.

"I told them that if they killed you, everyone would say Ta-Kumsaw and the Prophet kidnapped these boys and murdered them. I told them that if they marked you in any way, when you went home everybody would say we tortured you."

"And I say I want a fair chance to prove I'm not a coward!"

"The gatlopp is a stupid idea, for men who forget their duty."

Measure reached down and grabbed a club from a Red man's hand.

He struck his own thighs with it, again, again, trying to draw blood. It hurt, but not very bad, because whether he wanted to or not, his arms flinched at causing pain to his own self. So he thrust the branch back into the warrior's arms and demanded, "Hit me!"

"The bigger a man is, the more people he serves," said the Prophet. "A small man serves himself. Bigger is to serve your family. Bigger is to serve your tribe. Then your people. Biggest of all, to serve all men, and all lands. For yourself, you show courage. For your family, your tribe, your people, my people—for the land and all people in it, you walk this gatlopp with no mark on you."

Slowly, Measure turned around, walked up the dune to Ta-Kumsaw, untouched. Again Ta-Kumsaw spat on the ground, this time at Measure's feet.

"I ain't no coward," said Measure.

Ta-Kumsaw walked away. Walked, slipped, slid down the dune. The warriors of the gatlopp also walked away. Measure stood at the top of the hill, feeling ashamed, angry, used.

"Go!" shouted the Prophet. "Walk south from here!"

He handed a pouch to Alvin, who scrambled up the dune and gave it to Measure. Measure opened it. It contained pemmican and dried corn, so he could suck on it on his way.

"You coming with me?" Measure asked.

"I'm going with Ta-Kumsaw," said Alvin.

"I could've made it through the gatlopp," said Measure.

"I know," said Alvin.

"If he wasn't going to let me go through it," said Measure, "how come the Prophet allowed it to happen at all?"

"He ain't telling," said Alvin. "But something terrible's going to happen. And he *wants* it to happen. If you'd've went before, when I told you to run away—"

"They would've caught me, Al."

"It was worth a try. Now when you leave, you're doing just what he wants."

"He plans for me to get killed or something?"

"He promised me you'd live through this, Measure. And all the family. Him and Ta-Kumsaw, too."

"Then what's so terrible?"

"I don't know. I'm just scared of what's going to happen. I think he's sending me with Ta-Kumsaw to save my life."

One more time, it was worth a try. "Alvin, if you love me, come with me now."

Alvin started to cry. "Measure, I love you, but I can't go." Still crying, he ran down the dune. Not wanting to watch him out of sight, Measure started walking. Almost due south, a little bit east. He wouldn't have no trouble finding the way. But he felt sick with dread, and with shame for having let them talk him into leaving without his brother. I failed at everything here. I'm pretty near useless.

He walked the rest of that day and spent the night in a pile of leaves in a hollow. Next day he walked till late afternoon, when he came to a south-flowing creek. It would flow into the Tippy-Canoe or the Wobbish, one or the other. It was too deep to walk down the middle, and too overgrown to walk alongside. So he just kept the stream within earshot and made his own way through the forest. He wasn't no Red, that was for sure. He got scratched up by bushes and branches and bit by insects, none of which felt too good on his sunburnt skin. He also kept running into thickets and having to back out. Like the land was his enemy, slowing him down. He kept wishing for a horse and a good road.

Hard as it was to go through the woods, though, he *was* up to it. Partly cause Alvin toughened up his feet for him. Partly cause of the way he seemed to breathe deeper than ever before. But it was more than that. Strength was wound in among his muscles in a way he never felt in his life. Never so alive as now. And he thought, If I had a horse right now, I think maybe I'd be wishing I was on foot.

It was late afternoon on the second day when he heard a splashing sound in the river. There was no mistaking it—horses were being walked in the stream. That meant White men, maybe even folks from Vigor Church, still searching for him and Alvin.

He scrambled his way to the stream, getting scratched something awful on the way. They were headed downstream, away from him, four men on horseback. It wasn't till he was already out into the stream, yelling to bust his head off that he noticed they were wearing the green uniform of the U.S. Army. He never heard of them coming up in these parts. This was the country where White folks didn't go much, on account of not wanting to rile up the French at Fort Chicago.

They heard him right off, and wheeled their horses around to see him. Almost quick as they saw him, three of them had their muskets up to the ready.

"Don't shoot!" Measure cried.

The soldiers rode toward him, making pretty slow progress as their horses had some trouble breasting the water.

"Don't shoot, for heaven's sake," Measure said. "You can see I ain't armed, I don't even have a knife."

"He talks English real good, don't he?" said one soldier to another.

"Of course I do! I'm a White man."

"Now don't that beat all," said another soldier. "First time I ever heard one of them claim to be White."

Measure looked down at his own skin. It was a vivid red color from his sunburn, much lighter than any true Red man. He *was* wearing a loincloth, and he looked pretty wild and dirty. But his beard was growing somewhat, wasn't it? For the first time Measure found himself wishing he was a hairy man, with thick heavy beard and lots of chest hair. Then there'd be no mistake, since Reds didn't grow much. As it was, though, they wouldn't see his light-colored mustache hair or the few little hairs on his chin till they were up close.

And they weren't taking no chances, either. Only one rode right up to him. The others hung back, their muskets out, ready to open fire in case Measure had some boys lying in ambush on the riverbank. He could see that the man riding toward him was plumb scared to death, looking this way and that, waiting to see a Red man flitch an arrow at him. Kind of an idiot, Measure decided, since there wasn't no chance of seeing a Red man in the woods till his arrow was already in you.

The soldier didn't come right to him. He circled around, got beside him. Then he looped a rope and tossed it to Measure. "You hitch this around your chest, under your arms," said the soldier.

"What for?"

"So I can lead you along."

"The hell I will," said Measure. "If I thought you were going to drag me along by a rope in the middle of a creek, I'd've stayed on dry land and walked home myself."

"If you don't put this rope around you in five seconds, them boys are going to blow your head off."

"What are you talking about?" Measure demanded. "I'm Measure Miller. I was captured with my little brother, Alvin, almost a week ago, and I'm just going home to Vigor Church."

"Well, ain't that a real pretty story?" said the soldier. He drew back the rope, sopping wet, and cast it again. This time it hit Measure in the face. Measure caught at it, held it in his hand. The soldier drew his sword. "Get ready to shoot, boys!" shouted the soldier. "It's that renegade, all right!"

"Renegade! I—" Then it finally occurred to Measure that something had gone real bad with this. They knew who he was, and they still wanted to take him prisoner. With three muskets and a sword close by, they had a fair chance of maybe even killing him if he tried to run away. This was the U.S. Army, wasn't it? Once they got him to an officer, he could explain and all this would get cleared up. So he put the rope over his head, and pulled the loop around his chest.

It wasn't too bad as long as they were in the water; sometimes he just floated along. But pretty soon they got out and then they made him walk along behind as they picked their way through the woods. They were looping east, around behind Vigor Church.

Measure tried talking, but they told him to shut up. "I tell you, we been told we can bring in renegades like you alive or dead. White man dressed like a Red—we know what you are."

From their conversation he was able to gather a few things. They were on a scout-around from General Harrison. It made Measure sick, to think things had got to the point where they'd call on that likker-dealing scoundrel to come north. And he got here awful fast, too.

They spent the night camped in a clearing. They made so much noise that Measure thought it was a wonder they didn't have every Red in the whole country nosing around before morning.

The next day, he flat refused to be dragged along on a rope. "I'm near naked, I got no weapons, and you can kill me or let me ride." They could talk about bringing him in alive or dead and not caring which, but he knew that that was talk. These were a crude bunch, but they didn't hanker much after killing white men in cold blood. So he ended up on horseback, holding one of them around the waist. Pretty soon they reached country that had some roads and trails, and they made good time.

Just after noon they reached an army camp. Not much of an army, maybe a hundred in uniform and another two hundred marching and drilling on a parade ground that used to be a pasture. Measure couldn't remember the name of the family that lived here. They were new folks, just come up from the area around Carthage. Turned out it didn't matter who they were, though. It was General Harrison had their house for his headquarters, and these scouts led him straight to Harrison.

"Ah," said Harrison. "One of the renegades."

"I'm no renegade," said Measure. "They been treating me like a prisoner this whole way. I swear the Reds treated me better than your White soldiers."

"I ain't surprised much," said Harrison. "They treated you real nice, I'm sure. Where's the other renegade?"

"Other renegade? You mean my brother Alvin? You know who I am, and you ain't letting me go home?"

"You answer *my* questions, and then I'll give some thought to answering yours."

"My brother Alvin ain't here, and he ain't coming, and from what I see before me I'm real glad he didn't come."

"Alvin? Ah, yes, they told me you were claiming to be Measure Miller. Well, we know that Measure Miller was murdered by Ta-Kumsaw and the Prophet."

Measure spat on the floor. "You *know* that? From a few tore-up bloody clothes? Well you don't fool me. Do you think I don't see what you're doing?"

"Take him to the cellar," said Harrison. "Be real gentle with him."

"You don't *want* folks to know I'm alive, cause then they'll see they don't need you up here!" shouted Measure. "I wouldn't be surprised if you got them Chok-Taw to capture us in the first place!"

"If that's true," said Harrison, "then if I were you I'd watch how I talked and what I said. I'd be real worried about getting home alive, *ever*. Now look at yourself, boy. Skin red as a redbird, wearing a loin-cloth, looking wild as a real bad dream. No, I reckon if it turned out you was shot dead by mistake, nobody'd blame us, not a soul."

"My father'd know," said Measure. "You can't fool him with a lie like that, Harrison. And Armor-of-God, he'll—"

"Armor-of-God? That pathetic weakling? The one who keeps telling people that Ta-Kumsaw and the Prophet are innocent, and we shouldn't be getting ready to wipe them out? Nobody listens to him no more, Measure."

"They will. Alvin's alive, and you'll never catch *him*."

"Why not?"

"Cause he's with Ta-Kumsaw."

"Ah, and where is that?"

"Not around *here*, you can bet."

"You've seen him? And the Prophet?"

The hungry look in Harrison's eyes made Measure kind of step back and hold his tongue. "I seen what I seen," said Measure. "And I'll say what I say."

"Say what I ask, or you'll be dead," said Harrison.

"Kill me, and I won't say nothing at all. But I'll tell you this. I saw the Prophet call a tornado out of a storm. I saw him walk on water. I saw him prophesy, and his prophecies all come true. He knows every thing you plan to do. You think you're doing what *you* want, but you'll end up serving his purpose, you watch and see."

"What an idea," said Harrison, chucking. "By that reckoning, boy, it serves his purpose for you to be in my hands, don't it?" He waved his hands, and the soldiers dragged him out of the house and down into the root cellar. They treated him real gentle on the way—kicked him and knocked him down and all they could before they threw him down the steps and barred the door behind him.

Since these folks came from Carthage country, the cellar door had a lock, as well as the bar. Down with the carrots, potatoes, and spiders, Measure tested that door as best he could. His whole body was one big ache. All the scratches and the sunburn were nothing compared to the raw skin inside his thighs from riding behind with bare legs. And that was nothing compared to the pain from the kicks and bashes they gave him on the way here.

Measure didn't waste no more time. He knew what was going on well enough to know Harrison couldn't let him out alive. He had those scouts out *looking* for him and Alvin. If they turned up alive, it would undo all his plans, and that'd be a real shame, cause things were going just right for Harrison. After all these years, here he was at Vigor Church, training the local men to be soldiers, while nobody was listening to Armor-of-God at all. Measure didn't much like the Prophet, but compared to Harrison the Prophet was a saint.

Or was he? The Prophet had him wait for the gatlopp—why? So he'd leave in the afternoon two days ago, instead of morning. So he'd reach the Tippy-Canoe just when them soldiers were riding down. Otherwise he would've come to Prophetstown and then hopped on over into Vigor Church without seeing a soldier. They'd never have found him, if he hadn't heard them and called out to them himself. Was this all part of the Prophet's plan?

Well, so what if it was? Maybe the Prophet's plan was a good thing, and maybe it wasn't—so far Measure didn't think too highly of it. But he sure wasn't going to sit around in a root cellar waiting to see how the plan worked out.

He burrowed his way through the potatoes to the back of the cellar. There was more spiderwebs in his face and hair than he cared for, but this wasn't a time to worry about tidiness. Pretty soon he cleared him a space at the back, with the potatoes pushed mostly to the front. When they opened the doors, they'd just see a lot of potatoes. Not a sign of his digging.

The root cellar was the normal kind. Dug out, timbered over, roofed, and then the roof covered up with all the dirt from the hole. He could dig into the back wall and come up behind the cellar, and they couldn't see a thing from the house at all. It was bare-hands digging, but this was rich Wobbish soil. He'd come out looking more like a Black than a Red, but he didn't much care.

Trouble was, the back wall wasn't dirt, it was wood. They'd walled it in, right to the bottom. Tidy folks. The floor was dirt, all right. But that meant digging down under the wall before he could tunnel up. Instead of being something he could do overnight, it'd take days. And any time, they might catch him digging. Or just plain drag him out and shoot him. Or maybe even bring back them Chok-Taws, to do what they started—leave him looking like Ta-Kumsaw and the Prophet had him tortured. All possible.

Home wasn't ten miles away. That's what plain drove him crazy. So close to home, and they didn't even guess it, had no idea they ought to come to help. He remembered that torch girl from Hatrack River, years ago, the one who saw them stuck in the river and sent help. That's who I need right now, I need me a torch, somebody who'd find me and send help.

But that wasn't too likely. Not for Measure. If it was Alvin, now, there'd be eight miracles, whatever it took to get him out safe. But for Measure, there'd be just whatever he could work up for hisself.

He broke a fingernail half off in the first ten minutes of digging. The pain was real bad, and he knew he was bleeding. If they dragged him out now, they'd know he was making a tunnel. But it was his only chance. So he kept digging, pain and all, every now and then stopping to toss out a potato that rolled down into the hole.

Pretty soon he took off his loincloth and used it in his work. He'd loosen up the soil with his hands, then pile it onto the cloth and use that to hoist it up out of the hole. It wasn't as good as having a spade, but it sure beat moving the dirt out one handful at a time. What did he have, days? Hours?

11

Red Boy

It wasn't an hour after Measure left. Ta-Kumsaw stood atop a dune, the White boy Alvin beside him. And in front of him, Tenskwa-Tawa. Lolla-Wossiky. His brother, the boy who once cried for the death of bees. A prophet, supposedly. Speaking the will of the land, supposedly. Speaking words of cowardice, surrender, defeat, destruction.

"This is the oath of the land at peace," said the Prophet. "To take none of the White man's weapons, none of the White man's tools, none of the White man's clothing, none of the White man's food, none of the White man's drink, and none of the White man's promises. Above all, never to take a life that doesn't offer itself to die."

The Reds who heard him had heard it all before, as had Ta-Kumsaw. Most of those who had come to Mizogan with them had already refused the Prophet's covenant of weakness. They took a different oath, the oath of the land's anger, the oath that Ta-Kumsaw offered them. Every White must live under Red man's law, or leave the land, or die. A White man's weapons can be used, but only to defend Reds against murder and theft. No Red man will torture or kill a prisoner—man, woman, or child. Above all, the death of no Red will go unavenged.

Ta-Kumsaw knew that if all the Reds of America took his oath, they could still defeat the White man. Whites had only made such inroads because the Reds could never unite under one leader. The Whites could always ally themselves with a tribe or two, who would lead them through the trackless forest and help them find their enemy. If Reds had not turned renegade—like the unspeakable Irrakwa, the half-White Cherriky—then the White man could not have survived here in the land. They would have been swallowed up, lost, as had happened to every other group that came from the old world.

When the Prophet finished his challenge, there were only a handful who took his oath, who would go back with him. He seemed sad, Ta-Kumsaw thought. Weighed down. He turned his back on the ones who remained—on the warriors, who would fight the White man.

"Those men are yours," said the Prophet. "I wish there weren't so many."

"Mine, yes, but I wish there weren't so few."

"Oh, you'll find allies enough. Chok-Taw, Cree-Ek, Chicky-Saw, the vicious Semmy-Noll of the Oky-Fenoky. Enough to raise the greatest army of Reds ever seen in this land, all thirsting for White man's blood."

"Stand at my side in that battle," said Ta-Kumsaw.

"You'll lose your cause by killing," said the Prophet. "I'll win my cause."

"By dying."

"If the land calls for my death, I'll answer."

"And all you people with you."

The Prophet shook his head. "I've seen what I've seen. The people of my oath are as much a part of the land as the bear or the buffalo, the squirrel or the beaver, the turkey or the pheasant or the grouse. All those animals have stood still to take your arrow, haven't they? Or stretched out their neck for your knife. Or lain down their head for your tommy-hawk."

"They're animals, meant to be meat."

"They're alive, meant to live until they die, and when they die, die so that others can live."

"Not me. Not *my* people. We won't stretch out our neck for the White man's knife."

The Prophet took Ta-Kumsaw by the shoulders, tears streaming down his face. He pressed his cheek against Ta-Kumsaw's cheek, putting his tears on his brother's face.

"Come find me across the Mizzipy, when all this is done," said the Prophet.

"I'll never let the land be divided," said Ta-Kumsaw. "The east doesn't belong to the White man."

"The east will die," said the Prophet. "Follow me west, where the White man will never go."

Ta-Kumsaw said nothing.

The White boy Alvin touched the Prophet's hand. "Tenskwa-Tawa, does that mean I can never go west?"

The Prophet laughed. "Why do you think I'm sending you with Ta-Kumsaw? If anyone can turn a White boy Red, Ta-Kumsaw can."

"I don't want him," said Ta-Kumsaw.

"Take him or die," said the Prophet.

Then the Prophet walked down the slope of the dune, to the dozen men who waited for him, their palms dripping blood to seal the covenant. They walked off along the shore of the lake, to where their families waited. Tomorrow they'd be back in Prophetstown. Ripe to be slaughtered.

Ta-Kumsaw waited until the Prophet had disappeared behind a dune. Then he cried out to the hundreds who remained. "When will the White man have peace?"

"When he leaves!" they shouted. "When he dies!"

Ta-Kumsaw laughed and held out his arms. He felt their love and trust like the heat of the sun on a winter's day. Lesser men had felt that heat before, but it had oppressed them, because they weren't worthy of the trust they had been given. Not Ta-Kumsaw. He had measured himself, and he knew that there was no task ahead of him that he couldn't accomplish. Only treachery could keep him from victory. And Ta-Kumsaw was very good at knowing a man's heart. Knowing if he could be trusted. Knowing if he was a liar. Hadn't he known Governor Harrison from the beginning? A man like that couldn't hide from him.

They left only minutes later. A few dozen men led the women and children to the new place where their wandering village would settle. They stayed no more than three days in any place—a permanent village like Prophetstown was an invitation to a massacre. The only thing that kept the Prophet safe was sheer numbers. Ten thousand Reds lived there now, more than had ever lived in any one place before. And it *was* a miraculous place, Ta-Kumsaw knew it. The maize grew up six ears to the stalk, thicker and milkier than any corn had ever been before. Buffalo and deer wandered into the city from a hundred miles around, walked to the cooking fires, and lay down waiting for the knife. When the geese flew overhead, a few from every flock would come to land on the Wobbish and the Tippy-Canoe, waiting for the arrow. The fish swam up from the Hio to leap into the nets of Prophetstown.

All that would mean nothing, if the White man ever brought his cannons to fire grapeshot and shrapnel through the fragile wigwams and lodges of the Red city. The searing metal would cut through the delicate walls—that deadly driven rain would not be held out by sticks and mud. Every Red man in Prophetstown would regret his oath on that day.

Ta-Kumsaw led them through the forest. The White boy ran directly behind him. Ta-Kumsaw deliberately set a killing pace, twice as fast as they had run before, bringing the boy and his brother to Mizogan. They had two hundred miles to Fort Detroit, and Ta-Kumsaw was determined to cover that distance in a single day. No White man could do it—no White man's horse, either. A mile every five minutes, on and on, the wind whipping through the top-knot of his hair. It would kill a man to run so fast for half an hour, except that the Red man called on the strength of the land to help him. The ground pushed back against his feet, adding to his strength. The bushes parted, making paths; space appeared where there was no space; Ta-Kumsaw raced across streams and rivers so quickly that his feet did not touch the bottom of the stream, merely sank just deep enough to find purchase on the water itself. His hunger to arrive at Fort Detroit was so strong that the land answered by feeding him, giving him strength. And not just Ta-Kumsaw, but every man behind him, every Red man who knew the feel of the land within him, he found the same strength as his leader, stepped in the same path, footfall by footfall, like one great soul walking a long slender highway through the wood.

I will have to carry the White boy, thought Ta-Kumsaw. But the footsteps behind him—for Whites made noise when they ran—kept up, falling into a rhythm identical with his own.

That, of course, was not possible. The boy's legs were too short, he had to take more strides to cover the same ground. Yet each step of Ta-Kumsaw's was matched so closely that he heard the sound of the White boy's feet as if they were his own.

Minute after minute, mile after mile, hour after hour, the boy kept on.

The sun set behind them, over the left shoulder. The stars came out, but no moon, and the night was dark under the trees. Still they didn't slow, found their way easily through the wood, because it wasn't their own eyes or their own mind finding the way, it was the land itself drawing them through the safe places in the darkness. Several times in the night, Ta-Kumsaw noticed that the boy was no longer making noise. He called out in Shaw-Nee to the man who ran behind the White boy Alvin, and always the man answered, "He runs."

The moon came up, casting patches of dim light onto the forest floor. They overtook a storm—the ground grew moist under their feet, then wet; they ran through showers, heavy rain, showers again, and then the land was dry. They never slackened their pace. The sky in the east turned grey, then pink, then blue, and the sun leapt upward. The day was warming and the sun already three hands above the horizon when they saw the smoke of cookfires, then the slack fleur-de-lis flag, and finally the cross of the cathedral. Only then did they slow down. Only then did they break the perfect unison of their step, loose the grip of the land in their minds, and come to rest in a meadow so near the town that they could hear the organ playing in the cathedral.

Ta-Kumsaw stopped, and the boy stopped behind him. How had Alvin, a White boy, traveled like a Red man through the night? Ta-Kumsaw knelt before the boy. Though Alvin's eyes were open, he seemed not to see anything. "Alvin," said Ta-Kumsaw, speaking English. The boy didn't answer. "Alvin, are you asleep?"

Several warriors gathered around. They were all somewhat quiet and spent from the journey. Not exhausted, because the land replenished them along the way. Their quiet was more from awe at having been so closely tied to the land; such a journey was known to be a holy thing, a gift from the land to its noblest children. Many a Red had set out on such a journey and been turned away, forced to stop and sleep and rest and eat, stopped by darkness or bad weather, because his need for the journey wasn't great enough, or his journey was contrary to what the land itself needed. Ta-Kumsaw, though, had never been refused; they all knew it. This was much of the reason Ta-Kumsaw was held in as high esteem as his brother. The Prophet did miraculous things, but no one saw his visions; he could only tell about them. What Ta-Kumsaw did, though, his warriors did with him, felt with him.

Now, though, they were as puzzled by the White boy as Ta-Kumsaw was. Had Ta-Kumsaw sustained the boy by his own power? Or had the land, unbelievably, reached out and supported a White child for his own sake?

"Is he White like his skin, or Red in his heart?" asked one. He spoke Shaw-Nee, and not in the quick way, but rather in the slow and holy language of the shamans.

To Ta-Kumsaw's surprise, Alvin responded to his words, looking at the man who spoke instead of staring straight ahead. "White," murmured Alvin. He spoke English.

"Does he speak our language?" asked a man.

Alvin appeared confused by the question. "Ta-Kumsaw," he said. He looked up to see the angle of the sun. "It's morning. Was I asleep?"

"Not asleep," said Ta-Kumsaw in Shaw-Nee. Now the boy appeared not to understand at all. "Not asleep," Ta-Kumsaw repeated in English.

"I feel like I was asleep," he said. "Only I'm standing up."

"You don't feel tired? You don't want to rest?"

"Tired? Why would I be tired?"

Ta-Kumsaw didn't want to explain. If the boy didn't know what he had done, then it was a gift of the land. Or perhaps there was something to what the Prophet had said about him. That Ta-Kumsaw should teach him to be Red. If he could match grown Shaw-Nee, step for step, in such a run as that, perhaps this boy of all Whites could learn to feel the land.

Ta-Kumsaw stood and spoke to the others. "I'm going into the city, with only four others."

"And the boy," said one. Others repeated his words. They all knew the Prophet's promise to Ta-Kumsaw, that as long as the boy was with him he wouldn't die. Even if he were tempted to leave the boy behind, they'd never let him do it.

"And the boy," Ta-Kumsaw agreed.

Detroit was not a fort like the pathetic wooden stockades of the Americans. It was made of stone, like the cathedral, with huge cannon pointing outward toward the river that connected Lake Huron and Lake St. Clair with Lake Canada, and smaller cannon aimed inland, ready to fend off attackers on land.

But it was the city, not the fort, that impressed them. A dozen streets of houses, wooden ones, with shops and stores, and in the center of all, a cathedral so massive that it made a mockery of Reverend Thrower's church. Black-robed priests went about their business like crows in the streets. The swarthy Frenchmen didn't show the same hostility toward Reds that Americans often seemed to have. Ta-Kumsaw understood that this was because the French in Detroit weren't there to settle. They didn't think of Reds as rivals for possession of the land. The French here were all biding their time till they went back to Europe, or at least back to the White-settled lands of Quebec and Ontario across the river; except the trappers, of course, and for them the Reds were not enemies, either. Trappers held Reds in awe, trying to learn how Reds found game so easily, when the trappers had such a devilish time knowing where to lay their snares. They thought, as White men always do, that it was some kind of trick the Reds performed, and if they only studied Red men long enough, these White trappers would learn how to do it. They would never learn. How could the land accept the kind of man who would kill every beaver in a pond, just for the pelts, leaving the meat to rot, and no beaver left to bear young? No wonder the bears killed these trappers whenever they could. The land rejected them.

When I have driven the Americans from the land west of the mountains, thought Ta-Kumsaw, then I will drive out the Yankees from New England, and the Cavaliers from the Crown Colonies. And when they're all gone, I'll turn to the Spanish of Florida and the French of Canada. Today I'll make use of you for my own purpose, but tomorrow I'll drive you out, too. Every White face that stays in this land will stay here because it's dead. And in that day, beavers will die only when the land tells them it's the time and place to die.

The French commander in Detroit was officially de Maurepas, but Ta-Kumsaw avoided him whenever he could. It was only the second man, Napoleon Bonaparte, who was worth talking to.

"I heard you were at Lake Mizogan," said Napoleon. He spoke in French, of course, but Ta-Kumsaw had learned French at the same time he was learning English, and from the same person. "Come, sit down." Napoleon looked with vague interest at the White boy Alvin, but said nothing to him.

"I was there," said Ta-Kumsaw. "So was my brother."

"Ah. But was there an army?"

"The seed of one," said Ta-Kumsaw. "I gave up arguing with Tenskwa-Tawa. I'll make an army out of other tribes."

"When!" demanded Napoleon. "You come here two, three times each year, you tell me you're going to have an army. Do you know how long I've waited? Four years, four miserable years of exile."

"I know how many years," said Ta-Kumsaw. "You'll have your battle."

"Before my hair turns grey? Tell me that! Do I have to be dying of old age before you'll call out a general rising of the Reds? You know how helpless I am. La Fayette and de Maurepas won't let me go more than fifty miles from here, won't give me any troops at all. There has to be an army first, they say. The Americans have to have some main force that you can fight with. Well, the only thing that will cause those miserably independent bastards to unite is *you*."

"I know," said Ta-Kumsaw.

"You promised me an army of ten thousand Reds, Ta-Kumsaw. Instead I keep hearing about a city of ten thousand *Quakers*!"

"Not Quakers."

"If they renounce war it amounts to the same thing." Suddenly Napoleon let his voice become soft, loving, persuasive. "Ta-Kumsaw, I need you, I depend on you, don't fail me."

Ta-Kumsaw laughed. Napoleon learned long ago that his tricks worked on White men, but not half so well on Reds, and on Ta-Kumsaw not at all. "You care nothing for me, and I care nothing for you," said Ta-Kumsaw. "You want one battle and a victory, so you can go home a hero to Paris. I want one battle and a victory, so I can strike terror into White men's hearts and bring together an even greater army of Reds under my command, to sweep the land south of here and drive the Englishmen back across the mountains. One battle, one victory— that's why we work together, and when that's done I'll never think of you again, and you'll never think of me."

Napoleon was angry, but he laughed. "Half true," he said. "I won't care about you, but I'll think of you. I've learned from you, Ta-Kumsaw. That love of a commander makes men fight better than love of country, and love of country better than the hope of glory, and the hope of glory better than looting, and looting better than wages. But best of all is to fight for a cause. A great and noble dream. I've always had the love of my men. They would die for me. But for a cause, they'd let their wives and children die and think it was worth the price.''

''How did you learn that from me?'' said Ta-Kumsaw. ''That's my brother's talk, not mine.''

''Your brother? I thought he didn't think anything was worth dying for.''

''No, he's very free with dying. It's killing he won't do.''

Napoleon laughed, and Ta-Kumsaw laughed with him. ''You're right, you know. We're not friends. But I do like you. What puzzles me is this—when you've won, and all the White men are gone, you really mean to walk away and let all the tribes go back to the way they were before, separate, quarreling, weak.''

''Happy. That's how we were before. Many tribes, many languages, but one living land.''

''Weak,'' said Napoleon again. ''If I ever brought all of *my* land under my flag, Ta-Kumsaw, I'd hold them together so long and so tightly that they'd become one great people, great and strong. And if I ever do that, you can count on this. We'll be back, and take your land away from you, just like every other land on Earth. Count on it.''

''That's because you are evil, General Bonaparte. You want to bend everything and everybody to your obedience.''

''That isn't evil, foolish savage. If everybody obeyed me, then they'd be happy and safe, at peace, and, for the first time in all of history, free.''

''Safe, unless they opposed you. Happy, unless they hated you. Free, unless they wanted something contrary to your will.''

''Imagine, a Red man philosophizing. Do those peasant squatters south of here know that you've read Newton, Voltaire, Rousseau, and Adam Smith?''

''I don't think they know I can read their languages.''

Napoleon leaned across his desk. ''We'll destroy them, Ta-Kumsaw, you and I together. But you have to bring me an army.''

''My brother prophesies that we'll have that army before the year ends.''

''A prophecy?''

''All his prophecies come true.''

''Does he say we'll win?''

Ta-Kumsaw laughed. "He says you'll be known as the greatest European general who ever lived. And I will be known as the greatest Red."

Napoleon ran his fingers through his hair and smiled, almost boyish now; he could pass from menacing to friendly to adorable in moments. "That seems to dodge the question. Dead men can be called great, too."

"But men who lose battles are never called great, are they? Noble, perhaps, even heroic. But not great."

"True, Ta-Kumsaw, true. But your brother is being coy. Oracular. Delphic."

"I don't know those words."

"Of course you don't. You're a savage." Napoleon poured wine. "I forget myself. Wine?"

Ta-Kumsaw shook his head.

"I suppose none for the boy," said Napoleon.

"He's only ten," said Ta-Kumsaw.

"In France, that means we water the wine half and half. What are you doing with a White boy, Ta-Kumsaw? Are you capturing children now?"

"This White boy," said Ta-Kumsaw, "he's more than he seems."

"In a loincloth he doesn't look like much. Does he understand French?"

"Not a word," said Ta-Kumsaw. "I came to ask you—can you give us guns?"

"No," said Napoleon.

"We can't fight bullets with arrows," said Ta-Kumsaw.

"La Fayette refuses to authorize us to issue you any guns. Paris agrees with him. They don't trust you. They're afraid any guns they give you might someday be turned against us."

"Then what good will it do me to raise an army?"

Napoleon smiled, sipped his wine. "I've been speaking to some Irrakwa traders."

"The Irrakwa are the urine of sick dogs," said Ta-Kumsaw. "They were cruel, vicious animals before the White man came, and they are worse now."

"Odd. The English seemed to find them to be kindred spirits. And La Fayette adores them. All that matters now, though, is this: They manufacture guns, in large numbers, cheaply. Not the most *reliable* weapons, but they use exactly the same size ammunition. It means they can make balls that fit the barrel more tightly, with better aim. And yet they sell them for less."

"You'll buy them for us?"

"No. *You'll* buy them."

"We don't have money."

"Pelts," said Napoleon. "Beaver pelts. Minks. Deerhides and buffalo leather."

Ta-Kumsaw shook his head. "We can't ask these animals to die for the sake of guns."

"Too bad," said Napoleon. "You Reds have a knack for hunting, I've been told."

"True Reds do. The Irrakwa don't. They've used White man's machines so long now that they're dead to the land, just like White men. Or they'd go and get the pelts they want for themselves."

"There's something else they want. Besides pelts," said Napoleon.

"We don't have anything they want."

"Iron," said Napoleon.

"We don't have iron."

"No. But they know where it is. In the upper reaches of the Mizzipy, and along the Mizota. Up near the west end of High Water Lake. All they want is your promise that you won't harm their boats bringing iron ore back to Irrakwa, or their miners as they dig it out of the earth."

"Peace for the future, in exchange for guns now?"

"Yes," said Napoleon.

"Aren't they afraid that I'll turn the guns against *them*?"

"They ask you to promise that you won't."

Ta-Kumsaw considered this. "Tell them this. I promise that if they give us guns, not one of the guns will ever be used against any Irrakwa. All my men will take this oath. And we will never attack any of their boats on the water, or their miners as they dig in the earth."

"You mean that?" asked Napoleon.

"If I said it, I meant it," said Ta-Kumsaw.

"As much as you hate them?"

"I hate them because the land hates them. When the White man is gone, and the land is strong again, not sick, then earthquakes can swallow up miners, and storms can sink boats, and the Irrakwa will become true Red men again or they will die. Once the White man is gone, the land will be stern with its children who remain."

The meeting was soon finished after that. Ta-Kumsaw got up and shook hands with the general. Alvin surprised them both by also stepping forward and offering his hand.

Napoleon shook hands with him, amused. "Tell the boy he keeps dangerous company," he said.

Ta-Kumsaw translated. Alvin looked at him with wide eyes. "Does he mean *you*?" he asked.

"I think so," said Ta-Kumsaw.

"But *he's* the most dangerous man in the world," said Alvin.

Napoleon laughed when Ta-Kumsaw translated the boy's words. "How can I be dangerous? A little man stuck away out here in the middle of the wilderness, when the center of the world is Europe, great wars are fought there and I have no part in them!"

Ta-Kumsaw didn't need to translate—the boy understood from Napoleon's tone and expression. "He's so dangerous because he makes people love him without deserving it."

Ta-Kumsaw felt the truth in the boy's words. That was what Napoleon did to White men, and it *was* dangerous, dangerous and evil and dark. Is this the man I rely on to help me? To be my ally? Yes, he is, because I have no choice. Ta-Kumsaw didn't translate what the boy said, even though Napoleon insisted. So far the French general had not attempted to cast his spell on the boy. If he knew the boy's words, he might try, and it just might capture Alvin. Ta-Kumsaw was coming to appreciate what the boy was. Perhaps the boy was too strong for Napoleon to charm him. Or perhaps the boy would become an adoring slave like de Maurepas. Better not to find out. Better to take the boy away.

Alvin insisted on seeing the cathedral. One priest looked horrified to see men in loincloths come into the place, but another rebuked him and welcomed them inside. Ta-Kumsaw was always amused by the statues of the saints. Whenever possible, the statues were shown being tortured in the most gruesome ways. White could talk all day about how barbaric it was, the Red practice of torturing captives so they could show courage. Yet whose statues did they kneel at to pray? People who showed courage under torture. There was no making sense of White men.

He and Alvin talked about this on their way out of the city, not hurrying at all now. He also explained to the boy something of how they were able to run so far, so quickly. And how remarkable it was for a White boy to keep up with them.

Alvin seemed to understand how Red men lived within the land; at least he tried. "I think I felt that. While I was running. It's like I'm not in myself. My thoughts are wandering all over. Like dreaming. And while I'm gone, something else is telling my body what to do. Feeding it, using it, taking it wherever it wants to go. Is that what you feel?"

That wasn't at all what Ta-Kumsaw felt. When the land came into *him*, it was like he was more alive than ever; not absent from his body, but more strongly present in it than at any other time. But he didn't explain this to the boy. Instead he turned the question back to Alvin. "You say it's like dreaming. What did you dream last night?"

"I dreamed again about a lot of the visions I saw when I was in the crystal tower with the Shining—with the Prophet."

"The Shining Man. I know you call him that—he told me why."

"I dreamed those things again. Only it was different. I could see some things more clearly now, and other things I forgot."

"Did you dream anything you *hadn't* seen before?"

"*This* place. The statues in the cathedral. And that man we visited, the general. And something even stranger. A big hill, almost round—no, with eight sides. I remember that, it was real clear. A hill with eight straight sides to it, sloping down. Inside it there was a whole city, lots of little rooms, like in anthills, only people-sized. Or anyway bigger than ants. And I was on top of it, wandering around in all these strange trees—they had silver leaves, not green—and I was looking for my brother. For Measure."

Ta-Kumsaw said nothing for a long time. But he thought many things. No White man had ever seen that place—the land was still strong enough to keep them from finding *that*. Yet this boy had dreamed of it. And a dream of Eight-Face Mound never came by chance. It always meant something. It always meant the same thing.

"We have to go there," Ta-Kumsaw said.

"Where?"

"To the hill you dreamed of," said Ta-Kumsaw.

"There *is* such a place?"

"No White man has ever seen it. For a White man to stand there would be—filthy." Alvin didn't answer that. What could he say? Ta-Kumsaw swallowed hard. "But if you dream of it, you have to go."

"What is it?"

Ta-Kumsaw shook his head. "The place you dreamed of. That's all. If you want to know more, dream again."

It was near night when they reached the camp; wigwams had been erected, because it looked like more rain tonight. The others insisted that Ta-Kumsaw share a hut with Alvin, for his safety's sake. But Ta-Kumsaw didn't want to. The boy made him afraid. The land was doing things with this boy, and not giving Ta-Kumsaw any idea what was happening.

But when you saw yourself at the Eight-Face Mound in your dreams, you had no choice but to go. And since Alvin could never find the way alone, Ta-Kumsaw had to take him.

He could never explain it to the others, and even if he could, he wouldn't do it. Word would get out that Ta-Kumsaw had taken a White to the ancient holy place, and then many Reds would refuse to listen to Ta-Kumsaw anymore.

So in the morning he told the others he was taking the boy off to teach him, as the Prophet had told him he must. "Meet me in five days where the Pickawee flows into the Hio," he told them. "From there we'll go south to talk to the Chok-Taw and the Chicky-Saw."

Take us with you, they said. You won't be safe alone. But he didn't answer them, and soon enough they gave up. He set off at a run, and once again Alvin fell in step behind him, matching him stride for stride. It was almost as far again as the journey from Mizogan to Detroit. By nightfall they would be at the edge of the Land of Flints. Ta-Kumsaw planned to sleep there, and find dreams of his own, before daring to lead a White boy to Eight-Face Mound.

12

Cannons

Measure heard them coming only seconds before the door swung open and light flooded the root cellar. Time enough to dump out the dirt and tuck his loincloth into the deerhide belt, then scramble forward onto the potatoes. The breechclout was so filthy it was like wearing dirt, but this wasn't a time to get finicky.

They didn't waste no time on prison inspection, so they didn't see the hole that was now reaching a good two feet under the back wall. Instead they reached in and drug him out by the armpits, slamming the root cellar doors shut behind him. The light was so sudden it dazzled him, and he couldn't make out who had him, or how many they were. Didn't much matter. Anyone local would have known him right off, so they had to be Harrison's boys, and once he knew that, he knew it wasn't nothing good going to happen to him.

"Like a pig," said Harrison. "Disgusting. You look like a Red."

"You put me in a hole in the ground," said Measure. "I ain't about to come out clean."

"I gave you one long night to think about it, boy," said Harrison. "Now you got to make up your mind. There's two ways you can be useful to me. One is alive, you telling all about how they tortured your brother to death, him screaming every second. You make it a good story, and you tell all about how Ta-Kumsaw and the Prophet were there, getting their own hands into the boy's blood. You tell a story like that, and it's worth keeping you alive."

"Ta-Kumsaw saved my life from *your* Chok-Taw Reds," said Measure. "That's the only story I'll tell. Except to mention how you *wanted* me to tell another story."

"That's what I thought," said Harrison. "Fact is, even if you lied to me and promised to tell the story my way, I reckon I wouldn't've believed you. So we both agree—it's the other choice."

Measure knew Harrison meant to produce his body, with the evidence of torture on it. Dead, he couldn't tell anybody who did the cutting and burning. Well, thought Measure, you'll see I die as brave as any man.

But because he wasn't one to welcome death with both hands, he thought he'd give talking a bit more of a try. "You let me go and call off this war, Harrison, and I'll keep my mouth shut. Just let me wander in, and you allow as how it was all a terrible mistake and take your boys on home and leave Prophetstown in peace, and I won't tell a word otherwise. That's a lie I'm glad to tell."

Harrison hesitated just a moment, and Measure allowed himself to hope he might actually have some spark of godliness left in him, to turn away from the sin of murder before it was fully done. Then Harrison smiled, shook his head, and waved his hand at a big ugly riverman standing right up against the wall.

"Mike Fink, this here's a renegade White boy, who has joined in with all the evil doings of Ta-Kumsaw and his gang of child-killers and wife-rapers. I hope you'll break several of his bones."

Fink stood there, contemplating. "I reckon he'll make a powerful lot of noise, Gov."

"Well, jam in a gag on him." Harrison took a kerchief out of his own coat pocket. "Here, stuff this in his mouth and tie it there."

Fink complied. Measure tried to keep his eyes off him, tried to calm the dread that made his belly so tight and his bladder so full. The kerchief filled his mouth so full he choked on it. He only got control of himself by breathing slow and steady through his nose. Fink tied his own red scarf so tight around Measure's face that it forced the gag down into his throat even farther; again it took all his concentration just to breathe evenly and stop from gagging and retching. If he did that, he'd sure breathe that kerchief right down into his lungs, and then he *would* die.

Which was a crazy thought, seeing as how Harrison meant to have him dead no matter what. Maybe choking on a kerchief would be better than the pain Fink meant to cause. But Measure had too strong a spark of life to choose to die like that. Pain or not, when he died he'd go out gasping, not smothering himself just to get off easy.

"Breaking his bones ain't the way Reds do it." Fink was being helpful. "They usually cut and burn."

"Well, we don't have time for cutting, and you can burn the body after he's dead. The point of this is to have a colorful corpse, Mike, not to cause this boy pain. We're not savages, or at least some of us aren't."

Mike chuckled, then reached out, took Measure by the shoulder, and kicked his feet out from under him. Measure never felt so helpless in his life as in that moment when he fell. Fink didn't have an inch of height or reach on him, and Measure knew a few wrassling tricks, but Fink never even tried to grapple with him. Just a grab and a kick, and Measure was on the floor.

"Don't you need to tie him first?" asked Harrison.

In answer, Fink picked up Measure's left leg so fast and high that Measure slid across the floor and his buttocks lifted right into the air. No chance to get leverage, no chance to kick. Then Fink brought Measure's leg down across his own thigh hard and sharp. His leg bones snapped like dry kindling wood. Measure screamed into the gag, then nearly inhaled the kerchief gasping for breath. He never felt pain like that in all his life. For one crazy moment he thought, This is how Alvin felt when that millstone fell on his leg.

"Not in here," said Harrison. "Take him out back. Do it in the root cellar."

"How many bones you want me to break?" asked Fink.

"All of them."

Fink picked Measure up by an arm and a leg and practically tossed him up over his shoulders. Despite the pain, Measure tried to lay in a punch or two, but Fink jerked down on his arm, breaking it right at the elbow.

Measure was barely conscious the rest of the way outside. He heard somebody in the distance call, "Who you got there!"

Fink yelled back, "Caught us a Red spy, sneaking around!"

The voice from the distance sounded familiar to Measure, but he couldn't concentrate well enough to remember who it was. "Tear him apart!" he shouted.

Fink didn't answer. He didn't set Measure down to open the root cellar doors, even though they were low and at a slant, so you had to reach out and down, then pull them up. Fink just hooked the toe of his boot under the door and flipped it up. It moved so fast it banged on the ground and rebounded so as to nearly close again, but by then Fink was already stepping into the cellar; the door hit his thigh and bounced right open again. Measure just heard it as banging and a little jostling, which made his leg and his elbow hurt all the more. Why haven't I fainted yet, he wondered. Now's as good a time as any.

But he never did faint. Both legs broken above and below the knee, his fingers bent back and disjointed, his hands crushed, his arms broken above and below the elbows—through all that he stayed awake, though the pain eventually got kind of far away, more like the memory of pain than pain itself. If you hear one cymbal crash, it's loud; two or three cymbal crashes at once are louder yet. But along about the twentieth cymbal crash, it don't get louder, you just get deafer, and you hardly hear any of them at all. That's how it was for Measure.

There was a sound of cheering in the distance.

Somebody ran up. "Governor says finish up real quick, he wants you right away."

"I'll be done in a minute," said Fink. "Except for the burning."

"Save it till later," the man said. "Hurry!"

Fink dropped Measure, then stomped his chest till his ribs were pretty much broke, bending in and out any which way. Then he picked him up by the arm and the hair and bit off his ear. Measure felt it tear away with one last desperate surge of anger. Then Fink gave his head a sharp twist. Measure heard his own neck snap. Fink flung him onto the potatoes. He rolled down the backside and into the hole he dug. Only when his face was in the dirt did the pain stop and darkness come.

Fink flipped the doors shut with his foot, slid the bar into place, and headed back to the house. The cheering out front was louder. Harrison met him coming out of his office. "Never mind about that now," Harrison said. "There's no need for a corpse to keep things hot around here. The cannon just got here, and we'll attack in the morning."

Harrison rushed out to the front porch, and Mike Fink followed him. Cannon? What did cannons have to do with needing or not needing a corpse? What did he think Mike was, an assassin? Killing Hooch was one thing, and killing a man in a fair fight was something else. But killing a young man with a gag in his mouth, that was altogether different. When he bit off that ear it just didn't feel right. It wasn't no trophy of a fair fight. Took the heart right out of him. He didn't even bother biting off the other ear.

Mike stood there beside Harrison, watching the horses pull the four cannon right along, brisk as you please. He knew how Harrison would use the guns, he'd heard him planning it. Two here, two there, so they rake the whole Red city from both sides. Grape and canister, to rip and tear the bodies of the Reds, women and children right along with the men.

It ain't my kind of a fight, thought Mike. Like that man out back. No challenge at all, like stomping baby frogs. You can do it, and not think twice. But you don't pick up the dead frogs, stuff them, and hang them on the wall, you just don't do that.

It ain't my kind of fight.

13

Eight-Face Mound

There was a different feel to the land around Licking River. Alvin didn't notice right off, mostly cause he was running with his wick trimmed, so to speak. Didn't notice much at all. It was one long dream as he ran. But as Ta-Kumsaw led him into the Land of Flints, there was a change in the dream. All around him, no matter what he saw in his dream, there was little sparks of deep-black fire. Not like the nothingness that always lurked at the edges of his vision. Not like the deep black that sucked light into itself and never let it go. No, this black shone, it gave off sparks.

And when they stopped running, and Alvin came to hisself again, those black fires may have faded just a bit but they were still there. Without so much as thinking, Alvin walked toward one, a black blaze in a sea of green, reached down and picked it up. A flint. A good big one.

"A twenty-arrow flint," said Ta-Kumsaw.

"It shines black and burns cold," said Alvin.

Ta-Kumsaw nodded. "You want to be a Red boy? Then make arrowheads with me."

Alvin caught on quick. He had worked with stone before. When he cut a millstone, he wanted smooth, flat surfaces. With flint, it was the edge, not the face that counted. His first two arrowheads were clumsy, but then he was able to feel his way into the stone and find the natural creases and folds, and then break them apart. For his fourth arrowhead, he didn't chip at all. Just used his fingers and gently pulled the arrowhead away from the flint.

Ta-Kumsaw's face showed no expression. That's what most White folks thought he looked like all the time. They thought Red men, and most especially Ta-Kumsaw, never *felt* nothing cause they never let nobody *see* their feelings. Alvin had seen him laugh, though, and cry, and all the other faces that a man can show. So he knowed that when Ta-Kumsaw showed nothing on his face, that meant he was feeling a whole lot of things.

"I worked with stone a lot before," said Alvin. He felt like he was sort of apologizing.

"Flint isn't *stone*," said Ta-Kumsaw. "Pebbles in the river, boulders, those are stone. This is living rock, rock with fire in it, the hard earth that the land gives to us freely. Not hewn out and tortured the way White men do with iron." He held up Alvin's fourth arrowhead, the one he cajoled out of the flint with his fingers. "Steel can never have an edge this sharp."

"It's just about as perfect an edge as I ever saw," said Al.

"No chip marks," said Ta-Kumsaw. "No pressing. A Red man would see this flint and say, The land grew the flint this way."

"But you know better," said Al. "You know it's just a knack I got."

"A *knack* bends the land," said Ta-Kumsaw. "Like a snag in the river churns the water on the river's face. So it is with the land when a White uses his knack. Not you."

Alvin puzzled on that for a minute. "You mean you can see where other folks did their doodlebug or beseeching or hex or charm?"

"Like the bad stink when a sick man loosens his bowel," said Ta-Kumsaw. "But you—what you do is clean. Like part of the land. I thought I would teach you how to be Red. Instead the land gives you arrowheads like a gift."

Again, Alvin felt like apologizing. It seemed to make Ta-Kumsaw angry, that he could do the things he did. "It ain't like I asked anybody for this," he said. "I was just the seventh son of a seventh son, and the thirteenth child."

"These numbers—seven, thirteen—you Whites care about them, but they're nothing in the land. The land has true numbers. One, two, three, four, five, six—these numbers you can find when you stand in the forest and look around you. Where is seven? Where is thirteen?"

"Maybe that's why they're so strong," said Alvin. "Maybe cause they ain't natural."

"Then why does the land love this unnatural thing that you do?"

"I don't know, Ta-Kumsaw. I'm only ten going on eleven."

Ta-Kumsaw laughed. "Ten? Eleven? Very weak numbers."

They spent the night there, in the borders of the Land of Flints. Ta-Kumsaw told Alvin the story of that place, how it was the best flint country in the whole land. No matter how many flints the Reds came and took away, more always came out of the ground, just lying there to get picked up. In years gone by, every now and then some tribe would try to own the place. They'd bring their warriors and kill anyone else who came for flints. That way they figured they'd have arrows and the other tribes wouldn't have any. But it never worked right. Cause as soon as that tribe won its battles and held the land, the flints just plain disappeared. Not a one. Members of that tribe would search and search, and never find a thing. They'd go away, and another tribe would come in, and there'd be flints again, as many as ever.

"It belongs to everybody, this place. All Reds are at peace here. No killing, no war, no quarrels—or the tribe has no flints."

"I wish the whole world was a place like that," said Alvin.

"Listen to my brother long enough, White boy, and you'll start to think it is. No, no, don't explain to me. Don't defend him. He takes his road, I take mine. I think his way will kill more people, Red or White, than mine."

In the night, Alvin dreamed. He saw himself walk all the way around Eight-Face Mound, until he found a place where a path seemed to lead up the steep hill. He climbed, then, and came to the top. The silver-leafed trees shook in the breeze, blinding him as the sun shone off them. He walked to one tree, and in it there was a nest of redbirds. Every tree the same, a single redbird nest.

Except one tree. It was different from the others. It was older, gnarled, with spreading branches instead of the up-reaching kind. Like a fruit tree. And the leaves were gold, not silver, so they didn't shine so bright, but they were soft and deep. In the tree, he saw round white fruit, and he knew that it was ripe. But when he reached out his hand to take the fruit, and eat it, he could hear laughter, jeering. He looked around him and saw everybody he ever knowed in his whole life, laughing at him. Except one—Taleswapper. Taleswapper was standing there, and he said, "Eat." Alvin reached up and plucked a single fruit out of the tree and took it to his lips and bit into it. It was juicy and firm, and the taste was sweet and bitter, salt and sour all at once, so strong it made him tingle all over—but good, a taste he wanted to hold inside him forever.

He was about to take a second bite when he saw that the fruit was gone from his hand, and not a one hung from the tree. "One bite is all you need for now," said Taleswapper. "Remember how it tastes."

"I'll never forget," said Alvin.

Everybody was still laughing, louder than ever; but Alvin paid them no mind. He'd took him a bite of the fruit, and all he wanted now was to bring his family to the same tree, and let them eat; to bring everybody he ever knowed, and even strangers, too, and let them taste it. If they'd just taste it, Alvin figured, they'd know.

"What would they know?" asked Taleswapper.

Al couldn't think what it was. "Just know," he said. "Know everything. Everything that's good."

"That's right," said Taleswapper. "With the first bite, you *know*."

"What about the second bite?"

"With the second bite, you live forever," said Taleswapper. "And that isn't a thing you'd better plan on doing, my boy. Don't ever imagine you can live forever."

Alvin woke up that morning with the taste of the fruit still in his mouth. He had to force himself to believe that it was just a dream. Ta-Kumsaw was already up. He had a low fire going, and he had called two fish out of the Licking River. Now they were spitted with sticks down their mouths. He handed one to Alvin.

But Alvin didn't want to eat. If he did, the taste of the fruit would go out of his mouth. He'd begin to forget, and he wanted to remember. Oh, he knowed that he'd have to eat sometime—a body can get remarkable thin saying no to food all the time. But today, for now, he didn't want to eat.

Still, he held the spit and watched the trout sizzle. Ta-Kumsaw talked, telling him about calling fish and other animals when you need to eat. Asking them to come. If the land wants you to eat, then they come; or maybe some other animal, it doesn't matter, just so you eat what the land gives you. Alvin thought about the fish he was roasting. Didn't the land know he wasn't going to eat this morning? Or did it send this fish to tell him he ought to eat after all?

Neither one. Because just at the moment the fish were ready to eat, they heard the crashing and thumping that told them a White man was coming.

Ta-Kumsaw sat very still, but he didn't so much as pull out his knife. "If the land brings a White man *here*, then he isn't my enemy," said Ta-Kumsaw.

In a few seconds, the White man stepped into the clearing. His hair was white, where he wasn't bald. He was carrying his hat. He had a slack-looking pouch over his shoulder, and no weapon at all. Alvin knew right off what was in that pouch. A change of clothes, a few snatches of food, and a book. A third of the book contained single sentences, where folks had written down the most important thing they ever saw happen with their own eyes. The last two-thirds of the book, though, were sealed with a leather strap. That was where Taleswapper wrote down his own stories, the ones he believed and thought were important.

Cause that's who it was, Taleswapper, who Alvin never thought to see again in his life. And suddenly, seeing that old friend, Alvin knew why two fish came at Ta-Kumsaw's call. "Taleswapper," Alvin said, "I hope you're hungry, cause I got a fish here that I roasted for you."

Taleswapper smiled. "I'm right glad to see you, Alvin, and right glad to see that fish."

Alvin handed him the spit. Taleswapper sat him down in the grass, across the fire from Alvin and Ta-Kumsaw. "Thank you kindly, Alvin," said Taleswapper. He pulled out his knife and neatly began flaking off slices of fish. They sizzled his lips, but he just licked and smacked and made short work of the trout. Ta-Kumsaw also ate his, and Alvin watched them both. Ta-Kumsaw never took his eyes off Taleswapper.

"This is Taleswapper," Alvin said. "He's the man who taught me how to heal."

"I didn't teach you," said Taleswapper. "I just gave you some idea how to teach yourself. And persuaded you that you ought to try." Taleswapper directed his next sentence at Ta-Kumsaw. "He was set to let himself die before he'd use his knack to heal himself, can you believe that?"

"And this is Ta-Kumsaw," said Alvin.

"Oh, I knew that the minute I saw you. Do you know what a legend you are among White people? You're like Saladin during the Crusade—they admire you more than they admire their own leaders, even though they know you're sworn to fight until you've driven the last White man out of America."

Ta-Kumsaw said nothing.

"I've met maybe two dozen children named after you, most of them boys, all of them White. And stories—about you saving White captives from being burned to death, about you bringing food to people you drove out of their homes, so they wouldn't starve. I even believe some of those stories."

Ta-Kumsaw finished his fish and laid the spit in the fire.

"I also heard a story as I was coming here, about how you captured two Whites from Vigor Church and sent their bloody torn-up clothes to their parents. How you tortured them to death to show how you meant to destroy every White—man, woman, and child. How you said the time for being civilized was past, and now you'd use pure terror to drive the White man out of America."

For the first time since Taleswapper arrived, Ta-Kumsaw spoke. "Did you believe *that* story?"

"Well, I didn't," said Taleswapper. "But that's because I already knew the truth. You see, I got a message from a girl I knew—a young lady now, she is. It was a letter." He took a folded letter from his coat, three sheets of paper covered with writing. He handed them to Ta-Kumsaw.

Without looking at it, Ta-Kumsaw handed the letter to Alvin. "Read it to me," he said.

"But you can read English," said Alvin.

"Not here," said Ta-Kumsaw.

Alvin looked at the letter, at all three pages of it, and to his surprise he couldn't read it either. The letters all looked familiar. When he studied them out, he could even name them—T-H-E-M-A-K-E-R-N-E-E-D-S-Y-O-U, that's how it started, but it made no sense to Al at all, he couldn't even say for sure what language it was in. "I can't read it either," he said, and handed it back to Taleswapper.

Taleswapper studied it for a minute, then laughed and put it back into his coat pocket. "Well, that's a story for my book. A place where a man can't read."

To Alvin's surprise, Ta-Kumsaw smiled. "Even you?"

"I know what it says, because I read it before," said Taleswapper. "But I can't make out a single word of it today. Even when I know what the word is supposed to be. What *is* this place?"

"We're in the Land of Flints," said Alvin.

"We're in the shadow of Eight-Face Mound," said Ta-Kumsaw.

"I didn't think a White man could get here," said Taleswapper.

"Neither did I," said Ta-Kumsaw. "But here is a White boy, and there is a White man."

"I dreamed you last night," said Alvin. "I dreamed I was on top of Eight-Face Mound, and you were with me, explaining things to me."

"Don't count on it," said Taleswapper. "I doubt there's a thing on Eight-Face Mound that I could explain to anybody."

"How did you come here," asked Ta-Kumsaw, "if you didn't know you were coming to the Land of Flints?"

"She told me to come up the Musky-Ingum, and when I saw a white boulder on the right, I should take the fork that led left. She said I'd find Alvin Miller Junior sitting with Ta-Kumsaw by a fire, roasting fish."

"Who told you all this?" asked Alvin.

"A woman," said Taleswapper. "A torch. She told me you saw her in a vision, Alvin, inside a crystal tower, not more than a week ago by now. She was the one who pulled the caul from your face, when you were born. She's been watching you ever since, in the way a torch sees. She went inside that tower with you and saw out of your eyes."

"The Prophet *said* someone was with us," said Alvin.

"She looked out of *his* eye, too," said Taleswapper, "and she saw all his futures. The Prophet will die. Tomorrow morning. Shot by your own father's gun, Alvin."

"No!" cried Alvin.

"Unless," said Taleswapper. "Unless Measure comes in time to show your father that he's alive, that Ta-Kumsaw and the Prophet never harmed him, or you either."

"But Measure left days ago!"

"That's right, Alvin. But he got captured by Governor Harrison's men. Harrison has him, and today, maybe even right now, one of Harrison's men is killing him. Breaking his bones, breaking his neck. Tomorrow Harrison will attack Prophetstown with his cannon, killing everybody. Every soul. So much blood that the Tippy-Canoe will flow scarlet and the Wobbish will flow red clear to the Hio."

Ta-Kumsaw leaped to his feet. "I have to go back. I have to—"

"You know how far you are," said Taleswapper. "You know where your warriors are. Even if you ran all night and all day, as fast as you Reds can go—"

"Noon tomorrow," said Ta-Kumsaw.

"He'll be dead already," said Taleswapper.

Ta-Kumsaw shouted in anguish, so loud that several birds cried out and flew away from the meadow.

"Now, hold your horses, just wait a minute. If there were nothing we could do, she wouldn't very well have sent me on this chase, now, would she? Don't you see we're acting out a plan that's bigger than all of us? Why did it happen that Alvin and Measure were the two boys that Harrison's hired Chok-Taw kidnapped? How do you happen to be here, and me also, at the very day when we're most needed?"

"They need us *there*," said Ta-Kumsaw.

"I don't think so," said Taleswapper. "I think that if they needed us there, then there we'd be. They need us *here*."

"You're like my brother, trying to make me fit into his plans!"

"I wish I *were* like your brother. He has visions and sees what's going on, while all I get is a letter from a torch. But here I am, and here you are, and if we weren't supposed to be here, we just plain wouldn't, whether you like it or not."

Alvin didn't like this talk of what was supposed to happen. Who was doing all this supposing? What did Taleswapper mean—they were all poppets on sticks? Was somebody making them move any old way, whatever he felt ought to happen? "If somebody's so all-fired in charge of everything," said Alvin, "he hasn't been doing too good a job of it, getting us into a fix like this."

Taleswapper grinned. "You really don't take to religion, do you, boy?"

"I just don't think anybody's making us do anything."

"Nor did I say so," said Taleswapper. "I'm just saying things never get so bad we can't do something to make them better."

"Well I'll be glad to take suggestions. What did this torch lady think I ought to do?" asked Alvin.

"She said you're supposed to climb the mountain and heal Measure. Don't ask me more than that—that's all she said. There isn't a mountain worthy of the name in these parts, and Measure's in the root cellar behind Vinegar Riley's house—"

"I know that place," said Alvin. "I been there. But I can't—I mean I've never tried to heal somebody who wasn't right there in front of me."

"Enough talking," said Ta-Kumsaw. "Eight-Face Mound called you in a dream, White boy. This man came to tell you to go up the mountain. Everything begins when you climb the Mound. If you can."

"Some things end on Eight-Face Mound," said Taleswapper.

"What does a White man know about this place?" asked Ta-Kumsaw.

"Not a thing," said Taleswapper. "But I knelt by the bed of a dying Irrakwa woman, many years ago, and she told me that the most important thing in her life was, she was the last Irrakwa ever to stand inside Eight-Face Mound."

"The Irrakwa have all turned White in their hearts," said Ta-Kumsaw. "Eight-Face Mound would never let them in now."

"But I'm White," said Alvin.

"Very good problem," said Ta-Kumsaw. "The Mound will tell you the answer. Maybe the answer is you don't go up and everybody dies. Come."

He led them along the path the land opened up for them, until they came to a steep hill, thickly grown with trees and brambles. There was no path. "This is Red Man's Face," said Ta-Kumsaw. "This is where Red men climb. The path is gone. You can't climb here."

"Where, then?" asked Alvin.

"How do I know?" said Ta-Kumsaw. "The story is that if you climb a different face, you find a different Mound. The story is that if you climb the Builders' Face, you find their ancient city, still alive on the Mound. If you climb the Beasts' Face, you find a land where a giant buffalo is king, a strange animal with horns that come out of his mouth and a nose like a terrible snake, and huge cougars with teeth as long as spears all bow before him and worship. Who knows if these stories are true? No one climbs those faces now.''

"Is there a White Man's Face?" asked Alvin.

"Red Man, Medicine, Builder, Beast. Four other faces we don't know their names," said Ta-Kumsaw. "Maybe one of them is White Man's Face. Come.''

He led them around the hill. The Mound rose on their left hand. No path opened. Alvin recognized everything they saw. His dream last night was true, at least this much: Taleswapper was with him, and he circled the Mound before climbing.

They came to the last of the unknown faces. No path. Alvin made as if to go on to the next face.

"No use," said Ta-Kumsaw. "All eight faces, none will let us up. The next is Red Man's Face again.''

"I know," said Alvin. "But here's the path.''

There it was, straight as an arrow. Right on the edge shared by Red Man's Face and the unknown face beside it.

"You *are* half Red," said Ta-Kumsaw.

"Go on up," said Taleswapper.

"In my dream you were with me up there," said Alvin.

"Maybe so," said Taleswapper. "But the fact is, I can't see this path the two of you are talking about. It looks just like all the rest of the faces. So I reckon I'm not invited.''

"Go," said Ta-Kumsaw. "Hurry.''

"You come with me, then," said Alvin. "You see the path, don't you?''

"I didn't dream of the Mound," said Ta-Kumsaw. "And what you see there, it will be half what the Red man sees, and half a new place that I should never see. Go now, don't waste time anymore. My brother and your brother will die unless you do whatever it is the land brought you here to do.''

"I'm thirsty," said Al.

"Drink there," said Ta-Kumsaw, "if the Mound offers you water. Eat if the Mound offers you food.''

Al set his feet on the path and scrambled up the hill. It was steep, but there were roots to grab, plenty of footholds, and before long the path crested, leveled, and the underbrush ended.

He had thought the Mound was a single hill, with eight slopes. Now, though, he could see that each of the eight slopes was a separate Mound, arranged to form a deep bowl in the middle. The valley seemed much too large, the farthest Mounds much too far away. Hadn't Alvin walked around the entire Mound this morning with Ta-Kumsaw and Taleswapper? Eight-Face Mound was much more inside than it seemed to be outside.

He walked carefully down the grassy slope. It was tufted, irregular, the grass cool, the soil moist and firm. It seemed much farther going down than it had been going up. When he finally reached the valley floor, he stood on the verge of a meadow, with silver-leafed trees, just like in his dream. So his dream had been true, showing him a real place that he could not have imagined.

But how was he supposed to find Measure and heal him? What did the Mound have to do with anything at all? It was afternoon now, they'd taken so long circling the Mound—Measure might already be dying, and he didn't have any idea how to go about helping him.

He couldn't think of anything to do but walk. He thought he'd cross the valley and see one of the other mounds, but it was the strangest thing. No matter how far he walked, no matter how many silver-leafed trees he passed, the mound he walked toward was always just as far away. It made him afraid—would he be trapped up here forever?— and he hurried back in the direction he started from. In just a few minutes he reached the place where his footprints came down the slope. Surely he had walked away from that spot for much longer than that. A couple more tries convinced him that the valley went on forever in every direction except the one he came from. In *that* direction, it was just like he was always in the very center of the Mound, no matter how far he'd walked to get where he was.

Alvin looked for the gold-leafed tree with the pure white fruit, but he couldn't find it, and he wasn't surprised. The taste of the fruit was still in his mouth from the dream the night before. He wouldn't get another taste of it, waking or dreaming, because the second bite would make him live forever. He didn't mind much, not getting that bite. Death didn't breathe all that heavy down the neck of a boy his age.

He heard water. A brook, clear cold water flowing rapidly over stones. It was impossible, of course. The valley of Eight-Face Mound was completely enclosed. If water ran so fast here, why didn't the valley fill right up to make a lake? Why wasn't there a single stream running off the mound outside? Where would such a stream come from, anyway? The mound was man-made, like all the other mounds scattered all through the country, though none of the others was so old. You don't get springs coming out of man-made hills. It made him suspicious of this water, to have it be so impossible. Come to think of it, though, quite a few impossible things had happened to him in his life, and this was far from being the most peculiar.

Ta-Kumsaw said to drink if the mound offered him water, so he knelt and drank, plunging his face right into the water and sucking the water straight into his mouth. It didn't take away the taste of the fruit. If anything, it was stronger after he drank.

He knelt on the bank, studying the opposite shore of the brook. The water was flowing differently there. In fact, it was lapping the shore like ocean waves, and once that thought occurred to Alvin he saw that the *shape* of the opposite shore was just like the map of the east coast that Armor-of-God showed him. The memory came back clear and sharp. Here where the shore bowed outward, that was Carolina in the Crown Colonies. This deep bay was the Chase-a-pick, and here was the mouth of the Potty-Mack, which made the border between the United States and the Crown Colonies.

Alvin stood and stepped across the stream.

It was just grass. He didn't see no rivers or towns, no boundaries, no roads. But from the coast, he could pretty much guess where the Hio country was, and where this very mound would be. He took two steps, and all of a sudden there he saw Ta-Kumsaw and Taleswapper, setting on the ground in front of him, looking up at him as surprised as could be.

"You climbed up after all," said Alvin.

"Nothing of the sort," said Taleswapper. "We've been right here since you left."

"Why did you come back down?" asked Ta-Kumsaw.

"But I ain't down at all," said Alvin. "I'm down here in the valley of the mound."

"Valley?" asked Ta-Kumsaw.

"We're down here below the mound," said Taleswapper.

Then Alvin understood. Not so as to put it into words, but well enough to use it, to use what the mound had given him. He could travel across the face of the land like this, a hundred miles in a step, and see the people that he needed to see. The people that he knew. Measure. Alvin touched his forehead in salute to the two men who waited for him, then took a small step. They disappeared.

He found the town of Vigor Church easy enough. First person he saw was Armor-of-God, kneeling in prayer. Alvin didn't say nothing to him, for fear Armor might take it as a vision of the dead. Where would Armor be, though? In his own house? In that case Vinegar Riley's place would be back this way, east of town. He turned around.

He saw his own father, setting with Mother. Pa was smoothing out some musket balls he'd cast. And Ma was whispering to him, all urgent. She was angry, and so was Pa. "Women and children, that's what they are in that town. Even if the Prophet and Ta-Kumsaw killed our boys, them women and children there didn't do it. You'll be no better than them if you raise a hand against them. I won't see you come back into this house, I'll never see you again if you kill one soul of them. I swear it, Alvin Miller."

Pa just kept on polishing, except once when he said, "They killed my boys."

Alvin tried to answer, opened his mouth to say, "But I ain't dead, Pa!"

It didn't work. He couldn't say a word. He wasn't brought up here to give a vision to his parents, neither. It was Measure he had to find, or Pa's own musket ball would kill the Shining Man.

It wasn't far, not even a step. Alvin just inched his feet forward, and Ma and Pa disappeared. He caught a glimpse of Calm and David, shooting their guns—probably at targets. And Wastenot and Wantnot, ramming something—ramming shot down the barrel of a cannon. Glimpses of other folks, though because he didn't know or care about them he didn't see them clear. Finally he saw Measure.

He had to be dead. His neck was broke, judging from the angle of his head, and his arms and legs were all broke, too. Alvin didn't dare move, or he'd travel a mile in an instant, and Measure would disappear just like the others. Alvin just stood there, and sent his spark out into the body of his brother, lying before him on the ground.

Alvin never felt such pain in all his life. It wasn't Measure's pain, it was his own. It was Alvin's sense of how things ought to be, of the right shape of things; inside Measure's body, nothing was going right. Parts of him were dying, the blood was packed into his belly and crushing his own life out, his brain wasn't connected to his body no more, it was the most terrible mess Alvin ever saw, everything wrong, so wrong that it hurt him to see it, a pain so sharp he cried out. But Measure didn't hear him. Measure was beyond hearing. If Measure wasn't dead he was half an inch from being dead, and that was sure.

Alvin went to his heart first. It was still pumping, but there wasn't much blood left in the veins; it was all lost in Measure's chest and belly. That was the first thing Alvin had to mend, heal up the blood vessels and get the blood back where it belonged, flowing it in its channels.

Time, it all took time. All the broken ribs, the cut-up organs. All the bones, joining them without so much as a hand to help move something into the right place—some of the bones were so out of line that he couldn't heal them at all. He'd have to wait until Measure woke up enough to help him.

So Alvin got inside Measure's brain, the nerves running down his spine, and healed it all, put it back the way it had to be.

Measure woke with one long, terrible scream of agony. He was alive and the pain was back, sharper and clearer than it ever was before. I'm sorry, Measure. I can't heal you up without letting the pain come back. And I got to heal you, or too many innocent folks are dead.

Alvin didn't even notice that it was already night, and half his work still lay ahead of him.

14

Tippy-Canoe

In Prophetstown, no one but the children slept that night. The adults all felt the circling White army; the hidings and hexes cast by the White troops were like trumpets and banners to the land-sense of the Reds.

Not all of them found they had the courage to keep their oath, now that iron-and-fire death was hours away. But they kept the oath this far: They gathered their families and slipped out of Prophetstown, passing silently between companies of White soldiers, who neither heard nor saw them. Knowing they could not die without defending themselves, they left, so that not one Red would mar the perfection of the Prophet's refusal to fight.

Tenskwa-Tawa was not surprised that some left; he was surprised that so many stayed. Almost all. So many who believed in him, so many who would prove that trust in blood. He dreaded the morning; the pain of a single murder close at hand had cursed him with the black noise for many years. True, it was his father who was killed, so the pain was more; but did he love the people of Prophetstown any less than he had loved his father?

Yet he had to fend off the black noise, keep his wits about him, or all their deaths would be in vain. If their dying accomplished nothing, he wouldn't have them do it. So many times he had searched the crystal tower, trying to find some way to approach this day, some path that would lead to something good. The best that he could find was the land divided, Red west of the Mizzipy, White to the east. Even that, though, could be found only through the narrowest of paths. So much depended on the White boys, so much on Tenskwa-Tawa, so much on White Murderer Harrison himself. For in all the paths in which Harrison showed any mercy, the massacre of Tippy-Canoe did nothing to stop the destruction of the Reds, and, with them, the land. In all those paths, the Red men dwindled, confined to tiny preserves of desolate land, until the whole land was White, and therefore brutalized into submission, stripped and cut and ravished, giving vast amounts of food that was only in imitation of the true harvest, poisoned into life by alchemical trickery. Even the White man suffered in those visions of the future, but it would be many generations before he realized what he had done. Yet here—Prophetstown—there was a day—tomorrow—when the future could be turned onto an unlikely path, but a better one. One that would lead to a living land after all, even if it was truncated; one that would lead someday to a crystal city catching sunlight and turning it into visions of truth for all who lived within it.

That was Tenskwa-Tawa's hope, that he could cling to the bright vision through all of tomorrow's pain, and so turn that pain, that blood, that black noise of murder, to an event that would change the world.

Even before the first detectable rays of light rose above the horizon, Tenskwa-Tawa felt the coming dawn. He felt it partly in the stirring of life to the east. He could feel it from farther off than any other Red. He felt it also, though, from the movements among the Whites as they prepared to light the matches for their cannon. Four fires, hidden and therefore revealed by spells and witchery. Four cannon, poised to rake the city, end to end.

Tenskwa-Tawa walked through the city, humming softly. They heard him, and awakened their children. The White men thought to kill them in their sleep, faceless within their wigwams and lodges. Instead, they emerged in the darkness, walking surefooted to the broad meadow of the meeting ground. There wasn't room enough for all of them even to sit. They stood, families together, father and mother with their children in the circle of their embrace, waiting for the White man to spill their blood.

"The earth will not soak up your blood," Tenskwa-Tawa had promised them. "It will flow into the river, and I will hold it there, all the power of all your lives and all your deaths, and I will use it to keep the land alive, and bind the White man to the lands he has already captured and begun to kill."

So now Tenskwa-Tawa made his way to the bank of the Tippy-Canoe, watching the meadow fill up with his people, of whom so many would die before him because they believed in his words. "Stand with me today, Mr. Miller," said General Harrison. "It's your kin whose blood we'll avenge today. I want you to have the honor of firing the first bullet in this war."

Mike Fink watched as the hot-eyed miller carefully rammed wad and shot down his musket barrel. Mike knew the thirst for murder in his eyes. It was a kind of madness that came on a man, and it made him dangerous, made him able to do things beyond his normal reach. Mike was just as glad that Miller didn't know just when and how his boy had died. Oh, Governor Bill hadn't never told him right out who that young man was, but Mike Fink wasn't a boy in short pants, and he knew all right. Harrison played a deep game, but one thing was sure. He'd do anything to raise himself higher and put more land and people under his control. And Mike Fink knew that Harrison would only keep him around as long as he was useful.

The funny thing was, you see, that Mike Fink didn't think of himself as a murderer. He thought of life as a contest, and dying was what happened to those who came out second best, but it wasn't the same as murder, it was a fair fight. Like how he killed Hooch—Hooch didn't have to be so careless. Hooch could have noticed Mike wasn't on the shore with the other poleboys, Hooch could have been watchful and wary, and if he had been, why, Mike Fink might well have died. So Hooch lost his life because he lost the contest—the contest he and Mike were both playing for.

But that boy yesterday, he wasn't a player. He wasn't in the contest at all. He just wanted to go home. Mike Fink never wrassled a man who didn't want a fight, and he never killed a man who wasn't set to kill him first if he got a chance. Yesterday was the first time he had ever killed somebody just cause he was told to, and he didn't like it, didn't like it one bit. Mike could see now that Governor Bill *thought* he had killed Hooch that same way, just because he was told to. But it wasn't so. And today Mike Fink looked at the young man's father, with all that rage in his eyes, and he said to that man—but silently, so nobody could hear—he said, I'm with you, I agree with you that the man who killed your boy should die.

Trouble was, Mike Fink was that man. And he was plain ashamed.

Same thing with them Red men in Prophetstown. What kind of contest was it, to wake them up with grapeshot whistling through their own houses, setting them afire, cutting into their bodies, the bodies of children and women and old men?

Not my kind of fight, thought Mike Fink.

The first light of dawn came into the sky. Prophetstown was still nothing but shadows, but it was time. Alvin Miller aimed his musket right into the thick of the houses, and then he fired.

A few seconds later, the cannons banged out their answer. Maybe a few more seconds, and the first flame appeared in the town.

The cannons fired again. Yet not a soul ran screaming out of the wigwams. Not even the ones that were afire.

Didn't anybody else notice it? Didn't they realize that the Reds were all gone out of Prophetstown? And if they were gone, that meant they knew all about this morning's attack. And if they knew, that meant they might be ready, lying in ambush. Or maybe they all escaped, or maybe—

Mike Fink's lucky amulet was nearly burning him, it felt so hot. He knew what that meant. Time to go. Something real bad was going to happen to him if he stayed.

So he slid off down the line of soldiers—or what passed for soldiers, since there hadn't been more than a day or two for training some of these raw farmers. Nobody paid no heed to Mike Fink. They were too busy watching the wigwams burn. Some of them had finally noticed that nobody seemed to be in the Red city, and they were talking about it, worried. Mike said nothing, kept moving along the line, down toward the creek.

The cannon were all on the high ground; they sounded farther away. Mike emerged from the trees into the cleared ground that ran down to the river. There he stopped short and stared. The dawn was still just a grey streak in the distance, but there was no mistaking what he saw. Thousands and thousands of Reds, standing shoulder to shoulder in the meadow. Some were crying softly—no doubt stray shrapnel and musket balls had come this far, since two of the cannons were on the opposite side of the city from here, firing this direction. But they weren't making a move to defend themselves. It wasn't an ambush. They had no weapons. These Red folks were all lined up to die.

There was maybe a dozen canoes up and down the bank of the river. Mike Fink pushed one out into the water and rolled himself aboard. Downstream, that's where he'd go, all the way down the Wobbish to the Hio. It wasn't war today, it was massacre, and that just wasn't Mike Fink's kind of fight. Nearly everybody's got a thing so bad he just won't do it. In the darkness of the root cellar, Measure couldn't see if Alvin was really there or not. But he could hear his voice, soft but urgent, riding in over the crest of the pain. "I'm trying to fix you, Measure, but I need your help."

Measure couldn't answer. Speech wasn't one of the things he could manage right at the moment.

"I've fixed your neck, and some of your ribs, and the guts that got tore up," said Alvin. "And your left arm bones were pretty much in a line, so they're all right, can you feel that?"

It was true that there wasn't no pain coming from Measure's left arm.

He moved it. It jostled the whole rest of his body, but it could move, it had some strength in it.

"Your ribs," said Alvin. "Poking out. You got to push them back in place."

Measure pushed on one and nearly fainted from the pain. "I can't."

"You got to."

"Make it not hurt."

"Measure, I don't know how. Not without making it so you can't *move*. You just got to stand it. Everything you get back in place, I can fix it, and then it won't hurt no more, but first you got to straighten it, you got to."

"You do it."

"I can't."

"Just reach out and do it, Alvin, you're big for ten, you can do it."

"I can't."

"I once cut your bone for you, to save your life, I once did that."

"Measure, I can't do it cause I ain't *there*."

This made no sense to Measure. So he knew he was dreaming. Well, if he was dreaming, why didn't he come up with some dream where things didn't hurt so bad?

"Push on the bone, Measure."

Alvin just wouldn't go away. So Measure pushed, and it hurt him. But Alvin was as good as his word. Soon after, the place where he straightened out the bone didn't hurt no more.

It took so long. He was so tore up that it seemed there just wasn't no end to the pain. But in between times, while Alvin was making things heal up where he just fixed the bones, Measure explained to Alvin what had happened to him, and Alvin told him what *he* knew, and pretty soon Measure understood that there was a lot more to this than saving the life of one young man in a root cellar.

Finally, finally it was over. Measure couldn't hardly believe it. He had hurt so much for so many hours that it felt downright strange not to hurt anywhere.

He heard the thump, thump of cannon firing. "Can you hear that, Alvin?" he asked.

Alvin couldn't.

"The shooting's started. The cannon."

"Then run, Measure. Go as fast as you can."

"Alvin, I'm in a root cellar. They barred the door."

Alvin cussed with a couple of words that Measure didn't know the boy had ever heard.

"Alvin, I got me a hole half-dug here in the back. You got such a knack with stone, I wondered if you could loosen things up for me here, so I could dig out real fast.''

And that's how it worked out. Measure rolled himself into the hole and just closed his eyes and pawed at the dirt above his head. It was nothing like digging the day before, rubbing his fingers raw on the dirt. It just fell away, slid off him; when he reached up to dig more, the dirt slipped under his shoulders, and *there* it firmed right up, so that he didn't even have to think about moving the dirt out of the hole, it was just filling up underneath him. He kicked, and his legs jostled the dirt loose, so his whole body was rising up the same way.

Swimming through dirt, that's what I'm doing, he thought, and he started to laugh, it was so easy and so strange.

His laugh was finished in the open air. He was on top, just behind the root cellar. The sky was pretty light—the sun would be up in just a minute or so. The booming of the cannon had stopped. Did that mean it was over, too late? Maybe, though, they were just letting the guns cool. Or moving them to another place. Or maybe the Reds even managed to capture the guns—

But would that be good news? Right or wrong, his brothers and his father were with them guns, and if the Reds won this battle, some of his kin might die. It was one thing to know that the Reds were in the right and the Whites in the wrong; it was something else to wish defeat on your own family, defeat and maybe death. He had to stop the battle, and so he ran, like he never done before. Alvin's voice was gone, now, but Measure didn't need to be encouraged. He fair to flew down that road.

He met two people on the way. One was Mrs. Hatch, who was driving her wagon along the road, loaded down with supplies. When she saw Measure, she screamed—he was wearing a loincloth and filthy as could be, and she couldn't be blamed for thinking he was a Red all set to scalp her. She was off that wagon and running before Measure could so much as call her name. Well, that was fine with him. He nearly tore the horse from the wagon, he worked so fast, and then he was riding bareback, galloping along the road hoping that the horse wouldn't trip and spill him.

The other person he met along the way was Armor-of-God. Armor was kneeling in the middle of the common green, out front of his store, praying his heart out while the cannon roared and the muskets crackled across the river. Measure hailed him, and Armor looked up with a face like as if he'd seen Jesus resurrected. "Measure!" he shouted. "Stop, stop!"

Measure was all set to go on, to say he had no time, but then Armor was out in the middle of the way, and the horse was shy to go around him, so he *did* stop. "Measure, are you an angel or alive?"

"Alive, no thanks to Harrison. Tried to murder me, he did. I'm alive and so is Alvin. This whole thing was Harrison's doing, and I've got to put a stop to it."

"Well you can't go like that," said Armor. "Wait, I said! You can't just show up wearing a loincloth and covered up with dirt like that, somebody's going to think you're a Red and shoot you on the spot!"

"Then hop on this horse behind me, and give me your clothing on the way!"

So Measure hoisted Armor-of-God onto the horse behind him, and they rode out to the river crossing.

Peter Ferryman's wife was there to run the winch. One look at Measure was enough to tell her all she needed to know. "Hurry," she said. "It's so bad, the river's running scarlet."

On the ferry, Armor stripped off his clothes while Measure ducked himself in the water, blood and all, to wash some of the dirt away. He didn't come out clean, but at least he looked somewhat like a White man. Still wet, he put on Armor's shirt and trousers, and then his waistcoat. They didn't fit too good, Armor being a smaller man, but Measure shrugged on the coat all the same. While he did, he said, "Sorry to leave you with just your summerjohns."

"I'd stand naked half the day in front of all the ladies in church if it would stop this massacre," said Armor. If he said more, Measure didn't hear it, cause he was already on his way. Nothing was the way Alvin Miller Senior thought that it would be. He'd imagined shooting his musket at the same screaming savages who cut up and killed his boys. But the city turned up empty, and they found the Reds all gathered in Speaking Meadow, just like they was ready for a sermon from the Prophet. Miller never knowed there was so many Reds in Prophetstown, cause he never seen them all in the same place like this. But they were Reds, weren't they? So he shot his musket all the same, just like the other men, firing and reloading, hardly looking at whether his shot hit anything. How could he miss, them all standing together so close? The bloodlust was on him then, he was crazy with anger and the power to kill. He didn't notice how some of the other men were getting quieter. Shooting less often. He just loaded and fired, loaded and fired, stepping a yard or two closer every time, out from the cover of the forest, out into the open; only when the cannon got moved into place did he stop shooting, make way for them, watched them mow great swaths through the mass of Reds.

That was the first time he really noticed what all was happening to the Reds, what they were doing, what they *weren't* doing. They weren't screaming. They weren't fighting back. They were just standing there, men and women and children, just looking out at the White men who were killing them. Not a one even turned his back to the hail of shrapnel. Not a parent tried to shield a child from the blast. They just stood, waited, died.

The grapeshot carved gaps in the crowd; the only thing to stop the spray of metal was human bodies. Miller saw them fall. Them as could, got up again, or at least knelt, or raised their heads above the mass of corpses so that the next blast would take them and kill them.

What is it, do they want to die?

Miller looked around him. He and the men with him were standing in a sea of corpses—they had already walked out to where the outer edges of the crowd of Reds had been. Right at his feet, the body of a boy no older than Alvin lay curled, his eye blown out by a musket ball. Maybe my own musket ball, thought Miller. Maybe I killed this boy.

During the lulls between cannon volleys, Miller could hear men crying. Not the Reds, the ones still living, huddled in an ever-smaller mass down toward the river. No, the men crying were his neighbors, White men standing beside him, or behind the line. Some of them were talking, pleading. Stop it, they said. Please, stop it.

Please stop. Were they talking to the cannon? Or to the Red men and women, who insisted on standing there, not trying to escape, not crying out in fear? Or to their children, who faced the guns as bravely as their parents? Or did they speak to the terrible gnawing pain in their own hearts, to see what they had done, were doing, would yet do?

Miller noticed that the blood didn't soak into the grass of the meadow. As it poured out of the wounds of those most recently hit, it formed rivulets, streams, great sheets of blood flowing down the slope of the meadow, toward the Tippy-Canoe Creek. The morning sunlight on this bright clear day shone vivid red from the water of the creek.

While he was watching, all at once the water of the creek went smooth as glass. The sunlight didn't dance on the water now, it reflected like a mirror, near blinding him. But he could still see a solitary Red man walking on the water, just like Jesus in the story, standing on the water in the middle of the creek.

It wasn't just a whimper behind him anymore. It was a shout, from more and more men. Stop shooting! Stop it! Put down your guns! And then others, talking about the man standing on the water.

A bugle sounded. The men fell silent. "Time to finish them, men!" shouted Harrison. He was on a prancing stallion at the head of the meadow, leading the way down the blood-slick hill. None of the farmer folk were with him, but his uniformed soldiers formed a line and came along, bayonets fixed. Where once ten thousand Reds had stood, there was just a field of bodies, and maybe a thousand, a ragged remnant, gathered near the water at the bottom of the hill.

That was the moment when a tall young White man ran from the wood at the bottom of the hill, dressed in a suit too small, his feet bare, his coat and waistcoat all unbuttoned, his hair wet and tousled, and face grimy and wet. But Miller knew him, knew him before he heard his voice.

"Measure!" he cried. "It's my boy Measure!"

He threw down his musket and ran out into the field of corpses, down the hill toward his son.

"My boy Measure! He's alive! You're alive!"

Then he slipped in the blood, or maybe he tripped on a body, but whatever happened he fell, his hands splashing into a river of blood, spattering his chest and face.

He heard Measure's voice, not ten yards away, shouting out so every man could hear him. "The Reds who captured me were hired by Harrison. Ta-Kumsaw and Tenskwa-Tawa saved me. When I came home two days ago, Harrison's soldiers captured me and wouldn't let me tell you the truth. He even tried to kill me." Measure spoke slow and clear, so every word carried, every sound was understood. "He knew all the time. This whole thing, Harrison planned it all along. The Reds are innocent. You're killing innocent people."

Miller stood up from the bloody field and raised his hands high over his head, thick blood running from his scarlet hands. A cry was wrung from his throat, forced out by anguish, by despair. "What have I done! What have I done!" The cry was echoed by a dozen, a hundred, three hundred voices.

And there was General Harrison on his prancing horse, out in front of everybody. Even his own soldiers had thrown down their guns by now.

"It's a lie!" cried Harrison. "I never saw this boy! Someone has played a terrible trick on me!"

"It ain't no trick!" shouted Measure. "Here's his kerchief—they stuffed it in my mouth yesterday, to gag me while they broke my bones!"

Miller could see the kerchief clearly in his son's hand. It had the WHH embroidered in large, clear letters in the corner. Every man in that army had seen his handkerchiefs.

And now some of Harrison's own soldiers spoke up. "It's true! We brought this boy to Harrison two days ago."

"We didn't know he was one of the boys they all said the Reds had killed!"

A high, howling cry floated over the meadow. They all looked down to where the one-eyed Prophet stood on the solid, scarlet water of the Tippy-Canoe.

"Come to me, my people!" he said.

The surviving Reds walked, slowly, steadily toward the water. They walked across it, then gathered on the other side.

"All my people, come!"

The corpses rustled, moved. The White men standing among them cried out in terror. But the dead were not rising up to walk—only the wounded who still breathed, they were the ones who rose up, staggered. Some of them tried to carry children, babies—they had no strength for it.

Miller saw and felt the blood on his own hands. He had to do something, didn't he? So he reached out to a struggling woman, whose husband leaned against her for support, meaning to take the baby from her arms and carry it for her. But when he came near, she looked into his face, and he saw his own reflection in her eyes—his face haggard, White, spattered with blood, his hands dripping with blood. Tiny as it was, he saw that reflection as clear as if it had been on a mirror held in front of his own face. He couldn't touch her baby, not with hands like his.

Some of the other White men on the hill also tried to help, but they must have seen something like what Miller saw, and they recoiled as if they had been burned.

Maybe a thousand wounded got up and tried to reach the creek. Many of them collapsed and died before they got there. Those that reached the water walked, staggered, crawled across; they were helped by the Reds on the other side.

Miller noticed something peculiar. All those wounded Reds, all the uninjured ones, they had walked on this meadow, they had walked across the blood-red river, and yet there wasn't a spot of blood on their hands or feet.

"All my people, all who died—Come home, says the land!"

All around them, the meadow was strewn with bodies—by far the majority of those who had stood there as living families only an hour before. Now, at the Prophet's words, these bodies seemed to shudder, to crumble; they collapsed and sank into the grass of the meadow. It took perhaps a minute, and they were gone, the grass springing up lush and green. The last of the blood skittered down the slope like beads of water on a hot griddle and became part of the bright red creek.

"Come to me, my friend Measure." The Prophet spoke quietly, and held out his hand.

Measure turned his back on his father and walked down the grassy slope to the water's edge.

"Walk to me," said the Prophet.

"I can't walk on the blood of your people," he said.

"They gave their blood to lift you up," said the Prophet. "Come to me, or take the curse that will fall on every White man in that meadow."

"I reckon I'll stay here, then," said Measure. "If I'd've been in their place, I don't figure I'd've done a thing different than what they did. If they're guilty, so am I."

The Prophet nodded.

Every White man there felt something warm and wet and sticky on his hands. Some of them cried out when they saw. From elbow to hands, they dripped with blood. Some tried to wipe it off on their shirts. Some searched for wounds that might be bleeding, but there were no wounds. Just bloody hands.

"Do you want your hands to be clean of the blood of my people?" asked the Prophet. He wasn't shouting anymore, but they all heard him, every word. And yes, yes, they wanted their hands to be clean.

"Then go home and tell this story to your wives and children, to your neighbors, to your friends. Tell the whole story. Leave nothing out. Don't say that someone fooled you—you all knew when you fired on people who had no weapons that what you did was murder. No matter whether you thought some of us might have committed some crime. When you shot at babies in their mothers' arms, little children, old men and women, you were murdering us because we were Red. So tell the story as it happened, and if you tell it true, your hands will be clean."

There wasn't a man on that meadow who wasn't weeping or trembling or faint with shame. To tell of this day's work to their wives and children, their parents, their brothers and sisters, that seemed unbearable. But if they didn't, these bloody hands would tell the story for them. It was more than they could bear to think of.

But the Prophet wasn't through. "If some stranger comes along, and you don't tell him the whole story before you sleep, then the blood will come back on your hands, and stay there until you do tell him. That's how it will be for the rest of your lives—every man and woman that you meet will have to hear the true story from your lips, or your hands will be filthy again. And if you ever, for any reason, kill another human being, then your hands and face will drip with blood forever, even in the grave."

They nodded, they agreed. It was justice, simple justice. They couldn't give back the lives of those they killed, but they could make sure no lie was ever told about the way that they were killed. No one could ever claim that Tippy-Canoe was a victory, or even a battle. It was a massacre, and White men committed it, and not one Red raised a hand in violence or defense. No excuse, no softening; it would be known.

Only one thing remained—the guilt of the man on the prancing stallion.

"White Murderer Harrison!" called the Prophet. "Come to me!"

Harrison shook his head, tried to turn his horse; the reins slipped from his bloody hands, and the horse walked briskly down the hill. All the White men watched him silently, hating him for how he lied to them, stirred them up, found the murder in their hearts and called it forth. The horse brought him to the water's edge. He looked downward at the one-eyed Red who had once sat under his table and begged for drops of whiskey from his cup.

"Your curse is the same," said the Prophet, "except that your story is much longer and uglier to tell. And you won't wait for strangers to come along before you speak—every day of your life you'll have to find someone who has never heard the story from your lips before, and tell it to him—every day!—or your hands will drip with blood. And if you decide to hide, and live with blood-soaked hands rather than find new people to tell, you'll feel the pain of my people's wounds, one new wound each day, until you tell the story again, once for every day you missed. Don't try to kill yourself, either—you can't do it. You'll wander from one end of this White man's land to the other. People will see you coming and hide, dreading the sound of your voice; you'll beg them to stop and listen to you. They'll even forget your old name, and call you by the name you earned today. Tippy-Canoe. That's your new name, White Murderer Harrison. Your true name, till you die a natural death as an old, old man."

Harrison bent onto the mane of the horse and wept into his bloody hands. But his were tears of fury, not grief or shame. Tears of rage that all his plans had gone awry. He would kill the Prophet even now, if he could. He would search far and wide for some witch or wizard who could break this curse. He couldn't bear to let this miserable one-eyed Red defeat him.

Measure spoke to the Prophet from the shore. "Where will you go now, Tenskwa-Tawa?"

"West," said Tenskwa-Tawa. "My people, all who still believe in me, we'll go west of the Mizzipy. When you tell your story, tell White men this—that west of the Mizzipy is Red man's land. Don't come there. The land can't bear the touch of a White man's foot. You breathe out death; your touch is poison; your words are lies; the living land won't have you.''

He turned his back, walked to the Reds waiting for him on the other shore, and helped an injured child walk up the far slope into the trees. Behind him, the water of the Tippy-Canoe began to flow again.

Miller walked down the slope to where his son stood on the bank of the creek. ''Measure,'' he said, ''Measure, Measure.''

Measure turned and reached out his hands to embrace his father. ''Alvin's alive, Father, far to the east of us. He's with Ta-Kumsaw, and he—''

But Miller hushed him, held his son's hands out. They dripped blood, just like Miller's own. Miller shook his head. ''It's my fault,'' he said. ''All my fault.''

''Not all, Father,'' said Measure. ''There's fault enough for everyone to share.''

''But not for you, Son. That's *my* shame on your hands.''

''Well, then, maybe you'll feel it less, for having two of us to carry it.'' Measure reached out and took his father by the shoulders, held him close. ''We've seen the worst that men can do, Pa, and been the worst that men can be. But that don't mean that someday we won't see the best, too. And if we can never be perfect after this, well, we can still be pretty good, can't we?''

Maybe, thought Miller. But he doubted it. Or maybe he just doubted that he'd ever believe it, even if it were true. He'd never look into his own heart again and like what he found there.

They waited there on the riverbank for Miller's other sons. They came with bloody hands—David, Calm, Wastenot, Wantnot. David held his hands in front of him and wept. ''I wish that I had died with Vigor in the Hatrack River!''

''No you don't,'' said Calm.

''I'd be dead, but I'd be clean.''

The twins said nothing, but held each other's cold and slimy hands.

''We need to go home,'' said Measure.

''No,'' said Miller.

''They'll be worried,'' said Measure. ''Ma, the girls, Cally.''

Miller remembered his parting from Faith. ''She said that if I—if this—''

''I know how Ma talks, but I also know your children need their pa, and she won't keep you out.''

''I'll have to tell her. What we did.''

''Yes, and the girls and Cally, too. We each have to tell them, and

Calm and David have their wives to tell. Best do it now, and clean our hands, and get on with our lives. All of us at once, all of us together. And I have a story to tell you, too, about me and Alvin. When we've done with this tale, I'll tell mine, is that good? Will you stay for that?''

Armor met them at the Wobbish. The ferry was already on the other side, still unloading, and other men had took all the boats they used for crossing last night. So they stood and waited.

Measure stripped off his bloody coat and trousers, but Armor wouldn't put them on. Armor didn't make no accusations, but none of the others would look at their brother-in-law. Measure took him aside and told him about the curse while the ferry was slowly drawn back across the river. Armor listened, then walked to Miller, whose back was to him, looking at the far shore.

"Father," said Armor-of-God.

"You were right, Armor," said Miller, still not looking at him. He held up his hands. "Here it is, the proof that you were right."

"Measure tells me that I have to hear the story once from all of you," said Armor, turning to include them all in his speech. "But then you'll never hear another word of it from me. I'm still your son and brother, if you'll have me; my wife is your daughter and your sister, and you're the only kin I have out here."

"To your shame," whispered David.

"Don't punish me because my hands are clean," said Armor.

Calm held out a bloody hand. Armor took it without hesitation, shook firmly, then let go.

"Look at that," said Calm. "You touch us, it comes off on you."

In answer, Armor held out that same stained hand to Miller. After a while, Miller took it. The handshake lasted till the ferry came. Then they headed on home.

15

Two-Soul Man

Taleswapper woke at dawn, instantly aware that something was wrong.
It was Ta-Kumsaw, sitting on the grass, his face toward the west, rocking back and forth and breathing heavily, as if he was enduring a dull
and heavy ache. Was he ill?

No. Alvin had failed. The slaughter had begun. Ta-Kumsaw's pain
was not from his own body. It was Ta-Kumsaw's people dying, somewhere afar off, and what he felt was not grief or pity, it was the pain
of their deaths. Even for a Red man as gifted as Ta-Kumsaw, to feel
death from so far away meant that many, many souls had gone on to
their reward.

As he had so many times before, Taleswapper addressed a few silent
words to God, which always came down to this question: Why do you
put us to so much trouble, when it all comes to nought in the end?
Taleswapper couldn't bear the futility of it. Ta-Kumsaw and Alvin rac-
ing across country in their way, Taleswapper making the best time a
White man can make, and Alvin going onto Eight-Face Mound, and
what does it come to? Does it save a life? So many are dying now that
Ta-Kumsaw can feel it from clear away by the Wobbish.

And, as usual, God had nothing much to say to Taleswapper when
his questioning was done.

Taleswapper had no wish to interrupt Ta-Kumsaw. Or rather he
guessed that Ta-Kumsaw had no particular wish to get into conversation
with a White man at this particular moment. Yet he felt a vision growing
within him. Not a vision such as prophets were rumored to see, not a
vision of inward eyes. To Taleswapper visions came as words, and he
did not know what the vision was until his own words told him. Even
then, he knew that he was not a prophet; his visions were never such

as would change the world, only the sort of thing that records it, that *understands* the world. Now, however, he took no thought of whether his visions were worthy or not. It came, and he must record it. Yet because the writing of words had been taken from him in this place, he could not write it down. What was there, then, but to speak the words aloud?

So Taleswapper spoke, forming the words into couplets as he said them because that was how visions ought to be expressed, in poetry. It was a confusing tale at first, and Taleswapper could not decide whether it was God or Satan whose terrible light blinded him as the words tumbled forth. He only knew that whichever one it was, whichever one had brought such slaughter to the world, he richly deserved Taleswapper's anger, and so he wasn't bashful about lashing him with language.

It all came down to these words rushing forth in a stream so intense that Taleswapper hardly breathed, certainly made no sensible break in the rhythms of his speech, his voice growing louder and louder as the lines were wrung from him and dashed out against the harsh wall of air around him, as if he dared God to hear him and resent his resentment:

> When I had my defiance given
> The sun stood trembling in heaven
> The moon that glowed remote below
> Became leprous and white as snow
> And every soul of men on the earth
> Felt affliction and sorrow and sickness and dearth
> God flamed in my path and the Sun was hot
> With the bows of my mind and the arrows of thought
> My bowstring fierce with ardor breathes
> My arrows glow in their golden sheaves
> My brothers and father march before
> The heavens drop with human gore—

"Stop!"

It was Ta-Kumsaw. Taleswapper waited with his mouth open, more words, more anguish waiting to pour from him. But Ta-Kumsaw was not to be disobeyed.

"It's finished," said Ta-Kumsaw.

"All dead?" whispered Taleswapper.

"I can't feel life from here," said Ta-Kumsaw. "I can feel death—the world is torn like an old cloth, it can never be mended." Despair gave way immediately to cold hate. "But it can be cleaned."

"If I could have prevented it, Ta-Kumsaw—"

"Yes, you're a good man, Taleswapper. There are others, too, among your kind. Armor-of-God Weaver is such a man. And if all White men came like you, to learn this land, then there'd be no war between us."

"There *is* no war between you and me, Ta-Kumsaw."

"Can you change the color of your skin? Can I change mine?"

"It isn't our skin, but our hearts—"

"When we stand with all the Red men on one side of the field, and all the White men on the other side of the field, where will you stand?"

"In the middle, pleading with both sides to—"

"You will stand with your people, and I will stand with mine."

How could Taleswapper argue with him? Perhaps he would have the courage to refuse such a choice. Perhaps not. "Pray God it never comes to such a pass."

"It already has, Taleswapper." Ta-Kumsaw nodded. "From this day's work, I will have no trouble gathering my army of Red men at last."

The words leapt from Taleswapper before he could stop them: "Then it's a terrible work you've chosen, if the death of so many good folk helps it along!"

Ta-Kumsaw answered with a roar, springing on Taleswapper all at once, knocking him back, flat on the grass of the meadow. Ta-Kumsaw's right hand clutched Taleswapper's hair; his left pressed against Taleswapper's throat. "All White men will die, all who don't escape across the sea!"

Yet it was not murder he intended. Even in his rage, Ta-Kumsaw did not press so hard as to strangle Taleswapper. After a moment the Red man pushed off and rolled away, burying his face in the grass, his arms and legs spread out to touch the earth with as much of his body as he could.

"I'm sorry," Taleswapper whispered. "I was wrong to say that."

"Lolla-Wossiky!" cried Ta-Kumsaw. "I did not want to be right, my brother!"

"Is he alive?" asked Taleswapper.

"I don't know," said Ta-Kumsaw. He turned his head to press his cheek against the grass; his eyes, though, bored at Taleswapper as if to kill him with a look. "Taleswapper, the words you were saying. What did they mean? What did you see?"

"I saw nothing," said Taleswapper. And then, though he only learned the truth as the words came out, he said, "It was Alvin's vision I was speaking. It's what *he* saw. My brothers and father march before. The heavens drop with human gore. His vision, my poem."

"And where is the boy?" asked Ta-Kumsaw. "All night on that

Mound, and where is he now?'' Ta-Kumsaw jumped to his feet, orienting himself toward Eight-Face Mound, toward the very center of it. ''No one stays there through the whole night, and now the sun is rising and he hasn't come.'' Ta-Kumsaw abruptly turned to face Taleswapper. ''He can't come down.''

''What do you mean?''

''He needs me,'' said Ta-Kumsaw. ''I can feel it. A terrible wound is in him. All his strength is bleeding into the earth.''

''What's on that hill! What wounded him?''

''Who knows what a White boy finds inside?'' said Ta-Kumsaw. Then he turned to face the Mound again, as if he had felt a new summoning. ''Yes,'' he said, then walked quickly toward the Mound.

Taleswapper followed, saying nothing about the incongruity—Ta-Kumsaw vowing to make war against Whites until all were dead or gone from this land, and yet hurrying back to Eight-Face Mound to save a White boy.

They stood together at the place where Alvin climbed.

''Can you see the place?'' asked Taleswapper.

''There is no path,'' said Ta-Kumsaw.

''But you saw it yesterday,'' said Taleswapper.

''Yesterday there was a path.''

''Then some other way,'' said Taleswapper. ''Your own way onto the Mound.''

''Another way would not take me to the same place.''

''Come now, Ta-Kumsaw, the Mound is big, but not so big you can't find someone up there in an hour of looking.''

Ta-Kumsaw gazed disdainfully at Taleswapper.

Abashed, Taleswapper spoke less confidently. ''So you have to take the same path to reach the same place?''

''How do I know?'' asked Ta-Kumsaw. ''I never heard of one going up the Mound, and another following by the same path.''

''Don't you ever go here in twos or threes?''

''This is the place where the land speaks to all creatures who live here. The speech of the land is grass and trees; the adornment is beasts and birds.''

Taleswapper noted that when he wished to, Ta-Kumsaw could speak the English language like any White man. No: like a well-educated White man. Adornment. Where in the Hio country could he learn a word like that? ''So we can't get in?''

Ta-Kumsaw's face showed no expression.

''Well, I say we go up anyway. We know the road he took—let's take it, whether we can see it or not.''

Ta-Kumsaw said nothing.

"Are you just going to stand here, then, and let him die up there?"

In answer, Ta-Kumsaw took a single step that brought him face to face—no, breast to breast—with Taleswapper. Ta-Kumsaw gripped his hand, threw his other arm around Taleswapper, held him close. Their legs were tangled; Taleswapper for a moment imagined how they must look, if there had been anyone to see them—whether someone would know which leg belonged to which man, they were so close together. He felt the Red man's heart beating, its rhythm more commanding within Taleswapper's body than the unsensed beat of his own hot pulse. "We are not two men," whispered Ta-Kumsaw. "Not Red and White men here, with blood between us. We are one man with two souls, a Red soul and a White soul, one man."

"All right," said Taleswapper. "Let it be as you say."

Still holding Taleswapper tightly, Ta-Kumsaw turned within the embrace; their heads pressed against each other, their ears so close-joined Taleswapper could hear nothing but Ta-Kumsaw's pulse like the pounding of ocean waves inside his ear. But now, their bodies so tightly joined that they seemed to have a single heartbeat, Taleswapper could see a clear path leading up the face of the Mound.

"Do you—" began Ta-Kumsaw.

"I see it," said Taleswapper.

"Stay this close to me," said Ta-Kumsaw. "Now we are like Alvin— a Red soul and a White soul in a single body."

It was awkward, even ridiculous, to attempt to climb the Mound this way. Yet when their movement up the path jostled them apart, even the tiniest fraction, the path seemed to grow more difficult, hidden behind an errant growth of some vine, some bush, some dangling limb. So Taleswapper clung to Ta-Kumsaw as tightly as the Red man clung to him, and together they made their difficult way up the hill.

At the top Taleswapper was astonished to see that instead of a single Mound, they were at the crest of a ring of eight separate Mounds, with an octagonal valley between them. More important, Ta-Kumsaw was also surprised. He seemed uncertain; his grip on Taleswapper was not as tight; he was no longer in control.

"Where does a White man go in this place?" asked Ta-Kumsaw.

"Down, of course," said Taleswapper. "When a White man sees a valley, he goes down into it, to find what's there."

"Is this how it always is for you?" asked Ta-Kumsaw. "Not knowing where you are, where anything is?"

Only then did Taleswapper realize that Ta-Kumsaw lacked his land-sense here. He was as blind as a White man in this place.

"Let's go down," said Taleswapper. "And look—we don't have to cling so tightly now. It's a grassy hill, and we don't need a path."

They crossed a stream and found him in a meadow, with a mist low on the ground around them. Alvin was not injured, but he lay trembling—as if fevered, though his brow was cool—and his breathing was shallow and quick. As Ta-Kumsaw had said: dying.

Taleswapper touched him, caressed him, then shook him, trying to wake the boy. Alvin showed no sign that he was aware of them. Ta-Kumsaw was no help. He sat beside the boy, holding his hand, whining so softly that Taleswapper doubted he knew he was making a sound.

But Taleswapper was not one to give in to despair, if in fact that was what Ta-Kumsaw was feeling. He looked around. Nearby was a tree, looking like spring, its leaves so yellow-green that in the light of dawn they might have been made on thin-hammered gold. Hanging from the tree was a light-colored fruit. No, a *white* fruit. And suddenly, as soon as he saw it, Taleswapper smelled it, pungent and sweet, so that he could almost taste it.

He acted, not thinking what he would do, but doing it. He walked to the tree, plucked the fruit, carried it back to Alvin where he lay on the ground, a child so small. Taleswapper passed it under Alvin's nose, so the odor of it might be like smelling salts, and revive him. Alvin's breathing suddenly became great deep gasps. His eyes opened, his lips parted, and from gritted teeth came a whine almost exactly like Ta-Kumsaw's keening; almost exactly like a kicked dog.

"Take a bite," said Taleswapper.

Ta-Kumsaw reached out, snatched Alvin's lower jaw in one hand and upper jaw in the other, his fingers interlaced at Alvin's teeth, and with great effort prised Alvin's jaws apart. Taleswapper thrust the fruit between Alvin's teeth; Ta-Kumsaw forced the jaws closed again. The fruit broke open, spilling clear fluid into Alvin's mouth and dribbling down his cheek into the grass. Slowly, with great effort, Alvin began to chew. Tears flowed from his eyes. He swallowed. Suddenly he reached out his hands, caught Taleswapper by the neck and Ta-Kumsaw by the hair, and pulled himself up to a sitting position. Clinging to them both, drawing their faces so close to his that they all breathed each other's breath, Alvin wept until their faces all were wet, and because Ta-Kumsaw and Taleswapper were also weeping, none could be sure whose tears cast a glaze across the skin of each man's face.

Alvin said little, but enough. He told them all that happened at Tippy-Canoe Creek that day, of blood in the river, a thousand survivors crossing on the water made smooth and hard; blood on White men's hands, and on one man's hands in particular.

"Not enough," said Ta-Kumsaw.

Taleswapper offered no argument. It was not for a White man to tell Ta-Kumsaw that the killers of his people had received a punishment exactly proportioned to their sin. Besides, Taleswapper wasn't sure he believed it himself.

Alvin told them how he had spent the evening and the night before, restoring Measure from the edge of death; and how he spent the morning, taking away the immeasurable agony as nine thousand innocent deaths shouted in the Prophet's mind—nine thousand times that one black shout that years before had maddened him. Which was harder—healing Measure or healing Lolla-Wossiky? "It was like you said," Alvin whispered to Taleswapper. "I just can't build that brick wall faster than it breaks down." Then, exhausted but at peace now, Alvin slept.

Taleswapper and Ta-Kumsaw faced each other, Alvin curled between them, his breathing soft and slow.

"I know his wound now," Ta-Kumsaw said. "His grief is for his own people, with their bloody hands."

"His grief was for the dead and the living too," said Taleswapper. "If I know Alvin, his deepest wound was thinking that he failed, that if he'd just tried harder, he might have got Measure there in time to stop it before the first shot was fired."

"White men grieve for White men," Ta-Kumsaw said.

"Lie to yourself if you like," said Taleswapper, "but lies don't fool me."

"But Red men don't grieve at all," said Ta-Kumsaw. "Red men will put White blood into the ground for the blood spilled today."

"I thought you served the land," said Taleswapper. "Don't you realize what happened today? Don't you remember where we are? You've seen a part of Eight-Face Mound you never knew existed, and why? Because the land let us into this place together, because—"

Ta-Kumsaw held up one hand. "To save this boy."

"Because Red and White can share this land if we—"

Ta-Kumsaw reached out his hand and touched his fingers to Taleswapper's lips.

"I'm not a farmer who wants to hear stories of faraway places," Ta-Kumsaw said. "Go tell your tales to someone who wants to hear them."

Taleswapper slapped Ta-Kumsaw's hand away. He had meant merely to push the Red man's arm, but instead he struck with too much force, throwing Ta-Kumsaw off balance. Ta-Kumsaw immediately leapt to his feet; Taleswapper did the same.

"Here is where it starts!" shouted Ta-Kumsaw.

Between them, at their feet, Alvin stirred.

"A Red man angered you, and you struck him, just like a White man, no patience—"

"You told me to be silent, you said my tales were—"

"Words, that's what I gave you, words and a soft touch, and you answered me with a blow." Ta-Kumsaw smiled. It was a terrifying smile, like a tiger's teeth out of the darkness of the jungle, his eyes glowing, his skin bright as flame.

"I'm sorry, I didn't mean—"

"White man never means anything, just couldn't help himself, it was all a *mistake*. That's what you think, isn't it, White Liar! Alvin's people killed my people because of a *mistake*, because they thought two White boys were dead. For the sake of two White boys they lashed out, just like you did, and they killed nine thousand of my people, babies and mothers, old men and stripling boys, their cannon—"

"I heard what Alvin said."

"Don't you like *my* story? Don't you want to hear it? You are White, Taleswapper. You are like all White men, quick to ask forgiveness, slow to give it; always expecting patience, but flaring up like a spark when the wind rises—you burn down a forest because you tripped on a root!" Ta-Kumsaw turned and began to walk quickly back the way they came.

"How can you leave without me!" cried Taleswapper after him. "We have to leave here together!"

Ta-Kumsaw stopped, turned around, tipped back his head, and laughed without mirth. "I don't need a path to get *down*, White Liar!" Then he was off again, running.

Alvin was awake, of course.

"I'm sorry, Alvin," said Taleswapper. "I didn't mean—"

"No," said Alvin. "Let me guess what he did. He touched you like this." Alvin touched Taleswapper's lips, just as Ta-Kumsaw had.

"Yes."

"That's what a Shaw-Nee mama does to shut up a little boy who's making too much noise. But I'll bet if one Red man did that to another—he was provoking you."

"I shouldn't have hit him."

"Then he would've done something else till you did."

Taleswapper had nothing to answer to that. Seemed to him the boy was probably right. Certainly right. The one thing Ta-Kumsaw could not bear today was being a White man's companion in peace.

Alvin slept again. Taleswapper explored, but found nothing strange. Just stillness and peace. He couldn't even tell now which tree it was the fruit came from. They all looked silvery green to him now, and no matter how far he walked in any direction, he ended up no farther from Alvin than a few minutes' walk. A strange place, not a place a man could map in his mind, not a place that a man could master. Here the land gives you what it wants to give, and no more.

It was near sunset when Alvin roused again, and Taleswapper helped him to his feet.

"I'm walking like a newborn colt," said Alvin. "I feel so weak."

"You only did half the labors of Hercules in the last twenty-four hours," said Taleswapper.

"Her what?"

"Hercules. A Greek."

"I got to find Ta-Kumsaw," said Alvin. "I shouldn't have let him go, but I was so tired."

"You're White, too," said Taleswapper. "Think he'll want you with him?"

"Tenskwa-Tawa prophesied," said Alvin. "As long as I'm with him, Ta-Kumsaw won't die."

Taleswapper supported Alvin as they walked to the one place that let them approach; they climbed the gentle grassy rise between Mounds and crested the hill. They stopped and looked down. Taleswapper saw no path—just thorns, vines, bushes, brambles. "I can't get down through that."

Alvin looked up at him, puzzled. "There's a path as plain as day."

"For you, maybe," said Taleswapper. "Not for me."

"You got in here," said Alvin.

"With Ta-Kumsaw," said Taleswapper.

"He got out."

"I'm no Red man."

"I'll lead."

Alvin started out with a few bold steps, as easy as if he was on a Sunday jaunt on the commons. But to Taleswapper it looked like the briars opened wide for him and closed up tight right after. "Alvin!" he called. "Stay with me!"

Alvin came and took him by the hand. "Follow tight behind," he said.

Taleswapper tried, but still the brambles snapped back and tore at his face, cut him sore. With Alvin going before, Taleswapper could make his way, but he felt like he was being flayed from behind. Even deerskin was no match for thorns like daggers, limbs that snapped back at him like a bo'sun's lash. He could feel blood running down his arms, his back, his legs. "I can't go any more, Alvin!" said Taleswapper.

"I see him," said Alvin.

"Who?"

"Ta-Kumsaw. Wait here."

He let go of Taleswapper's hand; he was gone for a moment, and Taleswapper was alone with the brambles. He tried not to move, but even his breathing seemed to provoke more stings and stabs.

Alvin was back. He took Taleswapper by the hand. "Follow me tight. One more step."

Taleswapper steeled himself and took the step.

"Down," said Alvin.

Taleswapper obeyed Alvin's tugging and knelt, though he feared that he'd never be able to rise again through the briars that closed over his head.

Then Alvin led his hand until it touched another hand, and suddenly the brambles cleared a little, and Taleswapper could see Ta-Kumsaw lying there, blood seeping from hundreds of wounds on his nearly naked body. "He got this far alone," said Alvin.

Ta-Kumsaw opened his eyes, rage burning. "Leave me here," he whispered.

In answer, Taleswapper cradled Ta-Kumsaw's head in his other arm. As more of their bodies touched, the briars seemed to sag and fall away; now Taleswapper could see a kind of path where he hadn't seen one before.

"No," said Ta-Kumsaw.

"We can't get down from here without each other's help," said Taleswapper. "Like it or not, if you're going to get your vengeance against the White man, you need a White man's help."

"Then leave me here," whispered Ta-Kumsaw. "Save your people by leaving me to die."

"I can't get down without you," said Taleswapper.

"Good," said Ta-Kumsaw.

Taleswapper noticed that Ta-Kumsaw's wounds looked much fewer. And those that were left were scabbed over, nearly healed. Then he realized that his own injuries didn't hurt anymore. He looked around. Alvin sat nearby, leaning against a tree trunk, his eyes closed, looking like somebody just flogged him, he was so spent and dreary.

"Look what we cost him, healing us," said Taleswapper.

Ta-Kumsaw's face showed his surprise, for once; surprise, then anger. "I didn't ask you to heal me!" he cried. He tore himself out of Taleswapper's grasp and tried to reach toward Alvin. But suddenly there were brambles twining around his arm, and Ta-Kumsaw cried out, not in pain, but in fury. "I won't be forced!" he cried.

"Why should you be the only man who isn't?" said Taleswapper.

"I'll do what I set out to do, and nothing else, whatever the land say!"

"The words of the blacksmith in his forge," said Taleswapper. "The farmer cutting down the trees, he says that."

"Don't you dare compare me to a White man!"

But the brambles bound him tight, till Taleswapper again made his painful way to Ta-Kumsaw, and embraced him. Again Taleswapper felt his own wounds heal, saw Ta-Kumsaw's vanish as quickly as the vines themselves had let go and dropped away. Alvin was looking at them with such pleading, as if to say, How much more strength will you steal from me, before you do what you know you have to do?

With a final anguished cry, Ta-Kumsaw turned and embraced Taleswapper as fully as before. Together they made their way down a wide path to the bottom of the Mound. Alvin stumbled after them.

They slept that night where they had the night before, but it was a troubled sleep. In the morning, Taleswapper wordlessly packed up his few goods, including the book whose letters made no sense. Then he kissed Alvin on the head and walked away. He said nought to Ta-Kumsaw, and Ta-Kumsaw said no more to him. They both knew what the land had said, and they both knew that for the first time in his life, Ta-Kumsaw was going against what was good for the land and satisfying a different need. Taleswapper didn't even try to argue against him anymore. He knew that Ta-Kumsaw would follow his path no matter what, no matter if it left him pierced with a thousand bleeding wounds. He only hoped that Alvin had the strength to stay with him all the way, and keep him alive when all hope was gone.

About noon, after walking almost due west all morning, Taleswapper stopped and pulled his book out of his pack. To his relief, he could read the words again. He unsealed the back two-thirds of the book, the pages where he did his own writing, and spent the rest of the afternoon writing all that had happened to him, all that Alvin had told him, all that he feared for the future. He also wrote the words of the poem that had come to him the morning before, the verses that came from his mouth but Alvin's vision. The poem was still right and true, but even as he read the words in his book, the power of them faded. It was the closest he had ever come to being a prophet himself; but now the gift had left him. It was never his gift at all, anyway. Just as he and Ta-Kumsaw had walked on the meadow without seeing anything special, never guessing that for Alvin it had been a map of the whole continent, so now Taleswapper had the words written down in his book and had no notion anymore of the power behind them.

Taleswapper couldn't travel like a Red man, through the night, sleeping on his feet. So it took him more than a few days to get all the way west to the town of Vigor Church, where he knew there'd be a lot of folks with a long and bitter tale to tell him. If ever a folk needed such a man as Taleswapper to hear their tale, it was them. Yet if ever there was a story that Taleswapper was loath to listen to, it was theirs. Still, he didn't shy from calling on them. He could bear it. There'd be plenty more dark tales to tell before Ta-Kumsaw was through; might as well get started now, so as not to fall behind.

16

La Fayette

Gilbert de La Fayette sat at his vast table, looking into the grain of the wood. Several letters lay before him. One was a letter from de Maurepas to King Charles. Obviously, Freddie had been won over by Napoleon. The letter was full of praise for the little general and his brilliant strategy.

> So soon we are going to win the decisive victory, Your Majesty, and glorify your name. General Bonaparte refuses to be bound by European military tradition. He is training our troops to fight like Reds, even as he lures the so-called Americans into fighting in the open field, like Europeans. As Andrew Jackson gathers his American army, we also gather an army of men who have better claim to the name American. Ta-Kumsaw's ten thousand will stand with us as we destroy the ten thousand of Old Hickory. Ta-Kumsaw will thus avenge the blood of the slaughter at Tippy-Canoe, while we destroy the American army and subjugate the land from the Hio to Huron Lake. In all this, we loyally give the glory to Your Majesty, for it was your insight in sending General Bonaparte here that has made this great conquest possible. And if you now send us two thousand more Frenchmen, to stiffen our line and provoke the Americans into further rashness, your act will be seen as the key intervention in our battle.

It was an outrageous letter for a mere Comte—and one out of favor—to send to his King. Yet Gilbert knew how the letter would be received.

For King Charles was also under Napoleon's spell, and he would read praise of the little Corsican with agreement, with joy.

If only Napoleon were only a vain posturer with a gift for seducing the loyalty of his betters. Then La Fayette could watch his inevitable destruction without soiling his own hands. Napoleon and de Maurepas would lead the French army to disaster, such a disaster as might well bring down a government, and lead to a curbing of the King's authority, even an expulsion of the monarchy, as the English so wisely did a century and a half before.

But Napoleon was exactly what he seduced Freddie and Charlie into thinking he was: a brilliant general. Gilbert knew that Napoleon's plan would succeed. The Americans would march northward, convinced that they faced only Reds. At the last moment, they would find themselves in combat with the French army, disciplined, well-armed, and fanatically loyal to Napoleon. The Americans would be forced to array themselves like a European army. Under their attack, the French would slowly, carefully retreat. When American discipline collapsed in the pursuit, *then* the Reds would attack in devastating numbers, completely surrounding the Americans. Not one American would escape alive—and almost no French lives would be lost.

It was audacious. It was dangerous. It involved exposing French troops to serious risk of destruction, as they would be vastly outnumbered by the Americans. It required implicit trust in the Reds. But Gilbert knew that Napoleon's trust in Ta-Kumsaw was justified.

Ta-Kumsaw would have his revenge. De Maurepas would have his escape from Detroit. Even La Fayette could probably claim enough credit from such a victory to come home and live in comfort and dignity on his ancestral lands. Above all, Napoleon would become the most loved and trusted figure in the military. King Charles would surely grant him a title and lands, and send him out a-conquering in Europe, making King Charles ever richer and more powerful and the people ever more willing to endure his tyranny.

So Gilbert carefully tore de Maurepas's letter into tiny fragments.

The second letter was from Napoleon himself to Gilbert. It was candid, even brutal, in its assessment of the situation. Napoleon had come to realize that while Gilbert de La Fayette was immune to his intoxicating charm, he was a sincere admirer and, indeed, a friend. I *am* your friend, Napoleon. Yet I am more a friend of France than of any man. And the path I have in mind for you is far greater than being the mere toady of a stupid King.

Gilbert reread the key paragraph of Napoleon's letter.

De Maurepas merely echoes what I say, which is comfortable but tedious. I shudder to think what would happen if he were ever in command. His idea of alliance with the Reds is to put them in uniform and stand them in rows like ninepins. What foolishness! How can King Charles consider himself anything but a halfwit, forcing me to serve *under* such an idiot as Freddie? But to Charles, Freddie no doubt seems like the soul of wit—after all, he does know how to appreciate the ballet. In Spain I won a victory for Charles that he did not deserve, and yet he is so spineless that he lets his jealous courtiers maneuver me to Canada, where my allies are savages and my officers are fools. Charlie doesn't deserve the victory I'll bring him. But then, Gilbert my friend, the royal blood has grown thin and weak in the years since Louis Fourteen. I'd urge you to burn this letter, except that Charlie loves me so well that I think he could read it word for word and not take offense! And if he did take offense, how would he dare punish me? What would his stature be in Europe, if I hadn't helped old Wooden-head to a case of dysentery so I could win the war in Spain, instead of losing it, as would surely have happened without me?

Napoleon's vanity was insufferable, but primarily because it was so fully justified. Every word in this letter was true, if rash; but Gilbert had carefully cultivated this candor in Napoleon. Napoleon had obviously longed for someone to admire him sincerely, without Napoleon diddling with his affections. He had found such a one—truly he had—in Gilbert, the only real friend Napoleon would ever have. And yet. And yet.

Gilbert carefully folded Napoleon's letter and enclosed it in his own, a simple note that said:

> Your Majesty, please do not be harsh with this gifted young man. He has the arrogance of youth; there is no treason in his heart, I know it. Nevertheless, I will be guided by you, as always, for you will always know the proper balance between justice and mercy. Your humble servant, Gilbert.

King Charles would be livid, of course. Even if Napoleon was right, and Charlie was inclined to be indulgent, the courtiers would never let such an opportunity pass. There would be such a howl for Napoleon's head that even King Charles could not resist cashiering the boy.

Another letter, the most painful one, was again in Gilbert's own hand, this time addressed to Frederic, Comte de Maurepas. Gilbert had written it long ago, almost as soon as Napoleon arrived in Canada. Soon it would be time to send it.

> On the eve of such momentous events, my dear Freddie, I think you should wear this amulet. It was given me by a holy man to fend the lies and deceptions of Satan. Wear it at all times, my friend, for I think your need for it is greater far than mine.

Freddie need not know that the "holy man" was Robespierre—de Maurepas would certainly never wear it then. Gilbert drew the amulet from the bosom of his shirt, where it dangled on a golden chain. What will de Maurepas do when Napoleon has no power over him? Why, he will act his true self again, that is what he will do.

Gilbert had sat thus for half an hour, knowing that the time of decision had arrived. The amulet would not be sent yet—only at the cusp of events would Napoleon suddenly lose his influence over Freddie. But the letter to the King must be sent now, if there was to be time for it to reach Versailles, and the inevitable response to return to Canada before the springtime battle with the Americans.

Am I a traitor, to work for the defeat of my King and country? No, I am not, most certainly I am not. For if I thought it would do my beloved France even an ounce of good, I would help Napoleon win his victory over the Americans, even if it meant crippling the cause of liberty in this new land. For though I am a Feuillant, a democrat, even a Jacobin in my darkest heart, and even though my love for America is greater than that of any man save perhaps Franklin or Washington, who are dead, or Jefferson among the living—despite all that, I am a Frenchman first, and what care I for liberty in any corner of God's world, if there is none in France?

No, I do this because a terrible, humiliating defeat in Canada is exactly what France needs, especially if it can be seen that the defeat is caused by King Charles's direct intervention. Such a direct intervention as removing popular and brilliant Bonaparte from command on the eve of battle, and replacing him with an ass like de Maurepas, all for the sake of Charlie's own vanity.

For there was one last letter, this one in code, seemingly innocuous in its babbling about hunting and the tedium of life in Niagara. But hidden within it was the entire text of both Napoleon's and Frederic's letters, to be published to withering effect as soon as the news of French defeat reached Paris. Almost as quickly as Napoleon's original letter reached the King, Robespierre would have this ciphered letter in his hands.

But what of my oath to the king? What sort of plotting is this? I was meant to be a general, to lead armies in battle; or a Governor, to move the machinery of state for the good of the people. Instead I am reduced to plotting, backstabbing, deception, betrayal. I am a Brutus, willing to betray all for the sake of a loyalty to the people. And yet—I pray that history will be kind to me, and let it be known that but for me King Charles would have called himself Charlemagne Second and used Napoleon to subjugate Europe in a new French Empire. Instead, with God's help, because of me France will set an example of peacefulness and liberty to all the world.

He lit his wax candle, let it drip to fasten closed the letter to the King and the letter to his trusted neighbor, and then pressed his seal into both. He called in his aide, who put them in the mail pouch, then left to carry them to the ship—the last ship that was sure to make it down the river and on to France before winter.

Only the letter to de Maurepas remained, that and the amulet. How I regret having you, he said to the amulet. If only I, too, could have been deceived by Napoleon, and rejoiced as he made his inevitable way into history. Instead I am thwarting him, for how can a general, be he as brilliant as Caesar, possibly thrive in the democracy Robespierre and I will create in France?

All seeds are planted, all traps are set.

For another hour Gilbert de La Fayette sat trembling in his chair. Then he arose, dressed in his finest clothing, and spent the evening watching a wretched farce by a fifth-rate company, the finest that poor Niagara could get from Mother France. At the end he stood and applauded, which, because he was Governor, guaranteed the company financial success in Canada; applauded long and vigorously, as the rest of the audience was forced to keep applauding with him; clapped his hands until his arms were sore, until the amulet was slick with sweat on his chest, until he felt the heat of his exertion burning through his shoulders and back, until he could clap no more.

17

Becca's Loom

Winter'd been going on half Alvin's life, it seemed like. Used to be he liked snowy times, peeking out his window through the craze of frost, looking at the sun dazzling off the smooth unbroken sea of snow. But then, in those days he could always get inside where it was warm, eat Ma's cooking, sleep in a soft bed. Not that he was suffering so much now; what with learning Red ways for doing things, Alvin wasn't bad off.

It had just been going on for too many months. Almost a year since that spring morning when Alvin set out with Measure for the trip to Hatrack River. That had seemed such a long journey then; now, to Alvin, it was no more than a day's jaunt by comparison with the traveling he had done. They been south so far the Reds spoke Spanish more than English when they talked White man talk. They been west to the foggy bottom lands near the Mizzipy. They talked to Cree-Ek, Chok-Taw, the "uncivilized" Cherriky folk of the bayou country. And north to the highest reaches of the Mizzipy where the lakes were so many and all hooked on that you could go everywhere by canoe.

It went the same with every village they visited. "We know about you, Ta-Kumsaw, you come to talk war. We don't want war. But—if the White man comes here, we fight."

And then Ta-Kumsaw explaining that by the time the White man comes to their village, it's too late, they'll be alone, and the Whites will be like a hailstorm, pounding them into the dirt. "We must make ourselves into one army. We still can be stronger than they are if we do."

It was never enough. A few young men would nod, would wish to say yes, but the old men, they didn't want war, they didn't want glory, they wanted peace and quiet, and the White man was still far away, still a rumor.

Then Ta-Kumsaw would turn to Alvin, and say, "Tell them what happened at Tippy-Canoe."

By the third telling, Alvin knew what would happen when he told the tale the tenth time, the hundredth time, every time. Knew it as soon as the Reds seated around the fire turned to look at him, with distaste because he was White, with interest because he was the White boy who traveled with Ta-Kumsaw. No matter how simple he made the tale, no matter how he included the fact that the Whites of Wobbish Territory thought that Ta-Kumsaw had kidnapped and tortured him and Measure, the Reds still listened to it with grief and grim fury. And at the end, the old men would be gripping handfuls of soil in their hands, tearing at the ground as if to turn loose some terrible beast inside the earth; and the young men would be drawing their flint-edged knives gently across their own thighs, drawing faint lines of blood, teaching their knives to be thirsty, teaching their own bodies to seek out pain and love it.

"When the snow is gone from the banks of the Hio," said Ta-Kumsaw.

"We will be there," said the young men, and the old men nodded their consent. The same in every village, every tribe. Oh, sometimes a few spoke of the Prophet and urged peace; they were scorned as "old women"; though as far as Alvin could see, the old women seemed most savage of all in their hate.

Yet Alvin never complained that Ta-Kumsaw was using him to heat up anger against his own race. After all, the story Alvin had to tell was true, wasn't it? He couldn't deny to tell it, not to anybody, not for any reason, no more than his family could deny to speak under the Prophet's curse. Not that blood would appear on Alvin's hands if he refused to tell. He just felt like the same burden was on him like it was on all the Whites who beheld the massacre at Tippy-Canoe. The story of Tippy-Canoe was true, and if every Red who heard that tale became filled with hate and wanted vengeance, wanted to kill every White man who didn't sail back to Europe, why, would that be a reason for Alvin to try to keep them from knowing? Or wasn't that their natural right, to know the truth so as to be able to let the truth lead them to do good or evil, as they chose?

Not that Alvin could talk about natural rights and such out loud. There wasn't much chance for conversation. Sure enough, he was always with Ta-Kumsaw, never more than an arm's length off. But Ta-Kumsaw almost never spoke to Alvin, and when he did it was things like "Catch a fish" or "Come with me now." Ta-Kumsaw made it plain that he had no friendship for Alvin now, and in fact he didn't much want a White along with him. Ta-Kumsaw walked fast, in his Red man's way, and never looked back to see if Alvin was with him or not. The only time he ever seemed to care that Alvin was there was when he turned to him and said, "Tell what happened at Tippy-Canoe."

One time, after they left a village so het up against Whites they were looking with interest at Alvin's own scalp, Alvin got to feeling defiant and he said, "Why don't you have me tell them about how you and I and Taleswapper all got into Eight-Face Mound?" Ta-Kumsaw's only answer was to walk so fast that Alvin had to run all day just keeping up.

Traveling with Ta-Kumsaw was like traveling alone, when it came to company. Alvin couldn't remember ever being so lonely in his life. So why don't I leave, he asked himself. Why do I keep going with him? It ain't like it's fun, and I'm helping him start a war against my own folks, and it's getting colder all the time, like as if the sun gave up shining and the world was supposed to be grey bare trees and blinding snow from one end to the other, and he don't even want me here.

Why did Alvin go on? It was partly Tenskwa-Tawa's prophecy that Ta-Kumsaw never would die if Alvin stuck close by. Alvin might not like Ta-Kumsaw's company, but Alvin knew he was a great and good man, and if Alvin could somehow help keep him alive, then it was his duty to give it a try as best he could.

But it was also more than that, more than the duty he felt to the Prophet, to care for his brother; more than the need he felt to act out the terrible punishment of his family by telling the tale of Tippy-Canoe all over the Red man's country. Alvin couldn't exactly find it in words to tell himself inside his head as he ran along through the woods, lost in a halfway dream, the green of the forest guiding his footsteps and filling his head with the music of the earth. No, that wasn't a word time. But it was a time of understanding without words, of having a sense of rightness about what he was doing, a feeling that Alvin was like the oil on the axle of a wagon wheel that was carrying great events forward. I might just get myself all used up, I might get burned away by the heat of the wheel rubbing on the axle, but the world is changing, and somehow I'm part of what's helping it go forward. Ta-Kumsaw's building something, bringing together Red men to make something out of them.

It was the first time Alvin understood that something could be built out of people, that when Ta-Kumsaw talked them Reds into feeling with one heart and acting with one mind, they became something bigger than just a few people; and building something like that, it was against the Unmaker, wasn't it? Just like Alvin always used to make little baskets by weaving grass. The grass was nothing but grass by itself, but all wove together it was something more than grass.

Ta-Kumsaw's making something new where there wasn't nothing, but the new thing won't come to be without me.

That filled him with fear of helping make something he didn't understand; but it also filled him with eagerness to see the future. So he pressed on, pushed forward, wore himself down, talked to Reds who started out suspicious and ended up filled with hate, and stared most of every day at the back of Ta-Kumsaw, running ahead of him ever deeper into the forest. The green of the wood turned gold and red, then black with the rains of autumn on the bare trees, and finally grey and white and still. And all his worry, all his discouragement, all his confusion, all his grief for the terrible things he saw coming and the terrible things he'd seen in the past—all turned into a weary distaste for winter, an impatience for the season to change, for the snow to melt and spring to come, and then summer.

Summer, when he could look back and think of all this as the past. Summer, when he'd know pretty much how it all turned out, for good or ill, and not have this sickening snow-white dread in the back of his mind, masking all his other feelings the way snow masked the earth beneath it.

Until one day Alvin noticed that the air *was* somewhat warm, and the snow had slacked off the grass and dirt and was purely gone from the tree limbs, and there was a flash of red where a certain bird was getting itself ready to find him a wife and nestle in for egg season. And on that very day, Ta-Kumsaw turned eastward, up over a ridge of hills, and stood perched atop a rock looking down on a valley of White men's farms in the northern part of the White man's state of Appalachee.

It was a sight Alvin had never seen before in his life. Not like the French city of Detroit, people all packed in together, nor like the sparse settlements of the Wobbish country, with each farm carved out like a gouge in the greenwood forest. Here the trees were all disciplined, lined up in rows to mark off one farmer's field from another. Only on the hills skirting the valley were the trees somewhat wild again. And as the ground softened today, there were farmers out cutting the earth open with their plows, just as gentle and shallow on the face of the earth as those Red warriors' flint knives against their thighs, teaching the blade to thirst, teaching the earth to bear, so that like the blood that seeped upward under the Red men's knives, the wheat or maize or rye or oats would seep upward, make a thin film of life across the skin of the earth, an open wound all summer until harvest blades made another kind of cut. Then the snow again, it would form like a scab, to heal the earth until the next year's injury. This whole valley was like that, broken like an old horse.

I shouldn't feel like this, thought Alvin. I should be glad to see White lands again. There was curls of smoke from a hundred chimneys up and down the valley. There was folks there, children getting outside to play after being penned up the whole of winter, men sweating into the chilly air of early spring as they did their tasks, hard-working animals raising a steam from their nostrils and off their hot, heaving flanks. This was like home, wasn't it? This was what Armor and Father and every other White man wanted to turn the Wobbish country into, wasn't it? This was civilization, one household butting up into the next one, all elbows jostling, all the land parceled out till nobody had no doubt at all who owned every inch of it, who had the right to use it and who was trespassing and better move along.

But after this year of being with Reds practically every minute and hardly seeing a White man except for Measure, for a while, and Taleswapper for a day or two, why, Alvin didn't see that valley with White eyes. He saw it like a Red man, and so to Alvin it looked like the end of the world.

"What're we doing here?" Alvin asked Ta-Kumsaw.

In answer, Ta-Kumsaw just walked right down from the mountain and on into the White man's valley, just like he had a right. Alvin couldn't figure, but he followed tight.

To Alvin's surprise, as they traipsed right through a field half-plowed, the farmer didn't so much as yell at them to mind the furrows, he just looked up, squinted at them, and then waved. "Howdy, Ike!" he called.

Ike?

And Ta-Kumsaw raised his hand in greeting and walked on.

Alvin like to laughed out loud. Ta-Kumsaw, being known to civilized farmers in a place like this, known so well that a White man could tell who he was at such a distance! Ta-Kumsaw, the most ferocious hater of Whites in all the woodland, being called by a White man's name?

But Alvin knew better than to ask for explanation. He just followed close behind till Ta-Kumsaw finally came to where he was going.

It looked to be a house like any other house, maybe a speck older. Big, anyway, and added onto in a jumbly way. Maybe that corner of the house was the original cabin, with a stone foundation, and then they added that wing onto it bigger than the log house, so the cabin no doubt got turned into a kitchen, and then another wing across the front of the cabin, only this time two stories high, with an attic, and then an add-on in the back of the cabin, right across the roof of it, keeping the gable shape and framing it with shaped timbers, which were white-washed clean enough once, but now were peeling off the paint and showing grey wood through. The whole history of this valley in that house—desperately just throwing up enough of a cabin to keep rain off between battling the forest; then a measure of peace to add a room or two for comfort; then some prosperity, and more children, and a need to put a grand two-story face on things, and finally three generations in that house, and building not for pride but just for space, just for rooms to put folks into.

Such a house it was, a house that held the whole story of the White man's victorious war against the land in its shape.

And up walks Ta-Kumsaw to a small and shabby-looking door in the back, and he doesn't so much as knock, he just opens the door and goes inside.

Well, Alvin saw that, and for the first time he didn't know what to do. By habit he wanted to follow Ta-Kumsaw right into the house, the way he'd followed him into a hundred mud-daubed Red man's huts. But by even older habit he knew you don't just walk right into a house like *this*, with a proper door and all. You go round to the front and knock polite, and wait for folks to invite you in.

So Alvin stood at the back door, which Ta-Kumsaw of course didn't even bother to close, watching the first flies of spring wander into the hallway. He could almost hear his mother yelling about people leaving doors open so the flies would come in and drive everybody crazy all night, buzzing when folks are trying to sleep. And so Alvin, thinking that way, did what Ma always had them do: he stepped inside and closed the door behind him.

But he dared go no farther into the house than that back hall, with some heavy coats on pegs and dirt-crusted boots in a jumble by the door. It felt too strange to move. He'd been hearing the greensong of the forest for so many months that it was deafening, the silence when it was near gone, near completely killed by the cacophony of the jammering life on a White man's farm in spring.

"Isaac," said a woman's voice.

One of the White noises stopped. Only then did Alvin realize that it had been an actual noise he was hearing with his ears, not the life-noises he heard with his Red senses. He tried to remember what it was. A rhythm, and banging, regular rhythm like—like a loom. It was a loom he'd been hearing. Ta-Kumsaw must've just walked hisself right into the room where some woman was weaving. Only he wasn't no stranger here, she knew him by the same name as that farmer fellow out in the fields. Isaac.

"Isaac," she said again, whoever she was.

"Becca," said Ta-Kumsaw.

A simple name, no reason for Alvin's heart to start a-pounding. But the *way* Ta-Kumsaw said it, the way he spoke—it was such a tone of voice that was meant to make hearts pound. And more: Ta-Kumsaw spoke it, not with the strange-twisted vowels of Red men talking English, but with as true an accent as if he was from England. Why, he sounded more like Reverend Thrower than Alvin would have thought possible.

No, no, it wasn't Ta-Kumsaw at all, it was another man, a White man in the same room with the White woman, that's all. And Alvin walked softly down the hall to find where the voices were, to see the White man whose presence would explain all.

Instead he stood in an open door and looked into a room where Ta-Kumsaw stood holding a White woman by her shoulders, looking down into her face, and her looking up into his. Saying not a word, just looking at each other. Not a White man in the room.

"My people are gathering at the Hio," said Ta-Kumsaw, in his strange English-sounding voice.

"I know," said the woman. "It's already in the fabric." Then she turned to look at Alvin in the doorway. "And you didn't come alone."

Alvin never saw eyes like hers before. He was still too young to hanker after women like he remembered Wastenot and Wantnot doing when they both hit fourteen at a gallop. So it wasn't any kind of man-wishing-for-a-woman feeling that he had, looking at her eyes. He just looked into them like he sometimes looked into a fire, watching the flames dance, not asking for them to make sense, just watching the sheer randomness of it. That was what her eyes were like, as if those eyes had seen a hundred thousand things happen, and they were all still swirling around inside those eyes, and no one had ever bothered or maybe even known how to get those visions out and make sensible stories out of them.

And Alvin feared mightily that she had some power of witchery that she used to turn Ta-Kumsaw into a White man.

"My name is Becca," said the woman.

"His name is Alvin," said Ta-Kumsaw; or rather, said Isaac, for it sure didn't sound like Ta-Kumsaw anymore. "He's a miller's son from the Wobbish country."

"He's that thread I saw running through the fabric out of place." She smiled at Alvin. "Come here," she said. "I want to see the legendary Boy Renegado."

"Who's that?" asked Alvin. "The Boy Rainy God—"

"Renegado. There are stories all through Appalachee, don't you know that? About Ta-Kumsaw, who appears one day in the Osh-Kontsy country and the next day in a village on the banks of the Yazoo, stirring up Reds to do massacre and torture. And always with him is a White boy who urges the Reds to be ever more brutal, who teaches them the secret methods of torture that used to be practiced by the Papist Inquisitions in Spain and Italy."

"That ain't so," said Alvin.

She smiled. The flames of her eyes danced.

"They must hate me," said Alvin. "I don't even know what a Inkyzitchum is."

"Inquisition," said Isaac.

Alvin felt a sick dread in his heart. If folks were telling such tales about him, why, folks would regard him as a criminal, a monster, practically. "I'm only going along with—"

"I know what you're doing, and why," said Becca. "Around here we all know Isaac well enough to disbelieve such lies about him and you both."

But Alvin didn't care about "around here." What he cared about was back home in Wobbish country.

"Don't worry yourself," said Becca. "Nobody knows who this legendary White boy is. Certainly not one of the two Innocents that Ta-Kumsaw chopped to bits in the forest. Certainly not Alvin or Measure. Which one *are* you, by the way?"

"Alvin," said Isaac.

"Oh, yes," said Becca. "You already told me that. I have such a hard time holding people's names in my head."

"Ta-Kumsaw didn't chop nobody up."

"As you might guess, Alvin, we didn't believe that story here, either."

"Oh." Alvin didn't know what to say, and since he'd been living like a Red for so long, he did what Reds do when they have nothing to say, something that a White man hardly ever thinks of doing. He said nary a thing at all.

"Bread and cheese?" asked Becca.

"You're too kind. Thank you," said Isaac.

If that didn't beat all. Ta-Kumsaw saying thank you like a fine gentleman. Not that he wasn't noble and fair-spoke among his kind. But in White man's language he was always so cold, so unflowered in his talk. Till now. Witchery.

Becca rang a little bell.

"It's simple fare, but we live simply in this house. And I especially in this room. Which is fitting—it's such a simple place."

Alvin looked around. She was right. It only just now occurred to him that this room was the original log cabin, with its one remaining window casting southern light into the room. Around it the walls were all still rough old wood; he just hadn't noticed, from all the cloth draped here and there, hanging on hooks, piled up on furniture, rolled up in bolts. A strange kind of cloth, lots of color in it but the color making no pattern or sense, just weaving this way, that way, changing shades and colors, a broad streak of blue, a few narrow strands of green, all twisting in and out of each other.

Somebody came into the room to answer Becca's bell, an older man from the sound of his voice; she sent him for food, but Alvin didn't even know what he looked like, he couldn't take his eyes off the cloth. What was so much cloth for? Why would somebody make it such a bright and ugly unorganized set of colors?

And where did it end?

He walked over to where maybe a dozen bolts of cloth were standing in a corner, leaning on each other, and he realized that each bolt grew out of the one before. Somebody'd taken the end of cloth from one bolt and wrapped it around itself to start the next one, so the cloth spooled off the end of one bolt, then leapt up and plunged right down into the center of the next, one after the other, making a chain of fabric. It wasn't a bunch of different cloths, it was all one cloth, rolled up until it was almost too heavy to move, and then the next bolt started right up, with never a scissor touching the cloth. Alvin began to wander around the room, his fingers tracing the pattern of the cloth, following its path up over hooks on the wall, down into folds stacked up on the floor. He followed, he followed, until finally, just as the old man returned with the bread and cheese, he found the end of the cloth. It was feeding out the front of Becca's loom.

All that time, Ta-Kumsaw had been talking to Becca in his Isaac voice, and she to him in her deep melodious way of speech, which had just the slightest hint of foreignness to it, like some of the Dutch in the area around Vigor Church, who'd been in America all their lives but still had a trace of the old country in their talk. Only now, with Alvin standing by the loom and the food on a low table with three chairs around it, only now did he pay attention to what they were saying, and that only because he wanted so badly to ask Becca what all this cloth was *for*, seeing as how she must have been weaving at it for more than a year, to have it so long, without never once taking shears to it to make something out of it. It was what Ma always called a shameful waste, to have something and make no use of it, like Dally Framer's pretty singing voice, which she sang with all day at home but wouldn't ever join in singing hymns at church.

"Eat," said Ta-Kumsaw. And when he spoke so bluntly to Alvin, his voice lost that Englishness; he was the real Ta-Kumsaw again. It set Alvin's mind to rest, knowing that there wasn't some witchery at work, that Ta-Kumsaw just had two different ways of talking; but of course that also set more questions into Alvin's mind, about how Ta-Kumsaw ever learned such talk. Alvin never even heard so much as a rumor about Ta-Kumsaw having White friends in Appalachee, and you'd think a tale like that would be known. Though it wasn't hard to guess why Ta-Kumsaw wouldn't want it noised around much. What would all those het-up Reds think if they saw Ta-Kumsaw here and now? What would it do to Ta-Kumsaw's war?

And come to think of it, how could Ta-Kumsaw wage such a war, if he had true White friends like the folk of this valley? Surely the land was dead here, at least as the Reds knew it. How could Ta-Kumsaw bear it? It left such a hunger in Alvin that even though he packed bread and cheese down his throat till his belly poked out, he still felt a gnawing inside him, a need to get back to the woodland and feel the song of the land inside himself.

The meal was filled with Becca's pleasant chatter about doings in the valley, her saying names that meant nothing to Alvin, except any one of them could have been the name of a body back in Vigor Church—there was even folks named Miller, which was natural, seeing how a valley this size no doubt had more than one miller's worth of grain to grind.

The old man came back to clear away.

"Did you come to see my cloth?" asked Becca.

Ta-Kumsaw nodded. "That's half why I came."

Becca smiled, and led him to the loom. She sat on her weaving stool and gathered the newest cloth up into her lap. She started about three yards from the lip of the loom. "Here," she said. "The gathering of your folk to Prophetstown."

Alvin saw how she passed her hand over a whole bunch of threads that seemed to climb out of their proper warp and migrate across the cloth to gather up near the edge.

"Reds from every tribe," she said. "The strongest of your people."

Even though the fibers tended to be greenish, they were indeed heavier than most threads, strong and taut. Becca fed the cloth farther down her lap. The gathering grew stronger and clearer, and the threads turned brighter green. How could threads change color that way? And how with the machinery of the loom could the warp shift like that?

"And now the Whites that gathered against them," she said.

And sure enough, another group of threads, tighter to start with, but gathering, knotting up a little. To Alvin's eyes it looked like the cloth was a ruin, the threads all tangled and bunched—who'd wear a shirt made of such stuff as that?—and the colors made no sense, all jumbled together without no effort to make a pattern or any kind of regular order.

Ta-Kumsaw reached out his hand and pulled the cloth toward himself. Pulled until he exposed a place were all those pure green threads just went slack and then stopped, most of them. The warp of the cloth was spare and thin, then, maybe one thread for every ten there used to be, like a worn-down raggedy patch in the elbow of an old shirt, so when you bent your elbow maybe a dozen threads made lines across your skin one direction, and no threads at all the other way.

If the green threads stood for Prophetstown, there couldn't be no mistake what was going on here. "Tippy-Canoe," Alvin murmured. Now he knew the order of this cloth.

Becca bent over the cloth and tears dropped from her eyes straight down on it.

Tearless, Ta-Kumsaw pulled the cloth again, steadily. Alvin saw the rest of the green threads, the few that remained from the massacre at Tippy-Canoe, migrate to the edge of the cloth and stop. The cloth was narrower by that many threads. Only now there was another gathering, and the threads were not green. They were mostly black.

"Black with hate," said Becca. "You are gathering your people with hate."

"Can you imagine conducting a war with love?" asked Ta-Kumsaw.

"That's a reason to refuse to make war at all," she said gently.

"Don't talk like a White woman," said Ta-Kumsaw.

"But she is one," said Alvin, who thought she made perfect sense.

They both looked at Alvin, Ta-Kumsaw impassively, Becca with— amusement? Pity? Then they returned to the cloth.

Very quickly they came to where the cloth hung over the beam, then fed out of the loom. Along the way, the black threads of Ta-Kumsaw's army worked closer together, knotted, intertwined. And other threads, some blue, some yellow, some black, all gathered in another place, the fabric bunching up something awful. It was thicker, but it didn't seem to Alvin that it was a speck stronger. Weaker, if anything. Less useful. Less trustworthy.

"This cloth ain't going to be worth much, if this goes on," said Alvin.

Becca smiled grimly. "Truer words were never spoken, lad."

"If this is about a year's worth of story," said Alvin, "you must have two hundred years all gathered up here."

Becca cocked her head. "More than that," she said.

"How do you find out all that's going on, to make it all go into the cloth?"

"Oh, Alvin, there's some things folks just do, without knowing how," she said.

"And if you change the threads around, can't you make things go different?" Alvin had in mind a careful rearrangement, spreading the threads out more even-like, and getting those black threads farther apart from each other.

"It doesn't work like that," she said. "I don't make things happen, with what I do here. Things that happen, they change *me*. Don't fret about it, Alvin."

"But there wasn't even White folks in this part of America more than two hundred years ago. How can this cloth go farther back?"

She sighed. "Isaac, why did you bring him to plague me with questions?"

Ta-Kumsaw smiled at her.

"Lad, will you tell no one?" she asked. "Will you keep it secret who I am and what I do?"

"I promise."

"I weave, Alvin. That's all. My whole family, from before we even remember, we've been weavers."

"That your name, then? Becca Weaver? My brother-in-law, Armor-of-God, his pa's a Weaver, and—"

"Nobody *calls* us weavers," said Becca. "If they had any name for us at all, they'd call us—no."

She wouldn't tell him.

"No, Alvin, I can't put such a burden on you. Because you'd want to come. You'd want to come and see—"

"See what?" asked Alvin.

"Like Isaac here. I should never have told him, either."

"He kept the secret, though. Never breathed a word."

"He didn't keep it secret from himself, though. He came to see."

"See what?" Alvin asked again.

"See how long are the threads a-flowing up into my loom."

Only then did Alvin notice the back end of the loom, where the warp threads were gathered into place by a rack of fine steel wires. The threads weren't colored at all. They were raw white. Cotton? Surely not wool. Linen, maybe. With all the colors in the finished cloth, he hadn't really noticed what it was made of.

"Where do the colors come from?" asked Alvin.

No one answered.

"Some of the threads go slack."

"Some of them end," said Ta-Kumsaw.

"Many of them end," said Becca. "And many begin. It's the pattern of life."

"What do you see, Alvin?" asked Ta-Kumsaw.

"If these black threads are your folk," said Alvin, "then I'd say there's a battle coming, and a lot are going to die. Not like Tippy-Canoe, though. Not as bad."

"That's what I see, too," said Ta-Kumsaw.

"And these other colors all bunched up, what are they? An army of White folk?"

"Word is that a man named Andrew Jackson of the western Tennizy country is gathering up an army. They call him Old Hickory."

"I know the man," said Ta-Kumsaw. "He doesn't stay in the saddle too well."

"He's been doing with White folks what you've been doing with Red, Isaac. He's been going up and down the western country, rousting people out and haranguing them about the Red Menace. About *you*, Isaac. For every Red soldier you've gathered, he's recruited two Whites. And he figures you'll go north, to join with a French army. He knows all your plans."

"He knows nothing," said Ta-Kumsaw. "Alvin, tell me, how many threads of this White army end?"

"A lot. More, maybe. I don't know. It's about even."

"Then it tells me nothing."

"It tells you that you'll have your battle," said Becca. "It tells you that there'll be more blood and suffering in the world, thanks to you."

"But it says nothing of victory," said Ta-Kumsaw.

"It never does."

Alvin wondered if you could just tie another thread onto the end of one of the broken ones, and save somebody's life. He looked for the spools of thread from which the warp was formed, but he couldn't find them. The threads hung down from the back beam of the loom, taut like there was a heavy weight hanging on them, but Alvin couldn't see where the threads came from. They didn't touch the floor. They didn't exactly stop, either. He looked this far, and there they were, hanging tight and long; and he looked this much farther, and there weren't no threads, nothing there at all. The threads were just coming out of nowhere, and there was no way the human eye could see or make sense of how they started.

But Alvin, he could see with other eyes, inward eyes, the way he studied into the tiny workings of the human body, into the cold inward currents of stone. And with that hidden vision he looked into a single thread and traced its shape, following how the fibers wound around and through, twisting and gripping each other to make the strength of the yarn. This time he could just keep following the thread. Just keep on following until finally, far beyond the place where the threads all disappeared to natural eyes, the thread ended. Whosoever soul that thread bespoke, he had a good long life ahead of him, before he died.

All these threads must end, when the person dies. And somehow a new thread must start up when a baby got born. Another thread coming out of nowhere.

"It never ends," said Becca. "I'll grow old and die, Alvin, but the cloth will go on."

"Do you know which thread is you?"

"No," she said. "I don't want to know."

"I reckon I'd like to see. I want to know how many years I got."

"Many," said Ta-Kumsaw. "Or few. All that matters is what you do with however many years you have."

"It does too matter how long I live," said Alvin. "Don't go saying it don't, cause you don't believe that yourself."

Becca laughed.

"Miss Becca," said Alvin, "what do you do this for, if you don't make things happen?"

She shrugged. "It's a work. Everybody has a work to do, and this is mine."

"You could go out and weave things for folks to wear."

"To wear and then wear out," she said. "And no, Alvin, I can't go out."

"You mean you stay indoors all the time?"

"I stay here, always," she said. "In this room, with my loom."

"I begged you once to go with me," said Isaac.

"And I begged you once to stay." She smiled up at him.

"I can't live forever where the land is dead."

"And I can't live a moment away from my cloth. The way the land lives in your mind, Isaac, that is how the lives of all the souls of America live in mine. But I love you. Even now."

Alvin felt like he shouldn't be there. It was like they forgot he was there, even though he'd just been talking to them. It finally dawned on him that they'd probably rather be alone. So he moved away, walked over to the cloth again, and again began tracing its path, the opposite direction this time, scanning quickly but carefully, up the walls, through the bolts and piles, searching for the earliest end of the cloth.

Couldn't find it. In fact, he must have been looking the wrong direction or got himself twisted up, because pretty soon he found himself on the same familiar path he had followed, the path that first led him to the loom. He reversed direction, and after a short time he found himself again on the path to the loom. He could no more search backward to find the oldest end of the cloth than he could search forward to find where the newest threads were coming from.

He turned again to Ta-Kumsaw and Becca. Whatever whispered conversation they had carried on was over. Ta-Kumsaw sat cross-legged on the floor in front of her, his head bowed. She was stroking his hair with gentle hands.

"This cloth is older than the oldest part of this house," said Alvin.

Becca didn't answer.

"This cloth's been going on forever."

"As long as men and women have known how to weave, this cloth has passed through the loom."

"But not this loom. This loom's new," said Alvin.

"We change looms from time to time. We build the new one around the old. It's what the men of our kind do."

"This cloth is older than the oldest White settlements in America," said Alvin.

"It was once a part of a larger cloth. But one day, back in our old country, we saw a large portion of the threads moving off the edge of the cloth. My great-great-great-great-great-great-grandfather built a new loom. We had the threads we needed. They pulled away from the old cloth; we continued it from there. It's still connected up—that's what you're seeing."

"But now it's here."

"It's here *and* there. Don't try to understand it, Alvin. I gave up long ago. But isn't it good to know that all of the threads of life are being woven into one great cloth?"

"Who's weaving the cloth for the Red folk that went west with Tenskwa-Tawa?" asked Alvin. "Those threads went off the cloth."

"That's not your business," said Becca. "We'll just say that another loom was built, and carried west."

"But Ta-Kumsaw said no White folk would ever cross the river to the west. The Prophet said it, too."

Ta-Kumsaw turned slowly on the floor, without getting up. "Alvin," he said, "you're only a boy."

"And I was only a girl," Becca reminded him, "when I first loved

438 HATRACK RIVER

you." She turned to Alvin. "It's my daughter who carried the loom into the west. She could go because she's only half White." She again stroked Ta-Kumsaw's hair. "Isaac is my husband. My daughter Wieza is his daughter."

"Mana-Tawa," said Ta-Kumsaw.

"I thought for a time that Isaac would choose to stay here, to live with us. But then I watched as his thread moved away from us, even though his body still was with us. I knew he would go to be with his people. I knew why he had come to us, alone from the forest. There is a hunger deeper than the Red man's hunger for the song of the living forest, deeper than a blacksmith's yearning for the hot wet iron, deeper even than a doodlebug's longing for the hollow heart of the earth. That hunger brought Ta-Kumsaw to our house. My mother was still the weaver at the loom then. I taught Ta-Kumsaw to read and write; he rushed through my father's library, and read every other book in the valley, and we sent for more books from Philadelphia and he read those. He chose his own name, then, for the man who wrote the *Principia*. When we came of age, he married me. I had a baby. He left. When Wieza was three, he came back, built a loom, and took her west over the mountain to live with his people."

"And you let your own daughter go?"

"Just like one of my ancestors sat at her old loom and let her daughter go, across the ocean to this land, her with a new loom and her watchful father beside her, yes, I let her go." Becca smiled sadly at Alvin. "We all have our work, but there's no good work that doesn't have its cost. By the time Isaac took her, I was already in this room. Everything that happened has been good."

"You didn't even ask how your daughter was doing when he got here! You still haven't asked."

"I didn't have to ask," said Becca. "No harm comes to the keepers of the loom."

"Well, if your daughter's gone, who's going to take your place?"

"Perhaps another husband will come here, by and by. One who'll stay in this house, and make another loom for me, and yet another for a daughter not yet born."

"And what happens to you then?"

"So many questions, Alvin," said Ta-Kumsaw. But his voice was soft and tired and English-sounding; Alvin wasn't in awe of the Ta-Kumsaw who read White men's books, and so he paid no heed to the mild rebuke.

"What happens to you when your daughter takes your place?"

"I don't know," said Becca. "But the story is that we go to the place where the threads come from."

"What do you do there?"

"We spin."

Alvin tried to imagine Becca's mother, and her grandmother, and the women before that, all in a line, he tried to imagine how many there'd be, all of them working their spinning wheels, winding out threads from the spindle, yarn all raw and white, which would just go somewhere, go on and disappear somewhere until it broke. Or maybe when it broke they held the whole thing, a whole human life, in their hands, and then tossed it upward until it was caught by a passing wind, and then dropped down and got snagged up in somebody's loom. A life afloat on the wind, then caught and woven into the cloth of humanity; born at some arbitrary time, then struggling to find its way into the fabric, weaving into the strength of it.

And as he imagined this, he also imagined that he understood something about that fabric. About the way it grew stronger the more tightly woven in each thread became. The ones that skipped about over the top of the cloth, dipping into the weft only now and then, they added little to the strength, though much to the color, of the cloth. While some whose color hardly showed at all, they were deeply wound among the threads, holding all together. There was a goodness in those hidden binding threads. Forever from then on, Alvin would see some quiet man or woman, little noticed and hardly thought of by others, who nevertheless went a-weaving through the life of village, town, or city, binding up, holding on, and Alvin would silently salute such folk, and do them homage in his heart, because he knew how their lives kept the cloth strong, the weave tight.

He also remembered the many threads that ended at the point where Ta-Kumsaw's battle was to take place. It was as if Ta-Kumsaw had taken shears to the cloth.

"Ain't there a way to heal things up?" asked Alvin. "Ain't there a hope of keeping this battle from ever happening, so those threads don't all get broke?"

Becca shook her head. "Even if Isaac refused to go, the battle would take place without him. No, the threads aren't broken by anything Isaac did. They broke the moment some Red man chose a course of action that would surely end in his death in battle; you and Isaac weren't going around spreading death, if that's what worries you. No more than Old Hickory's been killing people. You were just going spreading choices. They didn't have to believe in you. They didn't have to choose to die."

"But they didn't know that's what they was choosing."

"They knew," said Becca. "We always know. We don't admit it to ourselves, not until the very moment of death, but in that moment, Alvin, we see all the life before us and we understand how we chose, every day of our lives, the manner of our death."

"What if something just happens to fall on somebody's head and mashes him?"

"He chose to be in a place where such things happen. And he wasn't looking up."

"I don't believe it," said Alvin. "I think folks can always change what's coming, and I think some things happen that ain't nobody ever chose to happen."

Becca smiled at him, reached out her arm. "Come here, Alvin. Let me hold you close to me. I love your simple faith, child. I want to hold on to that faith, even if I can't believe it."

So she held him for a time, and her arm around him felt so much like his own mama's, strong and gentle, that he cried a little. In fact he cried a good deal more than he would ever have meant to cry, if he'd meant to cry at all. And he knew better than to ask to see his own thread, even though he imagined his thread would be easy to find—the one thread born in the White man's section of the cloth, but migrating over and becoming green. Surely becoming green, like the Prophet's people did.

One thing he was also sure of, so sure that he didn't even ask, though heaven knows he wasn't shy about asking any question popped into his head: He was sure that Becca knew which thread was Ta-Kumsaw's, and knew as well that his and Ta-Kumsaw's threads were all bound up with each other, for a while at least. As long as Alvin was with him, Ta-Kumsaw'd be alive. Alvin knew that there was two endings to the prophecy: the one in which Alvin died first, leaving Ta-Kumsaw by himself, in which case he'd die too; or the one in which neither one of them died and their threads went on until they disappeared. There might've been a third way it could come out: Alvin might just up and leave Ta-Kumsaw. But then if he did that, he wouldn't be Alvin anymore, so there wasn't no point in considering that as a possibility, cause it wasn't one.

Alvin slept the night on a mat on the library floor, after reading a few pages in a book by a man named Adam Smith. Where Ta-Kumsaw saw slept, Alvin didn't know or care to ask. What a man does with his wife is no affair for children, Alvin knew; but he wondered if the main reason Ta-Kumsaw had come back here wasn't his wish to see the loom, but the hungering that Becca spoke of. The need to make another daughter to care for Becca's loom. It wasn't a bad idea, in Alvin's mind, to have the cloth of White America in the hands of a Red man's daughter.

In the morning Ta-Kumsaw led him away, back into the forest. They did not speak of Becca, or anything else; it was back to the old way, with Ta-Kumsaw speaking only to get things done. Alvin never heard him speak in his Isaac voice again, so that Alvin began to wonder if he really heard it.

On the north bank of the Hio, near where the Wobbish empties into it, the Red army gathered, more Reds than Alvin knew existed in the whole world. More people than Alvin had ever imagined together in the same place at the same time.

Because such a company was bound to get hungry, the animals also came to them, sensing their need and fulfilling what they all was born for. Did the forest know that all its hopes of withstanding White men's axes depended on Ta-Kumsaw's victory?

No, Alvin decided, the forest was just doing what it always did— making shift to feed its own.

It was raining and the breeze was cool on the morning they set out from the Hio, bound northward. But what was rain to Red men? The messenger had come from the French in Detroit. It was time to join forces, and lure Old Hickory's army north.

18

Detroit

It was a glorious time for Frederic, Comte de Maurepas. Far from living in hell here in Detroit, with none of the amenities of Paris, he found the exhilaration of, for once, being part of something larger than himself. War was afoot, the fort was stirring, the heathen Reds were gathering from the far corners of the wilderness, and soon, under de Maurepas's command, the French would destroy the ragtag American army Old Chestnut had brought north of the Maw-Mee. Old Willow? Whatever they called him.

Of course a part of him was rather unnerved by all this. Frederic had never been a man of action, and now so much action was going on that he could hardly fathom it. It bothered him sometimes that Napoleon was letting the savages fight from behind trees. Surely Europeans, even the barbarous Americans, should be courteous enough not to let the Reds take unfair advantage of their ability to hide in the woods. But never mind. Napoleon was sure it would work out. What could go wrong, really? Everything was working as Napoleon said it would. Even Governor La Fayette, traitorous effete Feuillant dog that he was, seemed enthusiastic about the battle ahead. He had even sent another ship with more troops, which Frederic had seen pull into harbor not ten minutes ago.

"My lord," said Whoever-it-was, the servant who handled things in the evening. He was announcing somebody, of all things.

"Who?" Who is it visiting at such an ungodly hour?

"A messenger from the Governor."

"In," said Frederic. He was feeling too pleasant to bother keeping the man cooling his heels for a while. After all, it was evening—no need to pretend to be hard at work at an hour like this. After four o'clock, in fact!

The man came in, smart in his uniform. A major officer, in fact. Frederic should know his name, probably, but then he wasn't anybody, hadn't even a cousin with a title. So Frederic waited, not greeting him.

The major held two letters in his hand. He laid one on Frederic's table.

"Is the other for me as well?"

"Yes, sir. But I have the Governor's instructions to give you that one first, to wait while you read it in my presence, and then decide whether to give you the other."

"The Governor's instructions! To make me wait to receive my mail until I've read his letter first?"

"The second letter is not addressed to you, my lord," said the major. "So it is not your mail. But I think you will want to see it."

"What if I'm weary of work, and choose to read the letter tomorrow?"

"Then I have still another letter, which I will read to your soldiers if you don't read the first letter within five minutes. That third letter relieves you of command and places me in charge of Fort Detroit, under the authority of the Governor."

"Audacious! Offensive! To address me in this manner!"

"I but repeat the words of the Governor, my lord. I urge you, read his letter. It can do you no harm, and not reading it will have devastating effect."

Unbearable. Who did the Governor think he was? Well, in fact, he was a Marquis. But then, La Fayette was actually farther out of favor with the King than—"

"Five minutes, my lord."

Seething, Frederic opened the letter. It was heavy; when he unfolded it, a metal amulet on a chain spilled onto the desk, clattering.

"What is *this*?"

"The letter, my lord."

Frederic scanned it quickly. "An amulet! Holy man! What am I to make of this? Has La Fayette become superstitious?" Yet despite his bravado, Frederic knew at once that he would put on the amulet. A ward against Satan! He had heard of such amulets, priceless beyond compare, for all had been touched by the finger of the Holy Mother herself, giving them their power. Could this be such a one? He opened the chain and lowered it over his head.

"Inside," said the major.

Frederic looked at him a moment in bafflement, then realized what was expected and tucked the amulet into his shirt. Now it was out of sight.

"There," he said. "I'm wearing it."

"Excellent, my lord," said the major. He held out the other letter.

It was not fastened shut, but it *had* been sealed, and Frederic was astonished to see that it was His Majesty's great seal imprinted in the wax. It was addressed to the Marquis de La Fayette. It contained the order for Napoleon Bonaparte to be placed under immediate arrest, to be returned to Paris in irons to stand trial for treason, sedition, disloyalty, and malfeasance.

"Do you think your pleading moves me?" said de Maurepas.

"I should hope that the justice of my arguments would move you," said Napoleon. "Tomorrow will be the battle. Ta-Kumsaw expects to take his orders from me; only I understand fully what is expected of the French army in this engagement."

"Only you? What is this sudden vanity of yours, to believe that only you are capable of command, that only you understand?"

"But of course *you* understand, my lord de Maurepas. Only it is for you to be concerned with the broader picture, while I—"

"Save your breath," said de Maurepas. "I am no longer deceived. Your witchery, your satanic influence, it floats past me like bubbles in the air, it means nothing to me. I am stronger than you thought. I have secret strengths!"

"It's good that you do, since all you have in public is idiocy," said Napoleon. "The defeat you will suffer without me will mark you as the champion fool in the history of the French army. Whenever anyone suffers an ignominious and avoidable disaster, they will laugh at him and say that he committed a Maurepas!"

"Enough," said de Maurepas. "Treason, sedition, malfeasance, *and* if that weren't enough, now insubordination. M. Guillotin will have business with you, I'm quite certain, my vain little bantam cock. Go, try your spurs on His Majesty, see how deep they dig when your limbs are in irons and your head is forfeit."

The betrayal was not obvious till morning, but then it was swift and complete. It began when the French quartermaster refused to issue gunpowder to Ta-Kumsaw's people. "I have my orders," he said.

When Ta-Kumsaw tried to see Napoleon, they laughed at him. "He won't see you now, or ever," he was told.

What about de Maurepas, then?

"He is a Comte. He does not treat with savages. He is not a lover of beasts, like little Napoleon."

Only then did Alvin notice that all the Frenchman they were dealing with today were the very ones that Napoleon had been circumventing; all the officers Napoleon preferred and trusted were not to be found. Napoleon had fallen.

"Bows and arrows," said an officer. "That's what your braves excel with, isn't it? With bullets you would cause more damage to your own men than to the enemy."

Ta-Kumsaw's scouts told him that the American army would arrive by noon. Ta-Kumsaw immediately deployed his men to harass the enemy. But now, without the range of muskets, they could do little more than annoy Old Hickory's army with the stings of feeble arrows fired from too far off, where they had meant to cripple the Americans with an irresistible storm of metal. And because the bowmen had to come so close to the Americans in order to fire, many of them were killed.

"Don't stand near me," Ta-Kumsaw told Alvin. "They all know of the prophecy. They'll think my courage only comes because I know I cannot die."

So Alvin stood farther off, but never so far that he didn't see deeply into Ta-Kumsaw's body, ready to heal any wound. What he could not heal was the fear and anger and despair that already gathered in Ta-Kumsaw's soul. Without gunpowder, without Napoleon, the sure victory had become a chancy thing at best.

The basic tactics were successful. Old Hickory spotted the trap at once, but the terrain forced him to fall into it or retreat, and he knew that retreat would be disaster. So he marched his army boldly between the hills filled with Reds, funneling into the narrow ground where French cannon and musketry would rake the Americans while the Reds killed any who tried to flee. The victory would be complete. Except that the Americans were supposed to be demoralized, confused, and their numbers deeply reduced by the Red men shooting at them all the way here.

The tactics were successful, except that when the American army came in view of the French, and hesitated before the muzzles of nine cannon loaded with canister, and two thousand muskets arrayed to sweep and double-sweep the field, the French incomprehensibly began to move back. It was as if they did not trust the impregnability of their own position. They did not even try to withdraw the cannon. They retreated as if they feared immediate destruction.

The course of the battle was predictable, then. Old Hickory knew what to do with opportunity. His soldiers ignored the Reds and fell on the retreating Frenchmen, slaughtering all who did not run, seizing their cannon and muskets, their powder and shot. Within an hour they had used the French artillery to break down the fortress walls in three places; Americans streamed into Detroit; there was bloody fighting in the streets.

Ta-Kumsaw should have left then. He should have let the Americans destroy the French, should have taken his men to safety. Perhaps he felt a duty to help the French, even after they had betrayed him. Perhaps he saw a glimmer of hope that with the Americans involved in battle, his army of Reds might win a victory after all. Or perhaps he knew that never again would he have the power to gather all the fighting men of every tribe; if he retreated now, with the battle unfought, who would follow him again? And if they would not follow him, they would follow no one, and the White men would nibble their way to conquest, devouring now this tribe, now that. Ta-Kumsaw surely knew that it was either victory now, however unlikely, or the struggle would be over for all time, and any of his people who weren't slaughtered outright would either escape into the west, a strange land to them, lacking in forest; or would remain as a diminished people, living like White men instead of Red, the forest forever silent. Whether he hoped for victory or not, he could not surrender to such a future, not without a fight.

So armed with bows and arrows, clubs and knives, the Reds attacked the American army from behind. At first they reaped the Whites in bloody harvest, clubbing them to the ground, piercing them with flints. Ta-Kumsaw shouted at them to take muskets, powder, ammunition from the dead, and many Reds obeyed. But then Old Hickory got the disciplined core of his men into action. The guns were turned. And the Reds, exposed on the open field, were felled in great swathes of grapeshot.

By evening, the sun going down, Detroit was on fire and the smoke filled the nearby wood. In that choking darkness stood Ta-Kumsaw with a few hundred of his own Shaw-Nee. Other tribes made isolated stands here and there; most despaired and fled into the forest, where no White man could follow. Old Hickory himself led the final assault against Ta-Kumsaw's wooded fortress, bringing with him the thousand Americans who weren't busy looting the French city and smashing the idols in the Papist cathedral.

The bullets came from all directions, it seemed. But through it all Ta-Kumsaw stood upright, shouting to his men, urging them to fight on with muskets stolen from fallen Americans in the first attack. For fifteen minutes that seemed like forever, Ta-Kumsaw fought like a madman, and his Shaw-Nee fought and died beside him. Ta-Kumsaw's body blossomed with scarlet wounds; blood streaked down his back and belly;

one arm hung limp by his side. No one knew how he found the strength to stand, he had so many wounds in him. But Ta-Kumsaw was made of flesh like any other man, and at last he fell in the smoky dusk, bearing half a dozen wounds, any one of which would surely have been fatal by itself.

When Ta-Kumsaw fell, the firing slackened. It was as if the Americans knew that they had only to kill that one man, and they would break the spirit of the Red man, now and forever. The dozen surviving Shaw-Nee warriors crept away in the smoke and the darkness, to bear the bitter news of Ta-Kumsaw's death to every Shaw-Nee village, and eventually to every hut where Red men and women lived. The great battle was hopeless; White men could not be trusted, French or American, and so Ta-Kumsaw's great plan could never have succeeded. Yet the Red men remembered that at least for a time they had united under one great man, had become a single people, had dreamed of victory. So Ta-Kumsaw was remembered in song as Red villages and families moved west across the Mizzipy to join the Prophet; he was remembered in stories told beside brick hearths, by families who wore clothing and worked at jobs like white men, but still remembered that once there was another way to live, and the greatest of all the forest Reds had been a man called Ta-Kumsaw, who died trying to save the woodland and the ancient, doomed Red way of life.

It was not only Reds who remembered Ta-Kumsaw. Even as they fired muskets at his shadowy figure in the woods, the American soldiers admired him. He was a great hero out of olden times. Americans were all farmers and shopkeepers at heart; Ta-Kumsaw lived a story like Achilles or Odysseus, Caesar or Hannibal, David or the Maccabees. "He can't die," they murmured as they saw him take bullets and still not fall. And when at last he did fall, they searched for his body and did not find it.

"The Shaw-Nee dragged him off," said Old Hickory, and that was that. He wouldn't even let them search for the Renegado Boy, figuring that such a White traitor was no doubt as faithless as the French and snuck off during the fight. Leave be, said Old Hickory, and who was going to argue with the old man? He won them the victory, didn't he? He broke the back of Red resistance once and for all, didn't he? Old Hickory, Andy Jackson—they wanted to make him King but they'd have to settle for President someday. Yet in the meantime they could not forget Ta-Kumsaw, and rumors spread that he was alive somewhere, crippled by his wounds, waiting to get healed up and lead a great Red invasion from across the Mizzipy, from the swamps of the South, or from some secret hidden fastness in the Appalachee Mountains.

*　　　*　　　*

All through the battle Alvin worked with all his might to keep Ta-Kumsaw alive. As each new bullet tore through flesh, Alvin mended broken arteries, trying to hold Ta-Kumsaw's blood inside him. The pain he had no time for, but Ta-Kumsaw seemed not to mind the savage injuries he took. Alvin crouched down in his hiding place between a standing tree and a fallen one, his eyes closed, watching Ta-Kumsaw only with his inward eyes, seeing his flesh from the inside out. Alvin saw none of the images that would haunt Ta-Kumsaw's legends. Alvin never even noticed as bullets sent a spray of leaf bits and chips of wood falling on him. He even took a sharp stinging bullet in the back of his left hand and hardly felt it, he was concentrating so hard on keeping Ta-Kumsaw on his feet.

But one thing Alvin saw: Beyond the edges of his vision, just out of reach, there was the Unmaker like a transparent shadow, shimmering fingers slicing through the wood. Ta-Kumsaw, him Alvin could heal. But who could heal the greenwood? Who could heal the tearing apart of tribe from tribe, Red from Red? All that Ta-Kumsaw had built was shivered apart in that single fraction of an hour, and all Alvin could do was keep a single man alive. A great man, true, a man who had changed the world, who had built something, even if it was something that in the end led to more harm and suffering; Ta-Kumsaw was a builder, and yet even as Alvin saved his life, he knew that Ta-Kumsaw's building days were done. Likely enough the Unmaker didn't begrudge Alvin his friend's life. What was Ta-Kumsaw, compared to what the Unmaker was consuming at this feast? Just like Taleswapper had said so long ago, the Unmaker could tear down, eat through, use up, and crush things faster than any one man could ever hope to build.

All the time, though Alvin scarcely noticed *where* Ta-Kumsaw was what with worrying about what was going on inside him, the Red man circled Alvin's hiding place like he was a dog tied to a tree, winding around and getting closer and closer. So when the bullets finally became too much for Alvin and the blood flowed so fast from dozens of wounds that Alvin couldn't stanch them all, it was into Alvin's sheltered place that Ta-Kumsaw fell, sprawling across Alvin's body, knocking the wind out of the boy.

Alvin scarce heard the search go on around him. He was too busy healing wounds, binding up torn flesh, connecting severed nerves and straightening broken bones. In desperation to save Ta-Kumsaw's life he opened his eyes and cut into the Red man's flesh with his own flint knife, prying bullets out and then healing up where he had cut. And all the time it was like the smoke gathered above them, making it impossible for anyone to see into the little sheltered place where the Unmaker had got Alvin holed up in hiding.

It was afternoon next day when Alvin awoke. Ta-Kumsaw lay beside him, weak and spent, but whole. Alvin was filthy and itchy and he had to void himself; gingerly he pulled himself out from under Ta-Kumsaw, who felt so light, as if he was half made of air. The smoke was gone now, but Alvin still felt invisible, walking around in broad daylight dressed like a Red man. He could hear drunken singing from the American camp near the ruins of Detroit. Stray smoke still drifted through the trees. And everywhere Alvin walked were the bodies of Red men cast like wet straw on the forest floor. It stank of death.

Alvin found a brook and drank, trying not to imagine some dead body lying in it upstream. He washed his face and hands, dipped his head into the water to cool his brain, the way he used to do at home after a hard day's work. Then he went back to wake Ta-Kumsaw and bring him here to drink.

Ta-Kumsaw was already awake. Already standing over the body of a fallen friend. His head was tipped back, his mouth open, as if he uttered a cry so deep and loud that human ears couldn't hear the sound of it, could only feel the earth trembling with the vibration of the shout. Alvin ran to him and flung his arms around him, clinging to him like the child he was, only it was Alvin doing the comforting, Alvin whispering, "You done your best, you done all that could be done."

And Ta-Kumsaw answered not at all, though his silence was an answer, too, like as if he was saying, I'm alive, which means I didn't do enough.

They walked away in the afternoon, not even bothering to conceal themselves. Some White men later woke up with hangovers, swearing they saw visions of Ta-Kumsaw and the Renegado Boy walking through the corpses of the Red army, but nobody paid them mind. And what did it matter? Ta-Kumsaw wasn't no danger to the Whites now. He'd broken against them like a great wave, but they stood against him; he thought to shatter them, but they broke him and his people into spray, and if some drops of it still clung, what did that matter? They had no power anymore. It was all spent in one brutal, futile blow.

Alvin spoke not a word to Ta-Kumsaw all the way south to the headwaters of the My-Ammy, and Ta-Kumsaw spoke nary a word to him as they dug out a canoe together. Alvin made the wood soft in the right places, so it took scarce half an hour, and another half hour to shape a good paddle. Then they dragged the canoe to the river's edge. Only with the canoe half in the water did Ta-Kumsaw stop and turn to Alvin, reach out a hand and touch his face. "If all White men were true like you, Alvin, I would never have been their enemy."

And as Alvin watched Ta-Kumsaw paddle steadily down the river out of sight, it occurred to him that it just didn't feel like Ta-Kumsaw had lost. It was as if the battle wasn't *about* Ta-Kumsaw. It was about White men, and their worthiness to have this land. They might think they won, they might think the Red man slunk away or bowed his head in defeat, but in fact it was the White man who lost, because when Ta-Kumsaw paddled down the Wobbish to the Hio, down the Hio to the Mizzipy, and crossed the fogs of the river to the other side, he was taking the land with him, the greensong; what the White man had won with so much blood and dishonesty was not the living land of the Red man, but the corpse of that land. It was decay that the White man won. It would turn to dust in his hands, Alvin knew it.

But I'm a White man, not a Red, whatever anybody might say. And rotting underfoot or not, this land is all the land we have, and our people all the people that we've got. So Alvin walked along the shore of the Wobbish, heading downriver, knowing that where the Tippy-Canoe discharged itself into the larger stream, there he'd find his pa and ma, his brothers and his sisters, all a-waiting there to find out what had happened to him in the year since he set out to become a prentice blacksmith back at Hatrack River.

19

Homecoming

Napoleon did not wear irons on his way back to France. He slept in the second cabin, and ate at table with Governor La Fayette, who was only too glad to have him. In the hot afternoons of the Atlantic crossing, La Fayette confided all his plans of revolution to Napoleon, his dearest friend, and Napoleon offered helpful advice on how to make the revolution go much faster and more effectively.

"The best thing about all these sad events," said La Fayette the day the lookout first spied the coast of Bretagne, "is that we are friends now, and the revolution is assured of success because you are a part of it. To think that once I mistrusted you, figuring you to be a tool of the King. A tool of Charles! But soon all France will know you for the hero that you are, and blame the King and Freddie for the sacking of Detroit. All that territory in the hands of Protestants and savages, while we are here to offer a better way, a truer leadership to the people of France. Ah, Napoleon, I have yearned for such a man as you through all my years of planning for democracy. All we have needed, we Feuillants, was a leader, a man who could guide us, a man who could lead France to true freedom." And La Fayette sighed and sank deeper into the cushions of his chair.

Through all this Napoleon listened with satisfaction, yes, but also sadness. For he had thought that La Fayette was immune to his charm because of some great inward strength. Now he knew that it was only a foolish amulet, that La Fayette was like any ordinary man when it came to resisting Napoleon; and now that the amulet lay buried in a mass grave outside Detroit, no doubt still chained to the moldering vertebrae of Frederic de Maurepas, Napoleon knew that he would never find his equal in this world, unless it was God himself, or Nature. There would be no man to deny him, that much was sure. So he listened to La Fayette's babbling with a wistful longing for the kind of man he once thought La Fayette could be.

The men on deck bustled and hurried and made ten thousand clumbing noises, for they were heaving in to land; Napoleon was home in France at last.

Ta-Kumsaw did not need to fear the thick fog that descended as he reached the Hio's mouth, pouring into the Mizzipy and getting lost in those stronger currents. He knew the way: west, and any shore would be his refuge, his safety, the end of his life.

For that's all that he could see ahead of him now. The land west of the Mizzipy was his brother's land, the place where White man would not come. The land itself, the water, every living thing would work to bar those White who were foolish enough to think that the Red men could be defeated again. But it was the Prophet's gifts the Red folk needed now, not those of a warrior like Ta-Kumsaw. He might be a figure of legend in the east, among fallen Reds and foolish Whites, but in the west they would know him for what he was. A failure, a bloody-handed man who led his people to destruction.

The water lapped at his canoe. He heard a redbird singing not far off. The fog grew whiter, dazzling; then broke, and the sun shone bright, blinding him. In three paddlestrokes his canoe nosed the shore, and there, to his surprise, was a man silhouetted in the late afternoon sun, standing on the bank. The man sprang down and took the end of Ta-Kumsaw's canoe and pulled it tight against the riverbank, then helped Ta-Kumsaw out of the little boat. Ta-Kumsaw couldn't see his face, his eyes were so bedazzled; but he knew who it was all the same, from the touch of the hand. And then the voice, murmuring, "Let the canoe drift away. There'll be no more crossing to the other side, my brother."

"Lolla-Wossiky," cried Ta-Kumsaw. Then he wept and knelt at his brother's feet, clinging to his knees. All the anguish, all the grief spilled out of him, while above him Lolla-Wossiky, called Tenskwa-Tawa, called the Prophet, sang to him a song of melancholy, a song about the death of bees.

Things were changed somewhat when Alvin got to town. There was a sign right out on the Wobbish Road, saying:

> *Pass by, stranger, if you can.*
> *Or hear a tale unfit for ears of man.*

Well Alvin knew the purpose of that sign. But he was no stranger here.

Or was he? As he made his way along the little spur of the road toward Vigor Church, he saw that new buildings had been put up, new houses built. Folks were living pretty much cheek-by-jowl here now, and Vigor Church was a proper town. But no one greeted him in the road, and even the children a-playing in the commons had no word for him; no doubt their parents taught them not to welcome strangers, or maybe they just were sick of hearing their fathers and older brothers telling their awful tale to whatever stranger came to call. Better not to welcome any man or woman here.

And the past year had changed Alvin. He was taller, yes, but also he knew that his walk was different, more like a Red man, unaccustomed to the feel of a White man's road beneath his feet, wishing for the greenwood song, which was near extinguished in these parts. Maybe I *am* a stranger here these days. Maybe I seen and done too much this last year to ever come back and be Alvin Junior anymore.

Even with the changes in the town, Alvin knew his way. This much hadn't changed: there was still bridges over every little stream on the roadway up to his father's house. Alvin tried to feel the old way, feel the anger of the water against him. But the black evil that once was his enemy, it hardly knew him either, now that he walked like a Red man, all at one with the living world. Never mind, thought Alvin. As the land gets tame and broken, I'll be White again in my step, and the Unmaker will find me. Just as he broke the Red man's healing hold on this land, he'll try to break me too, and if Ta-Kumsaw wasn't strong enough or Tenskwa-Tawa wise enough to stand against the old Unmaker, what will I ever do?

Just make my way, day by day, like the old hymn said. Make my way, day by day, Lord above, light and love, in my grief bring relief, fill my cup, lift me up, heal my soul, make me whole. Amen. Amen.

Cally was a-standing there right on the porch, doing nothing, like as if he was just watching out in case Alvin Junior should come home today, and maybe that's what he was doing, maybe it was. Anyway it was Cally shouted out, Cally who knew him at once despite all changes in him.

"Alvin! Ally! Alvin Junior! He's home! You're home!"

First one to come at his call, running around the house with his sleeves up and the ax still trailing from his hand, was Measure. Soon as he saw it was truly Alvin, he dropped the ax and took Alvin Junior by the shoulders, looked him over for any harm, and Alvin done the same, looking for any scars on Measure. None at all, healed proper. But

Measure found some deeper injuries in Alvin, and softly said, ''You got older, Al.'' To which Alvin had nary a thing to say, it being true, and for a moment they just stared into each other's eyes, each knowing how far down the long road of the Red man's suffering and exile the other had walked; no other White man could ever know what they knew.

Then Ma came out onto the porch and Pa out of the mill and up to the house, and oh, there was hugging and kissing and crying and laughing and shouting and silence. They didn't kill the fatted calf, but there was a young pig didn't see another sunrise. Cally ran to the brothers' farms and Armor-of-God's store and gave notice what was up, and soon all the family was gathered to greet Alvin Junior, who they knew wasn't dead but had given up hope of seeing again.

And then, as it was getting late, there came a time when Pa hid his hands in his pockets, and the other menfolk all grew still, and then the womenfolk, till Alvin nodded and said, ''I know the tale you have to tell. So tell it now, all of you, and then I'll tell you my part in it.''

They did, and he did, and there was more weeping, of grief this time instead of joy. This valley of the Wobbish was all the home they'd ever know now; it was the only way they could bear to live, all the folk who'd done murder at Tippy-Canoe, was right among each other and seeing no strangers. Where could they go and live in peace, what with having to tell all comers what it was they done? ''So we got to stay, Al Junior. But not you or Cally, you know. And maybe your apprenticeship is still a thing that we can do, what do you think?''

''Time to think of that later,'' said Ma. ''Time for all those questions later. He's home, that's all for now, you hear me? He's home, who I never thought to lay eyes on again. Thank the Lord God that he didn't make me a prophet, when I said I'd never lay eyes on my sweet little Alvin anymore.''

Alvin hugged his ma back just as hard as she hugged him. He didn't tell her that her prophecy was true. That it wasn't her sweet little Alvin who'd come home this time. Let her find that out on her own. Right now it was enough that the year was over, that he'd seen the unwinding of all the great changes, that now, however different it might be, however bitter, life could go on in a steady path, with no more breaking of the ground underfoot.

At night in his own bed, Alvin listened to the distant greensong, still warm and beautiful, still bright and hopeful even though the forest was getting so sparse, even though the future was so dim. Cause there's no fear of future in the song of life, just the ever-joyful present moment. That's all I want right now, thought Alvin. The present moment, which is good enough.

PRENTICE ALVIN

For all my good teachers, especially:

Fran Schroeder,
fourth grade, Millikin Elementary, Santa Clara, California,
for whom I wrote my first book.

Ida Huber,
tenth-grade English, Mesa High School, Arizona,
who believed in my future more than I did.

Charles Whitman,
playwriting, Brigham Young University,
who made my scripts look better than they deserved.

Norman Council,
literature, University of Utah,
for Spenser and Milton, alive.

Edward Vasta,
literature, University of Notre Dame,
for Chaucer and for friendship.

And always François.

ACKNOWLEDGMENTS

In the preparation of this volume of the Tales of Alvin Maker I have, as always, depended on others for help. For immeasurable help on the opening chapters of this book, my thanks go to the gentlefolk of the second Sycamore Hill Writers Workshop, to wit: Carol Emshwiller, Karen Joy Fowler, Gregg Keizer, James Patrick Kelly, John Kessel, Nancy Kress, Shariann Lewitt, Jack Massa, Rebecca Brown Ore, Susan Palwick, Bruce Sterling, Mark L. Van Name, Connie Willis, and Allen Wold.

Thanks also to the Utah State Institute of Fine Arts for awarding a prize to my narrative poem "Prentice Alvin and the No-Good Plow." That encouragement led to my developing the story in prose and at greater length; this is the first volume to include part of the story recounted in that poem.

For details of frontier life and crafts, I have used John Seymour's wonderful book *The Forgotten Crafts* (New York City: Knopf, 1984) and Douglass L. Brownstone's *A Field Guide to America's History* (New York City: Facts On File, Inc., 1984).

I'm grateful that Gardner Dozois has kindly allowed pieces of the Tales of Alvin Maker to appear in the pages of *Isaac Asimov's Science Fiction Magazine*, allowing it to find an audience before the books appeared.

Beth Meacham at Tor is one of that vanishing breed of editors with a golden touch; her advice is never intrusive, always wise; and (rarest editorial trait of all) she returns my telephone calls. For that alone she may be sainted.

Thanks to my writing class in Greensboro in the winter and spring of 1988 for suggestions that led to important improvements in the book; and to my sister, friend, and editorial assistant, Janice, for her work on keeping story details fresh in mind.

Thanks most of all to Kristine A. Card, who listens to me ramble through the many versions of each as-yet-unwritten book, reads the dot-matrix printouts of the early drafts, and is my second self through every page of everything I write.

CONTENTS

1

The Overseer

Let me start my history of Alvin's prenticeship where things first began to go wrong. It was a long way south, a man that Alvin had never met nor never would meet in all his life. Yet he it was who started things moving down the path that would lead to Alvin doing what the law called murder—on the very day that his prenticeship ended and he rightly became a man.

It was a place in Appalachee, in 1811, before Appalachee signed the Fugitive Slave Treaty and joined the United States. It was near the borders where Appalachee and the Crown Colonies meet, so there wasn't a White man but aspired to own a passel of Black slaves to do his work for him.

Slavery, that was a kind of alchemy for such White folk, or so they reckoned. They calculated a way of turning each bead of a Black man's sweat into gold and each moan of despair from a Black woman's throat into the sweet clear sound of a silver coin ringing on the money-changer's table. There was buying and selling of souls in that place. Yet there was nary a one of them who understood the whole price they paid for owning other folk.

Listen tight, and I'll tell you how the world looked from inside Cavil Planter's heart. But make sure the children are asleep, for this is a part of my tale that children ought not to hear, for it deals with hungers they don't understand too well, and I don't aim for this story to teach them.

Cavil Planter was a godly man, a church-going man, a tithepayer. All his slaves were baptized and given Christian names as soon as they understood enough English to be taught the gospel. He forbade them to practice their dark arts—he never allowed them to slaughter so much as a chicken themselves, lest they convert such an innocent act into a sacrifice to some hideous god. In all ways Cavil Planter served the Lord as best he could.

So, how was the poor man rewarded for his righteousness? His wife, Dolores, she was beset with terrible aches and pains, her wrists and fingers twisting like an old woman's. By the time she was twenty-five she went to sleep most nights crying, so that Cavil could not bear to share the room with her.

He tried to help her. Packs of cold water, soaks of hot water, powders and potions, spending more than he could afford on those charlatan doctors with their degrees from the University of Camelot, and bringing in an endless parade of preachers with their eternal prayers and priests with their hocum pocus incantations. All of it accomplished nigh onto nothing. Every night he had to lie there listening to her cry until she whimpered, whimper until her breath became a steady in and out, whining just a little on the out-breath, a faint little wisp of pain.

It like to drove Cavil mad with pity and rage and despair. For months on end it seemed to him that he never slept at all. Work all day, then at night lie there praying for relief. If not for her, then for him.

It was Dolores herself who gave him peace at night. "You have work to do each day, Cavil, and can't do it unless you sleep. I can't keep silent, and you can't bear to hear me. Please—sleep in another room."

Cavil offered to stay anyway. "I'm your husband, I belong here"— he said it, but she knew better.

"Go," she said. She even raised her voice. "Go!"

So he went, feeling ashamed of how relieved he felt. He slept that night without interruption, a whole five hours until dawn, slept well for the first time in months, perhaps years—and arose in the morning consumed with guilt for not keeping his proper place beside his wife.

In due time, though, Cavil Planter became accustomed to sleeping alone. He visited his wife often, morning and night. They took meals together, Cavil sitting on a chair in her room, his food on a small side table, Dolores lying in bed as a Black woman carefully spooned food into her mouth while her hands sprawled on the bedsheets like dead crabs.

Even sleeping in another room, Cavil wasn't free of torment. There would be no babies. There would be no sons to raise up to inherit Cavil's fine plantation. There would be no daughters to give away in magnificent weddings. The ballroom downstairs—when he brought Dolores into the fine new house he had built for her, he had said, "Our daughters will meet their beaux in this ballroom, and first touch their hands, the way our hands first touched in your father's house." Now

Dolores never saw the ballroom. She came downstairs only on Sundays to go to church and on those rare days when new slaves were purchased, so she could see to their baptism.

Everyone saw her on such occasions, and admired them both for their courage and faith in adversity. But the admiration of his neighbors was scant comfort when Cavil surveyed the ruins of his dreams. All that he prayed for—it's as if the Lord wrote down the list and then in the margin noted ''no, no, no'' on every line.

The disappointments might have embittered a man of weaker faith. But Cavil Planter was a godly, upright man, and whenever he had the faintest thought that God might have treated him badly, he stopped whatever he was doing and pulled the small psaltery from his pocket and whispered aloud the words of the wise man.

> *In thee, O Lord, do I put my trust;*
> *Bow down thine ear to me;*
> *Be thou my strong rock.*

He concentrated his mind firmly, and the doubts and resentments quickly fled. The Lord was with Cavil Planter, even in his tribulations.

Until the morning he was reading in Genesis and he came upon the first two verses of chapter 16.

> *Now Sarai Abram's wife bore him no children: and she had*
> *an handmaid, an Egyptian, whose name was Hagar. And Sarai*
> *said unto Abram, Behold now, the Lord hath restrained me*
> *from bearing: I pray thee, go in unto my maid: it may be that*
> *I may obtain children by her.*

At that moment the thought came into his mind, Abraham was a righteous man, and so am I. Abraham's wife bore him no children, and mine likewise has no hope. There was an African slavewoman in their household, as there are such women in mine. Why shouldn't I do as Abraham did, and father children by one of these?

The moment the thought came into his head, he shuddered in horror. He'd heard gossip of White Spaniards and French and Portuguese in the jungle islands to the south who lived openly with Black women— truly they were the lowest kind of creature, like men who do with beasts. Besides, how could a child of a Black woman ever be an heir to him? A mix-up boy could no more take possession of an Appalachee plantation than fly. Cavil just put the thought right out of his mind.

But as he sat at breakfast with his wife, the thought came back. He found himself watching the Black woman who fed his wife. Like Hagar, this woman is Egyptian, isn't she? He noticed how her body twisted lithely at the waist as she bore the spoon from tray to mouth. Noticed how as she leaned forward to hold the cup to the frail woman's lips, the servant's breasts swung down to press against her blouse. Noticed how her gentle fingers brushed crumbs and drops from Dolores's lips. He thought of those fingers touching *him*, and trembled slightly. Yet it felt like an earthquake inside him.

He rushed from the room with hardly a word. Outside the house, he clutched his psaltery.

> *Wash me thoroughly from mine iniquity,*
> *And cleanse me from my sin.*
> *For I acknowledge my transgressions:*
> *And my sin is ever before me.*

Yet even as he whispered these words, he looked up and saw the field women washing themselves at the trough. There was the young girl he had bought only a few days before, six hundred dollars even though she was small, since she was probably breeding stock. So fresh from the boat she was that she hadn't learned a speck of Christian modesty. She stood there naked as a snake, leaning over the trough, pouring cups of water over her head and down her back.

Cavil stood transfixed, watching her. What had only been a brief thought of evil in his wife's bedroom now became a trance of lust. He had never seen anything so graceful as her blue-black thighs sliding against each other, so inviting as her shiver when the water ran down her body.

Was this the answer to his fervent psalm? Was the Lord telling him that it was indeed with him as it had been with Abraham?

Just as likely it was witchery. Who knew what knacks these fresh-from-Africa Blacks mights have? She knows I'm here a-watching, and she's tempting me. These Blacks are truly the devil's own children, to excite such evil thoughts in me.

He tore his gaze from the new girl and turned away, hiding his burning eyes in the words of the book. Only somehow the page had turned—when did he turn it?—and he found himself reading in the Song of Solomon.

> *Thy two breasts are like two young roes*
> *That are twins, which feed among the lilies.*

"God help me," he whispered. "Take this spell from me."

Day after day he whispered the same prayer, yet day after day he found himself watching his slavewomen with desire, particularly that newbought girl. Why was it God seemed to be paying him no mind? Hadn't he always been a righteous man? Wasn't he good to his wife? Wasn't he honest in business? Didn't he pay tithes and offerings? Didn't he treat his slaves and horses well? Why didn't the Lord God of Heaven protect him and take this Black spell from him?

Yet even when he prayed, his very confessions became evil imaginings. O Lord, forgive me for thinking of my newbought girl standing in the door of my bedroom, weeping at the caning she got from the overseer. Forgive me for imagining myself laying her on my own bed and lifting her skirts to anoint them with a balm so powerful the welts on her thighs and buttocks disappear before my eyes and she begins to giggle softly and writhe slowly on the sheets and look over her shoulder at me, smiling, and then she turns over and reaches out to me and—O Lord, forgive me, save me!

Whenever this happened, though, he couldn't help but wonder—why do such thoughts come to me even when I pray? Maybe I'm as righteous as Abraham; maybe it's the Lord who sent these desires to me. Didn't I first think of this while I was reading scripture? The Lord can work miracles—what if I went in unto the newbought girl and she conceived, and the Lord worked a miracle and the baby was born White? All things are possible to God.

This thought was both wonderful and terrible. If only it were true! Yet Abraham heard the voice of God, so he never had to wonder about what God might want of him. God never said a word to Cavil Planter.

And why not? Why didn't God just tell him right out? Take the girl, she's yours! Or, Touch her not, she is forbidden! Just let me hear your voice, Lord, so I'll know what to do!

> *O Lord my rock;*
> *Unto thee will I cry,*
> *Be not silent to me,*
> *Lest, if thou be silent to me,*
> *I become like them*
> *That go down into the pit.*

On a certain day in 1810 that prayer was answered.

Cavil was kneeling in the curing shed, which was mostly empty, seeing how last year's burly crop was long since sold and this year's was still a-greening in the field. He'd been wrestling in prayer and confession and dark imaginings until at last he cried out, "Is there no one to hear my prayer?"

"Oh, I hear you right enough," said a stern voice.

Cavil was terrified at first, fearing that some stranger—his overseer, or a neighbor—had overheard some terrible confession. But when he looked, he saw that it wasn't anyone he knew. Still, he knew at once *what* the man was. From the strength in his arms, his sun-browned face, and his open shirt—no jacket at all—he knew the man was no gentleman. But he was no White trash, either, nor a tradesman. The stern look in his face, the coldness of his eye, the tension in his muscles like a spring tight-bound in a steel trap: He was plainly one of those men whose whip and iron will keep discipline among the Black fieldworkers. An overseer. Only he was stronger and more dangerous than any overseer Cavil had ever seen. He knew at once that *this* overseer would get every ounce of work from the lazy apes who tried to avoid work in the fields. He knew that whoever's plantation was run by *this* overseer would surely prosper. But Cavil also knew that he would never dare to hire such a man, for this overseer was so strong that Cavil would soon forget who was man and who was master.

"Many have called me their master," said the stranger. "I knew that you would recognize me at once for what I am."

How had the man known the words that Cavil thought in the hidden reaches of his mind? "Then you *are* an overseer?"

"Just as there was one who was once called, not *a* master, but simply Master, so am I not *an* overseer, but *the* Overseer."

"Why did you come here?"

"Because you called for me."

"How could I call for you, when I never saw you before in my life?"

"If you call for the unseen, Cavil Planter, then of course you will see what you never saw before."

Only now did Cavil fully understand what sort of vision it was he saw, there in his own burly curing shed. A man whom many called their master, come in answer to his prayer.

"Lord Jesus!" cried Cavil.

At once the Overseer recoiled, putting up his hand as if to fend off Cavil's words. "It is forbidden for any man to call me by that name!" he cried.

In terror, Cavil bowed his head to the dirt. "Forgive me, Overseer! But if I am unworthy to say your name, how is it I can look upon your face? Or am I doomed to die today, unforgiven for my sins?"

"Woe unto you, fool," said the Overseer. "Do you really believe that you have looked upon my *face*?"

Cavil lifted his head and looked at the man. "I see your eyes even now, looking down at me."

"You see the face that you invented for me in your own mind, the body conjured out of your own imagination. Your feeble wits could never comprehend what you saw, if you saw what I truly am. So your sanity protects itself by devising its own mask to put upon me. If you see me as an Overseer, it is because that is the guise you recognize as having the greatness and power I possess. It is the form that you at once love and fear, the shape that makes you worship and recoil. I have been called by many names. Angel of Light and Walking Man, Sudden Stranger and Bright Visitor, Hidden One and Lion of War, Unmaker of Iron and Water-bearer. Today you have called me Overseer, and so, to you, that is my name."

"Can I ever know your true name, or see your true face, Overseer?"

The Overseer's face became dark and terrible, and he opened his mouth as if to howl. "Only one soul alive in all the world has ever seen my true shape, and that one will surely die!"

The mighty words came like dry thunder and shook Cavil Planter to his very root, so that he gripped the dirt of the shed floor lest he fly off into the air like dust whipped away in the wind before the storm. "Do not strike me dead for my impertinence!" cried Cavil.

The Overseer's answer came gentle as morning sunlight. "Strike you dead? How could I, when you are a man I have chosen to receive my most secret teachings, a gospel unknown to priest or minister."

"Me?"

"Already I have been teaching you, and you understood. I know you desire to do as I command. But you lack faith. You are not yet completely mine."

Cavil's heart leapt within him. Could it be that the Overseer meant to give him what he gave to Abraham? "Overseer, I am unworthy."

"Of course you are unworthy. None is worthy of me, no, not one soul upon this earth. But still, if you obey, you may find favor in my eyes."

Oh, he will! cried Cavil in his heart, yes, he will give me the woman! "Whatever you command, Overseer."

"Do you think I would give you Hagar because of your foolish lust and your hunger for a child? There is a greater purpose. These Black people are surely the sons and daughters of God, but in Africa they lived under the power of the devil. That terrible destroyer has polluted their blood—why else do you think they are Black? I can never save them as long as each generation is born pure Black, for then the devil owns them. How can I reclaim them as my own, unless you help me?"

"Will my child be born White then, if I take the girl?"

"What matters to me is that the child will not be born pure Black. Do you understand what I desire of you? Not one Ishmael, but many children; not one Hagar, but many women."

Cavil hardly dared to name the secretest desire of his heart. "All of them?"

"I give them to you, Cavil Planter. This evil generation is your property. With diligence, you can prepare another generation that will belong to me."

"I will, Overseer!"

"You must tell no one that you saw me. I speak only to those whose desires already turn toward me and my works, the ones who already thirst for the water I bring."

"I'll speak no word to any man, Overseer!"

"Obey me, Cavil Planter, and I promise that at the end of your life you will meet me again and know me for what I truly am. In that moment I will say to you, You are mine, Cavil Planter. Come and be my true slave forever."

"Gladly!" cried Cavil. "Gladly! Gladly!"

He flung out his arms and embraced the Overseer's legs. But where he should have touched the visitor, there was nothing. He had vanished.

From that night on, Cavil Planter's slavewomen had no peace. As Cavil had them brought to him by night, he tried to treat them with the strength and mastery he had seen in the face of the fearful Overseer. They must look at me and see His face, thought Cavil, and it's sure they did.

The first one he took unto himself was a certain newbought slavegirl who had scarce a word of English. She cried out in terror until he raised the welts upon her that he had seen in his dreams. Then, whimpering, she permitted him to do as the Overseer had commanded. For a moment, that first time, he thought her whimpering was like Dolores's voice when she wept so quietly in bed, and he felt the same deep pity that he had felt for his beloved wife. Almost he reached out tenderly to the girl as he had once reached out to comfort Dolores. But then he remembered the face of the Overseer and thought, this Black girl is His enemy; she is my property. As surely as a man must plow and plant the land God gave to him, I must not let this Black womb lie fallow.

Hagar, he called her that first night. You do not understand how I am blessing you.

In the morning he looked in the mirror and saw something new in his face. A kind of fierceness. A kind of terrible hidden strength. Ah, thought Cavil, no one ever saw what I truly am, not even me. Only now do I discover that what the Overseer is, I also am.

He never felt another moment's pity as he went about his nightly work. Ashen cane in hand, he went to the women's cabin and pointed at the one who was to come with him. If any hung back, she learned from the cane how much reluctance cost. If any other Black, man or woman, spoke in protest, the next day Cavil saw to it that the Overseer took it out of them in blood. No White guessed and no Black dared accuse him.

The newbought girl, his Hagar, was first to conceive. He watched her with pride as her belly began to grow. Cavil knew then that the Overseer had truly chosen him, and he took fierce joy in having such mastery. There would be a child, *his* child. And already the next step was clear to him. If his White blood was to save as many Black souls as possible, then he could not keep his mix-up babes at home, could he? He would sell them south, each to a different buyer, to a different city, and then trust the Overseer to see that they in turn grew up and spread his seed throughout all the unfortunate Black race.

And each morning he watched his wife eat her breakfast. "Cavil, my love," she said one day, "is something wrong? There's something darker in your face, a look of—rage, perhaps, or cruelty. Have you quarreled with someone? I would not speak except you—you frighten me."

Tenderly he patted his wife's twisted hand as the Black woman watched him under heavy-lidded eyes. "I have no anger against any man or woman," said Cavil gently. "And what you call cruelty is nothing more than mastery. Ah, Dolores, how can you look in my face and call me cruel?"

She wept. "Forgive me," she cried. "I imagined it. You, the kindest man I've ever heard of—the devil put such a vision in my mind, I know it. The devil can give false visions, you know, but only the wicked are deceived. Forgive me for my wickedness, Husband!"

He forgave her, but she wouldn't stop her weeping until he had sent for the priest. No wonder the Lord chose only men to be his prophets. Women were too weak and compassionate to do the work of the Overseer.

That's how it began. That was the first footfall on this dark and terrible path. Nor Alvin nor Peggy ever knew this tale until I found it out and told them both long after, and they recognized at once that it was the start of all.

But I don't want you to think this was the whole cause of all the evil that befell, for it wasn't. There were other choices made, other mistakes, other lies and other willing cruelties done. A man might have plenty of help finding the short path to hell, but no one else can make him set foot upon it.

2

Runaway

Peggy woke up in the morning with a dream of Alvin Miller filling her
heart with all kinds of terrible desires. She wanted to run from that boy,
and to stay and wait for him; to forget she knew him, and to watch him
always. She lay there on her bed with her eyes almost closed, watching the
grey dawnlight steal into the attic room where she slept. I'm holding
something, she noticed. The corners of it clenched into her hands so
tight that when she let go her palm hurt like she been stung. But she
wasn't stung. It was just the box where she kept Alvin's birth caul. Or
maybe, thought Peggy, maybe she *had* been stung, stung deep, and only
just now did she feel the pain of it.

Peggy wanted to throw that box just as far from her as she could,
bury it deep and forget where she buried it, drown it underwater and
pile rocks on so it wouldn't float.

Oh, but I don't mean that, she said silently, I'm sorry for thinking
such a thing, I'm plain sorry, but he's coming now, after all these years
he's coming to Hatrack River and he won't be the boy I seen in all the
paths of his future, he won't be the man I see him turning into. No,
he's still just a boy, just eleven years old. He's seen him enough of life
that somewise maybe he's a man inside, he's seen grief and pain enough
for someone five times his age, but it's still an eleven-year-old boy he'll
be when he walks into this town.

And I don't want to see no eleven-year-old Alvin come here. He'll
be looking for me, right enough. He knows who I am, though he never
saw me since he was two weeks old. He knows I saw his future on the
rainy dark day when he was born, and so he'll come, and he'll say to
me, "Peggy, I know you're a torch, and I know you wrote in Tale-

swapper's book that I'm to be a Maker. So tell me what I'm supposed
to be.'' Peggy knew just what he'd say, and every way he might choose
to say it—hadn't she seen it a hundred times, a thousand times? And
she'd teach him and he'd become a great man, a true Maker, and—

And then one day, when he's a handsome figure of twenty-one and
I'm a sharp-tongued spinster of twenty-six he'll feel so *grateful* to me,
so *obligated*, that he'll propose himself for marriage to me as his
bounden duty. And I, being lovesick all these years, full of dreams of
what he'll do and what we'll be together, I'll say yes, and saddle him
with a wife he wished he didn't have to marry, and his eyes will hunger
for other women all the days of our lives together—

Peggy wished, oh she wished so deep, that she didn't know for certain
things would be that way. But Peggy was a torch right enough, the
strongest torch she'd ever heard of, stronger even than the folk hereabouts in Hatrack River ever guessed.

She sat up in bed and did not throw the box or hide it or break it or
bury it. She opened it. Inside lay the last scrap of Alvin's birth caul, as
dry and white as paper ash in a cold hearth. Eleven years ago when
Peggy's mama served as midwife to pull baby Alvin out of the well of
life, and Alvin first sucked for breath in the damp air of Papa's Hatrack
River roadhouse, Peggy peeled that thin and bloody caul from the baby's
face so he could breathe. Alvin, the seventh son of a seventh son, and
the thirteenth child—Peggy saw at once what the paths of his life would
be. Death, that was where he was headed, death from a hundred different
accidents in a world that seemed bent on killing him even before he
was hardly alive.

She was Little Peggy then, a girl of five, but she'd been torching for
two years already, and in that time she never did a seeing on a birthing
child who had so many paths to death. Peggy searched up all the paths
of his life, and found in all of them but one single way that boy could
live to be a man.

That was if she kept that birth caul, and watched him from afar off,
and whenever she saw death reaching out to take him, she'd use that
caul. Take just a pinch of it and grind it between her fingers and whisper
what had to happen, see it in her mind. And it would happen just the
way she said. Hadn't she held him up from drowning? Saved him from
a wallowing buffalo? Caught him from sliding off a roof? She even split
a roof beam once, when it was like to fall from fifty feet up and squash
him on the floor of a half-built church; she split that beam neat as you
please, so it fell on one side of him and the other, with just a space for
him to stand there in between. And a hundred other times when she

acted so early that nobody ever even guessed his life had been saved, even those times she saved him, using the caul.

How did it work? She hardly knew. Except that it was his own power she was using, the gift born right in him. Over the years he'd learned somewhat about his knack for making things and shaping them and holding them together and splitting them apart. Finally this last year, all caught up in the wars between Red men and White, he'd taken charge of saving his own life, so she hardly had to do a thing to save him anymore. Good thing, too. There wasn't much of that caul left.

She closed the lid of the box. I don't want to see him, thought Peggy. I don't want to know any more about him.

But her fingers opened that lid right back up, cause of course she had to know. She'd lived half her life, it seemed like, touching that caul and searching for his heartfire away far off in the northwest Wobbish country, in the town of Vigor Church, seeing how he was doing, looking up the paths of his future to see what danger lay in ambush. And when she was sure he was safe, she'd look farther ahead, and see him coming back one day to Hatrack River, where he was born, coming back and looking into her face and saying, it was you who saved me all those times, you who saw I was a Maker back afore a living soul thought such a thing was possible. And then she'd watch him learn the great depths of his power, the work he had to do, the crystal city he had to build; she saw him sire babies on her, and saw him touch the nursing infants she held in her arms; she saw the ones they buried and the ones that lived; and last of all she saw him—

Tears came down her face. I don't want to know, she said. I don't want to know all the roads of the future. Other girls can dream of love, the joys of marriage, of being mothers to strong healthy babes; but all my dreams have dying in them, too, and pain, and fear, because my dreams are true dreams, I know more than a body can know and still have any hope inside her soul.

Yet Peggy *did* hope. Yes sir, you can be sure of it—she still clung to a kind of desperate hope, because even knowing what's likely to come down the pathways of a body's life, she still caught her some glimpses, some clear plain visions of certain days, certain hours, certain passing moments of joy so great it was worth the grief just to get there.

Trouble was those glimpses were so rare and small in the spreading futures of Alvin's life that she couldn't find a road that led there. All the pathways she could find easily, the plain ones, the ones most likely to become real, those all led to Alvin wedding her without love, out of gratitude and duty, a miserable marriage. Like the story of Leah in the Bible, whose beautiful husband Jacob hated her even though she loved him dear and bore him more babies than his other wives and would've died for him if he'd as much as asked her.

It's an evil thing God did to women, thought Peggy, to make us hanker after husband and children till it leads us to a life of sacrifice and misery and grief. Was Eve's sin so terrible, that God should curse all women with that mighty curse? You will groan and bear children, said Almighty Merciful God. You will be eager for your husband, and he will rule over you.

That was what was burning in her—eagerness for her husband. Even though he was only an eleven-year-old boy who was looking, not for a wife, but for a teacher. He may be just a boy, thought Peggy, but I'm a woman, and I've seen the man he'll be, and I yearn for him. She pressed one hand against her breast; it felt so large and soft, still somewhat out of place on her body, which used to be all sticks and corners like a shanty cabin, and now was softening, like a calf being fattened up for the return of the prodigal.

She shuddered, thinking what happened to the fatted calf, and once again touched the caul, and *looked*:

In the distant town of Vigor Church, young Alvin was breakfasting his last morning at his mother's table. The pack he was to carry on his journey to Hatrack River lay on the floor beside the table. His mother's tears flowed undisguised across her cheeks. The boy loved his mother, but never for a moment did he feel sorry to be leaving. His home was a dark place now, stained with too much innocent blood for him to hanker to stay. He was eager to be off, to start his life as a prentice boy to the blacksmith of Hatrack River, and to find the torch girl who saved his life when he was born. He couldn't eat another bite. He pushed back from the table, stood up, kissed his mama—

Peggy let go the caul and closed the lid of the box as tight and quick as if she was trying to catch a fly inside.

Coming to find me. Coming to start a life of misery together. Go ahead and cry, Faith Miller, but not because your little boy Alvin's on his way east. You cry for me, the woman whose life your boy will wreck. You shed your tears for one more woman's lonely pain.

Peggy shuddered, shook off the bleak mood of the grey dawn, and dressed herself quickly, ducking her head to avoid the low sloping crossbeams of the attic roof. Over the years she'd learned ways to push thoughts of Alvin Miller Junior clean out of her mind, long enough to do her duty as daughter in her parents' household and as torch for the people of the country hereabouts. She could go hours without thinking about that boy, when she set her mind to it. And though it was harder now, knowing he was about to set his foot on the road toward her that very morning, she still put thoughts of him aside.

Peggy opened the curtain of the south-facing window and sat before it, leaning on the sill. She looked out over the forest that still stretched from the roadhouse, down the Hatrack River and on to the Hio, with only a few pig farms here and there to block the way. Of course she couldn't *see* the Hio, not that many miles from here, not even in the clear cool air of springtime. But what her natural eyes couldn't see, the burning torch in her could find easy enough. To see the Hio, she had only to search for a far-off heartfire, then slip herself inside that fellow's flame, and see out of his eyes as easy as she could see out of her own. And once there, once she had ahold of someone's heartfire, she could see other things, too, not just what he saw, but what he thought and felt and wished for. And even more: Flickering away in the brightest parts of the flame, often hidden by all the noise of the fellow's present thought and wishes, she could see the paths ahead of him, the choices coming to him, the life he'd make for himself if he chose this or that or another way in the hours and days to come.

Peggy could see so much in other people's heartfires that she hardly was acquainted with her own.

She thought of herself sometimes like that lone lookout boy at the tip-top of a ship's mast. Not that she ever saw her a ship in her whole life, except the rafts on the Hio and one time a canal boat on the Irrakwa Canal. But she read some books, as many as ever she could get Doctor Whitley Physicker to bring back to her from his visits to Dekane. So she knew about the lookout on the mast. Clinging to the rigging, arms half-wrapped in the lines so he didn't fall if there was a sudden roll or pitch of the boat, or a gust of wind unlooked-for; froze blue in winter, burnt red in summer; and nothing to do all day, all the long long hours of his watch, but look out onto the empty blue ocean. If it was a pirate ship, the lookout watched for victims' sails. If it was a whaler, he looked for blows and breaches. Most ships, he just looked for land, for shoals, for hidden sand bars; looked for pirates or some sworn enemy of his nation's flag.

Most days he never saw a thing, not a thing, just waves and dipping sea birds and fluffy clouds.

I am on a lookout perch, thought Peggy. Sent up aloft some sixteen years ago the day I was born, and kept here ever since, never once let down below, never once allowed to rest within the narrow bunkspace of the lowest deck, never once allowed to so much as close a hatch over my head or a door behind my back. Always, always I'm on watch, looking far and near. And because it isn't my natural eyes I look through, I can't shut them, not even in sleep.

No escape from it at all. Sitting here in the attic, she could see without trying:

Mother, known to others as Old Peg Guester, known to herself as Margaret, cooking in the kitchen for the slew of guests due in for one of her suppers. Not like she has any particular knack for cooking, either, so kitchen work is hard, she isn't like Gertie Smith who can make salt pork taste a hundred different ways on a hundred different days. Peg Guester's knack is in womenstuff, midwifery and house hexes, but to make a good inn takes good food and now Oldpappy's gone she has to cook, so she thinks only of the kitchen and couldn't hardly stand interruption, least of all from her daughter who mopes around the house and hardly speaks at all and by and large that girl is the most unpleasant, ill-favored child even though she started out so sweet and promising, everything in life turns sour somehow. . . .

Oh, that was such a joy, to know how little your own mama cared for you. Never mind that Peggy also knew the fierce devotion that her mama had. Knowing that a portion of love abides in your mama's heart doesn't take away but half the sting of knowing her dislike for you as well.

And Papa, known to others as Horace Guester, keeper of the Hatrack River Roadhouse. A jolly fellow, Papa was, even now out in the dooryard telling tales to a guest who was having trouble getting away from the inn. He and Papa always seemed to have something more to talk about, and oh, that guest, a circuit lawyer from up Cleveland way, he fancied Horace Guester was just about the finest most upstanding citizen he ever met, if all folks was as good-hearted as old Horace there'd be no more crime and no more lawyering in the upriver Hio country. Everybody felt that way. Everybody loved old Horace Guester.

But his daughter, Peggy the torch, she saw into his heartfire and knew how he felt about it. He saw those folks a-smiling at him and he said to himself, if they knew what I really was they'd spit in the road at my feet and walk away and forget they ever saw my face or knew my name.

Peggy sat there in her attic room and all the heartfires glowed, all of them in town. Her parents' most, cause she knew them best; the lodgers who stayed in the roadhouse; and then the people of the town.

Makepeace Smith and his wife Gertie and their three snot-nose children planning devilment when they weren't puking or piddling—Peggy saw Makepeace's pleasure in the shaping of iron, his loathing for his own children, his disappointment as his wife changed from a fascinating unattainable vision of beauty into a stringy-haired hag who screamed at the children first and then came to use the same voice to scream at Makepeace.

Pauley Wiseman, the sheriff, loving to make folks a-scared of him; Whitley Physicker, angry at himself because his medicine didn't work more than half the time, and every week he saw death he couldn't do a thing about. New folks, old folks, farmers and professionals, she saw through their eyes and into their hearts. She saw the marriage beds that were cold at night and the adulteries kept secret in guilty hearts. She saw the thievery of trusted clerks and friends and servants, and the honorable hearts inside many who were despised and looked down on.

She saw it all, and said nothing. Kept her mouth shut. Talked to no one. Cause she wasn't going to lie. She promised years before that she'd never lie, and kept her word by keeping still.

Other folks didn't have her problem. They could talk and tell the truth. But Peggy couldn't tell the truth. She knew these folks too well. She knew what they all were scared of, what they all wanted, what they all had done that they'd kill her or theirself if they once got a notion that she knew. Even the ones who never done a bad thing, they'd be so ashamed to think she knew their secret dreams or private craziness. So she never could speak frankly to these folks, or something would slip out, not even a word maybe, it might be just the way she turned her head, the way she sidestepped some line of talk, and they'd know that she knew, or just fear that she knew, or just fear. Just fear alone, without even naming what it was, and it could undo them, some of them, the weakest of them.

She was a lookout all the time, alone atop the mast, hanging to the lines, seeing more than she ever wanted to, and never getting even a minute to herself.

When it wasn't some baby being born, so she had to go and do a seeing, then it was some folks in trouble somewhere that had to be helped. It didn't do her no good to sleep, neither. She never slept all the way. Always a part of her was looking, and saw the fire burning, saw it flash.

Like now. Now this very moment, as she looked out over the forest, there it was. A heartfire burning ever so far off.

She swung herself close in—not her body, of course, her flesh stayed right there in the attic—but being a torch she knew how to look *close* at far-off heartfires.

It was a young woman. No, a girl, even younger than herself. And strange inside, so she knew right off this girl first spoke a language that wasn't English, even though she spoke and thought in English now. It made her thoughts all twisty and queer. But some things run deeper than

the tracks that words leave in your brain; Little Peggy didn't need no
help understanding that baby the girl held in her arms, and the way she
stood at the riverbank knowing she would die, and what a horror waited
for her back at the plantation, and what she'd done last night to get
away.

See the sun there, three fingers over the trees. This runaway Black
slavegirl and her little bastard half-White boy-baby, see them standing
on the shore of the Hio, half hid up in trees and bushes, watching as
the White men pole them rafts on down. She a-scared, she know them
dogs can't find her but very soon they get them the runaway finder,
very worse thing, and how she ever cross that river with this boy-baby?

She cotch her a terrible thought: I leave this boy-baby, I hide him in
this rotten log, I swim and steal the boat and I come back to here. That
do the job, yes sir.

But then this Black girl who nobody never teach how to be a mama,
she know a good mama don't leave this baby who still gots to suck
two-hand times a day. She whisper, Good mama don't leave a little boy-
baby where old fox or weasel or badger come and nibble off little parts
and kill him dead. No ma'am not me.

So she just set down here a-hold of this baby, and watch the river
flow on, might as well be the seashore cause she never get across.

Maybe some White folks help her? Here on the Appalachee shore the
White folk hang them as help a slavegirl run away. But this runaway
Black slavegirl hear stories on the plantation, about Whites who say
nobody better be own by nobody else. Who say this Black girl better
have that same right like the White lady, she say no to any man be not
her true husband. Who say this Black girl better can keep her baby, not
let them White boss promise he sell it on weaning day, they send this
boy-baby to grow up into a house slave in Drydenshire, kiss a White
man's feet if he say boo.

"Oh, your baby is so *lucky*," they say to this slavegirl. "He'll grow
up in a fine lord's mansion in the Crown Colonies, where they still have
a king—he might even *see* the King someday."

She don't say nothing, but she laugh inside. She don't set no store to
see a king. Her pa a king back in Africa, and they shoot him dead.
Them Portuguese slavers show her what it mean to be a king—it mean
you die quick like everybody, and spill blood red like everybody, and
cry out loud in pain and scared—oh, *fine* to be a king, and *fine* to see
one. Do them White folk believe this lie?

I don't believe them. I say I believe them but I lie. I never let them
take him my boy-baby. A king grandson him, and I tell him every day

he growing up. When he the tall king, ain't nobody hit him with the stick or he hit them back, and nobody take his woman, spread her like a slaughterpig and stick this half-White baby in her but he can't do nothing, he sit in his cabin and cry. No ma'am, no sir.

So she do the forbidden evil ugly bad thing. She steal two candles and hot them all soft by the cookfire. She mash them like dough, she mash in milk from her own teat after boy-baby suck, and she mash some of her spit in the wax too, and then she push it and poke it and roll it in ash till she see a poppet shape like Black slavegirl. Her very own self.

Then she hide this Black slavegirl poppet and she go to Fat Fox and beg him feathers off that big old blackbird he cotch him.

"Black slavegirl don't need her no feathers," say Fat Fox.

"I make a boogy for my boy-baby," she say.

Fat Fox laugh, he know she lie. "Ain't no blackfeather boogy. I never heared of such a thing."

Black slavegirl, she say, "My papa king in Umbawana. I know all secret thing."

Fat Fox shake his head, he laugh, he laugh. "What do you know, anyway? You can't even talk English. I'll give you all the blackbird feathers you want, but when that baby stops sucking you come to me and I'll give you another one, all Black this time."

She hate Fat Fox like White Boss, but he got him blackbird feathers so she say, "Yes sir."

Two hands she fill up with feathers. She laugh inside. She far away and dead before Fat Fox never put him no baby in her.

She cover Black slavegirl poppet with feathers till she little girl-shape bird. Very strong thing, this poppet with her own milk and spit in it, blackbird feathers on. Very strong, suck all her life out, but boy-baby, he never kiss no White Boss feet, White Boss never lay no lash on him.

Dark night, moon not showing yet. She slip out her cabin. Boy-baby suck so he make no sound. She tie that baby to her teat so he don't fall. She toss that poppet on the fire. Then all the power of the feather come out, burning, burning, burning. She feel this fire pour into her. She spread her wings, oh so wide, spread them, flap like she see that big old blackbird flap. She rise up into the air, high up in that dark night, she rise and fly, far away north she fly, and when that moon he come up, she keep him at her right hand so she get this boy-baby to land where White say Black girl never slave, half-White boy-baby never slave.

Come morning and the sun and she don't fly no more. Oh, like dying, like dying she think, walking her feet on the ground. That bird with her wing broke, she pray for Fat Fox to find her, she know that now. After you fly, make you sad to walk, hurt you bad to walk, like a slave with chains, that dirt under your feet.

But she walk with that boy-baby all morning and now she come to this wide river. This close I come, say runaway Black slavegirl. I fly this far, yes I fly this river across. But that sun come up and I come down before this river. Now I never cross, old finder find me somehow, whup me half dead, take my boy-baby, sell him south.

Not me. I trick them. I die first.

No, I die second.

Other folks could argue about whether slavery was a mortal sin or just a quaint custom. Other folks could bicker on about how Emancipationists were too crazy to put up with even though slavery was a real bad thing. Other folks could look at Blacks and feel sorry for them but still be somewhat glad they were mostly in Africa or in the Crown Colonies or in Canada or somewhere else far and gone. Peggy couldn't afford the luxury of having opinions on the subject. All she knew was that no heartfire ever was in such pain as the soul of a Black who lived in the thin dark shadow of the lash.

Peggy leaned out the attic window, called out: "Papa!"

He strode out from the front of the house, walked into the road, where he could look up and see her window. "You call me, Peggy?"

She just looked at him, said naught, and that was all the signal that he needed. He good-byed and fare-thee-welled that guest so fast the poor old coot was halfway into the main part of town before he knew what hit him. Pa was already inside and up the stairs.

"A girl with a babe," she told him. "On the far side of the Hio, scared and thinking of killing herself if she's caught."

"How far along the Hio?"

"Just down from the Hatrack Mouth, near as I can guess. Papa, I'm coming with you."

"No you're not."

"Yes I am, Papa. You'll never find her, not you nor ten more like you. She's too scared of White men, and she's got cause."

Papa looked at her, unsure what to do. He'd never let her come before, but usually it was Black men what ran off. But then, usually she found them this side the Hio, lost and scared, so it was safer. Crossing into Appalachee, it was prison for sure if they were caught helping a Black escape. Prison if it wasn't a quick rope on a tree. Emancipationists didn't fare well south of the Hio, and still less the kind of Emancipa-

tionist who helped run-off bucks and ewes and pickaninnies get north
to French country up in Canada.

"Too dangerous across the river," he said.

"All the more reason you need me. To find her, and to spot if anyone
else happens along."

"Your mother would kill me if she knew I was taking you."

"Then I'll leave now, out the back."

"Tell her you're going to visit Mrs. Smith—"

"I'll tell her nothing or I'll tell the truth, Papa."

"Then I'll stay up here and pray the good Lord saves my life by not
letting her notice you leaving. We'll meet up at Hatrack Mouth come
sundown."

"Can't we—"

"No we can't, not a minute sooner," he said. "Can't cross the river
till dark. If they catch her or she dies afore we get there then it's just
too bad, cause we can't cross the Hio in the daylight, bet your life on
that."

Noise in the forest, this scare Black slavegirl very bad. Trees grab
her, owls screech out telling where they find her, this river just laugh
at her all along. She can't move cause she fall in the dark, she hurt this
baby. She can't stay cause they find her sure. Flying don't fool them
finders, they look far and see her even a hand of hands away off.

A step for sure. Oh, Lord God Jesus save me from this devil in the
dark.

A step, and breathing, and branches they brush aside. But no lantern!
Whatever come it see me in the dark! Oh, Lord God Moses Savior
Abraham.

"Girl."

That voice, I hear that voice, I can't breathe. Can you hear it, little
boy-baby? Or do I dream this voice? This lady voice, very soft lady
voice. Devil got no lady voice, everybody know, ain't that so?

"Girl, I come to take you across the river and help you and your
baby get north and free."

I don't find no words no more, not slave words or Umbawa talk.
When I put on feathers do I lose my words?

"We got a good stout rowboat and two strong men to row. I know
you understand me and I know you trust me and I know you want to
come. So you just set there, girl, you hold my hand, there, that's my
hand, you don't have to say a word, you just hold my hand. There's
some White men but they're my friends and they won't touch you.

Nobody's going to touch you except me, you believe that, girl, you just believe it.''

Her hand it touch my skin very cool and soft like this lady voice. This lady angel, this Holy Virgin Mother of God.

Lots of steps, heavy steps, and now lanterns and lights and big old White men but this lady she just hold on my hand.

"Scared plumb to death.''

"Look at this girl. She's most wasted away to nothing.''

"How many days she been without eating?''

Big men's voices like White Boss who give her this baby.

"She only left her plantation last night,'' said the Lady.

How this White lady know? She know everything, Eve the mama of all babies. No time to talk, no time to pray, move very quick, lean on this White lady, walk and walk and walk to this boat it lie waiting in the water just like I dream, O! here the boat little boy-baby, boat lift us cross the Jordan to the Promise Land.

They were halfway across the river when the Black girl started shaking and crying and chattering.

"Hush her up,'' said Horace Guester.

"There's nobody near us,'' answered Peggy. "No one to hear.''

"What's she babbling about?'' asked Po Doggly. He was a pig farmer from near Hatrack Mouth and for a moment Peggy thought he was talking about *her*. But no, it was the Black girl he meant.

"She's talking in her African tongue, I reckon,'' said Peggy. "This girl is really something, how she got away.''

"With a baby and all,'' agreed Po.

"Oh, the baby,'' said Peggy. "I've got to hold the baby.''

"Why's that?'' asked Papa.

"Because you're both going to have to carry her,'' she said. "From shore to the wagon, at least. There's no way this child can walk another step.''

When they got to shore, they did just that. Po's old wagon was no great shakes for comfort—one old horseblanket was about as soft as it was going to get—but they laid her out and if she minded she didn't say so. Horace held the lantern high and looked at her. "You're plumb right, Peggy.''

"What about?'' she asked.

"Calling her a child. I swear she couldn't be thirteen. I swear it. And her with a baby. You sure this baby's hers?''

"I'm sure,'' said Peggy.

Po Doggly chuckled. "Oh, you know them guineas, just like bunny rabbits, the minute they can they do.'' Then he remembered that Peggy was there. ''Begging your pardon, ma'am. We don't never have ladies along till tonight.''

''It's *her* pardon you have to beg,'' said Peggy coldly. ''This child is a mixup. Her owner sired this boy without a by-your-leave. I reckon you understand me.''

''I won't have you discussing such things,'' said Horace Guester. His temper was hot, all right. ''Bad enough you coming along on this without you knowing all this kind of thing about this poor girl, it ain't right telling her secrets like that.''

Peggy fell silent and stayed that way all the ride home. That was what happened whenever she spoke frankly which is why she almost never did. The girl's suffering made her forget herself and talk too much. Now Papa was thinking on about how much his daughter knew about this Black girl in just a few minutes, and worrying how much she knew about *him*.

Do you want to know what I know, Papa? I know why you do this. You're not like Po Doggly, Papa, who doesn't think much of Blacks but hates seeing any wild thing cooped up. He does this, helping slaves make their way to Canada, cause he's just got that need in him to set them free. But you, Papa, you do it to pay back your secret sin. Your pretty little secret who smiled at you like heartbreak in person and you could've said no but you didn't, you said yes oh yes. While Mama was expecting me, it was, and you were off in Dekane buying supplies, you stayed there a week and had that woman must be ten times in six days, I remember every one of those times as clear as you do, I can feel you dreaming about her in the night. Hot with shame, hotter with desire, I know just how a man feels when he wants a woman so bad his skin itches and he can't hold still. All these years you've hated yourself for what you did and hated yourself all the more for loving that memory, and so you pay for it. You risk going to jail or getting hung up in a tree somewhere for the crows to pick, not because you love the Black man but because you hope maybe doing good for God's children might just set you free of your own secret love of evil.

And here's the funny thing, Papa. If you knew I knew your secret you would probably die, it might just kill you on the spot. And yet if I could tell you, just tell you that I know, then I could tell you something else on top of that, I could say, Papa, don't you see that it's your knack? You who thinks he never had no knack, but you got one. It's the knack for making folks feel loved. They come to your inn and they feel right to home. Well you saw her, and she was hungry, that woman in Dekane, she needed to feel the way you make folks feel, needed you so bad.

And it's hard, Papa, hard not to love a body who loves you so powerful, who hangs onto you like clouds hanging onto the moon, knowing you're going to go on, knowing you'll never stay, but hungering, Papa. I looked for that woman, looked for her heartfire, far and wide I searched for her, and I found her. I know where she is. She ain't young now like you remember. But she's still pretty, pretty as you recall her, Papa. And she's a good woman, and you done her no harm. She remembers you fondly, Papa. She knows God forgave her and you both. It's you who won't forgive, Papa.

Such a sad thing, Peggy thought, coming home in that wagon. Papa's doing something that would make him a hero in any other daughter's eyes. A great man. But because I'm a torch, I know the truth. He doesn't come out here like Hector afore the gates of Troy, risking death to save other folks. He comes slinking like a whipped dog, cause he *is* a whipped dog inside. He runs out here to hide from a sin that the good Lord would have forgave long ago if he just allowed forgiveness to be possible.

Soon enough, though, Peggy stopped thinking it was sad about her Papa. It was sad about most *everybody*, wasn't it? But most sad people just kept right on being sad, hanging onto misery like the last keg of water in a drouth. Like the way Peggy kept waiting here for Alvin even though she knew he'd bring no joy to her.

It was that girl in the back of the wagon who was different. She had a terrible misery coming on her, going to lose her boy-baby, but she didn't just set and wait for it to happen so she could grieve. She said no. Plain no, just like that, I won't let you sell this boy south on me, even to a good rich family. A rich man's slave is still a slave, ain't he? And down south means he'll be even farther away from where he can run off and make it north. Peggy could feel those feelings in that girl, even as she tossed and moaned in the back of the wagon.

Something more, though. That girl was more a hero than Papa or Po Doggly either one. Because the only way she could think to get away was to use a witchery so strong that Peggy never even heard of it before. Never dreamed that Black folks had such lore. But it was no lie, it was no dream neither. That girl flew. Made a wax poppet and feathered it and burnt it up. Burnt it right up. It let her fly all this way, this long hard way till the sun came up, far enough that Peggy saw her and they took her across the Hio. But what a price that runaway had paid for it.

When they got back to the roadhouse, Mama was just as angry as Peggy ever saw her. "It's a crime you should have a whipping for, taking your sixteen-year-old daughter out to commit a crime in the darkness."

But Papa didn't answer. He didn't have to, once he carried that girl inside and laid her on the floor before the fire.

"She can't have ate a thing for days. For weeks!" cried Mama.

"And her brow is like to burn my hand off just to touch her. Fetch me a pan of water, Horace, to mop her brow, while I het up the broth for her to sip—"

"No, Mama," said Peggy. "Best you find some milk for the baby."

"The baby won't die, and this girl's likely to, don't you tell me my business, I know physicking for *this*, anyway—"

"No, Mama," said Peggy. "She did a witchery with a wax poppet. It's a Black sort of witchery, but she had the know-how and she had the power, being the daughter of a king in Africa. She knew the price and now she can't help but pay."

"Are you saying this girl's bound to die?" asked Mama.

"She made a poppet of herself, Mama, and put it on the fire. It gave her the wings to fly one whole night. But the cost of it is the rest of her life."

Papa looked sick at heart. "Peggy, that's plain crazy. What good would it do her to escape from slavery if she was just going to die? Why not kill herself there and save the trouble?"

Peggy didn't have to answer. The baby she was a-holding started to cry right then, and that was all the answer there was.

"I'll get milk," said Papa. "Christian Larsson's bound to have a gill or so to spare even this time of the night."

Mama stopped him, though. "Think again, Horace," she said. "It's near midnight now. What'll you tell him you need the milk *for*?"

Horace sighed, laughed at his own foolishness. "For a runaway slave-girl's little pickaninny baby." But then he turned red, getting hot with anger. "What a crazy thing this Black girl done," he said. "She came all this way, knowing that she'd die, and now what does she reckon we'll do with a little pickaninny like that? We sure can't take it north and lay it across the Canadian border and let it bawl till some Frenchman comes to take it."

"I reckon she just figures it's better to die free than live slave," said Peggy. "I reckon she just knew that whatever life that baby found here had to be better than what it was there."

The girl lay there before the fire, breathing soft, her eyes closed.

"She's asleep, isn't she?" asked Mama.

"Not dead yet," said Peggy, "but not hearing us."

"Then I'll tell you plain, this is a bad piece of trouble," said Mama. "We can't have people knowing you bring runaway slaves through here. Word of that would spread so fast we'd have two dozen finders camped here every week of the year, and one of them'd be bound to take a shot at you sometime from ambush.''

"Nobody has to know," said Papa.

"What are you going to do, tell folks you happened to trip over her dead body in the woods?''

Peggy wanted to shout at them, she ain't dead yet, so mind how you talk! But the truth was they had to get some things planned, and quick. What if one of the guests woke up in the night and came downstairs? There'd be no keeping this secret then.

"How soon will she die?" Papa asked. "By morning?''

"She'll be dead before sunrise, Papa.''

Papa nodded. "Then I better get busy. The girl I can take care of. You women can think of something to do with that pickaninny, I hope.''

"Oh, we can, can we?" said Mama.

"Well I know I can't, so you'd better.''

"Well then maybe I'll just tell folks it's my own babe.''

Papa didn't get mad. Just grinned, he did, and said, "Folks ain't going to believe that even if you dip that boy in cream three times a day.''

He went outside and got Po Doggly to help him dig a grave.

"Passing this baby off as born around here ain't such a bad idea,'' said Mama. "That Black family that lives down in that boggy land— you remember two years back when some slaveowner tried to prove he used to own them? What's their name, Peggy?''

Peggy knew them far better than any other White folks in Hatrack River did; she watched over them the same as everyone else, knew all their children, knew all their names. "They call their name Berry,'' she said. "Like a noble house, they just keep that family name no matter what job each one of them does.''

"Why couldn't we pass this baby off as theirs?''

"They're poor, Mama," said Peggy. "They can't feed another mouth.''

"We could help with that," said Mama. "We have extra.''

"Just think a minute, Mama, how that'd look. Suddenly the Berrys get them a light-colored baby like this, you *know* he's half-White just to look at him. And then Horace Guester starts bringing gifts down to the Berry house.''

Mama's face went red. "What do you know about such things?'' she demanded.

"Oh, for heaven's sake, Mama, I'm a torch. And you know people would start to talk, you know they would.''

Mama looked at the Black girl lying there. "You got us into a whole lot of trouble, little girl.''

The baby started fussing.

Mama stood up and walked to the window, as if she could see out into the night and find some answer writ on the sky. Then, abruptly, she headed for the door, opened it.

"Mama," said Peggy.

"There's more than one way to pluck a goose," said Mama.

Peggy saw what Mama had thought of. If they couldn't take the baby down to the Berry place, they could maybe keep the baby here at the roadhouse and say they were taking care of it for the Berrys cause they were so poor. As long as the Berry family went along with the tale, it would account for a half-Black baby showing up one day. And nobody'd think the baby was Horace's bastard—not if his wife brought it right into the house.

"You realize what you're asking them, don't you?" said Peggy. "Everybody's going to think somebody else has been plowing with Mr. Berry's heifer."

Mama looked so surprised Peggy almost laughed out loud. "I didn't think Blacks cared about such things," she said.

Peggy shook her head. "Mama, the Berrys are just about the best Christians in Hatrack River. They have to be, to keep forgiving the way White folks treat them and their children."

Mama closed the door again and stood inside, leaning on it. "How *do* folks treat their children?"

It was a pertinent question, Peggy knew, and Mama had thought of it only just in time. It was one thing to look at that scrawny fussing little Black baby and say, I'm going to take care of this child and save his life. It was something else again to think of him being five and seven and ten and seventeen years old, a young buck living right there in the house.

"I don't think you have to fret about that," said Little Peggy, "not half so much as how *you* plan to treat this boy. Do you plan to raise him up to be your servant, a lowborn child in your big fine house? If that's so, then this girl died for nothing, she might as well have let them sell him south."

"I never hankered for no slave," said Mama. "Don't you go saying that I did."

"Well, what then? Are you going to treat him as your own son, and stand with him against all comers, the way you would if you'd ever borne a son of your own?"

Peggy watched as Mama thought of that, and suddenly she saw all kinds of new paths open up in Mama's heartfire. A son—that's what this half-White boy could be. And if folks around here looked cross-

eyed at him on account of him not being all White, they'd have to
reckon with Margaret Guester, they would, and it'd be a fearsome day
for them, they'd have no terror at the thought of hell, not after what
she'd put them through.

Mama hadn't felt such a powerful grim determination in all the years
Peggy'd been looking into her heart. It was one of those times when
somebody's whole future changed right before her eyes. All the old
paths had been pretty much the same; Mama had no choices that would
change her life. But now, this dying girl had brought a transformation.
Now there were hundreds of new paths open, and all of them had a
little boychild in them, needing her the way her daughter'd never needed
her. Set upon by strangers, cruelly treated by the boys of the town, he'd
come to her again and again for protection, for teaching, for toughening,
the kind of thing that Peggy'd never done.

That's why I disappointed you, wasn't it, Mama? Cause I knew too
much, too young. You wanted me to come to you in my confusion, with
my questions. But I never had no questions, Mama, cause I knew from
childhood up. I knew what it meant to be a woman from the memories
in your own head. I knew about married love without you telling me. I
never had a tearful night pressed up against your shoulder, crying cause
some boy I longed for wouldn't look at me; I never longed for any boy
around here. I never did a thing you dreamed your little girl would do,
cause I had a torch's knack, and I knew everything and needed nothing
that you wanted to give me.

But this half-Black boy, he'll need you no matter what his knack
might be. I see down all those paths, that if you take him in, if you
raise him up, he'll be more son to you than I ever was your daughter,
though your blood is half of mine.

"Daughter," said Mama, "if I go through this door, will it turn out
well for the boy? And for us, too?"

"Are you asking me to See for you, Mama?"

"I am, Little Peggy, and I never asked for that before, never on my
own behalf."

"Then I'll tell you." Peggy hardly needed to look far down the paths
of Mama's life to find how much pleasure she'd have in the boy. "If
you take him in, and treat him like your own son, you'll never regret
doing it."

"What about your papa? Will he treat him right?"

"Don't you know your own husband?" asked Peggy.

Mama walked a step toward her, her hand all clenched up even
though she never laid a hand on Peggy. "Don't get fresh with me," she
said.

"I'm talking the way I talk when I See," said Peggy. "You come to me as a torch, I talk as a torch to you."

"Then say what you have to say."

"It's easy enough. If you don't know how your husband will treat this boy, you don't know that man at all."

"So maybe I don't," said Mama. "Maybe I don't know him at all. Or maybe I do, and I want you to tell me if I'm right."

"You're right," said Peggy. "He'll treat him fair, and make him feel loved all the days of his life."

"But will he really love him?"

There wasn't no chance that Peggy'd answer that question. Love wasn't even in the picture for Papa. He'd take care of the boy because he ought to, because he felt a bounden duty, but the boy'd never know the difference, it'd feel like love to him, and it'd be a lot more dependable than love ever was. But to explain that to Mama would mean telling her how Papa did so many things because he felt so bad about his ancient sins, and there'd never be a time in Mama's life when she was ready to hear *that* tale.

So Peggy just looked at Mama and answered her the way she answered other folks who pried too deep into things they didn't really want to know. "That's for him to answer," Peggy said. "All you need to know is that the choice you already made in your heart is a good one. Already just deciding that has changed your life."

"But I haven't even decided yet," said Mama.

In Mama's heart there wasn't a single path left, not a single one, in which she didn't get the Berrys to say it was their boy, and leave him with her to raise.

"Yes you have," said Peggy. "And you're glad of it."

Mama turned and left, closing the door gentle behind her, so as not to wake the traveling preacher who was sleeping in the room upstairs of the door.

Peggy had just one moment's unease, and she wasn't even sure why. If she'd thought about it a minute, she'd have known it was on account of how she cheated her Mama without even knowing it. When Peggy did a Seeing for anybody else, she always took care to look far down the paths of their life, looking for darkness from causes not even guessed at. But Peggy was so sure she knew her Mama and Papa, she didn't even bother looking except at what was coming up right away. That's how it goes within a family. You think you know each other so well, and so you don't bother hardly getting to know each other at all. It wouldn't be years yet till Peggy would think back on this day, and try to figure why she didn't See what was coming. Sometimes she'd even imagine that her knack failed her. But it didn't. She failed her own knack. She wasn't the first to do so, nor the last, nor even the worst, but there's few ever lived to regret it more.

The moment of unease passed, and Peggy forgot it as her thoughts turned to the Black girl on the common-room floor. She was awake, her eyes open. The baby was still mewling. Without the girl saying a thing, Peggy knew she was willing for the babe to suckle, if she had anything in her breasts to suck on out. The girl hadn't even strength to open up her faded cotton shirt. Peggy had to sit beside her, cradling the child against her own thighs while she fumbled the girl's buttons open with her free hand. The girl's chest was so skinny, her ribs so stark and bare, that her breasts looked to be saddlebags tossed onto a rail fence. But the nipple still stood up for the baby to suck, and a white froth soon appeared around the baby's lips, so there was something there, even now, even at the very end of his mama's life.

The girl was far too weak to talk, but she didn't need to; Peggy heard what she wanted to say, and answered her. "My own mama's going to keep your boy," said Peggy. "And no wise is she going to let any man make a slave of him."

That was what the girl wanted most to hear—that and the sound of her greedy boy-baby slurping and humming and squealing at her breast.

But Peggy wanted her to know more than that before she died. "Your boy-baby's going to know about you," she told the girl. "He's going to hear how you gave your life so you could fly away and take him here to freedom. Don't you think he'll ever forget you, cause he won't."

Then Peggy looked into the child's heartfire, searched there for what he'd be. Oh, that was a painful thing, because the life of a half-White boy in a White town was hard no matter which of the paths of his life he chose. Still, she saw enough to know the nature of the babe whose fingers scratched and clutched at his mama's naked chest. "And he'll be a man worth dying for, too, I promise you that."

The girl was glad to hear it. It brought her peace enough that she could sleep again. After a time the babe, satisfied, also fell asleep. Peggy picked him up, wrapped him in a blanket, and laid him in the crook of his mama's arm. Every last moment of your mama's life you'll be with her, she told the boychild silently. We'll tell you that, too, that she held you in her arms when she died.

When she died. Papa was out with Po Doggly, digging her grave; Mama was off at the Berrys, to persuade them to help her save the baby's life and freedom; and here was Peggy, thinking as if the girl was already dead.

But she wasn't dead, not yet. And all of a sudden it came to Peggy, with a flash of anger that she was too stupid to think of it before, that there was one soul she knew of who had the knack in him to heal the sick. Hadn't he knelt by Ta-Kumsaw at the battle of Detroit, that great Red man's body riddled with bullet holes, hadn't Alvin knelt there and healed him up? Alvin could save this girl, if he was here.

She cast off in the darkness, searching for the heartfire that burned so bright, the heartfire she knew better than any in the world, better even than her own. And there he was, running in the darkness, traveling the way Red men did, like he was asleep, and the land around him was his soul. He was coming faster than any White could ever come, even with the fastest horse on the best road between the Wobbish and the Hatrack, but he wouldn't be here till noon tomorrow, and by then this runaway slavegirl would be dead and in the ground up in the family graveyard. By twelve hours at most she'd miss the one man in this country who could have saved her life.

Wasn't that the way of it? Alvin could save her, but he'd never know she needed saving. While Peggy, who couldn't do a thing, she knew all that was happening, knew all the things that might happen, knew the one thing that *should* happen if the world was good. It wasn't good. It wouldn't happen.

What a terrible gift it was, to be a torch, to know all these things a-coming, and have so little power to change them. The only power she'd ever had was just the words of her mouth, telling folks, and even then she couldn't be sure what they'd choose to do. Always there'd be some choice they could make that would set them down a path even worse than the one she wanted to save them from—and so many times in their wickedness or cantankerousness or just plain bad luck, they'd make that terrible choice and then things'd be worse for them than if Peggy'd just kept still and never said a thing. I wish I didn't know. I wish I had some hope that Alvin would come in time. I wish I had some hope this girl would live. I wish that I could save her life myself.

And then she thought of the many times she *had* saved a life. Alvin's life, using Alvin's caul. At that moment hope *did* spark up in her heart, for surely, just this once, she could use a bit of the last scrap of Alvin's caul to save this girl, to restore her.

Peggy leapt up and ran clumsily to the stairs, her legs so numb from sitting on the floor that she couldn't hardly feel her own footsteps on the bare wood. She tripped on the stairs and made some noise, but none of the guests woke up, as far as she noticed right off like that. Up the stairs, then up the attic ladderway that Oldpappy made into a proper stairway not three months afore he died. She threaded her way among the trunks and old furniture until she reached her room up against the west end of the house. Moonlight came in through her south-facing window, making a squared-off pattern on the floor. She pried up the floorboard and took the box from the place where she hid it whenever she left the room.

She walked too heavy or this one guest slept too light, but as she came down the ladderway, there he stood, skinny white legs sticking out from under his longshirt, a-gazing down the stairs, then back toward his room, like as if he couldn't make up his mind whether to go in or out, up or down. Peggy looked into his heartfire, just to find out whether he'd been downstairs and seen the girl and her baby—if he had, then all their thought and caution had been in vain.

But he hadn't—it was still possible.

"Why are you still dressed for going out?" he asked. "At this time of the morning, too?"

She gently laid her finger against his lips. To silence him, or at least that's how the gesture began. But she knew right away that she was the first woman ever to touch this man upon the face since his mama all those many years ago. She saw that in that moment his heart filled, not with lust, but with the vague longings of a lonely man. He was the minister who'd come day before yesterday morning, a traveling preacher—from Scotland, he said. She'd hardly paid him no mind, her being so preoccupied with knowing Alvin was on his way back. But now all that mattered was to send him back into his room, quick as could be, and she knew one sure way to do it. She put her hands on his shoulders, getting a strong grip behind his neck, and pulled him down to where she could kiss him fair on the lips. A good long buss, like he never had from a woman in all his days.

Just like she expected, he was back into his room almost before she let go of him. She might've laughed at that, except she knew from his heartfire it wasn't her kiss sent him back, like she planned. It was the box she still held in one hand, which she had pressed up against the back of his neck when she held him. The box with Alvin's caul inside.

The moment it touched him, he felt what was inside. It wasn't no knack of his, it was something else—just being so near something of Alvin's done it to him. She saw the vision of Alvin's face loom up inside his mind, with such fear and hatred like she never seen before. Only then did she realize that he wasn't just any minister. He was Reverend Philadelphia Thrower, who once had been a preacher back in Vigor Church. Reverend Thrower, who once had tried to kill the boy, except Alvin's pa prevented him.

The fear of a woman's kiss was nothing to him compared to his fear of Alvin Junior. The trouble was that now he was *so* afraid he was already thinking of leaving right this minute and getting out of this roadhouse. If he did that, he'd have to come downstairs and then he'd see all, just what she meant to fend off. This was how it went so often—she tried to stave off a bad thing and it turned out worse, something so unlikely she didn't see it. How could she not have reckonized who he was? Hadn't she seen him through Alvin's eyes all those many times in years past? But he'd changed this last year, he looked thin and haunted and older. Besides, she wasn't looking for him here, and anyhow it was too late to undo what she already done. All that mattered now was to keep him in his room.

So she opened his door and followed him inside and looked him square in the face and said, "He was born here."

"Who?" he said. His face was white as if he'd just seen the devil himself. He knew who she meant.

"And he's coming back. Right now he's on his way. You're only safe if you stay in your room tonight, and leave in the morning at first light."

"I don't know—know what you're talking about."

Did he really think he could fool a torch? Maybe he didn't know she was—no, he knew, he knew, he just didn't believe in torching and hexing and knacks and suchlike. He was a man of science and higher religion. A blamed fool. So she'd have to prove to him that what he feared most was so. She knew him, and she knew his secrets. "You tried to kill Alvin Junior with a butchery knife," she said.

That did it, right enough. He fell to his knees. "I'm not afraid to die," he said. Then he began to murmur the Lord's prayer.

"Pray all night, if you like," she said, "but stay in your room to do it."

Then she stepped through the door and closed it. She was halfway down the stairs when she heard the bar fall into place across the door. Peggy didn't even have time to care whether she caused him undue misery—he wasn't really a murderer in his heart. All she cared for now was to get the caul down to where she could use it to help the runaway, if by any chance Alvin's power was really hers to use. So much time that minister had cost her. So many of the slavegirl's precious breaths.

She was still breathing, wasn't she? Yes. No. The babe lay sleeping beside her, but her chest didn't move even as much as him, her lips didn't make even so much as a baby's breath on Peggy's hand. But her heartfire still burned! Peggy could see that plain enough, still burned bright because she was so strong-hearted, that slavegirl was. So Peggy opened up the box, took out the scrap of caul, and rubbed a dry corner of it to dust between her fingers, whispering to her, "Live, get strong."

She tried to do what Alvin did when he healed, the way he could feel the small broken places in a person's body, set them right. Hadn't she watched him as he did it so many times before? But it was different, doing it herself. It was strange to her, she didn't have the vision for it, and she could feel the life ebbing away from the girl's body, the heart stilled, the lungs slack, the eyes open but unlighted, and at last the heartfire flashed like a shooting star, all sudden and bright, and it was gone.

Too late. If I hadn't stopped in the hall upstairs, hadn't had to deal with the minister—

But no, no, she couldn't blame herself, it wasn't her power anyway, it was too late before she began. The girl had been dying all through her body. Even Alvin himself, if he was here, even he couldn't have done it. It was never more than a slim hope. Never even hope enough that she could see a single pathway where it worked. So she wouldn't do like so many did, she wouldn't endlessly blame herself when after all she'd done her best at a task that had little hope in it from the start.

Now that the girl was dead, she couldn't leave the baby there to feel his mama's arm grow cold. She picked him up. He stirred, but slept on in the way that babies do. Your mama's dead, little half-White boy, but you'll have *my* mama, and my papa too. They got love enough for a little one; you won't starve for it like some children I seen. So you make the best of it, boy-baby. Your mama died to bring you here—you make the best of it, and you'll be something, right enough.

You'll be something, she heard herself whispering. You'll be something, and so will I.

She made her decision even before she realized there was even a decision to be made. She could feel her own future changing even though she couldn't see rightly what it was going to be.

That slavegirl guessed at the likeliest future—you don't have to be a torch to see *some* things plain. It was an ugly life ahead, losing her baby, living as a slave till the day she dropped. Yet she saw just the faintest glimmer of hope for her baby, and once she saw it, she didn't hold back, no sir, that glimmer was worth paying her life for.

And now look at me, thought Peggy. Here I look down the paths of Alvin's life and see misery for myself—nowhere near as bad as that slavegirl's, but bad enough. Now and then I catch the shine of a bright chance for happiness, a strange and backward way to have Alvin and have him love me, too. Once I seen it, am I going to sit on my hands and watch that bright hope die, just because I'm not sure how to get to it from here?

If that beat-down child can make her own hope out of wax and ash and feathers and a bit of herself, then I can make my own life, too. Somewhere there's a thread that if I just lay hold on it, it'll lead me to happiness. And even if I never find that particular thread, it'll be better than the despair waiting for me if I stay. Even if I never become a part of Alvin's life when he comes to manhood, well, that's still not as steep a price as that slavegirl paid for freedom.

When Alvin comes tomorrow, I won't be here.

That was her decision, just like that. Why, she could hardly believe she never thought of it before. Of all people in the whole of Hatrack River, she ought to have knowed that there's *always* another choice. Folks talked on about how they were forced into misery and woe, they didn't have no choice at all—but that runaway girl showed that there's always a way out, long as you remember even death can be a straight smooth road sometimes.

I don't even have to get no blackbird feathers to fly, neither.

Peggy sat there holding the baby, making bold and fearsome plans for how she'd leave in the morning afore Alvin could arrive. Whenever she felt a-scared of what she'd set herself to do, she cast her gaze down on that girl, and the sight of her was comfort, it truly was. I might someday end up like you, runaway girl, dead in some stranger's house. But better that unknown future than one I knew all along I'd hate, and then did nothing to avoid.

Will I do it, will I really do it in the morning, when the time's come and no turning back? She touched Alvin's caul with her free hand, just snaking her fingers into the box, and what she saw in Alvin's future made her feel like singing. Used to be most paths showed them meeting up and starting out her life of misery. Now only a few of those paths were there—in most of Alvin's futures, she saw him come to Hatrack River and search for the torch girl and find her gone. Just changing her mind tonight had closed down most of the roads to misery.

Mama came back with the Berrys before Papa came in from grave-digging. Anga Berry was a heavyset woman with laughter lines outnumbering the lines of worry on her face, though both kinds were plain enough. Peggy knew her well and liked her better than most folks in Hatrack River. She had a temper but she also had compassion, and Peggy wasn't surprised at all to see her rush to the body of the girl and take up that cold limp hand and press it to her bosom. She murmured words almost like a lullaby, her voice was so low and sweet and kind.

"She's dead," said Mock Berry. "But that baby's strong I see."

Peggy stood up and let Mock see the baby in her arms. She didn't like him half so well as she liked his wife. He was the kind of man who'd slap a child so hard blood flowed, just cause he didn't like what was said or done. It was almost worse cause he didn't rage when he did it. Like he felt nothing at all, to hurt somebody or not hurt somebody made no powerful difference in his mind. But he worked hard, and even though he was poor his family got by; and nobody who knew Mock paid heed to them crude folks what said there wasn't a buck who wouldn't steal or a ewe you couldn't tup.

"Healthy," said Mock. Then he turned to Mama. "When he grow up to be a big old buck, ma'am, you still aim to call him your boy? Or you make him sleep out back in the shed with the animals?"

Well, he wasn't one to pussyfoot around the issue, Peggy saw.

"Shut your mouth, Mock," said his wife. "And you give me that baby, Miss. I just wish I'd knowed he was coming or I'd've kept my youngest on the tit to keep the milk in. Weaned that boy two months back and he's been nothing but trouble since, but you ain't no trouble, baby, you ain't no trouble at all." She cooed to the baby just like she cooed to his dead mama, and he didn't wake up either.

"I told you. I'll raise him as my son," said Mama.

"I'm sorry, ma'am, but I just never heard of no White woman doing such a thing," said Mock.

"What I say," said Mama, "that's what I do."

Mock thought on that a moment. Then he nodded. "I reckon so," he said. "I reckon I never heard you break your word, not even to Black folks." He grinned. "Most White folk allow as how lying to a buck ain't the same as *lying*."

"We'll do like you asked," said Anga Berry. "I'll tell anybody who ask me this is my boy, only we gave him to you cause we was too poor."

"But don't you ever go forgetting that it's a lie," said Mock. "Don't you ever go thinking that if it really was our own baby, we'd ever give him up. And don't you ever go thinking that my wife here ever would let some White man put a baby in her, and her being married to me."

Mama studied Mock for a minute, taking his measure in the way she had. "Mock Berry, I hope you come and visit me any day you like while this boy is in my house, and I'll show you how one White woman keeps her word."

Mock laughed. "I reckon you a regular Mancipationist."

Papa came in then, covered with sweat and dirt. He shook hands with the Berrys, and in a minute they told him the tale they all would tell. He made his promises too, to raise the boy like his own son. He even thought of what never entered Mama's head—he said a few words to Peggy, to promise her that they wouldn't give no preference to the boy, neither. Peggy nodded. She didn't want to say much, cause anything she said would either be a lie or give her plans away; she knew she had no intention to be in this house for even a single day of this baby's future here.

"We go on home now, Mrs. Guester," said Anga. She handed the baby to Mama. "If one of my children wake up with a boogly dream I best be there or you hear them screams clear up here on the high road."

"Ain't you going have no preacher say words at her grave?" said Mock.

Papa hadn't thought of it. "We do have a minister upstairs," he said.

But Peggy didn't let him hold that thought for even a moment. "No," she said, sharp as she could.

Papa looked at her, and knew that she was talking as a torch. Wasn't no arguing that point. He just nodded. "Not this time, Mock," he said. "Wouldn't be safe."

Mama fretted Anga Berry clear to the door. "Is there anything I ought to know?" said Mama. "Is there anything different about Black babies?"

"Oh, powerful different," said Anga. "But that baby, he half White I reckon, so you just take care of that White half, and I reckon the Black half take care of hisself."

"Cow's milk from a pig bladder?" Mama insisted.

"You know all them things," said Anga. "I learnt everything I know from you, Mrs. Guester. All the women round here do. How come you asking me now? Don't you know I need my sleep?"

Once the Berrys were gone, Papa picked up the girl's body and carried her outside. Not even a coffin, though they would overlay the corpse with stones to keep the dogs off. "Light as a feather," he said when first he hoisted her. "Like the charred carcass of a burnt log."

Which was apt enough, Peggy had to admit. That's what she was now. Just ashes. She'd burnt herself right up.

Mama held the pickaninny boy while Peggy went up into the attic and fetched down the cradle. Nobody woke up this time, except that minister. He was *wide* awake behind his door, but he wasn't coming out for any reason. Mama and Peggy made up that little bed in Mama's and Papa's room, and laid the baby in it. "Tell me if this poor orphan baby's got him a name," said Mama.

"She never gave him one," said Peggy. "In her tribe, a woman never got her a name till she married, and a man had no name till he killed him his first animal."

"That's just awful," said Mama. "That ain't even Christian. Why, she died unbaptized."

"No," said Peggy. "She was baptized right enough. Her owner's wife saw to that—all the Blacks on their plantation were baptized."

Mama's face went sour. "I reckon she thought that made her a Christian. Well, I'll have a name for you, little boy." She grinned wickedly. "What do you think your papa would do if I named this baby Horace Guester Junior?"

"Die," said Peggy.

"I reckon so," said Mama. "I ain't ready to be a widow yet. So for now we'll name him—oh, I can't think, Peggy. What's a Black man's name? Or should I just name him like any White child?"

"Only Black man's name I know is Othello," said Peggy.

"That's a queer name if I ever heard one," said Mama. "You must've got that out of one of Whitley Physicker's books."

Peggy said nothing.

"I know," said Mama. "I know his name. Cromwell. The Lord Protector's name."

"You might better name him Arthur, after the King," said Peggy.

Mama just cackled and laughed at that. "That's your name, little boy. Arthur Stuart! And if the King don't like such a namesake, let him send an army and I still won't change it. His Majesty will have to change his own name first."

Even though she got to bed so late, Peggy woke early next morning. It was hoofbeats woke her—she didn't have to go to the window to recognize his heartfire as the minister rode away. Ride on, Thrower, she said silently. You won't be the last to run away this morning, fleeing from that eleven-year-old boy.

It was the north-facing window she looked out of. She could see between the trees to the graveyard up the hill. She tried to see where the grave was dug last night, but there wasn't no sign her natural eyes could see, and in a graveyard there wasn't no heartfires neither, nothing to help her. Alvin will see it though, she knew that sure. He'd head for that graveyard first thing he did, cause his oldest brother's body lay there, the boy Vigor, who got swept away in the Hatrack River saving Alvin's mother's life in the last hour before she gave birth to her seventh son. But Vigor hung on to life just long enough, in spite of the river's strongest pulling at him, hung on just long enough that when Alvin was born he was the seventh of seven living sons. Peggy herself had watched his heartfire flicker and die right after the babe was born. He would've heard that story a thousand times. So he'd come to that graveyard, and *he* could feel his way through the earth and find what lay hidden there. He'd find that unmarked grave, that wasted body so fresh buried there.

Peggy took the box with the caul in it, put it deep in a cloth bag along with her second dress, a petticoat, and the most recent books Whitley Physicker had brought. Just because she didn't want to meet him face to face didn't mean she could forget that boy. She'd touch the caul again tonight, or maybe not till morning, and then she'd stand with him in memory and use his senses to find that nameless Black girl's grave.

Her bag packed, she went downstairs.

Mama had drug the cradle into the kitchen and she was singing to the baby while she kneaded bread, rocking the cradle with one foot, even though Arthur Stuart was fast asleep. Peggy set her bag outside the kitchen door, walked in and touched her Mama's shoulder. She hoped a little that she'd see her Mama grieving something awful when she found out Peggy'd gone off. But it wasn't so. Oh, she'd carry on and rage at first, but in the times to come she'd miss Peggy less than she might've guessed. It was the baby'd take her mind off worrying about her daughter. Besides, Mama knew Peggy could take care of herself. Mama knew Peggy wasn't a one to need to hold a body's hand. While Arthur Stuart needed her.

If this was the first time Peggy noticed how her Mama felt about her, she'd have been hurt deep. But it was the hundredth time, and she was used to it, and looked behind it to the reason, and loved her Mama for being a better soul than most, and forgave her for not loving Peggy more.

"I love you, Mama," said Peggy.

"I love you too, baby," said Mama. She didn't even look up nor guess what Peggy had in mind.

Papa was still asleep. After all, he dug a grave last night and filled it too.

Peggy wrote a note. Sometimes she took care to put in a lot of extra letters in the fancy way they did in books, but this time she wanted to make sure Papa could read it for hisself. That meant putting in no more letters than it took to make the sounds for reading out loud.

I lov you Papa and Mama but I got to leav I no its rong to lev Hatrak with out no torch but I bin torch sixtn yr. I seen my fewchr and ile be saf donte you fret on my acown.

She walked out the front door, carried her bag to the road, and waited only ten minutes before Doctor Whitley Physicker came along in his carriage, bound on the first leg of a trip to Philadelphia.

"You didn't wait on the road like this just to hand me back that Milton I lent you," said Whitley Physicker.

She smiled and shook her head. "No sir, I'd like you take me with you to Dekane. I plan to visit with a friend of my father's, but if you don't mind the company I'd rather not spend the money for a coach."

Peggy watched him consider for a minute, but she knew he'd let her come, and without asking her folks, neither. He was the kind of man thought a girl had as much worth as any boy, and more than that, he plain liked Peggy, thought of her as something like a niece. And he knew that Peggy never lied, so he had no need to check with her folks.

And she hadn't lied to him, no more than she ever lied when she left off without telling all she knew. Papa's old lover, the woman he dreamed of and suffered for, she lived there in Dekane—widowed for the last few years, but her mourning time over so she wouldn't have to turn away company. Peggy knew that lady well, from watching far off for all these years. If I knock on her door, thought Peggy, I don't even have to tell her I'm Horace Guester's girl, she'd take me in as a stranger, she would, and care for me, and help me on my way. But maybe I *will* tell her whose daughter I am, and how I knew to come to her, and how Papa still lives with the aching memory of his love for her.

The carriage rattled over the covered bridge that Alvin's father and older brothers had built eleven years before, after the river drowned the oldest son. Birds nested in the rafters. It was a mad, musical, happy sound they made, at least to her ears, chirping so loud inside the bridge that it sounded like she imagined grand opera ought to be. They had opera in Camelot, down south. Maybe someday she'd go and hear it, and see the King himself in his box.

Or maybe not. Because someday she might just find the path that led to that brief but lovely dream, and then she'd have more important things to do than look at kings or hear the music of the Austrian court played by lacy Virginia musicians in the fancy opera hall in Camelot. Alvin was more important than any of these, if he could only find his way to all his power and what he ought to do with it. And she was born to be part of it. That's how easily she slipped into her dreams of him. Yet why not? Her dreams of him, however brief and hard to find, were true visions of the future, and the greatest joy and the greatest grief she could find for herself both touched this boy who wasn't even a man yet, who had never seen her face to face.

But sitting there in the carriage beside Doctor Whitley Physicker, she forced those thoughts, those visions from her mind. What comes will come, she thought. If I find that path I find it, and if not, then not. For now, at least, I'm free. Free of my watch aloft for the town of Hatrack, and free of building all my plans around that little boy. And what if I end up free of him forever? What if I find another future that doesn't even have him in it? That's the likeliest end of things. Give me time enough, I'll even forget that scrap of a dream I had, and find my own good road to a peaceful end, instead of bending myself to fit his troubled path.

The dancing horses pulled the carriage along so brisk that the wind caught and tossed her hair. She closed her eyes and pretended she was flying, a runaway just learning to be free.

Let him find his path to greatness now without me. Let me have a happy life far from him. Let some other woman stand beside him in his glory. Let another woman kneel a-weeping at his grave.

3

Lies

Eleven-year-old Alvin lost half his name when he came to Hatrack River. Back home in the town of Vigor Church, not far from where the Tippy-Canoe poured its waters into the Wobbish, everybody knowed his father was Alvin, miller for the town and the country round about. Alvin Miller. Which made his namesake, his seventh son, Alvin *Junior*. Now, though, he was going to live in a place where there wasn't six folks who so much as ever met his pa. No need for names like Miller and Junior. He was just Alvin, plain Alvin, but hearing that lone name made him feel like only half hisself.

He came to Hatrack River on foot, hundreds of miles across Wobbish and Hio territories. When he set out from home it was with a pair of sturdy broke-in boots on and a pack of supplies on his back. He did five miles that way, before he stopped up at a poor cabin and gave his food to the folk there. After another mile or so he met a poor traveling family, heading on west to the new lands in the Noisy River country. He gave them the tent and blanket in his pack, and because they had a thirteen-year-old boy about Alvin's size, he pulled off them new boots and gave them straight out, just like that, socks too. He kept only his clothes and the empty pack on his back.

Why, them folks were wide-eyed and silly-faced over it, worrying that Alvin's pa might be mad, him giving stuff away like that, but he allowed as how it was his to give.

"You sure I won't be meeting up with your pa with a musket and a possy-come-and-take-us?" asked the poor man.

"I'm sure you won't, sir," said young Alvin, "on account of I'm from the town of Vigor Church, and the folks there won't see you at all unless you force them."

It took them near ten seconds to realize where they'd heard the name of Vigor Church before. "Them's the folk of the Tippy-Canoe massacre," they said. "Them's the folk what got blood on their hands."

Alvin just nodded. "So you see they'll leave you be."

"Is it true they make every traveler listen to them tell that terrible gory tale of how they killed all them Reds in cold blood?"

"Their blood wasn't cold," said Alvin, "and they only tell travelers who come right on into town. So just stay on the road, leave them be, ride on through. Once you cross the Wobbish, you'll be in open land again, where you'll be glad to meet up with settled folk. Not ten mile on."

Well, they didn't argue no more, nor even ask him how he came not to have to tell the tale hisself. The name of the Massacre of Tippy-Canoe was enough to put a silence on folks like setting in a church, a kind of holy, shameful, reverent attitude. Cause even though most Whites shunned the bloody-handed folk who shed Red men's blood at Tippy-Canoe, they still knew that if they'd stood in the same place, they'd've done the same thing, and it'd be their hands dripping red till they told a stranger about the wretched deed they done. That guilty knowledge didn't make many travelers too keen on stopping in Vigor Church, or any homes in the upper Wobbish country. Them poor folks just took Alvin's boots and gear and moved on down the road, glad of a stretch of canvas over their heads and a slice of leather on their big boy's feet.

Alvin betook him off the road soon after, and plunged into woodland, into the deepest places. If he'd been wearing boots, he would've stumbled and crunched and made more noise than a rutting buffalo in the woods—which is about what most White folks did in the natural forest. But because he was barefoot, his skin touching the forest floor, he was like a different person. He had run behind Ta-Kumsaw through the forests of this whole land, north and south, and in that running young Alvin learned him how the Red man ran, hearing the greensong of the living woodland, moving in perfect harmony to that sweet silent music. When he ran that way, not thinking about where to step, the ground became soft under young Alvin's feet, and he was guided along, no sticks breaking when he stepped, no bushes swishing or twigs snapping off with his onward push. Behind him he left nary a footprint or a broken branch.

Just like a Red man, that was how he moved. And pretty soon his White man's clothing chafed on him, and he stopped and took it off, stuffed it into the pack on his back, and then ran naked as a jaybird, feeling the leaves of the bushes against his body. Soon he was caught up in the rhythm of his own running, forgetting anything about his own body, just part of the living forest, moving onward, faster and stronger, not eating, not drinking. Like a Red man, who could run forever through the deep forest, never needing rest, covering hundreds of miles in a single day.

This was the natural way to travel, Alvin knew it. Not in creaking wooden wagons, rattling over dry ground, sucking along on muddy roads. And not on horseback, a beast sweating and heaving under you, slave to your hurry, not on any errand of its own. Just a man in the woods, bare feet on the ground, bare face in the wind, dreaming as he ran.

All that day and all that night he ran, and well into the morning. How did he find his way? He could feel the slash of the well-traveled road off on his left, like a prickle or an itch, and even though that road led through many a village and many a town, he knew that after a while it'd fetch him up at the town of Hatrack. After all, that was the road his own folks followed, bridging every stream and creek and river on the way, carrying him as a newborn babe in the wagon. Even though he never traveled it before, and wasn't looking at it now, he knew where it led.

So on the second morning he fetched up at the edge of the wood, on the verge of a field of new green maize billowing over rolling ground. There was so many farms in this settled country that the forest was too weak to hold him in his dream much longer anyhow.

It took a while, just standing there, to remember who he was and where he was bound. The music of the greenwood was strong behind him, weak afore. All he could know for sure was a town ahead, and a river maybe five mile on, that's all he could *feel* for sure. But he knew it was the Hatrack River yonder, and so the town could be no other than the one he was bound for.

He had figured to run the forest right up to the edge of town. Now, though, he had no choice but to walk those last miles on White man's feet or not go at all. That was a thought he had never thought of—that there might be places in the world so settled that one farm butted right against the next, with only a row of trees or a rail fence to mark the boundary, farm after farm. Was this what the Prophet saw in his visions of the land? All the forest killed back and these fields put in their place, so a Red man couldn't run no more, nor a deer find cover, nor a bear find him where to sleep come wintertime? If that was so, no wonder he took all the Reds who'd follow him out west, across the Mizzipy. There was no living for a Red man here.

That made Alvin a little sad and a little scared, to leave behind the living lands he'd come to know as well as a man knows his own body. But he wasn't no philosopher. He was a boy of eleven, and he also hankered to see an eastern town, all settled up and civilized. Besides, he had business here, business he'd waited a year to take up, ever since he first learned there was such a body as the torch girl, and how she looked for him to be a Maker.

He pulled his clothes out of his pack and put them on. He walked the edge of the farmland till he came to a road. First time the road crossed a stream, there was proof it was the right road: a covered bridge stood over that little one-jump brooklet. His own pa and older brothers built that bridge, and others like it all the way along that road from Hatrack to Vigor Church. Eleven years ago they built it, when Alvin was a baby sucking on his mama while the wagon rattled west.

He followed the road, and it wasn't awful far. He'd just run hundreds of miles through virgin forest without harm to his feet, but the White man's road had no part of the greensong and it didn't yield to Alvin's feet. Within a couple of miles he was footsore and dusty and thirsty and hungry. Alvin hoped it wasn't too many miles on White man's road, or he'd sure be wishing he'd kept his boots.

The sign beside the road said, Town of Hatrack, Hio.

It was a good-sized town, compared to frontier villages. Of course it didn't compare to the French city of Detroit, but that was a foreign place, and this town was, well, American. The houses and buildings were like the few rough structures in Vigor Church and other new settlements, only smoothed out and growed up to full size. There was four streets that crossed the main road, with a bank and a couple of shops and churches and even a county courthouse and some places with shingles saying Lawyer and Doctor and Alchemist. Why, if there was professional folk here, it was a town *proper*, not just a hopeful place like Vigor Church before the massacre.

Less than a year ago he'd seen a vision of the town of Hatrack. It was when the Prophet, Lolla-Wossiky, caught him up in the tornado that he called down onto Lake Mizogan. The walls of the whirlwind turned to crystal that time, and in the crystal Alvin had seen many things. One of them was the town of Hatrack the way it was when Alvin was born. It was plain that things hadn't stayed the same in these eleven years. He didn't recognize a thing, walking through the town. Why, this place was so big now that not a soul even seemed to notice he was a stranger to give him howdy-do.

He was most of the way through the built-up part of town before he realized that it wasn't the town's bigness that made folks pay him no mind. It was the dust on his face, his bare feet, the empty pack on his back. They looked, they took him in at a glance, and then they looked away, like as if they were halfway scared he'd come up and ask them for bread or a place to stay. It was something Alvin never met up with before, but he knowed it right away for what it was. In the last eleven years, the town of Hatrack, Hio, had learned the difference between rich and poor.

The built-up part was over. He was through the town, and he hadn't seen a single blacksmith's shop, which was what he was supposed to be looking for, nor had he seen the roadhouse where he was born, which was what he was really looking for. All he saw right now was a couple of pig farms, stinking the way pig farms do, and then the road bent a bit south and he couldn't see more.

The smithy had to still be there, didn't it? It was only a year and a half ago that Taleswapper had carried the prentice contract Pa wrote up for Makepeace, the blacksmith of Hatrack River. And less than a year ago that Taleswapper hisself told Alvin that he delivered that letter, and Makepeace Smith was amenable—that was the word he used, *amenable*. Since Taleswapper talked in his halfway English manner, with the *R*s dropped off the ends of words, it sounded to Alvin like old Taleswapper said Makepeace Smith was "a meaner bull," till Taleswapper wrote it down for him. Anyway, the smith was here a year ago. And the torch girl in the roadhouse, the one he visioned in Lolla-Wossiky's crystal tower, she *must* be here. Hadn't she written in Taleswapper's book, "A Maker is born"? When he looked at those words the letters burned with light like as if they been conjured, like the message writ by the hand of God on the wall in that Bible story: "Mean, mean, take all apart, son," and sure enough, it came to pass, Babylon was took all apart. Words of prophecy was what turned letters bright like that. So if that Maker was Alvin himself, and he knowed it was, then she must see more in her torchy way. She must know what a Maker really *is* and how to be one.

Maker. A name folks said with a hush. Or spoke of wistful, saying that the world had done with Makers, there'd be no more. Oh, some said Old Ben Franklin was a Maker, but he denied being so much as a wizard till the day he died. Taleswapper, who knew Old Ben like a father, he said Ben only made one thing in his life, and that was the American Compact, that piece of paper that bound the Dutch and Swedish colonies with the English and German settlements of Pennsylvania and Suskwahenny and, most important of all, the Red nation of Irrakwa, altogether forming the United States of America, where Red and White, Dutchman, Swede and Englishman, rich and poor, merchant and laborer, all could vote and all could speak and no one could say, I'm a better man than you. Some folks allowed as how that made Ben as true a

Maker as ever lived, but no, said Taleswapper, that made Ben a binder, a knotter, but not a Maker.

I am the Maker that torch girl wrote about. She touched me as I was a-borning, and when she did she saw that I had Maker-stuff in me. I've got to find that girl, growed up to be sixteen years old by now, and she's got to tell me what she saw. Cause the powers I've found inside me, the things that I can do, I know they've got a purpose bigger than just cutting stone without hands and healing the sick and running through the woods like any Red man can but no White man ever could. I've got a work to do in my life and I don't have the first spark of an idea how to get ready for it.

Standing there in the road, with a pig farm on either hand, Alvin heard the sharp *ching ching* of iron striking iron. The smith might as well have called out to him by name. Here I am, said the hammer, find me up ahead along the road.

Before he ever got to the smithy, though, he rounded the bend and saw the very roadhouse where he was born, just as plain as ever in the vision in the crystal tower. Whitewashed shiny and new with only the dust of this summer on it, so it didn't look quite the same, but it was as welcome a sight as any weary traveler could hope for.

Twice welcome, cause inside it, with any decent luck, the torch girl could tell him what his life was supposed to be.

Alvin knocked at the door cause that's what you do, he thought. He'd never stayed in a roadhouse before, and had no notion of a public room. So he knocked once, and then twice, and then hallooed till finally the door opened. It was a woman with flour on her hands and her checked apron, a big woman who looked annoyed beyond belief—but he knew her face. This was the woman in his crystal tower vision, the one what pulled him out of the womb with her own fingers around his neck.

"What in the world are you thinking of, boy, to knock my door like that and start hullaballooing like there was a fire! Why can't you just come on in and set like any other folk, or are you so powerful important that you got to have a servant come and open doors for you?"

"Sorry, ma'am," said Alvin, about as respectful as could be.

"Now what business could you have with us? If you're a beggar then I got to tell you we'll have no scraps till after dinner, but you're welcome to wait till then, and if you got a conscience, why, you can chop some wood for us. Except for look at you, I can't believe you're more than fourteen years old—"

"Eleven, ma'am."

"Well, then, you're right big for your age, but I still can't figure what business you got here. I won't serve you no liquor even if you got money, which I doubt. This is a Christian house, in fact more than mere Christian because we're true-blue Methodist and that means we don't touch a drop nor serve it neither, and even if we did we wouldn't serve children. And I'd stake ten pound of porkfat on a wager that you don't have the price of a night's lodging.''

"No ma'am,'' said Alvin, "but—''

"Well then here you are, dragging me out of my kitchen with the bread half-kneaded and a baby who's bound to cry for milk any minute, and I reckon you don't plan to stand at the head of the table and explain to all my boarders why their dinner is late, on account of a boy who can't open a door his own self, no, you'll leave me to make apologies myself as best I can, which is right uncivil of you if you don't mind my saying, or even if you do.''

"Ma'am,'' said Alvin, "I don't want food and I don't want a room.'' He knew enough courtesy *not* to add that travelers had always been welcome to stay in his father's house whether they had money or not, and a hungry man didn't get afternoon scraps, he set down at Pa's own table and ate with the family. He was catching on to the idea that things were different here in civilized country.

"Well, all we deal in here is food and rooms,'' said the roadhouse lady.

"I come here, ma'am, cause I was born in this house almost twelve years ago.''

Her whole demeanor changed at once. She wasn't a roadhouse mistress now, she was a midwife. "Born in this house?''

"Born on the day my oldest brother Vigor died in the Hatrack River. I thought as how you might even remember that day, and maybe you could show me the place where my brother lies buried.''

Her face changed again. "You,'' she said. "You're the boy who was born to that family—the seventh son of—''

"Of a seventh son,'' said Alvin.

"Well what's become of you, tell me! Oh, it was a portentous thing. My daughter stood there and looked afar off and saw that your big brother was still alive as you came out of the womb—''

"Your daughter,'' said Alvin, forgetting himself so much that he interrupted her clean in the middle of a sentence. "She's a torch.''

The lady turned cold as ice. "*Was*,'' she said. "She don't torch no more.''

But Alvin hardly noticed how the lady changed. "You mean she lost her knack for it? I never heard of a body losing their knack. But if she's here, I'd like to talk to her.''

"She ain't here no more,'' said the lady. Now Alvin finally caught on that she didn't much care to talk about it. "There ain't no torch now in Hatrack River. Babies will be born here without a body touching them to see how they lie in the womb. That's the end of it. I won't say another word about such a girl as that who'd run off, just run right off—"

Something caught in the lady's voice and she turned her back to him. "I got to finish my bread," said the lady. "The graveyard is up the hill there." She turned around again to face him, with nary a sign of the anger or grief or what-all that she felt a second before. "If my Horace was here I'd have him show you the way, but you'll see it anyhow, there's a kind of path. It's just a family graveyard, with a picket fence around it." Her stern manner softened. "When you're done up there you come on back and I'll serve you better than scraps." She hurried on into the kitchen. Alvin followed her.

There was a cradle by the kitchen table, with a babe asleep in it but wiggling somewhat. Something funny about the baby but Alvin couldn't say right off what it was.

"Thank you for your kindness, ma'am, but I don't ask for no hand-outs. I'll work to pay for anything I eat."

"That's rightly said, and like a true man—your father was the same, and the bridge he built over the Hatrack is still there, strong as ever. But you just go now, see the graveyard, and then come back by and by."

She bent over the huge wad of dough on the kneading table. Alvin got the notion for just a moment that she was crying, and maybe he did and maybe he didn't see tears drop from her eyes straight down into the dough. It was plain she wanted to be alone.

He looked again at the baby and realized what was different. "That's a pickaninny baby, isn't it?" he said.

She stopped kneading, but left her hands buried to the wrist in dough. "It's a baby," she said, "and it's *my* baby. I adopted him and he's mine, and if you call him a pickaninny I'll knead your face like dough."

"Sorry, ma'am, I meant no harm. He just had a sort of cast to his face that gave me that idea, I reckon—"

"Oh, he's half-Black all right. But it's the White half of him I'm raising up, just as if he was my own son. We named him Arthur Stuart."

Alvin got the joke of that right off. "Ain't nobody can call the King a pickaninny, I reckon."

She smiled. "I reckon not. Now get, boy. You owe a debt to your dead brother, and you best pay it now."

The graveyard was easy to find, and Alvin was gratified to see that his brother Vigor had a stone, and his grave was as well-tended as any other. Only a few graves here. Two stones with the same name—"Baby

Missy''—and dates that told of children dying young. Another stone
that said ''Oldpappy'' and then his real name, and dates that told of a
long life. And Vigor.

He knelt by his brother's grave and tried to picture what he might
have been like. The best he could do was imagine his brother Measure,
who was his favorite brother, the one who was captured by Reds along
with Alvin. Vigor must have been like Measure. Or maybe Measure
was like Vigor. Both willing to die if need be, for their family's sake.
Vigor's death saved my life before I was born, thought Alvin, and yet
he hung on to the last breath so that when I was born I was still the
seventh son of a seventh son, with all my brothers ahead of me alive.
The same kind of sacrifice and courage and strength that it took when
Measure, who hadn't killed a single Red man, who near died just trying
to stop the Tippy-Canoe massacre from happening, took on himself the
same curse as his father and his brothers, to have blood on his hands if
he failed to tell any stranger the true story of the killing of all them
innocent Reds. So when he knelt there at Vigor's grave, it was like he
was kneeling at Measure's grave, even though he knew Measure wasn't
dead.

Wasn't wholly dead, anyway. But like the rest of the folk of Vigor
Church, he'd never leave that place again. He'd live out all his days
where he wouldn't have to meet too many strangers, so that for days
on end he could forget the slaughter on that day last summer. The whole
family, staying together there, with all the folks in the country roundabout, living out their days of life until them as had the curse all died,
sharing each other's shame and each other's loneliness like they was all
kin, every one of them.

All them together, except for me. I didn't take no curse on me. I left
them all behind.

Kneeling there, Alvin felt like an orphan. He might as well be. Sent
off to be a prentice here, knowing that whatever he did, whatever he
made, his kin could never come on out to see. He could go home to
that bleak sad town from time to time, but that was more like a graveyard than this grassy living place, because even with dead folks buried
here, there was hope and life in the town nearby, people looking forward
instead of back.

Alvin had to look forward, too. Had to find his way to what he was
born to be. You died for me, Vigor, my brother that I never met. I just
haven't figured out yet why it was so important for me to be alive.
When I find out, I hope to make you proud of me. I hope you'll think
that I was worth dying for.

When his thoughts was all spent and gone, when his heart had filled up and then emptied out again, Alvin did something he never thought to do. He looked under the ground.

Not by digging, mind you. Alvin's knack was such that he could get the feel of underground without using his eyes. Like the way he looked into stone. Now it might seem to some folk like a kind of grave-robbing, for Al to peek inside the earth where his brother's body lay. But to Al it was the only way he'd ever see the man who died to save him.

So he closed his eyes and gazed under the soil and found the bones inside the rotted wooden box. The size of him—Vigor was a big boy, which is about what it would take to roll and yaw a full-sized tree in a river's current. But the soul of him, that wasn't there, and even though he knowed it wouldn't be Al was somewhat disappointed.

His hidden gaze wandered to the small bodies barely clinging to their own dust, and then to the gnarled old corpse of Oldpappy, whoever that was, fresh in the earth, only a year or so buried.

But not so fresh as the other body. The unmarked body. One day dead at most, she was, all her flesh still on her and the worms hardly working at her yet.

He cried out in the surprise of it, and the grief at the next thought that came to mind. Could it be the torch girl buried there? Her mother said that she run off, but when folks run off it ain't unusual for them to come back dead. Why else was the mother grieving so? The innkeeper's own daughter, buried without a marker—oh, that spoke of terrible bad things. Did she run off and get herself shamed so bad her own folks wouldn't mark her burying place? Why else leave her there without a stone?

"What's wrong with you, boy?"

Alvin stood, turned, faced the man. A stout fellow who was right comfortable to look upon; but his face wasn't too easy right now.

"What are you doing here in this graveyard, boy?"

"Sir," said Alvin, "my brother's buried here."

The man thought a moment, his face easing. "You're one of that family. But I recall all their boys was as old as you even back then—"

"I'm the one what was born here that night."

At that news the man just opened up his arms and folded Alvin up inside. "They named you Alvin, didn't they," said the man, "just like your father. We call him Alvin Bridger around here, he's something of legend. Let me see you, see what you've become. Seventh son of a seventh son, come home to see your birthplace and your brother's grave. Of course you'll stay in my roadhouse. I'm Horace Guester, as you might guess, I'm pleased to meet you, but ain't you somewhat big for—what, ten, eleven years old?"

"Almost twelve. Folks say I'm tall."

"I hope you're proud of the marker we made for your brother. He was admired here, even though we all met him in death and never in life."

"I'm suited," said Alvin. "It's a good stone." And then, because he couldn't help himself, though it wasn't a particularly wise thing to do, he up and asked the question most burning in him. "But I wonder, sir, why one girl got herself buried here yesterday, and no stone nor marker tells her name."

Horace Guester's face turned ashen. "Of course you'd see," he whispered. "Doodlebug or something. Seventh son. God help us all."

"Did she do something shameful, sir, not to have no marker?" asked Alvin.

"Not shame," said Horace. "As God is my witness, boy, this girl was noble in life and died a virtuous death. She stays unmarked so this house can be a shelter to others like her. But oh, lad, say you'll never tell what you found buried here. You'd cause pain to dozens and hundreds of lost souls along the road from slavery to freedom. Can you believe me that much, trust me and be my friend in this? It'd be too much grief, to lose my daughter and have this secret out, all in the same day. Since I can't keep the secret from you, you have to keep it with me, Alvin, lad. Say you will."

"I'll keep a secret if it's honorable, sir," said Alvin, "but what honorable secret leads a man to bury his own daughter without a stone?"

Horace's eyes went wide, and then he laughed like he was calling loony birds. When he got control of hisself, he clapped Alvin on the shoulder. "That ain't my daughter in the ground there, boy, what made you think it was? It's a Black girl, a runaway slave, who died last night on her way north."

Now Alvin realized for the first time that the body was way too small to be no sixteen-year-old, anyhow. It was a child-size body. "That baby in your kitchen, it's her brother?"

"Her son," said Horace.

"But she's so small," said Alvin.

"That didn't stop her White owner from getting her with child, boy. I don't know how you stand on the question of slavery, or if you even thought about it, but I beg you do some thinking now. Think about how slavery lets a White man steal a girl's virtue and still go to church on Sunday while she groans in shame and bears his bastard child."

"You're a Mancipationist, ain't you?" said Alvin.

"Reckon I am," said the innkeeper, "but I reckon all good Christian folk are Mancipationists in their hearts."

"I reckon so," said Alvin.

"I hope *you* are, cause if word gets out that I was helping a slavegirl run off to Canada, there'll be finders and cotchers from Appalachee and the Crown Colonies a-spying on me so I can't help no others get away."

Alvin looked back at the grave and thought about the babe in the kitchen. "You going to tell that baby where his mama's grave is?"

"When he's old enough to know, and not to tell it," said the man.

"Then I'll keep your secret, if you keep mine."

The man raised his eyebrows and studied Alvin. "What secret *you* got, Alvin, a boy as young as you?"

"I don't have no partickler wish to have it known I'm a seventh son. I'm here to prentice with Makepeace Smith, which I reckon is the man I hear a-hammering at the forge down yonder."

"And you don't want folks knowing you can see a body lying in an unmarked grave."

"You caught my drift right enough," said Alvin. "I won't tell your secret, and you won't tell mine."

"You have my word on it," said the man. Then he held out his hand.

Took that hand and shook it, gladly. Most grownup folk wouldn't think of making a bargain like that with a mere child like him. But this man even offered his hand, like they were equals. "You'll see I know how to keep my word, sir," said Alvin.

"And anyone around here can tell you Horace Guester keeps a promise, too." Then Horace told him the story that they were letting out about the baby, how it was the Berrys' youngest, and they gave it up for Old Peg Guester to raise, cause they didn't need another child and she'd always hankered to have her a son. "And that part is true enough," said Horace Guester. "All the more, with Peggy running off."

"Your daughter," said Alvin.

Suddenly Horace Guester's eyes filled up with tears and he shuddered with a sob like Alvin never heard from a growed man in his life. "Just ran off this morning," said Horace Guester.

"Maybe she's just a-calling on somebody in town or something," said Alvin.

Horace shook his head. "I beg your pardon, crying like that, I just beg your pardon, I'm awful tired, truth to tell, up all night last night, and then this morning, her gone like that. She left us a note. She's gone all right."

"Don't you know the man she run off with?" asked Alvin. "Maybe they'll get married, that happened once to a Swede girl out in the Noisy River country—"

Horace turned a bit red with anger. "I reckon you're just a boy so you don't know better than to say such a thing. So I'll tell you now, she didn't run off with no *man*. She's a woman of pure virtue, and no one ever said otherwise. No, she run off alone, boy.''

Alvin thought he'd seen all kinds of strange things in his life—a tornado turned into a crystal tower, a bolt of cloth with all the souls of men and women woven in it, murders and tortures, tales and miracles, Alvin knew more of life than most boys at eleven years of age. But this was the strangest thing of all, to think of a girl of sixteen just up and leaving her father's house, without no husband or nothing. In all his life he never saw a woman go *nowhere* by herself beyond her own dooryard.

"Is she—is she *safe*?"

Horace laughed bitterly. "Safe? Of course she's safe. She's a torch, Alvin, the best torch I ever heard of. She can see folks miles off, she knows their hearts, ain't a man born can come near her with evil on his mind without she knows exactly what he's planning and just how to get away. No, I ain't *worried* about her. She can take care of herself better than any man. I just—''

"Miss her," said Alvin.

"I guess it don't take no torch to guess that, am I right, lad? I miss her. And it hurt my feelings somewhat that she up and left with no warning. I could've given her God bless to send her on her way. Her mama could've worked up some good hex, not that Little Peggy'd need it, or anyhow just pack her a cold dinner for on the road. But none of that, no fare-thee-well nor God-be-with-you. It was like as if she was running from some awful boogly monster and had no time to take but one spare dress in a cloth bag and rush on out the door.''

Running from some monster—those words stung right to Alvin's soul. She was such a torch that it might well be she saw Alvin coming. Up and ran away the morning he arrived. If she wasn't no torch then maybe it was just chance that took her off the same day he come. But she *was* a torch. She saw him coming. She knew he came all this way a-hoping to meet her and beg her to help him find his way into becoming whatever it was that he was born to be. She saw all that, and ran away.

"I'm right sorry that she's gone," said Alvin.

"I thank you for your pity, friend, it's good of you. I just hope it won't be for long. I just hope she'll do whatever she left to do and come on back in a few days or maybe a couple of weeks." He laughed again, or maybe sobbed, it was about the same sound. "I can't even go ask the Hatrack torch to tell a fortune about her, cause the Hatrack River torch is gone.''

Horace cried outright again, for just a minute. Then he took Alvin by the shoulders and looked him in the eye, not even hiding the tears on his cheeks. "Alvin, you just remember how you seen me crying all unmanlike, and you remember that's how fathers feel about their children when they're gone. That's how your own pa feels right now, having you so far away."

"I know he does," said Alvin.

"Now if you don't mind," said Horace Guester, "I need to be alone here."

Alvin touched his arm just a moment and then he went away. Not down to the house to have his noon meal like Old Peg Guester offered. He was too upset to sit and eat with them. How could he explain that he was nigh on to being as heartbroke as them, to have that torch girl gone? No, he'd have to keep silence. The answers he was looking for in Hatrack, they were gone off with a sixteen-year-old girl who didn't want to meet him when he came.

Maybe she seen my future and she hates me. Maybe I'm as bad a boogly monster as anybody ever dreamed of on an evil night.

He followed the sound of the blacksmith's hammer. It led him along a faint path to a springhouse straddling a brook that came straight out of a hillside. And down the stream, along a clear meadow slope, he walked until he came to the smithy. Hot smoke rose from the forge. Around front he walked, and saw the blacksmith inside the big sliding door, hammering a hot iron bar into a curving shape across the throat of his anvil.

Alvin stood and watched him work. He could feel the heat from the forge clear outside; inside must be like the fires of hell. His muscles were like fifty different ropes holding his arm on under the skin. They shifted and rolled across each other as the hammer rose into the air, then bunched all at once as the hammer came down. Close as he was now, Alvin could hardly bear the bell-like crash of iron on iron, with the anvil like a sounding fork to make the sound ring on and on. Sweat dripped off the blacksmith's body, and he was naked to the waist, his white skin ruddy from the heat, streaked with soot from the forge and sweat from his pores. I've been sent here to be prentice to the devil, thought Alvin.

But he knew that was a silly idea even as he thought it. This was a hardworking man, that's all, earning his living with a skill that every town needed if it hoped to thrive. Judging from the size of the corrals for horses waiting to be shod, and the heaps of iron bars waiting to be made into plows and sickles, axes and cleavers, he did a good business, too. If I learn this trade, I'll never be hungry, thought Alvin, and folks will always be glad to have me.

And something more. Something about the hot fire and the ruddy iron. What happened in this place was akin somehow to making. Alvin knew from the way he'd worked with stone in the granite quarry, when he carved the millstone for his father's mill, he knew that with his knack he could probably reach inside the iron and make it go the way he wanted it to go. But he had something to learn from the forge and the hammer, the bellows and the fire and the water in the cooling tubs, something that would help him become what he was born to become.

So now he looked at the blacksmith, not as a powerful stranger, but as Alvin's future self. He saw how the muscles grew on the smith's shoulders and back. Alvin's body was strong from chopping wood and splitting rails and all the hoisting and lifting that he did earning pennies and nickels on neighbors' farms. But in that kind of work, your whole body went into every movement. You rared back with the axe and when it swung it was like your whole body was part of the axhandle, so that legs and hips and back all moved into the chop. But the smith, he held the hot iron in the tongs, held it so smooth and exact against the anvil that while his right arm swung the hammer, the rest of his body couldn't move a twitch, that left arm stayed as smooth and steady as a rock. It shaped the smith's body differently, forced the arms to be much stronger by themselves, muscles rooted to the neck and breastbone standing out in a way they never did on a farmboy's body.

Alvin felt inside himself, the way his own muscles grew, and knew already where the changes would have to come. It was part of his knack, to find his way within living flesh most as easily as he could chart the inner shapes of living stone. So even now he was hunkering down inside, teaching his body to change itself to make way for the new work.

"Boy," said the smith.

"Sir," said Alvin.

"Have you got business for me? I don't know you, do I?"

Alvin stepped forward, held out the note his father writ.

"Read it to me, boy, my eyes are none too good."

Alvin unfolded the paper. "From Alvin Miller of Vigor Church. To Makepeace, Blacksmith of Hatrack River. Here is my boy Alvin what you said could be your prentice till he be seventeen. He'll work hard and do what all you say, and you teach him what all a man needs to be a good smith, like in the articles I signed. He is a good boy."

The smith reached for the paper, held it close to his eyes. His lips moved as he repeated a few phrases. Then he slapped the paper down on the anvil. "This is a fine turn," said the smith. "Don't you know you're a year late, boy? You was supposed to come last spring. I turned away three offers for prentice cause I had your pa's word you was coming, and here I've been without help this whole year cause he *didn't* keep his word. Now I'm supposed to take you in with a year less on your contract, and not even a by-your-leave or beg-your-pardon.''

"I'm sorry, sir," said Alvin. "But we had the war last year. I was on my way here but I got captured by Choc-Taw.''

"Captured by—oh, come now, boy, don't tell me tales like that. If the Choc-Taw caught you, you wouldn't have such a dandy head of hair now, would you! And like as not you'd be missing a few fingers.''

"Ta-Kumsaw rescued me," said Alvin.

"Oh, and no doubt you met the Prophet hisself and walked on water with him.''

As a matter of fact, Alvin done just that. But from the smith's tone of voice, he reckoned that it wouldn't be wise to say so. So Alvin said nothing.

"Where's your horse?" asked the smith.

"Don't have one," said Alvin.

"Your father wrote the date on this letter boy, two days ago! You must've rode a horse.''

"I ran." As soon as Alvin said it, he knew it was a mistake.

"Ran?" said the smith. "With *bare feet?* It must be nigh four hundred mile or more to the Wobbish from here! Your feet ought to be ripped to rags clear up to your knees! Don't tell me tales, boy! I won't have no liars around me!''

Alvin had a choice, and he knew it. He could explain about how he could run like a Red man. Makepeace Smith wouldn't believe him, and so Alvin would have to show him some of what he could do. It would be easy enough. Bend a bar of iron just by stroking it. Make two stones mash together to form one. But Alvin already made up his mind he didn't want to show his knacks here. How could he be a proper prentice, if folks kept coming around for him to cut them hearthstones or fix a broken wheel or all the other fixing things he had a knack for? Besides, he never done such a thing, showing off just for the sake of proving what he could do. Back home he only used his knack when there was need.

So he stuck with his decision to keep his knack to himself, pretty much. Not tell what he could do. Just learn like any normal boy, working the iron the way the smith himself did, letting the muscles grow slowly on his arms and shoulders, chest and back.

"I was joking," Alvin said. "A man gave me a ride on his spare mount.''

"I don't like that kind of joke," said the smith. "I don't like it that you lied to me so easy like that.''

What could Alvin say? He couldn't even claim that he hadn't lied—

he had, when he told about a man letting him ride. So he was as much a liar as the smith thought. The only confusion was about *which* statement was a lie.

"I'm sorry," said Alvin.

"I'm not taking you, boy. I don't have to take you anyway, a year late. And here you come lying to me the first thing. I won't have it."

"Sir, I'm sorry," said Alvin. "It won't happen again. I'm not known for a liar back home, and you'll see I'll be known for square dealing here, if you give me a chance. Catch me lying or not giving fair work all the time, and you can chuck me, no questions asked. Just give me a chance to prove it, sir."

"You don't look like you're eleven, neither, boy."

"But I am, sir. You know I am. You yourself with your own arms pulled my brother Vigor's body from the river on the night that I was born, or so my pa told me."

The smith's face went distant, as if he was remembering. "Yes, he told you true, I was the one who pulled him out. Clinging to the roots of that tree even in death, so I thought I'd have to cut him free. Come here, boy."

Alvin walked closer. The smith poked and pushed the muscles of his arms.

"Well, I can see you're not a lazy boy. Lazy boys get soft, but you're strong like a hardworking farmer. Can't lie about *that*, I reckon. Still, you haven't seen what real work is."

"I'm ready to learn."

"Oh, I'm sure of that. Many a boy would be glad to learn from me. Other work might come and go, but there's always a need for a blacksmith. That'll never change. Well, you're strong enough in body, I reckon. Let's see about your brain. Look at this anvil. This here's the bick, on the point, you see. Say that."

"Bick."

"And then the throat here. And this is the table—it ain't faced with blister steel, so when you ram a cold chisel into it the chisel don't blunt. Then up a notch onto the steel face, where you work the hot metal. And this is the hardie hole, where I rest the butt of the fuller and the flatter and the swage. And this here's the pricking hole, for when I punch holes in strap iron—the hot punch shoots right through into this space. You got all that?"

"I think so, sir."

"Then name me the parts of the anvil."

Alvin named them as best he could. Couldn't remember the job each one did, not all of them, anyways, but what he did was good enough, cause the blacksmith nodded and grinned. "Reckon you ain't a half-wit, anyhow, you'll learn quick enough. And big for your age is good. I won't have to keep you on a broom and the bellows for the first four years, the way I do with smaller boys. But your age, that's a sticking point. A term of prentice work is seven year, but my written-up articles with your pa, they only say till you're seventeen."

"I'm almost twelve now, sir."

"So what I'm saying is, I want to be able to hold you the full seven years, if need be. I don't want you whining off just when I finally get you trained enough to be useful."

"Seven years, sir. The spring when I'm nigh on nineteen, then my time is up."

"Seven years is a long time, boy, and I mean to hold you to it. Most boys start when they're nine or ten, or even seven years old, so they can make a living, start looking for a wife at sixteen or seventeen years old. I won't have none of that. I expect you to live like a Christian, and no fooling with any of the girls in town, you understand me?"

"Yes sir."

"All right then. My prentices sleep in the loft over the kitchen, and you eat at table with my wife and children and me, though I'll thank you not to speak until spoken to inside the house—I won't have my prentices thinking they have the same rights as my own children, cause you don't."

"Yes sir."

"And as for now, I need to het up this strap again. So you start to work the bellows there."

Alvin walked to the bellows handle. It was T-shaped, for two-handed working. But Alvin twisted the end piece so it was at the same angle as the hammer handle when the smith lifted it into the air. Then he started to work the bellows with one arm.

"What are you doing, boy!" shouted Alvin's new master. "You won't last ten minutes working the bellows with one arm."

"Then in ten minutes I'll switch to my left arm," said Alvin. "But I won't get myself ready for the hammer if I bend over every time I work the bellows."

The smith looked at him angrily. Then he laughed. "You got a fresh mouth, boy, but you also got sense. Do it your way as long as you can, but see to it you don't slack on wind—I need a hot fire, and that's more important than you working up strength in your arms right now."

Alvin set to pumping. Soon he could feel the pain of this unaccustomed movement gnawing at his neck and chest and back. But he kept going, never breaking the rhythm of the bellows, forcing his body to endure. He could have made the muscles grow right now, teaching them the pattern with his hidden power. But that wasn't what Alvin was here for, he was pretty sure of that. So he let the pain come as it would, and his body change as it would, each new muscle earned by his own effort.

Alvin lasted fifteen minutes with his right hand, ten minutes with his left. He felt the muscles aching and liked the way it felt. Makepeace Smith seemed pleased enough with what he did. Alvin knew that he'd be changed here, that his work would make a strong and skillful man of him.

A man, but not a Maker. Not yet fully on the road to what he was born to be. But since there hadn't been a Maker in the world in a thousand years or more, or so folks said, who was he going to prentice himself to in order to learn *that* trade?

4

Modesty

Whitley Physicker helped Peggy down from the carriage in front of a fine-looking house in one of the best neighborhoods of Dekane. "I'd like to see you to the door, Peggy Guester, just to make sure they're home to greet you," said he, but she knew he didn't expect her to allow him to do that. If anybody knew how little she liked to have folks fussing over her, it was Doctor Whitley Physicker. So she thanked him kindly and bid him farewell.

She heard his carriage rolling off, the horse clopping on the cobblestones, as she rapped the knocker on the door. A maid opened the door, a German girl so fresh off the boat she couldn't even speak enough English to ask Peggy's name. She invited her in with a gesture, seated her on a bench in the hall, and then held out a silver plate.

What was the plate *for*? Peggy couldn't hardly make sense at all of what she saw inside this foreign girl's mind. She was expecting something—what? A little slip of paper, but Peggy didn't have a notion why. The girl thrust the salver closer to her, insisting. Peggy couldn't do a thing but shrug.

Finally the German girl gave up and went away. Peggy sat on the bench and waited. She searched for heartfires in the house, and found the one she looked for. Only then did she realize what the plate was for—her calling card. Folks in the city, rich folks anyway, they had little cards they put their name on, to announce theirself when they came to visit. Peggy even remembered reading about it in a book, but it was a book from the Crown Colonies and she never thought folks in free lands kept such formality.

Soon the lady of the house came, the German girl shadowing her, peering from behind her fine day gown. Peggy knew from the lady's heartfire that she didn't think herself dressed in any partickler finery today, but to Peggy she was like the Queen herself.

Peggy looked into her heartfire and found what she had hoped for. The lady wasn't annoyed a bit at seeing Peggy there, merely curious. Oh, the lady was judging her, of course—Peggy never met a soul, least of all herself, what didn't make some judgment of every stranger—but the judgment was kind. When the lady looked at Peggy's plain clothes, she saw a country girl, not a pauper; when the lady looked at Peggy's stern, expressionless face, she saw a child who had known pain, not an ugly girl. And when the lady imagined Peggy's pain, her first thought was to try to heal her. All in all, the lady was *good*. Peggy made no mistake in coming here.

"I don't believe I've had the pleasure to meet you," said the lady. Her voice was sweet and soft and beautiful.

"I reckon not, Mistress Modesty," said Peggy. "My name is Peggy. I think you had some acquaintance with my papa, years ago."

"Perhaps if you told me his name?"

"Horace," said Peggy. "Horace Guester, of Hatrack, Hio."

Peggy saw the turmoil in her heartfire at the very sound of his name— glad memory, and yet a glimmer of fear of what this strange girl might intend. Yet the fear quickly subsided—her husband had died several years ago, and so was beyond hurt. And none of these emotions showed in the lady's face, which held its sweet and friendly expression with perfect grace. Modesty turned to the maid and spoke a few words of fluent German. The maid curtsied and was gone.

"Did your father send you?" asked the lady. Her unspoken question was: Did your father tell you what I meant to him, and he to me?

"No," said Peggy. "I come here on my own. He'd die if he found out I knew your name. You see I'm a torch, Mistress Modesty. He has no secrets, not from me. Nobody does."

It didn't surprise Peggy one bit how Modesty took that news. Most folks would've thought right off about all the secrets they hoped she wouldn't guess. Instead, the lady thought at once how awful it must be for Peggy, to know things that didn't bear knowing. "How long has it been that way?" she said softly. "Surely not when you were just a little girl. The Lord is too merciful to let such knowledge fill a child's mind."

"I reckon the Lord didn't concern himself much with me," said Peggy.

The lady reached out and touched Peggy's cheek. Peggy knew the lady had noticed she was somewhat dirty from the dust of the road. But what the lady mostly thought of wasn't clothes or cleanliness. A torch, she was thinking. That's why a girl so young wears such a cold, forbidding face. Too much knowledge has made this girl so hard.

"Why have you come to me?" asked Modesty. "Surely you don't mean harm to me or your father, for such an ancient transgression."

"Oh, no ma'am," said Peggy. Never in her life did her own voice sound so harsh to her, but compared to this lady she was squawking like a crow. "If I'm torch enough to know your secret, I'm torch enough to know there was some good in it as well as sin, and as far as the sin goes, Papa's paying for it still, paying double and treble every year of his life."

Tears came into Modesty's eyes. "I had hoped," she murmured, "I had hoped that time would ease the shame of it, and he'd remember it now with joy. Like one of the ancient faded tapestries in England, whose colors are no longer bright, but whose image is the very shadow of beauty itself."

Peggy might've told her that he felt more than joy, that he relived all his feelings for her like it happened yesterday. But that was Papa's secret, and not hers to tell.

Modesty touched a kerchief to her eyes, to take away the tears that trembled there. "All these years I've never spoken to a mortal soul of this. I've poured out my heart only to the Lord, and he's forgiven me; yet I find it somehow exhilarating to speak of this to someone whose face I can see with my eyes, and not just my imagination. Tell me, child, if you didn't come as the avenging angel, have you come perhaps as a forgiving one?"

Mistress Modesty spoke with such elegance that Peggy found herself reaching for the language of the books she read, instead of her natural talking voice. "I'm a—a supplicant," said Peggy. "I come for help. I come to change my life, and I thought, being how you loved my father, you might be willing to do a kindness for his daughter."

The lady smiled at her. "And if you're half the torch you claim to be, you already know my answer. What kind of help do you need? My husband left me a good deal of money when he died, but I think it isn't money that you need."

"No ma'am," said Peggy. But what was it that she wanted, now that she was here? How could she explain why she had come? "I didn't like the life I saw for myself back in Hatrack. I wanted to—"

"Escape?"

"Somewhat like that, I reckon, but not exactly."

"You want to become something other than what you are," said the lady.

"Yes, Mistress Modesty."

"What is it that you wish to be?"

Peggy had never thought of words to describe what she dreamed of, but now, with Mistress Modesty before her, Peggy saw how simply those dreams might be expressed. "You, ma'am."

The lady smiled and touched her own face, her own hair. "Oh, my child, you must have higher aims than that. Much of what is best in me, your father gave me. The way he loved me taught me that perhaps— no, not *perhaps*—that I *was* worth loving. I have learned much more since then, more of what a woman is and ought to be. What a lovely symmetry, if I can give back to his daughter some of the wisdom he brought to me." She laughed gently. "I never imagined myself taking a pupil."

"More like a disciple, I think, Mistress Modesty."

"Neither pupil nor disciple. Will you stay here as a guest in my home? Will you let me be your friend?"

Even though Peggy couldn't rightly see the paths of her own life, she still felt them open up inside her, all the futures she could hope for, waiting for her in this place. "Oh, ma'am," she whispered, "if you will."

5

Dowser

Hank Dowser'd seen him prentice boys a-plenty over the years, but never a one as fresh as this. Here was Makepeace Smith bent over old Picklewing's left forehoof, all set to drive in the nail, and up spoke his boy.

"Not that nail," said the blacksmith's prentice boy. "Not there."

Well, that was as fine a moment as Hank ever saw for the master to give his prentice boy a sharp cuff on the ear and send him bawling into the house. But Makepeace Smith just nodded, then looked at the boy.

"You think you can nail this shoe, Alvin?" asked the master. "She's a big one, this mare, but I see you got you some inches since last I looked."

"I can," said the boy.

"Now just hold your horses," said Hank Dowser. "Picklewing's my only animal, and I can't just up and buy me another. I don't want your prentice boy learning to be a farrier and making his mistakes at my poor old nag's expense." And since he was already speaking his mind so frank like, Hank just rattled right on like a plain fool. "Who's the master here, anyway?" said he.

Well, that was the wrong thing to say. Hank knew it the second the words slipped out of his mouth. You don't say Who's the master, not in front of the prentice. And sure enough, Makepeace Smith's ears turned red and he stood up, all six feet of him, with arms like oxlegs and hands that could crush a bear's face, and he said, "I'm the master here, and when I say my prentice is good enough for the job, then he's good enough, or you can take your custom to another smith."

"Now just hold your horses," said Hank Dowser.

"I *am* holding your horse," said Makepeace Smith. "Or at least your horse's leg. In fact, your horse is leaning over on me something heavy. And now you start asking if I'm master of my own smithy.''

Anybody whose head don't leak knows that riling the smith who's shoeing your horse is about as smart as provoking the bees on your way in for the honey. Hank Dowser just hoped Makepeace would be somewhat easier to calm down. "Course you are," said Hank. "I meant nothing by it, except I was surprised when your prentice spoke up so smart and all.''

"Well that's cause he's got him a knack," said Makepeace Smith. "This boy Alvin, he can tell things about the inside of a horse's hoof— where a nail's going to hold, where it's going into soft hurting flesh, that kind of thing. He's a natural farrier. And if he says to me, Don't drive that nail, well I know by now that's a nail I don't want to drive, cause it'll make the horse crazy or lame.''

Hank Dowser grinned and backed off. It was a hot day, that's all, that's why tempers were so high. "I have respect for every man's knack," said Hank. "Just like I expect them to have respect for mine.''

"In that case, I've held up your horse long enough," said the smith. "Here, Alvin, nail this shoe.''

If the boy had swaggered or simpered or sneered, Hank would've had a reason to be so mad. But Prentice Alvin just hunkered down with nails in his mouth and hooked up the left forehoof. Picklewing leaned on him, but the boy was right tall, even though his face had no sign of beard yet, and he was like a twin of his master, when it come to muscle under his skin. It wasn't one minute, the horse leaning that way, before the shoe was nailed in place. Picklewing didn't so much as shiver, let alone dance the way he usually did when the nails went in. And now that Hank thought about it a little, Picklewing always *did* seem to favor that leg just a little, as if something was a mite sore inside the hoof. But he'd been that way so long Hank hardly noticed it no more.

The prentice boy stepped back out of the way, still not showing any brag at all. He wasn't doing a thing that was the tiniest bit benoctious, but Hank still felt an unreasonable anger at the boy. "How old is he?'' asked Hank.

"Fourteen," said Makepeace Smith. "He come to me when he was eleven.''

"A mite old for a prentice, wouldn't you say?" asked Hank.

"A year late in arriving, he was, because of the war with the Reds and the French—he's from out in the Wobbish country.''

"Them was hard years," said Hank. "Lucky me I was in Irrakwa the whole time. Dowsing wells for windmills the whole way along the railroad they were building. Fourteen, eh? Tall as he is, I reckon he lied about his age even so.''

If the boy disliked being named a liar, he didn't show no sign of it. Which made Hank Dowser all the more annoyed. That boy was like a burr under his saddle, just made him mad whatever the boy did. ''No,'' said the smith. ''We know his age well enough. He was born right here in Hatrack River, fourteen years ago, when his folks were passing through on their way west. We buried his oldest brother up on the hill. Big for his age though, ain't he?''

They might've been discussing a horse instead of a boy. But Prentice Alvin didn't seem to mind. He just stood there, staring right through them as if they were made of glass.

''You got four years left of his contract, then?'' asked Hank.

''Bit more. Till he's near nineteen.''

''Well, if he's already this good, I reckon he'll be buying out early and going journeyman.'' Hank looked, but the boy didn't brighten up at this idea, neither.

''I reckon not,'' said Makepeace Smith. ''He's good with the horses, but he gets careless with the forge. Any smith can do shoes, but it takes a *real* smith to do a plow blade or a wheel tire, and a knack with horses don't help a bit with that. Why, for my masterpiece I done me an anchor! I was in Netticut at the time, mind you. There ain't much call for anchors *here*, I reckon.''

Picklewing snorted and stamped—but he didn't dance lively, the way horses do when their new shoes are troublesome. It was a good set of shoes, well shod. Even *that* made Hank mad at the prentice boy. His own anger made no sense to him. The boy had put on Picklewing's last shoe, on a leg that might have been lamed in another farrier's hands. The boy had done him *good*. So why this wrath burning just under the surface, getting worse whatever the boy did or said?

Hank shrugged off his feelings. ''Well, that's work well done,'' he said. ''And so it's time for me to do my part.''

''Now, we both know a dowsing's worth more than a shoeing,'' said the smith. ''So if you need any more work done, you know I owe it to you, free and clear.''

''I *will* come back, Makepeace Smith, next time my nag needs shoes.'' And because Hank Dowser was a Christian man and felt ashamed of how he disliked the boy, he added praise for the lad. ''I reckon I'll be sure to come back while this boy's still under prentice bond to you, him having the knack he's got.''

The boy might as well not've heard the good words, and the master smith just chuckled. "You ain't the only one who feels like that," he said.

At that moment Hank Dowser understood something that he might've missed otherwise. This boy's knack with hooves was good for trade, and Makepeace Smith was just the kind of man who'd hold that boy to every day of his contract, to profit from the boy's name for clean shoeing with no horses lost by laming. All a greedy master had to do was claim the boy wasn't good at forgework or something like, then use that as a pretext to hold him fast. In the meantime the boy'd make a name for this place as the best farriery in eastern Hio. Money in Makepeace Smith's pocket, and nothing for the boy at all, not money nor freedom.

The law was the law, and the smith wasn't breaking it—he had the right to every day of that boy's service. But the custom was to let a prentice go as soon as he had the skill and had sense enough to make his way in the world. Otherwise, if a boy couldn't hope for early freedom, why should he work hard to learn as quick as he could, work as hard as he could? They said even the slaveowners in the Crown Colonies let their best slaves earn a little pocket money on the side, so's they could buy their freedom sometime before they died.

No, Makepeace Smith wasn't breaking no law, but he was breaking the custom of masters with their prentice boys, and Hank thought ill of him for it; it was a mean sort of master who'd keep a boy who'd already learned everything the master had to teach.

And yet, even knowing that it was the boy who was in the right, and his master in the wrong—even knowing that, he looked at that boy and felt a cold wet hatred in his heart. Hank shuddered, tried to shake it off.

"You say you need a well," said Hank Dowser. "You want it for drinking or for washing or for the smithy?"

"Does it make a difference?" asked the smith.

"Well, I think so," said Hank. "For drinking you need pure water, and for washing you want water that got no disease in it. But for your work in the smithy, I reckon the iron don't give no never mind whether it cools in clear or murky water, am I right?"

"The spring up the hill is giving out, slacking off year by year," said the smith. "I need me a well I can count on. Deep and clean and pure."

"You know why the stream's going slack," said Hank. "Everybody else is digging wells, and sucking out the water before it can seep out the spring. Your well is going to be about the last straw."

"I wouldn't be surprised," said the smith. "But I can't undig their wells, and I got to have my water, too. Reason I settled here was because of the stream, and now they've dried it up on me. I reckon I could move on, but I got me a wife and three brats up at the house, and I like it here, like it well enough. So I figure I'd rather draw water than move.''

Hank went on down to the stand of willows by the stream, near where it came out from under an old springhouse, which had fallen into disrepair. "Yours?" asked Hank.

"No, it belongs to old Horace Guester, him who owns the roadhouse up yonder.''

Hank found him a thin willow wand that forked just right, and started cutting it out with his knife. "Springhouse doesn't get much use now, I see.''

"Stream's dying, like I said. Half the time in summer there ain't enough water in it to keep the cream jars cool. Springhouse ain't no good if you can't count on it all summer.''

Hank made the last slice and the willow rod pulled free. He shaved the thick end to a point and whittled off all the leaf nubs, making it as smooth as ever he could. There was some dowsers who didn't care how smooth the rod was, just broke off the leaves and left the ends all raggedy, but Hank knew that the water didn't always want to be found, and then you needed a good smooth willow wand to find it. There was others used a clean wand, but always the same one, year after year, place after place, but that wasn't no good neither, Hank knew, cause the wand had to be from willow or, sometimes, hickory that grew up sucking the water you were hoping to find. Them other dowsers were mountebanks, though it didn't do no good to say so. They found water most times because in most places if you dig down far enough there's *bound* to be water. But Hank did it right, Hank had the true knack. He could feel the willow wand trembling in his hands, could feel the water singing to him under the ground. He didn't just pick the first sign of water, either. He was looking for clear water, high water, close to the surface and easy to pull. He took *pride* in his work.

But it wasn't like that prentice boy—what was his name?—Alvin. Wasn't like him. Either a man could nail horseshoes without ever laming the horse, or he couldn't. If he *ever* lamed a horse, folks thought twice before they went to that farrier again. But with a dowser, it didn't seem to make no difference if you found water every time or not. If you called yourself a dowser and had you a forked stick, folks would pay you for dowsing wells, without bothering to find out if you had any knack for it at all.

Thinking that, Hank wondered if maybe that was why he hated this boy so much—because the boy already had a name for his good work, while Hank got no fame at all even though he was the only true dowser likely to pass through these parts in a month of Sundays.

Hank set down on the grassy bank of the stream and pulled off his boots. When he leaned to set the second boot on a dry rock where it wouldn't be so like to fill up with bugs, he saw two eyes blinking in the shadows inside a thick stand of bushes. It gave him such a start, cause he thought to see a bear, and then he thought to see a Red man hankering after dowser's scalp, even though both such was gone from these parts for years. No, it was just a little light-skinned pickaninny hiding in the bushes. The boy was a mixup, half-White, half-Black, that was plain to see once Hank got over the surprise. "What're you looking at?" demanded Hank.

The eyes closed and the face was gone. The bushes wiggled and whispered from something crawling fast.

"Never you mind him," said Makepeace Smith. "That's just Arthur Stuart."

Arthur Stuart! Not a soul in New England or the United States but knew that name as sure as if they lived in the Crown Colonies. "Then you'll be glad to hear that I'm the Lord Protector," said Hank Dowser. "Cause if the King be that partickler shade of skin, I got some news that'll get me three free dinners a day in any town in Hio and Suskwahenny till the day I die."

Makepeace laughed brisk at that idea. "No, that's Horace Guester's joke, naming him thate way. Horace and Old Peg Guester, they're raising that boy, seeing how his natural ma's too poor to raise him. Course I don't think that's the whole reason. Him being so light-skinned, her husband, Mock Berry, you can't blame him if he don't like seeing that child eat at table with his coal-black children."

Hank Dowser started pulling off his stockings. "You don't suppose old Horace Guester took him in on account of he's the party responsible for causing the boy's skin to be so light."

"Hush your mouth with a pumpkin, Hank, before you say such a thing," said Makepeace. "Horace ain't that kind of a man."

"You'd be surprised who I've known turn out to be that kind of a man," said Hank. "Though I don't think it of Horace Guester, mind."

"Do you think Old Peg Guester'd let a half-Black bastard son of her husband into the house?"

"What if she didn't know?"

"She'd know. Her daughter Peggy used to be torch here in Hatrack River. And everybody knowed that Little Peggy Guester never told a lie."

"I used to hear tell about the Hatrack River torch, afore I ever come here. How come I never seen her?"

"She's gone, that's why," said Makepeace. "Left three years ago.

Just run off. You'd be wise never to ask about her up to Guester's roadhouse. They're a mite ticklish on the subject.''

Barefoot now, Hank Dowser stood up on the bank of the stream. He happened to glance up, and there off in the trees, just a-watching him, stood that Arthur Stuart boy again. Well, what harm could a little pickaninny do? Not a bit.

Hank stepped into the stream and let the ice-cold water pour over his feet. He spoke silently to the water: I don't mean to block your flow, or slack you down even further. The well I dig ain't meant to do you no harm. It's like giving you another place to flow through, like giving you another face, more hands, another eye. So don't you hide from me, Water. Show me where you're rising up, pushing to reach the sky, and I'll tell them to dig there, and set you free to wash over the earth, you just see if I don't.

"This water pure enough?" Hank asked the smith.

"Pure as it can be," said Makepeace. "Never heard of nobody taking sick from it.''

Hank dipped the sharp end of the wand into the water, upstream of his feet. Taste it, he told the wand. Catch the flavor of it, and remember, and find me more just this sweet.

The wand started to buck in his hands. It was ready. He lifted it from the stream; it settled down, calmer, but still shaking just the least bit, to let him know it was alive, alive and searching.

Now there was no more talking, no more thinking. Hank just walked, eyes near closed because he didn't want his vision to distract from the tingling in his hands. The wand never led him astray; to *look* where he was going would be as much as to admit the wand had no power to find.

It took near half an hour. Oh, he found a few places right off, but not good enough, not for Hank Dowser. He could tell by how sharp the wand bucked and dropped whether the water was close enough to the surface to do much good. He was so good at it now that most folks couldn't make no difference between him and a doodlebug, which was about as fine a knack as a dowser could ever have. And since doodlebugs were right scarce, mostly being found among seventh sons or thirteenth children, Hank never wished anymore that he was a doodlebug instead of just a dowser, or not often, anyway.

The wand dropped so hard it buried itself three inches deep in the earth. Couldn't do much better than that. Hank smiled and opened his eyes. He wasn't thirty feet back of the smithy. Couldn't have found a better spot with his eyes open. No doodlebug could've done a nicer job.

The smith thought so, too. "Why, if you'd asked me where I wished the well would be, this is the spot I'd pick."

Hank nodded, accepting the praise without a smile, his eyes half-closed, his whole body still a-tingle with the strength of the water's call to him. "I don't want to lift this wand," said Hank, "till you've dug a trench all round this spot to mark it off."

"Fetch a spade!" cried the smith.

Prentice Alvin jogged off in search of the tool. Hank noticed Arthur Stuart toddling after, running full tilt on them short legs so awkward he was bound to fall. And fall he did, flat down on his face in the grass, moving so fast he slid a yard at least, and came up soaking wet with dew. Didn't pause him none. Just waddled on around the smithy building where Prentice Alvin went.

Hank turned back to Makepeace Smith and kicked at the soil just underfoot. "I can't be sure, not being a doodlebug," said Hank, as modest as he could manage, "but I'd say you won't have to dig ten feet till you strike water here. It's fresh and lively as I ever seen."

"No skin off my nose either way," said Makepeace. "I don't aim to dig it."

"That prentice of yours looks strong enough to dig it hisself, if he doesn't lazy off and sleep when your back is turned."

"He ain't the lazying kind," said Makepeace. "You'll be staying the night at the roadhouse, I reckon."

"I reckon not," said Hank. "I got some folks about six mile west who want me to find them some *dry* ground to dig a good deep cellar."

"Ain't that kind of *anti*-dowsing?"

"It is, Makepeace, and it's a whole lot harder, too, in wettish country like this."

"Well, come back this way, then," said Makepeace, "and I'll save you a sip of the first water pulled up from your well."

"I'll do that," said Hank, "and gladly." That was an honor he wasn't often offered, that first sip from a well. There was power in that, but only if it was freely given, and Hank couldn't keep from smiling now. "I'll be back in a couple of days, sure as shooting."

The prentice boy come back with the spade and set right to digging. Just a shallow trench, but Hank noticed that the boy squared it off without measuring, each side of the hole equal, and as near as Hank could guess, it was true to the compass points as well. Standing there with the wand still rooted into the ground, Hank felt a sudden sickness in his stomach, having the boy so close. Only it wasn't the kind of sickness where you hanker to chuck up what you ate for breakfast. It was the kind of sickness that turns to pain, the sickness that turns to violence; Hank felt himself yearning to snatch the spade out of the boy's hands and smack him across the head with the sharp side of the blade.

Till finally it dawned on him, standing there with the wand a-trembling in his hand. It wasn't *Hank* who hated this boy, no sir. It was the *water* that Hank served so well, the *water* that wanted this boy dead.

The moment that thought entered Hank's head, he fought it down, swallowed back the sickness inside him. It was the plain craziest idea that ever entered his head. Water was water. All it wanted was to come up out of the ground or down out of the clouds and race over the face of the earth. It didn't have no malice in it. No desire to kill. And anyway, Hank Dowser was a Christian, and a Baptist to boot—a natural dowser's religion if there ever was one. When he put folks under the water, it was to baptize them and bring them to Jesus, not to drownd them. Hank didn't have murder in his heart, he had his Savior there, teaching him to love his enemies, teaching him that even to hate a man was like murder.

Hank said a silent prayer to Jesus to take this rage out of his heart and make him stop wishing for this innocent boy's death.

As if in answer, the wand leapt right out of the ground, flew clear out of his hands and landed in the bushes most of two rods off.

That never happened to Hank in all his days of dowsing. A wand taking off like that! Why, it was as if the water had spurned him as sharp as a fine lady spurns a cussing man.

"Trench is all dug," said the boy.

Hank looked sharp at him, to see if he noticed anything funny about the way the wand took off like that. But the boy wasn't even looking at him. Just looking at the ground inside the square he'd just ditched off.

"Good work," said Hank. He tried not to let his voice show the loathing that he felt.

"Won't do no good to dig here," said the boy.

Hank couldn't hardly believe his ears. Bad enough the boy sassing his own master, in the trade he knew, but what in tarnation did this boy know about dowsing?

"What did you say, boy?" asked Hank.

The boy must have seen the menace in Hank's face, or caught the tone of fury in his voice, because he backed right down. "Nothing, sir," he said. "None of my business anyhow."

Such was Hank's built-up anger, though, that he wasn't letting the boy off so easy. "You think you can do my job too, is that it? Maybe your master lets you think you're as good as he is cause you got your knack with *hooves*, but let me tell you, boy, I am a true dowser and my wand tells me there's water here!''

"That's right," said the boy. He spoke mildly, so that Hank didn't really notice that the boy had four inches on him in height and probably more than that in reach. Prentice Alvin wasn't so big you'd call him a giant, but you wouldn't call him no dwarf, neither.

"That's *right*? It ain't for you to say right or wrong to what my wand tells me!''

"I know it, sir, I was out of turn."

The smith came back with a wheelbarrow, a pick, and two stout iron levers. "What's all this?" he asked.

"Your boy here got smart with me," said Hank. He knew as he said it that it wasn't quite fair—the boy had already apologized, hadn't he?

Now at last Makepeace's hand lashed out and caught the boy a blow like a bear's paw alongside his head. Alvin staggered under the cuffing, but he didn't fall. "I'm sorry, sir," said Alvin.

"He said there wasn't no water here, where I said the well should be." Hank just couldn't stop himself. "I had respect for *his* knack. You'd think he'd have respect for mine."

"Knack or no knack," said the smith, "he'll have respect for my customers or he'll learn how long it takes to be a smith, oh sir! he'll learn."

Now the smith had one of the heavy iron levers in his hand, as if he meant to cane the boy across the back with it. That would be sheer murder, and Hank hadn't the heart for it. He held out his hand and caught the end of the lever. "No, Makepeace, wait, it's all right. He did tell me he was sorry."

"And is that enough for you?"

"That and knowing you'll listen to me and not to him," said Hank. "I'm not so old I'm ready to hear boys with hoof-knacks tell me I can't dowse no more."

"Oh, the well's going to be dug right here, you can bet your life. And this boy's going to dig it all himself, and not have a bite to eat until he strikes water."

Hank smiled. "Well, then, he'll be glad to discover that I know what I'm doing—he won't have to dig far, that's for sure."

Makepeace rounded on the boy, who now stood a few yards off, his hands slack at his side, showing no anger on his face, nothing at all, really. "I'm going to escort Mr. Dowser back to his new-shod mare, Alvin. And this is the last I want to see of you until you can bring me a bucket of clean water from this well. You won't eat a bite or have a sip of water until you drink it from here!''

"Oh, now," said Hank, "have a heart. You know it takes a couple of days sometimes for the dirt to settle out of a new well."

"Bring me a bucket of water from the new well, anyway," said Makepeace. "Even if you work all night."

They headed back for the smithy then, to the corral where Picklewing waited. There was some chat, some work at saddling up, and then Hank Dowser was on his way, his nag riding smoother and easier under him, just as happy as a clam. He could see the boy working as he rode off. There wasn't no flurry of dirt, just methodical lifting and dumping, lifting and dumping. The boy didn't seem to stop to rest, either. There wasn't a single break in the sound of his labor as Hank rode off. The *shuck* sound of the spade dipping into the soil, then the *swish-thump* as the dirt slid off onto the pile.

Hank didn't calm down his anger till he couldn't hear a sound of the boy, or even remember what the sound was like. Whatever power Hank had as a dowser, this boy was the enemy of his knack, that much Hank knew. He had thought his rage was unreasonable before, but now that the boy had spoke up, Hank knew he had been right all along. The boy thought he was a master of water, maybe even a doodlebug, and that made him Hank's enemy.

Jesus said to give your enemy your own cloak, to turn the other cheek—but what about when your enemy aims to take away your livelihood, what then? Do you let him ruin you? Not this Christian, thought Hank. I learned that boy something this time, and if it doesn't take, I'll learn him more later.

6

Masquerade

Peggy wasn't the belle of the Governor's Ball, but that was fine with her. Mistress Modesty had long since taught her that it was a mistake for women to compete with each other. "There is no single prize to be won, which, if one woman attains it, must remain out of reach for all the others."

No one else seemed to understand this, however. The other women eyed each other with jealous eyes, measuring the probable expense of gowns, guessing at the cost of whatever amulet of beauty the other woman wore; keeping track of who danced with whom, how many men arranged to be presented.

Few of them turned a jealous eye toward Peggy—at least not when she first entered the room in mid-afternoon. Peggy knew the impression she was making. Instead of an elegant coiffure, her hair was brushed and shining, pulled up in a style that looked well-tended, but prone to straying locks here and there. Her gown was simple, almost plain—but this was by calculation. "You have a sweet young body, so your gown must not distract from the natural litheness of youth." Moreover, the gown was unusually modest, showing less bare flesh than any other woman's dress; yet, more than most, it revealed the free movement of the body underneath it.

She could almost hear Mistress Modesty's voice, saying, "So many girls misunderstand. The corset is not an end in itself. It is meant to allow old and sagging bodies to imitate the body that a healthy young woman naturally has. A corset on *you* must be lightly laced, the stays only for comfort, not containment. Then your body can move freely, and you can breathe. Other girls will marvel that you have the courage to appear in public with a natural waistline. But men don't measure the

cut of a woman's clothes. Instead they pleasure in the naturalness of a
lady who is comfortable, sure of herself, enjoying life on this day, in
this place, in his company.''

Most important, though, was the fact that she wore no jewelry. The
other ladies all depended on beseemings whenever they went out in
public. Unless a girl had a knack for beseemings herself, she had to
buy—or her parents or husband had to buy—a hex engraven on a ring
or amulet. Amulets were preferred, since they were worn nearer the
face, and so one could get by with a much weaker—and therefore
cheaper—hex. Such beseemings had no effect from far off, but the
closer you came to a woman with a beseeming of beauty, the more you
began to feel that her face was particularly beautiful. None of her fea-
tures was transformed; you still saw what was actually there. It was
your judgment that changed. Mistress Modesty laughed at such hexes.
''What good does it do to fool someone, when he knows that he's being
fooled?'' So Peggy wore no such hex.

All the other women at the ball were in disguise. Though no one's
face was hidden, this ball was a masquerade. Only Peggy and Mistress
Modesty, of all the women here, were not in costume, were not pretending to some unnatural ideal.

She could guess at the other girls' thoughts as they watched her enter
the room: Poor thing. How plain. No competition there. And their es-
timation was true enough—at least at first. No one took particular notice
of Peggy.

But Mistress Modesty carefully selected a few of the men who approached her. ''I'd like you to meet my young friend Margaret,'' she
would say, and then Peggy would smile the fresh and open smile that
was not artificial at all—her natural smile, the one that spoke of her
honest gladness at meeting a friend of Mistress Modesty's. They would
touch her hand and bow, and her gentle echoing courtesy was graceful
and unmeasured, an honest gesture; her hand squeezed his as a friendly
reflex, the way one greets a hoped-for friend. ''The art of beauty is the
art of truth,'' said Mistress Modesty. ''Other women pretend to be
someone else; you will be your loveliest self, with the same natural
exuberant grace as a bounding deer or a circling hawk.'' The man would
lead her onto the floor, and she would dance with him, not worrying
about correct steps or keeping time or showing off her dress, but rather
enjoying the dance, their symmetrical movement, the way the music
flowed through their bodies together.

The man who met her, who danced with her, remembered. Afterward
the other girls seemed stilted, awkward, unfree, artificial. Many men,
themselves as artificial as most of the ladies, did not know themselves

well enough to know they enjoyed Peggy's company more than any other young lady's. But then, Mistress Modesty did not introduce Peggy to such men. Rather she only allowed Peggy to dance with the kind of man who could respond to her; and Mistress Modesty knew which men *they* were because they were genuinely fond of Mistress Modesty.

So as the hours passed by at the ball, hazy afternoon giving way to bright evening, more and more men were circling Peggy, filling up her dance card, eagerly conversing with her during the lulls, bringing her refreshment—which she ate if she was hungry or thirsty, and kindly refused if she was not—until the other girls began to take note of her. There were plenty of men who took no notice of Peggy, of course; no other girl lacked because of Peggy's plenty. But they didn't see it that way. What they saw was that Peggy was always surrounded, and Peggy could guess at their whispered conversations.

"What kind of spell does she have?"

"She wears an amulet under her bodice—I'm sure I saw its shape pressing against that cheap fabric."

"Why don't they see how thick-waisted she is?"

"Look how her hair is awry, as if she had just come in from the barnyard."

"She must flatter them dreadfully."

"Only a certain *kind* of man is attracted to her, I hope you notice."

Poor things, poor things. Peggy had no power that was not already born within any of these girls. She used no artifice that they would have to buy.

Most important to her was the fact that she did not even use her own knack here. All of Mistress Modesty's other teachings had come easily to her over the years, for they were nothing more than the extension of her natural honesty. The one difficult barrier was Peggy's knack. By habit, the moment she met someone she had always looked into his heartfire to see who he was; and, knowing more about him than she knew about herself, she then had to conceal her knowledge of his darkest secrets. It was this that had made her so reserved, even haughty-seeming.

Mistress Modesty and Peggy both agreed—she could not tell others how much she knew about them. Yet Mistress Modesty assured her that as long as she was concealing something so important, she could not become her most beautiful self—could not become the woman that Alvin would love for herself, and not out of pity.

The answer was simple enough. Since Peggy could not tell what she knew, and could not hide what she knew, the only solution was not to know it in the first place. That was the real struggle of these past three years—to train herself *not* to look into the heartfires around her. Yet by hard work, after many tears of frustration and a thousand different tricks to try to fool herself, she had achieved it. She could enter a crowded ballroom and remain oblivious to the heartfires around her. Oh, she *saw* the heartfires—she could not blind herself—but she paid no attention to them. She did not find herself drawing close to see deeply. And now she was getting skilled enough that she didn't even have to *try* not to see into the heartfire. She could stand this close to someone, conversing, paying attention to their words, and yet see no more of his inner thoughts than any other person would.

Of course, years of torchery had taught her more about human nature—the kinds of thoughts that go behind certain words or tones of voice or expressions or gestures—that she was very good at guessing others' present thoughts. But good people never minded when she seemed to know what was on their mind right at the moment. She did not have to hide that knowledge. It was only their deepest secrets that she could not know—and those secrets were now invisible to her unless she chose to see.

She did not choose to see. For in her new detachment she found a kind of freedom she had never known before in all her life. She could take other people at face value now. She could rejoice in their company, not knowing and therefore not feeling responsible for their hidden hungers or, most terribly, their dangerous futures. It gave a kind of exhilarating madness to her dancing, her laughter, her conversation; no one else at the ball felt so free as Modesty's young friend Margaret, because no one else had ever known such desperate confinement as she had known all her life till now.

So it was that Peggy's evening at the Governor's Ball was glorious. Not a *triumph*, actually, since she vanquished no one—whatever man won her friendship was not conquered, but liberated, even victorious. What she felt was pure joy, and so those who were with her also rejoiced in her company. Such good feelings could not be contained. Even those who gossiped nastily about her behind their fans nevertheless caught the joy of the evening; many told the governor's wife that this was the best ball ever held in Dekane, or for that matter in the whole state of Suskwahenny.

Some even realized who it was who brought such gladness to the evening. Among them were the governor's wife and Mistress Modesty. Peggy saw them talking once, as she turned gracefully on the floor, returning to her partner with a smile that made him laugh with joy to be dancing with her. The governor's wife was smiling and nodding, and she pointed with her fan toward the dance floor, and for a moment

Peggy's eyes met hers. Peggy smiled in warm greeting; the governor's wife smiled and nodded back. The gesture did not go unremarked. Peggy would be welcome at any party she wanted to attend in Dekane—two or three a night, if she desired, every night of the year.

Yet Peggy did not glory in this achievement, for she recognized how small it really was. She had won her way into the finest events in Dekane—but Dekane was merely the capital of a state on the edge of the American frontier. If she longed for social victories, she would have to make her way to Camelot, to win the accolades or royalty—and from there to Europe, to be received in Vienna, Paris, Warsaw, or Madrid. Even then, though, even if she had danced with every crowned head, it would mean nothing. She would die, they would die, and how would the world be any better because she had danced?

She had seen true greatness in the heartfire of a newborn baby fourteen years ago. She had protected the child because she loved his future; she had also come to love the boy because of who he was, the kind of soul he had. Most of all, though, more important than her feelings for Prentice Alvin, most of all she loved the work that lay ahead of him. Kings and queens built kingdoms, or lost them; merchants made fortunes, or squandered them; artists made works that time faded or forgot. Only Prentice Alvin had in him the seeds of Making that would stand against time, against the endless wasting of the Unmaker. So as she danced tonight, she danced for him, knowing that if she could win the love of these strangers, she might also win Alvin's love, and earn a place beside him on his pathway to the Crystal City, that place in which all the citizens can see like torches, build like makers, and love with the purity of Christ.

With the thought of Alvin, she cast her attention to his distant heartfire. Though she had schooled herself not to see into nearby heartfires, she never gave up looking into his. Perhaps this made it harder for her to control her knack, but what purpose was it to learn anything, if by learning she lost her connection to that boy? So she did not have to search for him; she knew always, in the back of her mind, where his heartfire burned. In these years she had learned not to see him constantly before her, but still she could see him in an instant. She did so now.

He was digging in the ground behind his smithy. But she hardly noticed the work, for neither did he. What burned strongest in his heartfire was anger. Someone had treated him unfairly—but that could hardly be new, could it? Makepeace, once the most fairminded of masters, had become steadily more envious of Alvin's skill at ironwork, and in his jealousy he had become unjust, denying Alvin's ability more fervently the further his prentice boy surpassed him. Alvin lived with injustice every day, yet never had Peggy seen such rage in him.

"Is something wrong, Mistress Margaret?" The man who danced with her spoke in concern. Peggy had stopped, there in the middle of the floor. The music still played, and couples still moved through the dance, but near her the dancers had stopped, were watching her.

"I can't—continue," she said. It surprised her to find that she was out of breath with fear. What was she afraid of?

"Would you like to leave the ballroom?" he asked. What was his name? There was only one name in her mind: Alvin.

"Please," she said. She leaned on him as they walked toward the open doors leading onto the porch. The crowd parted; she didn't see them.

It was as if all the anger Alvin had stored up in his years of working under Makepeace Smith now was coming out, and every dig of his shovel was a deep cut of revenge. A dowser, an itinerant water-seeker, that's who had angered him, that's the one he meant to harm. But the dowser was none of Peggy's concern; nor was his provocation, however mean or terrible. It was Alvin. Couldn't he see that when he dug so deep in hatred it was an act of destruction? And didn't he know that when you work to destroy, you invite the Destroyer? When your labor is unmaking, the Unmaker can claim you.

The air outside was cooler in the gathering dusk, the last shred of the sun throwing a ruddy light across the lawns of the Governor's mansion. "Mistress Margaret, I hope I did nothing to cause you to faint."

"No, I'm not even fainting. Will you forgive me? I had a thought, that's all. One that I must think about."

He looked at her strangely. Any time a woman needed to part with a man, she always claimed to be near fainting. But not Mistress Margaret—Peggy knew that he was puzzled, uncertain. The etiquette of fainting was clear. But what was a gentleman's proper manner toward a woman who "had a thought"?

She laid her hand on his arm. "I assure you, my friend—I'm quite well, and I delighted in dancing with you. I hope we'll dance again. But for now, for the moment, I need to be alone."

She could see how her words eased his concern. Calling him "my friend" was a promise to remember him; her hope to dance with him again was so sincere that he could not help but believe her. He took her words at face value, and bowed with a smile. After that she didn't even see him leave.

Her attention was far away, in Hatrack River, where Prentice Alvin was calling to the Unmaker, not guessing what he was doing. Peggy searched and searched in his heartfire, trying to find something she might do to keep him safe. But there was nothing. Now that Alvin was being driven by anger, all paths led to one place, and that place terrified her, for she couldn't see what was there, couldn't see what would happen. And there were no paths out.

What was I doing at this foolish ball, when Alvin needed me? If I had been paying proper attention, I would have seen this coming, would have found some way to help him. Instead I was dancing with these men who mean less than nothing to the future of this world. Yes, they delight in me. But what is that worth, if Alvin falls, if Prentice Alvin is destroyed, if the Crystal City is unmade before its Maker begins to build it?

7

Wells

Alvin didn't need to look up when the dowser left. He could feel where the man was as he moved along, his anger like a black noise in the midst of the sweet green music of the wood. That was the curse of being the only White, man or boy, who could feel the life of the greenwood— it meant that he was also the only White who knew how the land was dying.

Not that the soil wasn't rich—years of forest growth had made the earth so fertile that they said the *shadow* of a seed could take root and grow. There was life in the fields, life in the towns even. But it wasn't part of the land's own song. It was just noise, whispering noise, and the green of the wood, the life of the Red man, the animal, the plant, the soil all living together in harmony, that song was quiet now, inter- mittent, sad. Alvin heard it dying and he mourned.

Vain little dowser. Why was he so mad? Alvin couldn't figure. But he didn't press it, didn't argue, because almost as soon as the dowser came along, Al could see the Unmaker shadowing the edges of his vision, as if Hank Dowser'd brought him along.

Alvin first saw the Unmaker in his nightmares as a child, a vast nothingness that rolled invisibly toward him, trying to crush him, to get inside him, to grind him into pieces. It was old Taleswapper who first helped Alvin give his empty enemy a name. The Unmaker, which longs to undo the universe, break it all down until everything is flat and cold and smooth and dead.

As soon as he had a name for it and some notion what it *was*, he started seeing the Unmaker in daylight, wide awake. Not right out in the open, of course. Look *at* the Unmaker and most times you can't see him. He goes all invisible behind all the life and growth and upbuilding in the world. But at the edges of your sight, as if he was sneaking up behind, that's where the sly old snake awaited, that's where Alvin saw him.

When Alvin was a boy he learned a way to make that Unmaker step back a ways and leave him be. All he had to do was use his hands to build something. It could be as simple as weaving grass into a basket, and he'd have some peace. So when the Unmaker showed up around the blacksmith's shop not long after Alvin got there, he wasn't too worried. There was plenty of chance for making things in the smithy. Besides, the smithy was full of fire—fire and iron, the hardest earth. Alvin knew from childhood on that the Unmaker hankered after water. Water was its servant, did most of its work, tearing things down. So it was no wonder that when a water man like Hank Dowser came along, the Unmaker freshened up and got lively.

Now, though, Hank Dowser was on his way, taking his anger and his unfairness with him, but the Unmaker was still there, hiding out in the meadow and the bushes, lurking in the long shadows of the evening.

Dig with the shovel, lever up the earth, hoist it to the lip of the well, dump it aside. A steady rhythm, a careful building of the pile, shaping the sides of the hole. Square the first three feet of the hole, to set the shape of the well house. Then round and gently tapered inward for the stonework of the finished well. Even though you know this well will never draw water, do it careful, dig as if you thought that it would last. Build smooth, as near to perfect as you can, and it'll be enough to hold that sly old spy at bay.

So why didn't Alvin feel a speck more brave about it?

Alvin knew it was getting on toward evening, sure as if he had him a watch in his pocket, cause here came Arthur Stuart, his face just scrubbed after supper, sucking on a horehound and saying not a word. Alvin was used to him by now. Almost ever since the boy could walk, he'd been like Alvin's little shadow, coming every day it didn't rain. Never had much to say, and when he did it wasn't too easy to understand his baby talk—he had trouble with his Rs and Ss. Didn't matter. Arthur never wanted nothing and never did no harm, and Alvin usually half-forgot the boy was around.

Digging there with the evening flies out, buzzing in his face, Alvin had nothing to do with his brain but think. Three years he been in Hatrack, and all that time he hadn't got him one inch closer to knowing what his knack was for. He hardly used it, except for the bit he done with the horses, and that was cause he couldn't bear to know how bad they suffered when it was so easy a thing for him to make the shoeing go right. That was a good thing to do, but it didn't amount to much up-building, compared to the ruination of the land all around him.

The White man was the Unmaker's tool in this forest land, Alvin knew that, better even than water at tearing things down. Every tree that fell, every badger, coon, deer, and beaver that got used up without consent, each death was part of the killing of the land. Used to be the Reds kept the balance of things, but now they were gone, either dead or moved west of the Mizzipy—or, like the Irrakwa and the Cherriky, turned White at heart, sleeves rolled up and working hard to unmake the land even faster than the White. No one left to try to keep things whole.

Sometimes Alvin thought he was the only one left who hated the Unmaker and wanted to build against him. And he didn't know how to do it, didn't have any idea what the next step ought to be. The torch who touched him at his birthing, she was the only one who might've taught him how to be a true Maker, but she was gone, run off the very morning that he came. Couldn't be no accident. She just didn't want to teach him aught. He had a destiny, he knew it, and not a soul to help him find the way.

I'm willing, thought Alvin. I got the power in me, when I can figure how to use it straight, and I got the desire to be whatever it is I'm meant to be, but somebody's got to teach me.

Not the blacksmith, that was sure. Profiteering old coot. Alvin knew that Makepeace Smith tried to teach him as little as he could. Even now Alvin reckoned Makepeace didn't know half how much Alvin had learned himself just by watching when his master didn't guess that he was alert. Old Makepeace never meant to let him go if he could help it. Here I got a destiny, a real honest-to-goodness Work to do in my life, just like the old boys in the Bible or Ulysses or Hector, and the only teacher I got is a smith so greedy I have to *steal* learning from him, even though it's mine by right.

Sometimes it burned Alvin up inside, and he got a hankering to do something spetackler to show Makepeace Smith that his prentice wasn't just a boy who didn't know he was being cheated. What would Make-peace Smith do if he saw Alvin split iron with his fingers? What if he saw that Al could straighten a bent nail as strong as before, or heal up brittle iron that shattered under the hammer? What if he saw that Al could beat iron so thin you could see sunlight through it, and yet so strong you couldn't break it?

But that was plain dumb when Alvin thought that way, and he knowed it. Makepeace Smith might gasp the first time, he might even faint dead away, but inside ten minutes he'd be figuring an angle how to make money from it, and Alvin'd be less likely than ever to get free ahead of time. And his fame would spread, yes sir, so that by the time he turned nineteen and Makepeace Smith had to let him go, Alvin would already have too much notice. Folks'd keep him busy healing and doodlebugging and fixing and stone shaping, work that wasn't even halfway toward what he was born for. If they brought him the sick and lame to heal, how would he ever have time to be aught but a physicker? Time enough for healing when he learned the whole way to be a Maker.

The Prophet Lolla-Wossiky showed him a vision of the Crystal City only a week before the massacre at Tippy-Canoe. Alvin knew that someday in the future it was up to him to build them towers of ice and light. That was his destiny, not to be a country fixit man. As long as he was bound to Makepeace Smith's service, he had to keep his real knack secret.

That's why he never ran off, even though he was big enough now that nobody'd take him for a runaway prentice. What good would freedom do? He had to learn first how to be a Maker, or it wouldn't make no difference if he went or stayed.

So he never spoke of what he could do, and scarce used his gifts more than to shoe horses and feel the death of the land around him. But all the time in the back of his brain he recollected what he really was. A Maker. Whatever that is, I'm it, which is why the Unmaker tried to kill me before I was born and in a hundred accidents and almost-murders in my childhood back in Vigor Church. That's why he lurks around now, watching me, waiting for a chance to get me, waiting maybe for a time like tonight, all alone out here in the darkness, just me and the spade and my anger of having to do work that won't amount to nothing.

Hank Dowser. What kind of man won't listen to a good idea from somebody else? Sure the wand went down hard—the water was like to bust up through the earth at that place. But the reason it *hadn't* busted through was on account of a shelf of rock along there, not four feet under the soil. Why else did they think this was a natural meadow here? The big trees couldn't root, because the water that fell here flowed right off the stone, while the roots couldn't punch through the shelf of rock to get to the water underneath it. Hank Dowser could find water, but he sure couldn't find what lay *between* the water and the surface. It wasn't Hank's fault he couldn't see it, but it sure was his fault he wouldn't entertain no notion it might be there.

So here was Alvin, digging as neat a well as you please, and sure enough, no sooner did he have the round side wall of the well defined than *clink, clank, clunk*, the spade rang against stone.

At the new sound, Arthur Stuart ran right up to the edge of the hole and looked in. "Donk donk," he said. Then he clapped his hands.

"Donk donk is right," said Alvin. "I'll be donking on solid rock the whole width of this hole. And I ain't going in to tell Makepeace Smith about it, neither, you can bet on that, Arthur Stuart. He told me I couldn't eat nor drink till I got water, and I ain't about to go in afore dark and start pleading for supper just cause I hit rock, no sir."

"Donk," said the little boy.

"I'm digging every scrap of dirt out of this hole till the rock is bare."

He carefully dug out all the dirt he could, scraping the spade along the bumpy face of the rock. Even so, it was still brown and earthy, and Alvin wasn't satisfied. He wanted that stone to shine white. Nobody was watching but Arthur Stuart, and he was just a baby anyhow. So Alvin used his knack in a way he hadn't done since leaving Vigor Church. He made all the soil flow away from the bare rock, slide right across the stone and fetch up tight against the smooth-edge earthen walls of the hole.

It took almost no time till the stone was so shiny and white you could think it was a pool reflecting the last sunlight of the day. The evening birds sang in the trees. Sweat dripped off Alvin so fast it left little black spots when it fell on the rock.

Arthur stood at the edge of the hole. "Water," he said.

"Now you stand back, Arthur Stuart. Even if this ain't all that deep, you just stand back from holes like this. You can get killed falling in, you know."

A bird flew by, its wings rattling loud as could be. Somewhere another bird gave a frantic cry.

"Snow," said Arthur Stuart.

"It ain't snow, it's rock," said Alvin. Then he clambered up out of the hole and stood there, laughing to himself. "There's your well, Hank Dowser," Alvin said. "You ride on back here and see where your stick drove into the dirt."

He'd be sorry he got Al a blow from his master's hand. It wasn't no joke when a blacksmith hit you, specially one like his master, who didn't go easy even on a little boy, and sure not on a man-size prentice like Alvin.

Now he could go on up to the house and tell Makepeace Smith the well was dug. Then he'd lead his master back down here and show him this hole, with the stone looking up from the bottom, as solid as the heart of the world. Alvin heard himself saying to his master, "You show me how to drink that and I'll drink it." It'd be pure pleasure to hear how Makepeace'd cuss himself blue at the sight of it.

Except now that he could show them how wrong they were to treat him like they did, Alvin knew it didn't matter in the long run whether he taught them a lesson or not. What mattered was Makepeace Smith really did need this well. Needed it bad enough to pay out a dowser's cost in free ironwork. Whether it was dug where Hank Dowser said or somewhere else, Alvin knew he had to dig it.

That would suit Alvin's pride even better, now he thought of it. He'd come in with a bucket, just like Makepeace ordered him to—but from a well of his own choosing.

He looked around in the ruddy evening light, thinking where to start looking for a diggable spot. He heard Arthur Stuart pulling at the meadow grass, and the sound of birds having a church choir practice, they were so loud tonight.

Or maybe they were plain scared. Cause now he was looking around, Alvin could see that the Unmaker was lively tonight. By rights digging the first hole should've been enough to send it headlong, keep it off for days. Instead it followed him just out of sight, every step he took as he hunted for the place to dig the true well. It was getting more and more like one of his nightmares, where nothing he did could make the Unmaker go away. It was enough to send a thrill of fear right through him, make him shiver in the warm spring air.

Alvin just shrugged off that scare. He knew the Unmaker wasn't going to touch him. For all the years of his life till now, the Unmaker'd tried to kill him by setting up accidents, like water icing up where he was bound to step, or eating away at a riverbank so he slipped in. Now and then the Unmaker even got some man or other to take a few swipes at Alvin, like Reverend Thrower or them Choc-Taw Reds. In all his life, outside his dreams, that Unmaker never did anything direct.

And he won't now either, Alvin told hisself. Just keep searching, so you can dig the *real* well. The false one didn't drive that old deceiver off, but the real one's bound to, and I won't see him shimmering at the edges of my vision for three months after that.

With that thought in mind, Alvin hunkered down and kept his mind on searching for a break in the hidden shelf of stone.

How Alvin searched things out underground wasn't like *seeing*. It was more like he had another hand that skittered through the soil and rock as fast as a waterdrop on a hot griddle. Even though he'd never met him a doodlebug, he figured doodling couldn't be much different than how he done it, sending his bug scouting along under the earth, feeling things out all the way. And if he *was* doodlebugging, then he had to wonder if folks was right who allowed as how it was the doo-dlebug's very *soul* that slithered under the ground, and there was tales about doodlebugs whose souls got lost and the doodler never said another word or moved a muscle till he finally died. But Alvin didn't let such tales scare him off from doing what he ought to. If there was a need for stone, he'd find him the natural breaks to make it come away without hardly chipping at it. If there was a need for water, he'd find him a way to dig on down to get it.

Finally he found him a place where the shelf of stone was thin and crumbled. The ground was higher here, the water deeper down, but what counted was he could get through the stone to it.

This new spot was halfway between the house and the smithy—which would be less convenient for Makepeace, but better for his wife Gertie, who had to use the same water. Alvin set to with a will, because it was getting on to dark, and he was determined to take no rest tonight until his work was done. Without even thinking about it he made up his mind to use his power like he used to back on his father's land. He never struck stone with his spade; it was like the earth turned to flour and jumped out of the hole instead of him having to heft it. If any grownup happened to see him right then they'd think they was likkered up or having a conniption fit, he dug so fast. But nobody was looking, except for Arthur Stuart. It was getting nightward, after all, and Al had no lantern, so nobody'd ever even notice he was there. He could use his knack tonight without fear of being found out.

From the house came the sound of shouting, loud but not clear enough for Alvin to make out the words.

"Mad," said Arthur Stuart. He was looking straight at the house, as steady as a dog on point.

"Can you hear what they're saying?" said Alvin. "Old Peg Guester always says you got ears like a dog, perk up at everything."

Arthur Stuart closed his eyes. "You got no right to starve that boy," he said.

Alvin like to laughed outright. Arthur was doing as perfect an imitation of Gertie Smith's voice as he ever heard.

"He's too big to thrash and I got to learn him," said Arthur Stuart. This time he sounded just like Alvin's master. "I'll be," murmured Alvin.

Little Arthur went right on. "Either Alvin eats this plate of supper Makepeace Smith or you'll wear it on your head. I'd like to see you try it you old hag I'll break your arms."

Alvin couldn't help himself, he just laughed outright. "Consarn it if you ain't a perfect mockingbird, Arthur Stuart."

The little boy looked up at Alvin and a grin stole across his face. Down from the house come the sound of breaking crockery. Arthur

Stuart started to laugh and run around in circles. "Break a dish, break a dish, break a dish!" he cried.

"If you don't beat all," said Alvin. "Now you tell me, Arthur, you didn't really understand all them things you just said, did you? I mean, you were just repeating what you heard, ain't that so?"

"Break a dish on his *head!*" Arthur screamed with laughter and fell over backward in the grass. Alvin laughed right along, but he couldn't take his eyes off the little boy. More to him than meets the eye, thought Alvin. Or else he's plain crazy.

From the other direction came another woman's voice, a full-throated call that floated over the moist darkening air. "*Arthur!* Arthur *Stuart!*"

Arthur sat right up. "Mama," he said.

"That's right, that's Old Peg Guester calling," said Alvin.

"Go to bed," said Arthur.

"Just be careful she don't give you a bath first, boy, you're a mite grimy."

Arthur got up and started trotting off across the meadow, up to the path that led from the springhouse to the roadhouse where he lived. Alvin watched him out of sight, the little boy flapping his arms as he ran, like as if he was flying. Some bird, probably an owl, flew right alongside the boy halfway across the meadow, skimming along the ground like as if to keep him company. Not till Arthur was out of sight behind the springhouse did Alvin turn back to his labor.

In a few more minutes it was full dark, and the deep silence of night came quick after that. Even the dogs were quiet all through town. It'd be hours before the moon came up. Alvin worked on. He didn't have to see; he could feel how the well was going, the earth under his feet. Nor was it the Red man's seeing now, their gift for hearing the green-wood song. It was his own knack he was using, helping him feel his way deeper into the earth.

He knew he'd strike rock twice as deep this time. But when the spade caught up on big chunks of rocks, it wasn't a smooth plate like it was at the spot Hank Dowser chose. The stones were crumbly and broke up, and with his knack Al hardly had to press his lever afore the stones flipped up easy as you please, and he tossed them out the well like clods.

Once he dug through that layer, though, the ground got oozy underfoot. If he wasn't who he was, he'd've had to set the work aside and get help to dredge it out in the morning. But for Alvin it was easy enough. He tightened up the earth around the walls of the hole, so water couldn't seep in so fast. It wasn't spadework now. Alvin used a dredge to scoop up the mucky soil, and he didn't need no partner to hoist it out on a rope, either, he just heaved it up and his knack was such that each scoop of ooze clung together and landed neat as you please outside the well, just like he was flinging bunny rabbits out the hole.

Alvin was master here, that was sure, working miracles in this hole in the ground. You tell me I can't eat or drink till the well is dug, thinking you'll have me begging for a cup of water and pleading for you to let me go to bed. Well, you won't see such a thing. You'll have your well, with walls so solid they'll be drawing water here after your house and smithy have crumbled into dust.

But even as he felt the sweet taste of victory, he saw that the Unmaker was closer than it had ever come in years. It flickered and danced, and not just at the edges of his vision anymore. He could see it right in front of him, even in the darkness, he could see it clearer than ever in daylight, cause now he couldn't see nothing real to distract him.

It was scary, all of a sudden, just like the nightmares of his childhood, and for a while Alvin stood in the hole, all froze with fear, as water oozed up from below, making the ground under him turn to slime. Thick slime a hundred feet deep, he was sinking down, and the walls of the well were getting soft, too, they'd cave in on him and bury him, he'd drown trying to breathe muck into his lungs, he knew it, he could feel it cold and wet around his thighs, his crotch; he clenched his fists and felt mud ooze between his fingers, just like the nothingness in all his nightmares—

And then he came to himself, got control. Sure, he was up to his waist in mud, and if he was any other boy in such a case he might have wiggled himself down deeper and smothered hisself, trying to struggle out. But this was Alvin, not some ordinary boy, and he was safe as long as he wasn't booglied up by fear like a child caught in a bad dream. He just made the slime under his feet harden enough to hold his weight, then made the hard place float upward, him out of the mud until he was standing on gravelly mud at the bottom of the well.

Easy as breaking a rat's neck. If that was all the Unmaker could think of doing, it might as well go on home. Alvin was a match for him, just like he was a match for Makepeace Smith and Hank Dowser both. He dug on, dredged up, hoisted, flung, then bent to dredge again.

He was pretty near deep enough now, a good six feet lower than the stone shelf. Why, if he hadn't firmed up the earthen sides of the well, it'd be full of water over his head already. Alvin took hold of the knotted rope he left dangling and walked up the wall, pulling himself hand over hand up the rope.

The moon was rising now, but the hole was so deep it wouldn't shine into the well until near moon-noon. Never mind. Into the pit Alvin dumped a barrowload of the stones he'd levered out only an hour before. Then he clambered down after it.

He'd been working rock with his knack since he was little, and he was never more sure-handed with it than tonight. With his bare hands he shaped the stone like soft clay, making it into smooth square blocks that he placed all around the walls of the well from the bottom up, braced firm against each other so that the pushing of soil and water wouldn't cave it in. Water would seep easily through the cracks between stones, but the soil wouldn't, so the well would be clean almost from the start.

There wasn't enough stone from the well itself, of course; Alvin made three trips to the stream to load the barrow with water-smoothed rocks. Even though he was using his knack to make the work easier, it was late at night and weariness was coming on him. But he refused to pay attention. Hadn't he learned the Red man's knack for running on long after weariness should have claimed him? A boy who followed Ta-Kumsaw, running without a rest from Detroit to Eight-Face Mound, such a boy had no need to give in to a single night of well-digging, and never mind his thirst or the pain in his back and thighs and shoulders, the ache of his elbows and his knees.

At last, at last, it was done. The moon past zenith, his mouth tasting like a horsehair blanket, but it was done. He climbed on out of the hole, bracing himself against the stone walls he'd just finished building. As he climbed he let go of his hold on the earth around the well, unsealed it, and the water, now tame, began to trickle noisily into the deep stone basin he'd built to hold it.

Still Alvin didn't go inside the house, didn't so much as walk to the stream and drink. His first taste of water would be from his well, just like Makepeace Smith had said. He'd stay here and wait until the well had reached its natural level, and then clear the water and draw up a bucket and carry it inside the house and drink a cup of it in front of his master. Afterward he'd take Makepeace Smith outside and show him the well Hank Dowser called for, the one Makepeace Smith had cuffed him for, and then point out the one where you could drop a bucket and it was splash, not clatter.

He stood there at the lip of the well, imagining how Makepeace Smith would sputter, how he'd cuss. Then he sat down, just to ease his feet, picturing Hank Dowser's face when he saw what Al had done. Then he lay right down to ease his aching back, and closed his eyes for just a minute, so he didn't have to pay no heed to the fluttering shadows of unmaking that kept pestering him out the corners of his eyes.

8

Unmaker

Mistress Modesty was stirring. Peggy heard her breathing change rhythm. Then she came awake and sat up abruptly on her couch. At once Mistress Modesty looked for Peggy in the darkness of the room.

"Here I am," Peggy murmured.

"What has happened, my dear? Haven't you slept at all?"

"I dare not," said Peggy.

Mistress Modesty stepped onto the portico beside her. The breeze from the southwest billowed the damask curtains behind them. The moon was flirting with a cloud; the city of Dekane was a shifting pattern of roofs down the hill below them. "Can you see him?" asked Mistress Modesty.

"Not him," said Peggy. "I see his heartfire; I can see through his eyes, as he sees; I can see his futures. But himself, no, I can't see him."

"My poor dear. On such a marvelous night, to have to leave the Governor's Ball and watch over this faraway child in grave danger." It was Mistress Modesty's way of asking what the danger was without actually *asking*. This way Peggy could answer or not, and neither way would any offense be given or taken.

"I wish I could explain," said Peggy. "It's his enemy, the one with no face—"

Mistress Modesty shuddered. "No face! How ghastly."

"Oh, he has a face for *other* men. There was a minister once, a man who fancied himself a scientist. He saw the Unmaker, but could not see him truly, not as Alvin does. Instead he made up a manshape for him in his mind, and a name—called him 'the Visitor,' and thought he was an angel."

"An angel!"

"I believe that when most of us see the Unmaker, we can't comprehend him, we haven't the strength of intellect for that. So our minds come as close as they can. Whatever shape represents naked destructive power, terrible and irresistible force, that is what we see. Those who *love* such evil power, they make themselves see the Unmaker as beautiful. Others, who hate and fear it, they see the worst thing in the world."

"What does your Alvin see?"

"I could never see it myself, it's so subtle; even looking through his eyes I wouldn't have noticed it, if *he* hadn't noticed it. I saw that he was seeing something, and only then did I understand what it was he saw. Think of it as—the feeling when you think you saw some movement out of the corner of your eye, only when you turn there's nothing there."

"Like someone always sneaking up behind you," said Mistress Modesty.

"Yes, exactly."

"And it's sneaking up on Alvin?"

"Poor boy, he doesn't realize that he's calling to it. He has dug a deep black pit in his heart, just the sort of place where the Unmaker flows."

Mistress Modesty sighed. "Ah, my child, these things are all beyond me. I never had a knack; I can barely comprehend the things you do."

"You? No knack?" Peggy was amazed.

"I know—hardly anyone ever admits to not having one, but surely I'm not the only one."

"You misunderstand me, Mistress Modesty," said Peggy. "I was startled, not that you had no knack, but that you *thought* you had no knack. Of course you have one."

"Oh, but I don't mind not having one, my dear—"

"You have the knack of seeing potential beauty as if it were already there, and by seeing, you let it come to be."

"What a lovely idea," said Mistress Modesty.

"Do you doubt me?"

"I don't doubt that you believe what you say."

There was no point in arguing. Mistress Modesty believed her, but was afraid to believe. It didn't matter, though. What mattered was Alvin, finishing his second well. He had saved himself once; he thought the danger was over. Now he sat at the edge of the well, just to rest a moment; now he lay down. Didn't he see the Unmaker moving close to him? Didn't he realize that his very sleepiness opened himself wide for the Unmaker to enter him?

"No!" whispered Peggy. "Don't sleep!"

"Ah," said Mistress Modesty. "You speak to him. Can he hear you?"

"Never," said Peggy. "Never a word."

"Then what can you do?"

"Nothing. Nothing I can think of."

"You told me you used his caul—"

"It's a part of his power, that's what I use. But even his knack can't send away what came at his own call. I never had the knowledge to fend off the Unmaker itself, anyway, even if I had a yard of his caulflesh, and not just a scrap of it."

Peggy watched in desperate silence as Alvin's eyes closed. "He sleeps."

"If the Unmaker wins, will he die?"

"I don't know. Perhaps. Perhaps he'll disappear, eaten away to nothing. Or perhaps the Unmaker will own him—"

"Can't you see the future, torch girl?"

"All paths lead into darkness, and I see no path emerging."

"Then it's over," whispered Mistress Modesty.

Peggy could feel something cold on her cheeks. Ah, of course: her own tears drying in the cool breeze.

"But if Alvin were awake, *he* could fend off this invisible enemy?" Mistress Modesty asked. "Sorry to bother you with questions, but if I know how it works, perhaps I can help you think of something."

"No, no, it's beyond us, we can only watch—" Yet even as Peggy rejected Mistress Modesty's suggestion, her mind leapt ahead to ways of using it. I must waken him. I don't have to fight the Unmaker, but if I waken him, then he can do his fighting for himself. Weak and weary though he is, he might still find a way to victory. At once Peggy turned and rushed back into her room, scrabbled through her top drawer until she found the carven box that held the caul.

"Should I leave?" Mistress Modesty had followed her.

"Stay with me," said Peggy. "Please, for company. For comfort, if I fail."

"You won't fail," said Mistress Modesty. "*He* won't fail, if he's the man you say he is."

Peggy barely heard her. She sat on the edge of her bed, searching in Alvin's heartfire for some way to waken him. Normally she could use his senses even when he slept, hearing what he heard, seeing his memory of the place around him. But now, with the Unmaker seeping in, his senses were fading. She could not trust them. Desperately she cast about for some other plan. A loud noise? Using what little was left of

Alvin's sense of the life around him, she found a tree, then rubbed a tiny bit of the caul and tried—as she had seen Alvin do it—to picture in her mind how the wood in the branch would come apart. It was painfully slow—Alvin did it so quickly!—but at last she made it fall. Too late. He barely heard it. The Unmaker had undone so much of the air around him that the trembling of sound could not pass through it. Perhaps Alvin noticed; perhaps he came a bit closer to wakefulness. Perhaps not.

How can I waken him, when he is so insensible that nothing can disturb him? Once I held this caul as a ridgebeam tumbled toward him; I burned a childsize gap in it, so that the hair of his head wasn't even touched. Once a millstone fell toward his leg; I split it in half. Once his own father stood in a loft, pitchfork in hand, driven by the Unmaker's madness until he had decided to murder his own most beloved son; I brought Taleswapper down the hill to him, distracting the father from his dark purpose and driving off the Unmaker.

How? How did Taleswapper's coming drive off the Destroyer? Because he would have seen the hateful beast and given the cry against it, that's why the Unmaker left when Taleswapper arrived. Taleswapper isn't anywhere near Alvin now, but surely there's someone I can waken and draw down the hill; someone filled with love and goodness, so that the Unmaker must flee before him.

With agonizing fear she withdrew from Alvin's heartfire even as the blackness of the Unmaker threatened to drown it, and searched in the night for another heartfire, someone she could waken and send to him in time. Yet even as she searched, she could sense in Alvin's heartfire a certain lightening, a hint of shadows within shadows, not the utter emptiness she had seen before where his future ought to be. If Alvin had any chance, it was from her searching. Even if she found someone, she had no notion how to waken them. But she would find a way, or the Crystal City would be swallowed up in the flood that came because of Alvin's foolish, childish rage.

9

Redbird

Alvin woke up hours later, the moon low in the west, the first scant light appearing in the east. He hadn't meant to sleep. But he was tired, after all, and his work was done, so of course he couldn't close his eyes and hope to stay awake. There was still time to take a bucketful of water and carry it inside.

Were his eyes open even now? The sky he could see, light grey to the left, light grey to the right. But where were the trees? Shouldn't they have been moving gently in the morning breeze, just at the fringes of his vision? For that matter, there was no breeze; and beyond the sight of his eyes, and touch on his skin, there were other things he could not feel. The green music of the living forest. It was gone; no murmur of life from the sleeping insects in the grass, no rhythm of the heartbeats of the dawn-browsing deer. No birds roosting in the trees, waiting for the sun's heat to bring out the insects.

Dead. Unmade. The forest was gone.

Alvin opened his eyes.

Hadn't they already been open?

Alvin opened his eyes again, and still he couldn't see; without closing them, he opened them still again, and each time the sky seemed darker. No, not darker, simply farther away, rushing up and away from him, like as if he was falling into a pit so deep that the sky itself got lost.

Alvin cried out in fear, and opened his already-open eyes, and saw:

The quivering air of the Unmaker, pressing down on him, poking itself into his nostrils, between his fingers, into his ears.

He couldn't feel it, no sir, except that he knew what *wasn't* there now; the outermost layers of his skin, wherever the Unmaker touched, his own body was breaking apart, the tiniest bits of him dying, drying, flaking away.

"No!" he shouted. The shout didn't make a sound. Instead, the Unmaker whipped inside his mouth, down into his lungs, and he couldn't close his teeth hard enough, his lips tight enough to keep that slimy uncreator from slithering on inside him, eating him away from the inside out.

He tried to heal himself the way he done with his leg that time the millstone broke it clean in half. But it was like the old story Taleswapper told him. He couldn't build things up half so fast as the Unmaker could tear them down. For every place he healed, there was a thousand places wrecked and lost. He was a-going to die, he was half-gone already, and it wouldn't be just death, just losing his flesh and living on in the spirit, the Unmaker meant to eat him body and spirit both alike, his mind and his flesh together.

A splash. He heard a splashing sound. It was the most welcome thing he ever heard in his life, to hear a sound at all. It meant that there *was* something beyond the Unmaker that surrounded and filled him.

Alvin heard the sound echo and ring inside his own memory, and with that to cling to, with that touch of the real world there to hang on to, Alvin opened his eyes.

This time for real, he knew, cause he saw the sky again with its proper fringe of trees. And there was Gertie Smith, Makepeace's missus, standing over him with a bucket in her hands.

"I reckon this is the first water from this well," she said.

Alvin opened his mouth, and felt cool moist air come inside. "Reckon so," he whispered.

"I never would've thought you could dig it all out and line it proper with stones, all in one night," she said. "That mixup boy, Arthur Stuart, he come to the kitchen where I was making breakfast biscuits, and he told me your well was done. I had to come and see."

"He gets up powerful early," said Alvin.

"And you stay up powerful late," said Gertie. "If I was a man your size I'd give my husband a proper licking, Al, prentice or no."

"I just did what he asked."

"I'm certain you did, just like I'm certain he wanted you to excavate that there circle of stone off by the smithy, am I right?" She cackled with delight. "That'll show the old coot. Sets such a store by that dowser, but his own prentice has a better dowsing knack than that old fraud—"

For the first time Alvin realized that the hole he dug in anger was like a signboard telling folks he had more than a hoof-knack in him. "Please, ma'am," he said.

"Please what?"

"My knack ain't dowsing, ma'am, and if you start saying so, I'll never get no peace."

She eyed him cool and steady. "If you ain't got the dowser's knack, boy, tell me how come there's clear water in this well you dug."

Alvin calculated his lie. "The dowser's stick dipped here, too, I saw it, and so when the first well struck stone, I tried here."

Gertie had a suspicious nature. "Do you reckon you'd say the same if Jesus was standing here judging your eternal soul depending on the truth of what you say?"

"Ma'am, I reckon if Jesus was here, I'd be asking forgiveness for my sins, and I wouldn't care two hoots about any old well."

She laughed again, cuffed him lightly on the shoulder. "I like your dowsing story. You just happened to be watching old Hank Dowser. Oh, that's a good one. I'll tell that tale to everybody, see if I don't."

"Thank you, ma'am."

"Here. Drink. You deserve first swallow from the first bucket of clear water from this well."

Alvin knew that the custom was for the owner to get first drinks. But she was offering, and he was so dry he couldn't have spit two bits' worth even if you paid him five bucks an ounce. So he set the bucket to his lips and drank, letting it splash out onto his shirt.

"I'd wager you're hungry, too," she said.

"More tired than hungry, I think," said Alvin.

"Then come inside to sleep."

He knew he should, but he could see the Unmaker not far off, and he was afeared to sleep again, that was the truth. "Thank you kindly, Ma'am, but anyhow, I'd like to be off by myself a few minutes."

"Suit yourself," she said, and went on inside.

The morning breeze chilled him as it dried off the water he spilled on his shirt. Was his ravishment by the Unmaker only a dream? He didn't think so. He was awake right enough, and it was real, and if Gertie Smith hadn't come along and dunked that bucket in the well, he would've been unmade. The Unmaker wasn't hiding out no more. He wasn't sneaking in backways nor roundabout. No matter where he looked, there it was, shimmering in the greyish morning light.

For some reason the Unmaker picked this morning for a face-to-face. Only Alvin didn't know how he was supposed to fight. If digging a well and building it up so fine wasn't making enough to drive off his enemy, he didn't know what else to do. The Unmaker wasn't like the men he wrestled with in town. The Unmaker had nothing he could take ahold of.

One thing was sure. Alvin'd never have a night of sleep again if he didn't take this Unmaker down somehow and wrestle him into the dirt.

I'm supposed to be your master, Alvin said to the Unmaker. So tell me, Unmaker, how do I undo *you*, when all you are is Undoing? Who's going to teach me how to win this battle, when you can sneak up on me in my sleep, and I don't have the faintest idea how to get to you?

As he spoke these words inside his head, Alvin walked to the edge of the woods. The Unmaker backed away from him, always out of reach. Al knew without looking that it also closed up behind him, so it had him on all sides.

This is the middle of the uncut wood where I ought to feel most at home, but the greensong, it's gone silent here, and all around me is my enemy from birth, and me here with no plan at all.

The Unmaker, though, he had a plan. He didn't need to waste no time a-dithering about what to do, Alvin found that out real quick.

Cause while Alvin was a-standing there in the cool heavy breeze of a summer morning, the air suddenly went chill, and blamed if snow-flakes didn't start to fall. Right down on the green-leaf trees they came, settling on the tall thick grass between them. Thick and cold it piled up, not the wet heavy flakes of a warm snow, but the tiny icy crystals of a deep winter blizzard blow. Alvin shivered.

"You can't do this," he said.

But his eyes weren't closed *now*, he knew that. This wasn't no half-asleep dream. This was real snow, and it was so thick and cold that the branches of summer-green trees were snapping, the leaves were tearing off and falling to the ground in a tinkle of broken ice. And Alvin himself was like to freeze himself clear to death if he didn't get out of there somehow.

He started to walk back the way he came, but the snow was coming down so thick he couldn't see more than five or six feet ahead of him, and he couldn't feel his way because the Unmaker had deadened the greensong of the living woods. Pretty soon he wasn't walking, he was running. Only he didn't run surefooted like Ta-Kumsaw taught him; he ran as noisy and stupid as any oaf of a White man, and like most Whites would've, he slipped on a patch of ice-covered stone and sprawled out face down across a reach of snow.

Snow that caught up in his mouth and nose and into his ears, snow that clung between his fingers, just like the slime last night, just like the Unmaker in his dream, and he choked and sputtered and cried out—

"I know it's a lie!"

His voice was swallowed up in the wall of snow.

"It's summer!" he shouted.

His jaw ached from the cold and he knew it'd hurt too much to speak again, but still he screamed through numb lips, "I'll make you stop!"

And then he realized that he could never make anything out of the Unmaker, could never make the Unmaker do or be anything because it was only Undoing and Unbeing. It wasn't the Unmaker he needed to call to, it was all the living things around him, the trees, the grass, the earth, the air itself. It was the greensong that he needed to restore.

He grabbed ahold of that idea and used it, spoke again, his voice scarce more than a whisper now, but he called to them, and not in anger.

"Summer," he whispered.

"Warm air!" he said.

"Leaves green!" he shouted. "Hot wind out of the southwest. Thunderheads in the afternoon, mist in the morning, sunlight hotting it up, burning off the fog!"

Did it change, just a little? Did the snowfall slacken? Did the drifts on the ground melt lower, the heaps on the treelimbs tumble off, baring more of the branch?

"It's a hot morning, dry!" he cried. "Rain may drift in later like the gift of the Wise Men, coming from a long way off, but for now sunlight beating on the leaves, waking you up, you're *growing*, putting out leaves, that's right! That's right!"

There was gladness in his voice because the snowfall was just a spatter of rain now, the snow on the ground was melted back to patches here and there, the broke-off leaves were sprouting on the branch again as quick as militia in a doubletime march.

And in the silence after his last shout, he heard birdsong.

Song like he'd never heard before. He didn't know this bird, this sweet melody that changed with every whistle and never played the same tune again. It was a weaving song, but one whose pattern you couldn't find, so you couldn't ever sing it again, but you also couldn't ravel it, spin it out and break it down. It was all of one piece, all of one single Making, and Alvin knew that if he could just find the bird with that song in his throat he'd be safe. His victory would be complete.

He ran, and now the greensong of the forest was with him, and his feet found the right places to step without him looking. He followed that song until he came to the clearing where the singing was.

Perched on an old log with a patch of snow still in the northwest shadow—a redbird. And sitting in front of that log, almost nose to nose as he listened to it sing—Arthur Stuart.

Alvin walked around the two of them real slow, walking a clean circle before he come much closer. Arthur Stuart like to never noticed he was there, he never took his eyes off that bird. The sunlight dazzled on the two of them, but neither bird nor boy so much as blinked. Alvin didn't say nothing, either. Just like Arthur Stuart, he was all caught up in the redbird song.

It wasn't no different from all the other redbirds, the thousand scarlet songbirds Alvin had seen since he was little. Except that from its throat came music that no other bird had ever sung before. This wasn't *a* redbird. Nor was it *the* redbird. There was no single bird had some gift the other redbirds lacked. It was just Redbird, the one picked for this moment to speak in the voice of all the birds, to sing the song of all the singers, so that this boy could hear.

Alvin knelt down on the new-grown grass not three feet from Red bird, and listened to its song. He knew from what Lolla-Wossiky once told him that Redbird's song was all the stories of the Red man, every-thing they ever done that was worth doing. Alvin halfway hoped to understand that ancient tale, or at least to hear how Redbird told of things that he took part in. The Prophet Lolla-Wossiky walking on wa-ter; Tippy-Canoe River all scarlet with Red folks' blood; Ta-Kumsaw standing with a dozen musketballs in him, still crying out for his men to stand, to fight, to drive the White thieves back.

But the sense of the song eluded him no matter how he listened. He might run the forest with a Red man's legs and hear the greensong with a Red man's ears, but Redbird's song wasn't meant for him. The saying told the truth: No one girl gets all the suitors, and no boy gets all the knacks. There was much that Alvin could do already, and much ahead of him to learn, but there'd be far more that was always out of his ken, and Redbird's song was part of that.

Yet Alvin was sure as shucks that Redbird wasn't here by accident. Come like this at the end of his face-to-face with the Unmaker, Redbird had to have some purpose. He had to get some answers out of Redbird's song.

Alvin was just about to speak, just about to ask the question burning in him ever since he first learned what his destiny might be. But it wasn't his voice that broke into Redbird's song. It was Arthur Stuart's.

"I don't know days coming up," said the mixup boy. His voice was like music and the words were clearer than any Alvin ever heard that three-year-old say before. "I only know days gone."

It took a second for Alvin to hitch himself to what was going on here. What Arthur said was the answer to Alvin's question. Will I ever be a Maker like the torch girl said? That was what Alvin would've asked, and Arthur's words were the answer.

But not Arthur Stuart's own answer, that was plain. The little boy no more understood what he was saying than he did when he was mimicking Makepeace's and Gertie's quarrel last night. He was giving Redbird's answer. Translating from birdsong into speech that Alvin's ears were fit to understand.

Alvin knew now that he'd asked the wrong question. He didn't need Redbird to tell him he was supposed to be a Maker—he knowed that firm and sure years ago, and knew it still in spite of all doubts. The real question wasn't whether, it was *how* to be a Maker.

Tell me how.

Redbird changed his song to a soft and simple tune, more like normal birdsong, quite different from the thousand-year-old Red man's tale that he'd been singing up to now. Alvin didn't understand the sense of it, but he knew all the same what it was about. It was the song of Making. Over and over, the same tune repeating, only a few moments of it—but they were blinding in their brightness, a song so true that Alvin saw it with his eyes, felt it from his lips to his groin, tasted it and smelled it. The song of Making, and it was his own song, he knew it from how sweet it tasted on his tongue.

And when the song was at its peak, Arthur Stuart spoke again in a voice that was hardly human it piped so sharp, it sang so clear.

"The Maker is the one who is part of what he makes," said the mixup boy.

Alvin wrote the words in his heart, even though he didn't understand them. Because he knew that someday he *would* understand them, and when he did, he would have the power of the ancient Makers who built the Crystal City. He would understand, and use his power, and find the Crystal City and build it once again.

The Maker is the one who is part of what he makes.

Redbird fell silent. Stood still, head cocked; and then became, not Redbird, but any old bird with scarlet feathers. Off it flew.

Arthur Stuart watched the bird out of sight. Then he called out after it in his own true childish voice, "Bird! Fly bird!" Alvin knelt beside the boy, weak from the night's work, the grey dawn's fear, this bright day's birdsong.

"I flied," said Arthur Stuart. For the first time, it seemed, he took notice Alvin was there, and turned to him.

"Did you now?" whispered Alvin, reluctant to destroy the child's dream by telling him that folks don't fly.

"Big blackbird tote me," said Arthur. "Fly and fly." Then Arthur reached up his hands and pressed in on Alvin's cheeks. "Maker," he said. Then he laughed and laughed with joy.

So Arthur wasn't just a mimic. He really understood Redbird's song, some of it, at least. Enough to know the name of Alvin's destiny.

"Don't you tell nobody," Alvin said. "I won't tell nobody you can talk to birds, and you don't tell nobody I'm a Maker. Promise?"

Arthur's face grew serious. "Don't talk birds," he said. "Birds talk *me*." And then: "I *flied*."

"I believe you," Alvin said.

"I beeve *you*," said Arthur. Then he laughed again.

Alvin stood up and so did Arthur. Al took him by the hand. "Let's go on home," he said.

He took Arthur to the roadhouse, where Old Peg Guester was full of scold at the mixup boy for running off and bothering folks all morning. But it was a loving scold, and Arthur grinned like an idiot at the voice of the woman he called Mama. As the door closed with Arthur Stuart on the other side, Alvin told himself, I'm going to tell that boy what he done for me. Someday I'll tell him what this meant.

Alvin came home by way of the springhouse path and headed on down toward the smithy, where Makepeace was no doubt angry at him for not being ready for work, even though he dug a well all night.

The well. Alvin found himself standing by the hole that he had dug as a monument to Hank Dowser, with the white stone bright in the sunlight, bright and cruel as scornful laughter.

In that moment Alvin knew why the Unmaker came to him that night. Not because of the true well that he dug. Not because he had used his knack to hold the water back, not because he had softened the stone and bent it to his need. It was because he had dug that first hole down to the stone for one reason only—to make Hank Dowser look the fool.

To punish him? Yes sir, to make him a laughingstock to any man who saw the stone-bottomed well on the spot that Hank had marked. It would destroy him, take away his name as a dowser—and unfairly so, because he *was* a good dowser who got hisself fooled by the lay of the land. Hank made an honest mistake, and Al had got all set to punish him as if he was a fool, which surely he was not.

Tired as he was, weak from labor and the battle with the Unmaker, Alvin didn't waste a minute. He fetched the spade from where it lay by the working well, then stripped off his shirt and set to work. When he dug this false well, it was a work of evil, to unmake an honest man for no reason better than spite. Filling it in, though, was a Maker's work. Since it was daylight, Alvin couldn't even use his knack to help—he did full labor on it till he thought he was so tired he might just die.

It was noon, and him without supper or breakfast either one, but the well was filled right up, the turves set back on so they'd grow back, and if you didn't look close you'd never know there'd been a hole at all. Alvin *did* use his knack a little, since no one was about, to weave the grassroots back together, knit them into the ground, so there'd be no dead patches to mark the spot.

All the time, though, what burned worse than the sun on his back or the hunger in his belly was his own shame. He was so busy last night being angry and thinking how to make a fool of Hank Dowser that it never once occurred to him to do the right thing and use his knack to break right through the shelf of stone in the very spot Hank picked. No one ever would've known save Alvin hisself that there'd been aught wrong with the place. That would've been the Christian thing, the charitable thing to do. When a man slaps your face, you answer by shaking his hand, that's what Jesus said to do, and Alvin just plain wasn't listening, Alvin was too cussed proud.

That's what called the Unmaker to me, thought Alvin. I could've used my knack to build up, and I used it to tear down. Well, never again, never again, never again. He made that promise three times, and even though it was a silent promise and no one'd ever know, he'd keep it better than any oath he might take before a judge or even a minister.

Well, too late now. If he'd thought of this before Gertie ever saw the false well or drew water from the true, he might've filled up the other well and made this one good after all. But now she'd seen the stone, and if he dug through it then all his secrets would be out. And once you've drunk water from a good new well, you can't never fill it up till it runs dry on its own. To fill up a living well is to beg for drouth and cholera to dog you all the days of your life.

He'd undone all he could. You can be sorry, and you can be forgiven, but you can't call back the futures that your bad decisions lost. He didn't need no philosopher to tell him that.

Makepeace wasn't a-hammering in the forge, and there wasn't no smoke from the smithy chimney, either. Must be Makepeace was up at the house, doing some chores there, Alvin figured. So he put the spade away back in the smithy and then headed on toward the house.

Halfway there, he come to the good well, and there was Makepeace Smith setting on the low wall of footing stones Al had laid down to be foundation for the wellhouse.

"Morning, Alvin," said the master.

"Morning, sir," said Alvin.

"Dropped me the tin and copper bucket right down to the bottom here. You must've dug like the devil hisself, boy, to get it so deep."

"Didn't want it to run dry."

"And lined it with stone already," said the smith. "It's a wonderment, I say."

"I worked hard and fast."

"You also dug in the right place, I see."

Alvin took a deep breath. "The way I figure, sir, I dug right where the dowser said to dig."

"I saw another hole just yonder," said Makepeace Smith. "Stone as thick and hard as the devil's hoof all along the bottom. You telling me you don't aim for folks to guess why you dug there?"

"I filled that old hole up," said Alvin. "I wish I'd never dug such a well. I don't want nobody telling stories on Hank Dowser. There was water there, right enough, and no dowser in the world could've guessed about the stone."

"Except you," said Makepeace.

"I ain't no dowser, sir," said Alvin. And he told the lie again: "I just saw that his wand dipped over here, too."

Makepeace Smith shook his head, a grin just creeping out across his face. "My wife told me that tale already, and I like to died a-laughing at it. I cuffed your head for saying he was wrong. You telling me now you want him to get the credit?"

"He's a true dowser," said Alvin. "And I *ain't* no dowser, sir, so I reckon since he *is* one, he ought to get the name for it."

Makepeace Smith drew up the copper bucket, put it to his lips, and drank a few swallows. Then he tipped back his head and poured the rest of the water straight onto his face and laughed out loud. "That's the sweetest water I ever drunk in my life, I swear."

It wasn't the same as promising to go along with his story and let Hank Dowser think it was his well, but Al knew it was the best he'd get from his master. "If it's all right, sir," said Al, "I'm a mite hungry."

"Yes, go eat, you've earned it."

Alvin walked by him. The smell of new water rose up from the well as he passed.

Makepeace Smith spoke again behind him. "Gertie tells me you took first swallow from the well."

Al turned around, fearing trouble now. "I did, sir, but not till she give it to me."

Makepeace studied on that notion awhile, as if he was deciding whether to make it reason for punishing Al or not. "Well," he finally said, "well, that's just like her, but I don't mind. There's still enough of that first dip in the wooden bucket for me to save a few swallows for Hank Dowser. I promised him a drink from the first bucket, and I'll keep my word when he comes back around.''

''When he comes, sir,'' said Alvin, ''and I hope you won't mind, but I think I'd like it best and so would he if I just didn't happen to be at home, if you see what I mean. I don't think he cottoned to me much.''

The smith eyed him narrowly. ''If this is just a way for you to get a few hours off work when that dowser comes on back, why''—he broke into a grin—''why, I reckon that you've earned it with last night's labor.''

''Thank you sir,'' said Alvin.

''You heading back to the house?''

''Yes sir.''

''Well, I'll take those tools and put them away—you carry this bucket to the missus. She's expecting it. A lot less way to tote the water than the stream. I got to thank Hank Dowser special for choosing this very exact spot.'' The smith was still chuckling to himself at his wit when Alvin reached the house.

Gertie Smith took the bucket, set Alvin down, and near filled him to the brim with hot fried bacon and good greasy biscuits. It was so much food that Al had to beg her to stop. ''We've already finished one pig,'' said Alvin. ''No need to kill another just for my breakfast.''

''Pigs are just corn on the hoof,'' said Gertie Smith, ''and you worked two hogs' worth last night, I'll say that.''

Belly full and belching, Alvin climbed the ladder into the loft over the kitchen, stripped off his clothes, and burrowed into the blankets on his bed.

The Maker is the one who is part of what he makes.

Over and over he whispered the words to himself as he went to sleep. He had no dreams or troubles, and slept clear through till suppertime, and then again all night till dawn.

When he woke up in the morning, just before dawn, there was a faint grey scarce brighter than moonlight sifting into the house through the windows. Hardly none of it got up into the loft where Alvin lay, and instead of springing up bright like he did most mornings, he felt logey from sleep and a little sore from his labors. So he lay there quiet, a faint sort of birdsong chirping in the back of his mind. He didn't think on the phrase Arthur Stuart told him from Redbird's song. Instead he got to wondering how things happened yesterday. Why did hard winter turn to summertime again, just from him shouting?

''Summer,'' he whispered. ''Warm air, leaves green.'' What was it about Alvin that when he said *summer*, summer came? Didn't always work that way, for sure—never when he was a-working the iron or slipping through stone to mend or break it. Then he had to hold the shape of it firm in his mind, understand the way things lined up, find the natural cracks and creases, the threads of the metal or the grain of the rock. And when he was a-healing, that was so hard it took his whole mind to find how the body ought to be, and mend it. Things were so small, so hard to see—well, not *see*, but whatever it was he did. Sometimes he had to work so hard to understand the way things were inside.

Inside, down deep, so small and fine, and always the deepest secrets of the way things worked skittered away like roaches when you bring a lamp into the room, always getting smaller, forming themselves up in strange new ways. Was there some particle that was smallest of all? Some place at the heart of things where what he saw was real, instead of just being made up out of lots of smaller pieces, and them out of smaller pieces still?

Yet he hadn't understood how the Unmaker made winter. So how did his desperate cries make the summer come back?

How can I be a Maker if I can't even guess how I do what I do?

The light came stronger from outside, shining through the wavering glass of the windows, and for a moment Alvin thought he saw the light like little balls flying so *fast*, like they was hit with a stick or shot from a gun, only even faster than that, bouncing around, most of them getting stuck in the tiny cracks of the wooden walls or the floor or the ceiling, so only a precious few got up into the loft where they got captured by Alvin's eyes.

Then that moment passed, and the light was just fire, pure fire, drifting into the room like the gentle waves washing against the shore of Lake Mizogan, and wherever they passed, the waves turned things warm— the wood of the walls, the massive kitchen table, the iron of the stove— so that they all quivered, they all danced with life. Only Alvin could see it, only Alvin knew how the whole room awoke with the day.

That fire from the sun, that's what the Unmaker hates most. The life it makes. Put that fire out, that's what the Unmaker says inside himself. Put all fires out, turn all water into ice, the whole world smooth with ice, the whole sky black and cold like night. And to oppose the Unmaker's desire, one lone Maker who can't do right even when he's digging a well.

The Maker is the one who is part of—part of what? What do I make? How am I part of it? When I work the iron, am I part of the iron? When I shiver stone, am I part of the stone? It makes no sense, but I got to make sense of it or I'll lose my war with the Unmaker. I could fight him all my days, every way I know how, and when I died the world would be farther along his downhill road than it was when I got born.

There's got to be some secret, some key to everything, so I can build it all at once. Got to find that key, that's all, find the secret, and then I can speak a word and the Unmaker will shy back and cower and give up and die, maybe even die, so that life and light go on forever and don't fade.

Alvin heard Gertie begin to stir in the bedroom, and one of the children uttered a soft cry, the last noise before waking. Alvin flexed and stretched and felt the sweet delicious pain of sore muscles waking up, getting set for a day at the forge, a day at the fire.

10

Goodwife

Peggy did not sleep as long or as well as Alvin. His battle was over; he could sleep a victor's sleep. For her, though, it was the end of peace.

It was still midafternoon when Peggy tossed herself awake on the smooth linen sheets of her bed in Mistress Modesty's house. She felt exhausted; her head hurt. She wore only her shift, though she didn't remember undressing. She remembered hearing Redbird singing, watching Arthur Stuart interpret the song. She remembered looking into Alvin's heartfire, seeing all his futures restored to him—but still did not find herself in any of them. Then her memory stopped. Mistress Modesty must have undressed her, put her to bed with the sun already nearing noon.

She rolled over; the sheet clung to her, and then her back went cold from sweat. Alvin's victory was won; the lesson was learned; the Unmaker would not find another such opening again. She saw no danger in Alvin's future, not soon. The Unmaker would doubtless lie in wait for another time, or return to working through his human servants. Perhaps the Visitor would return to Reverend Thrower, or some other soul with a secret hunger for evil would receive the Unmaker as a welcome teacher. But that wasn't the danger, not the immediate danger, Peggy knew.

For as long as Alvin had no notion how to be a Maker or what to do with his power, then it made no difference how long they kept the Unmaker at bay. The Crystal City would never be built. And it must be built, or Alvin's life—and Peggy's life, devoted to helping him—both would be in vain.

It seemed so clear now to Peggy, coming out of a feverish exhausted sleep. Alvin's labor was to prepare himself, to master his own human frailties. If there was some knowledge somewhere in the world about the art of Making, or the science of it, Alvin would have no chance to learn it. The smithy was his school, the forge his master, teaching him— what?—to change other men only by persuasion and long-suffering, gentleness and meekness, unfeigned love and kindness. Someone else, then, would have to acquire that pure knowledge which would raise Alvin up to greatness.

I am done with all my schooling in Dekane.

So many lessons, and I have learned them all, Mistress Modesty. All so I would be ready to bear the title you taught me was the finest any lady could aspire to.

Goodwife.

As her mother had been called Goody Guester all these years, and other women Goody this or Goody that, any woman could have the name. But few deserved it. Few there were who inspired others to call her by the name in full: Goodwife, not just Goody; the way that Mistress Modesty was never called Missus. It would demean her name to be touched by a diminished, a common title.

Peggy got up from the bed. Her head swam for a moment; she waited, then got up. Her feet padded on the wooden floor. She walked softly, but she knew she would be heard; already Mistress Modesty would be coming up the stairs.

Peggy stopped at the mirror and looked at herself. Her hair was tousled by sleep, stringy with sweat. Her face was imprinted, red and white, with the creases in the pillowcase. Yet she saw there the face that Mistress Modesty had taught her how to see.

"Our handiwork," said Mistress Modesty.

Peggy did not turn. She knew her mentor would be there.

"A woman should know that she is beautiful," said Mistress Modesty. "Surely God gave Eve a single piece of glass, or flat polished silver, or at least a still pool to show her what it was that Adam saw."

Peggy turned and kissed Mistress Modesty on the cheek. "I love what you've made of me," she said.

Mistress Modesty kissed her in return, but when they drew apart, there were tears in the older woman's eyes. "And now I shall lose your company."

Peggy wasn't used to others guessing what *she* felt, especially when she didn't realize that she had already made the decision.

"Will you?" asked Peggy.

"I've taught you all I can," said Mistress Modesty, "but I know after last night that you need things that I never dreamed of, because you have work to do that I never thought that anyone could do."

"I meant only to be Goodwife to Alvin's Goodman."

"For me that was the beginning and the end," said Mistress Modesty.

Peggy chose her words to be true, and therefore beautiful, and therefore good. "Perhaps all that some men need from a woman is for her to be loving and wise and careful, like a field of flowers where he can play the butterfly, drawing sweetness from her blossoms."

Mistress Modesty smiled. "How kindly you describe me."

"But Alvin has a sturdier work to do, and what he needs is not a beautiful woman to be fresh and loving for him when his work is done. What he needs is a woman who can heft the other end of his burden."

"Where will you go?"

Peggy answered before she realized that she knew the answer. "Philadelphia, I think."

Mistress Modesty looked at her in surprise, as if to say, You've already decided? Tears welled in her eyes.

Peggy rushed to explain. "The best universities are there—free ones, that teach all there is to know, not the crabbed religious schools of New England or the effete schools for lordlings in the South."

"This isn't sudden," said Mistress Modesty. "You've been planning this for long enough to find out where to go."

"It *is* sudden, but perhaps I *was* planning, without knowing it. I've listened to others talk, and now there it is already in my mind, all sorted out, the decision made. There's a school for women there, but what matters is the libraries. I have no formal schooling, but somehow I'll persuade them to let me in."

"It won't take much persuasion," Mistress Modesty said, "if you arrive with a letter from the governor of Suskwahenny. And letters from other men who trust my judgment well enough."

Peggy was not surprised that Mistress Modesty still intended to help her, even though Peggy had determined so suddenly, so ungracefully to leave. And Peggy had no foolish notion of pridefully trying to do without such help. "Thank you, Mistress Modesty!"

"I've never known a woman—or a man, for that matter—with such ability as yours. Not your knack, remarkable as it is; I don't measure a person by such things. But I fear that you are wasting yourself on this boy in Hatrack River. How could any man deserve all that you've sacrificed for him?"

"Deserving it—that's his labor. Mine is to have the knowledge when he's ready to learn it."

Mistress Modesty was crying in earnest now. She still smiled—for she had taught herself that love must always smile, even in grief—but the tears flowed down her cheeks. "Oh, Peggy, how could you have learned so well, and yet make such a mistake?"

A mistake? Didn't Mistress Modesty trust her judgment, even now? " 'A woman's wisdom is her gift to women,' " Peggy quoted. " 'Her beauty is her gift to men. Her love is her gift to God.' "

Mistress Modesty shook her head as she listened to her own maxim from Peggy's lips. "So why do you intend to inflict your wisdom on this poor unfortunate man you say you love?"

"Because some men are great enough that they can love a whole woman, and not just a part of her."

"Is *he* such a man?"

How could Peggy answer? "He will be, or he won't have me."

Mistress Modesty paused for a moment, as if trying to find a beautiful way to tell a painful truth. "I always taught you that if you become completely and perfectly yourself, then good men will be drawn to you and love you. Peggy, let us say this man has great needs—but if you must become something that is *not* you in order to supply him, then you will not be perfectly yourself, and he will *not* love you. Isn't that why you left Hatrack River in the first place, so he would love you for yourself, and not for what you did for him?"

"Mistress Modesty, I want him to love me, yes. But I love the work he must accomplish even more than that. What I am today would be enough for the man. What I will go and do tomorrow is not for the man, it is for his work."

"But—" began Mistress Modesty.

Peggy raised an eyebrow and smiled slightly. Mistress Modesty nodded and did not interrupt.

"If I love his work more than I love the man, then to be perfectly myself, I must do what his work requires of me. Won't I, then, be even more beautiful?"

"To me, perhaps," said Mistress Modesty. "Few men have vision clear enough for *that* subtle beauty."

"He loves his work more than he loves his life. Won't he, then, love the woman who shares in it more than a woman who is merely beautiful?"

"You may be right," said Mistress Modesty, "for I have never loved work more than I have loved the person doing it, and I have never known a man who truly loved his work more than his own life. All that I have taught you is true in the world I know. If you pass from my world into another one, I can no longer teach you anything."

"Maybe I can't be a perfect woman and also live my life as it must be lived."

"Or perhaps, Mistress Margaret, even the best of the world is not fit to recognize a perfect woman, and so will accept me as a fair counterfeit, while you pass by unknown."

That was more than Peggy could bear. She cast aside decorum and threw her arms around Mistress Modesty and kissed her and cried, assuring her that there was nothing counterfeit about her. But when all the weeping was done, nothing had changed. Peggy was finished in Dekane, and by next morning her trunk was packed.

Everything she had in the world was a gift from Mistress Modesty, except for the box Oldpappy gave her long ago. Yet what was in that box was a heavier burden by far than any other thing that Peggy carried.

She sat in the northbound train, watching the mountains drift by outside her east-facing window. It wasn't all that long ago that Whitley Physicker had brought her to Dekane in his carriage. Dekane had seemed the grandest place at first; at the time it seemed to her that she was discovering the world by coming here. Now she knew that the world was far too large for one person to discover it. She was leaving a very small place and going to another very small place, and perhaps from there to other small places. The same size heartfires blazed in every city, no brighter for having so much company.

I left Hatrack River to be free of you, Prentice Alvin. Instead I found a larger, far more entangling net outside. Your work is larger than yourself, larger than me, and because I know of it I'm bound to help. If I didn't, I'd be a vile person in my own eyes.

So if you end up loving me or not, that doesn't matter all that much. Oh, yes, to *me* it matters, but the course of the world won't change one way or the other. What matters is that we both prepare you to do your work. Then if love comes, then if you can play Goodman to my Goodwife, we'll take that as an unlooked-for blessing and be glad of it as long as we can.

11

Wand

It was a week before Hank Dowser found his way back to Hatrack River. A miserable week with no profit in it, because try as he would he couldn't find decent dry ground for them folks west of town to dig their cellar. "It's all wet ground," he said. "I can't help it if it's all watery."

But they held him responsible just the same. Folks are like that. They act like they thought the dowser *put* the water where it sets, instead of just pointing to it. Same way with torches—blamed them half the time for *causing* what they saw, when all they did was see it. There was no gratitude or even simple understanding in most folks.

So it was a relief to be back with somebody half-decent like Makepeace Smith. Even if Hank wasn't too proud of the way Makepeace was dealing with his prentice boy. How could Hank criticize him? He himself hadn't done much better—oh, he was pure embarrassed now to think how he railed on that boy and got him a cuffing, and for nothing, really, just a little affront to Hank Dowser's pride. Jesus stood and took whippings and a crown of thorns in silence, but I lash out when a prentice mumbles a few silly words. Oh, thoughts like that put Hank Dowser in a dark mood, and he was aching for a chance to apologize to the boy.

But the boy wasn't there, which was too bad, though Hank didn't have long to brood about it. Gertie Smith took Hank Dowser up to the house and near jammed the food down his throat with a ramrod, just to get in an extra half-loaf of bread, it felt like. "I can't hardly walk," said Hank, which was true; but it was also true that Gertie Smith cooked just as good as her husband forged and that prentice boy shod and Hank dowsed, which is to say, with a true knack. Everybody has his talent, everybody has his gift from God, and we go about sharing gifts with each other, that's the way of the world, the best way.

So it was with pleasure and pride that Hank drank the swallows of water from the first clear bucket drawn from the well. Oh, it was fine water, sweet water, and he loved the way they thanked him from their hearts. It wasn't till he was out getting mounted on his Picklewing again that he realized he hadn't seen the well. Surely he should've seen the well—

He rounded the smithy on horseback and looked where he thought he had dowsed the spot, but the ground didn't appear like it had been troubled in a hundred years. Not even the trench the prentice dug while he was standing there. It took him a minute to find where the well actually was, sort of halfway between smithy and house, a fine little roof over the windlass, the whole thing finished with smoothed-worked stone. But surely he hadn't been so near the house when the wand dipped—

"Oh, Hank!" called Makepeace Smith. "Hank, I'm glad you ain't gone yet!"

Where was the man? Oh, there, back in the meadow just up from the smithy, near where Hank had first looked for the well. Waving a stick in his hand—a forked stick—

"Your wand, the one you used to dowse this well—you want it back?"

"No, Makepeace, no thanks. I never use the same wand twice. Doesn't work proper when it isn't fresh."

Makepeace Smith pitched the wand back over his head, walked back down the slope and stood exactly in the place where Hank *thought* he had dowsed the well to be. "What do you think of the well house we built?"

Hank glanced back toward the well. "Fine stonework. If you ever give up the forge, I bet there's a living for you in stonecutting."

"Why, thank you, Hank! But it was my prentice boy did it all."

"That's some boy you got," said Hank. But it left a bad taste in his mouth, to say those words. There was something made him uneasy about this whole conversation. Makepeace Smith meant something sly, and Hank didn't know rightly what it was. Never mind. Time to be on his way. "Good-bye, Makepeace!" he said, walking his nag back toward the road. "I'll be back for shoes, remember!"

Makepeace laughed and waved. "I'll be glad to see your ugly old face when you come!"

With that, Hank nudged old Picklewing and headed off right brisk for the road that led to the covered bridge over the river. That was one of the nicest things about the westbound road out of Hatrack. From there to the Wobbish the track was as sweet as you please, with covered bridges over every river, every stream, every rush and every rivulet. Folks were known to camp at night on the bridges, they were so tight and dry.

There must've been three dozen redbird nests in the eaves of the Hatrack Bridge. The birds were making such a racket that Hank allowed as how it was a miracle they didn't wake the dead. Too bad redbirds were too scrawny for eating. There'd be a banquet on that bridge, if it was worth the trouble.

"Ho there, Picklewing, my girl, ho," he said. He sat astride his horse, a-standing in the middle of the bridge, listening to the redbird song. Remembering now as clear as could be how the wand had leapt clean out of his hands and flung itself up into the meadow grass. Flung itself northeast of the spot he dowsed. And that's just where Makepeace Smith picked it up when he was saying good-bye.

Their fine new well wasn't on the spot he dowsed at all. The whole time he was there, they all were lying to him, pretending he dowsed them a well, but the water they drank was from another place.

Hank knew, oh yes, he knew who chose the spot they used. Hadn't the wand as much as told him when it flew off like that? Flew off because the boy spoke up, that smart-mouth prentice. And now they made mock of him behind his back, not saying a thing to his face, of course, but he knew that Makepeace was laughing the whole time, figuring he wasn't even smart enough to notice the switch.

Well, I noticed, yes sir. You made a fool of me, Makepeace Smith, you and that prentice boy of yours. But I noticed. A man can forgive seven times, or even seven times seven. But then there comes the fiftieth time, and even a good Christian can't forget.

"Gee-ap," he said angrily. Picklewing's ears twitched and she started forward in a gentle walk, new shoes clopping loud on the floorboards of the bridge, echoing from the walls and ceiling. "Alvin," whispered Hank Dowser. "Prentice Alvin. Got no respect for any man's knack except his own."

12

School Board

When the carriage pulled up in front of the inn, Old Peg Guester was upstairs hanging mattresses half out the windows to let them air, so she saw. She recognized Whitley Physicker's rig, a new-fangled closed car that kept the weather and most of the dust out; Physicker could use a carriage like that, now that he could afford to pay a man just to drive for him. It was things like that carriage that had most folks calling him *Dr. Physicker* now, instead of just Whitley.

The driver was Po Doggly, who used to have a farm of his own till he got to likkering up after his wife died. It was a good thing, Physicker hiring him when other folks just thought of old Po as a drunk. Things like that made most plain folks think well of Dr. Physicker, even if he did show off his money more than was seemly among Christians.

Anyway, Po hopped down from his seat and swung around to open the door of the carriage. But it wasn't Whitley Physicker got out first—it was Pauley Wiseman, the sheriff. If ever a man didn't deserve his last name, it was Pauley Wiseman. Old Peg felt herself wrinkle up inside just seeing him. It was like her husband Horace always said—any man who *wants* the job of sheriff is plainly unfit for the office. Pauley Wiseman wanted his job, wanted it more than most folks wanted to breathe. You could see it in the way he wore his stupid silver star right out in the open, on the outside of his coat, so nobody'd forget they was talking to the man who had the keys to the town jail. As if Hatrack River needed a jail!

Then Whitley Physicker got out of the carriage, and Old Peg knew exactly what business they were here for. The school board had made its decision, and these two were come to make sure she settled for it without making any noise about it in public. Old Peg tossed the mattress she was holding, tossed it so hard it near to flew clean out the window; she caught it by a corner and pulled it back so it'd hang proper and get a good airing. Then she ran down the stairs—she wasn't so old yet she couldn't run a flight of stairs when she wanted. Downward, anyways.

She looked around a bit for Arthur Stuart, but of course he wasn't in the house. He was just old enough for chores, and he did them, right enough, but after that he was always off by himself, over in town sometimes, or sometimes bothering around that blacksmith boy, Prentice Alvin. "What you do that for, boy?" Old Peg asked him once. "What you always have to be with Prentice Alvin for?" Arthur just grinned and then put his arms out like a street rassler all set to grab and said, "Got to learn how to throw a man twice my size." What made it funny was he said it just exactly in Alvin's own voice, complete with the way Alvin would've said it—with a joke in his voice, so you'd know he didn't take himself all that serious. Arthur had that knack, to mimic folks like as if he knew them right to the soul. Sometimes it made her wonder if he didn't have something of the torchy knack, like her runaway daughter Little Peggy; but no, it didn't seem like Arthur actually understood what he was doing. He was just a mimic. Still, he was smart as a whip, and that's why Old Peg knew the boy deserved to be in school, probably more than any other child in Hatrack River.

She got to the front door just as they started in to knock. She stood there, panting a little from her run down the stairs, waiting to open it even though she saw their shadows through the lace-curtain windows on the door. They were kind of shifting their weight back and forth, like they was nervous—as well they should be. Let 'em sweat.

It was just like them folks on the school board, to send Whitley Physicker of all people. It made Old Peg Guester mad just to see his shadow at her door. Wasn't he the one who took Little Peggy off six years ago, and then wouldn't tell her where the girl went? Dekane was all he said, to folks she seemed to know. And then Peg's husband Horace reading the note over and over, saying, If a torch can't see her own future safe, none of us can look out for her any better. Why, if it hadn't been for Arthur Stuart needing her so bad, Old Peg would have up and left. Just up and left, and see how they liked that! Take her daughter away and tell her it's all for the best—such a thing to tell a mother! Let's see what they think when *I* leave. If she hadn't had Arthur to look after, she would have gone so fast her shadow would've been stuck in the door.

And now they send Whitley Physicker to do it again, to set her grieving over another child, just like before. Only worse this time, because Little Peggy really *could* take care of herself, while Arthur Stuart couldn't, he was just a six-year-old boy, a boy with no future at all unless Old Peg fought for it tooth and nail.

They knocked again. She opened the door. There was Whitley Physicker, looking all cheerful and dignified, and behind him Pauley Wiseman, looking all important and dignified. Like two masts on the same ship, with sails all puffed out and bossy-looking. All full of wind. Coming to tell me what's right and proper, are you? We'll see.

"Goody Guester," said Dr. Physicker. He doffed his hat proper, like a gentleman. That's what's wrong with Hatrack River these days, thought Old Peg. Too many folks putting on like gentlemen and ladies. Don't they know this is Hio? All the high-toned folks are down in the Crown Colonies with His Majesty, the other Arthur Stuart. The long-haired White king, as opposed to her own short-haired Black boy Arthur. Anybody in the state of Hio who thinks he's a gentleman is just fooling himself and nobody but the other fools.

"I suppose you want to come in," said Old Peg.

"I hoped you'd invite us," said Physicker. "We come from the school board."

"You can turn me down on the porch as easy as you can inside my house."

"Now see here," said Sheriff Pauley. He wasn't used to folks leaving him standing on porches.

"We didn't come to turn you down, Goody Guester," said the doctor.

Old Peg didn't believe it for a minute. "You telling me that stiff-necked bunch of high-collar hypocrites is going to let a Black child into the new school?"

That set Sheriff Pauley off like gunpowder in a bucket. "Well, if you're so all-fired sure you know the answer, Old Peg, why'd you bother asking the question?"

"Cause I wanted you all down on record as being Black-hating slavers in your hearts! Then someday when the Emancipationists have their way and Black people have all their rights everywhere, you'll have to wear your shame in public like you deserve."

Old Peg didn't even hear her husband coming up behind her, she was talking so loud.

"Margaret," said Horace Guester. "No man stands on my porch without a welcome."

"*You* welcome them yourself, then," said Old Peg. She turned her back on Dr. Physicker and Sheriff Pauley and walked on into the kitchen. "I wash my hands of it," she shouted over her shoulder.

But once she was in the kitchen she realized that she wasn't cooking yet this morning, she was doing the upstairs beds. And as she stood there, kind of confused for a second, she got to thinking it was Pontius Pilate who did that first famous hand-washing. Why, she'd confessed herself unrighteous with her own words. God wouldn't look kindly on her if she once started in imitating someone as killed the Lord Jesus, like Pilate did. So she turned around and walked back into the common room and sat down near the hearth. It being August there wasn't no fire in it, which made it a cool place to sit. Not like the kitchen hearth, which was hot as the devil's privy on summer days like this. No reason she should sweat her heart out in the kitchen while these two decided the fate of Arthur Stuart in the coolest spot in the house.

Her husband and the two visitors looked at her but didn't say a thing about her storming out and then storming back in. Old Peg knew what was said behind her back—that you might as well try to set a trap for a cyclone as to tangle with Old Peg Guester—but she didn't mind a bit if men like Whitley Physicker and Pauley Wiseman walked a little wary around her. After a second or two, waiting for her to settle down, they went right on with their talk.

"As I was saying, Horace, we looked at your proposal seriously," Physicker said. "It would be a great convenience to us if the new teacher could be housed in your roadhouse instead of being boarded here and there the way it usually happens. But we wouldn't consider having you do it for free. We have enough students enrolled and enough basis in the property tax to pay you a small stipend for the service."

"How much does a sty pen come to in money?" asked Horace.

"The details remain to be worked out, but the sum of twenty dollars for the year was mentioned."

"Well," said Horace, "that's a mite low, if you're thinking you're paying the actual cost."

"On the contrary, Horace, we know that we're underpaying you by considerable. But since you offered to do it free, we hoped this would be an improvement on the original offer."

Horace was all set to agree, but Peg wouldn't stand for all this pretending. "I know what it is, Dr. Physicker, and it's no improvement. We didn't offer to put up the schoolteacher for *free*. We offered to put up *Arthur Stuart's* teacher for free. And if you figure twenty dollars is going to make me change my mind about that, you better go back and do your figuring again."

Dr. Physicker got a pained look on his face. "Now, Goody Guester. Don't get ahead of yourself on this. There was not a man on the school board who had any personal objection to having Arthur Stuart attend the new school."

When Physicker said that, Old Peg took a sharp look at Pauley Wise-

man. Sure enough, he squirmed in his chair like he had a bad itch in a
place where a gentleman doesn't scratch. That's right, Pauley Wiseman.
Dr. Physicker can say what he likes, but *I* know *you*, and there was one,
at least, who had all kinds of objections to Arthur Stuart.

Whitley Physicker went on talking, of course. Since he was pretending that everybody loved Arthur Stuart dearly, he couldn't very well
take notice of how uncomfortable Sheriff Pauley was. "We know Arthur has been raised by the two oldest settlers and finest citizens of
Hatrack River, and the whole town loves him for his own self. We just
can't think what benefit a school education would give the boy."

"It'll give him the same benefit it gives any other boy or girl," said
Old Peg.

"Will it? Will his knowing how to read and write get him a place in
a counting house? Can you imagine that even if they let him take the
bar, any jury would listen to a Black lawyer plead? Society has decreed
that a Black child will grow up to be a Black man, and a Black man,
like ancient Adam, will earn his bread by the sweat of his body, not by
the labors of his mind."

"Arthur Stuart is smarter than any child who'll be in that school and
you know it."

"All the more reason we shouldn't build up young Arthur's hopes,
only to have them dashed when he's older. I'm talking about the way
of the world, Goody Guester, not the way of the heart."

"Well why don't you wise men of the school board just say, To hell
with the way of the world, we'll do what's right! I can't make you do
what you don't want to do, but I'll be damned if I let you pretend it's
for Arthur's own good!"

Horace winced. He didn't like it to hear Old Peg swear. She'd only
taken it up lately, beginning with the time she cussed Millicent Mercher
right in public for insisting on being called "Mistress Mercher" instead
of "Goody Mercher." It didn't sit well with Horace, her using those
words, especially since she didn't seem to ken the time and place for it
like a man would, or at least so he said. But Old Peg figured if you
can't cuss at a lying hypocrite, then what was cussing invented for?

Pauley Wiseman started turning red, barely controlling a stream of
his own favorite cusswords. But Whitley Physicker was now a gentleman, so he merely bowed his head for a moment, like as if he was
saying a prayer—but Old Peg figured it was more likely he was waiting
till he calmed down enough for his words to come out civil. "Goody
Guester, you're right. We didn't think up that story about it being for
Arthur's own good till after the decision was made."

His frankness left her without a word, at least for the moment. Even

Sheriff Pauley could only give out a kind of squeak. Whitley Physicker wasn't sticking to what they all agreed to say; he sounded espiciously close to telling the truth, and Sheriff Pauley didn't know what to do when people started throwing the truth around loose and dangerous. Old Peg enjoyed watching Pauley Wiseman look like a fool, it being something for which old Pauley had a particular knack.

"You see, Goody Guester, we want this school to work proper, we truly do," said Dr. Physicker. "The whole idea of public schools is a little strange. The way they do schools in the Crown Colonies, it's all the people with titles and money who get to attend, so that the poor have no chance to learn or rise. In New England all the schools are religious, so you don't come out with bright minds, you come out with perfect little Puritans who all stay in their place like God meant them to. But the public schools in the Dutch states and Pennsylvania are making people see that in America we can do it different. We can teach every child in every wildwood cabin to read and write and cipher, so that we have a whole population educated enough to be fit to vote and hold office and govern ourselves."

"All this is well and good," said Old Peg, "and I recollect hearing you give this exact speech in our common room not three months ago before we voted on the school tax. What I can't figure, Whitley Physicker, is why you figure my son should be the exception."

At this, Sheriff Pauley decided it was time to put an oar in. And since the truth was being used so recklessly, he lost control of himself and spoke truthfully himself. It was a new experience, and it went to his head a little. "Begging your pardon, Old Peg, but there isn't a drop of your blood in that boy, so he's no-wise your son, and if Horace here has some part of him, it isn't enough to turn him White."

Horace slowly got to his feet, as if he was preparing to invite Sheriff Pauley outside to punch some caution into him. Pauley Wiseman must have known he was in trouble the second he accused Horace of maybe being the father of a half-Black bastard. And when Horace stood up so tall like that, Pauley remembered he wasn't no match for Horace Guester. Horace wasn't exactly a small man and Pauley wasn't exactly a large one. So old Pauley did what he always did when things got out of hand. He turned kind of sideways so his badge was facing straight at Horace Guester. Take a lick at me, that badge said, and you'll be facing a trial for assaulting an officer of the law.

Still, Old Peg knew that Horace wouldn't hit a man over a word; he hadn't even knocked down that river rat who accused Horace of unspeakable crimes with barnyard animals. Horace just wasn't the kind to lose control of himself in anger. In fact, Old Peg could see that as

Horace stood there, he'd already forgotten about his anger at Pauley Wiseman and was thinking over an idea.

Sure enough, Horace turned to Old Peg as if Wiseman didn't even exist. "Maybe we should give it up, Peg. It was fine when Arthur was a sweet little baby, but . . ."

Horace, who was looking right at Old Peg's face, he knew better than to finish his sentence. Sheriff Pauley wasn't half so bright. "He just gets blacker every day, Goody Guester."

Well, what do you say to that kind of thing, anyway? At least now it was plain what was going on—that it was Arthur Stuart's color and nothing else that was keeping him out of the new Hatrack River School.

Whitley Physicker sighed into the silence. Nothing that happened with Sheriff Pauley there ever went according to plan. "Don't you see?" said Physicker. He sounded mild and reasonable, which he was good at. "There's some ignorant and backward folks"—and at this he took a cool look at Sheriff Pauley—"who can't abide the thought of a Black child getting the same education as their own boys and girls. What's the advantage of schooling, they figure, if a Black has it the same as a White? Why, the next thing you know, Blacks would be wanting to vote or hold office."

Old Peg hadn't thought of that. It just never entered her mind. She tried to imagine Mock Berry being governor, and trying to give orders to the militia. There wasn't a soldier in Hio who'd take orders from a Black man. It'd be as unnatural as a fish jumping out of the river to kill him a bear.

But Old Peg wasn't going to give up so easy, just because Whitley Physicker made one point like that. "Arthur Stuart's a good boy," she said. "He wouldn't no more try to vote than I would."

"I know that," said Physicker. "The whole school board knows that. But it's the backwoods people who won't know it. They're the ones who'll hear there's a Black child in the school and they'll keep their children home. And here we'll be paying for a school that won't be doing its job of educating the citizenry of our republic. We're asking Arthur to forgo an education that will do him no good anyway, in order to allow others to receive an education that will do them and our nation a great deal of good."

It all sounded so logical. After all, Whitley Physicker was a doctor, wasn't he? He'd even been to college back in Philadelphia, so he had a deeper understanding than Old Peg would ever have. Why did she think even for a moment that she could disagree with a man like Physicker and not be wrong?

Yet even though she couldn't think of a single argument against him, she couldn't get rid of a feeling deep in her guts that if she said yes to Whitley Physicker, she'd be stabbing a knife right into little Arthur's heart. She could imagine him asking her, "Mama, why can't I go to school like all my friends?" And then all these fine words from Dr. Physicker would fly away like she'd never heard them, and she'd just sit there and say, "It's because you're Black, Arthur Stuart Guester."

Whitley Physicker seemed to take her silence as surrender, which it nearly was. "You'll see," said Physicker. "Arthur won't mind not going to school. Why, the White boys'll all be jealous of *him*, when he can be outside in the sun while they're cooped up in a classroom."

Old Peg Guester knew there was something wrong with all this, that it wasn't as sensible as it sounded, but she couldn't think what it was.

"And someday things might be different," said Physicker. "Someday maybe society will change. Maybe they'll stop keeping Blacks as slaves in the Crown Colonies and Appalachee. Maybe there'll be a time when . . ." His voice trailed off. Then he shook himself. "I get to wondering sometimes, that's all," he said. "Silly things. The world is the way the world is. It just isn't natural for a Black man to grow up like a White."

Old Peg felt a bitter hatred inside her when he said those words. But it wasn't a hot rage, to make her shout at him. It was a cold, despairing hate, that said, Maybe I *am* unnatural, but Arthur Stuart is my true son, and I won't betray him. No I won't.

Again, though, her silence was taken to mean consent. The men all got up, looking relieved, Horace most of all. It was plain they never figured Old Peg would listen to reason so fast. The visitors' relief was to be expected, but why was Horace looking so happy? Old Peg had a nasty suspicion and she knew at once that it had to be the truth—Horace Guester and Dr. Physicker and Sheriff Pauley had already worked things out between them before they ever come a-calling today. This whole conversation was pretend. Just a show put on to make Old Peg Guester happy.

Horace didn't want Arthur Stuart in school any more than Whitley Physicker or anybody else in Hatrack River.

Old Peg's anger turned hot, but now it was too late. Physicker and Pauley was out the door, Horace following on out after them. No doubt they'd all pat each other on the back and share a smile out of Old Peg's sight. But Old Peg wasn't smiling. She remembered all too clear how Little Peggy had done a seeing for her that last night before she run off, a Seeing about Arthur Stuart's future. Old Peg had asked Little Peggy if Horace would ever love little Arthur, and the girl refused to answer. That *was* an answer, sure enough. Horace might go through the motions of treating Arthur like his own son, but in fact he thought of him as just a Black boy that his wife had taken a notion to care for. Horace was no papa to Arthur Stuart.

So Arthur's an orphan all over again. Lost his father. Or, rightly speaking, never had a father. Well, so be it. He's got two mothers: the one who died for him when he was born, and me. I can't get him in the school. I knew I couldn't, knew it from the start. But I can get him an education all the same. A plan for it sprung into her head all at once. It all depended on the schoolmistress they hired, this teacher lady from Philadelphia. With luck she'd be a Quaker, with no hate for Blacks and so the plan would work out just fine. But even if the schoolmistress hated Blacks as bad as a finder watching a slave stand free on the Canadian shore, it wouldn't make a bit of difference. Old Peg would find a way. Arthur Stuart was the only family she had left in the world, the only person she loved who didn't lie to her or fool her or do things behind her back. She wasn't going to let him be cheated out of anything that might do him good.

13

Springhouse

Alvin first knew something was up when he heard Horace and Old Peg Guester yelling at each other up at the old springhouse. It was so loud for a minute there that he could hear them clear over the sound of the forgefire and his own hammering. Then they quietened themselves down a mite, but by then Alvin was so curious he kind of laid off the hammer. Laid it right down, in fact, and stepped outside to hear better.

No, no, he wasn't *listening*. He was just going to the well to fetch more water, some to drink and some for the cooling barrel. If he happened to hear them somewhat, he couldn't be blamed, now, could he?

"Folks'll say I'm a bad innkeeper, making the teacher live in the springhouse instead of putting her up proper."

"It's just an empty building, Horace, and we'll put it to use. And it'll leave us the rooms in the inn for paying customers."

"I won't have that schoolmistress living off alone by herself. It ain't decent!"

"Why, Horace? Are you planning to make advances?"

Alvin could hardly believe his ears. Married people just didn't say such things to each other. Alvin half expected to hear the sound of a slap. But instead Horace must've just took it. Everybody said he was henpecked, and this was about all the proof a body'd need, to have his wife accuse him of hankering after adultery and him not hit her or even say boo.

"It doesn't matter, anyway," said Old Peg. "Maybe you'll have your way and she'll say no. But we'll fix it up, anyway, and offer it to her."

Horace mumbled something that Alvin couldn't hear.

"I don't care if Little Peggy *built* this springhouse. She's gone of her own free will, left without so much as a word to me, and I'm not about to keep this springhouse like a monument just because she used to come here when she was little. Do you hear me?"

Again Alvin couldn't hear what Horace said.

On the other hand, he could hear Old Peg right fine. Her voice just sailed right out like a crack of thunder. "You're telling *me* who loved who? Well let me tell you, Horace Guester, all your love for Little Peggy didn't keep her here, *did* it? But my love for Arthur Stuart is going to get him an education, do you understand me? And when it's all said and done, Horace Guester, we'll just see who does better at loving their children!"

There wasn't exactly a slap or nothing, but there was a slammed door which like to took the door of the springhouse off its hinges. Alvin couldn't help craning his neck a little to see who did the slamming. Sure enough, it was Old Peg stalking away.

A minute later, maybe even more, the door opened real slow. Alvin could barely make it out through the brush and leaves that had grown up between the well and the springhouse. Horace Guester came out even slower, his face downcast in a way Alvin had never seen him before. He stood there awhile, his hand on the door. Then he pushed it closed, as gentle as if he was tucking a baby into bed. Alvin always wondered why they hadn't tore down that springhouse years ago, when Alvin dug the well that finally killed the stream that used to go through it. Or at least why they never put it to some use. But now Alvin knew it had something to do with Peggy, that torch girl who left right before Alvin showed up in Hatrack River. The way Horace touched that door, the way he closed it, it made Alvin see for the first time how much a man might dote on a child of his, so that even when she was gone, the places that she loved were like holy ground to her old dad. For the first time Alvin wondered if he'd ever love a child of his own like that. And then he wondered who the mother of that child might be, and if she'd ever scream at him the way Old Peg screamed at Horace, and if he'd ever have at her the way Makepeace Smith had at his wife Gertie, him flailing with his belt and her throwing the crockery.

"Alvin," said Horace.

Well, Alvin like to died with embarrassment, to be caught staring at Horace like that. "I beg pardon, sir," said Alvin. "I shouldn't ought to've been listening."

Horace smiled wanly. "I reckon as you'd have to be a deaf mute not to hear that last bit."

"It got a mite loud," said Alvin, "but I didn't exactly go out of my way not to hear, neither."

"Well, I know you're a good boy, and I never heard of no one carrying tales from you."

The words "good boy" rankled a bit. Alvin was eighteen now, less than a year to being nineteen, long since ready to be a journeyman smith out on his own. Just because Makepeace Smith wouldn't release him early from his prenticeship didn't make it right for Horace Guester to call him a *boy*. I may be Prentice Alvin, and not a man yet afore the law, but no woman yells *me* to shame.

"Alvin," said Horace, "you might tell your master we'll be needing new hinges and fittings for the springhouse doors. I reckon we're fixing it up for the new schoolteacher to live here, if she wants."

So that was the way of it. Horace had lost the battle with Old Peg. He was giving in. Was that the way of marriage, then? A man either had to be willing to hit his wife, like Makepeace Smith, or he'd be bossed around like poor Horace Guester. Well, if that's the choices, I'll have none of it, thought Alvin. Oh, Alvin had an eye for girls in town. He'd see them flouncing along the street, their breasts all pushed up high by their corsets and stays, their waists so small he could wrap his great strong hands right around and toss them every which way, only he never thought of tossing or grabbing, they just made him feel shy and hot at the same time, so he looked down when they happened to look at him, or got busy loading or unloading or whatever business brought him into town.

Alvin knew what they saw when they looked at him, those town girls. They saw a man with no coat on, just in his shirt-sleeves, stained and wet from his labor. They saw a poor man who'd never keep them in a fine white clapboard house like their papa, who was no doubt a lawyer or a judge or a merchant. They saw him *low*, a mere prentice still, and him already more than eighteen years old. If by some miracle he ever married one such girl, he knew how it would be, her always looking down at him, always expecting him to give way for her because she was a lady.

And if he married a girl who was as low as himself, it would be like Gertie Smith or Old Peg Guester, a good cook or a hard worker or whatever, but a hellion when she didn't get her way. There was no woman in Alvin Smith's life, that was sure. He'd never let himself be showed up like Horace Guester.

"Did you hear me, Alvin?"

"I did, Mr. Horace, and I'll tell Makepeace Smith first off when I see him. All the fittings for the springhouse."

"And nice work, too," said Horace. "It's for the schoolmistress to live there." But Horace wasn't so whipped that he couldn't get a curl to his lip and a nasty tone to his voice as he said, "So she can give *private* lessons."

The way he said "private lessons" made it sound like it'd be a whorehouse or something, but Alvin knew right off, by putting things together, exactly who would be getting private lessons. Didn't everybody know how Old Peg had asked to have Arthur Stuart accepted at the school?

"Well, so long," said Horace.

Alvin waved him good-bye, and Horace ambled away along the path to the inn.

Makepeace Smith didn't come in that afternoon. Alvin wasn't surprised. Now that Alvin had his full mansize on him, he could do the whole work of the smithy, and faster and better than Makepeace. Nobody said aught about it, but Alvin noticed back last year that folks took to dropping in during the times when Makepeace *wasn't* at the forge. They'd ask Alvin to do their ironwork quicklike, while they was there waiting. "Just a little job," they'd say, only sometimes the job wasn't all that little. And pretty soon Alvin realized that it wasn't just chance brought them by. They wanted *Alvin* to do the work they needed.

It wasn't because Alvin did anything peculiar to the iron, either, except a hex or two where it was called for, and every smith did that. Alvin knew it wouldn't be right to best his master using some secret knack—it'd be like slipping a knife into a rassling match. It'd just bring him trouble anyway, if he used his knack to give *his* iron any peculiar strength. So he did his work natural, with his own strong arm and good eye. He'd earned every inch of muscle in his back and shoulders and arms. And if people liked his work better than Makepeace Smith's, why, it was because Alvin was a better blacksmith, not because his knack gave him the advantage.

Anyhow, Makepeace must've caught on to what was happening, and he took to staying away from the forge more and more. Maybe it was because he knew it was better for business, and Makepeace was humble enough to give way before his prentice's skill—but Alvin never quite believed that. More likely Makepeace stayed away so folks wouldn't see how he snuck a look over Alvin's shoulder now and then, trying to figure out what Al did better than his master. Or maybe Makepeace was plain jealous, and couldn't bear to watch his prentice at work. Could be, though, that Makepeace was just lazy, and since his prentice boy was doing the work just fine, why *shouldn't* Makepeace go out to drink himself silly with the river rats down at Hatrack Mouth?

Or perhaps, by some strange twist of chance, Makepeace was actually ashamed of how he kept Alvin to his prentice contract even though

Alvin was plainly ready to take to the road as a journeyman. It was a low thing for a master to hold a prentice after he knew his trade, just to get the benefit of his labor without having to pay him a fair wage. Alvin brought good money into Makepeace Smith's household, everybody knew that, and all the while Alvin stayed dirt poor, sleeping in a loft and never two coins in his pocket to make a jingle when he walked to town. Sure, Gertie fed him proper—best food in town, Al knew well, having eaten a bite now and then with one of the town boys. But good food wasn't the same thing as a good wage. Food you ate and it was gone. Money you could use to buy things, or to do things—to have *freedom*. That contract Makepeace Smith kept in the cupboard up to the house, the one signed by Alvin's father, it made Alvin a slave as sure any Black in the Crown Colonies.

Except for one difference. Alvin could count the days till freedom. It was August. Not even a year left. Next spring he'd be free. No slave in the South ever knew such a thing; nary such a hope would ever enter their heads. Alvin had thought on that often enough over the years, when he was feeling most put upon; he'd think, if they can keep on living and working, having no hope of freedom, then I can hold out for another five years, three years, one year, knowing that it'll come to an end someday.

Anyway, Makepeace Smith didn't show up that afternoon, and when Alvin finished his assigned work, instead of doing chores and cleaning up, instead of getting ahead, he went on up to the springhouse and took the measure of the doors and windows. It was a place built to keep in the cool of the stream, so the windows didn't open, but the schoolmistress wouldn't cotton to *that*, never having a breath of air, so Alvin took the measure there, too. Not that he exactly decided to make new window frames himself, seeing how he wasn't no carpenter particularly, except what woodworking skill any man learns. He was just taking the measure of the place, and when he got to the windows he kept going.

He took the measure of a lot of things. Where a little pot-bellied stove would have to go, if the place was going to be warm in the winter; and figuring that, he also figured how to lay in the right foundation under the heavy stove, and how to put the flaring around the chimney, all the things it'd take to make the springhouse into a tight little cabin, fit for a lady to live in.

Alvin didn't write down the measures. He never did. He just knew them, now that he'd put his fingers and hands and arms into all the places; and if he forgot, and took the measure wrong somehow, he knew that in a pinch he could make it fit even so. It was a kind of laziness, he knew, but he got precious little advantage from his knack these days, and there was no shame in such small fidging.

Arthur Stuart wandered along when Al was just about done at the springhouse. Alvin didn't say nothing, nor did Arthur; you don't greet somebody who belongs where you are, you hardly notice them. But when Alvin needed to get the measure of the roof, he just said so and then tossed Arthur up onto the roof as easy as Peg Guester tossed the feather mattresses from the inn beds.

Arthur walked like a cat on top of the roof, paying no heed to being up so high. He paced off the roof and kept his own count, and when he was done he didn't even wait to make sure Alvin was ready to catch him, he just took a leap into the air. It was like Arthur believed he could fly. And with Alvin there to catch him below, why, it might as well be true, since Alvin had such arms on him that he could catch Arthur easy and let him down as gentle as a mallard settling onto a pond.

When Al and Arthur was done with measuring, they went back to the smithy. Alvin took a few bars of iron from the pile, het up the forge, and set to work. Arthur set in to pumping the bellows and fetching tools—they'd been doing this so long that it was like Arthur was Alvin's own prentice, and it never occurred to either of them that there was anything wrong with it. They just did this together, so smooth that to other folks it looked like a kind of dance.

A couple of hours later, Alvin had all the fittings. It should've taken less time by half, only for some reason Alvin got it into his head that he ought to make a lock for the door, and then he got it into his head that it ought to be a real lock, the kind that a few rich folks in town ordered from back east in Philadelphia—with a proper key and all, and a catch that shut all by itself when you closed the door, so you'd never forget to lock the door behind you.

What's more, he put secret hexes on all the fittings, perfect six-point figures that spoke of safety, and no one with harm in his heart being about to turn the lock. Once the lock was closed and fastened in place on the door, nobody'd see those hexes, but they'd do the work sure, since when Alvin made a hex the measure was so perfect it cast a network of hexes like a wall for many yards on every side.

It occurred to Alvin to wonder why a hex should work at all. Of course he knew why it was such a magical shape, being twice three; and he knew how you could lay hexes down on a table and they'd fit snug together, as perfect as squares, only stronger, woven not with warp and weft, but with warp and weft and hax. It wasn't like squares, which were hardly ever found in nature, being too simple and weak; there was hexes in snowflakes and crystals and honeycombs. Making a single hex was the same as making a whole fabric of hexes, so that the perfect hexes he hid up inside the lock would wrap all the way around the house, sealing it from outside harm as surely as if he forged a net of iron and wove it right in place.

But that didn't answer the question *why* it worked. Why his hidden hexes should bar a man's hand, turn a man's mind away from entering. Why the hex should invisibly repeat itself as far as it could, and the more perfect the hex, the farther the net it threw. All these years of puzzling things out, and he still knew so little. Knew so near to nothing that he despaired, and even now, holding the springhouse fittings in his hands, he wondered if in fact he shouldn't content himself to be a good smith and forget these tales of Makering.

With all his wondering and questioning, Alvin never did ask himself what should have been the plainest question of all. Why would a schoolmistress need such a perfectly hexed, powerful lock? Alvin didn't even try to guess. He wasn't thinking like that. Instead he just knew that such a lock was something fine, and this little house had to be as fine as he could make it. Later on he'd wonder about it, wonder if he knew even then, before he met her, what this schoolmistress would mean to him. Maybe he already had a plan in the back of his mind, just like Old Peg Guester did. But he sure didn't know about it yet, and that was the truth. When he made all those fancy fittings, with patterns cut in them so the door would look pretty, he most likely was doing it for Arthur Stuart; maybe he was halfway thinking that if the schoolmistress had a right pretty little place to live, she'd be more inclined to give Arthur Stuart his private lessons.

It was time to quit for the day, but Alvin didn't quit. He pushed all the fittings up to the springhouse in a wheelbarrow, along with a couple of other tools he figured to need, and some scrap tin for the flaring of the chimney. He worked fast, and without quite meaning to, he used his knack to smooth the labor. Everything fit first time; the doors rehung as nice as could be, and the lock fitted exactly to the inside face of the door, bolted on so tight that it'd never come off. This was a door no man could force—easier to chop through the split-log wall than attack this door. And with the hexes inside, a man wouldn't dare to lift his axe against the house, or if he did, he'd be too weak to strike a telling blow—these were hexes that even a Red might not laugh at.

Al took another trip back to the shed outside the smithy and chose the best of the old broke-down pot-belly stoves that Makepeace had bought for the iron in them. Carrying a whole stove wasn't easy even for a man strong as a blacksmith, but it was sure the wheelbarrow couldn't handle such a load. So Alvin hefted it up the hill by main strength. He left it outside while he brought stones from the old stream-bed to make a foundation under the floor at the place where the stove would go. The floor of the springhouse was set on beams running the length of the house inside, but they hadn't planked over the strip where the stream used to go—it wouldn't have been much of a springhouse if they covered over the cold water. Anyway he put a tight stone foundation under an upstream corner where the floor was done but not too high off the ground, and then bolted sheets of thin-beat iron on top of the planks to make a fireproof floor. Then he hefted the stove into place and piped it up to the hole he knocked in the roof.

He set Arthur Stuart to work with a rasp, tearing the dead moss off the inside of the walls. It came off easy, but it mostly kept Arthur distracted so he didn't notice that Alvin was fixing things on that broke-down stove that couldn't be fixed by a natural man. Good as new, and all fittings tight.

"I'm hungry," said Arthur Stuart.

"Get on up to Gertie and tell her I'm working late and please send food down for both of us, since you're helping."

Arthur Stuart took off running. Alvin knew that he'd deliver the message word for word, and in Alvin's own voice, so that Gertie'd laugh out loud and give him a good supper in a basket. Probably such a good supper that Arthur'd have to stop and rest three or four times on the way back, it'd be so heavy.

All this time Makepeace Smith never so much as showed his face.

When Arthur Stuart finally got back, Alvin was on the roof putting the final touch on the flaring, and fixing some of the shingles while he was up there. The flaring fit so tight water'd never get into the house, he saw to that. Arthur Stuart stood below, waiting and watching, not asking if he could go ahead and eat, not even asking how long till Alvin'd come down; he wasn't the type of child to whine or complain. When Alvin was done, he dropped over the edge of the roof, caught himself on the lip of the eaves, then dropped to the ground.

"Cold chicken be mighty good after a hot day's work," said Arthur Stuart, in a voice that was exactly Gertie Smith's, except pitched in a child's high voice.

Alvin grinned at him and opened the basket. They fell to eating like sailors who'd been on short rations for half the voyage, and in no time they was both lying there on their backs, bellies packed full, belching now and then, watching the white clouds move like placid cattle grazing across the sky.

The sun was getting low toward the west now. Definitely time to pack in for the day, but Alvin just couldn't feel good about that. "Best you get home," he said. "Maybe if you just run that empty basket back up to Gertie Smith's, you can get in without your Ma gets too upset at you."

"What you doing now?"

"Got windows to frame and re-hang."

"Well I got walls to finish rasping down," said Arthur Stuart.

Alvin grinned, but he also knew that what he planned to do to the windows wasn't a thing he wanted witnesses for. He had no intention of actually doing a lot of carpentry, and he didn't ever let anybody watch him do something *obvious* with his knack. "Best you go home now," said Alvin.

Arthur sighed.

"You been a good help to me, but I don't want you getting in trouble."

To Alvin's surprise, Arthur just returned his own words back to him in his own voice. "You been a good help to me, but I don't want you getting in trouble."

"I mean it," said Alvin.

Arthur Stuart rolled over, got up, came over and sat down astride of Alvin's belly—which Arthur often did, but it didn't feel none too comfortable at the moment, there being about a chicken and a half inside that belly.

"Come on, Arthur Stuart," said Alvin.

"I never told nobody bout no redbird," said Arthur Stuart.

Well, that just sent a chill right through Alvin. Somehow he'd figured that Arthur Stuart was just too young that day more than three years ago to even remember that anything happened. But Alvin should've knowed that just because Arthur Stuart didn't talk about something didn't mean that he forgot. Arthur never forgot so much as a caterpillar crawling on a leaf.

If Arthur Stuart remembered the redbird, then he no doubt remembered that day when it was winter out of season, when Alvin's knack dug a well and made the stone come clean of dirt without using his hands. And if Arthur Stuart knew all about Alvin's knack, then what point was there in trying to sneak around and make it secret?

"All right then," said Alvin. "Help me hang the windows." Alvin almost added, "as long as you don't tell a soul what you see." But Arthur Stuart already understood that. It was just one of the things that Arthur Stuart understood.

They finished before dark, Alvin cutting into the wood of the window frames with his bare fingers, shaping what was just wood nailed into wood until it was windows that could slide free, up and down. He made little holes in the sides of the window frames and whittled plugs of wood to fit them, so the window would stay up as far as a body might want. Of course, he didn't quite whittle like a natural man, since each stroke of the knife took off a perfect arc. Each plug was done in about six passes of the knife.

Meantime Arthur Stuart finished the rasping, and then they swept out the house, using a broom of course, but Alvin helped with his knack so that every scrap of sawdust and iron filings and flakes of moss and ancient dust ended up outside the house. Only thing they didn't do was try to cover the strip of open dirt down the middle of the springhouse, where once the stream flowed. That'd take felling a tree to get the planks, and anyway Alvin was starting to get a little scared, seeing how much he'd done and how fast he'd done it. What if somebody came *tonight* and realized that all this work was done in a single long afternoon? There'd be questions. There'd be guesses.

"Don't tell anybody that we did this all in a day," said Alvin.

Arthur Stuart just grinned. He'd lost one of his front teeth recently, so there was a spot where his pink gums showed up. Pink as a White person's gums, Alvin thought. Inside his mouth he's no different from a White. Then Alvin had this crazy idea of God taking all the people in the world who ever died and flaying them and hanging up their bodies like pigs in the butcher's shop, just meat and bones hanging there by the heel, even the guts and the head gone, just meat. And then God would ask folks like the Hatrack River School Board to come in and pick out which was Black folks and which was Red and which was White. They couldn't do it. Then God would say, "Well why in hell did you say that this one and this one and this one couldn't go to school with this one and this one and this one?" What answer would they have then? Then God would say, "You people, you're all the same rare meat under the skin. But I tell you, I don't like your flavor. I'm going to toss your beefsteaks to the dogs."

Well, that was such a funny idea that Alvin couldn't help but tell it to Arthur Stuart, and Arthur Stuart laughed just as hard as Alvin. Only after it was all said and the laughing was done did Alvin remember that maybe nobody'd told Arthur Stuart about how his ma tried to get him into the school and the school board said no. "You know what this is all about?"

Arthur Stuart didn't understand the question, or maybe he understood it even better than Alvin did. Anyways, he answered, "Ma's hoping the teacher lady'll learn me to read and write here in this springhouse."

"Right," said Alvin. No point in explaining about the school, then. Either Arthur Stuart already knew how some White folks felt about

Blacks, or else he'd find out soon enough without Alvin telling him now.

"We're all the same rare meat," said Arthur Stuart. He used a funny voice that Alvin had never heard before.

"Whose voice was that?" asked Alvin.

"God, of course," said Arthur Stuart.

"Good imitation," said Alvin. He was being funny.

"Sure is," said Arthur Stuart. He wasn't.

Turned out nobody came to the springhouse for a couple of days and more. It was Monday of the next week when Horace ambled into the smithy. He came early in the morning, at a time when Makepeace was most likely to be there, ostentatiously "teaching" Alvin to do something that Alvin already knew how to do.

"*My* masterpiece was a ship's anchor," said Makepeace. "Course, that was back in Newport, afore I come west. Them ships, them whaling ships, they weren't like little bitty houses and wagons. They needed *real* ironwork. A boy like you, you do well enough out here where they don't know better, but you'd never make a go of it *there*, where a smith has to be a *man*."

Alvin was used to such talk. He let it roll right off him. But he was grateful anyway when Horace came in, putting an end to Makepeace's brag.

After all the *good-morning*s and *howdy-do*s, Horace got right to business. "I just come by to see when you'll have a chance to get started on the springhouse."

Makepeace raised an eyebrow and looked at Alvin. Only then did Alvin realize that he'd never mentioned the job to Makepeace.

"It's already done, sir," Alvin said to Makepeace—for all the world as if Makepeace's unspoken question had been, "Are you finished yet?" and not, "What is this springhouse job the man's talking about?"

"Done?" said Horace.

Alvin turned to him. "I thought you must've noticed. I thought you were in a hurry, so I did it right off in my free time."

"Well, let's go see it," said Horace. "I didn't even think to look on my way down here."

"Yes, I'm dying to look at it myself," said the smith.

"I'll just stay here and keep working," said Alvin.

"No," said Makepeace. "You come along and show off this work you done in your *free time*." Alvin didn't hardly notice how Makepeace emphasized the last two words, he was so nervous to show off what he done at the springhouse. He only barely had sense enough to drop the keys he made into his pocket.

They made their way up the hill to the springhouse. Horace was the kind of man who could tell when somebody did real good work, and wasn't shy to say so. He fingered the fancy new hingework and admired the lock afore he put in the key. To Alvin's pride it turned smooth and easy. The door swung open quiet as a leaf in autumn. If Horace noticed the hexes, he didn't let on. It was other things he noticed, not hexery.

"Why, you cleaned off the walls," said Horace.

"Arthur Stuart did that," said Alvin. "Rasped it off neat as you please."

"And this stove—I tell you, Makepeace, I didn't figure the price of a new stove in this."

"It isn't a new stove," said Alvin. "I mean, begging your pardon, but it was a brokedown stove we kept for the scrap, only when I looked it over I saw we could fix it up, so why not put it here?"

Makepeace gave Alvin a cool look, then turned back to Horace. "That don't mean it's free, of course."

"Course not," said Horace. "If you bought it for scrap, though . . ."

"Oh, the price won't be too terrible high."

Horace admired how it joined to the roof. "Perfect work," he said. He turned around. To Alvin he looked a little sad, or maybe just resigned. "Have to cover the rest of the floor, of course."

"Not our line of work," said Makepeace Smith.

"Just talking to myself, don't mind me." Horace went over to the east window, pushed against it with his fingers, then raised it. He found the pegs on the sill and put them into the third hole on each side, then let the window fall back down to rest against the pegs. He looked at the pegs, then out the window, then back at the pegs, for a long time. Alvin dreaded having to explain how he, not trained as a fine carpenter, managed to hang such a fine window. Worse yet, what if Horace guessed that this was the original window, not a new one? That could only be explained by Alvin's knack—no carpenter could get inside the wood to cut out a sliding window like that.

But all Horace said was, "You did some extra work."

"Just figured it needed doing," said Alvin. If Horace wasn't going to ask about how he did it, Alvin was just as happy not to explain.

"I didn't reckon to have it done so fast," said Horace. "Nor to have so much done. The lock looks to be an expensive one, and the stove—I hope I don't have to pay for all at once."

Alvin almost said, You don't have to pay for any of it, but of course that wouldn't do. It was up to Makepeace Smith to decide things like that.

But when Horace turned around, looking for an answer, he didn't face Makepeace Smith, he stood square on to Alvin. "Makepeace Smith here's been charging full price for your work, so I reckon I shouldn't pay you any less."

Only then did Alvin realize that he made a mistake when he said he did the work in his free time, since work a prentice did in his official free time was paid for direct to the prentice, and not the master. Makepeace Smith never gave Alvin free time—whatever work anyone wanted done, Makepeace would hire Alvin out to do, which was his right under the prentice contract. By calling it free time, Alvin seemed to be saying that Makepeace had given him time off to earn money for himself.

"Sir, I—"

Makepeace spoke up before Alvin could explain the mistake. "Full price wouldn't be right," said Makepeace. "Alvin getting so close to the end of his contract, I thought he should start trying things on his own, see how to handle money. But even though the work looks right to you, to me it definitely looks second rate. So half price is right. I figure it took at least twenty hours to do all this—right, Alvin?"

It was more like ten, but Alvin just nodded. He didn't know what to say, anyway, since his master was obviously not committed to telling the plain truth about this job. And the job he did would have been at least twenty hours—two full days' labor—for a smith without Alvin's knack.

"So," said Makepeace, "between Al's labor at half price and the cost of the stove and the iron and all, it comes to fifteen dollars."

Horace whistled and rocked back on his heels.

"You can have my labor free, for the experience," Alvin said.

Makepeace glared at him.

"Wouldn't dream of it," said Horace. "The Savior said the laborer is worthy of his hire. It's the sudden high price of iron I'm a little skeptical about."

"It's a *stove*," said Makepeace Smith.

Wasn't till I fixed it, Alvin said silently.

"You bought it as scrap iron," said Horace. "As you said about Al's labor, full price wouldn't be right."

Makepeace sighed. "For old times' sake, Horace, cause you brought me here and helped set me up on my own when I came west eighteen years ago. Nine dollars."

Horace didn't smile, but he nodded. "Fair enough. And since you

602   HATRACK RIVER

usually charge four dollars a day for Alvin's hire, I guess his twenty hours at *half* price comes to four bucks. You come by the house this afternoon, Alvin, I'll have it for you. And Makepeace, I'll pay you the rest when the inn fills up at harvest time.''

"Fair enough," said Makepeace.

"Glad to see that you're giving Alvin free time now," said Horace. "There's been a lot of folks criticizing you for being so tight with a good prentice, but I always told them, Makepeace is just biding his time, you'll see."

"That's right," said Makepeace. "I was biding my time."

"You don't mind if I tell other folks that the biding's done?"

"Alvin still has to do his work for me," said Makepeace.

Horace nodded wisely. "Reckon so," he said. "He works for you mornings, for himself afternoons—is that right? That's the way most fair-minded masters do it, when a prentice gets so near to journeyman."

Makepeace began to turn a little red. Alvin wasn't surprised. He could see what was happening—Horace Guester was being like a lawyer for him, seizing on this chance to shame Makepeace into treating Alvin fair for the first time in more than six years of prenticing. When Makepeace decided to pretend that Alvin really *did* have free time, why, that was a crack in the door, and Horace was muscling his way through by main force. Pushing Makepeace to give Alvin half days, no less! That was surely too much for Makepeace to swallow.

But Makepeace swallowed. "Half days is fine with me. Been meaning to do that for some time."

"So you'll be working afternoons yourself now, right, Makepeace?"

Oh, Alvin had to gaze at Horace with pure admiration. He wasn't going to let Makepeace get away with lazing around and forcing Alvin to do all the work at the smithy.

"When I work's my own business, Horace."

"Just want to tell folks when they can be sure to find the master in, and when the prentice."

"I'll be in *all day.*"

"Why, glad to hear it," said Horace. "Well, fine work, I must say, Alvin. Your master done a good job teaching you, and you been care-fuler than I ever seen before. You make sure to come by this evening for your four dollars."

"Yes sir. Thank you, sir."

"I'll just let you two get back to work now," said Horace. "Are these the only two keys to the door?"

"Yes sir," said Alvin. "I oiled them up so they won't rust."

"I'll keep them oiled myself. Thanks for the reminder."

Horace opened the door and pointedly held it open till Makepeace and Alvin came on out. Horace carefully locked the door, as they watched. He turned and grinned at Alvin. "Maybe first thing I'll have you do is make a lock this fine for *my* front door." Then he laughed out loud and shook his head. "No, I reckon not. I'm an innkeeper. My business is to let people in, not lock them out. But there's others in town who'll like the look of this lock."

"Hope so, sir. Thank you."

Horace nodded again, then took a cool gaze at Makepeace as if to say, Don't forget all you promised to do here today. Then he ambled off up the path to the roadhouse.

Alvin started down the hill to the smithy. He could hear Makepeace following him, but Alvin wasn't exactly hoping for a conversation with his master just now. As long as Makepeace said nothing, that was good enough for Alvin.

That lasted only till they were both inside the smithy.

"That stove was broke to hell and back," said Makepeace.

That was the last thing Alvin expected to hear, and the most fearful. No chewing-out for claiming free time; no attempt to take back what he'd promised in the way of work schedule. Makepeace Smith had remembered that stove better than Alvin expected.

"Looked real bad, all right," said Alvin.

"No way to fix it without recasting," said Makepeace. "If I didn't know it was impossible, I would've fixed it myself."

"I thought so, too," said Alvin. "But when I looked it over—"

The look on Makepeace Smith's face silenced him. He knew. There was no doubt in Alvin's mind. The master knew what his prentice boy could do. Alvin felt the fear of being found out right down to his bones; it felt just like hide-and-go-find with his brothers and sisters when he was little, back in Vigor Church. The worst was when you were the last one still hid and unfound, all the waiting and waiting, and then you hear the footsteps coming, and you tingle all over, you feel it in every part of your body, like as if your whole self was awake and itching to move. It gets so bad you want to jump out and scream, "Here I am! I'm here!" and then run like a rabbit, not to the haven tree, but just anywhere, just run full out until every muscle of your body was wore out and you fell down on the earth. It was crazy—no good came of such craziness. But that's how it felt playing with his brothers and sisters, and that's how it felt now on the verge of being found out.

To Alvin's surprise, a slow smile spread across his master's face. "So that's it," said Makepeace. "That's it. Ain't you full of surprises. I see it now. Your pa said when you was born, he's the seventh son of a seventh son. Your way with horses, sure, I knew about that. And what you done finding that well, sense like a doodlebug, I could see *that*, too. But now.'' Makepeace grinned. ''Here I thought you were a smith like never was born, and all the time you was fiddling with it like an alchemist.''

''No sir,'' said Alvin.

''Oh, I'll keep your secret,'' said Makepeace. ''I won't tell a soul.'' But he was laughing in the way he had, and Alvin knew that while Makepeace wouldn't tell straight out, he'd be dropping hints from here to the Hio. But that wasn't what bothered Alvin most.

''Sir,'' said Alvin, ''all the work I ever done for *you*, I done honest, with my own arms and skill.''

Makepeace nodded wisely, like he understood some secret meaning in Alvin's words. ''I get it,'' he said. ''Secret's safe with me. But I knew it all along. Knew you couldn't be as good a smith as you seemed.''

Makepeace Smith had no idea how close he was to death. Alvin wasn't a murderous soul—any lust for blood that might have been born in him was driven out of him on a certain day inside Eight-Face Mound near seven years ago. But during all the years of his prenticeship, he had never heard one word of praise from this man, nothing but complaints about how lazy Alvin was, and how second-rate his work was, and all the time Makepeace Smith was lying, all the time he knew Alvin was good. Not till Makepeace was convinced Alvin had used hidden knackery to do his smithwork, not till now did Makepeace ever let Alvin know that he was, in fact, a good smith. Better than good. Alvin knew it, of course, knew he was a natural smith, but never having it said out loud hurt him deeper than he guessed. Didn't his master know how much a word might have meant, even half an hour ago, just a word like, ''You've got some skill at this, boy,'' or, ''You have a right good hand with that sort of work''? But Makepeace couldn't do it, had to lie and pretend Alvin had no skill until now, when Makepeace believed that he didn't have a smith's skill after all.

Alvin wanted to reach out and take hold of Makepeace's head and ram it into the anvil, ram it so hard that the truth would be driven right through Makepeace's skull and into his brain. I never used my Maker's knack in any of my smithwork, not since I got strong enough to do it with my own strength and skill, so don't smirk at me like I'm just a trickster, and no real smith. Besides, even if I used my Maker's art, do you think that's easy, either? Do you think I haven't paid a price for that as well?

All the fury of Alvin's life, all these years of slavery, all these years of rage at the unfairness of his master, all these years of secrecy and disguise, all his desperate longing to know what to do with his life and having no one in the world to ask, all this was burning inside Alvin hotter than the forge fire. Now the itching and tingling inside him wasn't a longing to run. No, it was a longing to do violence, to stop that smile on Makepeace Smith's face, to stop it forever against the anvil's beak.

But somehow Alvin held himself motionless, speechless, as still as an animal trying to be invisible, trying not to be where he is. And in that stillness Alvin heard the greensong all around him, and he let the life of the woodland come into him, fill his heart, bring him peace. The greensong wasn't loud as it used to be, farther west in wilder times, when the Red man still sang along with the greenwood music. It was weak, and sometimes got near drowned out by the unharmonious noise of town life or the monotones of well-tended fields. But Alvin could still find the song at need, and sing silently along with it, and let it take over and calm his heart.

Did Makepeace Smith know how close he came to death? For it was sure he'd be no match for Alvin rassling, not with Al so young and tall and so much terrible righteous fire in his heart. Whether he guessed or not, the smile faded from Makepeace Smith's face, and he nodded solemnly. "I'll keep all I said, up there, when Horace pushed me so hard. I know you probably put him up to it, but I'm a fair man, so I'll forgive you, long as you still pull some weight here for me, till your contract's up."

Makepeace's accusation that Alvin conspired with Horace should have made Alvin angrier, but by now the greensong owned him, and Alvin wasn't hardly even in the smithy. He was in the kind of trance he learned when he ran with Ta-Kumsaw's Reds, where you forget who and where you are, and your body's just a far-off creature running through the woods.

Makepeace waited for an answer, but it didn't come. So he just nodded wisely and turned to leave. "I got business in town," he said. "Keep at it." He stopped at the wide doorway and turned back into the smithy. "While you're at it, you might as well fix those other broke-down stoves in the shed."

Then he was gone.

Alvin stood there a long time, not moving, not hardly even knowing he had a body to move. It was full noon before he came to himself and took a step. His heart was utterly at peace then, with not a spot of rage left in it. If he'd thought about it, he probably would've knowed that the anger was sure to come back, that he wasn't so much healed as soothed. But soothing was enough for now, it'd do. His contract would be up this spring, and then he'd be out of this place, a free man at last.

One thing, though. It never did occur to him to do what Makepeace Smith asked, and fix those other brokedown stoves. And as for Makepeace, he never brought it up again, neither. Alvin's knack wasn't a part of his prenticeship, and Makepeace Smith must've knowed that, deep down, must've knowed he didn't have the right to tell young Al what to do when he was a-Making.

A few days later Alvin was one of the men who helped lay the new floor in the springhouse. Horace took him aside and asked him why he never came by for his four dollars.

Alvin couldn't very well tell him the truth, that he'd never take money for work he did as a Maker. "Call it my share of the teacher's salary," said Alvin.

"You got no property to pay tax on," said Horace, "nor any children to go to the school, neither."

"Then say I'm paying you for my share of the land my brother's body sleeps in up behind the roadhouse," said Alvin.

Horace nodded solemnly. "That debt, if there *was* a debt, was paid in full by your father's and brothers' labor seventeen year gone, young Alvin, but I respect your wish to pay your share. So this time I'll consider you paid in full. But any other work you do for me, you take full wages, you hear me?"

"I will, sir," said Alvin. "Thank you sir."

"Call me Horace, boy. When a growed man calls me sir it just makes me feel old."

They went back to work then, and said nary another word about Alvin's work on the springhouse. But something stuck in Alvin's mind all the same: what Horace said when Alvin offered to let his wages be a share of the teacher's salary. "You got no property, nor any children to go to the school." There it was, right there, in just a few words. That was why even though Alvin had his full growth on him, even though Horace called him a growed man, he wasn't really a man yet, not even in his own eyes. Because he had no family. Because he had no property. Till he had those, he was just a big old boy. Just a child like Arthur Stuart, only taller, with some beard showing when he didn't shave.

And just like Arthur Stuart, he had no share in the school. He was too old. It wasn't built for the likes of him. So why did he wait so anxious for the schoolmistress to come? Why did he think of her with so all-fired much hope? She wasn't coming here for him, and yet he knew that he had done his work on the springhouse for her, as if to put her in his debt, or perhaps to thank her in advance for what he wanted her, so desperately, to do for him.

Teach me, he said silently. I got a Work to do in this world, but nobody knows what it is or how it's done. Teach me. That's what I want from you, Lady, to help me find my way to the root of the world or the root of myself or the throne of God or the Unmaker's heart, wherever the secret of Making lies, so that I can build against the snow of winter, or make a light to shine against the fall of night.

14

River Rat

Alvin was in Hatrack Mouth the afternoon the teacher came. Makepeace had sent him with the wagon, to fetch a load of new iron that come down the Hio. Hatrack Mouth used to be just a single wharf, a stop for riverboats unloading stuff for the town of Hatrack River. Now, though, as river traffic got thicker and more folks were settling out in the western lands on both sides of the Hio, there was a need for a couple of inns and shops, where farmers could sell provender to passing boats, and river travelers could stay the night. Hatrack Mouth and the town of Hatrack River were getting more important all the time, since this was the last place where the Hio was close to the great Wobbish Road—the very road that Al's own father and brothers cut through the wilderness west to Vigor Church. Folks would come downriver and unship their wagons and horses here, and then move west overland.

There was also things that folks wouldn't tolerate in Hatrack River itself: gaming houses, where poker and other games got played and money changed hands, the law not being inclined to venture much into the dens of river rats and other such scum. And upstairs of such houses, it was said there was women who wasn't ladies, plying a trade that decent folks scarcely whispered about and boys of Alvin's age talked of in low voices with lots of nervous laughter.

It wasn't the thought of raised skirts and naked thighs that made Alvin look forward to his trips to Hatrack Mouth. Alvin scarce noticed those buildings, knowing he had no business there. It was the wharf that drew him, and the porthouse, and the river itself, with boats and rafts going by all the time, ten going downstream for every one coming up. His favorite boats were the steamboats, whistling and spitting their way along at unnatural speeds. With heavy engines built in Irrakwa, these riverboats were wide and long, and yet they moved upstream against the current faster than rafts could float downstream. There was eight of them on the Hio now, going from Dekane down to Sphinx and back again. No farther than Sphinx, though, since the Mizzipy was thick with fog, and nary a boat dared navigate there.

Someday, thought Alvin, someday a body could get on such a boat as *Pride of the Hio* and just float away. Out to the West, to the wild lands, and maybe catch a glimpse of the place where Ta-Kumsaw and Tenskwa-Tawa live now. Or upriver to Dekane, and thence by the new stream train that rode on rails up to Irrakwa and the canal. From there a body could travel the whole world, oceans across. Or maybe he could stand on this bank and the whole world would someday pass him by.

But Alvin wasn't lazy. He didn't linger long at riverside, though he might want to. Soon enough he went into the porthouse and turned in Makepeace Smith's chit to redeem the iron packed in nine crates on the dock.

"Don't want you using my hand trucks to tote those, now," said the portmaster. Alvin nodded—it was always the same. Folks wanted iron bad enough, the portmaster included, and he'd be up to the smithy soon enough asking for this or that. But in the meantime, he'd let Alvin heft the iron all himself, and not let him wear out the portmaster's trucks moving such a heavy load. Nor did Makepeace ever give Alvin money enough to hire one of the river rats to help with the toting. Truth to tell, Alvin was glad enough of that. He didn't much like the sort of man who lived the river life. Even though the day of brigands and pirates was pretty much over, there being too much traffic on the water now for much to happen in secret, still there was thievery enough, and crooked dealing, and Alvin looked down hard on the men who did such things. To his way of thinking, such men counted on the trust of honest folks, and then betrayed them; and what could that do, except make it so folks would stop trusting each other at all? I'd rather face a man with raw fighting in him, and match him arm for arm, than face a man who's full of lies.

So wouldn't you know it, Alvin met the new teacher and matched himself with a river rat all in the same hour.

The river rat he fought was one of a gang of them lolling under the eaves of the porthouse, probably waiting for a gaming house to open. Each time Alvin came out of the porthouse with a crate of iron bars, they'd call out to him, taunting him. At first it was sort of good-natured, saying things like, "Why are you taking so many trips, boy? Just tuck one of those crates under each arm!" Alvin just grinned at remarks like that, since he knew that they knew just how heavy a load of iron was.

Why, when they unloaded the iron from the boat yesterday, the boatmen no doubt hefted two men to a crate. So in a way, teasing him about being lazy or weak was a kind of compliment, since it was only a joke because the iron was heavy and Alvin was really very strong.

Then Alvin went on to the grocer's, to buy the spices Gertie had asked him to bring home for her kitchen, along with a couple of Irrakwa and New England kitchen tools whose purpose Al could only half guess at.

When he came back, both arms full, he found the river rats still loitering in the shade, only they had somebody new to taunt, and their mockery was a little ugly now. It was a middle-aged woman, some forty years old by Alvin's guess, her hair tied up severe in a bun and a plain hat atop it, her dark dress right up to the neck and down the wrist as if she was afraid sunlight on her skin might kill her. She was staring stonily ahead while the river rats had words at her.

"You reckon that dress is sewed on, boys?"

They reckoned so.

"Probably never comes up for no man."

"Why no, boys, there's nothing *under* that skirt, she's just a doll's head and hands sewed onto a stuffed dress, don't you think?"

"No way could she be a *real* woman."

"I can tell a real woman when I see one, anyway. The minute they lay eyes on me, *real* women just naturally start spreading their legs and raising their skirts."

"Maybe if you helped her out a little, you could turn her into a real woman."

"This one? This one's carved out of wood. I'd get splinters in my oar, trying to row in such waters."

Well, that was about all Alvin could stand to hear. It was bad enough for a man to think such thoughts about a woman who invited it—the girls from the gaming houses, who opened their necklines down to where you could count their breasts as plain as a cow's teats and flounced along the streets kicking up their skirts till you could see their knees. But this woman was plainly a lady, and by rights oughtn't to have to hear the dirty thoughts of these low men. Alvin figured she must be waiting for somebody to fetch her—the stagecoach to Hatrack River was due, but not for a couple of hours yet. She didn't look fearful—she probably knew these men was more brag than action, so her virtue was safe enough. And from her face Alvin couldn't guess whether she was even listening, her expression was so cold and faraway. But the river rats' words embarrassed *him* so much he couldn't stand it, and couldn't feel right about just driving his wagon off and leaving her there.

So he put the parcels he got from the port grocer into the wagon and then walked up to the river rats and spoke to the loudest and crudest talker among them.

"Maybe you'd best speak to her like a lady," said Alvin. "Or perhaps not speak to her at all."

Alvin wasn't surprised to see the glint these boys all got in their eyes the minute he spoke. Provoking a lady was one kind of fun, but he knew they were sizing him up now to see how easy he'd be to whup. They always loved a chance to teach a lesson to a town boy, even one built up as strong as Alvin was, him being a blacksmith.

"Maybe you'd best not speak to us at all," said the loud one. "Maybe you already said more than you ought."

One of the river rats didn't understand, and thought the game was still talking dirty about the lady. "He's just jealous. He wants to pole her muddy river himself."

"I haven't said enough," said Alvin, "not while you still don't have the manners to know how to speak to a lady."

Only now did the lady speak for the first time. "I don't need protection, young man," she said. "Just go along, please." Her voice was strange-sounding. Cultured, like Reverend Thrower, with all the words clear. Like people who went to school in the East.

It would have been better for her not to speak, since the sound of her voice only encouraged the river rats.

"Oh, she's sweet on this boy!"

"She's making a move on him!"

"He wants to row our boat!"

"Let's show her who the real man is!"

"If she wants his little mast, let's cut it off and give it to him."

A knife appeared, then another. Didn't she know enough to keep her mouth shut? If they dealt with Alvin alone, they'd set up to have a single fight, one to one. But if they got to showing off for her, they'd be happy enough to gang up on him and cut him bad, maybe kill him, certainly take an ear or his nose or, like they said, geld him.

Alvin glared at her for a moment, silently telling her to shut her mouth. Whether she understood his look or just figured things out for herself or got plain scared to say more, she didn't offer any more conversation, and Alvin set to turning things in a direction he could handle.

"Knives," said Alvin, with all the contempt he could muster. "So you're afraid to face a blacksmith with bare hands?"

They laughed at him, but the knives got pulled back and put away.

"Blacksmith's *nothing* compared to the muscles we get poling the river."

"You don't pole the river no more, boys, and everybody knows that," said Alvin. "You just set back and get fat, watching the paddlewheel push the boat along."

The loudest talker got up and stepped out, pulling his filthy shirt off over his head. He was strongly muscled, all right, with more than a few scars making white and red marks here and there on his chest and arms. He was also missing an ear.

"From the look of you," said Alvin, "you've fought a lot of men."

"Damn straight," said the river rat.

"And from the look of you, I'd say most of them was better than you."

The man turned red, blushing under his tan clear down to his chest.

"Can't you give me somebody who's worth rassling? Somebody who mostly *wins* his fights?"

"I win my fights!" shouted the man—getting mad, so he'd be easy to lick, which was Al's plan. But the others, they started pulling him back.

"The blacksmith boy's right, you're no great shakes at rassling."

"Give him what he wants."

"Mike, you take this boy."

"He's yours, Mike."

From the back—the shadiest spot, where he'd been sitting on the only chair with a back to it—a man stood up and stepped forward.

"I'll take this boy," he said.

At once the loud one backed off and got out of the way. This wasn't what Alvin wanted at all. The man they called Mike was bigger and stronger than any of the others, and as he stripped his shirt off, Al saw that while he had a scar or two, he was mostly clean, and he had both his ears, a sure sign that if he ever lost a rassling match, he sure never lost *bad*.

He had muscles like a buffalo.

"My name is Mike Fink!" he bellowed. "And I'm the meanest, toughest son-of-a-bitch ever to walk on the water! I can orphan baby alligators with my bare hands! I can throw a live buffalo up onto a wagon and slap him upside the head until he's dead! If I don't like the bend of a river, I grab ahold of the end of it and give it a shake to straighten it out! Every woman I ever put down come up with triplets, if she come up at all! When I'm done with you, boy, your hair will hang down straight on both sides cause you won't have no more ears. You'll have to sit down to piss, and you'll never have to shave again!"

All the time Mike Fink was making his brag, Alvin was taking off his shirt and his knife belt and laying them on the wagon seat. Then he marked a big circle in the dirt, making sure he looked as calm and relaxed as if Mike Fink was a spunky seven-year-old boy, and not a man with murder in his eyes.

So when Fink was shut of boasting, the circle was marked. Fink walked to the circle, then rubbed it out with his foot, raising a dust. He walked all around the circle, rubbing it out. "I don't know who taught you how to rassle, boy," he said, "but when you rassle *me*, there ain't no lines and there ain't no rules."

Once again the lady spoke up. "Obviously there are no rules when you speak, either, or you'd know that the word *ain't* is a sure sign of ignorance and stupidity."

Fink turned to the woman and made as if to speak. But it was like he knew he had nothing to say, or maybe he figured that whatever he said would make him sound more ignorant. The contempt in her voice enraged him, but it also made him doubt himself. At first Alvin thought the lady was making it more dangerous for him, meddling again. But then he realized that she was doing to Fink what Alvin had tried to do to the loudmouth—make him mad enough to fight stupid. Trouble was, as Alvin sized up the river man, he suspected that Fink didn't fight stupid when he was mad—it just made him fight meaner. Fight to kill. Act out his brag about taking off parts of Alvin's body. This wasn't going to be a friendly match like the ones Alvin had in town, where the game was just to throw the other man, or if they was fighting on grass, to pin him down.

"You're not so much," Alvin said, "and you know it, or you wouldn't have a knife hid in your boot."

Fink looked startled, then grinned. He pulled up his pantleg and took a long knife out of his boot, tossed it to the men behind him. "I won't need a knife to fight *you*," he said.

"Then why don't you take the knife out of the *other* boot?" asked Alvin.

Fink frowned and raised the other pantleg. "Ain't no knife here," he said.

Alvin knew better, of course, and it pleased him that Fink was worried enough about this fight not to part with his most secret knife. Besides which, probably nobody else knew about that knife but Alvin, with his ability to see what others couldn't see. Fink didn't want to let on to the others that he had such a knife, or word would spread fast along the river and he'd get no advantage from it.

Still, Alvin couldn't afford to let Fink fight with the knife on him. "Then take off the boots and we'll fight barefoot," Alvin said. It was a good idea anyway, knife or no knife. Alvin knew that when the river rats fought, they kicked like mules with their boots. Fighting barefoot might take some of the spunk out of Mike Fink.

But if Fink lost any spunk, he didn't show it. Just sat down in the dust of the road and pulled off his boots. Alvin did the same, and his socks too—Fink didn't wear socks. So now the two of them had on nothing but their trousers, and already out in the sunlight there was enough dust and sweat that their bodies were looking a little streaked and cakey with clay.

Not so caked up, though, that Alvin couldn't feel a hex of protection drawn over Mike Fink's whole body. How could such a thing be? Did he have a hex on some amulet in his pocket? The pattern was strongest near his backside, but when Alvin sent his bug to search that pocket, there was nothing but the rough cotton canvas of Fink's trousers. He wasn't carrying so much as a coin.

By now a crowd was gathered. Not just the river rats who'd been resting in the porthouse shade, but a whole slew of others, and it was plain they all expected Mike Fink to win. He must be something of a legend on the river, Alvin realized, and no surprise, with this mysterious hex he had. Alvin could imagine folks poking a knife at Fink, only to twist at the last moment, or lose their grip, or somehow keep the knife from doing harm. It was a lot easier to win all your rassling if no man's teeth could bite into you, and if a knife couldn't do much more than graze your skin.

Fink tried all the obvious stuff first, of course, because it made the best show: Roaring, rushing at Alvin like a buffalo, trying to get a bear hug on him, trying to grab onto Alvin and give him a swing like a rock on a string. But Alvin wouldn't have none of that. He didn't even have to use knackery to get away, neither. He was younger and quicker than Fink, and the river man hardly so much as laid a hand on him, Al dodged away so sudden. At first the crowd hooted and called Alvin coward. But after a while of this, they began to laugh at Fink, since he looked so silly, rushing and roaring and coming up empty all the time.

In the meantime, Alvin was exploring to find the source of Fink's hex, for there was no hope of winning this fight if he couldn't get rid of that strong web. He found it soon enough—a pattern of dye embedded deep in the skin of Fink's buttock. It wasn't a perfect hex anymore, since the skin had changed shape somewhat as Fink grew over the years, but it was a clever pattern, with strong locks and links—good enough to cast a strong net over him, even if it was misshapen.

If he hadn't been in the middle of a rassling match with Fink, Alvin might have been more subtle, might have just weakened the hex a little, for he had no will to deprive Fink of the hex that had protected him for so long. Why, Fink might die of it, losing his hex, especially if he had let himself get careless, counting on it to protect him. But what choice did Alvin have? So he made the dyes in Fink's skin start to flow, seeping into his bloodstream and getting carried away. Alvin could do without full concentration—just set it to happening and let it glide on, while he worked on dodging out of Fink's way.

Soon enough Al could sense the hex weakening, fading, finally collapsing completely. Fink wouldn't know it, but Alvin did—he could now be hurt like any other man.

By this time, though, Fink was no longer making those rough and stupid rushes at him. He was circling, feinting, looking to grapple in a square, then use his greater bulk to throw Alvin. But Alvin had a longer reach, and there was no doubt his arms were stronger, so whenever Fink reached to grab, Alvin batted the river man's arms out of the way.

With the hex gone, however, Alvin didn't slap him away. Instead, he reached inside Fink's arms, so that as Fink grasped his arms, Alvin got his hands hooked behind Fink's neck.

Alvin pulled down hard, bowing Fink down so his head was even with Alvin's chest. It was too easy—Fink was letting him, and Alvin guessed why. Sure enough, Fink pulled Alvin closer and brought his head up fast, expecting to catch Alvin on the chin with the back of his head. He was so strong he might've broke Alvin's neck doing that— only Alvin's chin wasn't where Fink thought it would be. In fact, Alvin had already rared his own head back, and when Fink came up hard and out of control, Alvin rammed forward and smashed his forehead into Fink's face. He could feel Fink's nose crumple under the blow, and blood erupted down both their faces.

It wasn't all that surprising, for a man's nose to get broke during a rassle like this. It hurt like blazes, of course, and it would've stopped a friendly match—though of course a friendly match wouldn't have included head butts. Any other river rat would've shook his head, roared a couple of times, and charged back into the fight.

Instead, Fink backed away, a look of real surprise on his face, his hands gripping his nose. Then he let out a howl like a whupped dog.

Everybody else fell silent. It was such a funny thing to happen, a river rat like Mike Fink howling at a broke-up nose. No, it wasn't rightly funny, but it was strange. It wasn't how a river rat was supposed to act.

"Come on, Mike," somebody murmured.

"You can take him, Mike."

But it was a half-hearted sort of encouragement. They'd never seen Mike Fink act hurt or scared before. He wasn't good at hiding it, either. Only Al knew why. Only Al knew that Mike Fink had never in his life felt such a pain, that Fink had never once shed his own blood in a fight. So many times he'd broke the other fellow's nose and laughed at the pain—it was easy to laugh, because he didn't know how it felt. Now he knew. Trouble was, he was learning what others learned at six years old, and so he was acting like a six-year-old. Not crying, exactly, but howling.

For a minute Alvin thought that maybe the match was over. But Fink's fear and pain soon turned to rage, and he waded back into the fight. Maybe he'd learned pain, but he hadn't learned caution from it.

So it took a few more holds, a few more wrenches and twists, before Alvin got Fink down onto the ground. Even as frightened and surprised as Fink was, he was the strongest man Alvin had ever rassled. Till this fight with Fink, Alvin had never really had occasion to find out just how strong he was; he'd never been pushed to his limit. Now he was, and he found himself rolling over and over in the dust, hardly able to breathe it was so thick, Fink's own hot panting breath now above him, now below, knees ramming, arms pounding and gripping, feet scrabbling in the dust, searching for purchase enough to get leverage.

In the end it came down to Fink's inexperience with weakness. Since no man could ever break a bone of his, Fink had never learned to tuck his legs, never learned not to expose them to where a man could stomp them. When Alvin broke free and scrambled to his feet, Fink rolled over quick and, for just a moment, lying there on the ground, he drew one leg across the other like a pure invitation. Alvin didn't even think, he just jumped into the air and came down with both feet onto Fink's top leg, jamming downward with all his weight, so the bones of the top leg were bowed over the lower one. So sharp and hard was the blow that it wasn't just the top leg that shattered, but the bottom one, too. Fink screamed like a child in the fire.

Only now did Alvin realize what he'd done. Oh, yes, of course he'd ended the fight—nobody's tough enough to fight on with two broken legs. But Alvin could tell at once, without looking—or at least without looking with his *eyes*—that these were not clean breaks, not the kind that can heal easy. Besides, Fink wasn't a young man now, and sure he wasn't a boy. If these breaks healed at all, they'd leave him lame at best, outright crippled at the worst. His livelihood would be gone. Besides, he must have made a lot of enemies over the years. What would they do now, with him broken and halt? How long would he live?

So Alvin knelt on the ground beside where Mike Fink writhed—or rather, the upper half of him writhed, while he tried to keep his legs from moving at all—and touched the legs. With his hands in contact with Fink's body, even through the cloth of his pants, Alvin could find his way easier, work faster, and in just a few moments, he had knitted the bones together. That was all he tried to do, no more—the bruise, the torn muscle, the bleeding, he had to leave that or Fink might get up and attack him again.

He pulled his hands away, and stepped back from Fink. At once the river rats gathered around their fallen hero.

"Is his legs broke?" asked the loudmouth river rat.

"No," said Alvin.

"They're broke to pieces!" howled Fink.

By then, another man had slit right up the pantleg. Sure enough he found the bruise, but as he felt along the bone, Fink screeched and pulled away. "Don't touch it!"

"Didn't feel broke to me," said the man.

"Look how he's moving his legs. They ain't broke."

It was true enough—Fink was no longer writhing with just the top half of his body, his legs were wiggling now as much as any other part of him.

One man helped Fink to his feet. Fink staggered, almost fell, caught himself by leaning against the loudmouth, smearing blood from his nose on the man's shirt. The others pulled away from him.

"Just a boy," muttered one.

"Howling like a puppydog."

"Big old baby."

"Mike *Fink*." And then a chuckle.

Alvin stood by the wagon, putting on his shirt, then sat up on the wagon seat to pull on his shoes and socks. He glanced up to find the lady watching him. She stood not six feet off, since the smith's wagon was pulled right up against the loading dock. She had a look of sour distaste. Alvin realized she was probably disgusted at how dirty he was. Maybe he shouldn't have put his shirt right back on, but then, it was also impolite to go shirtless in front of a lady. In fact, the town men, especially the doctors and lawyers, they acted ashamed to be out in public without a proper coat and waistcoat and cravat. Poor folks usually didn't have such clothes, and a prentice would be putting on airs to dress like that. But a shirt—he had to have his shirt on, whether he was filthy with dust or not.

"Beg pardon, Ma'am," he said. "I'll wash when I get home."

"Wash?" she asked. "And when you do, will your brutality also wash away?"

"I reckon I don't know, since I never heard that word."

"I daresay you haven't," she said. "Brutality. From the word *brute*. Meaning beast."

Alvin felt himself redden with anger. "Maybe so. Maybe I should've let them go on talking to you however they liked."

"I paid no attention to them. They didn't bother me. You had no need to protect me, especially not that way. Stripping naked and rolling around in the dirt. You're covered with blood."

Alvin hardly knew what to answer, she was so snooty and boneheaded. "I wasn't naked," Alvin said. Then he grinned. "And it was *his* blood."

"And are you proud of that?"

Yes, he was. But he knew that if he said so, it would diminish him in her sight. Well, what of that? What did he care what she thought of him? Still, he said nothing.

In the silence between them, he could hear the river rats behind him, hooting at Fink, who wasn't howling anymore, but wasn't saying much, either. It wasn't just Fink they were thinking about now, though.

"Town boy thinks he's tough."

"Maybe we ought to show him a *real* fight."

"Then we'll see how uppity his ladyfriend is."

Alvin couldn't rightly tell the future, but it didn't take no torch to guess at what was going to happen. Al's boots were on, his horse was full-hitched, and it was time to go. But snooty as she was, he couldn't leave the lady behind. He knew she'd be the river rats' target now, and however little she thought she needed protection, he knew that these river men had just watched their best man get whupped and humbled, and all on account of her, which meant she'd likely end up lying in the dirt with her bags all dumped in the river, if not worse.

"Best you get in," Alvin said.

"I wonder that you dare to give me instructions like a common— What are you doing?"

Alvin was tossing her trunk and bags into the back of the wagon. It seemed so obvious to him that he didn't bother answering her.

"I think you're robbing me, sir!"

"I am if you don't get in," said Alvin.

By now the river rats were gathering near the wagon, and one of them had hold of the horse's harness. She glanced around, and her angry expression changed. Just a little. She stepped from the dock onto the wagon seat. Alvin took her hand and helped her arrange herself on the seat. By now, the loudmouth river rat was standing beside him, leaning on the wagon, grinning wickedly. "You beat one of us, blacksmith, but can you beat us all?"

Alvin just stared at him. He was concentrating on the man holding the horse, making his hand suddenly tingle with pain, like he was being punctured with a hundred pins. The man cried out and let go the horse. The loudmouth looked away from Alvin, toward the sound of the cry, and in that moment Alvin kicked him in the ear with his boot. It wasn't much of a kick, but then, it wasn't much of an ear, either, and the man ended up sitting in the dirt, holding his head.

"Gee-yap!" shouted Alvin.

The horse obediently lunged forward—and the wagon moved about an inch. Then another inch. Hard to get a wagonload of iron moving fast, at least all of a sudden. Alvin made the wheels turn smooth and easy, but he couldn't do a thing about the weight of the wagon or the strength of the horse. By the time the horse got moving, the wagon was a good deal heavier, with the weight of river rats hanging on it, pulling back, climbing aboard.

Alvin turned around and swung his whip at them. The whip was for show—it didn't hit a one. Still, they all fell off or let go of the wagon as if it *had* hit them, or scared them anyway. What really happened was that all of a sudden the wood of the wagon got as slick as if it was greased. There was no way for them to hold onto it. So the wagon lurched forward as they collapsed back into the dust of the road.

They weren't done, though. After all, Alvin had to turn around and head back *up* the road right past them in order to get to Hatrack River. He was trying to figure what to do next when he heard a musket go off, loud as a cannonshot, the sound hanging on in the heavy summer air. When he got the wagon turned around, he saw the portmaster standing on the dock, his wife behind him. He was holding one musket, and she was reloading the one he had just fired.

"I reckon we get along well enough most of the time, boys," said the portmaster. "But today you just don't seem to know when you been beat fair and square. So I guess it's about time you settled down in the shade, cause if you make another move toward that wagon, them as don't die from buckshot'll be standing trial in Hatrack River, and if you think you won't pay dear for assaulting a local boy and the new school-teacher, then you really are as dumb as you look."

It was quite a little speech, and it worked better than most speeches Alvin had heard in his life. Those river rats just settled right down in the shade, taking a couple of long pulls from a jug and watching Al and the lady with a real sullen look. The portmaster went back inside before the wagon even turned the corner onto the town road.

"You don't suppose the portmaster is in danger from having helped us, do you?" asked the lady. Alvin was pleased to hear that the arrogance was gone from her voice, though she still spoke as clear and even as the ringing of a hammer on iron.

"No," said Alvin. "They all know that if ever a portmaster got harmed, them as did it would never work again on the river, or if they did, they wouldn't live through a night ashore."

"What about you?"

"Oh, I got no such guarantee. So I reckon I won't come back to Hatrack Mouth for a couple of weeks. By then all those boys'll have jobs and be a hundred miles up or downstream from here." Then he remembered what the portmaster had said. "You're the new school-teacher?"

She didn't answer. Not directly, anyway. "I suppose there are men like that in the East, but one doesn't meet them in the open like this."

"Well, it's a whole lot better to meet them in the open than it is to meet them in private!" Al said, laughing.

She didn't laugh.

"I was waiting for Dr. Whitley Physicker to meet me. He expected my boat later in the afternoon, but he may be on his way."

"This is the only road, Ma'am," Alvin said.

"Miss," she said. "Not madame. That title is properly reserved for married women."

"Like I said, it's the only road. So if he's on his way, we won't *miss* him. Miss."

This time Alvin didn't laugh at his own joke. On the other hand, he thought, looking out of the corner of his eye, that he just might have caught a glimpse of her smiling. So maybe she wasn't as hoity-toity as she seemed, Alvin thought. Maybe she's almost human. Maybe she'll even consent to give private schooling to a certain little half-Black boy. Maybe she'll be worth the work I went to fixing up the springhouse.

Because he was facing forward, driving the wagon, it wouldn't be natural, let alone good manners, for him to turn and stare right at her like he wanted to. So he sent out his bug, his spark, that part of him that "saw" what no man or woman could rightly with their own eyes see. For Alvin this was near second nature by now, to explore people under the skin so to speak. Keep in mind, though, that it wasn't like he could see with his eyes. Sure enough he could tell what was under a body's clothes, but he still didn't see folks naked. Instead he just got a close-in experience of the surface of their skin, almost like he'd took up residence in one of their pores. So he didn't think of it like he was peeping in windows or nothing. It was just another way of looking at folks and understanding them; he wouldn't see a body's shape or color, but he'd see whether they was sweating or hot or healthy or tensed-up. He'd see bruises and old healed-up injuries. He'd see hidden money or secret papers—but if he was to read the papers, he had to discover the feel of the ink on the surface and then trace it until he could build up a picture of the letters in his mind. It was very slow. Not like seeing, no sir.

Anyhow, he sent his bug to "see" this high-toned lady that he couldn't exactly look at. And what he found caught him by surprise. Cause she was every bit as hexed-up as Mike Fink had been.

No, more. She was layers deep in it, from hexy amulets hanging around her neck to hexes stitched into her clothes, even a wire hex embedded in the bun of her hair. Only one of them was for protection, and it wasn't half so strong as Mike Fink's had been. The rest were all—for what? Alvin hadn't seen such work before, and it took some thought and exploration to figure out what these hexwork webs that covered her were doing. The best he could get, riding along in the wagon, keeping his eyes on the road ahead, was that somehow these hexes were doing a powerful beseeming, making her look to be something that she wasn't.

The first thought he had, as I suppose was natural, was to try to discover what she really was, under her disguise. The clothes she wore were real enough—the hexery was only changing the sound of her voice, the hue and texture of the surface of her skin. But Alvin had little practice with beseemings, and none at all with beseemings wove from hexes. Most folks did a beseeming with a word and a gesture, tied up with a drawing of what they wanted to seem to be. It was a working on other folks' minds, and once you saw through it, it didn't fool you at all. Since Alvin always saw through it, such beseemings had no hold on him.

But hers was different. The hex changed the way light hit her and bounced off, so that you weren't fooled into thinking you saw what wasn't there. Instead you really saw her different, the light actually struck your eyes that way. Since it wasn't a change made on Alvin's mind, knowing the trickery didn't help him see the truth. And using his bug, he couldn't tell much about what was hidden away behind the hexes, except that she wasn't quite so wrinkled-up and bony as she looked, which made him guess she might be younger.

It was only when he gave up trying to guess at what lay under the disguise that he came to the real question: Why, if a woman had the power to disguise herself and seem to be anything she wanted, why would she choose to look like *that?* Cold, severe, getting old, bony, unsmiling, pinched-up, angry, aloof. All the things a woman ought to hope she never was, this teacher lady *chose* to be.

Maybe she was a fugitive in disguise. But she was definitely a woman underneath the hexes, and Alvin never heard of a woman outlaw, so it couldn't be that. Maybe she was just young, and figured other folks wouldn't take her serious if she didn't look older. Alvin knew about *that* right enough. Or maybe she was pretty, and men kept thinking of her the wrong way—Alvin tried to conjure up in his mind what might've happened with those river rats if she'd been real beautiful. But truth to tell, the river men probably would've been polite as they knew how, if she was pretty. It was only ugly women they felt free to taunt, since ugly women probably reminded them of their mothers. So her plainness wasn't exactly protection. And it wasn't designed to hide a scar, neither, cause Alvin could see her skin wasn't pocked or blemished or marred.

Truth was he couldn't guess at why she was all hid up under so many layers of lies. She could be anything or anybody. He couldn't even ask her, since to tell her he saw through her disguise was the same as to tell her of his knack, and how could he know she could be trusted with such a secret as *that*, when he didn't even know who she really was or why she chose to live inside a lie?

He wondered if he ought to tell somebody. Shouldn't the school board know, before putting the town's children into her care, that she wasn't exactly what she seemed to be? But he couldn't tell them, either, without giving himself away; and besides, maybe her secret was her own business and no harm to anyone. Then if he told the truth on her, it would ruin both him and her, with no good done for anybody.

No, best to watch her, real careful, and learn who she was the only way a body can ever truly know other folks: by seeing what they do. That's the best plan Alvin could think of, and the truth is, now that he knew she had such a secret, how could he *keep* from paying special attention to her? Using his bug to explore around him was such a habit for him that he'd have to work *not* to check up on her, especially if she was living up at the springhouse. He half hoped she wouldn't, so he wouldn't be bothered so much by this mystery; but he just as much hoped she would, so he could keep watch and make sure she was a rightful sort of person.

And I could watch her even better if I studied from her. I could watch her with her own eyes, ask her questions, listen to her answers, and judge what kind of person she might be. Maybe if she taught me long enough, she'd come to trust me, and I her, and then I'd tell her I'm to be a Maker and she'd tell her deep secrets to me and we'd help each other, we'd be true friends the way I haven't had no true friend since I left my brother Measure behind me in Vigor Church.

He wasn't pushing the horse too hard, the load being so heavy, what with her trunk and bags on top of the iron—and herself, to boot. So after all their talk, and then all this silence as he tried to figure out who she really was, they were still only about a half a mile out of Hatrack Mouth when Dr. Physicker's fancy carriage came along. Alvin recognized the carriage right off, and hailed Po Doggly, who was driving. It took all of a couple of minutes to move the teacher and her things from wagon to carriage. Po and Alvin did all the lifting—Dr. Physicker used all his efforts to help the teacher lady into the carriage. Alvin had never seen the doctor act so elegant.

"I'm terribly sorry you had to suffer the discomforts of a ride in that wagon," said the doctor. "I didn't think that I was late."

"In fact you're early," she said. And then, turning graciously to Alvin, she added, "And the wagon ride was surprisingly pleasant."

Since Alvin hadn't said a word for most of the journey, he didn't rightly know whether she meant it as a compliment for him being good company, or as gratitude that he kept his mouth shut and didn't bother her. Either way, though, it made him feel a kind of burning in his face, and not from anger.

As Dr. Physicker was climbing into the carriage, the teacher asked him, "What is this young man's name?" Since she spoke to the doctor, Alvin didn't answer.

"Alvin," said the doctor, settling into his seat. "He was born here. He's the smith's apprentice."

"Alvin," she said, now directing herself to him through the carriage window. "I thank you for your gallantry today, and I hope you'll forgive the ungraciousness of my first response. I had underestimated the villainous nature of our unwelcome companions."

Her words were so elegant-sounding it was like music hearing her talk, even though Alvin could only half-guess what she was saying. Her expression, though, was about as kindly as her forbidding face could look, he reckoned. He wondered what her real visage might look like underneath.

"My pleasure, Ma'am," he said. "I mean Miss."

From the driver's bench, Po Doggly gee-ed the pair of mares and the carriage took off, still heading toward Hatrack Mouth, of course. It wasn't easy for Po to find a place on that road to turn around, either, so Alvin was well on his way before the carriage came back and passed him. Po slowed the carriage, and Dr. Physicker leaned over and tossed a dollar coin into the air. Alvin caught it, more by reflex than by thought.

"For your help for Miss Larner," said Dr. Physicker. Then Po gee-ed the horses again and they went on, leaving Alvin to chew on the dust in the road.

He felt the weight of the coin in his hand, and for a moment he wanted to throw it after the carriage. But that wouldn't do no good at all. No, he'd give it back to Physicker some other time, in some way that wouldn't get nobody riled up. But still it hurt, it stung deep, to be paid for helping a lady, like as if he was a servant or a child or something. And what hurt worst was wondering if maybe it was her idea to pay him. As if she thought he had earned a quarter-day's wages when he fought for her honor. It was sure that if he'd been wearing a coat and cravat instead of one filthy shirt, she'd have thought he done the service due a lady from any Christian gentleman, and she'd know she owed him gratitude instead of payment.

Payment. The coin burned in his hand. Why, for a few minutes there he'd almost thought she liked him. Almost he had hoped that maybe she'd agree to teach him, to help him work out some understanding of how the world works, of what he could do to be a true Maker and tame the Unmaker's terrible power. But now that it was plain she despised him, how could he even ask? How could he even pretend to be worthy of teaching, when he knew that all she saw about him was filth and blood and stupid poverty? She knew he meant well, but he was still a brute in her eyes, like she said first off. It was still in her heart. Brutality.

Miss Larner. That's what the doctor called her. He tasted the name as he said it. Dust in his mouth. You don't take animals to school.

15

Teacher

Miss Larner had no intention of giving an inch to these people. She had heard enough horror stories about frontier school boards to know that they would try to get out of keeping most of the promises they made in their letters. It was beginning already.

"In your letters you represented to me that I would have a residence provided as part of my salary. I do not regard an inn as a private residence."

"You'll have your own private room," said Dr. Physicker.

"And take all my meals at a common table? This is not acceptable. If I stay, I will be spending all my days in the company of the children of this town, and when that day's work is over, I expect to be able to prepare my own meals in private and eat them in solitude, and then spend the evening in the company of books, without distraction or annoyance. That is not possible in a roadhouse, gentlemen, and so a room in a roadhouse does *not* constitute a private residence."

She could see them sizing her up. Some were abashed by the mere precision of her speech—she knew perfectly well that country lawyers put on airs in their own towns, but they were no match for someone of real education. The only real trouble was going to come from the sheriff, Pauley Wiseman. How absurd, for a grown man still to use a child's nickname.

"Now see here, young lady," said the sheriff.

She raised an eyebrow. It was typical of such a man that, even though Miss Larner seemed to be on the greying side of forty, he would assume that her unmarried status gave him the right to call her "young lady," as one addresses a recalcitrant girlchild.

"What is 'here' that I am failing to see?"

"Well, Horace and Peg Guester *did* plan to offer you a small house off by yourself, but we said no to it, plain and simple, we said no to them, and we say no to you."

"Very well, then. I see that you do not, after all, intend to keep your word to me. Fortunately, gentlemen, I am not a common schoolteacher, grateful to take whatever is offered. I had a good position at the Penn School, and I assure you that I can return there at will. Good day."

She rose to her feet. So did all the men except the sheriff—but they weren't rising out of courtesy.

"Please."

"Sit down."

"Let's talk about this."

"Don't be hasty."

It was Dr. Physicker, the perfect conciliator, who took the floor now, after giving the sheriff a steady look to quell him. The sheriff, however, did not seem particularly quelled.

"Miss Larner, our decision on the private house was not an irrevocable one. But please consider the problems that worried us. First, we were concerned that the house would not be suitable. It's not really a house at all, but a mere room, made out of an abandoned springhouse—"

The old springhouse. "Is it heated?"

"Yes."

"Has it windows? A door that can be secured? A bed and table and chair?"

"All of that, yes."

"Has it a wooden floor?"

"A nice one."

"Then I doubt that its former service as a springhouse will bother me. Had you any other objections?"

"We damn well do!" cried Sheriff Wiseman. Then, seeing the horrified looks around the room, he added, "Begging the lady's pardon for my rough language."

"I am interested in hearing those objections," said Miss Larner.

"A woman alone, in a solitary house in the woods! It ain't proper!"

"It is the word *ain't* which is not proper, Mr. Wiseman," said Miss Larner. "As to the propriety of my living in a house to myself, I assure you that I have done so for many years, and have managed to pass that entire time quite unmolested. Is there another house within hailing distance?"

"The roadhouse to one side and the smith's place to the other," said Dr. Physicker.

"Then if I am under some duress or provocation, I can assure you that I will make myself heard, and I expect those who hear will come to my aid. Or are you afraid, Mr. Wiseman, that I may enter into some improper activity *voluntarily?*''

Of course that was exactly what he was thinking, and his reddening face showed it.

"I believe you have adequate references concerning my moral character," said Miss Larner. "But if you have any doubts on that score, it would be better for me to return to Philadelphia at once, for if at my age I cannot be trusted to live an upright life without supervision, how can you possibly trust me to supervise your young children?"

"It just ain't decent!" cried the sheriff. "Aren't."

"Isn't." She smiled benignly at Pauley Wiseman. "It has been my experience, Mr. Wiseman, that when a person assumes that others are eager to commit indecent acts whenever given the opportunity, he is merely confessing his own private struggle."

Pauley Wiseman didn't understand that she had just accused him, not until several of the lawyers started in laughing behind their hands.

"As I see it, gentlemen of the school board, you have only two alternatives. First, you can pay my boat passage back to Dekane and my overland passage to Philadelphia, plus the salary for the month that I will have expended in traveling."

"If you don't teach, you get no salary," said the sheriff.

"You speak hastily, Mr. Wiseman," said Miss Larner. "I believe the lawyers present will inform you that the school board's letters constitute a contract, of which you are in breach, and that I would therefore be entitled to collect, not just a month's salary, but the entire year's."

"Well, that's not *certain*, Miss Larner," began one of the lawyers.

"Hio is one of the United States now, sir," she answered, "and there is ample precedent in other state courts, precedent which is binding until and unless the government of Hio makes specific legislation to the contrary."

"Is she a schoolteacher or a lawyer?" asked another lawyer, and they all laughed.

"Your second alternative is to allow me to inspect this—this springhouse—and determine whether I find it acceptable, and if I do, to allow me to live there. If you ever find me engaging in morally reprehensible behavior, it is within the terms of our contract that you may discharge me forthwith."

"We can put you in *jail*, that's what we can do," said Wiseman.

"Why, Mr. Wiseman, aren't we getting ahead of ourselves, talking of jail when I have yet to select which morally hideous act I shall perform?"

"Shut up, Pauley," said one of the lawyers.

"Which alternative do you choose, gentlemen?" she asked.

Dr. Physicker was not about to let Pauley Wiseman have at the more weak-willed members of the board. He'd see to it there was no further debate. "We don't need to retire to consider this, do we, gentlemen? We may not be Quakers here in Hatrack River, so we aren't used to thinking of ladies as wanting to live by themselves and engage in business and preach and whatnot, but we're open-minded and willing to learn new ways. We want your services, and we'll keep to the contract. All in favor?"

"Aye."

"Opposed? The ayes have it."

"Nay," said Wiseman.

"The voting's over, Pauley."

"You called it too damn fast!"

"Your negative vote has been recorded, Pauley."

Miss Larner smiled coldly. "You may be sure I won't forget it, Sheriff Wiseman."

Dr. Physicker tapped the table with his gavel. "This meeting is adjourned until next Tuesday afternoon at three. And now, Miss Larner, I'd be delighted to escort you to the Guesters' springhouse, if this is a convenient hour. Not knowing when you would arrive, they have given me the key and asked me to open the cottage for you; they'll greet you later."

Miss Larner was aware, as they all were, that it was odd, to say the least, for the landlord not to greet his guest in person.

"You see, Miss Larner, it wasn't certain whether you'd accept the cottage. They wanted you to make your decision when you saw the place—and not in their presence, lest you feel embarrassed to decline it."

"Then they have acted graciously," said Miss Larner, "and I will thank them when I meet them."

It was humiliating, Old Peg having to walk out to the springhouse all by herself to plead with this stuck-up snooty old Philadelphia spinster. Horace ought to be going out there with her. Talk man to man with her—that's what this woman seemed to think she was, not a lady but a lord. Might as well come from Camelot, she might, thinks she's a princess giving orders to the common folk. Well, they took care of it in France, old Napoleon did, put old Louis the Seventeenth right in his place. But lordly women like this teacher lady, Miss Larner, they never got their comeuppance, just went on through life thinking folks what didn't talk perfect was too low to take much account of.

So where was Horace, to put this teacher lady in her place? Setting by the fire. Pouting. Just like a four-year-old. Even Arthur Stuart never got such a pout on him.

"I don't like her," says Horace.

"Well like her or not, if Arthur's to get an education it's going to be from her or nobody," says Old Peg, talking plain sense as usual, but does Horace listen? I should laugh.

"She can live there and she can teach Arthur if she pleases, or not if she don't please, but I don't like her and I don't think she belongs in that springhouse."

"Why, is it holy ground?" says Old Peg. "Is there some curse on it? Should we have built a palace for her royal highness?" Oh, when Horace gets a notion on him it's no use talking, so why did she keep on trying?

"None of that, Peg," said Horace.

"Then what? Or don't you need reasons anymore? Do you just decide and then other folks better make way?"

"Because it's Little Peggy's place, that's why, and I don't like having that benoctious woman living there!"

Wouldn't you know? It was just like Horace, to bring up their runaway daughter, the one who never so much as wrote to them once she ran away, leaving Hatrack River without a torch and Horace without the love of his life. Yes ma'am, that's what Little Peggy was to him, the love of his life. If I ran off, Horace, or, God forbid, if I died, would you treasure my memory and not let no other woman take my place? I reckon not. I reckon there wouldn't be time for my spot on the sheet to get cold afore you'd have some other woman lying there. Me you could replace in a hot minute, but Little Peggy, we have to treat the springhouse as a *shrine* and make me come out here all by myself to face this high-falutin old maid and beg her to teach a little Black child. Why, I'll be lucky if she doesn't try to buy him from me.

Miss Larner took her time about answering the door, too, and when she did, she had a handkerchief to her face—probably a perfumed one, so she wouldn't have to smell the odor of honest country folks.

"If you don't mind I've got a thing or two I'd like to discuss with you," said Old Peg.

Miss Larner looked away, off over Old Peg's head, as if studying some bird in a far-off tree. "If it's about the school, I was told I'd have a week to prepare before we actually registered students and began the autumn session."

From down below, Old Peg could hear the *ching-ching-ching* of one of the smiths a-working at the forge. Against her will she couldn't help thinking of Little Peggy, who purely hated that sound. Maybe Horace was right in his foolishness. Maybe Little Peggy haunted this spring-house.

Still, it was Miss Larner standing in the doorway now, and Miss Larner that Old Peg had to deal with. "Miss Larner, I'm Margaret Guester. My husband and I own this springhouse."

"Oh. I beg your pardon. You're my landlady, and I'm being ungracious. Please come in."

That was a bit more like it. Old Peg stepped up through the open door and stood there a moment to take in the room. Only yesterday it had seemed bare but clean, a place full of promise. Now it was almost homey, what with a doily and a dozen books on the armoire, a small woven rug on the floor, and two dresses hanging from hooks on the wall. The trunks and bags filled a corner. It looked a bit like somebody lived there. Old Peg didn't know what she'd expected. Of course Miss Larner had more dresses than this dark traveling outfit. It's just Old Peg hadn't thought of her doing something so ordinary as changing clothes. Why, when she's got one dress off and before she puts on another, she probably stands there in her underwear, just like anybody.

"Do sit down, Mrs. Guester."

"Around here we ain't much with Mr. and Mrs., except them lawyers, Miss Larner. I'm Goody Guester, mostly, except when folks call me Old Peg."

"Old Peg. What a—what an interesting name."

She thought of spelling out why she was called "Old" Peg—how she had a daughter what run off, that sort of thing. But it was going to be hard enough to explain to this teacher lady how she come to have a Black son. Why make her family life seem even more strange?

"Miss Larner, I won't beat around the bush. You got something that I need."

"Oh?"

"That is, not me, to say it proper, but my son, Arthur Stuart."

If she recognized that it was the King's proper name, she gave no sign. "And what might he need from me, Goody Guester?"

"Book-learning."

"That's what I've come to provide to all the children in Hatrack River, Goody Guester."

"Not Arthur Stuart. Not if those pin-headed cowards on the school board have their way."

"Why should they exclude your son? Is he over-age, perhaps?"

"He's the right age, Miss Larner. What he ain't is the right color."

Miss Larner waited, no expression on her face.

"He's Black, Miss Larner."

"Half-Black, surely," offered the teacher.

Naturally the teacher was trying to figure how the innkeeper's wife came to have her a half-Black boy-baby. Old Peg got some pleasure out of watching the teacher act polite while she must surely be cringing in horror inside herself. But it wouldn't do to let such a thought linger too long, would it? "He's adopted, Miss Larner," said Old Peg. "Let's just say that his Black mama got herself embarrassed with a half-White baby."

"And you, out of the goodness of your heart—"

Was there a nasty edge to Miss Larner's voice? "I wanted me a child. I ain't taking care of Arthur Stuart for pity. He's *my* boy now."

"I see," said Miss Larner. "And the good people of Hatrack River have determined that their children's education will suffer if half-Black ears should hear my words at the same time as pure White ears."

Miss Larner sounded nasty again, only now Old Peg dared to let herself rejoice inside, hearing the way Miss Larner said those words. "Will you teach him, Miss Larner?"

"I confess, Goody Guester, that I have lived in the City of Quakers too long. I had forgotten that there were places in this world where people of small minds would be so shameless as to punish a mere child for the sin of being born with skin of a tropical hue. I can assure you that I will refuse to open school at all if your adopted son is not one of my pupils."

"No!" cried Old Peg. "No, Miss Larner, that's going too far."

"I am a committed Emancipationist, Goody Guester. I will not join in a conspiracy to deprive any Black child of his or her intellectual heritage."

Old Peg didn't know what in the world an intellectual heritage was, but she knew that Miss Larner was in too much sympathy. If she kept up this way, she'd be like to ruin everything. "You got to hear me out, Miss Larner. They'll just get another teacher, and I'll be worse off, and so will Arthur Stuart. No, I just ask that you give him an hour in the evening, a few days a week. I'll make him study somewhat in the daytime, to learn proper what you teach him quick. He's a bright boy, you'll see that. He already knows his letters—he can A it and Z it better than my Horace. That's my husband, Horace Guester. So I'm not asking more than a few hours a week, if you can spare it. That's why we worked up this springhouse, so you could do it and none the wiser."

Miss Larner arose from where she sat on the edge of her bed, and walked to the window. "This is not what I ever imagined—to teach a child in secret, as if I were committing a crime."

"In *some* folks' eyes, Miss Larner—"

"Oh, I have no doubt of that."

"Don't you Quakers have silent meetings? All I ask is a kind of quiet meeting, don't you know—"

"I am not a Quaker, Goody Guester. I am merely a human being who refuses to deny the humanity of others, unless their own acts prove them unworthy of that noble kinship."

"Then you'll teach him?"

"After hours, yes. Here in my home, which you and your husband so kindly provided, yes. But in secret? Never! I shall proclaim to all in this place that I am teaching Arthur Stuart, and not just a few nights a week, but daily. I am free to tutor such pupils as I desire—my contract is quite specific on that point—and as long as I do not violate the contract, they must endure me for at least a year. Will that do?"

Old Peg looked at the woman in pure admiration. "I'll be jiggered," she said, "you're mean as a cat with a burr in its behind."

"I regret that I've never seen a cat in such an unfortunate situation, Goody Guester, so that I cannot estimate the accuracy of your simile."

Old Peg couldn't make no sense of the words Miss Larner said, but she caught something like a twinkle in the lady's eye, so it was all right.

"When should I send Arthur to you?" she asked.

"As I said when I first opened the door, I'll need a week to prepare. When school opens for the White children, it opens for Arthur Stuart as well. There remains only the question of payment."

Old Peg was taken aback for a moment. She'd come here prepared to offer money, but after the way Miss Larner talked, she thought there'd be no cost after all. Still, teaching was Miss Larner's livelihood, so it was only fair. "We thought to offer you a dollar a month, that being most convenient for us, Miss Larner, but if you need more—"

"Oh, not cash, Goody Guester. I merely thought to ask if you might indulge me by allowing me to hold a weekly reading of poetry in your roadhouse on Sunday evenings, inviting all in Hatrack River who aspire to improve their acquaintance with the best literature in the English language."

"I don't know as how there's all that many who hanker after poetry, Miss Larner, but you're welcome to have a go of it."

"I think you'll be pleasantly surprised at the number of people who wish to be thought educated, Goody Guester. We shall have difficulty finding seats for all the ladies of Hatrack River who compel their husbands to bring them to hear the immortal words of Pope and Dryden, Donne and Milton, Shakespeare and Gray and—oh, I shall be daring—

Wordsworth and Coleridge, and perhaps even an American poet, a wandering spinner of strange tales named Blake.''

"You don't mean old Taleswapper, do you?''

"I believe that is his most common sobriquet.''

"You've got some of his poems wrote down?''

"Written? Hardly necessary, for that dear friend of mine. I have committed many of his verses to memory.''

"Well, don't that old boy get around. Philadelphia, no less.''

"He has brightened many a parlor in that city, Goody Guester. Shall we hold our first soiree this Sunday?''

"What's a swore raid?''

"Soiree. An evening gathering, perhaps with ginger punch—''

"Oh, you don't have to teach me nothing about hospitality, Miss Larner. And if that's the price for Arthur Stuart's education, Miss Larner, I'm sore afraid I'm cheating you, because it seems to me you're doing *us* the favor both ways.''

"You're most kind, Goody Guester. But I must ask you one question.''

"Ask away. Can't promise I'm too good at answers.''

"Goody Guester,'' said Miss Larner. "Are you aware of the Fugitive Slave Treaty?''

Fear and anger stabbed right through Old Peg's heart, even to hear it mentioned. "A devilish piece of work!''

"Slavery is a devilish work indeed, but the treaty was signed to bring Appalachee into the Compact, and to keep our fragile nation from war with the Crown Colonies. Peace is hardly to be labeled devilish.''

"It is when it's a peace that says they can send their damned Finders into the free states and bring back captive Black people to be slaves!''

"Perhaps you're right, Goody Guester. Indeed, one could say that the Fugitive Slave Treaty is not so much a treaty of peace as it is an article of surrender. Nevertheless, it is the law of the land.''

Only now did Old Peg realize what this teacher just done. What could it mean, her bringing up the Fugitive Slave Treaty, excepting to make sure Old Peg knew that Arthur Stuart wasn't safe here, that Finders could still come from the Crown Colonies and claim him as the property of some family of White so-called Christians? And that also meant that Miss Larner didn't believe a speck of her story about where Arthur Stuart come from. And if she saw through the lie so easy-like, why was Old Peg fool enough to think everybody else believed it? Why, as far as Old Peg knew, the whole town of Hatrack River had long since guessed that Arthur Stuart was a slave boy what somehow run off and got hisself a White mama.

And if everybody knew, what was to stop somebody from giving report on Arthur Stuart, sending word to the Crown Colonies about a runaway slavechild living in a certain roadhouse near the Hatrack River? The Fugitive Slave Treaty made her adoption of Arthur Stuart plain illegal. They could take the boy right out of her arms and she'd never have the right to see him again. In fact, if she ever went south they could arrest her and hang her under the slave-poaching laws of King Arthur. And thinking of that monstrous King in his lair in Camelot made her remember the unkindest thing of all—that if they ever took Arthur Stuart south, they'd change his name. Why, it'd be high treason in the Crown Colonies, having a slavechild named with the same name as the King. So all of a sudden poor Arthur would find hisself with some other name he never heard of afore. She couldn't help thinking of the boy all confused, somebody calling him and calling him, and whipping him for not coming, but how could he know to come, since nobody called him by his right name?

Her face must've painted a plain picture of all the thoughts going through her head, because Miss Larner walked behind her and put her hands on Old Peg's shoulders.

"You've nought to fear from me, Goody Guester. I come from Philadelphia, where people speak openly of defying that treaty. A young New Englander named Thoreau has made quite a nuisance of himself, preaching that a bad law must be defied, that good citizens must be prepared to go to jail themselves rather than submit to it. It would do your heart good to hear him speak."

Old Peg doubted that. It only froze her to the heart to think of the treaty at all. Go to jail? What good would that do, if Arthur was being whipped south in chains? No matter what, it was none of Miss Larner's business. "I don't know why you're saying all this, Miss Larner. Arthur Stuart is the freeborn son of a free Black woman, even if she got him on the wrong side of the sheets. The Fugitive Slave Treaty means nothing to me."

"Then I shall think no more of it, Goody Guester. And now, if you'll forgive me, I'm somewhat weary from traveling, and I had hoped to retire early, though it's still light outside."

Old Peg sprang to her feet, mighty relieved at not talking anymore about Arthur and the treaty. "Why, of course. But you ain't hopping into bed without taking a bath, are you? Nothing like a bath for a traveler."

"I quite agree, Goody Guester. However, I fear my luggage was not copious enough for me to bring my tub along."

"I'll send Horace over with my spare tub the second I get back, and if you don't mind hotting up your stove there, we can get water from Gertie's well yonder and set it to steaming in no time.''

''Oh, Goody Guester, I fear you'll convince me before the evening's out that I'm in Philadelphia after all. It shall be almost disappointing, for I had steeled myself to endure the rigors of primitive life in the wilderness, and now I find that you are prepared to offer all the convivial blessings of civilization.''

''I'll take it that what you said mostly means thank you, and so I say you're welcome, and I'll be back in no time with Horace and the tub. And don't you dare fetch your own water, at least not today. You just set there and read or philosophate or whatever an educated person does instead of dozing off.''

With that Old Peg was out of the springhouse. She like to flew along the path to the inn. Why, this teacher lady wasn't half so bad as she seemed at first. She might talk a language that Old Peg couldn't hardly understand half the time, but at least she was willing to talk to folks— and she'd teach Arthur at no cost and hold poetry readings in the road-house to boot. Best of all, though, best of all she might even be willing to talk to Old Peg sometimes and maybe some of that smartness might rub off on her. Not that smartness was all that much good to a woman like Old Peg, but then, what good was a jewel on a rich lady's finger, either? And if being around this educated eastern spinster gave Old Peg even a jigger more understanding of the great world outside Hatrack River, it was more than Old Peg had dared to hope for in her life. Like daubing just a spot of color on a drab moth's wing. It don't make the moth into a butterfly, but maybe now the moth won't despair and fly into the fire.

Miss Larner watched Old Peg walk away. Mother, she whispered. No, didn't even whisper. Didn't even open her mouth. But her lips pressed together a bit tighter with the *M*, and her tongue shaped the other sounds inside her mouth.

It hurt her, to deceive. She had promised never to lie, and in a sense she wasn't lying even now. The name she had taken, *Larner*, meant nothing more than *teacher*, and since she *was* a teacher, it was as truly her name as Father's name was Guester and Makepeace's name was Smith. And when people asked her questions, she never lied to them, though she did refuse to answer questions that might tell them more than they ought to know, that might set them wondering.

Still, despite her elaborate avoidance of an open lie, she feared that she merely deceived herself. How could she believe that her presence here, so disguised, was anything but a lie?

And yet surely even that deception was the truth, at its root. She was no longer the same person she had been when she was torch of Hatrack River. She was no longer connected to these people in the former ways. If she claimed to be Little Peggy, that would be a deeper lie than her disguise, for they would suppose that she was the girl they once knew, and treat her accordingly. In that sense, her disguise was a reflection of who she really was, at least here and now—educated, aloof, a deliberate spinster, and sexually unavailable to men.

So her disguise was not a lie, surely it was not; it was merely a way to keep a secret, the secret of who she used to be, but was no longer. Her vow was still unbroken.

Mother was long since out of sight in the woods between the spring-house and the inn, but still Peggy looked after her. And if she wanted, Peggy could have seen her even yet, not with her eyes, but with her torch sight, finding Mother's heartfire and moving close, looking tight. Mother, don't you know you have no secrets from your daughter Peggy?

But the fact was that Mother could keep all the secrets she desired. Peggy would not look into her heart. Peggy hadn't come home to be the torch of Hatrack River again. After all these years of study, in which Peggy had read so many books so rapidly that she feared once that she might run out, that there might not be books enough in America to satisfy her—after all these years, there was only one skill she was certain of. She had finally mastered the ability *not* to see inside the hearts of other people unless she wanted to. She had finally tamed her torchy sight.

Oh, she still looked inside other people when she needed to, but she rarely did. Even with the school board, when she had to tame them, it took no more than her knowledge of human nature to guess their present thoughts and deal with them. And as for the futures revealed in the heartfire, she no longer noticed them.

I am not responsible for your futures, none of you. Least of all you, Mother. I have meddled enough in your life, in everyone's lives. If I know all your futures, all you people in Hatrack River, then I have a moral imperative to shape my own actions to help you achieve the happiest possible tomorrow. Yet in so doing, I cease to exist myself. My own future becomes the only one with no hope, and why should that be? By shutting my eyes to what *will* happen, I become like you, able to live my life according to my guesses at what *may* happen. I couldn't guarantee you happiness anyway, and this way at least I also have a chance of it myself.

Even as she justified herself, she felt the same sour guilt well up inside her. By rejecting her knack, she was sinning against the God that gave it to her. That great magister Erasmus, he had taught as much: Your knack is your destiny. You'll never know joy except through following the path laid out before you by what is inside you. But Peggy refused to submit to that cruel discipline. Her childhood had already been stolen from her, and to what end? Her mother disliked her, the people of Hatrack River feared her, often hated her, even as they came to her again and again, seeking answers to their selfish, petty questions, blaming her if any seeming ill came into their lives, but never thanking her for saving them from dire events, for they never knew how she had saved them because the evils never happened.

It wasn't gratitude she wanted. It was freedom. It was a lightening of her burden. She had started bearing it too young, and they had shown her no mercy in their exploitation. Their own fears always outweighed her need for a carefree girlhood. Did any of them understand that? Did any of them know how gratefully she left them all behind?

Now Peggy the torch was back, but they'd never know it. I did not come back for *you*, people of Hatrack River, nor did I come to serve your children. I came back for one pupil only, the man who stands even now at the forge, his heartfire burning so brightly that I can see it even in my sleep, even in my dreams. I came back having learned all that the world can teach, so I in turn can help that young man achieve a labor that means more than any one of us. *That* is my destiny, if I have one.

Along the way I'll do what other good I can—I'll teach Arthur Stuart, I'll try to fulfill the dreams his brave young mother died for; I'll teach all the other children as much as they're willing to learn, during those certain hours of the day that I've contracted for; I'll bring such poetry and learning into the town of Hatrack River as you're willing to receive.

Perhaps you don't desire poetry as much as you would like to have my torchy knowledge of your possible futures, but I daresay poetry will do you far more good. For knowing the future only makes you timid and complacent by turns, while poetry can shape you into the kind of souls who can face any future with boldness and wisdom and nobility, so that you need not know the future at all, so that any future will be an opportunity for greatness, if you have greatness in you. Can I teach you to see in yourselves what Gray saw?

> *Some heart once pregnant with celestial fire,*
> *Hands that the rod of empire might have swayed,*
> *Or waked to ecstasy the living lyre.*

But she doubted that any of these ordinary souls in Hatrack River were really mute, inglorious Miltons. Pauley Wiseman was no secret Caesar. He might wish for it, but he lacked the wit and self-control. Whitley Physicker was no Hippocrates, however much he tried to be a healer and conciliator—his love of luxury undid him, and like many another well-meaning physician he had come to work for what the fee could buy, and not for joy of the work itself.

She picked up the water bucket that stood by the door. Weary as she was, she would not allow herself to seem helpless even for a moment. Father and Mother would come and find Miss Larner had already done for herself all that she could do before the tub arrived.

Ching-ching-ching. Didn't Alvin rest? Didn't he know the sun was boiling the western sky, turning it red before sinking out of sight behind the trees? As she walked down the hill toward the smithy, she felt as if she might suddenly begin to run, to fly down the hill to the smithy as she had flown the day that Alvin was born. It was raining that day, and Alvin's mother was stuck in a wagon in the river. It was Peggy who saw them all, their heartfires off in the blackness of the rain and the flooding river. It was Peggy who gave alarm, and then Peggy who stood watch over the birthing, seeing Alvin's futures in his heartfire, the brightest heartfire she had ever seen or would ever see in all her life. It was Peggy who saved his life then by peeling the caul away from his face; and, by using bits of that caul, Peggy who had saved his life so many times over the years. She might turn her back on being torch of Hatrack River, but she'd never turn her back on *him.*

But she stopped herself halfway down the hill. What was she thinking of? She could not go to him, not now, not yet. He had to come to *her.* Only that way could she become his teacher; only that way was there a chance of becoming anything more than that.

She turned and walked across the face of the hill, slanting down and eastward toward the well. She had watched Alvin dig the well—both wells—and for once she was helpless to help him when the Unmaker came. Alvin's own anger and destructiveness had called his enemy, and there was nothing Peggy could do with the caul to save him that time. She could only watch as he purged the unmaking that was inside himself, and so defeated, for a time, the Unmaker who stalked him on the outside. Now this well stood as a monument both to Alvin's power and to his frailty.

She dropped the copper bucket into the well, and the windlass clattered as the rope unwound. A muffled splash. She waited a moment for the bucket to fill, then wound it upward. It arrived brimming. She meant to pour it out into the wooden bucket she brought with her, but instead she brought the copper bucket to her lips and drank from the cold heavy load of water that it bore. So many years she had waited to taste that water, the water that Alvin tamed the night he tamed himself. She had been so afraid, watching him all night, and when at last in the morning he filled up the first vengeful hole he dug, she wept in relief. This water wasn't salty, but still it tasted to her like her own tears.

The hammer was silent. As always, she found Alvin's heartfire at once, without even trying. He was leaving the smithy, coming outside. Did he know she was there? No. He always came for water when he finished his work for the day. Of course she could not turn to him, not yet, not until she actually heard his step. Yet, though she knew he was coming and listened for him, she couldn't hear him; he moved as silently as a squirrel on a limb. Not until he spoke did he make a sound.

"Pretty good water, ain't it?"

She turned around to face him. Turned too quickly, too eagerly—the rope still held the bucket, so it lurched out of her hands, splashed her with water, and clattered back down into the well.

"I'm Alvin, you remember? Didn't mean to frighten you, Ma'am. Miss Larner."

"I foolishly forgot the bucket was tied," she said. "I'm used to pumps and taps, I'm afraid. Open wells are not common in Philadelphia."

She turned back to the well to draw the bucket up again.

"Here, let me," he said.

"There's no need. I can wind it well enough."

"But why should you, Miss Larner, when I'm glad to do it for you?"

She stepped aside and watched as he cranked the windlass with one hand, as easily as a child might swing a rope. The bucket fairly flew to the top of the well. She looked into his heartfire, just dipped in, to see if he was showing off for her. He was not. He could not see how massive his own shoulders were, how his muscles danced under the skin as his arm moved. He could not even see the peacefulness of his own face, the same quiet repose that one might see in the face of a fearless stag. There was no watchfulness in him. Some people had darting eyes, as if they had to be alert for danger, or perhaps for prey. Others looked intently at the task at hand, concentrating on what they were doing. But Alvin had a quiet distance, as if he had no particular concern about what anyone else or he himself might be doing, but instead dwelt on inward thoughts that no one else could hear. Again the words of Gray's *Elegy* played out in her mind.

Far from the madding crowd's ignoble strife,
Their sober wishes never learned to stray;

> *Along the cool, sequestered vale of life*
> *They kept the noiseless tenor of their way.*

Poor Alvin. When I'm done with you, there'll be no cool sequestered vale. You'll look back on your prenticeship as the last peaceful days of your life.

He gripped the full, heavy bucket with one hand on the rim, and easily tipped it to pour it out into the bucket she had brought, which he held in his other hand; he did it as lightly and easily as a housewife pours cream from one cup into another. What if those hands as lightly and easily held my arms? Would he break me without meaning to, being so strong? Would I feel manacled in his irresistible grasp? Or would he burn me up in the white heat of his heartfire?

She reached out for her bucket.

"Please let me carry it, Ma'am. Miss Larner."

"There's no need."

"I know I'm dirtied up, Miss Larner, but I can carry it to your door and set it inside without messing anything."

Is my disguise so monstrously aloof that you think I refuse your help out of excessive cleanliness? "I only meant that I didn't want to make you work anymore today. You've helped me enough already for one day."

He looked straight into her eyes, and now he lost that peaceful expression. There was even a bit of anger in his eyes. "If you're afraid I'll want you to pay me, you needn't have no fear of that. If this is your dollar, you can have it back. I never wanted it." He held out to her the coin that Whitley Physicker had tossed him from the carriage.

"I reproved Dr. Physicker at the time. I thought it insulting that *he* should presume to pay you for the service you did me out of pure gallantry. It cheapened both of us, I thought, for him to act as if the events of this morning were worth exactly one dollar."

His eyes had softened now.

Peggy went on in her Miss Larner voice. "But you must forgive Dr. Physicker. He is uncomfortable with wealth, and looks for opportunities to share it with others. He has not yet learned how to do it with perfect tact."

"Oh, it's no never mind now, Miss Larner, seeing how it didn't come from you." He put the coin back in his pocket and started to carry the full bucket up the hill toward the house.

It was plain he was unaccustomed to walking with a lady. His strides were far too long, his pace too quick, for her to keep up with him. She couldn't even walk the same route he took—he seemed oblivious to the degree of slope. He was like a child, not an adult, taking the most direct route even if it meant unnecessary clambering over obstacles.

And yet I'm barely five years older than he is. Have I come to believe my own disguise? At twenty-three, am I already thinking and acting and living like a woman of twice that age? Didn't I once love to walk just as he does, over the most difficult ground, for the sheer love of the exertion and accomplishment?

Nevertheless, she walked the easier path, skirting the hill and then climbing up where the slope was longer and gentler. He was already there, waiting at the door.

"Why didn't you open the door and set the bucket inside? The door isn't locked," she said.

"Begging your pardon, Miss Larner, but this is a door that asks not to be opened, whether it's locked or not."

So, she thought, he wants to make sure I know about the hidden hexes he put in the locks. Not many people could see a hidden hex—nor could she, for that matter. She wouldn't have known about them if she hadn't watched him put the hexes in the lock. But of course she couldn't very well tell him *that*. So she asked, "Oh, is there some protection here that I can't see?"

"I just put a couple of hexes into the lock. Nothing much, but it should make it fairly safe here. And there's a hex in the top of the stove, so I don't think you have to worry much about sparks getting free."

"You have a great deal of confidence in your hexery, Alvin."

"I do them pretty good. Most folks knows a few hexes, anyway, Miss Larner. But not many smiths can put them into the iron. I just wanted you to know."

He wanted her to know more than that, of course. So she gave him the response he hoped for. "I take it, then, that you did some of the work on this springhouse."

"I done the windows, Miss Larner. They glide up and down sweet as you please, and there's pegs to hold them in place. And the stove, and the locks, and all the iron fittings. And my helper, Arthur Stuart, he scraped down the walls."

For a young man who seemed artless, he was steering the conversation rather well. For a moment she thought of toying with him, of pretending not to make the connections he was counting on, just to see how he handled it. But no—he was only planning to ask her to do what she came here to do. There was no reason to make it hard for him. The teaching itself would be hard enough. "Arthur Stuart," she said. "He must be the same boy that Goody Guester asked me to teach privately."

"Oh, did she already ask you? Or shouldn't I ask?"

"I have no intention of keeping it a secret, Alvin. Yes, I'll be teaching Arthur Stuart."

"I'm glad of that, Miss Larner. He's the smartest boy you ever knew. And a mimic! Why, he can hear anything once and say it back to you in your own voice. You'll hardly believe it even when he's a-doing it."

"I only hope he doesn't choose to play such a game when I'm teaching him."

Alvin frowned. "Well, it isn't rightly a game, Miss Larner. It's just something he does without meaning to in particular. I mean to say, if he starts talking back to you in your own voice, he isn't making fun or nothing. It's just that when he hears something he remembers it voice and all, if you know what I mean. He can't split them up and remember the words without the voice that gave them."

"I'll keep that in mind."

In the distance, Peggy heard a door slam closed. She cast out and looked, finding Father's and Mother's heartfires coming toward her. They were quarreling, of course, but if Alvin was to ask her, he'd have to do it quickly.

"Was there something else you wanted to say to me, Alvin?"

This was the moment he'd been leading up to, but now he was turning shy on her. "Well, I had some idea of asking you—but you got to understand, I didn't carry the water for you so you'd feel obliged or nothing. I would've done that anyway, for anybody, and as for what happened today, I didn't rightly know that you were the teacher. I mean maybe I might've guessed, but I just didn't think of it. So what I done was just itself, and you don't owe me nothing."

"I think I'll decide how much gratitude I owe, Alvin. What did you want to ask me?"

"Of course you'll be busy with Arthur Stuart, so I can't expect you to have much time free, maybe just one day a week, just an hour even. It could be on Saturdays, and you could charge whatever you want, my master's been giving me free time and I've saved up some of my own earnings, and—"

"Are you asking me to tutor you, Alvin?"

Alvin didn't know what the word meant.

"Tutor you. Teach you privately."

"Yes, Miss Larner."

"The charge is fifty cents a week, Alvin. And I wish you to come at the same time as Arthur Stuart. Arrive when he does, and leave when he does."

"But how can you teach us both at once?"

"I daresay you could benefit from some of the lessons I'll be giving him, Alvin. And when I have him writing or ciphering, I can converse with you."

"I just don't want to cheat him out of his lesson time."

"Think clearly, Alvin. It would not be proper for you to take lessons with me alone. I may be somewhat older than you, but there are those who will search for fault in me, and giving private instruction to a young bachelor would certainly give cause for tongues to wag. Arthur Stuart will be present at all your lessons, and the door of the springhouse will stand open."

"We could go up and you could teach me at the roadhouse."

"Alvin. I have told you the terms. Do you wish to engage me as your tutor?"

"Yes, Miss Larner." He dug into his pocket and pulled out a coin. "Here's a dollar for the first two weeks."

Peggy looked at the coin. "I thought you meant to give this dollar back to Dr. Physicker."

"I wouldn't want to make him uncomfortable about having so much money, Miss Larner." He grinned.

Shy he may be, but he can't stay serious for long. There'll always be a tease in him, just below the surface, and eventually it will always come out.

"No. I imagine not," said Miss Larner. "Lessons will begin next week. Thank you for your help."

At that moment, Father and Mother came up the path. Father carried a large tub over his head, and he staggered under the weight. Alvin immediately ran to help—or, rather, to simply take the tub and carry it himself.

That was how Peggy saw her father's face for the first time in more than six years—red, sweating, as he puffed from the labor of carrying the tub. And angry, too, or at least sullen. Even though Mother had no doubt assured him that the teacher lady wasn't half so arrogant as she seemed at first, still Father was resentful of this stranger living in the springhouse, a place that belonged only to his long-lost daughter.

Peggy longed to call out to him, call him Father, and assure him that it *was* his daughter who dwelt here now, that all his labor to make a home of this old place was really a gift of love to her. How it comforted her to know how much he loved her, that he had not forgotten her after all these years; yet it also made her heart break for him, that she couldn't name herself to him truly, not yet, not if she was to accomplish all she needed to. She would have to do with him what she was already trying to do with Alvin and with Mother—not reclaim old loves and debts, but win new love and friendship.

She could not come home as a daughter of this place, not even to Father, who alone would purely rejoice at her coming. She had to come home as a stranger. For surely that's what she was, even if she had no disguise, for after three years of one kind of learning in Dekane and another three of schooling and study, she was no longer Little Peggy, the quiet, sharp-tongued torch; she had long since become something else. She had learned many graces under the tutelage of Mistress Modesty; she had learned many other things from books and teachers. She was not who she had been. It would be as much a lie to say, Father, I am your daughter Little Peggy, as it was to say what she said now: "Mr. Guester, I am your new tenant, Miss Larner. I'm very glad to meet you."

He huffed up to her and put out his hand. Despite his misgivings, despite the way he had avoided meeting her when first she arrived at the roadhouse an hour or so past, he was too much the consummate innkeeper to refuse to greet her with courtesy—or at least the rough country manners that passed for courtesy in this frontier town.

"Pleased to meet you, Miss Larner. I trust your accommodation is satisfactory?"

It made her a little sad, to hear him trying fancy language on her, the way he talked to those customers he thought of as "dignitaries," meaning that he believed their station in life to be above his. I've learned much, Father, and this above all: that no station in life is above any other, if it's occupied by someone with a good heart.

As to whether Father's heart was good, Peggy believed it but refused to look. She had known his heartfire far too well in years past. If she looked too closely now, she might find things a daughter had no right to see. She'd been too young to control herself when she explored his heartfire all those years ago; in the innocence of childhood she had learned things that made both innocence and childhood impossible. Now, though, with her knack better tamed, she could at last give him privacy in his own heart. She owed him and Mother that.

Not to mention that she owed it to herself not to know *exactly* what they thought and felt about everything.

They set up the tub in her little house. Mother had brought another bucket and a kettle, and now Father and Alvin both set to toting water up from the well, while Mother boiled some on the stove. When the bath was ready, she sent the men away; then Peggy sent Mother away as well, though not without considerable argument. "I am grateful for your solicitude," Peggy said, "but it is my custom to bathe in utter privacy. You have been exceptionally kind, and as I now take my bath, alone, you may be sure I will think of you gratefully every moment."

The stream of high-sounding language was more than even Mother could resist. At last the door was closed and locked, the curtains drawn. Peggy removed her traveling gown, which was heavy with dust and sweat, and then peeled away her chemise and her pantalets, which clung hotly to her skin. It was one of the benefits of her disguise, that she need not trouble herself with corsetry. No one expected a spinster of her supposed age to have the perversely slender waist of those poor young victims of fashion who bound themselves until they could not breathe.

Last of all she removed her amulets, the three that hung around her neck and the one enwrapped with her hair. The amulets were hard-won, and not just because they were the new, expensive ones that acted on what others actually saw, and not just on their opinion of it. It had taken four visits before the hexman believed that she really did want to appear ugly. "A girl so lovely as you, you don't need my art," he said it over and over again, until she finally took him by the shoulders and said, "That's why I need it! To make me *stop* being beautiful." He gave in, but kept muttering that it was a sin to cover what God created well.

God or Mistress Modesty, thought Peggy. I *was* beautiful in Mistress Modesty's house. Am I beautiful now, when no one sees me but myself, I who am least likely to admire?

Naked at last, herself at last, she knelt beside the tub and ducked her head to begin the washing of her hair. Immersed in water, hot as it was, she felt the same old freedom she had felt so long ago in the springhouse, the wet isolation in which no heartfires intruded, so she was truly herself alone, and had a chance of knowing what her self might actually be.

There was no mirror in the springhouse. Nor had she brought one. Nevertheless, she knew when her bath was done and she toweled herself before the stove, already sweating in the steamy room, in the early August evening—she knew that she *was* beautiful, as Mistress Modesty had taught her how to be; knew that if Alvin could see her as she really was, he would desire her, not for wisdom, but for the more casual and shallow love that any man feels for a woman who delights his eyes. So, just as she had once hidden from him so he wouldn't marry her for pity, now she hid from him so he wouldn't marry her for boyish love. This self, the smooth and youthful body, would remain invisible to him, so that her truer self, the sharp and well-filled mind, might entice the finest man in him, the man that would be, not a lover, but a Maker.

If only she could somehow disguise his body from her own eyes, so that she would not have to imagine his touch, as gentle as the touch of air on her skin as she moved across the room.

16

Property

The Blacks started in a-howling before the roosters got up. Cavil Planter didn't get up right away; the sound of it sort of fit into his dream. Howling Blacks figured in his dreams pretty common these days. Anyway it finally woke him, and he bounded up out of bed. Barely light outside; he had to open the curtain to get light enough to find his trousers. He could make out shadows moving down near the slave quarters, but couldn't see what all was going on. He thought the worst, of course, and pulled his shotgun down from the rack on his bedroom wall. Slaveowners, in case you didn't guess, always keep their firearms in the same room where they sleep.

Out in the hall, he nearly bumped into somebody. She screeched. It took Cavil a moment to realize it was his wife, Dolores. Sometimes he forgot she knew how to walk, seeing how she only left her room at certain times. He just wasn't used to seeing her out of bed, moving around the house without a slave or two to lean on.

"Hush now, Dolores, it's me, Cavil."

"Oh, what is it, Cavil! What's happening out there!" She was clinging to his arm, so he couldn't move on.

"Don't you think I can tell you better if you let me go find out?"

She hung on tighter. "Don't do it, Cavil! Don't go out there alone! They might kill you!"

"Why would they kill me? Am I not a righteous master? Will the Lord not protect me?" All the same, he felt a thrill of fear. Could this be the slave revolt that every master feared but none spoke of? He realized now that this very thought had been lingering at the back of his mind since he first woke up. Now Dolores had put it into words. "I have my shotgun," said Cavil. "Don't worry about me."

"I'm afraid," said Dolores.

"You know what *I'm* afraid of? That you'll stumble in the dark and really hurt yourself. Go back to bed, so I don't have to worry about you while I'm outside."

Somebody started pounding at the door.

"Master! Master!" cried a slave. "We need you, Master!"

"Now see? That's Fat Fox," said Cavil. "If it was a revolt, my love, they'd strangle him first off, before they ever came after me."

"Is that supposed to make me feel better?" she asked.

"Master! Master!"

"To bed," said Cavil.

For a moment her hand rested on the hard cold barrel of the shotgun. Then she turned and, like a pale grey ghost in the darkness of the hall, she disappeared into the shadows toward her room.

Fat Fox was near to jumping up and down he was so agitated. Cavil looked at him, as always, with disgust. Even though Cavil depended on Fat Fox to let him know which slaves talked ugly behind his back, Cavil didn't have to like him. There wasn't a hope in heaven of saving the soul of any full-blood Black. They were all born in deep corruption, like as if they embraced original sin and sucked more of it with their mother's milk. It's a wonder their milk wasn't black with all the foulness that must be in it. I wish it wasn't such a slow process, turning the Black race White enough to be worth trying to save their souls.

"It's that Salamandy girl, Master," said Fat Fox.

"Is her baby coming early?" said Cavil.

"Oh no," said Fat Fox. "No, no, it ain't coming, no Master. Oh please come on down. It ain't that gun you needing, Master. It's your big old buck knife I think."

"I'll decide that," said Cavil. If a Black suggests you ought to put your gun away, that's when you hang onto it tightest of all.

He strode toward the slave women's quarters. It was getting light enough by now that he could see the ground, could see the Blacks all slinking here and there in the dark, watching him, white eyes watching. That was a mercy from the Lord God, making their eyes white, else you couldn't see them at all in the shadows.

There was a passel of women all outside the door to the cabin where Salamandy slept. Her being so close to her time, she didn't have to do any field work these days, and she got a bed with a fine mattress. Nobody could say Cavil Planter didn't take care of his breeding stock.

One of the women—in the darkness he couldn't tell who, but from the voice he thought it was maybe Coppy, the one baptized as Agnes but who chose to call herself after the copperhead rattler—anyway she cried out, "Oh, Master, you got to let us bleed a chicken on this one!"

"No heathen abominations shall be practiced on my plantation," said Cavil sternly. But he knew now that Salamandy was dead. Only a month from delivery, and she was dead. It stabbed his heart deep. One child less. One breeding ewe gone. O God have mercy on me! How can I serve thee aright if you take away my best concubine?

It smelled like a sick horse in the room, from her bowel opening up as she died. She'd hung herself with the bedsheet. Cavil damned himself for a fool, giving her such a thing. Here he meant it as a sign of special favor, her being on her sixth half-White baby, to let her have a sheet on her mattress, and now she turned around and answered him like this.

Her feet dangled not three inches from the floor. She must have stood on the bed and then stepped off. Even now, as she swayed slightly in the breeze of his movement in the room, her feet bumped into the bedstead. It took a second or two for Cavil to realize what that meant. Since her neck wasn't broke, she must have been a long time strangling, and the whole time the bed was inches away, and she *knew* it. The whole time, she could have stopped strangling at any time. Could have changed her mind. This was a woman who wanted to die. No, wanted to *kill*. Murder that baby she was carrying.

Proof again how strong these Blacks were in their wickedness. Rather than give birth to a half-White child with a hope of salvation, she'd strangle to death herself. Was there no limit to their perversity? How could a godly man save such creatures?

"She kill herself, Master!" cried the woman who had spoke before. He turned to look at her, and now it was light enough to see for sure that it was Coppy talking. "She waiting for tomorrow night to kill somebody else, less we bleed a chicken on her!"

"It makes me ill, to think you'd use this poor woman's death as an excuse to roast a chicken out of turn. She'll have a decent burial, and her soul will *not* hurt anyone, though as a suicide she will surely burn in hell forever."

At his words Coppy wailed in grief. The other women joined in her keening. Cavil had Fat Fox set a group of young bucks digging a grave—not in the regular slaveyard, of course, since as a suicide she couldn't lie in consecrated ground. Out among the trees, with no marker, as befit a beast that took the life of her own young.

She was in the ground before nightfall. Since she was a suicide, Cavil couldn't very well ask the Baptist preacher or the Catholic priest to come help with it. In fact, he figured to say the words himself, only it happened that tonight was the night he'd already invited a traveling

preacher to supper. That preacher showed up early, and the house slaves
sent him around back where he found the burial in progress and offered
to help.

"Oh, you don't need to do that," said Cavil.

"Let it never be said that Reverend Philadelphia Thrower did not
extend Christian love to all the children of God—White or Black, male
or female, saint or sinner."

The slaves perked up at that, and so did Cavil—for the opposite
reason. That was Emancipationist talk, and Cavil felt a sudden fear that
he had invited the devil into his own house by bringing this Presbyterian
preacher. Nevertheless, it would probably do much to quiet the Blacks'
superstitious fears if he allowed the rites to be administered by a real
preacher. And sure enough, when the words were said and the grave
was covered, they all seemed right quiet—none of that ghastly howling.

At dinner, the preacher—Thrower, that was his name—eased Cavil's
fears considerably. "I believe that it is part of God's great plan for the
Black people to be brought to America in chains. Like the children of
Israel, who had to suffer years of bondage to the Egyptians, these Black
souls are under the Lord's own lash, shaping them to His own purposes.
The Emancipationists understand one truth—that God loves his Black
children—but they misunderstand everything else. Why, if they had
their way and freed all the slaves at once, it would accomplish the
devil's purpose, not God's, for without slavery the Blacks have no hope
of rising out of their savagery."

"Now, that sounds downright theological," said Cavil.

"Don't the Emancipationists understand that every Black who es-
capes from his rightful master into the North is doomed to eternal dam-
nation, him and all his children? Why, they might as well have remained
in Africa as go north. The Whites up north hate Blacks, as well they
should, since only the most evil and proud and stiff-necked dare to
offend God by leaving their masters. But you here in Appalachee and
in the Crown Colonies, you are the ones who truly love the Black man,
for only you are willing to take responsibility for these wayward children and help them progress on the road to full humanity."

"You may be a Presbyterian, Reverend Thrower, but you know the
true religion."

"I'm glad to know I'm in the home of a godly man, Brother Cavil."

"I hope I am your brother, Reverend Thrower."

And that's how the talk went on, the two of them liking each other
better and better as the evening wore. By nightfall, when they sat on
the porch cooling off, Cavil began to think he had met the first man to
whom he might tell some part of his great secret.

Cavil tried to bring it up casual. "Reverend Thrower, do you think the Lord God speaks to any men today?"

Thrower's voice got all solemn. "I know He does."

"Do you think He might even speak to a common man like me?"

"You mustn't hope for it, Brother Cavil," said Thrower, "for the Lord goes where He will, and not where we wish. Yet I do know that it's possible for even the humblest man to have a—Visitor."

Cavil felt a trembling in his belly. Why, Thrower sounded like he already knew Cavil's secret. But still he didn't blurt it out all at once. "You know what I think?" said Cavil. "I think that the Lord God can't appear in His true form, because His glory would kill a natural man."

"Oh, indeed," said Thrower. "As when Moses craved a vision of the Lord, and the Lord covered his eyes with His hand, only letting Moses see His back parts as he passed by."

"I mean, what if a man like me saw the Lord Jesus himself, only not looking like any painting of him, but instead looking like an overseer. I reckon that a man sees only what will make him understand the power of God, not the true majesty of the Lord."

Thrower nodded wisely. "It may well be," he said. "That's a plausible explanation. Or it might be that you only saw an angel."

There it was—that simple. From "what if a man like me" to Thrower saying "you saw an angel." That's how much alike these two men were. So Cavil told the whole story, for the first time ever, near seven years after it happened.

When he was done, Thrower took his hand and held it in a brotherly grip, looking him in the eye with a fierce-looking kind of expression. "To think of your sacrifice, mingling your flesh with that of these Black women, in order to serve the Lord. How many children?"

"Twenty-five that got born alive. You helped me bury the twenty-sixth inside Salamandy's belly this evening."

"Where are all these hopeful half-White youngsters?"

"Oh, that's half the labor I'm doing," said Cavil. "Till the Fugitive Slave Treaty, I used to sell them all south as soon as I could, so they'd grow up there and spread White blood throughout the Crown Colonies. Each one will be a missionary through his seed. Of course, the last few I've kept here. It ain't the safest thing, neither, Reverend Thrower. All my breeding-age stock is pure Black, and folks are bound to wonder where these mixup children come from. So far, though, my overseer, Lashman, he keeps his mouth shut if he notices, and nobody else ever sees them."

Thrower nodded, but it was plain his mind was on something else. "Only twenty-*five* of these children?"

"It's the best I could do," said Cavil. "Even a Black woman can't make a baby right off after a birthing."

"I meant—you see, I also had a—visitation. It's the reason why I came here, came touring through Appalachee. I was told that I would meet a farmer who also knew my Visitor, and who had produced twenty-six living gifts to God."

"Twenty-*six*."

"Living."

"Well, you see—well, ain't that just the way of it. You see, I wasn't including in my tally the very first one born, because his mother run off and stole him from me a few days before he was due to be sold. I had to refund the money in cash to the buyer, and it was no good tracking, the dogs couldn't pick up her scent. Word among the slaves was that she turned into a blackbird and *flew*, but you know the tales they tell."

"So—twenty-six then. And tell me this—is there some reason why the name 'Hagar' should mean anything to you?"

Cavil gasped. "No one knows I called the mother by that name!"

"My Visitor told me that Hagar had stolen away your first gift."

"It's Him. You've seen Him, too."

"To me He comes as—not an overseer. More like a scientist—a man of unguessable wisdom. Because *I* am a scientist, I imagine, besides my vocation as a minister. I have always supposed that He was a mere angel—listen to me, a *mere* angel—because I dared not hope that He was—was the Master himself. But now what you tell me—could it be that we have both entertained the presence of our Lord? Oh, Cavil, how can I doubt it? Why else would the Lord have brought us together like this? It means that I—that I'm forgiven."

"Forgiven?"

At Cavil's question, Thrower's face darkened.

Cavil hastened to reassure him. "No, you don't need to tell me if you don't want."

"I—it is almost unbearable to think of it. But now that I am clearly deemed acceptable—or at least, now that I've been given another chance—Brother Cavil, once I was given a mission to perform, one as dark and difficult and secret as your own. Except that where you have had the courage and strength to prevail, I failed. I tried, but I had not wit or vigor enough to overcome the power of the devil. I thought I was rejected, cast off. That's why I became a traveling preacher, for I felt myself unworthy to take a pulpit of my own. But now—"

Cavil nodded, holding the man's hands as tears flowed down his cheek.

At last Thrower looked up at him. "How do you suppose our— Friend—meant me to help you in your work?"

"I can't say," said Cavil. "But there's only one way I can think of, offhand."

"Brother Cavil, I'm not sure if I can take upon myself that loathsome duty."

"In my experience, the Lord strengthens a man, and makes it—bearable."

"But in my case, Brother Cavil—you see, I've never known a woman, as the Bible speaks of it. Only once have my lips touched a woman's, and that was against my will."

"Then I'll do my best to help you. How if we pray together good and long, and then I show you once?"

Well, that seemed like the best idea either of them could think of right offhand, and so they did it, and it turned out Reverend Thrower was a quick learner. Cavil felt a great sense of relief to have someone else join in, not to mention a kind of peculiar pleasure at having somebody watch him and then watching the other fellow in turn. It was a powerful sort of brotherhood, to have their seed mingled in the same vessel, so to speak. Like Reverend Thrower said, "When this field comes to harvest, Brother Cavil, we shall not guess whose seed came unto ripeness, for the Lord gave us this field together, for this time."

Oh, and then Reverend Thrower asked the girl's name. "Well, we baptized her as 'Hepzibah,' but she goes by the name 'Roach.'"

"Roach!"

"They all take animal names. I reckon she doesn't have too high an opinion of herself."

At that, Thrower just reached over and took Roach's hand and patted it, as kindly a gesture as if Thrower and Roach was man and wife, an idea that made Cavil almost laugh right out. "Now, Hepzibah, you must use your Christian name," said Thrower, "and not such a debasing animal name."

Roach just looked at him wide-eyed, lying there curled up on the mattress.

"Why doesn't she answer me, Brother Cavil?"

"Oh, they never talk during this. I beat that out of them early—they always tried to talk me out of doing it. I figure better to have no words than have them say what the devil wants me to hear."

Thrower turned back to the woman. "But now I ask you to speak to me, Roach. You won't say devil words, will you?"

In answer, Roach's eyes wandered upward to where part of a bedsheet was still knotted around a rafter. It had been raggedly hacked off below the knot.

Thrower's face got kind of sick-looking. "You mean this is the room where—the girl we buried—"

"This room has the best bed," said Cavil. "I didn't want us doing this on a straw pallet if we didn't have to."

Thrower said nothing. He just left the room, pretty quick, plunging outside into the darkness. Cavil sighed, picked up the lantern, and followed him. He found Thrower leaning over the pump. He could hear Roach skittering out of the room where Salamandy died, heading for her own quarters, but he didn't give no never mind to her. It was Thrower—surely the man wasn't so beside himself that he'd throw up on the drinking water!

"I'm all right," whispered Thrower. "I just—the same room—I'm not at all superstitious, you understand. It just seemed disrespectful to the dead."

These northerners. Even when they understood somewhat about slavery, they couldn't get rid of their notion of Blacks as if they was people. Would you stop using a room just because a mouse died there, or you once killed a spider on the wall? Do you burn down your stable just because your favorite horse died there?

Anyway, Thrower got himself together, hitched up his trousers and buttoned them up proper, and they went back in the house. Brother Cavil put Thrower in their guest room, which wasn't all that much used, so there was a cloud of dust when Cavil slapped the blanket. "Should have known the house slaves'd be slacking in this room," said Brother Cavil.

"No matter," said Thrower. "On a night this warm, I'll need no blanket."

On the way down the hall to his own bedroom, Cavil paused a moment to listen for his wife's breathing. As sometimes happened, he could hear her whimpering softly in her bedroom. The pain must be bad indeed. Oh Lord, thought Cavil, how many more times must I do Thy bidding before You'll have mercy and heal my Dolores? But he didn't go in to her—there was nothing he could do to help her, besides prayer, and he'd need his sleep. This had been a late night, and tomorrow had work enough.

Sure enough, Dolores had had a bad night—she was still asleep at breakfast time. So Cavil ended up eating with Thrower. The preacher put away an astonishingly large portion of sausage and grits. When his plate was clean for the third time, he looked at Cavil and smiled. "The Lord's service can give a man quite an appetite!" They both had a good laugh at that.

After breakfast, they walked outside. It happened they went near the woods where Salamandy had been buried. Thrower suggested looking at the grave, or else Cavil probably never would have known what the Blacks did in the night. There were footprints all over the grave itself, which was churned into mud. Now the drying mud was covered with ants.

"Ants!" said Thrower. "They can't possibly smell the body under the ground."

"No," said Cavil. "What they're finding is fresher and right on top. Look at that—cut-up entrails."

"They didn't—exhume her body and—"

"Not *her* guts, Reverend Thrower. Probably a squirrel or blackbird or something. They did a devil sacrifice last night."

Thrower immediately began murmuring a prayer.

"They know I forbid such things," said Cavil. "By evening, the proof of it would no doubt be gone. They're disobeying me behind my back. I won't have it."

"Now I understand the magnitude of the work you slaveowners have. The devil has an iron grip upon their souls."

"Well, never you mind. They'll pay for it today. They want blood dropped on her grave? It'll be their own. Mr. Lashman! Where are you! Mr. Lashman!"

The overseer had only just arrived for the day's work.

"A little half-holiday for the Blacks this morning, Mr. Lashman," said Thrower.

Lashman didn't ask why. "Which ones you want whipped?"

"All of them. Ten lashes each. Except the pregnant women, of course. But even they—one lash for each of them, across the thighs. And all to watch."

"They get a bit unruly, watching it, sir," said Lashman.

"Reverend Thrower and I will watch also," said Cavil.

While Lashman was off assembling the slaves, Thrower murmured something about not really wanting to watch.

"It's the Lord's work," said Cavil. "I have stomach enough to watch any act of righteousness. I thought after last night that you did too."

So they watched together as each slave in turn was whipped, the blood dripping down onto Salamandy's grave. After a while Thrower didn't even flinch. Cavil was glad to see it—the man wasn't weak, after all, just a little soft from his upbringing in Scotland and his life in the North.

Afterward, as Reverend Thrower prepared to be on his way—he had promised to preach in a town a half-day's ride south—he happened to ask Cavil a question.

"I noticed that all your slaves seem—not old, you understand, but not young, either."

Cavil shrugged. "It's the Fugitive Slave Treaty. Even though my farm's prospering, I can't buy or sell any slaves—we're part of the United States now. Most folks keep up by breeding, but you know all my pickaninnies ended up south, till lately. And now I've lost me another breeder, so I'm down to five women now. Salamandy was the best. The others don't have so many years of babies left in them."

"It occurs to me," said Thrower. He paused in thought.

"What occurs to you?"

"I've traveled a lot in the North, Brother Cavil, and in most every town in Hio and Suskwahenny and Irrakwa and Wobbish, there's a family or two of Blacks. Now, you know and I know that they didn't grow on northern trees."

"All runaways."

"Some, no doubt, have their freedom legally. But many—certainly there are many runaways. Now, I understand that it's a custom for every slaveowner to keep a cachet of hair and nail clippings and—"

"Oh, yes, we take them from the minute they're born or the minute we buy them. For the Finders."

"Exactly."

"But we can't exactly send the Finders to walk every foot of ground in the whole North, hoping to run into one particular runaway buck. It'd cost more than the price of the slave."

"It seems to me that the price of slaves has gone up lately."

"If you mean that we can't buy one at any price—"

"That's what I mean, Brother Cavil. And what if the Finders don't have to go blindly through the North, relying on chance? What if you arranged to hire people in the North to scour the papers and take note of the name and age of every Black they see there? Then the Finders could go armed with information."

Well, that idea was so good that it stopped Cavil right short. "There's got to be something wrong with that idea, or somebody'd already be doing it."

"Oh, I'll tell you why nobody's done it so far. There's a good deal of ill-feeling toward slaveowners in the North. Even though northerners hate their Black neighbors, their misguided consciences won't let them cooperate in any kind of slave search. So any southerner who ever went north searching for a runaway soon learned that if he didn't have his

Finder right with him, or if the trail was cold, then there was no use searching.''

"That's the truth of it. Like a bunch of thieves up North, conspiring to keep a man from recovering his run-off stock.''

"But what if you had northerners doing the searching for you? What if you had an agent in the North, a minister perhaps, who could enlist others in the cause, who could find people who could be trusted? Such an endeavor would be expensive, but given the impossibility of *buying* new slaves in Appalachee, don't you imagine people would be willing to pay enough to finance the work of recovering their runaways?''

"Pay? They'd pay double what you ask. They'd pay up front on the chance of you doing it.''

"Suppose I charged twenty dollars to register their runaway—birth-date, name, description, time and circumstances of escape—and then charged a thousand dollars if I provide them with information leading to recovery?''

"Fifty dollars to register, or they won't believe you're serious. And another fifty whenever you send them information, even if it doesn't turn out to be the right one. And *three* thousand for runaways recovered healthy.''

Thrower smiled slightly. "I don't wish to make an unfair profit from the work of righteousness.''

"Profit! You got a lot of folks up there to pay if you're going to do a good job. I tell you, Thrower, you write up a contract, and then get the printer in town to run you off a thousand copies. Then you just go around and tell what you plan to one slaveowner in each town you come to in Appalachee. I reckon you'll have to get a new printing done within a week. We're not talking profit here, we're talking a valuable service. Why, I'll bet you get contributions from folks what *never* had a run-away. If you can make it so the Hio River stops being the last barrier before they get away clean, it'll not only return old runaways, it'll make the other slaves lose hope and stay home!''

Not half an hour later, Thrower was back ouside and on his horse— but now he had notes written up for the contract and letters of intro-duction from Cavil to his lawyer and to the printer, along with letters of credit to the tune of five hundred dollars. When Thrower protested that it was too much, Cavil wouldn't even hear him out. "To get you started,'' said Cavil. "We both know whose work we're doing. It takes money. I have it and you don't, so take it and get busy.''

"That's a Christian attitude,'' said Thrower. "Like the saints in the early Church, who had all things in common.''

Cavil patted Thrower's thigh, where he sat stiff in the saddle—

northerners just didn't know how to sit a horse. "We've had more in common than any other two men alive," said Cavil. "We've had the same visions and done the same works, and if that don't make us two peas in a pod, I don't know what will."

"When next I see the Visitor, if I should be so fortunate, I know that he'll be pleased."

"Amen," said Cavil.

Then he slapped Thrower's horse and watched him out of sight. My Hagar. He's going to find my Hagar and her little boy. Nigh on seven years since she stole my firstborn child from me. Now she'll come back, and this time she'll stay in chains and give me more children until she can't have no more. And as for the boy, he'll be my Ishmael. That's what I'll call him, too. Ishmael. I'll keep him right here, and raise him up to be strong and obedient and a true Christian. When he's old enough I'll hire him out to other plantations, and during the nights he'll go and carry on my work, spreading the chosen seed throughout Appalachee. Then my children will surely be as numberless as the sands of the sea, just like Abraham.

And who knows? Maybe then the miracle will happen, and my own dear wife will be healed, and she'll conceive and bear me a pure White child, my Isaac, to inherit all my land and all my work. Lord my Overseer, be merciful to me.

17

Spelling Bee

Early January, with deep snow, and a wind sharp enough to slice your nose off—so of course that was a day for Makepeace Smith to decide *he* had to work in the forge all day, while Alvin went into town to buy supplies and deliver finished work. In the summer, the choice of jobs tended to go the other way.

Never mind, thought Alvin. He *is* the master here. But if I'm ever master of my own forge, and if I have me a prentice, you can bet he'll be treated fairer than I've been. A master and prentice ought to share the work alike, except for when the prentice plain don't know how, and then the master ought to teach him. That's the bargain, not to have a slave, not to always have the prentice take the wagon into town through the snow.

Truth to tell, though, Alvin knew he wouldn't have to take the wagon. Horace Guester's sleigh-and-two would do the job, and he knew Horace wouldn't mind him taking it, as long as Alvin did whatever errands the roadhouse needed doing in town.

Alvin bundled himself tight and pushed out into the wind—it was right in his face, from the west, the whole way up to the roadhouse. He took the path up by Miss Larner's house, it being the closest way with the most trees to break the wind. Course she wasn't in. It being school hours, she was with the children in the schoolhouse in town. But the old springhouse, it was Alvin's schoolhouse, and just passing by the door got him to thinking about his studies.

She had him learning things he never thought to learn. He was expecting more of ciphering and reading and writing, and in a way that's what she had him doing, right enough. But she didn't have him reading out of those primers like the children—like Arthur Stuart, who plugged away at his studies by lamplight every night in the springhouse. No, she talked to Alvin about ideas he never would've thought of, and all his writing and calculating was about such things.

Yesterday:

"The smallest particle is an atom," she said. "According to the theory of Demosthenes, everything is made out of smaller things, until you come to the atom, which is smallest of all and cannot be divided."

"What's it look like?" Alvin asked her.

"I don't know. It's too small to see. Do *you* know?"

"I reckon not. Never saw anything so small but what you could cut it in half."

"But can't you *imagine* anything smaller?"

"Yeah, but I can split that too."

She sighed. "Well, now, Alvin, think again. If there *were* a thing so small it couldn't be divided, what would it be like?"

"*Real* small, I reckon."

But he was joking. It was a problem, and he set out to answer it the way he answered any practical problem. He sent his bug out into the floor. Being wood, the floor was a jumble of things, the broke-up once-alive hearts of living trees, so Alvin quickly sent his bug on into the iron of the stove, which was mostly all one thing inside. Being hot, the bits of it, the tiniest parts he ever saw clear, they were a blur of movement; while the fire inside, it made its own outward rush of light and heat, each bit of it so small and fine that he could barely hold the idea of it in his mind. He never really *saw* the bits of fire. He only knew that they had just passed by.

"Light," he said. "And heat. They can't be cut up."

"True. Fire isn't like earth—it can't be cut. But it can be changed, can't it? It can be extinguished. It can cease to be itself. And therefore the parts of it must become something else, and so they were not the unchangeable and indivisible atoms."

"Well, there's nothing smaller than those bits of fire, so I reckon there's no such thing as an atom."

"Alvin, you've got to stop being so empirical about things."

"If I knowed what that was, I'd stop being it."

"If I knew."

"Whatever."

"You can't always answer every question by sitting back and doodle-bugging your way through the rocks outside or whatever."

Alvin sighed. "Sometimes I wish I never told you what I do."

"Do you want me to teach you what it means to be a Maker or not?"

"That's just *what* I want! And instead you talk about atoms and gravity and—I don't care what that old humbug Newton said, nor anybody else! I want to know how to make the—*place*." He remembered only just in time that there was Arthur Stuart in the corner, memorizing every word they said, complete with tone of voice. No sense filling Arthur's head with the Crystal City.

"Don't you understand, Alvin? It's been so long—thousands of years—that no one knows what a Maker really is, or what he does. Only that there were such men, and a few of the tasks that they could do. Changing lead or iron into gold, for instance. Water into wine. That sort of thing."

"I expect iron to gold'd be easier," said Alvin. "Those metals are pretty much all one thing inside. But wine—that's such a mess of different stuff inside that you'd have to be a—a—" He couldn't think of a word for the most power a man could have.

"Maker."

That was the word, right enough. "I reckon."

"I'm telling you, Alvin, if you want to learn how to do the things that Makers once did, you have to understand the nature of things. You can't change what you don't understand."

"And I can't understand what I don't see."

"Wrong! Absolutely false, Alvin Smith! It is what you *can* see that remains impossible to understand. The world you actually see is nothing more than an example, a special case. But the underlying principles, the order that holds it all together, *that* is forever invisible. It can only be discovered in the imagination, which is precisely the aspect of your mind that is most neglected."

Well, last night Alvin just got mad, which she said would only guarantee that he'd stay stupid, which he said was just fine with him as he'd stayed alive against long odds by being as pure stupid as he was without any help from *her*. Then he stormed on outside and walked around watching the first flakes of this storm start coming down.

He'd only been walking a little while when he realized that she was right, and he knowed it all along. Knew it. He always sent out his bug to see what was *there*, but then when he got set to make a change, he first had to think up what he *wanted* it to be. He had to think of something that wasn't there, and hold a picture of it in his mind, and then, in that way he was born with and still didn't understand, he'd say, See this? This is how you ought to be! And then, sometimes fast, sometimes slow, the bits of it would move around until they lined up right. That's how he always did it: separating a piece off of living rock; joining together two bits of wood; making the iron line up strong and true; spreading the heat of the fire smooth and even along the bottom of the crucible. So I do see what isn't there, in my mind, and that's what makes it *come* to be there.

For a terrible dizzying moment he wondered if maybe the whole world was maybe no more than what he imagined it to be, and if that was true then if he stopped imagining, it'd just go away. Of course, once he got his sense together he knew that if he'd been thinking it up, there wouldn't be so many strange things in the world that he never could've thought of himself.

So maybe the world was all dreamed up in the mind of God. But no, can't be that neither, because if God dreamed up men like White Murderer Harrison then God wasn't too good. No, the best Alvin could think of was that God worked pretty much the way Alvin did—told the rocks of the earth and the fire of the sun and stuff like that, told it all how it was supposed to be and then let it be that way. But when God told *people* how to be, why, they just thumbed their noses and laughed at him, mostly, or else they pretended to obey while they still went on and did what they pleased. The planets and the stars and the elements, they all might be thought up from the mind of God, but people were just too cantankerous to blame them on anybody but their own self.

Which was about the limit of Alvin's thinking last night, in the snow—wondering about what he could never know. Things like I wonder what God dreams about if he ever sleeps, and if all his dreams come true, so that every night he makes up a whole new world full of people. Questions that couldn't never get him a speck closer to being a Maker.

So today, slogging through the snow, pushing against the wind toward the roadhouse, he started thinking again about the original question—what an atom would be like. He tried to picture something so tiny that he couldn't cut it. But whenever he imagined something like that—a little box or a little ball or something—why, then he'd just up and imagine it splitting right in half.

The only way he couldn't split something in half was if it was so thin nothing could be thinner. He thought of it squished so flat it was thinner than paper, so thin that in that direction it didn't even *exist*, if you looked at it edge-on it would just plain not be there. But even then, he might not be able to split it along the edge, but he could still imagine turning it and slicing it across, just like paper.

So—what if it was squished up in another direction, too, so it was all edge, going on like the thinnest thread you ever dreamed of? Nobody could see it, but it would still be there, because it would stretch from here to there. He sure couldn't split that along the edge, and it didn't have any flat surface like paper had. Yet as long as it stretched like invisible thread from one spot to another, no matter how short the distance was, he could still imagine snipping it right in half, and each half in half again.

No, the only way something could be small enough to be an atom is if it had no size at all in any direction, not length nor breadth nor depth. That would be an atom all right—only it wouldn't even *exist*, it'd just be *nothing*. Just a place without anything in it.

He stood on the porch of the roadhouse, stamping snow off his feet, which did better than knocking for telling folks he was there. He could hear Arthur Stuart's feet running to open the door, but all he was thinking about was atoms. Because even though he'd just figured out that there couldn't be no atoms, he was beginning to realize it might be even crazier to imagine there *not* being atoms, so things could always get cut into smaller bits and *those* things into smaller bits, and those into even *smaller* bits, forever and ever. And when you think about it, it's got to be one or the other. Either you get to the bit that can't be split, and it's an atom, or you never do, and so it goes on *forever*, which is more than Alvin's head could hold.

Alvin found himself in the roadhouse kitchen, with Arthur Stuart piggyback, playing with Alvin's hat and scarf. Horace Guester was out in the barn stuffing straw into new bedticks, so Alvin asked Old Peg for use of the sleigh. It was hot in the kitchen, and Goody Guester didn't look to be in good temper. She allowed as how he could take the sled, but there was a price to pay.

"Save the life of a certain child, Alvin, and take Arthur Stuart with you," she said, "or I swear he'll do one more thing to rile me and end up in the pudding tonight."

It was true that Arthur Stuart seemed to be in a mood to make trouble—he was strangling Alvin with his own scarf and laughing like a fool.

"Let's do some lessons, Arthur," said Alvin. "Spell 'choking to death.' "

"C-H-O-K-I-N-G," said Arthur Stuart. "T-W-O. D-E-A-T-H."

Mad as she was, Goody Guester just had to break up laughing—not because he spelled "to" wrong, but because he'd spelled out the words in the most perfect imitation of Miss Larner's voice. "I swear, Arthur Stuart," she said, "you best never let Miss Larner hear you go on like that or your schooling days are over."

"Good! I hate school!" said Arthur.

"You don't hate school so much as you'd hate working with me in the kitchen every day," said Goody Guester. "All day every day, summer and winter, even swimming days."

"I might as well be a slave in Appalachee!" shouted Arthur Stuart.

Goody Guester stopped teasing and being mad, both, and turned solemn. "Don't even joke like that, Arthur. Somebody died once just to keep you from being such a thing."

"I know," said Arthur.

"No you don't, but you'd better just think before you—"

"It was my mama," said Arthur.

Now Old Peg started looking scared. She took a glance at Alvin and then said, "Never mind about that, anyway."

"My mama was a blackbird," said Arthur. "She flew so high, but then the ground caught her and she got stuck and died."

Alvin saw how Goody Guester looked at him, even more nervous-like. So maybe there was something to Arthur's story of flying after all. Maybe somehow that girl buried up beside Vigor, maybe somehow she got a blackbird to carry her baby somehow. Or maybe it was just some vision. Anyway, Goody Guester had decided to act like it was nothing after all—too late to fool Alvin, of course, but she wouldn't know that. "Well, that's a pretty story, Arthur," said Old Peg.

"It's true," said Arthur. "I remember."

Goody Guester started looking even more upset. But Alvin knew better than to argue with Arthur about this blackbird idea he had, and about him flying once. The only way to stop Arthur talking about it was to get his mind on something else. "Better come with me, Arthur Stuart," said Alvin. "Maybe you got a blackbird mama sometime in your past, but I have a feeling your mama here in this kitchen is about to knead you like dough."

"Don't forget what I need you to buy for me," said Old Peg.

"Oh, don't worry. I got a list," said Alvin.

"I didn't see you write a thing!"

"Arthur Stuart's my list. Show her, Arthur."

Arthur leaned close to Alvin's ear and shouted so loud it like to split Alvin's eardrums right down to his ankles. "A keg of wheat flour and two cones of sugar and a pound of pepper and a dozen sheets of paper and a couple of yards of cloth that might do for a shirt for Arthur Stuart."

Even though he was shouting, it was his mama's own voice.

She purely hated it when he mimicked her, and so here she came with the stirring fork in one hand and a big old cleaver in the other. "Hold still, Alvin, so I can stick the fork in his mouth and shave off a couple of ears!"

"Save me!" cried Arthur Stuart.

Alvin saved him by running away, at least till he got to the back door. Then Old Peg set down her instruments of boy-butchery and helped

Alvin bundle Arthur Stuart up in coats and leggings and boots and
scarves till he was about as big around as he was tall. Then Alvin
pitched him out the door into the snow and rolled him with his foot till
he was covered with snow.

Old Peg barked at him from the kitchen door. "That's right. Alvin
Junior, freeze him to death right before his own mother's eyes, you
irresponsible prentice boy you!"

Alvin and Arthur Stuart just laughed. Old Peg told them to be careful
and get home before dark and then she slammed the door tight.

They hitched up the sleigh, then swept out the new snow that had
blown in while they were hitching it and got in and pulled up the lap
robe. They first went on down to the forge again to pick up the work
Alvin had to deliver—mostly hinges and fittings and tools for carpenters
and leatherworkers in town, who were all in the midst of their busiest
season of the year. Then they headed out for town.

They didn't get far before they caught up to a man trudging townward—and none too well dressed, either, for weather like this. When
they were beside him and could see his face, Alvin wasn't surprised to
see it was Mock Berry.

"Get on this sleigh, Mock Berry, so I won't have your death on my
conscience," said Alvin.

Mock looked at Alvin like his words was the first Mock even noticed
somebody was there on the road, even though he'd just been passed by
the horses, snorting and stamping through the snow. "Thank you, Alvin," said the man. Alvin slid over on the seat to make room. Mock
climbed up beside him—clumsy, cause his hands were cold. Only when
he was sitting down did he seem to notice Arthur Stuart sitting on the
bench. And then it was like somebody slapped him—he started to get
right back down off the sleigh.

"Now hold on!" said Alvin. "Don't tell me you're just as stupid as
the White folks in town, refusing to sit next to a mixup boy! Shame on
you!"

Mock looked at Alvin real steady for a long couple of seconds before
he decided how to answer. "Look here, Alvin Smith, you know me
better than that. I know how such mixup children come to be, and I
don't hold against them what some White man done to their mama. But
there's a story in town about who's the real mama of this child, and it
does me no good to be seen coming into town with this child nearby."

Alvin knew the story well enough—how Arthur Stuart was supposedly the child of Mock's wife Anga, and how, since Arthur was plainly
fathered by some White man, Mock refused even to have the boy in his
own house, which led to Goody Guester taking Arthur in. Alvin also

knew the story wasn't true. But in a town like this it was better to have such a story believed than to have the true story guessed at. Alvin wouldn't put it past some folks to try to get Arthur Stuart declared a slave and shipped on south just to be rid of him so there'd be no more trouble about schools and such.

"Never mind about that," said Alvin. "Nobody's going to see you on a day like this, and even if they do, Arthur looks like a wad of cloth, and not a boy at all. You can hop off soon as we get into town." Alvin leaned out and took Mock's arm and pulled him onto the seat. "Now pull up the lap robe and snuggle close so I don't have to take you to the undertaker on account of having froze to death."

"Thank you kindly, you persnickety uppity prentice boy." Mock pulled the lap robe up so high that it covered Arthur Stuart completely. Arthur yelled and pulled it down again so he could see over the top. Then he gave Mock Berry such a glare that it might have burnt him to a cinder, if he hadn't been so cold and wet.

When they got into town, there was sleighs a-plenty, but none of the merriment of the first heavy snowfall. Folks just went about their business, and the horses stood and waited, stamping their feet and snorting and steaming in the cold wind. The lazier sort of folks—the lawyers and clerks and such—they were all staying at home on a day like this. But the people with real work to do, they had their fires hot, their workshops busy, their stores open for business. Alvin made his rounds a-dropping off ironwork with the folks who'd called for it. They all put their signature on Makepeace's delivery book—one more slight, that he wouldn't trust Alvin to take cash, like he was a nine-year-old prentice boy and not more than twice that age.

On those quick errands, Arthur Stuart stayed bundled up on the sleigh—Alvin never stayed indoors long enough to warm up from the walk between sleigh and front door. It wasn't till they got to Pieter Vanderwoort's general store that it was worth going inside and warming up for a spell. Pieter had his stove going right hot, and Alvin and Arthur wasn't the first to think of warming up there. A couple of boys from town were there warming their feet and sipping tea with a nip or two from a flask in order to keep warm. They weren't any of the boys Alvin spent much time with. He'd throwed them once or twice, but that was true of every male creature in town who was willing to rassle. Alvin knew that these two—Martin, that was the one with pimples, and the other one was Daisy—I know that sounds like a crazy name for anyone but a cow, but that was his name all right—anyway, Alvin knew that these two boys were the kind who like to set cats afire and make nasty jokes about girls behind their back. Not the kind that Alvin spent much time with, but not any that he had any partickler dislike for, neither. So he nodded them good afternoon, and they nodded him back. One of them held up his flask to share, but Alvin said no thanks and that was that.

At the counter, Alvin pulled off some of his scarves, which felt good because he was so sweaty underneath; then he set to unwinding Arthur Stuart, who spun around like a top while Alvin pulled on the end of each scarf. Arthur's laughing brought Mr. Vanderwoort out from the back, and he set to laughing, too.

"They're so cute when they're little, aren't they," said Mr. Vanderwoort.

"He's just my shopping list today, aren't you, Arthur?"

Arthur Stuart spouted out his list right off, using his Mama's voice again. "A keg of wheat flour and two cones of sugar and a pound of pepper and a dozen sheets of paper and a couple of yards of cloth that might do for a shirt for Arthur Stuart."

Mr. Vanderwoort like to died laughing. "I get such a kick out of that boy, the way he talks like his mama."

One of the boys by the stove gave a whoop.

"I mean his adopted mama, of course," said Vanderwoort.

"Oh, she's probably his mama all right!" said Daisy. "I hear Mock Berry does a *lot* of work up to the roadhouse!"

Alvin just set his jaw against the answer that sprang to mind. Instead he hotted up the flask in Daisy's hand, so Daisy whooped again and dropped it.

"You come on back with me, Arthur Stuart," said Vanderwoort.

"Like to burned my hand off!" muttered Daisy.

"You just say the list over again, bit by bit, and I'll get what's wanted," said Vanderwoort. Alvin lifted Arthur over the counter and Vanderwoort set him down on the other side.

"You must've set it on the stove like the blamed fool you are, Daisy," said Martin. "What is it, whiskey don't warm you up less it's boiled?"

Vanderwoort led Arthur into the back room. Alvin took a couple of soda crackers from the barrel and pulled up a stool near the fire.

"I didn't set it anywheres near the stove," said Daisy.

"Howdy, Alvin," said Martin.

"Howdy, Martin, Daisy," said Alvin. "Good day for stoves."

"Good day for nothing," muttered Daisy. "Smart-mouth pickaninnies and burnt fingers."

"What brings you to town, Alvin?" asked Martin. "And how come you got that baby buck with you? Or did you buy him off Old Peg Guester?''

Alvin just munched on his cracker. It was a mistake to punish Daisy for what he said before, and a worse mistake to do it again. Wasn't it trying to punish folks that brought the Unmaker down on him last summer? No, Alvin was working on curbing his temper, so he said nothing. Just broke off pieces of the cracker with his mouth.

"That boy ain't for sale," said Daisy. "Everybody knows it. Why, she's even trying to educate him, I hear."

"I'm educating my dog, too," said Martin. "You think that boy's learnt him how to beg or point game or anything useful?''

"But you got yourself the advantage there, Marty," said Daisy. "A dog's got him enough brains to know he's a dog, so he don't try to learn how to read. But you get one of these hairless monkeys, they get to thinking they're people, you know what I mean?''

Alvin got up and walked to the counter. Vanderwoort was coming back now, arms full of stuff. Arthur was tagging along behind.

"Come on behind the counter with me, Al," said Vanderwoort. "Best if you pick out the cloth for Arthur's shirt.''

"I don't know a thing about cloth," said Alvin.

"Well, I know about cloth but I don't know about what Old Peg Guester likes, and if she ain't happy with what you come home with, I'd rather it be your fault than mine.''

Alvin hitched his butt up onto the counter and swung his legs over. Vanderwoort led him back and they spent a few minutes picking out a plaid flannel that looked suitable enough and might also be tough enough to make patches on old trousers out of the leftover scraps. When they came back, Arthur Stuart was over by the fire with Daisy and Martin.

"Spell 'sassafras,' '' said Daisy.

"Sassafras," said Arthur Stuart, doing Miss Larner's voice as perfect as ever. "S-A-S-S-A-F-R-A-S.''

"Was he right?'' asked Martin.

"Beats hell out of me.''

"Now don't be using words like that around a child," said Vanderwoort.

"Oh, never you mind," said Martin. "He's our pet pickaninny. We won't do him no harm.''

"I'm not a pickaninny," said Arthur Stuart. "I'm a mixup boy.''

"Well, ain't that the truth!'' Daisy's voice went so loud and high that his voice cracked.

Alvin was just about fed up with them. He spoke real soft, so only

Vanderwoort could hear him. "One more whoop and I'll fill that boy's ears with snow."

"Now don't get riled," said Vanderwoort. "They're harmless enough."

"That's why I won't kill him." But Alvin was smiling, and so was Vanderwoort. Daisy and Martin were just playing, and since Arthur Stuart was enjoying it, why not?

Martin picked something off a shelf and brought it over to Vanderwoort. "What's this word?" he asked.

"Eucalyptus," said Vanderwoort.

"Spell 'eucalipidus,' mixup boy."

"Eucalyptus," said Arthur. "E-U-C-A-L-Y-P-T-U-S."

"Listen to that!" cried Daisy. "That teacher lady won't give time of day to us, but here we got her own voice spelling whatever we say."

"Spell 'bosoms,' " said Martin.

"Now that's going too far," said Vanderwoort. "He's just a boy."

"I just wanted to hear the teacher lady's voice saying it," said Martin.

"I know what you wanted, but that's behind-the-barn talk, not in my general store."

The door opened and, after a blast of cold wind, Mock Berry came in, looking tired and half-froze, which of course he was.

The boys took no notice. "Behind the barn don't got a stove," said Daisy.

"Then keep that in mind when you decide how to talk," said Vanderwoort.

Alvin watched how Mock Berry took sidelong glances at the stove, but made no move to go over there. No man in his right mind would choose not to go to the stove on a day like this—but Mock Berry knew there was worse things than being cold. So instead he just walked up to the counter.

Vanderwoort must've known he was there, but for a while he just kept on watching Martin and Daisy play spelling games with Arthur Stuart, paying no mind to Mock Berry.

"Suskwahenny," said Daisy.

"S-U-S-K-W-A-H-E-N-N-Y," said Arthur.

"I bet that boy could win any spelling bee he ever entered," said Vanderwoort.

"You got a customer," said Alvin.

Vanderwoort turned real slow and looked at Mock Berry without expression. Then, still moving slow, he walked over and stood in front of Mock without a word.

"Just need me two pounds of flour and twelve feet of that half-inch rope," said Mock.

"Hear that?" said Daisy. "He's a-fixing to powder his face white and then hang himself, I'll bet."

"Spell 'suicide,' boy," said Martin.

"S-U-I-C-I-D-E," said Arthur Stuart.

"No credit," said Vanderwoort.

Mock laid down some coins on the counter. Vanderwoort looked at them a minute. "Six feet of rope."

Mock just stood there.

Vanderwoort just stood there.

Alvin knew it was more than enough money for what Mock wanted to buy. He couldn't hardly believe Vanderwoort was raising his price for a man about as poor but hard-working as any in town. In fact, Alvin began to understand a little about why Mock stayed so poor. Now, Alvin knew there wasn't much he could do about it—but he could at least do what Horace Guester had once done for him with his master Makepeace—make Vanderwoort put things out in the open and stop pretending he wasn't being as unfair as he was being. So Alvin laid down the paper Vanderwoort had just written out for him. "I'm sorry to hear there's no credit," Alvin said. "I'll go fetch the money from Goody Guester."

Vanderwoort looked at Alvin. Now he could either make Alvin go fetch the money or say right out that there was credit for the *Guesters*, just not for Mock Berry.

Of course he chose another course. Without a word he went into the back and weighed out the flour. Then he measured out twelve feet of half-inch rope. Vanderwoort was known for giving honest measure. But then, he was also known for giving a fair price, which is why it took Alvin aback to see him do otherwise with Mock Berry.

Mock took his rope and his flour and started out.

"You got change," said Vanderwoort.

Mock turned around, looking surprised though he tried not to. He came back and watched as Vanderwoort counted out a dime and three pennies onto the counter. Then, hesitating a moment, Mock scooped them off the counter and dropped them into his pocket. "Thank you sir," he said. Then he went back out into the cold.

Vanderwoort turned to Alvin, looking angry or maybe just resentful. "I can't give credit to everybody."

Now, Alvin could've said something about at least he could give the same price to Blacks as Whites, but he didn't want to make an enemy out of Mr. Vanderwoort, who was after all a mostly good man. So Alvin grinned real friendly and said, "Oh, I know you can't. Them Berrys, they're almost as poor as me."

Vanderwoort relaxed, which meant it was Alvin's good opinion he wanted more than to get even for Alvin embarrassing him. "You got to understand, Alvin, it ain't good for trade if they come in here all the time. Nobody minds that mixup boy of yours—they're cute when they're little—but it makes folks stay away if they think they might run into one of them here."

"I always knowed Mock Berry to keep his word," said Alvin. "And nobody ever said he stole or slacked or any such thing."

"No, nobody ever told such a tale on him."

"I'm glad to know you count us both among your customers," said Alvin.

"Well, lookit here, Daisy," said Martin. "I think *Prentice* Alvin's gone and turned preacher on us. Spell 'reverend,' boy."

"R-E-V-E-R-E-N-D."

Vanderwoort saw things maybe turning ugly, so of course he tried to change the subject. "Like I said, Alvin, that mixup boy's bound to be the best speller in the county, don't you think? What I want to know is, why don't he go on and get into the county spelling bee next week? I think he'd bring Hatrack River the championship. He might even get the *state* championship, if you want my opinion."

"Spell 'championship,' " said Daisy.

"Miss Larner never said me that word," said Arthur Stuart.

"Well figure it out," said Alvin.

"C-H-A-M-P," said Arthur. "E-U-N-S-H-I-P."

"Sounds right to me," said Daisy.

"Shows what *you* know," said Martin.

"Can you do better?" asked Vanderwoort.

"*I'm* not going to be in the county spelling bee," said Martin.

"What's a spelling bee?" asked Arthur Stuart.

"Time to go," said Alvin, for he knew full well that Arthur Stuart wasn't a regular admitted student in the Hatrack River Grammar School, and so it was a sure thing he wouldn't be in no spelling bee. "Oh, Mr. Vanderwoort, I owe you for two crackers I ate."

"I don't charge my friends for a couple of crackers," said Vander-woort.

"I'm proud to know you count me one of your friends," said Alvin. Alvin meant it, too—it took a good man to get caught out doing something wrong, and then turn around and treat the one that caught him as a friend.

Alvin wound Arthur Stuart back into his scarves, and then wrapped himself up again, and plunged back into the snow, this time carrying all that he bought from Vanderwoort in a burlap sack. He tucked the sack under the seat of the sleigh so it wouldn't get snowed on. Then he lifted Arthur Stuart into place and climbed up after. The horses looked happy enough to get moving again—they only got colder and colder, standing in the snow.

On the way back to the roadhouse they found Mock Berry on the road and took him on home. Not a word did he say about what happened in the store, but Alvin knew it wasn't cause he didn't appreciate it. He figured Mock Berry was plain ashamed of the fact that it took an eighteen-year-old prentice boy to get him honest measure and fair price in Vanderwoort's general store—only cause the boy was White. Not the kind of thing a man loves to talk about.

"Give a howdy to Goody Berry," said Alvin, as Mock hopped off the sleigh up the lane from his house.

"I'll say you said so," said Mock. "And thanks for the ride." In six steps he was clean gone in the blowing snow. The storm was getting worse and worse.

Once everything was dropped off at the roadhouse, it was near time for Alvin's and Arthur's schooling at Miss Larner's house, so they headed on down there and threw snowballs at each other all the way. Alvin stopped in at the forge to give the delivery book to Makepeace. But Makepeace must've laid off early cause he wasn't there; Alvin tucked the book onto the shelf by the door, where Makepeace would know to look for it. Then he and Arthur went back to snowballs till Miss Larner came back.

Dr. Whitley Physicker drove her in his covered sleigh and walked her right up to her door. When he took note of Alvin and Arthur waiting around, he looked a bit annoyed. "Don't you boys think Miss Larner shouldn't have to do any more teaching on a day like this?"

Miss Larner laid a hand on Dr. Physicker's arm. "Thank you for bringing me home, Dr. Physicker," she said.

"I wish you'd call me Whitley."

"You're kind to me, Dr. Physicker, but I think your honored title suits me best. As for these pupils of mine, it's in bad weather that I do my best teaching, I've found, for they aren't wishing to be at the swimming hole."

"Not me!" shouted Arthur Stuart. "How do you spell 'championship'?"

"C-H-A-M-P-I-O-N-S-H-I-P," said Miss Larner. "Wherever did you hear that word?"

"C-H-A-M-P-I-O-N-S-H-I-P," said Arthur Stuart—in Miss Larner's voice.

"That boy is certainly remarkable," said Physicker. "A mockingbird, I'd say."

"A mockingbird copies the song," said Miss Larner, "but makes no sense of it. Arthur Stuart may speak back the spellings in my voice, but he truly knows the word and can read it or write it whenever he wishes."

"I'm not a mockingbird," said Arthur Stuart. "I'm a spelling bee championship."

Dr. Physicker and Miss Larner exchanged a look that plainly meant more than Alvin could understand just from watching.

"Very well," said Dr. Physicker. "Since I did in fact enroll him as a special student—at your insistence—he *can* compete in the county spelling bee. But don't expect to take him any farther, Miss Larner!"

"Your reasons were all excellent, Dr. Physicker, and so I agree. But *my* reasons—"

"Your reasons were overwhelming, Miss Larner. And I can't help but relish in advance the consternation of the people who fought to keep him out of school, when they watch him do as well as children twice his age."

"Consternation, Arthur Stuart," said Miss Larner.

"Consternation," said Arthur. "C-O-N-S-T-E-R-N-A-T-I-O-N."

"Good evening, Dr. Physicker. Come inside, boys. Time for school."

Arthur Stuart won the county spelling bee, with the word "celebratory." Then Miss Larner immediately withdrew him from further competition; another child would take his place at the state competition. As a result there was little note taken, except among the locals. Along with a brief notice in the Hatrack River newspaper.

Sheriff Pauley Wiseman folded up that page of the newspaper with a short note and put them in an envelope addressed to Reverend Philadelphia Thrower, The Property Rights Crusade, 44 Harrison Street, Carthage City, Wobbish. It took two weeks for that newspaper page to be spread open on Thrower's desk, along with the note, which said simply:

> *Boy turned up here summer 1811, only a few weeks old best guess. Lives in Horace Guester's roadhouse, Hatrack River. Adoption don't hold water I reckon if the boy's a runaway.*

No signature—but Thrower was used to that, though he didn't understand it. Why should people try to conceal their identity when they were taking part in works of righteousness? He wrote his own letter and sent it south.

A month later, Cavil Planter read Thrower's letter to a couple of Finders. Then he handed them the cachets he'd saved all these years, those belonging to Hagar and her stole-away Ishmael-child. "We'll be back before summer," said the black-haired Finder. "If he's yourn, we'll have him."

"Then you'll have earned your fee and a fine bonus as well," said Cavil Planter.

"Don't need no bonus," said the white-haired Finder. "Fee and costs is plenty."

"Well, then, as you wish," said Cavil. "I know God will bless your journey."

18

Manacles

It was early spring, a couple of months before Alvin's nineteenth birthday, when Makepeace Smith come to him and said, "About time you start working on a journeyman piece, Al, don't you think?"

The words sang like redbird song in Alvin's ears, so he couldn't hardly speak back except to nod.

"Well, what do you think you'll make?" asked the master.

"I been thinking maybe a plow," said Alvin.

"That's a lot of iron. Takes a perfect mold, and no easy one, neither. You're asking me to put a good bit of iron at risk, boy."

"If I fail, you can always melt it back."

Since they both knew that Alvin had about as much chance of failing as he did of flying, this was pretty much empty talk—just the last rags of Makepeace's old pretense about how Alvin wasn't much good at smithing.

"Reckon so," said Makepiece. "You just do your best, boy. Hard but not too brittle. Heavy enough to bite deep, but light enough to pull. Sharp enough to cut the earth, and strong enough to cast all stones aside."

"Yes sir." Alvin had memorized the rules of the tools back when he was twelve years old.

There were some other rules that Alvin meant to follow. He had to prove to himself that he was a good smith, and not just a half-baked Maker, which meant that he'd use none of his knack, only the skills that any smith has—a good eye, knowledge of the black metal, the vigor of his arms and the skill of his hands.

Working on his journeyman piece meant he had no other duties till it was done. He started from scratch on this one, as a good journeyman always does. No common clay for the mold—he went upriver on the Hatrack to the best white clay, so the face of the mold would be pure and smooth and hold its shape. Making a mold meant seeing things all inside-out, but Alvin had a good mind for shapes. He patted and stroked the clay into place on the wooden frame, all the time seeing how the different pieces of the mold would give the cooling iron its plow shape. Then he baked the mold dry and hard, ready to receive the iron.

For the metal, he took from the pile of scrap iron and then carefully filed the iron clean, getting rid of all dirt and rust. He scoured the crucible, too. Only then was he ready to melt and cast. He hotted up the coal fire, running the bellows himself, raising and lowering the bellows handle just like he done when he was a new prentice. At last the iron was white in the crucible—and the fire so hot he could scarce bear to come near it. But he came near it anyway, tongs in hand, and hoisted the crucible from the fire, then carried it to the mold and poured. The iron sparked and dazzled, but the mold held true, no buckling or breaking in the heat.

Set the crucible back in the fire. Push the other parts of the mold into place. Gently, evenly, getting no splash. He had judged the amount of liquid iron just right—when the last part of the form slipped into place, just a bit of iron squeezed out evenly all around the edges, showing there was just enough, and scarce any waste.

And it was done. Nothing for it but to wait for the iron to cool and harden. Tomorrow he'd know what he'd wrought.

Tomorrow Makepeace Smith would see his plow and call him a man—a journeyman, free to practice at any forge, though not yet ready to take on his own prentices. But to Alvin—well, he'd reached that point of readiness years ago. Makepeace would have only a few weeks short of the full seven years of Alvin's service—that's what he'd been waiting for, not for this plow.

No, Alvin's real journeyman work was yet to come. After Makepeace declared the plow good enough, then Alvin had yet another work to perform.

"I'm going to turn it gold," said Alvin.

Miss Larner raised an eyebrow. "And what then? What will you tell people about a golden plow? That you found it somewhere? That you happened to have some gold lying about, and thought—this is just enough to make a plow?"

"You're the one what told me a Maker was the one who could turn iron to gold."

"Yes, but that doesn't mean it's wise to do it." Miss Larner walked out of the hot forge into the stagnant air of late afternoon. It was cooler, but not much—the first hot night of spring.

"More than gold," said Alvin. "Or at least not normal gold."

"Regular gold isn't good enough for you?"

"Gold is dead. Like iron."

"It isn't dead. It's simply—earth without fire. It never *was* alive, so it can't be dead."

"You're the one who told me that if I can imagine it, then maybe I can make it come to be."

"And you can imagine living gold?"

"A plow that cuts the earth with no ox to draw it."

She said nothing, but her eyes sparkled.

"If I could make such a thing, Miss Larner, would you consider as how I'd graduated from your school of Makers?"

"I'd say you were no longer a prentice Maker."

"Just what I thought, Miss Larner. A journeyman blacksmith and a journeyman Maker, both, if I can do it."

"And can you?"

Alvin nodded, then shrugged. "I think so. It's what you said about atoms, back in January."

"I thought you gave up on that."

"No ma'am. I just kept thinking—what is it you can't cut into smaller pieces? And then I thought—why, if it's got any size at all, it can be cut. So an atom, it's nothing more than just a place, one exact place, with no width at all."

"Euclid's geometric point."

"Well, yes ma'am, except that you said his geometry was all imaginary, and this is real."

"But if it has no size, Alvin—"

"That's what I thought—if it's got no size, then it's nothing. But it *isn't* nothing. It's a place. Only then I thought, it *isn't* a place—it just *has* a place. If you see the difference. An atom can be in one place, one pure geometric point like you said, but then it can *move*. It can be somewhere else. So, you see, it not only has place, it has a past and a future. Yesterday it was there, today it's here, and tomorrow over yonder."

"But it isn't *anything*, Alvin."

"No, I know that, it isn't *anything*. But it ain't *nothing*, neither."

"Isn't. Either."

"I know all that grammar, Miss Larner, but I'm not thinking about that right now."

"You won't have good grammar unless you use it even when you're not thinking about it. But never mind."

"See, I start thinking, if this atom's got no size, how can anybody tell where it is? It's not giving off any light, because it's got no fire in it to give off. So here's what I come up with: Just suppose this atom's got no *size*, but it's still got some kind of mind. Some kind of tiny little wit, just enough to know where it is. And the only power it has is to move somewhere else, and know where it is *then*."

"How could that be, a memory in something that doesn't exist?"

"Just suppose it! Say you got thousands of them just lying around, just going any which way. How can any of them tell where they are? Since all the others are moving any which way, nothing around it stays the same. But then suppose somebody comes along—and I'm thinking about God here—somebody who can show them a pattern. Show them some way to set still. Like he says—you, there, you're the center, and all the rest of you, you just stay the same distance away from him all the time. Then what have you got?"

Miss Larner thought for a moment. "A hollow sphere. A ball. But still composed of nothing, Alvin."

"But don't you see? That's why I knew that this was true. I mean, if there's one thing I know from doodlebugging, it's that everything's mostly empty. That anvil, it looks solid, don't it? But I tell you it's mostly empty. Just little bits of ironstuff, hanging a certain distance from each other, all patterned there. But most of the anvil is the empty space between. Don't you see? Those bits are acting just like the atoms I'm talking about. So let's say the anvil is like a mountain, only when you get real close you see it's made of gravel. And then when you pick up the gravel, it crumbles in your hand, and you see it's made of dust. And if you could pick up a single fleck of dust you'd see that it was just like the mountain, made of even tinier gravel all over again."

"You're saying that what we see as solid objects are really nothing but illusion. Little nothings making tiny spheres that are put together to make your bits, and pieces made from bits, and the anvil made from pieces—"

"Only there's a lot more steps between, I reckon. Don't you see, this explains everything? Why it is that all I have to do is imagine a new shape or a new pattern or a new order, and show it in my mind, and if I think it clear and strong enough, and command the bits to change, why—they do. Because they're *alive*. They may be small and none too bright, but if I show them clear enough, they can do it."

"This is too strange for me, Alvin. To think that everything is really nothing."

"No, Miss Larner, you're missing the point. The point is that everything is *alive*. That everything is made out of living atoms, all obeying the commands that God gave them. And just following those commands, why, some of them get turned into light and heat, and some of them become iron, and some water, and some air, and some of them our own skin and bones. All those things are real—and so those atoms are real."

"Alvin, I told you about atoms because they were an interesting theory. The best thinkers of our time believe there are no such things."

"Begging your pardon, Miss Larner, but the best thinkers never saw the things I saw, so they don't know diddly. I'm telling you that this is the only idea I can think of that explains it all—what I see and what I do."

"But where did these atoms come from?"

"They don't come from anywhere. Or rather, maybe they come from everywhere. Maybe these atoms, they're just there. Always been there, always will be there. You can't cut them up. They can't die. You can't make them and you can't break them. They're forever."

"Then God didn't create the world."

"Of course he did. The atoms were nothing, just places that didn't even know where they were. It's God who put them all into places so he'd know where they were, and so *they'd* know where they were—and everything in the whole universe is made out of them."

Miss Larner thought about it for the longest time. Alvin stood there watching her, waiting. He knew it was true, or at least truer than anything else he'd ever heard of or thought of. Unless she could think of something wrong with it. So many times this year she'd done that, point out something he forgot, some reason why his idea wouldn't work. So he waited for her to come up with something. Something wrong.

Maybe she would've. Only while she was standing there outside the forge, thinking, they heard the sound of horses cantering up the road from town. Of course they looked to see who was coming in such a rush.

It was Sheriff Pauley Wiseman and two men that Alvin never saw before. Behind them was Dr. Physicker's carriage, with old Po Doggly driving. And they didn't just pass by. They stopped right there at the curve by the forge.

"Miss Larner," said Pauley Wiseman. "Arthur Stuart around here?"

"Why do you ask?" said Miss Larner. "Who are these men?"

"He's here," said one of the men. The white-haired one. He held up a tiny box between his thumb and forefinger. Both the strangers looked at it, then looked up the hill toward the springhouse. "In there," said the white-haired man.

"You need any more proof than that?" asked Pauley Wiseman. He was talking to Dr. Physicker, who was now out of his carriage and standing there looking furious and helpless and altogether terrible.

"Finders," whispered Miss Larner.

"That's us," said the white-haired one. "You got a runaway slave up there, Ma'am."

"He is not," she said. "He is a pupil of mine, legally adopted by Horace and Margaret Guester—"

"We got a letter from his owner, giving his birthdate, and we got his cachet here, and he's the very one. We're sworn and certified, Ma'am. What we Find is found. That's the law, and if you interfere, you're obstructing." The man spoke real nice and quiet and polite.

"Don't worry, Miss Larner," said Dr. Physicker. "I already have a writ from the mayor, and that'll hold him till the judge gets back to-morrow."

"Hold him in *jail*, of course," said Pauley Wiseman. "Wouldn't want anybody to try to run off with him, now, would we?"

"Wouldn't do much good if they tried," said the white-haired Finder. "We'd just follow. And then we'll probably shoot them dead, seeing how they was thieves escaping with stolen property."

"You haven't even told the Guesters, have you!" said Miss Larner.

"How could I?" said Dr. Physicker. "I had to stay with *them*, to make sure they didn't just take him."

"We obey the law," said the white-haired Finder.

"There he is," said the black-haired Finder.

Arthur Stuart stood in the open door of the springhouse.

"Just stay where you are, boy!" shouted Pauley Wiseman. "If you move a muscle I'll whip you to jelly!"

"You don't have to threaten him," said Miss Larner, but there wasn't nobody to listen, since they were all running up the hill.

"Don't hurt him!" cried Dr. Physicker.

"If he don't run, he won't get hurt," said the white-haired Finder.

"Alvin," said Miss Larner. "Don't do it."

"They ain't taking Arthur Stuart."

"Don't use your power like that. Not to hurt someone."

"I tell you—"

"Think, Alvin. We have until tomorrow. Maybe the judge—"

"Putting him in jail!"

"If anything happens to these Finders, then the nationals will be in it, to enforce the Fugitive Slave Treaty. Do you understand me? It's not a local crime like murder. You'd be taken off to Appalachee to be tried."

"I can't do *nothing*."

"Run and tell the Guesters."

Alvin waited just a moment. If it was up to him, he'd burn their hands right off before he let them take Arthur. But already the boy was between them, their fingers digging into Arthur's arms. Miss Larner was right. What they needed was a way to win Arthur's freedom for sure, not some stupid blunder that would end up making things worse.

Alvin ran for the Guesters' house. It surprised him how they took it— like they'd been expecting it all the time for the last seven years. Old Peg and Horace just looked at each other, and without a word Old Peg started in packing—her clothes *and* Arthur Stuart's.

"What's she packing *her* things for?" asked Alvin.

Horace smiled, a real tight smile. "She ain't going to let Arthur spend a night in jail alone. So she'll have them lock her up right alongside him."

It made sense—but it was strange to think of people like Arthur Stuart and Old Peg Guester in jail.

"What are *you* going to do?" asked Alvin.

"Load my guns," said Horace. "And when they're gone, I'll follow."

Alvin told him what Miss Larner had said about the nationals coming if somebody laid hand on a Finder.

"What's the worst they can do to me? Hang me. I tell you, I'd rather be hanged than live in this house a single day if they take Arthur Stuart away and I done nothing to stop them. And I can do it, Alvin. Hell, boy, I must've saved fifty runaway slaves in my time. Po Doggly and me, we used to pick them up this side of the river and send them on to safety in Canada. Did it all the time."

Alvin wasn't a bit surprised to hear of Horace Guester being an Emancipationist—and not a talker, neither.

"I'm telling you this, Alvin, cause I need your help. I'm just one man and there's two of them. I got no one I can trust—Po Doggly ain't gone with me on something like this in a week of Christmases, and I don't know where he stands no more. But you—I know you can keep a secret, and I know you love Arthur Stuart near as much as my wife does."

The way he said it gave Alvin pause. "Don't *you* love him, sir?"

Horace looked at Alvin like he was crazy. "They ain't taking a mixup boy right out from under my roof, Al."

Goody Guester come downstairs then, with two bundles in homespun bags under her arms. "Take me into town, Horace Guester."

They heard the horses riding by on the road outside.

"That's probably them," said Alvin.

"Don't worry, Peg," said Horace.

"Don't *worry*?" Old Peg turned on him in fury. "Only two things are likely to happen out of this, Horace. Either I lose my son to slavery in the South, or my fool husband gets himself probably killed trying to rescue him. Of course I won't worry." Then she burst into tears and hugged Horace so tight it near broke Alvin's heart to see it.

It was Alvin drove Goody Guester into town on the roadhouse wagon. He was standing there when she finally wore down Pauley Wiseman so he'd let her spend the night in the cell—though he made her take a terrible oath about not trying to sneak Arthur Stuart out of jail before he'd do it.

As he led the way to the jail cell, Pauley Wiseman said, "You shouldn't fret none, Goody Guester. His master's no doubt a good man. Folks here got the wrong idea of slavery, I reckon."

She whirled on him. "Then you'll go in his place, Pauley? Seeing how it's so fine?"

"Me?" He was no more than amused at the idea. "I'm *White*, Goody Guester. Slavery ain't my natural state."

Alvin made the keys slide right out of Pauley's fingers.

"I'm sure getting clumsy," said Pauley Wiseman.

Goody Guester's foot just naturally ended up right on top of the key ring.

"Just lift up your foot, Goody Guester," said the sheriff, "or I'll charge you with aiding and abetting, not to mention resisting."

She moved her foot. The sheriff opened the door. Old Peg stepped through and gathered Arthur Stuart into her arms. Alvin watched as Pauley Wiseman closed and locked the door behind them. Then he went on home.

Alvin broke open the mold and rubbed away the clay that still clung to the face of the plow. The iron was smooth and hard, as good a plow as Alvin ever saw cast till then. He searched inside it and found no flaws, not big enough to mar the plow, anyway. He filed and rubbed, rubbed and filed till it was smooth, the blade sharp as if he meant to use it in a butcher shop instead of some field somewhere. He sit it on top of the workbench. Then he sat there waiting while the sun rose and the rest of the world came awake.

In due time Makepeace came down from the house and looked at the plow. But Alvin didn't see him, being asleep. Makepeace woke him up enough to get him to walk back up to the house.

"Poor boy," said Gertie. "I bet he never even went to sleep last night. I bet he went on down and worked on that fool plow all night."

"Plow looks fair."

"Plow looks perfect, I'll bet, knowing Alvin."

Makepeace grimaced. "What do you know about ironwork?"

"I know Alvin and I know you."

"Strange boy. Ain't it the truth though? He does his best work when he stays up all night." Makepeace even had some affection in his voice, saying that. But Alvin was asleep in his bed by then and didn't hear.

"Sets such store by that mixup child," said Gertie. "No wonder he couldn't sleep."

"Sleeping now," said Makepeace.

"Imagine sending Arthur Stuart into slavery at his age."

"Law's the law," said Makepeace. "Can't say I like it, but a fellow has to live by the law or what then?"

"You and the law," said Gertie. "I'm glad we don't live on the other side of the Hio, Makepeace, or I swear you'd be wanting slaves instead of prentices—if you know the difference."

That was as pure a declaration of war as they ever gave each other, and they were all set for one of their rip-snorting knock-about break-dish fights, only Alvin was snoring up in the loft and Gertie and Makepeace just glared at each other and let this one go. Since all their quarrels came out the same, with all the same cruel things said and all the same hurts and harms done, it was like they just got tired and said, Pretend I just said all the things you hate worst in all the world to hear, and I'll pretend you said the things I hate worst back to me, and then let be.

Alvin didn't sleep all that long, nor all too well, neither. Fear and anger and eagerness all played through his body till he could hardly hold still, let alone keep his brain drifting with the currents of his dreams. He woke up dreaming of a black plow turned to gold. He woke up dreaming of Arthur Stuart being whipped. He woke up again thinking of aiming a gun at one of them Finders and pulling the trigger. He woke up again thinking of aiming at a Finder and *not* pulling the trigger, and then watching them go away dragging Arthur after them, him screaming all the time, Alvin, where are you! Alvin, don't let them take me.

"Wake up or hush up!" shouted Gertie. "You're scaring the children."

Alvin opened his eyes and leaned over the edge of the loft. "Your children ain't even here."

"Then you're scaring *me*. I don't know what you was dreaming, boy, but I hope that dream never comes even to my worst enemy—which happens to be my husband this morning, if you want to know the truth."

Her mentioning Makepeace made Alvin alert, yes sir. He pulled on his trousers, wondering when and how he got up to this loft and who pulled his pants and boots off. In just that little amount of time, Gertie somehow got food on the table—cornbread and cheese and a dollop of molasses. "I don't have time to eat, Ma'am," said Alvin. "I'm sorry, but I got to—"

"You got time."

"No Ma'am, I'm sorry—"

"Take the bread, then, you plain fool. You plan to work all day with an empty belly? After only a morning's sleep? Why, it ain't even noon yet."

So he was chewing on bread when he come down the hill to the forge. There was Dr. Physicker's carriage again, and the Finders' horses. For a second Alvin thought—they come here cause Arthur Stuart got away somehow, and the Finders lost him, and—

No. They had Arthur Stuart with them.

"Good morning, Alvin," said Makepeace. He turned to the other men. "I must be about the softest master I ever heard of, letting my prentice boy sleep till near noon."

Alvin didn't even notice how Makepeace was criticizing him and calling him a prentice *boy* when his journeyman piece stood there finished on the workbench. He just squatted down in front of Arthur Stuart and looked him in the eyes.

"Stand back now," said the white-haired Finder.

Alvin didn't hardly notice him. He wasn't really seeing Arthur Stuart, not with his eyes, anyhow. He was searching his body for some sign of harm. None. Not yet anyway. Just the fear in the boy.

"You haven't told us yet," said Pauley Wiseman. "Will you make them or not?"

Makepeace coughed. "Gentlemen, I once made a pair of manacles, back in New England. For a man convicted of treason, being shipped back to England in irons. I hope I never make a manacle for a seven-year-old boy who done no harm to a living soul, a boy who played around my forge and—"

"Makepeace," said Pauley Wiseman. "I told them that if you made the manacles, they wouldn't have to use this."

Wiseman held up the heavy iron-and-wood collar that he'd left leaning against his leg.

"It's the law," said the white-haired Finder. "We bring runaway slaves back home in that collar, to show the others what happens. But him being just a boy, and seeing how it was his mama what run away and not him, we agreed to manacles. But it don't make no difference to me. We get paid either way.''

"You and your damned Fugitive Slave Treaty!'' cried Makepeace. "You use that law to make slavers out of us, too.''

"I'll make them,'' said Alvin.

Makepeace looked at him in horror. "You!''

"Better than that collar,'' said Alvin. What he didn't say was, I don't intend for Arthur Stuart to wear those manacles a minute longer than tonight. He looked at Arthur Stuart. "I'll make you some manacles as don't hurt much, Arthur Stuart.''

"Wisely done,'' said Pauley Wiseman.

"Good to see somebody with sense here,'' said the white-haired Finder.

Alvin looked at him and tried to hold all his hatred in. He couldn't quite do it. So his spittle ended up spattering the dust at the Finder's feet.

The black-haired Finder looked ready to throw a punch at him for that, and Alvin wouldn't't've minded a bit to grapple with him and maybe rub his face in the dirt a minute or two. But Pauley Wiseman jumped right between them and he had sense enough to do his talking to the black-haired Finder, and not to Alvin. "You got to be a blame fool, setting to rassle with a blacksmith. Look at his arms.''

"I could take him,'' said the Finder.

"You folks got to understand,'' said the white-haired Finder. "It's our knack. We can no more help being Finders than—''

"There's some knacks,'' said Makepeace, "where it'd be better to die at birth than grow up and use it.'' He turned to Alvin. "I don't want you using my forge for this.''

"Don't make a nuisance of yourself, Makepeace,'' said Pauley Wiseman.

"Please,'' said Dr. Physicker. "You're doing the boy more harm than good.''

Makepeace backed off, but none too graciously.

"Give me your hands, Arthur Stuart,'' Alvin said.

Alvin made a show of measuring Arthur's wrists with a string. Truth was, he could see the measure of him in his mind, every inch of him, and he'd shape the iron to fit smooth and perfect, with rounded edges and no more weight than needed. Arthur wouldn't feel no pain from these manacles. Not with his body, anyhow.

They all stood and watched Alvin work. It was the smoothest, purest job they'd ever see. Alvin used his knack this time, but not so it'd show. He hammered and bent the scrap iron, cutting it exactly right. The two halves of each manacle fit snug, so they wouldn't shift and pinch the skin. And all the time he was thinking how Arthur used to pump the bellows for him, or just stand there and talk to him while he worked. Never again. Even after they saved him tonight, they'd have to take him to Canada or hide him somehow—as if you could hide from a Finder.

"Good work," said the white-haired Finder. "I never saw me a better blacksmith."

Makepeace piped up from the dark corner of the forge. "You should be proud of yourself, Alvin. Why, let's make those manacles your journeyman piece, all right?"

Alvin turned and faced him. "My journeyman piece is that plow setting on the workbench, Makepeace."

It was the first time Alvin ever called his master by his first name. It was as clear as Alvin could let him know that the days of Makepeace talking to him like that were over now.

Makepeace didn't want to understand him. "Watch how you talk to me, boy! Your journeyman piece is what I say it is, and—"

"Come on, boy, let's get these on you." The white-haired Finder wasn't interested in Makepeace's talk, it seemed.

"Not yet," said Alvin.

"They're ready," said the Finder.

"Too hot," said Alvin.

"Well dip them in that bucket there and cool them off."

"If I do that, they'll change shape just a little, and then they'll cut the boy's arms so they bleed."

The black-haired Finder rolled his eyes. What did he care about a little blood from a mixup boy?

But the white-haired Finder knew that nobody'd stand for it if he didn't wait. "No hurry," he said. "Can't take too long."

They sat around waiting without a word. Then Pauley started in talking about nothing, and so did the Finders, and even Dr. Physicker, just jawing away like as if the Finders were any old visitors. Maybe they thought they were making the Finders feel more kindly so they wouldn't take it out on the boy once they had him across the river. Alvin had to figure that so he wouldn't hate them.

Besides, an idea was growing in his mind. It wasn't enough to get Arthur Stuart away tonight—what if Alvin could make it so even the Finders couldn't find him again?

"What's in that cachet you Finders use?" he asked.

"Don't you wish you knew," said the black-haired Finder.

"It's no secret," said the white-haired Finder. "Every slaveowner makes up a box like this for each slave, soon as he's bought or born.

Scrapings from his skin, hair from his head, a drop of blood, things like that. Parts of his own flesh.''

"You get his scent from that?''

"Oh, it ain't a scent. We ain't *bloodhounds*, Mr. Smith.''

Alvin knew that calling him Mr. Smith was pure flattery. He smiled a little, pretending that it pleased him.

"Well then how does it help?''

"Well, it's our *knack*," said the white-haired Finder. "Who knows how it works? We just look at it, and we—it's like we see the shape of the person we're looking for.''

"It ain't like that," said the black-haired Finder.

"Well that's how it is for *me*."

"I just know where he is. Like I can see his soul. If I'm close enough, anyway. Glowing like a fire, the soul of the slave I'm searching for.'' The black-haired Finder grinned. "I can see from a long way off.''

"Can you show me?" asked Alvin.

"Nothing to see," said the white-haired Finder.

"I'll show you, boy," said the black-haired Finder. "I'll turn my back and y'all move that boy around in the forge. I'll point to him over my shoulder, perfect all the time.''

"Come on now," said the white-haired Finder.

"We got nothing to do anyway till the iron cools. Give me the cachet.''

The black-haired Finder did what he bragged—pointed at Arthur Stuart the whole time. But Alvin hardly saw that. He was busy watching from the inside of that Finder, trying to understand what he was doing, what he was *seeing*, and what it had to do with the cachet. He couldn't see how seven-year-old dried-up bits of Arthur Stuart's newborn body could show them where he was *now*.

Then he remembered that for a moment right at first the Finder hadn't pointed at all. His finger had wandered a little, and only after just that pause had he started pointing right at Arthur Stuart. Like as if he'd been trying to sort out which of the people behind him in the smithy was Arthur. The cachet wasn't for Finding—it was for recognizing. The Finders saw everybody, but they couldn't tell who was who without a cachet.

So what they were seeing wasn't Arthur's mind, or Arthur's soul. They were just seeing a body, like every other body unless they could sort it out. And what they were sorting was plain enough to Alvin— hadn't he healed enough people in his life to know that people were pretty much the same, except for some bits at the center of each living piece of their flesh? Those bits were different for every single person, yet the same in every part of that person's flesh. Like it was God's way of naming them right in their flesh. Or maybe it was the mark of the beast, like in the book of Revelation. Didn't matter. Alvin knew that the only thing in that cachet that was the same as Arthur Stuart's body was that signature that lived in every part of his body, even the dead and cast-off parts in the cachet.

I can change those bits, thought Alvin. Surely I can change them, change them in every part of his body. Like turning iron into gold. Like turning water into wine. And then their cachet wouldn't work at all. Wouldn't help them at all. They could search for Arthur Stuart all they liked, but as long as they didn't actually see his face and recognize him the regular way, they'd never find him.

Best of all, they wouldn't even realize what happened. They'd still have the cachet, same as ever, and they'd know it hadn't been changed a bit because Alvin wouldn't change it. But they could search the whole world over and never find a body just like those specks in their cachet, and they'd never guess why.

I'll do it, thought Alvin. Somehow I'll figure a way to change him. Even though there must be millions of those signatures all through his body, I'll find a way to change every one. Tonight I'll do it, and tomorrow he'll be safe forever.

The iron was cool. Alvin knelt before Arthur Stuart and gently put the manacles in place. They fit his flesh so perfectly he might have cast them in a mold taken from Arthur's own body. When they were locked into place, with a length of light chain strung between them, Alvin looked Arthur Stuart in the eye. "Don't be afraid," he said.

Arthur Stuart didn't say a thing.

"I won't forget you," said Alvin.

"Sure," said the black-haired Finder. "But just in case you get ideas about remembering him while he's on his way home to his rightful master, I ought to tell you square—we never both of us sleep at the same time. And part of being a Finder is, we know if anybody's coming. You can't sneak up on us. Least of all you, smith boy. I could see *you* ten miles away."

Alvin just looked at him. Eventually the Finder sneered and turned away. They put Arthur Stuart onto the horse in front of the white-haired Finder. But Alvin figured that as soon as they got across the Hio, they'd have Arthur walking. Not out of meanness, maybe—but it wouldn't do no good for Finders to show themselves being kindly to a runaway. Besides, they had to set an example for the other slaves, didn't they? Let them see a boy seven years old walking along, feet bleeding, head bowed, and they'd think twice about trying to run off with their children. They'd know that Finders have no mercy.

Pauley and Dr. Physicker rode away with them. They were seeing the Finders to the Hio River and watching them cross the river, to make sure they did no hurt to Arthur Stuart while he was in free territory. It was the best they could do.

Makepeace didn't have much to say, but what he said, he said plain. "A real man would never put manacles on his own friend," said Makepeace. "I'll go up to the house and sign your journeyman papers. I don't want you in my smithy or my house another night." He left Alvin alone by the forge.

He'd been gone no more than five minutes when Horace Guester got to the smithy.

"Let's go," he said.

"No," said Alvin. "Not yet. They can see us coming. They'll tell the sheriff if they're being followed."

"We got no choice. Can't lose their trail."

"You know something about what I am and what I can do," said Alvin. "I've got them even now. They won't get more than a mile from the Hio shore before they fall asleep."

"You can do that?"

"I know what goes on inside people when they're sleepy. I can make that stuff start happening inside them the minute they're in Appalachee."

"While you're at it, why don't you kill them?"

"I can't."

"They aren't men! It wouldn't be murder, killing them!"

"They *are* men," said Alvin. "Besides, if I kill them, then it's a violation of the Fugitive Slave Treaty."

"Are you a lawyer now?"

"Miss Larner explained it to me. I mean she explained it to Arthur Stuart while I was there. He wanted to know. Back last fall. He said, 'Why don't my pa just kill them if some Finders come for me?' And Miss Larner, she told him how there'd just be more Finders coming, only this time they'd hang you and take Arthur Stuart anyway."

Horace's face had turned red. Alvin didn't understand why for a minute, not till Horace Guester explained. "He shouldn't call me his pa. I never wanted him in my house." He swallowed. "But he's right. I'd kill them Finders if I thought it'd do good."

"No killing," said Alvin. "I think I can fix it so they'll never find Arthur again."

"I know. I'm going to ride him to Canada. Get to the lake and sail across."

"No sir," said Alvin. "I think I can fix it so they'll never find him *anywhere*. We just got to hide him till they go away."

"Where?"

"Springhouse, if Miss Larner'll let us."

"Why there?"

"I got it hexed up every which way from Tuesday. I thought I was doing it for the teacher lady. But now I reckon I was really doing it for Arthur Stuart."

Horace grinned. "You're really something, Alvin. You know that?"

"Maybe. Sure wish I knew *what*."

"I'll go ask Miss Larner if we can make use of her house."

"If I know Miss Larner, she'll say yes before you finish asking."

"When do we start, then?"

It took Alvin by surprise, having a grown man ask *him* when they should start. "Soon as it's dark, I reckon. Soon as those two Finders are asleep."

"You can really *do* that?"

"I can if I keep watching them. I mean sort of watching. Keeping track of where they are. So I don't go putting the wrong people to sleep."

"Well, are you watching them now?"

"I know where they are."

"Keep watching, then." Horace looked a little scared, almost as bad as he did near seven years ago, when Alvin told him he knew about the girl buried there. Scared because he knew Alvin could do something strange, something beyond any hexings or knacks in Horace's ken.

Don't you know me, Horace? Don't you know that I'm still Alvin, the boy you liked and trusted and helped so many times? Finding out that I'm stronger than you thought, in ways you didn't think of, that don't mean I'm a whit more dangerous to you. No reason to be a-scared.

As if Horace could hear his words, the fear eased away from his face. "I just mean—Old Peg and I are counting on you. Thank God you ended up in this place, right at this time when we needed you so bad. The good Lord's looking out for us." Horace smiled, then turned and left the smithy.

What Horace said, it left Alvin feeling good, feeling sure of himself. But then, that was Horace's knack, wasn't it—to give folks the view of theirselves they most needed to see.

Alvin turned his thoughts at once to the Finders, and sent out his bug to stay with them, to keep track of the way their bodies moved like small black storms through the greensong around them, with Arthur Stuart's small song bright and clear between them. Black and White don't have nothing to do with bright and dark at heart, I reckon, thought Alvin. His hands stayed busy doing work at the forge, but for the life of him he couldn't pay real attention to it. He'd never watched somebody so far off before—except for that time he got helped by powers he didn't understand, inside Eight-Face Mound.

And the worst thing of all would be if he lost them, if they got away with Arthur Stuart, all because Alvin didn't pay attention close enough and lost that boy among all the beat-down souls of slaves in Appalachee and on beyond, in the deep South where all White men were servants to the other Arthur Stuart, King of England, and so all Blacks were slaves of slaves. Ain't going to lose Arthur in a place so bad. Going to hold on tight to him, like as if he got a thread to connect him to me.

Almost as soon as he thought of it, almost as soon as he imagined a thin invisible thread connecting him and that mixup boy, why, there it was. There was a thread in the air, a thread about as thin as what he imagined once trying to understand what an atom might be. A thread that only had size in one direction—the direction that led toward Arthur Stuart, connecting them heart to heart. Stay with him, Alvin told the thread, like as if it really was alive. And in answer it seemed to grow brighter, thicker, till Alvin was sure anybody who come along could see it.

But when he looked with his eyes, he couldn't see the thread at all; it only appeared to him again when he looked without eyes. It plain astonished him, that such a thing could come to be, created—not out of nothing—but created without pattern except the pattern found in Alvin's own mind. This is a Making. My first, thin, invisible Making—but it's real, and it's going to lead me to Arthur Stuart tonight, so I can set him free.

In her little house, Peggy watched Alvin and Arthur Stuart both, looking back and forth from one to the other, trying to find some pathway that led for Arthur's freedom without costing Alvin's death or capture. No matter how closely and carefully she looked, there was no such path. The Finders were too skilled with their terrible knack; on some paths, Alvin and Horace might carry Arthur off, but he'd only be found again and recaptured—at the cost of Alvin's blood or Alvin's freedom.

So she watched despairing as Alvin spun his almost nonexistent thread. Only then, for the first time, did she see some glimmer of a possibility of freedom in Arthur Stuart's heartfire. It came, not from the fact that the thread would lead Alvin to the boy—on many paths before he spun the thread, she had seen Alvin finding the Finders and putting them to sleep. No, the difference now was that Alvin could make the thread at all. The possibility of it had been so small that there had been no path that showed it. Or perhaps—something she hadn't thought of before—the very act of Making was such a violation of the natural order that her own knack couldn't see paths that relied on it, not until it was actually accomplished.

Yet even at the moment of Alvin's birth, hadn't she seen his glorious future? Hadn't she seen him building a city made of the purest glass or ice? Hadn't she seen his city filled with people who spoke with the tongues of angels and saw with the eyes of God? The fact that Alvin would Make, that was always probable, provided he stayed alive. But any one particular act of Making, that was never likely, never natural enough for a torch—even an extraordinary torch like Peggy—to see it.

She saw Alvin put the Finders to sleep almost as soon as it was dark and they could find a stopping place on the far side of the Hio. She saw Alvin and Horace meet in the smithy, preparing to set out through the woods to the Hio, avoiding the road so they wouldn't meet the sheriff and Dr. Physicker coming back from Hatrack Mouth. But she paid little heed to them. Now that there was new hope, she gave her full attention to Arthur's future, studying how and where his slender new paths of freedom were rooted to the present action. She could not find the clear moment of choice and change. To her that fact was proof that all depended on Alvin becoming a Maker, truly, on this night.

"O God," she whispered, "if thou didst cause this boy to be born with such a gift, I pray thee teach him Making now, tonight."

Alvin stood beside Horace, masked by shadows at the riverbank, waiting for a well-lighted riverboat to pass. Out on the boat, musicians were playing, and people danced a fancy quadrille on the decks. It made Alvin angry, to see them playing like children when a real child was being carried off to slavery tonight. Still, he knew they meant no harm, and knew it wasn't fair to blame others for being happy while somebody they don't even know might be grieving. By that measure there'd be no happiness in all the world, Alvin figured. Life being how it is, Alvin thought, there's not a moment in the day when there ain't at least a few hundred people grieving about something.

The ship had no sooner passed around a bend than they heard a crashing in the woods behind them. Or rather, Alvin heard the sound, and it only seemed like crashing to *him* because of his sense of the right order of things in the greenwood song. It took more than a few minutes before Horace heard it at all. Whoever it was sneaking up on them, he was right stealthy for a White man.

"Now I'm wishing for a gun," whispered Horace.

Alvin shook his head. "Wait and watch," he whispered—so faint his lips barely moved.

They waited. After a while, they saw a man step out of the woods and slither down the bank to the muddy edge of the water, where the boat rocked on the water. Seeing nobody there, he looked around, then sighed and stepped out into the boat, turned around and sat down in the stern, glumly resting his chin on his hands.

Suddenly Horace started chuckling. "Play fetch with my bones when I'm dead, but I do think that's old Po Doggly."

At once the man in the boat leaned back and Alvin could finally see him clear in the moonlight. It *was* Dr. Physicker's driver, sure enough. But this didn't seem to bother Horace none. He was already slipping down the riverbank, to splash out to the boat, climb aboard, and give Po Doggly such a violent hug the boat took on water. In only a second they both noticed that the boat was rocking out of kilter, and without a word they both shifted exactly right to balance the load, and then again without a word Po got the oars into the locks while Horace took a flat tin baling cup out from under his bench and commenced to dipping it and pouring it out overboard, again and again.

Alvin marveled for a moment at how smooth the two of them fit together. He didn't even have to ask—he knew from how they acted that they'd done this sort of thing a good many times before. Each knew what the other was going to do, so they didn't even have to think about it anymore. One man did his part, and the other his, and neither even had to check to make sure both parts were getting done.

Like the bits and pieces that made up everything in the world; like the dance of atoms Alvin had imagined in his mind. He'd never realized it before, but people could be like those atoms, too. Most of the time people were all disorganized, nobody knowing who anybody else was, nobody holding still long enough to trust or be trusted, just like Alvin imagined atoms might have been before God taught them who they were and gave them work to do. But here were two men, men that nobody'd ever figure even knew each other hardly, except as how everybody in a town like Hatrack River knows everybody else. Po Doggly, a one-time farmer reduced to driving for Dr. Physicker, and Horace Guester, the first settler in this place, and still prospering. Who'd've thought they could fit together so smooth? But it was because each one knew who the other was, knew it pure and true, knew it as sure as an atom might know the name God gave him; each one in his place, doing his work.

All these thoughts rushed through Alvin's mind so fast he hardly noticed himself thinking them, yet in later years he'd remember right enough that this was when he first understood: These two men, together, made something between them that was just as real and solid as the dirt under his feet, as the tree he was leaning on. Most folks couldn't see it—they'd look at the two of them and see nothing but two men who happened to be sitting in a boat together. But then, maybe to other atoms it wouldn't seem like the atoms making up a bit of iron was anything more than two atoms as happened to be next to each other. Maybe you have to be far off, like God, or anyhow bigger by far in order to see what it is that two atoms make when they fit together in a certain way. But just because another atom don't see the connection don't mean it isn't real, or that the iron isn't as solid as iron can be.

And if I can teach these atoms how to make a string out of nothing, or maybe how to make iron out of gold, or even—let it be so—change Arthur's secret invisible signature all through his body so the Finders wouldn't know him no more—then why couldn't a Maker also do with people as he does with atoms, and teach them a new order, and once he finds enough that he can trust, build them together into something new, something strong, something as real as iron.

"You coming, Al, or what?"

Like I said, Alvin hardly knew what thought it was he had. But he didn't forget it, no, even sliding down the bank into the mud he knew that he'd never forget what he thought of just then, even though it'd take him years and miles and tears and blood before he really understood it all the way.

"Good to see you, Po," said Alvin. "Only I kind of thought we was doing something a mite secret."

Po rowed the boat closer in, slacking the rope and letting Alvin spider his way on board without getting his feet wet. Alvin didn't mind that. He had an aversion to water, which was natural enough seeing how often the Unmaker tried to use water to kill him. But the water seemed to be just water tonight; the Unmaker was invisible or far away. Maybe it was the slender string that still hooked Alvin to Arthur—maybe that was such a powerful Making that the Unmaker plain hadn't the strength to turn even this much water against Alvin.

"Oh, it's still secret, Alvin," said Horace. "You just don't know. Afore you ever got to Hatrack River—or anyway I mean afore you came back—me and Po, we used to go out and fetch in runaway slaves and help them on to Canada whenever we could."

"Didn't the Finders ever get you?" asked Alvin.

"Any slave got this far, that meant the Finders wasn't too close behind," said Po. "A good number that reached us stole their own cachet."

"Besides, that was afore the Fugitive Slave Treaty," said Horace. "Long as the Finders didn't kill us outright, they couldn't touch us."

"And in those days we had a torch," said Po.

Horace said nothing, just untied the rope from the boat and tossed it back onto shore. Po started in rowing the first second the rope was free—and Horace had already braced himself for the first lurch of the boat. It was a miracle, seeing how smooth they knew each other's next move before the move was even begun. Alvin almost laughed out loud in the joy of seeing such a thing, knowing it was possible, dreaming of what it might mean—thousands of people knowing each other that well, moving to fit each other just right, working together. Who could stand in the way of such people?

"When Horace's girl left, why, we had no way of knowing there was a runaway coming through here." Po shook his head. "It was over. But I knowed that with Arthur Stuart put in chains and dragged on south, why, there wasn't no way in hell old Horace wasn't going to cross the river and fetch him back. So once I dropped off them Finders and headed back away from the Hio a ways, I stopped the carriage and hopped on down."

"I bet Dr. Physicker noticed," said Alvin.

"Course he did, you fool!" said Po. "Oh, I see you're funning me. Well, he noticed. He just says to me, 'You be careful, them boys are dangerous.' And I said I'd be careful all right and then he says to me, 'It's that blame sheriff Pauley Wiseman. He didn't have to let them take him so fast. Might be we could've fought exerdiction if we could've held onto Arthur Stuart till the circuit judge come around. But Pauley, he did everything legal, but he moved so fast I just knew in my heart he wanted that boy gone, wanted him clean out of Hatrack River and never come back.' I believe him, Horace. Pauley Wiseman never did like that mixup boy, once Old Peg got the wind in her sails about him going to school."

Horace grunted; he turned the tiller just a little, exactly at the moment when Po slacked the oar on one side so the boat would turn slightly upstream to make the right landing on the far shore. "You know what I been thinking?" said Horace. "I been thinking your job just ain't enough to keep you busy, Po."

"I like my job good enough," said Po Doggly.

"I been thinking that there's a county election this fall, and the office of sheriff goes up for grabs. I think Pauley Wiseman ought to get turned out."

"And me get made sheriff? You think that's likely, me being a known drunk?"

"You ain't touched a drop the whole time you been with the doctor. And if we live through this and get Arthur back safe, why, you're going to be a hero."

"A hero hell! You crazy, Horace? We can't tell a soul about this or there'll be a reward out for our brains on rye bread from the Hio to Camelot."

"We ain't going to print up the story and sell copies, if that's what you mean. But you know how word spreads. Good folks'll know what you and me done."

"Then *you* be sheriff, Horace."

"Me?" Horace grinned. "Can you imagine me putting a man in jail?"

Po laughed softly. "Reckon not."

When they reached the shore, again their movements were swift and fit together just right. It was hard to believe it had been so many years since they worked together. It was like their bodies already knew what to do, so they didn't even have to think about it. Po jumped into the water—ankle deep is all, and he leaned on the boat so as not to splash much. The boat rocked a bit at *that*, of course, but without a bit of wasted motion Horace leaned against the rocking and calmed it down, hardly even noticing he was doing it. In a minute they had the bow dragged up onto the shore—sandy here, not muddy like the other side— and tied to a tree. To Alvin the rope looked old and rotten, but when he sent his bug inside to feel it out, he was sure it was still strong enough to hold the boat against the rocking of the river against the stern.

Only when all their familiar jobs was done did Horace present himself like militia on the town square, shoulders squared and eyes right on Alvin. "Well, now, Al, I reckon it's up to you to lead the way."

"Ain't we got to track them?" asked Po.

"Alvin knows where they are," said Horace.

"Well ain't that nice," said Po. "And does he know whether they got their guns aimed at our heads?"

"Yes," said Alvin. He said it in such a way as to make it plain that he didn't want no more questions.

It wasn't plain enough for Po. "You telling me this boy's a torch, or what? Most I heard was he got him a knack for shoeing horses."

Here was the bad part about having somebody else along. Alvin didn't have no wish to tell Po Doggly what all he could do, but he couldn't very well tell the man that he didn't trust him.

It was Horace came to the rescue. "Po, I got to tell you, Alvin ain't part of the story of this night."

"Looks to me like he's the biggest part."

"I tell you, Po, when this story gets told, it was you and me came along and happened to find the Finders asleep, you understand?"

Po wrinkled his brow, then nodded. "Just tell me this, boy. Whatever knack you got, you a Christian? I don't even ask that you be a Methodist."

"Yes sir," said Alvin. "I'm a Christian, I reckon. I hold to the Bible."

"Good then," said Po. "I just don't want to get myself all mixed up in devil stuff."

"Not with me," said Alvin.

"All right then. Best if I don't know what you do, Al. Just take a care not to get me killed because I don't know it."

Alvin stuck out his hand. Po shook it and grinned. "You blacksmiths got to be strong as a bear."

"Me?" said Alvin. "A bear gets in my way, I beat on his head till he's a wolverine."

"I like your brag, boy."

A moment's pause, and then Alvin led them off, following the thread that connected him to Arthur Stuart.

It wasn't all that far, but it took them an hour cutting through the woods in the dark—with all the leaves out, there wasn't much moonlight got to the ground. Without Alvin's sense of the forest around them, it would've taken three times as long and ten times the noise.

They found the Finders asleep in a clearing with a campfire dying down between them. The white-haired Finder was curled up on his bedroll. The black-haired Finder must've been left on watch; he was snoring away leaning against a tree. Their horses were asleep not far off. Alvin stopped them before they got close enough to disturb the animals.

Arthur Stuart was wide awake, sitting there staring into the fire.

Alvin sat there a minute, trying to figure how to do this. He wasn't sure how smart the Finders might be. Could they find scraps of dried skin, fallen-off hairs, something like that, and use it for a new cachet? Just in case, it wouldn't do no good to change Arthur right where he was; nor would it be too smart to head on out into the clearing where they might leave bits of their own selves, as proof of who stole Arthur away.

So from a distance, Alvin got inside the iron of the manacles and made cracks in all four parts, so they fell away to the ground at once, with a clank. The noise bothered the horses, who nickered a bit, but the Finders were still sleeping like the dead. Arthur, though, it didn't take him a second to figure out what was happening. He jumped to his feet all at once and started looking around for Alvin at the clearing's edge.

Alvin whistled, trying to match the song of a redbird. It was a pretty bad imitation, as birdcalls go, but Arthur heard it and knew that it was Alvin calling him. Without a moment's waiting or worrying, Arthur plunged right into the woods and not five minutes later, with a few more bad birdcalls to guide him, he was face to face with Alvin.

Of course Arthur Stuart made as if to give Alvin a big old hug, but Alvin held up a hand. "Don't touch anybody or anything," he whispered. "I've got to make a change in you, Arthur Stuart, so the Finders can't catch you again."

"I don't mind," said Arthur.

"I don't dare have a single scrap of the old way you used to be. You got hairs and skin and such all over in your clothes. So strip them off."

Arthur Stuart didn't hesitate. In a few moments his clothes were in a pile at his feet.

"Excuse me for not knowing a bit about this," said Po, "but if you leave those clothes a-lying there, them Finders'll know he come this way, and that points north to them sure as if we painted a big white arrow on the ground."

"Reckon you're right," said Alvin.

"So have Arthur Stuart bring them along and float them down the river," said Horace.

"Just make sure you don't touch Arthur or nothing," said Alvin. "Arthur, you just pick up your clothes and follow along slow and careful. If you get lost, give me a redbird whistle and I'll whistle back till you find us."

"I knew you was coming, Alvin," said Arthur Stuart. "You too, Pa."

"So did them Finders," said Horace, "and much as I wish we could arrange it, they ain't going to sleep forever."

"Wait a minute anyway," said Alvin. He sent his bug back into the manacles and drew them back together, fit them tight, joined the iron again as if it had been cast that way. Now they lay on the ground unbroken, fastened tight, giving no sign of how the boy got free.

"I don't suppose you're maybe breaking their legs or something, Alvin," said Horace.

"Can he *do* that from here?" asked Po.

"I'm doing no such thing," said Alvin. "What we want is for the Finders to give up searching for a boy who as far as they can tell doesn't exist no more."

"Well that makes sense, but I still like thinking of them Finders with their legs broke," said Horace.

Alvin grinned and plunged off into the forest, deliberately making enough noise and moving slow enough that the others could follow him in the near-darkness; if he wanted to, he could've moved like a Red man through the woods, making not a sound, leaving no whiff of a trail that anyone could follow.

They got to the river and stopped. Alvin didn't want Arthur getting into the boat in his present skin, leaving traces of himself all over. So if he was going to change him, he had to do it here.

"Toss them clothes, boy," said Horace. "Far as you can."

Arthur took a step or two into the water. It made Alvin scared, for with his inward eye he saw it as if Arthur, made of light and earth and air, suddenly got part of himself disappeared into the blackness of the water. Still, the water hadn't harmed them none on the trip here, and Alvin saw as how it might even be useful.

Arthur Stuart pitched his wad of clothes out into the river. The current wasn't all that strong; they watched the clothes turn lazily and float downstream, gradually drifting apart. Arthur stood there, up to his butt in water, watching the clothes. No, not watching them—he didn't turn a speck when they drifted far to the left. He was just looking at the north shore, the free side of the river.

"I been here afore," he said. "I seen this boat."

"Might be," said Horace. "Though you was a mite young to remember it. Po and I, we helped your mama into this very boat. My daughter Peggy held you when we got to shore."

"My sister Peggy," said Arthur. He turned around and looked at Horace, like as if it was really a question.

"I reckon so," said Horace, and that was the answer.

"Just stand there, Arthur Stuart," said Alvin. "When I change you, I got to change you all over, inside and out. Better to do that in the water, where all the dead skin with your old self marked in it can wash away."

"You going to make me White?" asked Arthur Stuart.

"Can you *do* that?" asked Po Doggly.

"I don't know what all is going to change," said Alvin. "I hope I don't make you White, though. That'd be like stealing away from you the part of you your mama gave you."

"They don't make White boys be slaves," said Arthur Stuart.

"They ain't going to make this partickler mixup boy a slave anyhow," said Alvin. "Not if I can help it. Now just stand there, stand right still, and let me figure this out."

They all stood there, the men and the boy, while Alvin studied inside Arthur Stuart, finding that tiny signature that marked every living bit of him.

Alvin knew he couldn't just go changing it willy-nilly, since he didn't rightly understand what all that signature was *for*. He just knew that it was somehow part of what made Arthur himself, and you don't just change that. Maybe changing the wrong thing might strike him blind, or make his blood turn to rainwater or something. How could Alvin know?

It was seeing the string still connecting them, heart to heart, that gave Alvin the idea—that and remembering what the Redbird said, using Arthur Stuart's own lips to say it. "The Maker is the one who is part of what he Makes." Alvin stripped off his own shirt and then stepped out into the water and knelt down in it, so he was near eye-to-eye with Arthur Stuart, cool water swirling gently around his waist. Then he put out his hands and pulled Arthur Stuart to him and held him there, breast to breast, hands on shoulders.

"I thought we wasn't supposed to touch the boy," said Po.

"Hush up you blame fool," said Horace Guester. "Alvin knows what he's doing."

I wish that was true, thought Alvin. But at least he had an idea what to do, and that was better than nothing. Now that their living skin was pressed together, Alvin could look and compare Arthur's secret signature with his own. Most of it was the same, exactly the same, and the way Alvin figured, that's the part that makes us both human instead of cows or frogs or pigs or chickens. That's the part I don't dare change, not a bit of it.

The rest—I can change that. But not any old how. What good to save him if I turn him bright yellow or make him stupid or something?

So Alvin did the only thing as made sense to him. He changed bits of Arthur's signature to be just like Alvin's own. Not *all* that was different—not all that much, in fact. Just a little. But even a little meant that Arthur Stuart had stopped being completely himself and started being partly Alvin. It seemed to Alvin that what he was doing was terrible and wonderful at the same time.

How much? How much did he have to change till the Finders wouldn't know the boy? Surely not all. Surely just *this* much, just *these* changes. There was no way to know. All that Alvin could do was guess, and so he took his guess and that was it.

That was only the beginning, of course. Now he started in changing all the other signatures to match the new one, each living bit of Arthur, one by one, as fast as he could. Dozens of them, hundreds of them; he found each new signature and changed it to fit the new pattern.

Hundreds of them, and hundreds more, and still he had changed no more than a tiny patch of skin on Arthur's chest. How could he hope to change the boy's whole body, going so slow?

"It hurts," whispered Arthur.

Alvin drew away from him. "I ain't doing nothing to hurt you, Arthur Stuart."

Arthur looked down at his chest. "Right here," he said, touching the spot where Alvin had been working.

Alvin looked in the moonlight and saw that indeed that spot seemed to be swollen, changed, darkened. He looked again, only not with his eyes, and saw that the rest of Arthur's body was attacking the part that Alvin changed, killing it bit by bit, fast as it could.

Of course. What did he expect? The signature was the way the body recognized itself—that's why every living bit of a body had to have that signature in it. If it wasn't there, the body knew it had to be a disease or something and killed it. Wasn't it bad enough that changing. Arthur was taking so long? Now Alvin knew that it wouldn't do no good to change him at all—the more he changed him, the sicker he'd get and the more Arthur Stuart's own body would try to kill itself until the boy either died or shed the new changed part.

It was just like Taleswapper's old story, about trying to build a wall so big that by the time you got halfway through building it, the oldest parts of it had already crumbled to dust. How could you build such a wall if it was getting broke down faster than you could build it up?

"I can't," said Alvin. "I'm trying to do what can't be done."

"Well if you can't do it," said Po Doggly, "I hope you can fly, cause that's the only way you can get that boy to Canada before the Finders catch up with you."

"I can't," said Alvin.

"You're just tired," said Horace. "We'll all just hush up so you can think."

"Won't do any good," said Alvin.

"My mama could fly," said Arthur Stuart.

Alvin sighed in impatience at this same old story coming back again.

"It's true, you know," said Horace. "Little Peggy told me. That little black slave girl, she diddled with some ash and blackbird feathers and such, and flew straight up here. That's what killed her. I couldn't believe it the first time I realized the boy remembers, and we always kept our mouths shut about it hoping he'd forget. But I got to tell you, Alvin, it'd be a pure shame if that girl died just so you could give up on us at this same spot in the river seven years later.''

Alvin closed his eyes. ''Just shut your mouth and let me think,'' he said.

''I *said* that's what we'd do,'' said Horace.

''So *do* it,'' said Po Doggly.

Alvin hardly even heard them. He was looking back inside Arthur's body, inside that patch that Alvin changed. The new signature wasn't bad in itself—only where it bordered on the skin with the old signature, that was the only place the new skin was getting sick and dying. Arthur'd be just fine if Alvin could somehow change him all at once, instead of bit by bit.

The way that the string came all at once, when Alvin thought of it, pictured where it started and where it ended and what it *was*. All the atoms of it moving into place at the same time. Like the way Po Doggly and Horace Guester fit together all at once, each doing his own task yet taking into account all that the other man did.

But the string was clean and simple. This was hard—like he told Miss Larner, turning water into wine instead of iron into gold.

No, can't think of it that way. What I did to make the string was teach all the atoms what and where to be, because each one of them was alive and each one could obey me. But inside Arthur's body I ain't dealing with atoms, I'm dealing with these living bits, and each one of *them* is alive. Maybe it's even the signature itself that makes them alive, maybe I can teach them all what they ought to be—instead of moving each part of them, one at a time, I can just say—Be like this—and they'll do it.

He no sooner thought of it than he tried it. In his mind he thought of speaking to all the signatures in Arthur's skin, all over his chest, all at once; he showed them the pattern he held in his mind, a pattern so complex he couldn't even understand it himself, except that he knew it was the same pattern as the signatures in this patch of skin he had changed bit by bit. And as soon as he showed them, as soon as he commanded them—Be like this! This is the way!—they changed. It all changed, all the skin on Arthur Stuart's chest, all at once.

Arthur gasped, then howled with pain. What had been a soreness in a patch of skin was now spread across his whole chest.

''Trust me,'' Alvin said. ''I'm going to change you sure now, and the pain will stop. But I'm doing it under the water, where all the old skin gets carried off at once. Plug your nose! Hold your breath!''

Arthur Stuart was panting from the pain, but he did what Alvin said. He pinched his nose with his right hand, then took a breath and closed his mouth. At once Alvin gripped Arthur's wrist in his left hand and put his right hand behind the boy and plunged him under the water. In that instant Alvin held Arthur's body whole in his mind, seeing all the signatures, not one by one, but all of them; he showed them the pattern, the new signature, and this time thought the words so strong his lips spoke them. "This is the way! Be like this!"

He couldn't feel it with his hands—Arthur's body didn't change a whit that he could sense with his natural senses. But Alvin could still see the change, all at once, all in an instant, every signature in the boy's body, in the organs, in the muscles, in the blood, in the brain; even his hair changed, every part of him that was connected to himself. And what wasn't connected, what didn't change, that was washed away and gone.

Alvin plunged himself under the water, to wash off any part of Arthur's skin or hair that might have clung to him. Then he rose up and lifted Arthur Stuart out of the water, all in one motion. The boy came up shedding waterdrops like a spray of cold pearls in the moonlight. He stood there gasping for breath and shaking from the cold.

"Tell me it don't hurt no more," said Alvin.

"Any more," said Arthur, correcting him just like Miss Larner always did. "I feel fine. Except cold."

Alvin scooped him up out of the water and carried him back to the bank. "Wrap him in my shirt and let's get out of here."

So they did. Not a one of them noticed that when Arthur imitated Miss Larner, he didn't use Miss Larner's voice.

Peggy didn't notice either, not right away. She was too busy looking inside Arthur Stuart's heartfire. How it changed when Alvin transformed him! So subtle a change it was that Peggy couldn't even tell what it was Alvin was changing—yet in the moment that Arthur Stuart emerged from the water, not a single path from his past remained—not a single path leading southward into slavery. And all the new paths, the new futures that the transformation had brought to him—they led to such amazing possibilities.

During all the time it took for Horace, Po, and Alvin to bring Arthur Stuart back across the Hio and through the woods to the smithy, Peggy did nothing more than explore in Arthur Stuart's heartfire, studying possibilities that had never before existed in the world. There was a new Maker abroad in the land; Arthur was the first soul touched by him, and everything was different. Moreover, most of Arthur's futures were inextricably tied with Alvin. Peggy saw possibilities of incredible journeys—on one path a trip to Europe where Arthur Stuart would be at

Alvin's side as the new Holy Roman Emperor Napoleon bowed to him; on another path a voyage into a strange island nation far to the south where Red men lived their whole lives on mats of floating seaweed; on another path a triumphant crossing into westward lands where the Reds hailed Alvin as the great unifier of all the races, and opened up their last refuge to him, so perfect was their trust. And always by his side was Arthur Stuart, the mixup boy—but now trusted, now himself gifted with some of the Maker's own power.

Most of the paths began with them bringing Arthur Stuart to her springhouse, so she was not surprised when they knocked at her door.

"Miss Larner," called Alvin softly.

She was distracted; reality was not half so interesting as the futures revealed now in Arthur Stuart's heartfire. She opened the door. There they stood, Arthur still wrapped in Alvin's shirt.

"We brought him back," said Horace.

"I can see that," said Peggy. She *was* glad of it, but that gladness didn't show up in her voice. Instead she sounded busy, interrupted, annoyed. As she was. Get on with it, she wanted to say. I've seen this conversation as Arthur overheard it, so get on with it, get it over with, and let me get back to exploring what this boy will be. But of course she could say none of this—not if she hoped to remain disguised as Miss Larner.

"They won't find him," said Alvin, "not as long as they don't actually see him with their eyes. Something—their cachet don't work no more."

"Doesn't work anymore," said Peggy.

"Right," said Alvin. "What we come for—came for—can we leave him with you? Your house, here, Ma'am, I've got it hexed up so tight they won't even think to come inside, long as you keep the door locked."

"Don't you have more clothes for him than this? He's been wet—do you want him to take a chill?"

"It's a warm night," said Horace, "and we don't want to be fetching clothes from the house. Not till the Finders come back and give up and go away again."

"Very well," said Peggy.

"We'd best be about our business," said Po Doggly. "I got to get back to Dr. Physicker's."

"And since I told Old Peg that I'd be in town, I'd better be there," said Horace.

Alvin spoke straight to Peggy. "I'll be in the smithy, Miss Larner. If something goes wrong, you give a shout, and I'll be up the hill in ten seconds.''

"Thank you. Now—please go on about your business.''

She closed the door. She didn't mean to be so abrupt. But she had a whole new set of futures. No one but herself had ever been so important in Alvin's work as Arthur was going to be. But perhaps that would happen with everyone that Alvin actually touched and changed— perhaps as a Maker he would transform everyone he loved until they all stood with him in those glorious moments, until they all looked out upon the world through the lensed walls of the Crystal City and saw all things as God must surely see them.

A knock on the door. She opened it.

"In the first place," said Alvin, "don't open the door without knowing who it is.''

"I knew it was you," she said. Truth was, though, she didn't. She didn't even think.

"In the second place, I was waiting to hear you lock the door, and you never did.''

"Sorry," she said. "I forgot.''

"We went to a lot of work to save this boy tonight, Miss Larner. Now it's all up to you. Just till the Finders go.''

"Yes, I know." She really was sorry, and let her voice reveal her regret.

"Good night then.''

He stood there waiting. For what?

Oh, yes. For her to close the door.

She closed it, locked it, then returned to Arthur Stuart and hugged him until he struggled to get away. "You're safe," she said.

"Of course I am," said Arthur Stuart. "We went to a lot of work to save this boy tonight, Miss Larner.''

She listened to him, and knew there was something wrong. What was it? Oh, yes, of course. Alvin had just said exactly those words. But what was wrong? Arthur Stuart was always imitating people.

Always imitating. But this time Arthur Stuart had repeated Alvin's words in his own voice, not Alvin's. She had never heard him do that. She thought it was his knack, that he was so natural a mimic he didn't even realize he was doing it.

"Spell 'cicada,' '' she said.

"C-I-C-A-D-A," he answered. In his own voice, not hers.

"Arthur Stuart," she whispered. "What's wrong?''

"Ain't nothing wrong, Miss Larner," he said. "I'm home.''

He didn't know. He didn't realize it. Never having understood how perfect a mimic he had been, now he didn't realize when the knack was gone. He still had the near-perfect memory of what others said—he still had all the words. But the voices were gone; only his own seven-year-old voice remained.

She hugged him again, for a moment, more briefly. She understood now. As long as Arthur Stuart remained himself, the Finders could have found him and taken him south into slavery. The only way to save him was to make him no longer completely himself. Alvin hadn't known, of course he hadn't, that in saving Arthur, he had taken away his knack, or at least part of it. The price of Arthur's freedom was making him cease to be fully Arthur. Did Alvin understand that?

"I'm tired, Miss Larner," said Arthur Stuart.

"Yes, of course," she said. "You can sleep here—in my bed. Take off that dirty shirt and climb in under the covers and you'll be warm and safe all night."

He hesitated. She looked into his heartfire and saw why; smiling, she turned her back. She heard a rustle of fabric and then a squeak of bedsprings and the swish of a small body sliding along her sheets into bed. Then she turned around, bent over him where he lay upon her pillow, and kissed him lightly on the cheek.

"Good night, Arthur," she said.

"Good night," he murmured.

In moments he was asleep. She sat at her writing table and pulled up the wick on her lamp. She would do some reading while she waited for the Finders to return. Something to keep her calm while she waited.

No, she wouldn't. The words were there on the page, but she made no sense of them. Was she reading Descartes or Deuteronomy? It didn't matter. She couldn't stay away from Arthur's new heartfire. Of course all the paths of his life changed. He wasn't the same person anymore. No, that wasn't quite true. He was still Arthur. Mostly Arthur.

Almost Arthur. Almost what he was. But not quite.

Was it worth it? To lose part of who he had been in order to live free? Perhaps this new self was better than the old; but that old Arthur Stuart was gone now, gone forever, even more surely than if he had gone south and lived the rest of his life in bitter slavery, with his time in Hatrack as a memory, and then a dream, and then a mythic tale he told the pickaninnies in the years just before he died.

Fool! she cried to herself in her heart. No one is the same person today that he was yesterday. No one had a body as young as it was, or a heart so naive, or a head so ignorant as it was. He would have been far more terribly transformed—malformed—by life in bondage than by Alvin's gentle changes. Arthur Stuart was more surely himself now than he would have been in Appalachee. Besides, she had seen all the dark paths that once dwelt in his heartfire, the taste of the lash, the stupefying sun beating down on him as he labored in the field, or the hanging rope that awaited him on the many paths that led to his leading or taking part in a slave revolt and slaughtering dozens of Whites as they lay in their beds. Arthur Stuart was too young to understand what had happened to him; but if he were old enough, if he could choose which future he'd prefer, Peggy had no doubt that he would choose the sort of future Alvin had just made possible.

In a way, he lost some of himself, some of his knack, and therefore some of the choices he might have had in life. But in losing those, he gained so much more freedom, so much more power, that he was clear winner in the bargain.

Yet as she remembered his bright face when he spelled words to her in her own voice, she could not keep herself from shedding a few tears of regret.

19

The Plow

The Finders woke up not long after Arthur Stuart's rescuers took him across the river.

"Look at this. Manacles still fastened tight. Good hard iron."

"Don't matter. They got them a good spell for sleeping and a good spell for slipping out of chains, but don't they know us Finders always find a runaway, once we got his scent?"

If you could've seen them, you'd think they was glad Arthur Stuart got loose. Truth was, these boys loved a good chase, loved showing folks that Finders just couldn't be shook loose. And if it so happened they put a fistful of lead shot through somebody's belly before the hunt was done, well, ain't that just the way of it? Like dogs on the trail of a bleeding deer.

They followed Arthur Stuart's path through the forest till they came to the water's edge. Only then did their cheerful looks give way to a kind of frown. They lifted up their eyes and looked across the water, searching for the heartfires of men abroad at this time of night, when all honest folk was bound to be asleep. The white-haired one, he just couldn't see far enough; but the black-haired one, he said, "I see a few, moving about. And a few not moving. We'll pick up the scent again in Hatrack River."

Alvin held the plow between his hands. He knew that he could turn it all to gold—he'd seen gold enough in his life to know the pattern, so he could show the bits of iron what they ought to be. But he also knew that it wasn't no ordinary gold that he wanted. That would be too soft, and as cold as any ordinary stone. No, he wanted something new, not just iron to gold like any alchemist could dream of, but a living gold, a gold that could hold its shape and strength better than iron, better than the finest steel. Gold that was awake, aware of the world around it—a plow that knew the earth that it would tear, to lay it open to the fires of the sun.

A golden plow that would know a man, that a man could trust, the way Po Doggly knew Horace Guester and each trusted the other. A plow that wouldn't need no ox to draw, nor added weight to force it downward into the soil. A plow that would know which soil was rich and which was poor. A sort of gold that never had been seen in all the world before, just like the world had never seen such a thin invisible string as Alvin spun between Arthur Stuart and himself today.

So there he knelt, holding the shape of the gold inside his mind. "Be like this," he whispered to the iron.

He could feel how atoms came from all around the plow and joined together with those already in the iron, forming bits much heavier than what the iron was, and lined up in different ways, until they fit the pattern that he showed them in his mind.

Between his hands he held a plow of gold. He rubbed his fingers over it. Gold, yes, bright yellow in the firelight from the forge, but still dead, still cold. How could he teach it to be alive? Not by showing it the pattern of his own flesh—that wasn't the kind of life it needed. It was the living atoms that he wanted to waken, to show them what they were compared to what they *could* be. To put the fire of life in them.

The fire of life. Alvin lifted the golden plow—much heavier now—and despite the heat of the slacking fire, he set it right amid the glowing charcoal of the forge.

They were back on their horses now, them Finders, walking them calmly up the road to Hatrack River, looking into every house and hut and cabin, holding up the cachet to match it with the heartfires that they found within. But nary a match did they find, nary a body did they recognize. They passed the smithy and saw that a heartfire burned inside, but it wasn't the runaway mixup boy. It was bound to be the smith what made the manacles, they knew it.

"I'd like to kill him," whispered the black-haired Finder. "I know he put that spell in the manacles, to make them so that boy could slip right out."

"Time enough for that after we find the pickaninny," said the white-haired Finder.

They saw two heartfires burning in the old springhouse, but neither one was like what they had in the cachet, so they went on, searching for a child that they might recognize.

*   *   *

The fire was deep within the gold now, but all it was doing was melting it. That wouldn't do at all—it was life the plow needed, not the death of metal in the fire. He held the plowshape in his mind and showed it plain as can be to every bit of metal in the plow; cried out silently to every atom, It ain't enough to be lined up in the little shapes of gold—you need to hold this larger shape yourselves, no matter the fire, no matter what other force might press or tear or melt or try to maim you.

He could sense that he was heard—there was movement in the gold, movement against the downward slipping of the gold as it turned to fluid. But it wasn't strong enough, it wasn't *sure* enough. Without thinking, Alvin reached his hands into the fire and clung to the gold, showing it the plowshape, crying to it in his heart, Like this! Be like this! This is what you are! Oh, the pain of it burned something fierce, but he knew that it was right for his hands to be there, for the Maker is a part of what he makes. The atoms heard him, and formed themselves in ways that Alvin never even thought of, but the result of it all was that the gold now took the heat of the fire into itself without melting, without losing shape. It was done; the plow wasn't alive, exactly, not the way he wanted—but it could stand in the forgefire without melting. The gold was more than gold now. It was gold that knew it was a plow and meant to stay that way.

Alvin pulled his hands away from the plow and saw flames still dancing on his skin, which was charred in places, peeling back away from the bone. Silent as death, he plunged his hands into the water barrel and heard the sizzle of the fire on his flesh as it went out. Then, before the pain could come in full force, he set to healing himself, sloughing away the dead skin and making new skin grow.

He stood there, weakened from all his body had to do to heal his hands, looking into the fire at the gold plow. Just setting there, knowing its shape and holding to it—but that wasn't enough to make the plow alive. It had to know what a plow was for. It had to know why it lived, so it could act to fulfill that purpose. That was Making, Alvin knew it now; that was what Redbird come to say three years ago. Making wasn't like carpentry or smithy work or any such, cutting and bending and melting to force things into new shapes. Making was something subtler and stronger—making things *want* to be another way, a new shape, so they just naturally flowed that way. It was something Alvin had done for years without knowing what it was he was doing. When he thought he was doing no more than finding the natural cracks in stone, he was really making those cracks; by imagining where he wanted them to be, and showing it to the atoms within the bits within the pieces of the rock, he taught them to want to fulfill the shape he showed them.

Now, with this plow, he had done it, not by accident, but on purpose; and he'd taught the gold to be something stronger, to hold better to its shape than anything he'd ever Made before. But how could he teach it more, teach it to act, to move in ways that gold was never taught to move?

In the back of his mind, he knew that this golden plow wasn't the real problem. The real problem was the Crystal City, and the building blocks of *that* weren't going to be simple atoms in a metal plow. The atoms of a city are men and women, and they don't believe the shape they're shown with the simple faith that atoms have, they don't understand with such pure clarity, and when they act, their actions are never half so pure. But if I can teach this gold to be a plow and to be alive, then maybe I can make a Crystal City out of men and women; maybe I can find people as pure as the atoms of this gold, who come to understand the shape of the Crystal City and love it the way I did the moment I saw it when I climbed the inside of that twister with Tenskwa-Tawa. Then they'll not only hold that shape but also make it act, make the Crystal City a living thing much larger and greater than any one of us who are its atoms.

The Maker is the one who is part of what he makes.

Alvin ran to the bellows and pumped up the fire till the charcoal was glowing hot enough to drive any regular smith outside into the night air to wait till the fire slacked. But not Alvin. Instead he walked right up to the forge and climbed right into the heat and the flame. He felt the clothes burning right off his body, but he paid no mind. He curled himself around that plow and then commenced to healing himself, not piecemeal, not bit by bit, but healing himself by telling his whole body, all at once, Stay alive! Put the fire that burns you into this plow!

And at the same time, he told the plow, Do as my body does! Live! Learn from every living bit of me how each part has its purpose, and acts on it. I can't show you the shape you've got to be, or how it's done, cause I don't know. But I can show you what it's like to be alive, by the pain of my body, by the healing of it, by the struggle to stay alive. Be like this! Whatever it takes, however hard it is for you to learn, this is you, be like me!

It took forever, trembling in the fire as his body struggled with the heat, finding ways to channel it the way a river channels water, pouring it out into the plow like it was an ocean of golden fire. And within the plow, the atoms struggled to do what Alvin asked, wanting to obey him, not knowing how. But his call to them was strong, too strong not to

hear; and it was more than a matter of hearing him, too. It was like
they could tell that what he wanted for them was good. They trusted
him, they wanted to be the living plow he dreamed of, and so in a
million flecks of time so small that a second seemed like eternity to
them, they tried this, they tried that, until somewhere within the golden
plow a new pattern was made that knew itself to be alive exactly as
Alvin wanted it to be; and in a single single moment the pattern passed
throughout the plow and it was alive.

Alive. Alvin felt it moving within the curve of his body as the plow
nestled down into the coals of the fire, cutting into it, plowing it as if
it were soil. And because it was a barren soil, one that could bear no
life, the plow rose quickly out of it and slipped outward, away from the
fire toward the lip of the forge. It moved by deciding to be in a different
place, and then being there; when it reached the brink of the forge it
toppled off and tumbled to the smithy floor.

In agony Alvin rolled from the fire and also fell, also lay pressed
against the cold dirt of the floor. Now that the fire no longer surrounded
him, his body gained against the death of his skin, healing him as he
had taught it to do, without him having to tell it what to do, without
need of direction at all. Become yourself, that had been Alvin's command, and so the signature within each living bit of him obeyed the
pattern it contained, until his body was whole and perfect, the skin new,
uncallused, and unburned.

What he couldn't remove was the memory of pain, or the weakness
from all the strength his body had given up. But he didn't care. Weak
as he was, his heart was jubilant, because the plow that lay beside him
on the ground was living gold, not because he made it, but because he
taught it how to make itself.

The Finders found nothing, nowhere in town—yet the black-haired
Finder couldn't see anyone running away, neither, not within the farthest
distance that any natural man or horse could possibly have gone since
the boy got taken back. Somehow the mixup boy was hiding from them,
a thing they knew full well was pure impossible—but it must be so.

The place to look was where the boy had lived for all these years.
The roadhouse, the springhouse, the smithy—places where folks were
up unnatural late at night. They rode to near the roadhouse, then tied
up their horses just off the road. They loaded their shotguns and pistols
and set off on foot. Passing by the roadhouse they searched again, ac-
counting for every heartfire; none of them was like the cachet.

"That cottage, with that teacher lady," said the white-haired Finder.
"That's where the boy was when we found him before."

The black-haired Finder looked over that way. Couldn't see the springhouse through the trees, of course, but what he was looking for he could see, trees or not. "Two people in there," he said.

"Could be the mixup boy, then," said the white-haired Finder.

"Cachet says not." Then the black-haired Finder grinned nastily. "Single teacher lady, living alone, got a visitor this time of night? I know what kind of company she's keeping, and it ain't no mixup boy."

"Let's go see anyhow," said the white-haired Finder. "If'n you're right, she won't be putting out any complaint on how we broke in her door, or we'll just tell what we saw going on inside when we done it."

They had a good little laugh about that, and set off through the moonlight toward Miss Larner's house. They meant to kick in the door, of course, and have a good laugh when the teacher lady got all huffy about it and made her threats.

Funny thing was, when they actually got near the cottage, that plan just clean went out of their heads. They forgot all about it. Just looked again at the heartfires within and compared them to the cachet.

"What the hell are we doing up here?" asked the white-haired Finder. "Boy's bound to be at the roadhouse. We *know* he ain't here!"

"You know what I'm thinking?" said the black-haired one. "Maybe they killed him."

"That's plain crazy. Why save him, then?"

"How else do you figure they made it so we can't see him, then?"

"He's in the roadhouse. They got some hex that hides him up, I'll bet. Once we open the right door there, we'll see him and that'll be that."

For a fleeting moment the black-haired Finder thought—well, why not look in this teacher lady's cottage, too, if they got a hex like that? Why not open *this* door?

But he no sooner had that thought than it just slipped away so he couldn't remember it, couldn't even remember *having* a thought. He just trotted away after the white-haired Finder. Mixup boy's bound to be in the roadhouse, that's for sure.

She saw their heartfires, of course, as the Finders came toward her cottage, but Peggy wasn't afraid. She had explored Arthur Stuart's heartfire all this time, and there was no path there which led to capture by these Finders. Arthur had dangers enough in the future—Peggy could see that—but no harm would come to the boy tonight. So she paid them little heed. She knew when they decided to leave; knew when the black-haired Finder thought of coming in; knew when the hexes blocked him and drove him away. But it was Arthur Stuart she was watching, searching out the years to come.

Then, suddenly, she couldn't hold it to herself any longer. She had to tell Alvin, both the joy and sorrow of what he had done. Yet how could she? How could she tell him that Miss Larner was really a torch who could see the million newborn futures in Arthur Stuart's heartfire? It was unbearable to keep all this to herself. She might have told Mistress Modesty, years ago, when she lived there and kept no secrets.

It was madness to go down to the smithy, knowing that her desire was to tell him things she couldn't tell without revealing who she was. Yet it would surely drive her mad to stay within these walls, alone with all this knowledge that she couldn't share.

So she got up, unlocked the door, and stepped outside. No one around. She closed the door and locked it; then again looked into Arthur's heartfire and again found no danger for the boy. He would be safe. She would see Alvin.

Only then did she look into Alvin's heartfire; only then did she see the terrible pain that he had suffered only minutes ago. Why hadn't she noticed? Why hadn't she seen? Alvin had just passed through the greatest threshold of his life; he had truly done a great Making, brought something new into the world, and she hadn't seen. When he faced the Unmaker while she was in far-off Dekane, she had seen his struggle—now, when she wasn't three rods off, why hadn't she turned to him? Why hadn't she known his pain when he writhed inside the fire?

Maybe it was the springhouse. Once before, near nineteen years ago, the day that Alvin was born, the springhouse had damped her gift and lulled her to sleep till she was almost too late. But no, it couldn't be that—the water didn't run through the springhouse anymore, and the forgefire was stronger than that.

Maybe it was the Unmaker itself, come to block her. But as she cast about with her torchy sight, she couldn't see any unusual darkness amid the colors of the world around her, not close at hand, anyway. Nothing that could have blinded her.

No, it had to be the nature of what Alvin himself was doing that blinded her to it. Just as she hadn't seen how he would extricate himself from his confrontation with the Unmaker years ago, just as she hadn't seen how he would change young Arthur at the Hio shore tonight, it was just the same way she hadn't seen what he was doing in the forge. It was outside the futures that her knack could see, the particular Making he performed tonight.

Would it always be like that? Would she always be blinded when his most important work was being done? It made her angry, it frightened her—what good is my knack, if it deserts me just when I need it most!

No. I didn't need it most just now. Alvin had no need of me or my sight when he climbed into the fire. My knack has never deserted me when it was *needed*. It's only my desire that's thwarted.

Well, he needs me now, she thought. She picked her way carefully down the slope; the moon was low, the shadows deep, so the path was treacherous. When she rounded the corner of the smithy, the light from the forgefire, spilling out onto the grass, was almost blinding; it was so red that it made the grass look shiny black, not green.

Inside the smithy Alvin lay curled on the ground, facing toward the forge, away from her. He was breathing heavily, raggedly. Asleep? No. He was naked; it took a moment to realize that his clothing must have burned off him in the forge. He hadn't noticed it in all his pain, and so had no memory of it; therefore she hadn't seen it happen when she searched for memories in his heartfire.

His skin was shockingly pale and smooth. Earlier today she had seen his skin a deep brown from the sun and the forgefire's heat. Earlier today he had been callused, with here and there a scar from some spark or searing burn, the normal accidents of life beside a fire. Now, though, his skin was as unmarked as a baby's, and she could not help herself; she stepped into the smithy, knelt beside him, and gently brushed her hand along his back, from his shoulder down to the narrow place above the hip. His skin was so soft it made her own hands feel coarse to her, as if she marred him just by touching him.

He let out a long breath, a sigh. She withdrew her hand.

"Alvin," she said. "Are you all right?"

He moved his arm; he was stroking something that lay within the curl of his body. Only now did she see it, a faint yellow in the double shadow of his body and of the forge. A golden plow.

"It's alive," he murmured.

As if in answer, she saw it move smoothly under his hand.

Of course they didn't knock. At this time of night? They would know at once it couldn't be some chance traveler—it could only be the Finders. Knocking at the door would warn them, give them a chance to try to carry the boy farther off.

But the black-haired Finder didn't so much as try the latch. He just let fly with his foot and the door crashed inward, pulling away from the upper hinge as it did. Then, shotgun at the ready, he moved quickly inside and looked around the common room. The fire there was dying down, so the light was scant, but they could see that there was no one there.

"I'll keep watch on the stairs," said the white-haired Finder. "You go out the back to see if anybody's trying to get out that way."

The black-haired Finder immediately made his way past the kitchen and the stairs to the back door, which he flung open. The white-haired Finder was halfway up the stairs before the back door closed again.

In the kitchen, Old Peg crawled out from under the table. Neither one had so much as paused at the kitchen door. She didn't know who they were, of course, but she hoped—hoped it was the Finders, sneaking back here because somehow, by some miracle, Arthur Stuart got away and they didn't know where he was. She slipped off her shoes and walked as quietly as she could from the kitchen to the common room, where Horace kept a loaded shotgun over the fireplace. She reached up and took it down, but in the process she knocked over a tin teakettle that someone had left warming by the fire earlier in the evening. The kettle clattered; hot water spilled over her bare feet; she gasped in spite of herself.

Immediately she could hear footsteps on the stairs. She ignored the pain and ran to the foot of the stairs, just in time to see the white-haired Finder coming down. He had a shotgun pointed straight at her. Even though she'd never fired a gun at a human being in her life, she didn't hesitate a moment. She pulled the trigger; the gun kicked back against her belly, driving the breath out of her and slamming her against the wall beside the kitchen door. She hardly noticed. All she saw was how the white-haired Finder stood there, his face suddenly relaxing till it looked as stupid as a cow's face. Then red blossoms appeared all over his shirt, and he toppled over backward.

You'll never steal another child away from his mama, thought Old Peg. You'll never drag another Black into a life of bowing under the whip. I killed you, Finder, and I think the good Lord rejoices. But even if I go to hell for it, I'm glad.

She was so intent on watching him that she didn't even notice that the door out back stood open, held in place by the barrel of the black-haired Finder's gun, pointed right at her.

Alvin was so intent on telling Peggy what he had done that he hardly noticed he was naked. She handed him the leather apron hanging from a peg on the wall, and he put it on by habit, without a thought. She hardly heard his words; all that he was telling her, she already knew from looking in his heartfire. Instead she was looking at him, thinking, Now he's a Maker, in part because of what I taught him. Maybe I'm finished now, maybe my life will be my own—but maybe not, maybe now I've just begun, maybe now I can treat him as a man, not as a pupil or a ward. He seemed to glow with an inner fire; and every step he took, the golden plow echoed, not by following him or tangling itself in his feet, but by slipping along on a line that could have been an orbit around him, well out of the way but close enough to be of use; as if it were a part of him, though unattached.

"I know," Peggy told him. "I understand. You *are* a Maker now."

"It's more than that!" he cried. "It's the Crystal City. I know how to build it now, Miss Larner. See, the city ain't the crystal towers that I saw, the city's the people inside it, and if I'm going to build the place I got to find the kind of folks who ought to be there, folks as true and loyal as this plow, folks who share the dream enough to want to build it, and keep on building it even if I'm not there. You see, Miss Larner? The Crystal City isn't a thing that a single Maker can make. It's a city of Makers; I got to find all kinds of folks and somehow make Makers out of them."

She knew as he said it that this was indeed the task that he was born for—and the labor that would break his heart. "Yes," she said. "That's true, I know it is." And in spite of herself, she couldn't sound like Miss Larner, calm and cool and distant. She sounded like herself, like her true feelings. She was burning up inside with the fire that Alvin lit there.

"Come with me, Miss Larner," said Alvin. "You know so much, and you're such a good teacher—I need your help."

No, Alvin, not those words. I'll come with you for those words, yes, but say the other words, the ones I need so much to hear. "How can I teach what only you know how to do?" she asked him—trying to sound quiet, calm.

"But it ain't just for the teaching, either—I can't do this alone. What I done tonight, it's so hard—I need to have you with me." He took a step toward her. The golden plow slipped across the floor toward her, behind her; if it marked the outer border of Alvin's largest self, then she was now well within that generous circle.

"What do you need me for?" asked Peggy. She refused to look within his heartfire, refused to see whether or not there was any chance that he might actually—no, she refused even to name to herself what it was she wanted now, for fear that somehow she'd discover that it couldn't possibly be so, that it could never happen, that somehow tonight all such paths had been irrevocably closed. Indeed, she realized, that was part of why she had been so caught up in exploring Arthur Stuart's new futures; he would be so close to Alvin that she could see much of Alvin's great and terrible future through Arthur's eyes, without ever having to know what she would know if she looked into Alvin's own heartfire: Alvin's heartfire would show her whether, in his many futures, there were any in which he loved her, and married her, and put that dear and perfect body into her arms to give her and get from her that gift that only lovers share.

"Come with me," he said. "I can't even think of going on out there without you, Miss Larner. I—" He laughed at himself. "I don't even know your first name, Miss Larner."

"Margaret," she said.

"Can I call you that? Margaret—will you come with me? I know you ain't what you seem to be, but I don't care what you look like under all that hexery. I feel like you're the only living soul who knows me like I really am, and I—"

He just stood there, looking for the word. And she stood there, waiting to hear it.

"I love you," he said. "Even though you think I'm just a boy."

Maybe she would've answered him. Maybe she would've told him that she knew he was a man, and that she was the only woman who could love him without worshipping him, the only one who could actually be a helpmeet for him. But into the silence after his words and before she could speak, there came the sound of a gunshot.

At once she thought of Arthur Stuart, but it only took a moment to see that his heartfire was undisturbed; he lay asleep up in her little house. No, the sound came from farther off. She cast her torchy sight to the roadhouse, and there found the heartfire of a man in the last moment before death, and he was looking at a woman standing down at the foot of the stairs. It was Mother, holding a shotgun.

His heartfire dimmed, died. At once Peggy looked into her mother's heartfire and saw, behind her thoughts and feelings and memories, a million paths of the future, all jumbling together, all changing before her eyes, all becoming one single path, which led to one single place. A flash of searing agony, and then nothing.

"Mother!" she cried. "Mother!"

And then the future became the present; Old Peg's heartfire was gone before the sound of the second gunshot reached the smithy.

Alvin could hardly believe what he was saying to Miss Larner. He hadn't known until this moment, when he said it, how he felt about her. He was so afraid she'd laugh at him, so afraid she'd tell him he was far too young, that in time he'd get over how he felt.

But instead of answering him, she paused for just a moment, and in that moment a gunshot rang out. Alvin knew at once that it came from the roadhouse; he followed the sound with his bug and found where it came from, found a dead man already beyond all healing. And then a moment later, another gunshot, and then he found someone else dying, a woman. He knew that body from the inside out; it wasn't no stranger. It had to be Old Peg.

"Mother!" cried Miss Larner. "Mother!"

"It's Old Peg Guester!" cried Alvin.

He saw Miss Larner tear open the collar of her dress, reach inside and pull out the amulets that hung there. She tore them off her neck, cutting herself bad on the breaking strings. Alvin could hardly take in what he saw—a young woman, scarce older than himself, and beautiful, even though her face was torn with grief and terror.

"It's my mother!" she cried. "Alvin, save her!"

He didn't wait a second. He just tore on out of the smithy, running barefoot on the grass, in the road, not caring how the rough dirt and rocks tore into his soft, unaccustomed feet. The leather apron caught and tangled between his knees; he tugged it, twisted it to the side, out of his way. He could see with his bug how Old Peg was already past saving, but still he ran, because he had to *try*, even though he knew there was no reason in it. And then she died, and still he ran, because he couldn't bear not to be running to where that good woman, his good friend was lying dead.

His good friend and Miss Larner's mother. The only way that could be is if she was the torch girl what run off seven years ago. But then if she was such a torch as folks around her said, why didn't she see this coming? Why didn't she look into her own mother's heartfire and foresee her death? It made no sense.

There was a man in front of him on the road. A man running down from the roadhouse toward some horses tied to trees just over yonder. It was the man who killed Old Peg, Alvin knew that, and cared to know no more. He sped up, faster than he'd ever run before without getting strength from the forest around him. The man heard him coming maybe thirty yards off, and turned around.

"You, smith!" cried the black-haired Finder. "Glad to kill you too!"

He had a pistol in his hand; he fired.

Alvin took the bullet in his belly, but he didn't care about that. His body started work at once fixing what the bullet tore, but it wouldn't've mattered a speck if he'd been bleeding to death. Alvin didn't even slow down; he flew into the man, knocking him down, landing on him and skidding with him ten feet across the dirt of the road. The man cried out in fear and pain. That single cry was the last sound he made; in his rage, Alvin caught the man's head in such a grip that it took only one sharp jab of his other hand against the man's jaw to snap his neckbone clean in half. The man was already dead, but Alvin hit his head again and again with his fists, until his arms and chest and his leather apron was all covered with the black-haired Finder's blood and the man's skull was broke up inside his head like shards of dropped pottery.

Then Alvin knelt there, his head stupid with exhaustion and spent anger. After a minute or so he remembered that Old Peg was still lying there on the roadhouse floor. He knowed she was dead, but where else did he have to go? Slowly he got to his feet.

He heard horses coming down the road from town. That time of night in Hatrack River, gunshots meant only trouble. Folks'd come. They'd find the body in the road—they'd come on up to the roadhouse. No need for Alvin to stay to greet them.

Inside the roadhouse, Peggy was already kneeling over her mother's body, sobbing and panting from her run up to the house. Alvin only knew for sure it was her from her dress—he'd only seen her face but once before, for a second there in the smithy. She turned when she saw Alvin come inside. "Where were you! Why didn't you save her! You could have saved her!"

"I never could," said Alvin. It was wrong of her to say such a thing. "There wasn't time."

"You should have looked! You should have seen what was coming."

Alvin didn't understand her. "I can't see what's coming," he said. "That's *your* knack."

Then she burst out crying, not the dry sobs like when he first came in, but deep, gut-wrenching howls of grief. Alvin didn't know what to do.

The door opened behind him.

"Peggy," whispered Horace Guester. "Little Peggy."

Peggy looked up at her father, her face so streaked with tears and twisted up and reddened with weeping that it was a marvel he could recognize her. "I killed her!" she cried. "I never should have left, Papa! I killed her!"

Only then did Horace understand that it was his wife's body lying there. Alvin watched as he started trembling, groaning, then keening loud and high like a hurt dog. Alvin never seen such grieving. Did my father cry like that when my brother Vigor died? Did he make such a sound as this when he thought that me and Measure was tortured to death by Red men?

Alvin reached out his arms to Horace, held him tight around the shoulders, then led him over to Peggy and helped him kneel there beside his daughter, both of them weeping, neither giving a sign that they saw each other. All they saw was Old Peg's body spread out on the floor; Alvin couldn't even guess how deeply, how agonizingly each one bore the whole blame for her dying.

After a while the sheriff came in. He'd already found the black-haired Finder's corpse outside, and it didn't take him long to understand exactly what happened. He took Alvin aside. "This is pure self-defense if I ever saw it," said Pauley Wiseman, "and I wouldn't make you spend three seconds in jail for it. But I can tell you that the law in Appalachee don't take the death of a Finder all that easy, and the treaty lets them come up here and get you to take back there for trial. What I'm saying, boy, is you better get the hell out of here in the next couple of days or I can't promise you'll be safe."

"I was going anyway," said Alvin.

"I don't know how you done it," said Pauley Wiseman, "but I reckon you got that half-Black pickaninny away from them Finders tonight and hid him somewhere around here. I'm telling you, Alvin, when you go, you best take that boy with you. Take him to Canada. But if I see his face again, I'll ship him south myself. It's that boy caused all this—makes me sick, a good White woman dying cause of some half-Black mixup boy."

"You best never say such a thing in front of me again, Pauley Wiseman."

The sheriff only shook his head and walked away. "Ain't natural," he said. "All you people set on a monkey like it was folks." He turned around to face Alvin. "I don't much care what you think of me, Alvin Smith, but I'm giving you and that mixup boy a chance to stay alive. I hope you have brains to take it. And in the meantime, you might go wash off that blood and fetch some clothes to wear."

Alvin walked on back to the road. Other folks was coming by then—he paid them no heed. Only Mock Berry seemed to understand what was happening. He led Alvin on down to his house, and there Anga washed him down and Mock gave him some of his own clothes to wear. It was nigh onto dawn when Alvin got him back to the smithy.

Makepeace was setting there on a stool in the smithy door, looking at the golden plow. It was resting on the ground, still as you please, right in front of the forge.

"That's one hell of a journeyman piece," said Makepeace.

"I reckon," said Alvin. He walked over to the plow and reached down. It fairly leapt into Alvin's hands—not heavy at all now—but if Makepeace noticed how the plow moved by itself just before Alvin touched it, he didn't say.

"I got a lot of scrap iron," said Makepeace. "I don't even ask for you to go halves with me. Just let me keep a few pieces when you turn them into gold.''

"I ain't turning no more iron into gold," said Alvin.

It made Makepeace angry. "That's *gold*, you fool! That there plow you made means never going hungry, never having to work again, living fine instead of in that rundown house up there! It means new dresses for Gertie and maybe a suit of clothes for me! It means folks in town saying Good morning to me and tipping their hats like I was a gentleman. It means riding in a carriage like Dr. Physicker, and going to Dekane or Carthage or wherever I please and not even caring what it costs. And you're telling me you ain't making no more *gold*?''

Alvin knew it wouldn't do no good explaining, but still he tried. "This ain't no common gold, sir. This is a living plow—I ain't going to let nobody melt it down to make coins out of it. Best I can figure, nobody could melt it even if they wanted to. So back off and let me go.''

"What you going to do, plow with it? You blame fool, we could be kings of the world together!" But when Alvin pushed on by, headed out of the smithy, Makepeace stopped his pleading and started getting ugly. "That's my iron you used to make that golden plow! That gold belongs to *me!* A journeyman piece always belongs to the master, less'n he gives it to the journeyman and I sure as hell don't! Thief! You're stealing from me!''

"You stole five years of my life from me, long after I was good enough to be a journeyman," Alvin said. "And this plow—making it was none of your teaching. It's alive, Makepeace Smith. It doesn't belong to you and it doesn't belong to me. It belongs to itself. So let me just set it down here and we'll see who gets it.''

Alvin set down the plow on the grass between them. Then he stepped back a few paces. Makepeace took one step toward the plow. It sank down into the soil under the grass, then cut its way through the dirt till it reached Alvin. When he picked it up, it was warm. He knew what that had to mean. "Good soil," said Alvin. The plow trembled in his hands.

Makepeace stood there, his eyes bugged out with fear. "Good Lord, boy, that plow *moved*.''

"I know it," said Alvin.

"What are you, boy? The devil?''

"I don't think so," said Alvin. "Though I might've met him once or twice.''

"Get on out of here! Take that thing and go away! I never want to see your face around here again!''

"You got my journeyman paper," said Alvin. "I want it."

Makepeace reached into his pocket, took out a folded paper, and threw it onto the grass in front of the smithy. Then he reached out and pulled the smithy doors shut, something he hardly ever did, even in winter. He shut them tight and barred them on the inside. Poor fool, as if Alvin couldn't break down them walls in a second if he really wanted to get inside. Alvin walked over and picked up the paper. He opened it and read it—signed all proper. It was legal. Alvin was a journeyman.

The sun was just about to show up when Alvin got to the springhouse door. Of course it was locked, but locks and hexes couldn't keep Alvin out, specially when he made them all himself. He opened the door and went inside. Arthur Stuart stirred in his sleep. Alvin touched his shoulder, brought the boy awake. Alvin knelt there by the bed and told the boy most all that happened in the night. He showed him the golden plow, showed him how it moved. Arthur laughed in delight. Then Alvin told him that the woman he called Mama all his life was dead, killed by the Finders, and Arthur cried.

But not for long. He was too young to cry for long. "You say she kilt one herself afore she died?"

"With your pa's own shotgun."

"Good for her!" said Arthur Stuart, his voice so fierce Alvin almost laughed, him being so small.

"I killed the other one myself. The one that shot her."

Arthur reached out and took Alvin's right hand and opened it. "Did you kill him with this hand?"

Alvin nodded.

Arthur kissed his open palm.

"I would've fixed her up if I could," said Alvin. "But she died too fast. Even if I'd been standing right there the second after the shot hit her, I couldn't've fixed her up."

Arthur Stuart reached out and hung onto Alvin around his neck and cried some more.

It took a day to put Old Peg into the ground, up on the hill with her own daughters and Alvin's brother Vigor and Arthur's mama who died so young. "A place for people of courage," said Dr. Physicker, and Alvin knew that he was right, even though Physicker didn't know about the runaway Black slave girl.

Alvin washed away the bloodstains from the floor and stairs of the roadhouse, using his knack to pull out what blood the lye and sand couldn't remove. It was the last gift he could give to Horace or to Peggy. Margaret. Miss Larner.

"I got to leave now," he told them. They were setting on chairs in the common room of the inn, where they'd been receiving mourners all day. "I'm taking Arthur to my folks' place in Vigor Church. He'll be safe there. And then I'm going on."

"Thank you for everything," said Horace. "You been a good friend to us. Old Peg loved you." Then he broke down crying again.

Alvin patted him on the shoulder a couple of times, and then moved over to stand in front of Peggy. "All that I am, Miss Larner, I owe to you."

She shook her head.

"I meant all I said to you. I still mean it."

Again she shook her head. He wasn't surprised. With her mama dead, never even knowing that her own daughter'd come home, why, Alvin didn't expect she could just up and go. Somebody had to help Horace Guester run the roadhouse. It all made sense. But still it stabbed him to the heart, because now more than ever he knew that it was true—he loved her. But she wasn't for him. That much was plain. She never had been. A woman like this, so educated and fine and beautiful—she could be his teacher, but she could never love him like he loved her.

"Well then, I guess I'm saying good-bye," said Alvin. He stuck out his hand, even though he knew it was kind of silly to shake hands with somebody grieving the way she was. But he wanted so bad to put his arms around her and hold her tight the way he'd held Arthur Stuart when he was grieving, and a handshake was as close as he could come to that.

She saw his hand, and reached up and took it. Not for a handshake, but just holding his hand, holding it tight. It took him by surprise. He'd think about that many times in the months and years to come, how tight she held to him. Maybe it meant she loved him. Or maybe it meant she only cared for him as a pupil, or thanked him for avenging her mama's death—how could he know what a thing like that could mean? But still he held onto that memory, in case it meant she loved him.

And he made her a promise then, with her holding his hand like that; made her a promise even though he didn't know if she even wanted him to keep it. "I'll be back," he said. "And what I said last night, it'll always be true." It took all his courage then to call her by the name she gave him permission last night to use. "God be with you, Margaret."

"God be with you, Alvin," she whispered.

Then he gathered up Arthur Stuart, who'd been saying his own good-byes, and led the boy outside. They walked out back of the roadhouse to the barn, where Alvin had hidden the golden plow deep in a barrel of beans. He took off the lid and held out his hand, and the plow rose upward until it glinted in the light. Then Alvin took it up, wrapped it double in burlap and put it inside a burlap bag, then swung the bag over his shoulder.

Alvin knelt down and held out his hand the way he always did when he wanted Arthur Stuart to climb up onto his back. Arthur did, thinking it was all for play—a boy that age, he can't be grieving for more than an hour or two at a time. He swung up onto Alvin's back, laughing and bouncing.

"This time it's going to be a long ride, Arthur Stuart," said Alvin. "We're going all the way to my family's house in Vigor Church."

"Walking the whole way?"

"*I'll* be walking. *You're* going to ride."

"Gee-yap!" cried Arthur Stuart.

Alvin set off at a trot, but before long he was running full out. He never set foot on that road, though. Instead he took off cross country, over fields, over fences, and on into the woods, which still stood in great swatches here and there across the states of Hio and Wobbish between him and home. The greensong was much weaker than it had been in the days when the Red men had it all to themselves. But the song was still strong enough for Alvin Smith to hear. He let himself fall into the rhythm of the greensong, running as the Red men did. And Arthur Stuart—maybe he could hear some of the greensong too, enough that it could lull him to sleep, there on Alvin's back. The world was gone. Just him, Arthur Stuart, the golden plow—and the whole world singing around him. I'm a journeyman now. And this is my first journey.

20

Cavil's Deed

Cavil Planter had business in town. He mounted his horse early on that fine spring morning, leaving behind wife and slaves, house and land, knowing all were well under his control, fully his own.

Along about noon, after many a pleasant visit and much business well done, he stopped in at the postmaster's store. There were three letters there. Two were from old friends. One was from Reverend Philadelphia Thrower in Carthage, the capital of Wobbish.

Old friends could wait. This would be news about the Finders he hired, though why the letter should come from Thrower and not from the Finders themselves, Cavil couldn't guess. Maybe there was trouble. Maybe he'd have to go north to testify after all. Well, if that's what it takes, I'll do it, thought Cavil. Gladly I'll leave the ninety and nine sheep, as Jesus said, in order to reclaim the one that strayed.

It was bitter news. Both Finders dead, and so also the innkeeper's wife who claimed to have adopted Cavil's stolen firstborn son. Good riddance to her, thought Cavil, and he spared not a second's grief for the Finders—they were hirelings, and he valued them less than his slaves, since they weren't *his*. No, it was the last news, the worst news, that set Cavil's hands to trembling and his breath to stop. The man who killed one of the Finders, a prentice smith named Alvin, he ran off instead of standing trial—and took with him Cavil's son.

He took my son. And the worst words from Thrower were these: "I knew this fellow Alvin when he was a mere child, and already he was an agent of evil. He is our mutual Friend's worst enemy in all the world, and now he has your most valued property in his possession. I wish I had better news. I pray for you, lest your son be turned into a dangerous and implacable foe of all our Friend's holy work."

With such news, how could Cavil go about the rest of the day's business? Without a word to the postmaster or to anybody, Cavil stuffed the letters into his pocket, went outside, mounted his horse, and headed home. All the way his heart was tossed between rage and fear. How could those northerner Emancipationist scum have let his slave, his son, get stole right out from under them, by the worst enemy of the Overseer? I'll go north, I'll make them pay, I'll find the boy, I'll—and then his thoughts would turn all of a sudden to what the Overseer would say, if ever He came again. What if He despises me now, and never comes again? Or worse, what if He comes and damns me for a slothful servant? Or what if He declares me unworthy and forbids me to take any more Black women to myself? How could I live if not in His service—what else is my life *for?*

And then rage again, terrible blasphemous rage, in which he cried out deep within his soul, O my Overseer! Why did You let this happen? You could have stopped it with a word, if You are truly Lord!

And then terror: Such a thing, to doubt the power of the Overseer! No, forgive me, I am truly Thy slave, O Master! Forgive me, I've lost everything, forgive me!

Poor Cavil. He'd find out soon enough what losing everything could mean.

He got himself home and turned the horse up that long drive leading to the house, only the sun being hot he stayed under the shade of the oaks along the south side of the road. Maybe if he'd rode out in the middle of the lane he would've been seen sooner. Maybe then he wouldn't have heard a woman cry out inside the house just as he was coming out from under the trees.

"Dolores!" he called. "Is something wrong?"

No answer.

Now, that scared him. It conjured up pictures in his mind of marauders or thieves or such, breaking into his house while he was gone. Maybe they already killed Lashman, and even now were killing his wife. He spurred his horse and raced around the house to the back.

Just in time to see a big old Black running from the back door of the house down toward the slave quarters. He couldn't see the Black man's face, on account of his trousers, which he didn't have on, nor any other clothing either—no, he was holding those trousers like a banner, flapping away in front of his face as he ran down toward the sheds.

A Black, no pants on, running out of my house, in which a woman was crying out. For a moment Cavil was torn between the desire to chase down the Black man and kill him with his bare hands and the need to go up and see to Dolores, make sure she was all right. Had he come in time? Was she undefiled?

Cavil bounded up the stairs and flung open the door to his wife's room. There lay Dolores in bed, her covers tight up under her chin, looking at him through wide-open, frightened eyes.

"What happened!" cried Cavil. "Are you all right?"

"Of course I am!" she answered sharply. "What are you doing home?"

That wasn't the answer you get from a woman who's just cried out in fear. "I heard you call out," said Cavil. "Didn't you hear me answer?"

"I hear everything up here," said Dolores. "I got nothing to do in my life but lie here and listen. I hear everything that's said in this house and everything that's done. Yes, I heard you call. But you weren't answering *me*."

Cavil was astonished. She sounded angry. He'd never heard her sound angry before. Lately he'd hardly heard a word from her at all—she was always asleep when he took breakfast, and their dinners together passed in silence. Now this anger—why? Why now?

"I saw a Black man running away from the house," said Cavil. "I thought maybe he—"

"Maybe he what?" She said the words like a taunt, a challenge.

"Maybe he hurt you."

"No, he didn't *hurt* me."

Now a thought began to creep into Cavil's mind, a thought so terrible he couldn't even admit he was thinking it. "What *did* he do, then?"

"Why, the same holy work that you've been doing, Cavil."

Cavil couldn't say a thing to that. She knew. She knew it all.

"Last summer, when your friend Reverend Thrower came, I lay here in my bed as you talked, the two of you."

"You were asleep. Your door was—"

"I heard everything. Every word, every whisper. I heard you go outside. I heard you talk at breakfast. Do you know I wanted to kill you? For years I thought you were the loving husband, a Christlike man, and all this time you were rutting with these Black women. And then sold all your own babies as slaves. You're a monster, I thought. So evil that for you to live another minute was an abomination. But my hands couldn't hold a knife or pull the trigger on a gun. So I lay here and thought. And you know what I thought?"

Cavil said nothing. The way she told it, it made him sound so bad. "It wasn't like that, it was holy."

"It was adultery!"

"I had a vision!"

"Yes, your vision. Well, fine and dandy, Mr. Cavil Planter, you had a vision that making half-White babies was a good thing. Here's some news for you. I can make half-White babies, too!"

It was all making sense now. "He raped you!"

"He didn't rape me, Cavil. I invited him up here. I told him what to do. I made him call me his vixen and say prayers with me before and after so it would be as *holy* as what you did. We prayed to your damned Overseer, but for some reason he never showed up."

"It never happened."

"Again and again, every time you left the plantation, all winter, all spring."

"I don't believe it. You're lying to hurt me. You *can't* do that—the doctor said—it hurts you too bad."

"Cavil, before I found out what you done with those Black women, I thought I knew what pain was, but all that suffering was nothing, do you hear me? I could live through that pain every day forever and call it a holiday. I'm pregnant, Cavil."

"He raped you. That's what we'll tell everybody, and we'll hang him as an example, and—"

"Hang *him?* There's only one rapist on this plantation, Cavil, and don't think for a moment that I won't tell. If you lay a hand on my baby's father, I'll tell the whole county what you've been doing. I'll get up on Sunday and tell the church."

"I did it in the service of the—"

"Do you think they'll believe that? No more than I do. The word for what you done isn't holiness. It's concupiscence. Adultery. Lust. And when word gets out, when my baby is born Black, they'll turn against you, all of them. They'll run you out."

Cavil knew she was right. Nobody would believe him. He was ruined. Unless he did one simple thing.

He walked out of her room. She lay there laughing at him, taunting him. He went to his bedroom, took the shotgun down from the wall, poured in the powder, wadded it, then dumped in a double load of shot and rammed it tight with a second wad.

She wasn't laughing when he came back in. Instead she had her face toward the wall, and she was crying. Too late for tears, he thought. She didn't turn to face him as he strode to the bed and tore down the covers. She was naked as a plucked chicken.

"Cover me!" she whimpered. "He ran out so fast, he didn't dress me. It's cold! Cover me, Cavil—"

Then she saw the gun.

Her twisted hands flailed in the air. Her body writhed. She cried out in the pain of trying to move so quickly. Then he pulled the trigger and her body just flopped right down on the bed, a last sigh of air leaking out of the top of her neck.

Cavil went back to his room and reloaded the gun.

He found Fat Fox fully dressed, polishing the carriage. He was such a liar, he thought he could fool Cavil Planter. But Cavil didn't even bother listening to his lies. "Your vixen wants to see you upstairs," he said.

Fat Fox kept denying it all the way until he got into the room and saw Dolores on the bed. Then he changed his tune. "She made me! What could I do, Master! It was like you and the women, Master! What choice a Black slave got? I got to obey, don't I? Like the women and you!"

Cavil knew devil talk when he heard it, and he paid no mind. "Strip off your clothes and do it again," he said. Fat Fox howled and Fat Fox whined, but when Cavil jammed him in the ribs with the barrel, he did what he was told. He closed his eyes so he didn't have to see what Cavil's shotgun done to Dolores, and he did what he was told. Then Cavil fired the gun again.

In a little while Lashman came in from the far field, all a-lather with running and fearing when he heard the gunshots. Cavil met him downstairs. "Lock down the slaves, Lashman, and then go fetch me the sheriff."

When the sheriff came, Cavil led him upstairs and showed him. The sheriff went pale. "Good Lord," he whispered.

"Is it murder, Sheriff? I did it. Are you taking me to jail?"

"No sir," said the sheriff. "Ain't nobody going to call this murder." Then he looked at Cavil with this twisted kind of expression on his face. "What kind of man are you, Cavil?"

For a moment Cavil didn't understand the question.

"Letting me see your wife like that. I'd rather die before I let somebody see my wife like that."

The sheriff left. Lashman had the slaves clean up the room. There was no funeral for either one. They both got buried out where Salamandy lay. Cavil was pretty sure a few chickens died over the graves, but by then he didn't care. He was on his tenth bottle of bourbon and his ten-thousandth muttered prayer to the Overseer, who seemed powerful standoffish at a time like this.

Along about a week later, or maybe longer, here comes the sheriff again, with the priest and the Baptist preacher both. The three of them woke Cavil up from his drunken sleep and showed him a draught for twenty-five thousand dollars. "All your neighbors took up a collection," the priest explained.

"I don't need money," Cavil said.

"They're buying you out," said the preacher.

"Plantation ain't for sale."

The sheriff shook his head. "You got it wrong, Cavil. What happened here, that was bad. But you letting folks see your wife like that—"

"I only let *you* see."

"You ain't no gentleman, Cavil."

"Also, there's the matter of the slave children," said the Baptist preacher. "They seem remarkably light-skinned, considering you have no breeding stock but what's black as night."

"It's a miracle from God," said Cavil. "The Lord is lightening the Black race."

The sheriff slid a paper over to Cavil. "This is the transfer of title of all your property—slaves, buildings, and land—to a holding company consisting of your former neighbors."

Cavil read it. "This deed says all the slaves here on the land," he said. "I got rights in a runaway slave boy up north."

"We don't care about that. He's yours if you can find him. I hope you noticed this deed also includes a stipulation that you will never return to this county or any adjoining county for the rest of your natural life."

"I saw that part," said Cavil.

"I can assure you that if you break that agreement, it will be the end of your natural life. Even a conscientious, hardworking sheriff like me couldn't protect you from what would happen."

"You said no threats," murmured the priest.

"Cavil needs to know the consequences," said the sheriff.

"I won't be back," said Cavil.

"Pray to God for forgiveness," said the preacher.

"That I will." Cavil signed the paper.

That very night he rode out on his horse with a twenty-five-thousand-dollar draught in his pocket and a change of clothes and a week's provisions on a pack horse behind him. Nobody bid him farewell. The slaves were singing jubilation songs in the sheds behind him. His horse manured the end of the drive. And in Cavil's mind there was only one thought. The Overseer hates me, or this all wouldn't have happened. There's only one way to win back His love. That's to find that Alvin Smith, kill him, and get back my boy, my last slave who still belongs to me.

Then, O my Overseer, will You forgive me, and heal the terrible stripes Thy lash has torn upon my soul?

21

Alvin Journeyman

Alvin stayed home in Vigor Church all summer, getting to know his family again. Folks had changed, more than a little—Cally was man-size now, and Measure had him a wife and children, and the twins Wastenot and Wantnot had married them a pair of French sisters from Detroit, and Ma and Pa was both grey-haired mostly, and moving slower than Alvin liked to see. But some things didn't change—there was playfulness in them all, the whole family, and the darkness that had fallen over Vigor Church after the massacre at Tippy-Canoe, it was—well, not *gone*—more like it had changed into a kind of shadow that was behind everything, so the bright spots in life seemed all the brighter by contrast.

They all took to Arthur Stuart right off. He was so young he could hear all the men of the town tell him the tale of Tippy-Canoe, and all that he thought of it was to tell them his own story—which was really a mish-mash of his real mama's story, and Alvin's story, and the story of the Finders and how his White mama killed one afore she died.

Alvin pretty much let Arthur Stuart's account of things stand uncorrected. Partly it was because why should he make Arthur Stuart out to be wrong, when he loved telling the tale so? Partly it was out of sorrow, realizing bit by bit that Arthur Stuart never spoke in nobody else's voice but his own. Folks here would never know what it was like to hear Arthur Stuart speak their own voice right back at them. Even so, they loved to hear the boy talk, because he still remembered all the words people said, never forgetting a scrap it seemed like. Why should Alvin mar what was left of Arthur Stuart's knack?

Alvin also figured that what he never told, nobody could ever repeat. For instance, there was a certain burlap parcel that nobody ever saw unwrapped. It wouldn't do no good for word to get around that a certain golden object had been seen in the town of Vigor Church—the town, which hadn't had many visitors since the dark day of the massacre at Tippy-Canoe, would soon have more company than they wanted, and all the wrong sort, looking for gold and not caring who got harmed along the way. So he never told a soul about the golden plow, and the only person who even knew he was keeping a secret was his close-mouthed sister Eleanor.

Alvin went to call on her at the store she and Armor-of-God kept right there on the town square, ever since before there *was* a town square. Once it had been a place where visitors, Red and White, came from far away to get maps and news, back when the land was still mostly forest from the Mizzipy to Dekane. Now it was still busy, but it was all local folks, come to buy or hear gossip and news of the outside world. Since Armor-of-God was the only grown-up man in Vigor Church who wasn't cursed with Tenskwa-Tawa's curse, he was also the only one who could easily go outside to buy goods and hear news, bringing it all back in to the farmers and tradesmen of Vigor Church. It happened that today Armor-of-God was away, heading up to the town of Mishy-Waka to pick up some orders of glass goods and fine china. So Alvin found only Eleanor and her oldest boy, Hector, there, tending the store.

Things had changed a bit since the old days. Eleanor, who was near as good a hexmaker as Alvin, didn't have to conceal her hexes in the patterns of hanging flower baskets and arrangements of herbs in the kitchen. Now some of the hexes were right out in the open, which meant they could be much clearer and stronger. Armor-of-God must've let up a little on his hatred of knackery and hidden powers. That was a good thing—it was a painful thing, in the old days, to know how Eleanor had to pretend not to be what she was or know what she knew.

"I got something with me," said Alvin.

"So I see," said Eleanor. "All wrapped in a burlap bag, as still as stone, and yet it seems to me there's something living inside."

"Never you mind about that," said Alvin. "What's here is for no other soul but me to see."

Eleanor didn't ask any questions. She knew from those words exactly why he brought his mysterious parcel by. She told Hector to wait on any customers as came by, and then led Alvin out into the new ware-room, where they kept such things as a dozen kinds of beans in barrels, salt meat in kegs, sugar in paper cones, powder salt in waterproof pots, and spices all in different kinds of jars. She went straight to the fullest of the bean barrels, filled with a kind of green-speckle bean that Alvin hadn't seen before.

"Not much call for these beans," she said. "I reckon we'll never see the bottom of this barrel."

Alvin set the plow, all wrapped in burlap, on top of the beans. And then he made the beans slide out of the way, flowing around the plow smooth as molasses, until it sank right down to the bottom. He didn't so much as ask Eleanor to turn away, since she knew Alvin had power to do *that* much since he was just a little boy.

"Whatever's living in there," said Eleanor, "it ain't going to die, being dry down at the bottom of the barrel, is it?"

"It won't ever die," said Alvin, "at least not the way folks grow old and die."

Eleanor gave in to curiosity just enough to say, "I wish you could promise me that if anybody ever knows what's in there, so will I."

Alvin nodded to her. That was a promise he could keep. At the time, he didn't know how or when he'd ever show that plow to anybody, but if anybody could keep a secret, silent Eleanor could.

So anyway he lived in Vigor Church, sleeping in his old bedroom in his parents' house, lived there a good many weeks, well on toward July, and all the while he kept most of what happened in his seven-year prenticeship to himself. In fact he talked hardly more than he had to. He went here and there, a-calling on folks with his Pa or Ma, and without much fuss healing such toothaches and broken bones and festering wounds and sickness as he found. He helped at the mill; he hired out to work in other farmers' fields and barns; he built him a small forge and did simple repairs and solders, the kind a smith can do without a proper anvil. And all that time, he pretty much spoke when people spoke to him, and said little more than what was needed to do business or get the food he wanted at table.

He wasn't glum—he laughed at a joke, and even told a few. He wasn't solemn, neither, and spent more than a few afternoons down in the square, proving to the strongest farmers in Vigor Church that they weren't no match for a blacksmith's arms and shoulders in a rassling match. He just didn't have any gossip or small talk, and he never told a story on himself. And if you didn't keep a conversation going, Alvin was content to let it fall into silence, keeping at his work or staring off into the distance like as if he didn't even remember you were there.

Some folks noticed how little Alvin talked, but he'd been gone a long time, and you don't expect a nineteen-year-old to act the same as an eleven-year-old. They just figured he'd grown up to be a quiet man.

But a few knew better. Alvin's mother and father had some words between the two of them, more than once. "The boy's had some bad things happen to him," said his mother; but his father took a different view. "I reckon maybe he's had bad and good mixed in together, like most folks—he just doesn't know us well enough yet, after being gone seven years. Let him get used to being a man in this town, and not a boy anymore, and pretty soon he'll talk his leg off."

Eleanor, she also noticed Alvin wasn't talking, but since she also knew he had a marvelous secret living thing hidden in her bean barrel, she didn't fuss for a minute about something being *wrong* with Alvin. It was like she said to her husband, Armor-of-God, when he mentioned about how Alvin just didn't seem to have five words altogether for nobody. "He's thinking deep thoughts," said Eleanor. "He's working out problems none of us knows enough to help him with. You'll see— he'll talk plenty when he figures it all out."

And there was Measure, Alvin's brother who got captured by Reds when Alvin was; the brother who had come to know Ta-Kumsaw and Tenskwa-Tawa near as well as Alvin himself. Of course Measure noticed how little Alvin had told them about his prentice years, and in due time he'd surely be one Alvin could talk to—that was natural, seeing how long Alvin had trusted Measure and all they'd been through together. But at first Alvin felt shy even around Measure, seeing how he had his wife, Delphi, and any fool could see how they hardly could stand to be more than three feet apart from each other; he was so gentle and careful with her, always looking out for her, turning to talk to her if she was near, looking for her to come back if she was gone. How could Alvin know whether there was room for him anymore in Measure's heart? No, not even to Measure could Alvin tell his tale, not at first.

One day in high summer, Alvin was out in a field building fences with his younger brother Cally, who was man-size now, as tall as Alvin though not as massive in the back and shoulders. The two of them had hired on for a week with Martin Hill. Alvin was doing the rail splitting—hardly using his knack at all, either, though truth to tell he could've split all the rails just by asking them to split themselves. No, he set the wedge and hammered it down, and his knack only got used to keep the logs from splitting at bad angles that wouldn't give full-length rails.

They must have fenced about a quarter mile before Alvin realized that it was peculiar how Cally never fell behind. Alvin split, and Cally got the posts and rails laid in place, never needing a speck of help to set a post into soil too hard or soft or rocky or muddy.

So Alvin kept his eye on the boy—or, more exactly, used his knack to keep watch on Cally's work—and sure enough, Alvin could see that Cally had something of Alvin's knack, the way it was long ago when he didn't half understand what he was doing with it. Cally would find just the right spot to set a post, then make the ground soft till he needed it to be firm. Alvin figured Cally wasn't exactly planning it. He probably thought he was finding spots that were naturally good for setting a post.

Here it is, thought Alvin. Here's what I know I've got to do: teach somebody else to be a Maker. If ever there was someone I should teach, it's Cally, seeing how he's got something of the same knack. After all, he's seventh son of a seventh son same as me, since Vigor was still alive when I was born, but long dead when Cally came along.

So Alvin just up and started talking as they worked, telling Cally all about atoms and how you could teach them how to be, and they'd be like that. It was the first time Alvin tried to explain it to anybody since the last time he talked to Miss Larner—Margaret—and the words tasted delicious in his mouth. This is the work I was born for, thought Alvin. Telling my brother how the world works, so he can understand it and get some control over it.

You can bet Alvin was surprised, then, when Cally all of a sudden lifted a post high above his head and threw it on the ground at his brother's feet. It had so much force—or Cally had so ravaged it with his knack—that it shivered into kindling right there where it hit. Alvin couldn't hardly even guess why, but Cally was plain filled with rage.

"What did I say?" asked Alvin.

"My name's Cal," said Cally. "I ain't been Cally since I was ten years old."

"I didn't know," said Alvin. "I'm sorry, and from now on you're Cal to me."

"I'm *nothing* to you," said Cal. "I just wish you'd go away!"

It was only right at this minute that Alvin realized that Cal hadn't exactly invited him to go along on this job—it was Martin Hill what asked for Alvin to come, and before that, the job had been Cal's alone.

"I didn't mean to butt into your work here," said Alvin. "It just never entered my head you wouldn't want my help. I know I wanted your company."

Seemed like everything Alvin said only made Cal seethe inside till now his face was red and his fists were clenched tight enough to strangle a snake. "I had a place here," said Cal. "Then you come back. All fancy school taught like you are, using all them big words. And *healing* people without so much as touching them, just walking into their house and talking a spell, and when you leave everybody's all healed up from whatever ailed them—"

Alvin didn't even know folks had noticed he was doing it. Since nobody said a thing about it, he figured they all thought it was natural healing. "I can't think how that makes you mad, Cal. It's a good thing to make folks better."

All of a sudden there were tears running down Cal's cheeks. "Even laying hands on them, I can't always fix things up," said Cal. "Nobody even asks me no more."

It never occurred to Alvin that maybe Cal was doing his own healings. But it made good sense. Ever since Alvin left, Cal had pretty much been what Alvin used to be in Vigor Church, doing all his works. Seeing how their knacks were so much alike, he'd come close to taking Alvin's place. And then he'd done things Alvin never did when he was small, like going about healing people as best he could. Now Alvin was back, not only taking back his old place, but also besting Cal at things that only Cal had ever done. Now who was there for Cal to be?

"I'm sorry," said Al. "But I can teach you. That's what I was starting to do."

"I never seen them bits and what-not you're talking about," said Cal. "I didn't understand a thing you talked about. Maybe I just ain't got a knack as good as yours, or maybe I'm too dumb, don't you see? All I can be is the best I figure out for myself. And I don't need you proving to me that I can't never measure up. Martin Hill asking for you on this job, cause he knows you can make a better fence. And there you are, not even using your knack to split the rails, though I know you can, just to show me that *without* your knack you're a match for me."

"That's not what I meant," said Alvin. "I just don't use my knack around—"

"Around people as dumb as *me*," said Cal.

"I was doing a bad job explaining," said Alvin, "but if you'll let me, Cal, I can teach you how to change iron into—"

"Gold," said Cal, his voice thick with scorn. "What do you think I am? Trying to fool me with an alchemist's tales! If you knew how to do *that*, you wouldn't've come home poor. You know I once used to think you were the beginning and end of the world. I thought, when Al comes home, it'll be like old times, the two of us playing and working together, talking all the time, me tagging on, doing everything together. Only it turns out you still think I'm just a little boy, you don't say nothing to me except 'here's another rail' and 'pass the beans, please.' You took over all the jobs folks used to look to me to do, even one as simple as making a stout rail fence."

"Job's yours," said Alvin, shouldering his hammer. There was no point in trying to teach Cal anything—even if he *could* learn it, he could never learn it from Alvin. "I got other work to do, and I won't detain you any longer."

"*Detain* me," said Cal. "Is that a word you learned in a book, or from that ugly old teacher lady in Hatrack River that your ugly little mixup boy talks about?"

Hearing Miss Larner and Arthur Stuart so scornfully spoken of, that made Alvin burn inside, especially since he had in fact learned to use phrases like "detain you any longer" from Miss Larner. But Alvin didn't say anything to show his anger. He just turned his back and walked off, back down the line of the finished fence. Cal could use his own knack and finish the fence himself; Alvin didn't even care about collecting the wages he'd earned in most of a day's work. He had other things on his mind—memories of Miss Larner, partly, but mostly he was upset about how Cal hadn't wanted Alvin to teach him. Here he was the person in the whole world who had the best chance to learn it all as easy as a baby learning to suck, since it was his natural knack—only he didn't want to learn it, not from Alvin. It was something Alvin never would have thought possible, to turn down the chance to learn something, just because the teacher was somebody you didn't like.

Come to think of it, though, hadn't Alvin hated going to school with Reverend Thrower, cause of how Thrower always made him feel like he was somehow bad or evil or stupid or something? Could it be that Cal hated Alvin the way Alvin had hated Reverend Thrower? He just couldn't understand why Cal was so angry. Of all people in the world, Cal had no reason to be jealous of Alvin, because he could come closest to doing all that Alvin did; yet for that very reason, Cal was so jealous he'd never learn it, not without going through every step of figuring it out for himself.

At this rate, I'll never build the Crystal City, cause I'll never be able to teach Making to another soul.

It was a few weeks after that when Alvin finally tried again to talk to somebody, to see if he really could teach Making. It was on a Sunday, in Measure's house, where Alvin and Arthur Stuart had gone to take their dinner. It was a hot day, so Delphi laid a cold table—bread and cheese and salt ham and smoked turkey—and they all went outside to take the afternoon in the shade of Measure's north-facing kitchen porch.

"Alvin, I invited you and Arthur Stuart here today for a reason," said Measure. "Delphi and me, we already talked it over, and said a few things to Pa and Ma, too."

"Sounds like it must be pretty terrible, if it took that much talking."

"Reckon not," said Measure. "It's just—well, Arthur Stuart, here, he's a fine boy, and a good hard worker, and good company to boot."

Arthur Stuart grinned. "I sleep solid, too," he said.

"Fine sleeper," said Measure. "But Ma and Pa ain't exactly young no more. I think Ma's used to doing things in the kitchen all her own way.''

"That she is," sighed Delphi, as if she had more than a little reason for knowing exactly how set in her ways Goody Miller was.

"And Pa, well, he's tiring out. When he gets home from the mill, he needs to lie down, have plenty of quiet around him."

Alvin thought he knew where the conversation was heading. Maybe his folks just weren't the quality of Old Peg Guester or Gertie Smith. Maybe they couldn't take a mixup boy into their home or their heart. It made him sad to think of such a thing about his own folks, but he knew right off that he wouldn't even complain about it. He and Arthur Stuart would just pack up and set out on a road leading—nowhere in particular. Canada, maybe. Somewhere that a mixup boy'd be full welcome.

"Mind you, they didn't say a thing like that to *me*," said Measure. "In fact, I sort of said it all to them. You see, me and Delphi, we got a house somewhat bigger than we need, and with three small ones Delphi'd be glad of a boy Arthur Stuart's age to help with kitchen chores like he does."

"I can make bread all myself," said Arthur Stuart. "I know Mama's recipe by heart. She's dead."

"You see?" said Delphi. "If he can make bread himself sometimes, or even just help me with the kneading, I wouldn't end up so worn out at the end of the week."

"And it won't be long before Arthur Stuart could help out in my work in the fields," said Measure.

"But we don't want you to think we're looking to hire him on like a servant," said Delphi.

"No, no!" said Measure. "No, we're thinking of him like another son, only growed up more than my oldest Jeremiah, who's only three and a half, which makes him still pretty much useless as a human being, though at least he isn't always trying to throw himself into the creek to drown like his sister Shiphrah—or like you when you were little, I might add."

Arthur Stuart laughed at that. "Alvin like to drowned *me* one time," said Arthur Stuart. "Stuck me right in the Hio."

Alvin felt pure ashamed. Ashamed of lots of things: The fact that he never told Measure the whole story of how he rescued Arthur Stuart from the Finders; the fact that he even thought for a minute that Measure and Ma and Pa might be trying to get rid of a mixup boy, when the truth was they were squabbling over who got to have him in their home.

"It's Arthur Stuart's choice where to live, once he's invited," said

Alvin. "He came home along with me, but I don't make such choices for him."

"Can I live here?" asked Arthur Stuart. "Cal doesn't much like me."

"Cal's got troubles of his own," said Measure, "but he likes you fine."

"Why didn't Alvin bring home something useful, like a horse?" said Arthur Stuart. "You eat like one, but I bet you can't even pull a two-wheel shay."

Measure and Delphi laughed. They knew Arthur Stuart was repeating something Cal had said, word for word. Arthur Stuart did it so often, folks came to expect it, and took delight in his perfect memory. But it made Alvin sad to hear it, because he knew that only a few months ago, Arthur Stuart would have said it in Cal's own voice, so even Ma couldn't't've known without looking that it wasn't Cal himself.

"Is Alvin going to live down here too?" asked Arthur Stuart.

"Well, see, that's what we're thinking," said Measure. "Why don't you come on down here, too, Alvin? We can put you up in the main room here, for a while. And when the summer work's done, we can set to fixing up our old cabin—it's still pretty solid, since we ain't moved out of it but two years now. You can be pretty much on your own then. I reckon you're too old now to be living in your pa's house and eating at your ma's table."

Why, Alvin never would've reckoned it, but all of a sudden he found his eyes full of tears. Maybe it was the pure joy of having somebody notice he wasn't the same old Alvin Miller Junior anymore. Or maybe it was the fact that it was Measure, looking out for him like in the old days. Anyway, it was at that moment that Alvin first felt like he'd really come home.

"Sure I'll come down here, if you want me," Alvin said.

"Well there's no reason to cry about it," said Delphi. "I already got three babies crying every time they think of it. I don't want to have to come along and dab your eyes and wipe your nose like I do with Keturah."

"Well at least he don't wear diapers," said Measure, and he and Delphi both laughed like that was the funniest thing they ever heard. But actually they were laughing with pleasure at how Alvin had gotten so sentimental over the idea of living with them.

So Alvin and Arthur Stuart moved on down to Measure's house, and Alvin got to know his best-loved brother all over again. All the old things that Alvin once loved were still in Measure as a man, but there were new things, too. The tender way Measure had with his children, even after a spanking or a stiff talking to. The way Measure looked after his land and buildings, seeing all that needed doing, and then doing it, so there was never a door that squeaked for a second day, never an animal that was off its feed for a whole day without Measure trying to account for what was wrong.

Above all, though, Alvin saw how Measure was with Delphi. She wasn't a noticeably pretty girl, though not particular ugly either; she was strong and stout and laughed loud as a donkey. But Alvin saw how Measure had a way of looking at her like the most beautiful sight he ever could see. She'd look up and there he'd be, watching her with a kind of dreamy smile on his face, and she'd laugh or blush or look away, but for a minute or two she'd move more graceful, walking partly on her toes maybe, like she was dancing, or getting set to fly. Alvin wondered then if he could ever give such a look to Miss Larner as would make *her* so full of joy that she couldn't hardly stay connected to the earth.

Then Alvin would lie there in the night, feeling all the subtle movements of the house, knowing without even using his doodlebug what the slow and gentle creaking came from; and at such times he remembered the face of the woman named Margaret who had been hiding inside Miss Larner all those months, and imagined her face close to his, her lips parted, and from her throat those soft cries of pleasure Delphi made in the silence of the night. Then he would see her face again, only this time twisted with grief and weeping. At such times his heart ached inside him, and he yearned to go back to her, to take her in his arms and find some place inside her where he could heal her, take her grief away, make her whole.

And because Alvin was in Measure's house, his wariness slipped away from him, so that his face again began to show his feelings. It happened, then, that once when Measure and Delphi exchanged such a look as they had between them, Measure happened to look at Alvin's face. Delphi was gone out of the room by then, and the children were long since in bed, so Measure was free to reach out a hand and touch Alvin's knee.

"Who is she?" Measure asked.

"Who?" asked Alvin, confused.

"The one you love till it takes your breath away just remembering."

For a moment Alvin hesitated, by long habit. But then the gateway opened, and all his story spilled out. He started with Miss Larner, and how she was really Margaret, who was the same girl who once was the torch in Taleswapper's stories, the one that looked out for Alvin from afar. But telling the story of his love for her led to the story of all she taught him, and by the time the tale was done, it was near dawn. Delphi was asleep on Measure's shoulder—she'd come back in sometime during the tale, but didn't last long awake, which was just as well, with her three children and Arthur Stuart sure to want breakfast on time no matter how late she stayed up in the night. But Measure was still awake, his eyes sparkling with the knowledge of what the Redbird said, of the living golden plow, of Alvin in the forgefire, of Arthur Stuart in the Hio. And also a deep sadness behind that light in Measure's eyes, for the murder Alvin had done with his own hands, however much it might have been deserved; and for the death of Old Peg Guester, and even for the death of a certain runaway Black slave girl Arthur Stuart's whole lifetime ago.

"Somehow I got to go out and find people I can teach to be Makers," said Alvin. "But I don't even know if somebody without a knack like mine can learn it, or how much they ought to know, or if they'd even want to know it."

"I think," said Measure, "that they ought to love the dream of your Crystal City before they ever know that they might learn to help in the making of it. If word gets out that there's a Maker who can teach Making, you'll get the sort of folks as wants to rule people with such power. But the Crystal City—ah, Alvin, think of it! Like living inside that twister that caught you and the Prophet all those years ago."

"Will you learn it, Measure?" asked Alvin.

"I'll do all I can to learn it," said Measure. "But first I make you a solemn promise, that I'll only use what you teach me to build up the Crystal City. And if it turns out I just can't learn enough to be a Maker, I'll help you any other way I can. Whatever you ask me to do, Alvin, that I'll do—I'll take my family to the ends of the Earth, I'll give up everything I own, I'll die if need be—anything to make the vision Tenskwa-Tawa showed you come true."

Alvin held him by both hands, held him for the longest time. Then Measure leaned forward and kissed him, brother to brother, friend to friend. The movement woke Delphi. She hadn't heard most of it, but she knew that something solemn was happening, and she smiled sleepily before she got up and let Measure take her off to bed for the last few hours till dawn.

That was the beginning of Alvin's true work. All the rest of that summer, Measure was his pupil and his teacher. While Alvin taught Making to Measure, Measure taught fatherhood, husbanding, manliness to Alvin. The difference was that Alvin didn't half realize what he was learning, while Measure won each new understanding, each tiny shred of the power of Makery, only after terrible struggle. Yet he *did* understand, bit by bit, and he did learn more than a little bit of Making; and

Alvin began to understand, after many failed efforts, how to go about teaching someone else to "see" without eyes, to "touch" without hands.

And now, when he lay awake at night, he did not yearn so often for the past, but rather tried to imagine the future. Somewhere out there was the place where he should build the Crystal City; and out there, too, were the folks he had to find and teach them to love that dream and show them how to make it real. Somewhere there was the perfect soil that his living plow was meant to delve. Somewhere there was a woman he could love and live with till he died.

Back in Hatrack River, that fall there was an election, and it happened that because of certain stories floating around about who was a hero and who was a snake, Pauley Wiseman lost his job and Po Doggly got him a new one. Along about that time, too, Makepeace Smith come in to file a complaint about how back last spring his prentice run off with a certain item that belonged to his master.

"That's a long time waiting to file such a charge," said Sheriff Doggly.

"He threatened me," said Makepeace Smith. "I feared for my family."

"Well, now, you just tell me what it was he stole."

"It was a plow," said Makepeace Smith.

"A common plow? I'm supposed to find a common plow? And why in tarnation would he steal such a thing?"

Makepeace lowered his voice and said it all secret-like. "The plow was made of gold."

Oh, Po Doggly just laughed his head off, hearing that.

"Well, it's true, I tell you," said Makepeace.

"Is it, now? Why, I think that I believe you, my friend. But if there was a gold plow in your smithy, I'll lay ten to one that it was Al's, not yours."

"What a prentice makes belongs to the master!"

Well, that's about when Po started getting a little stern. "You start telling tales like that around Hatrack River, Makepeace Smith, and I reckon other folks'll tell how you kept that boy when he long since was a better smith than you. I reckon word'll get around about how you wasn't a fair master, and if you start to charging Alvin Smith with stealing what only he in all this world could possibly make, I think you'd find yourself laughed to scorn."

Maybe he would and maybe he wouldn't. It was sure that Makepeace didn't try no legal tricks to try to get that plow back from Alvin—

wherever he was. But he told his tale, making it bigger every time he told it—how Alvin was always stealing from him, and how that golden plow was Makepeace Smith's inheritance, made plowshape and painted black, and how Alvin uncovered it by devil powers and carried it off. As long as Gertie Smith was alive she scoffed at all such tales, but she died not too long after Alvin left, from a blood vein popping when she was a-screaming at her husband for being such a fool. From then on, Makepeace had the story his own way, even allowing as how Alvin killed Gertie herself with a curse that *made* her veins pop open and bleed to death inside her head. It was a terrible lie, but there's always folks as like to hear such tales, and the story spread from one end of the state of Hio to the other, and then beyond. Pauley Wiseman heard it. Reverend Thrower heard it. Cavil Planter heard it. So did a lot of other folks.

Which is why when Alvin finally ventured forth from Vigor Church, there was plenty of folks with an eye for strangers carrying bundles about the size of a plowshare, looking for a glint of gold under burlap, measuring strangers to see if they might be a certain run-off prentice smith who stole his master's inheritance. Some of those folks even meant to take it back to Makepeace Smith in Hatrack River, if it happened they ever laid their hands upon the golden plow. On the other hand, with some of those folks such a thought never crossed their minds.